The Psammead

or, the Gifts

E. NESBIT

The Complete Trilogy

Five Children and It (1902)
The Phoenix and the Carpet (1904)
The Story of the Amulet (1906)

2012

Legere Bonum Litteris

Contents

The Psammead 1

FIVE CHILDREN AND IT 4

   CHAPTER 1 BEAUTIFUL AS THE DAY 4

   CHAPTER 2 GOLDEN GUINEAS..............................23

   CHAPTER 3 BEING WANTED 42

   CHAPTER 4 WINGS 62

      MY DEAR MOTHER DEAR, ...63

      DEAR REVEREND CLERGYMAN, ...75

   CHAPTER 5 NO WINGS...79

   CHAPTER 6 A CASTLE AND NO DINNER 89

   CHAPTER 7 A SIEGE AND BED.............................102

   CHAPTER 8 BIGGER THAN THE BAKER'S BOY 113

   CHAPTER 9 GROWN UP 130

   CHAPTER 10 SCALPS..143

   CHAPTER 11 THE LAST WISH..............................156

THE PHOENIX AND THE CARPET............................171

   CHAPTER 1. THE EGG...171

   CHAPTER 2. THE TOPLESS TOWER....................187

   CHAPTER 3. THE QUEEN COOK 204

   CHAPTER 4. TWO BAZAARS................................223

   CHAPTER 5. THE TEMPLE 241

   CHAPTER 6. DOING GOOD 259

   CHAPTER 7. MEWS FROM PERSIA 273

   CHAPTER 8. THE CATS, THE COW, AND THE BURGLAR
  288

CHAPTER 9. THE BURGLAR'S BRIDE..............................302

CHAPTER 10. THE HOLE IN THE CARPET........................317

CHAPTER 11. THE BEGINNING OF THE END 331

CHAPTER 12. THE END OF THE END 345

THE STORY OF THE AMULET 361

CHAPTER 1. THE PSAMMEAD 361

CHAPTER 2. THE HALF AMULET..375

CHAPTER 3. THE PAST 387

CHAPTER 4. EIGHT THOUSAND YEARS AGO.................397

CHAPTER 5. THE FIGHT IN THE VILLAGE......................411

CHAPTER 6. THE WAY TO BABYLON..............................423

CHAPTER 7. 'THE DEEPEST DUNGEON BELOW THE
CASTLE MOAT' 438

CHAPTER 8. THE QUEEN IN LONDON 456

CHAPTER 9. ATLANTIS 477

CHAPTER 10. THE LITTLE BLACK GIRL AND JULIUS
CAESAR..494

CHAPTER 11. BEFORE PHARAOH......................................509

CHAPTER 12. THE SORRY-PRESENT AND THE EXPELLED
LITTLE BOY 529

CHAPTER 13. THE SHIPWRECK ON THE TIN ISLANDS..548

CHAPTER 14. THE HEART'S DESIRE 564

Biography of Edith Bland, nee Nesbit 584

FIVE CHILDREN AND IT

CHAPTER 1. BEAUTIFUL AS THE DAY

The house was three miles from the station, but before the dusty hired fly had rattled along for five minutes the children began to put their heads out of the carriage window and to say, 'Aren't we nearly there?' And every time they passed a house, which was not very often, they all said, 'Oh, is THIS it?' But it never was, till they reached the very top of the hill, just past the chalk-quarry and before you come to the gravel-pit. And then there was a white house with a green garden and an orchard beyond, and mother said, 'Here we are!'

'How white the house is,' said Robert.

'And look at the roses,' said Anthea.

'And the plums,' said Jane.

'It is rather decent,' Cyril admitted.

The Baby said, 'Wanty go walky'; and the fly stopped with a last rattle and jolt.

Everyone got its legs kicked or its feet trodden on in the scramble to get out of the carriage that very minute, but no one seemed to mind. Mother, curiously enough, was in no hurry to get out; and even when she had come down slowly and by the step, and with no jump at all, she seemed to wish to see the boxes carried in, and even to pay the driver, instead of joining in that first glorious rush round the garden and the orchard and the thorny, thistly, briery, brambly wilderness beyond the broken gate and the dry fountain at the side of the house. But the children were wiser, for once. It was not really a pretty house at all; it was quite ordinary, and mother thought it was rather inconvenient, and was quite annoyed at there being no shelves, to speak of, and hardly a cupboard in the place. Father used to say that the ironwork on the roof and coping was like an architect's nightmare. But the house was deep in the country, with no other house in sight, and the children had been in London for two years, without so much as once going to the seaside even for a day by an excursion train, and so the White House seemed to them a sort of Fairy Palace set down in an Earthly Paradise. For London is like prison for children, especially if their relations are not rich.

Of course there are the shops and the theatres, and Maskelyne and Cook's, and things, but if your people are rather poor you don't get taken to the theatres, and you can't buy things out of the shops; and London has none of those nice things that children may play with without hurting the things or themselves - such as trees and sand and woods and waters. And nearly everything in London is the wrong sort of shape - all straight lines and flat streets, instead of being all sorts of odd shapes, like things are in the country. Trees are all different, as you know, and I am sure some tiresome person must have told you that there are no two blades of grass exactly alike. But in streets, where the blades of grass don't grow, everything is like everything else. This is why so many children who live in towns are so extremely naughty. They do not know what is the matter with them, and no more do their fathers and mothers, aunts, uncles, cousins, tutors, governesses, and nurses; but I know. And so do you now. Children in the country are naughty sometimes, too, but that is for quite different reasons.

The children had explored the gardens and the outhouses thoroughly before they were caught and cleaned for tea, and they saw quite well that they were certain to be happy at the White House. They thought so from the first moment, but when they found the back of the house covered with jasmine, an in white flower, and smelling like a bottle of the most expensive scent that is ever given for a birthday present; and when they had seen the lawn, all green and smooth, and quite different from the brown grass in the gardens at Camden Town; and when they had found the stable with a loft over it and some old hay still left, they were almost certain; and when Robert had found the broken swing and tumbled out of it and got a lump on his head the size of an egg, and Cyril had nipped his finger in the door of a hutch that seemed made to keep rabbits in, if you ever had any, they had no longer any doubts whatever.

The best part of it all was that there were no rules about not going to places and not doing things. In London almost everything is labelled 'You mustn't touch,' and though the label is invisible, it's just as bad, because you know it's there, or if you don't you jolly soon get told.

The White House was on the edge of a hill, with a wood behind it - and the chalk-quarry on one side and the gravel-pit on the other. Down at the bottom of the hill was a level plain, with queer-shaped white buildings where people burnt lime, and a big red brewery and other houses; and when the big chimneys were smoking and the sun was setting, the valley looked as if it was filled with golden mist, and the limekilns and oast-houses glimmered and glittered till they were like an enchanted city out of the Arabian Nights.

Now that I have begun to tell you about the place, I feel that I could go on and make this into a most interesting story about all the ordinary things that the children did - just the kind of things you do yourself, you know - and you would believe every word of it; and when I told about the children's being tiresome, as you are sometimes, your aunts would perhaps write in the margin of the story with a pencil, 'How true!' or 'How like life!'and you would see it and very likely be annoyed. So I will only tell you the really astonishing things that happened, and you may leave the book about quite safely, for no aunts and uncles either are likely to write 'How true!' on the edge of the story. Grown-up people find it very difficult to believe really wonderful things, unless they have what they call proof. But children will believe almost anything, and grown-ups know this. That is why they tell you that the earth is round like an orange, when you can see perfectly well that it is flat and lumpy; and why they say that the earth goes round the sun, when you can see for yourself any day that the sun gets up in the morning and goes to bed at night like a good sun as it is, and the earth knows its place, and lies as still as a mouse. Yet I daresay you believe all that about the earth and the sun, and if so you will find it quite easy to believe that before Anthea and Cyril and the others had been a week in the country they had found a fairy. At least they called it that, because that was what it called itself; and of course it knew best, but it was not at all like any fairy you ever saw or heard of or read about.

It was at the gravel-pits. Father had to go away suddenly on business, and mother had gone away to stay with Granny, who was not very well. They both went in a great hurry, and when they were gone the house seemed dreadfully quiet and empty, and the children wandered from one room to another and looked at the bits of paper and string on the floors left over from the packing, and not yet cleared up, and wished they had something to do. It was Cyril who said:

'I say, let's take our Margate spades and go and dig in the gravel-pits. We can pretend it's seaside.'

'Father said it was once,' Anthea said; 'he says there are shells there thousands of years old.'

So they went. Of course they had been to the edge of the gravel-pit and looked over, but they had not gone down into it for fear father should say they mustn't play there, and the same with the chalk-quarry. The gravel-pit is not really dangerous if you don't try to climb down the edges, but go the slow safe way round by the road, as if you were a cart.

Each of the children carried its own spade, and took it in turns to carry the Lamb. He was the baby, and they called him that because 'Baa' was the first thing he ever said. They called Anthea 'Panther', which seems silly when you read it, but when you say it it sounds a little like her name.

The gravel-pit is very large and wide, with grass growing round the edges at the top, and dry stringy wildflowers, purple and yellow. It is like a giant's wash-hand basin. And there are mounds of gravel, and holes in the sides of the basin where gravel has been taken out, and

7

high up in the steep sides there are the little holes that are the little front doors of the little sand-martins' little houses.

The children built a castle, of course, but castle-building is rather poor fun when you have no hope of the swishing tide ever coming in to fill up the moat and wash away the drawbridge, and, at the happy last, to wet everybody up to the waist at least.

Cyril wanted to dig out a cave to play smugglers in, but the others thought it might bury them alive, so it ended in all spades going to work to dig a hole through the castle to Australia. These children, you see, believed that the world was round, and that on the other side the little Australian boys and girls were really walking wrong way up, like flies on the ceiling, with their heads hanging down into the air.

The children dug and they dug and they dug, and their hands got sandy and hot and red, and their faces got damp and shiny. The Lamb had tried to eat the sand, and had cried so hard when he found that it was not, as he had supposed, brown sugar, that he was now tired out, and was lying asleep in a warm fat bunch in the middle of the half-finished castle. This left his brothers and sisters free to work really hard, and the hole that was to come out in Australia soon grew so deep that Jane, who was called Pussy for short, begged the others to Stop.

'Suppose the bottom of the hole gave way suddenly,' she said, 'and you tumbled out among the little Australians, all the sand would get in their eyes.'

'Yes,' said Robert; 'and they would hate us, and throw stones at us, and not let us see the kangaroos, or opossums, or blue-gums, or Emu Brand birds, or anything.'

Cyril and Anthea knew that Australia was not quite so near as all that, but they agreed to stop using the spades and go on with their hands. This was quite easy, because the sand at the bottom of the hole was very soft and fine and dry, like sea-sand. And there were little shells in it.

'Fancy it having been wet sea here once, all sloppy and shiny,' said Jane, 'with fishes and conger-eels and coral and mermaids.'

'And masts of ships and wrecked Spanish treasure. I wish we could find a gold doubloon, or something,' Cyril said.

'How did the sea get carried away?' Robert asked.

'Not in a pail, silly,' said his brother. 'Father says the earth got too hot underneath, like you do in bed sometimes, so it just hunched up its shoulders, and the sea had to slip off, like the blankets do off us, and the shoulder was left sticking out, and turned into dry land. Let's go and look for shells; I think that little cave looks likely, and I see something sticking out there like a bit of wrecked ship's anchor, and it's beastly hot in the Australian hole.'

The others agreed, but Anthea went on digging. She always liked to finish a thing when she had once begun it. She felt it would be a disgrace to leave that hole without getting through to Australia.

The cave was disappointing, because there were no shells, and the wrecked ship's anchor turned out to be only the broken end of a pickaxe handle, and the cave party were just making up their minds that the sand makes you thirstier when it is not by the seaside, and someone had suggested going home for lemonade, when Anthea suddenly screamed:

'Cyril! Come here! Oh, come quick! It's alive! It'll get away! Quick!'

They all hurried back.

'It's a rat, I shouldn't wonder,' said Robert. 'Father says they infest old places - and this must be pretty old if the sea was here thousands of years ago.'

9

'Perhaps it is a snake,' said Jane, shuddering.

'Let's look,' said Cyril, jumping into the hole. 'I'm not afraid of snakes. I like them. If it is a snake I'll tame it, and it will follow me everywhere, and I'll let it sleep round my neck at night.'

'No, you won't,' said Robert firmly. He shared Cyril's bedroom. 'But you may if it's a rat.'

'Oh, don't be silly!' said Anthea; 'it's not a rat, it's MUCH bigger. And it's not a snake. It's got feet; I saw them; and fur! No - not the spade. You'll hurt it! Dig with your hands.'

'And let IT hurt ME instead! That's so likely, isn't it?' said Cyril, seizing a spade.

'Oh, don't!' said Anthea. 'Squirrel, DON'T. I - it sounds silly, but it said something. It really and truly did.'

'What?'

'It said, "You let me alone".'

But Cyril merely observed that his sister must have gone off her nut, and he and Robert dug with spades while Anthea sat on the edge of the hole, jumping up and down with hotness and anxiety. They dug carefully, and presently everyone could see that there really was something moving in the bottom of the Australian hole.

Then Anthea cried out, 'I'M not afraid. Let me dig,' and fell on her knees and began to scratch like a dog does when he has suddenly remembered where it was that he buried his bone.

'Oh, I felt fur,' she cried, half laughing and half crying. 'I did indeed! I did!' when suddenly a dry husky voice in the sand made them all jump back, and their hearts jumped nearly as fast as they did.

'Let me alone,' it said. And now everyone heard the voice and looked at the others to see if they had too.

'But we want to see you,' said Robert bravely.

'I wish you'd come out,' said Anthea, also taking courage.

'Oh, well - if that's your wish,' the voice said, and the sand stirred and spun and scattered, and something brown and furry and fat came rolling out into the hole and the sand fell off it, and it sat there yawning and rubbing the ends of its eyes with its hands.

'I believe I must have dropped asleep,' it said, stretching itself.

The children stood round the hole in a ring, looking at the creature they had found. It was worth looking at. Its eyes were on long horns like a snail's eyes, and it could move them in and out like telescopes; it had ears like a bat's ears, and its tubby body was shaped like a spider's and covered with thick soft fur; its legs and arms were furry too, and it had hands and feet like a monkey's.

'What on earth is it?' Jane said. 'Shall we take it home?'

The thing turned its long eyes to look at her, and said: 'Does she always talk nonsense, or is it only the rubbish on her head that makes her silly?'

It looked scornfully at Jane's hat as it spoke.

'She doesn't mean to be silly,' Anthea said gently; we none of us do, whatever you may think! Don't be frightened; we don't want to hurt you, you know.'

'Hurt ME!' it said. 'ME frightened? Upon my word! Why, you talk as if I were nobody in particular.' All its fur stood out like a cat's when it is going to fight.

'Well,' said Anthea, still kindly, 'perhaps if we knew who you are in particular we could think of something to say that wouldn't make you cross. Everything we've said so far seems to have. Who are you? And don't get angry! Because really we don't know.'

'You don't know?' it said. 'Well, I knew the world had changed - but - well, really - do you mean to tell me seriously you don't know a Psammead when you see one?'

'A Sammyadd? That's Greek to me.'

'So it is to everyone,' said the creature sharply. 'Well, in plain English, then, a SAND-FAIRY. Don't you know a Sand-fairy when you see one?'

It looked so grieved and hurt that Jane hastened to say, 'Of course I see you are, now. It's quite plain now one comes to look at you.'

'You came to look at me, several sentences ago,' it said crossly, beginning to curl up again in the sand.

'Oh - don't go away again! Do talk some more,' Robert cried. 'I didn't know you were a Sand-fairy, but I knew directly I saw you that you were much the wonderfullest thing I'd ever seen.'

The Sand-fairy seemed a shade less disagreeable after this.

'It isn't talking I mind,' it said, 'as long as you're reasonably civil. But I'm not going to make polite conversation for you. If you talk nicely to me, perhaps I'll answer you, and perhaps I won't. Now say something.'

Of course no one could think of anything to say, but at last Robert thought of 'How long have you lived here?' and he said it at once.

'Oh, ages - several thousand years,' replied the Psammead.

'Tell us all about it. Do.'

12

'It's all in books.'

'You aren't!' Jane said. 'Oh, tell us everything you can about yourself! We don't know anything about you, and you are so nice.'

The Sand-fairy smoothed his long rat-like whiskers and smiled between them.

'Do please tell!' said the children all together.

It is wonderful how quickly you get used to things, even the most astonishing. Five minutes before, the children had had no more idea than you that there was such a thing as a sand-fairy in the world, and now they were talking to it as though they had known it all their lives. It drew its eyes in and said:

'How very sunny it is - quite like old times. Where do you get your Megatheriums from now?'

'What?' said the children all at once. It is very difficult always to remember that 'what' is not polite, especially in moments of surprise or agitation.

'Are Pterodactyls plentiful now?' the Sand-fairy went on.

The children were unable to reply.

'What do you have for breakfast?' the Fairy said impatiently, 'and who gives it you?'

'Eggs and bacon, and bread-and-milk, and porridge and things. Mother gives it us. What are Mega-what's-its-names and Ptero-what-do-you-call-thems? And does anyone have them for breakfast?'

'Why, almost everyone had Pterodactyl for breakfast in my time! Pterodactyls were something like crocodiles and something like birds - I believe they were very good grilled. You see it was like this: of course there were heaps of sand-fairies then, and in the morning early you went out and hunted for them, and when you'd found one it gave you your wish. People used to send their little boys down to the seashore early in the morning before breakfast to get the day's wishes, and very often the eldest boy in the family would be told to wish for a Megatherium, ready jointed for cooking. It was as big as an elephant, you see, so there was a good deal of meat on it. And if they wanted fish, the Ichthyosaurus was asked for - he was twenty to forty feet long, so there was plenty of him. And for poultry there was the Plesiosaurus; there were nice pickings on that too. Then the other children could wish for other things. But when people had dinner-parties it was nearly always Megatheriums; and Ichthyosaurus, because his fins were a great delicacy and his tail made soup.'

'There must have been heaps and heaps of cold meat left over,' said Anthea, who meant to be a good housekeeper someday.

'Oh no,' said the Psammead, 'that would never have done. Why, of course at sunset what was left over turned into stone. You find the stone bones of the Megatherium and things all over the place even now, they tell me.'

'Who tell you?' asked Cyril; but the Sand-fairy frowned and began to dig very fast with its furry hands.

'Oh, don't go!' they all cried; 'tell us more about it when it was Megatheriums for breakfast! Was the world like this then?'

It stopped digging.

'Not a bit,' it said; 'it was nearly all sand where I lived, and coal grew on trees, and the periwinkles were as big as tea-trays - you find them now; they're turned into stone. We sand-fairies used to live on the seashore, and the children used to come with their little flint-spades and flint-pails and make castles for us to live in. That's thousands of years ago, but I hear that children still build castles on the sand. It's difficult to break yourself of a habit.'

'But why did you stop living in the castles?' asked Robert.

'It's a sad story,' said the Psammead gloomily. 'It was because they WOULD build moats to the castles, and the nasty wet bubbling sea used to come in, and of course as soon as a sand-fairy got wet it caught cold, and generally died. And so there got to be fewer and fewer, and, whenever you found a fairy and had a wish, you used to wish for a Megatherium, and eat twice as much as you wanted, because it might be weeks before you got another wish.'

'And did YOU get wet?' Robert inquired.

The Sand-fairy shuddered. 'Only once,' it said; 'the end of the twelfth hair of my top left whisker - I feel the place still in damp weather. It was only once, but it was quite enough for me. I went away as soon as the sun had dried my poor dear whisker. I scurried away to the back of the beach, and dug myself a house deep in warm dry sand, and there I've been ever since. And the sea changed its lodgings afterwards. And now I'm not going to tell you another thing.'

'Just one more, please,' said the children. 'Can you give wishes now?'

'Of course,' said it; 'didn't I give you yours a few minutes ago? You said, "I wish you'd come out," and I did.'

'Oh, please, mayn't we have another?'

'Yes, but be quick about it. I'm tired of you.'

I daresay you have often thought what you would do if you had three wishes given you, and have despised the old man and his wife in the black-pudding story, and felt certain that if you had the chance you could think of three really useful wishes without a moment's hesitation. These children had often talked this matter over, but, now the chance had suddenly come to them, they could not make up their minds.

'Quick,' said the Sand-fairy crossly. No one could think of anything, only Anthea did manage to remember a private wish of her own and jane's which they had never told the boys. She knew the boys would not care about it - but still it was better than nothing.

'I wish we were all as beautiful as the day,' she said in a great hurry.

The children looked at each other, but each could see that the others were not any better-looking than usual. The Psammead pushed out its long eyes, and seemed to be holding its breath and swelling itself out till it was twice as fat and furry as before. Suddenly it let its breath go in a long sigh.

'I'm really afraid I can't manage it,' it said apologetically; 'I must be out of practice.'

The children were horribly disappointed.

'Oh, DO try again!' they said.

'Well,' said the Sand-fairy, 'the fact is, I was keeping back a little strength to give the rest of you your wishes with. If you'll be contented with one wish a day amongst the lot of you I daresay I can screw myself up to it. Do you agree to that?'

'Yes, oh yes!' said Jane and Anthea. The boys nodded. They did not believe the Sand-fairy could do it. You can always make girls believe things much easier than you can boys.

It stretched out its eyes farther than ever, and swelled and swelled and swelled.

'I do hope it won't hurt itself,' said Anthea.

'Or crack its skin,' Robert said anxiously.

Everyone was very much relieved when the Sand-fairy, after getting so big that it almost filled up the hole in the sand, suddenly let out its breath and went back to its proper size.

'That's all right,' it said, panting heavily. 'It'll come easier to-morrow.'

'Did it hurt much?' asked Anthea.

'Only my poor whisker, thank you,' said he, 'but you're a kind and thoughtful child. Good day.'

It scratched suddenly and fiercely with its hands and feet, and disappeared in the sand. Then the children looked at each other, and each child suddenly found itself alone with three perfect strangers, all radiantly beautiful.

They stood for some moments in perfect silence. Each thought that its brothers and sisters had wandered off, and that these strange children had stolen up unnoticed while it was watching the swelling form of the Sand-fairy. Anthea spoke first -

'Excuse me,' she said very politely to Jane, who now had enormous blue eyes and a cloud of russet hair, 'but have you seen two little boys and a little girl anywhere about?'

'I was just going to ask you that,' said Jane. And then Cyril cried:

'Why, it's YOU! I know the hole in your pinafore! You ARE Jane, aren't you? And you're the Panther; I can see your dirty handkerchief that you forgot to change after you'd cut your thumb! Crikey! The wish has come off, after all. I say, am I as handsome as you are?'

'If you're Cyril, I liked you much better as you were before,' said Anthea decidedly. 'You look like the picture of the young chorister, with your golden hair; you'll die young, I shouldn't wonder. And if that's Robert, he's like an Italian organ-grinder. His hair's all black.'

'You two girls are like Christmas cards, then - that's all - silly Christmas cards,' said Robert angrily. 'And jane's hair is simply carrots.'

It was indeed of that Venetian tint so much admired by artists.

'Well, it's no use finding fault with each other,' said Anthea; 'let's get the Lamb and lug it home to dinner. The servants will admire us most awfully, you'll see.'

Baby was just waking when they got to him, and not one of the children but was relieved to find that he at least was not as beautiful as the day, but just the same as usual.

'I suppose he's too young to have wishes naturally,' said Jane. 'We shall have to mention him specially next time.'

Anthea ran forward and held out her arms.

'Come to own Panther, ducky,' she said.

The Baby looked at her disapprovingly, and put a sandy pink thumb in his mouth, Anthea was his favourite sister.

'Come then,' she said.

'G'way long!' said the Baby.

'Come to own Pussy,' said Jane.

'Wants my Panty,' said the Lamb dismally, and his lip trembled.

'Here, come on, Veteran,' said Robert, 'come and have a yidey on Yobby's back.'

'Yah, narky narky boy,' howled the Baby, giving way altogether. Then the children knew the worst. THE BABY DID NOT KNOW THEM!

18

They looked at each other in despair, and it was terrible to each, in this dire emergency, to meet only the beautiful eyes of perfect strangers, instead of the merry, friendly, commonplace, twinkling, jolly little eyes of its own brothers and sisters.

'This is most truly awful,' said Cyril when he had tried to lift up the Lamb, and the Lamb had scratched like a cat and bellowed like a bull. 'We've got to MAKE FRIENDS with him! I can't carry him home screaming like that. Fancy having to make friends with our own baby! - it's too silly.'

That, however, was exactly what they had to do. It took over an hour, and the task was not rendered any easier by the fact that the Lamb was by this time as hungry as a lion and as thirsty as a desert.

At last he consented to allow these strangers to carry him home by turns, but as he refused to hold on to such new acquaintances he was a dead weight and most exhausting.

'Thank goodness, we're home!' said Jane, staggering through the iron gate to where Martha, the nursemaid, stood at the front door shading her eyes with her hand and looking out anxiously. 'Here! Do take Baby!'

Martha snatched the Baby from her arms.

'Thanks be, HE'S safe back,' she said. 'Where are the others, and whoever to goodness gracious are all of you?'

'We're US, of course,' said Robert.

'And who's US, when you're at home?' asked Martha scornfully.

'I tell you it's US, only we're beautiful as the day,' said Cyril. 'I'm Cyril, and these are the others, and we're jolly hungry. Let us in, and don't be a silly idiot.'

Martha merely dratted Cyril's impudence and tried to shut the door in his face.

'I know we LOOK different, but I'm Anthea, and we're so tired, and it's long past dinner-time.'

'Then go home to your dinners, whoever you are; and if our children put you up to this playacting you can tell them from me they'll catch it, so they know what to expect!' With that she did bang the door. Cyril rang the bell violently. No answer. Presently cook put her head out of a bedroom window and said:

'If you don't take yourselves off, and that precious sharp, I'll go and fetch the police.' And she slammed down the window.

'It's no good,' said Anthea. 'Oh, do, do come away before we get sent to prison!'

The boys said it was nonsense, and the law of England couldn't put you in prison for just being as beautiful as the day, but all the same they followed the others out into the lane.

'We shall be our proper selves after sunset, I suppose,' said Jane.

'I don't know,' Cyril said sadly; 'it mayn't be like that now - things have changed a good deal since Megatherium times.'

'Oh,' cried Anthea suddenly, 'perhaps we shall turn into stone at sunset, like the Megatheriums did, so that there mayn't be any of us left over for the next day.'

She began to cry, so did Jane. Even the boys turned pale. No one had the heart to say anything.

It was a horrible afternoon. There was no house near where the children could beg a crust of bread or even a glass of water. They were afraid to go to the village, because they had seen Martha go down there with a basket, and there was a local constable. True, they were all as beautiful as the day, but that is a poor comfort when you are as hungry as a hunter and as thirsty as a sponge.

Three times they tried in vain to get the servants in the White House to let them in and listen to their tale. And then Robert went alone, hoping to be able to climb in at one of the back windows and so open the door to the others. But all the windows were out of reach, and Martha emptied a toilet-jug of cold water over him from a top window, and said:

'Go along with you, you nasty little Eyetalian monkey."

It came at last to their sitting down in a row under the hedge, with their feet in a dry ditch, waiting for sunset, and wondering whether, when the sun did set, they would turn into stone, or only into their own old natural selves; and each of them still felt lonely and among strangers, and tried not to look at the others, for, though their voices were their own, their faces were so radiantly beautiful as to be quite irritating to look at.

'I don't believe we SHALL turn to stone,' said Robert, breaking a long miserable silence, 'because the Sand-fairy said he'd give us another wish to-morrow, and he couldn't if we were stone, could he?'

The others said 'No,' but they weren't at all comforted.

Another silence, longer and more miserable, was broken by Cyril's suddenly saying, 'I don't want to frighten you girls, but I believe it's beginning with me already. My foot's quite dead. I'm turning to stone, I know I am, and so will you in a minute.'

'Never mind,' said Robert kindly, 'perhaps you'll be the only stone one, and the rest of us will be all right, and we'll cherish your statue and hang garlands on it.'

But when it turned out that Cyril's foot had only gone to sleep through his sitting too long with it under him, and when it came to life in an agony of pins and needles, the others were quite cross.

'Giving us such a fright for nothing!' said Anthea.

The third and miserablest silence of all was broken by Jane. She said: 'If we DO come out of this all right, we'll ask the Sammyadd to make it so that the servants don't notice anything different, no matter what wishes we have.'

The others only grunted. They were too wretched even to make good resolutions.

At last hunger and fright and crossness and tiredness - four very nasty things - all joined together to bring one nice thing, and that was sleep. The children lay asleep in a row, with their beautiful eyes shut and their beautiful mouths open. Anthea woke first. The sun had set, and the twilight was coming on.

Anthea pinched herself very hard, to make sure, and when she found she could still feel pinching she decided that she was not stone, and then she pinched the others. They, also, were soft.

'Wake up,' she said, almost in tears of joy; 'it's all right, we're not stone. And oh, Cyril, how nice and ugly you do look, with your old freckles and your brown hair and your little eyes. And so do you all!' she added, so that they might not feel jealous.

When they got home they were very much scolded by Martha, who told them about the strange children.

'A good-looking lot, I must say, but that impudent.'

'I know,' said Robert, who knew by experience how hopeless it would be to try to explain things to Martha.

'And where on earth have you been all this time, you naughty little things, you?'

'In the lane.'

'Why didn't you come home hours ago?'

'We couldn't because of THEM,' said Anthea.

'Who?'

'The children who were as beautiful as the day. They kept us there till after sunset. We couldn't come back till they'd gone. You don't know how we hated them! Oh, do, do give us some supper - we are so hungry.'

'Hungry! I should think so,' said Martha angrily; 'out all day like this. Well, I hope it'll be a lesson to you not to go picking up with strange children - down here after measles, as likely as not! Now mind, if you see them again, don't you speak to them - not one word nor so much as a look - but come straight away and tell me. I'll spoil their beauty for them!'

'If ever we DO see them again we'll tell you,' Anthea said; and Robert, fixing his eyes fondly on the cold beef that was being brought in on a tray by cook, added in heartfelt undertones -

'And we'll take jolly good care we never DO see them again.'

And they never have.

CHAPTER 2. GOLDEN GUINEAS

Anthea woke in the morning from a very real sort of dream, in which she was walking in the Zoological Gardens on a pouring wet day without any umbrella. The animals seemed desperately unhappy because of the rain, and were all growling gloomily. When she awoke, both the growling and the rain went on just the same. The growling was the heavy regular breathing of her sister Jane, who had a slight cold and was still asleep. The rain fell in slow drops on to Anthea's face from the wet corner of a bath-towel which her brother Robert was gently squeezing the water out of, to wake her up, as he now explained.

'Oh, drop it!' she said rather crossly; so he did, for he was not a brutal brother, though very ingenious in apple-pie beds, booby-traps, original methods of awakening sleeping relatives, and the other little accomplishments which make home happy.

'I had such a funny dream,' Anthea began.

'So did I,' said Jane, wakening suddenly and without warning. 'I dreamed we found a Sand-fairy in the gravel-pits, and it said it was a Sammyadd, and we might have a new wish every day, and -'

'But that's what I dreamed,' said Robert. 'I was just going to tell you - and we had the first wish directly it said so. And I dreamed you girls were donkeys enough to ask for us all to be beautiful as the day, and we jolly well were, and it was perfectly beastly.'

'But CAN different people all dream the same thing?' said Anthea, sitting up in bed, 'because I dreamed all that as well as about the Zoo and the rain; and Baby didn't know us in my dream, and the servants shut us out of the house because the radiantness of our beauty was such a complete disguise, and -'

The voice of the eldest brother sounded from across the landing.

'Come on, Robert,' it said, 'you'll be late for breakfast again - unless you mean to shirk your bath like you did on Tuesday.'

'I say, come here a sec,' Robert replied. 'I didn't shirk it; I had it after brekker in father's dressing-room, because ours was emptied away.'

Cyril appeared in the doorway, partially clothed.

24

'Look here,' said Anthea, 'we've all had such an odd dream. We've all dreamed we found a Sand-fairy.'

Her voice died away before Cyril's contemptuous glance. 'Dream?' he said, 'you little sillies, it's TRUE. I tell you it all happened. That's why I'm so keen on being down early. We'll go up there directly after brekker, and have another wish. Only we'll make up our minds, solid, before we go, what it is we do want, and no one must ask for anything unless the others agree first. No more peerless beauties for this child, thank you. Not if I know it!'

The other three dressed, with their mouths open. If all that dream about the Sand-fairy was real, this real dressing seemed very like a dream, the girls thought. Jane felt that Cyril was right, but Anthea was not sure, till after they had seen Martha and heard her full and plain reminders about their naughty conduct the day before. Then Anthea was sure. 'Because,' said she, 'servants never dream anything but the things in the Dream-book, like snakes and oysters and going to a wedding - that means a funeral, and snakes are a false female friend, and oysters are babies.'

'Talking of babies,' said Cyril, 'where's the Lamb?'
'Martha's going to take him to Rochester to see her cousins. Mother said she might. She's dressing him now,' said Jane, 'in his very best coat and hat. Bread-and-butter, please.'

'She seems to like taking him too,' said Robert in a tone of wonder.

'Servants do like taking babies to see their relations,' Cyril said. 'I've noticed it before - especially in their best things.'

'I expect they pretend they're their own babies, and that they're not servants at all, but married to noble dukes of high degree, and they say the babies are the little dukes and duchesses,' Jane suggested dreamily, taking more marmalade. 'I expect that's what Martha'll say to her cousin. She'll enjoy herself most frightfully-'

'She won't enjoy herself most frightfully carrying our infant duke to Rochester,' said Robert, 'not if she's anything like me - she won't.'

'Fancy walking to Rochester with the Lamb on your back! Oh, crikey!' said Cyril in full agreement.

'She's going by carrier,' said Jane. 'Let's see them off, then we shall have done a polite and kindly act, and we shall be quite sure we've got rid of them for the day.'

So they did.

Martha wore her Sunday dress of two shades of purple, so tight in the chest that it made her stoop, and her blue hat with the pink cornflowers and white ribbon. She had a yellow-lace collar with a green bow. And the Lamb had indeed his very best cream-coloured silk coat and hat. It was a smart party that the carrier's cart picked up at the Cross Roads. When its white tilt and red wheels had slowly vanished in a swirl of chalk-dust -

'And now for the Sammyadd!' said Cyril, and off they went.

As they went they decided on the wish they would ask for. Although they were all in a great hurry they did not try to climb down the sides of the gravel-pit, but went round by the safe lower road, as if they had been carts. They had made a ring of stones round the place where the Sand-fairy had disappeared, so they easily found the spot. The sun was burning and bright, and the sky was deep blue - without a cloud. The sand was very hot to touch.

'Oh - suppose it was only a dream, after all,' Robert said as the boys uncovered their spades from the sand-heap where they had buried them and began to dig.

'Suppose you were a sensible chap,' said Cyril; 'one's quite as likely as the other!' 'Suppose you kept a civil tongue in your head,' Robert snapped.

'Suppose we girls take a turn,' said Jane, laughing. 'You boys seem to be getting very warm.'

'Suppose you don't come shoving your silly oar in,' said Robert, who was now warm indeed.

'We won't,' said Anthea quickly. 'Robert dear, don't be so grumpy - we won't say a word, you shall be the one to speak to the Fairy and tell him what we've decided to wish for. You'll say it much better than we shall.'

'Suppose you drop being a little humbug,' said Robert, but not crossly. 'Look out - dig with your hands, now!'

So they did, and presently uncovered the spider-shaped brown hairy body, long arms and legs, bat's ears and snail's eyes of the Sand-fairy himself. Everyone drew a deep breath of satisfaction, for now of course it couldn't have been a dream.

The Psammead sat up and shook the sand out of its fur.

'How's your left whisker this morning?' said Anthea politely.

'Nothing to boast of,' said it, 'it had rather a restless night.
But thank you for asking.'

'I say,' said Robert, 'do you feel up to giving wishes to-day, because we very much want an extra besides the regular one? The extra's a very little one,' he added reassuringly.

'Humph!' said the Sand-fairy. (If you read this story aloud, please pronounce 'humph' exactly as it is spelt, for that is how he said it.) 'Humph! Do you know, until I heard you being disagreeable to each other just over my head, and so loud too, I really quite thought I had dreamed you all. I do have very odd dreams sometimes.'

'Do you?'Jane hurried to say, so as to get away from the subject of disagreeableness. 'I wish,' she added politely, 'you'd tell us about your dreams - they must be awfully interesting.'

'Is that the day's wish?' said the Sand-fairy, yawning.

Cyril muttered something about 'just like a girl,' and the rest stood silent. If they said 'Yes,' then good-bye to the other wishes they had decided to ask for. If they said 'No,' it would be very rude, and they had all been taught manners, and had learned a little too, which is not at all the same thing. A sigh of relief broke from all lips when the Sand-fairy said:

'If I do I shan't have strength to give you a second wish; not even good tempers, or common sense, or manners, or little things like that.'

'We don't want you to put yourself out at all about these things, we can manage them quite well ourselves,' said Cyril eagerly; while the others looked guiltily at each other, and wished the Fairy would not keep all on about good tempers, but give them one good rowing if it wanted to, and then have done with it.

'Well,' said the Psammead, putting out his long snail's eyes so suddenly that one of them nearly went into the round boy's eyes of Robert, 'let's have the little wish first.'

'We don't want the servants to notice the gifts you give us.'

'Are kind enough to give us,' said Anthea in a whisper.

'Are kind enough to give us, I mean,' said Robert.

The Fairy swelled himself out a bit, let his breath go, and said -

'I've done THAT for you - it was quite easy. People don't notice things much, anyway. What's the next wish?'

'We want,' said Robert slowly, 'to be rich beyond the dreams of something or other.'

'Avarice,' said Jane.

'So it is,' said the Fairy unexpectedly. 'But it won't do you much good, that's one comfort,' it muttered to itself. 'Come - I can't go beyond dreams, you know! How much do you want, and will you have it in gold or notes?'

'Gold, please - and millions of it.'

'This gravel-pit full be enough?' said the Fairy in an off-hand manner.

'Oh YES!'

'Then get out before I begin, or you'll be buried alive in it.'

It made its skinny arms so long, and waved them so frighteningly, that the children ran as hard as they could towards the road by which carts used to come to the gravel-pits. Only Anthea had presence of mind enough to shout a timid 'Good-morning, I hope your whisker will be better to-morrow,' as she ran.

On the road they turned and looked back, and they had to shut their eyes, and open them very slowly, a little bit at a time, because the sight was too dazzling for their eyes to be able to bear it. It was something like trying to look at the sun at high noon on Midsummer Day. For the whole of the sand-pit was full, right up to the very top, with new shining gold pieces, and all the little sand-martins' little front doors were covered out of sight. Where the road for the carts wound into the gravel-pit the gold lay in heaps like stones lie by the roadside, and a great bank of shining gold shelved down from where it lay flat and smooth between the tall sides of the gravel-pit. And all the gleaming heap was minted gold. And on the sides and edges of these countless coins the midday sun shone and sparkled, and glowed and gleamed till the quarry looked like the mouth of a smelting furnace, or one of the fairy halls that you see sometimes in the sky at sunset.

The children stood with their mouths open, and no one said a word.

At last Robert stopped and picked up one of the loose coins from the edge of the heap by the cart-road, and looked at it. He looked on both sides. Then he said in a low voice, quite different to his own, 'It's not sovereigns.'

'It's gold, anyway,' said Cyril. And now they all began to talk at once. They all picked up the golden treasure by handfuls, and let it run through their fingers like water, and the chink it made as it fell was wonderful music. At first they quite forgot to think of spending the money, it was so nice to play with. Jane sat down between two heaps of gold and Robert began to bury her, as you bury your father in sand when you are at the seaside and he has gone to sleep on the beach with his newspaper over his face. But Jane was not half buried before she cried out, 'Oh, stop, it's too heavy! It hurts!

Robert said 'Bosh!' and went on.

'Let me out, I tell you,' cried Jane, and was taken out, very white, and trembling a little.

'You've no idea what it's like,' said she; 'it's like stones on you - or like chains.'

'Look here,' Cyril said, 'if this is to do us any good, it's no good our staying gasping at it like this. Let's fill our pockets and go and buy things. Don't you forget, it won't last after sunset. I wish we'd asked the Sammyadd why things don't turn to stone. Perhaps this will. I'll tell you what, there's a pony and cart in the village.'

'Do you want to buy that?' asked Jane.

30

'No, silly - we'll HIRE it. And then we'll go to Rochester and buy heaps and heaps of things. Look here, let's each take as much as we can carry. But it's not sovereigns. They've got a man's head on one side and a thing like the ace of spades on the other. Fill your pockets with it, I tell you, and come along. You can jaw as we go - if you must jaw.'

Cyril sat down and began to fill his pockets.
'You made fun of me for getting father to have nine pockets in my Norfolks,' said he, 'but now you see!'

They did. For when Cyril had filled his nine pockets and his handkerchief and the space between himself and his shirt front with the gold coins, he had to stand up. But he staggered, and had to sit down again in a hurry-

'Throw out some of the cargo,' said Robert. 'You'll sink the ship, old chap. That comes of nine pockets.'

And Cyril had to.

Then they set off to walk to the village. It was more than a mile, and the road was very dusty indeed, and the sun seemed to get hotter and hotter, and the gold in their pockets got heavier and heavier.

It was Jane who said, 'I don't see how we're to spend it all. There must be thousands of pounds among the lot of us. I'm going to leave some of mine behind this stump in the hedge. And directly we get to the village we'll buy some biscuits; I know it's long past dinner-time.' She took out a handful or two of gold and hid it in the hollows of an old hornbeam. 'How round and yellow they are,' she said. 'Don't you wish they were gingerbread nuts and we were going to eat them?'

'Well, they're not, and we're not,' said Cyril. 'Come on!'

But they came on heavily and wearily. Before they reached the village, more than one stump in the hedge concealed its little hoard of hidden treasure. Yet they reached the village with about twelve hundred guineas in their pockets. But in spite of this inside wealth they looked quite ordinary outside, and no one would have thought they could have more than a half-crown each at the outside. The haze of heat, the blue of the wood smoke, made a sort of dim misty cloud over the red roofs of the village. The four sat down heavily on the first bench they came to- It happened to be outside the Blue Boar Inn.

It was decided that Cyril should go into the Blue Boar and ask for ginger-beer, because, as Anthea said, 'It is not wrong for men to go into public houses, only for children. And Cyril is nearer to being a man than us, because he is the eldest.' So he went. The others sat in the sun and waited.

'Oh, hats, how hot it is!' said Robert. 'Dogs put their tongues out when they're hot; I wonder if it would cool us at all to put out ours?'

'We might try,'Jane said; and they all put their tongues out as far as ever they could go, so that it quite stretched their throats, but it only seemed to make them thirstier than ever, besides annoying everyone who went by. So they took their tongues in again, just as Cyril came back with the ginger-beer.

'I had to pay for it out of my own two-and-sevenpence, though, that I was going to buy rabbits with,' he said. 'They wouldn't change the gold. And when I pulled out a handful the man just laughed and said it was card-counters. And I got some sponge-cakes too, out of a glass jar on the bar-counter. And some biscuits with caraways in.'

The sponge-cakes were both soft and dry and the biscuits were dry too, and yet soft, which biscuits ought not to be. But the ginger-beer made up for everything.

'It's my turn now to try to buy something with the money,' Anthea said, 'I'm next eldest. Where is the pony-cart kept?'

It was at The Chequers, and Anthea went in the back way to the yard, because they all knew that little girls ought not to go into the bars of public-houses. She came out, as she herself said, 'pleased but not proud'.

'He'll be ready in a brace of shakes, he says,' she remarked, 'and he's to have one sovereign - or whatever it is - to drive us in to Rochester and back, besides waiting there till we've got everything we want. I think I managed very well.'

'You think yourself jolly clever, I daresay,' said Cyril moodily. 'How did you do it?'

'I wasn't jolly clever enough to go taking handfuls of money out of my pocket, to make it seem cheap, anyway,' she retorted. 'I just found a young man doing something to a horse's leg with a sponge and a pail. And I held out one sovereign, and I said, "Do you know what this is?" He said, "No," and he'd call his father. And the old man came, and he said it was a spade guinea; and he said was it my own to do as I liked with, and I said "Yes"; and I asked about the pony-cart, and I said he could have the guinea if he'd drive us in to Rochester. And his name is S. Crispin. And he said, "Right oh".'

It was a new sensation to be driven in a smart pony-trap along pretty country roads, it was very pleasant too (which is not always the case with new sensations), quite apart from the beautiful plans of spending the money which each child made as they went along, silently of course and quite to itself, for they felt it would never have done to let the old innkeeper hear them talk in the affluent sort of way they were thinking. The old man put them down by the bridge at their request.

'If you were going to buy a carriage and horses, where would you go?' asked Cyril, as if he were only asking for the sake of something to say.

'Billy Peasemarsh, at the Saracen's Head,' said the old man promptly. 'Though all forbid I should recommend any man where

33

it's a question of horses, no more than I'd take anybody else's recommending if I was a-buying one. But if your pa's thinking of a turnout of any sort, there ain't a straighter man in Rochester, nor a civiller spoken, than Billy, though I says it.'

'Thank you,' said Cyril. 'The Saracen's Head.'

And now the children began to see one of the laws of nature turn upside down and stand on its head like an acrobat. Any grown-up persons would tell you that money is hard to get and easy to spend. But the fairy money had been easy to get, and spending it was not only hard, it was almost impossible. The tradespeople of Rochester seemed to shrink, to a trades-person, from the glittering fairy gold ('furrin money' they called it, for the most part). To begin with, Anthea, who had had the misfortune to sit on her hat earlier in the day, wished to buy another. She chose a very beautiful one, trimmed with pink roses and the blue breasts of peacocks. It was marked in the window, 'Paris Model, three guineas'.

'I'm glad,' she said, 'because, if it says guineas, it means guineas, and not sovereigns, which we haven't got.'

But when she took three of the spade guineas in her hand, which was by this time rather dirty owing to her not having put on gloves before going to the gravel-pit, the black-silk young lady in the shop looked very hard at her, and went and whispered something to an older and uglier lady, also in black silk, and then they gave her back the money and said it was not current coin.

'It's good money,' said Anthea, 'and it's my own.'

'I daresay,' said the lady, 'but it's not the kind of money that's fashionable now, and we don't care about taking it.'

'I believe they think we've stolen it,' said Anthea, rejoining the others in the street; 'if we had gloves they wouldn't think we were so dishonest. It's my hands being so dirty fills their minds with doubts.'

34

So they chose a humble shop, and the girls bought cotton gloves, the kind at sixpence three-farthings, but when they offered a guinea the woman looked at it through her spectacles and said she had no change; so the gloves had to be paid for out of Cyril's two-and-sevenpence that he meant to buy rabbits with, and so had the green imitation crocodile-skin purse at ninepence-halfpenny which had been bought at the same time. They tried several more shops, the kinds where you buy toys and scent, and silk handkerchiefs and books, and fancy boxes of stationery, and photographs of objects of interest in the vicinity. But nobody cared to change a guinea that day in Rochester, and as they went from shop to shop they got dirtier and dirtier, and their hair got more and more untidy, and Jane slipped and fell down on a part of the road where a water-cart had just gone by. Also they got very hungry, but they found no one would give them anything to eat for their guineas. After trying two pastrycooks in vain, they became so hungry, perhaps from the smell of the cake in the shops, as Cyril suggested, that they formed a plan of campaign in whispers and carried it out in desperation. They marched into a third pastrycook's - Beale his name was - and before the people behind the counter could interfere each child had seized three new penny buns, clapped the three together between its dirty hands, and taken a big bite out of the triple sandwich. Then they stood at bay, with the twelve buns in their hands and their mouths very full indeed. The shocked pastrycook bounded round the corner.

'Here,' said Cyril, speaking as distinctly as he could, and holding out the guinea he got ready before entering the shop, 'pay yourself out of that.'

Mr Beale snatched the coin, bit it, and put it in his pocket.

'Off you go,' he said, brief and stern like the man in the song.

'But the change?' said Anthea, who had a saving mind.

'Change!' said the man. 'I'll change you! Hout you goes; and you may think yourselves lucky I don't send for the police to find out where you got it!'

In the Castle Gardens the millionaires finished the buns, and though the curranty softness of these were delicious, and acted like a charm in raising the spirits of the party, yet even the stoutest heart quailed at the thought of venturing to sound Mr Billy Peasemarsh at the Saracen's Head on the subject of a horse and carriage. The boys would have given up the idea, but Jane was always a hopeful child, and Anthea generally an obstinate one, and their earnestness prevailed.

The whole party, by this time indescribably dirty, therefore betook itself to the Saracen's Head. The yard-method of attack having been successful at The Chequers was tried again here. Mr Peasemarsh was in the yard, and Robert opened the business in these terms -

'They tell me you have a lot of horses and carriages to sell.' It had been agreed that Robert should be spokesman, because in books it is always the gentlemen who buy horses, and not ladies, and Cyril had had his go at the Blue Boar.

'They tell you true, young man,' said Mr Peasemarsh. He was a long lean man, with very blue eyes and a tight mouth and narrow lips.

'We should like to buy some, please,' said Robert politely.

'I daresay you would.'

'Will you show us a few, please? To choose from.' 'Who are you a-kiddin of?' inquired Mr Billy Peasemarsh. 'Was you sent here of a message?'

'I tell you,' said Robert, 'we want to buy some horses and carriages, and a man told us you were straight and civil spoken, but I shouldn't wonder if he was mistaken.'

'Upon my sacred!' said Mr Peasemarsh. 'Shall I trot the whole stable out for your Honour's worship to see? Or shall I send round to the Bishop's to see if he's a nag or two to dispose of?'

'Please do,' said Robert, 'if it's not too much trouble. It would be very kind of you.'

Mr Peasemarsh put his hands in his pockets and laughed, and they did not like the way he did it. Then he shouted 'Willum!'

A stooping ostler appeared in a stable door.

'Here, Willum, come and look at this 'ere young dook! Wants to buy the whole stud, lock, stock, and bar'l. And ain't got tuppence in his pocket to bless hisself with, I'll go bail!'

Willum's eyes followed his master's pointing thumb with contemptuous interest.

'Do 'e, for sure?' he said.

But Robert spoke, though both the girls were now pulling at his jacket and begging him to 'come along'. He spoke, and he was very angry; he said:

'I'm not a young duke, and I never pretended to be. And as for tuppence - what do you call this?' And before the others could stop him he had pulled out two fat handfuls of shining guineas, and held them out for Mr Peasemarsh to look at. He did look. He snatched one up in his finger and thumb. He bit it, and Jane expected him to say, 'The best horse in my stables is at your service.' But the others knew better. Still it was a blow, even to the most desponding, when he said shortly:

'Willum, shut the yard doors,' and Willum grinned and went to shut them.

'Good-afternoon,' said Robert hastily; 'we shan't buy any of your horses now, whatever you say, and I hope it'll be a lesson to you.' He had seen a little side gate open, and was moving towards it as he spoke. But Billy Peasemarsh put himself in the way.

'Not so fast, you young off-scouring!' he said. 'Willum, fetch the pleece.'

Willum went. The children stood huddled together like frightened sheep, and Mr Peasemarsh spoke to them till the pleece arrived. He said many things. Among other things he said:

'Nice lot you are, aren't you, coming tempting honest men with your guineas!'

'They ARE our guineas,' said Cyril boldly.

'Oh, of course we don't know all about that, no more we don't - oh no - course not! And dragging little gells into it, too. 'Ere - I'll let the gells go if you'll come along to the pleece quiet.'

'We won't be let go,' said Jane heroically; 'not without the boys. It's our money just as much as theirs, you wicked old man.'

'Where'd you get it, then?' said the man, softening slightly, which was not at all what the boys expected when Jane began to call names.

Jane cast a silent glance of agony at the others.

'Lost your tongue, eh? Got it fast enough when it's for calling names with. Come, speak up! Where'd you get it?'

'Out of the gravel-pit,' said truthful Jane.

'Next article,' said the man.

'I tell you we did,' Jane said. 'There's a fairy there - all over brown fur - with ears like a bat's and eyes like a snail's, and he gives you a wish a day, and they all come true.'

'Touched in the head, eh?' said the man in a low voice, 'all the more shame to you boys dragging the poor afflicted child into your sinful burglaries.'

'She's not mad; it's true,' said Anthea; 'there is a fairy. If I ever see him again I'll wish for something for you; at least I would if vengeance wasn't wicked - so there!'

'Lor' lumme,' said Billy Peasemarsh, 'if there ain't another on 'em!'

And now Willum came -back with a spiteful grin on his face, and at his back a policeman, with whom Mr Peasemarsh spoke long in a hoarse earnest whisper.

'I daresay you're right,' said the policeman at last. 'Anyway, I'll take 'em up on a charge of unlawful possession, pending inquiries. And the magistrate will deal with the case. Send the afflicted ones to a home, as likely as not, and the boys to a reformatory. Now then, come along, youngsters! No use making a fuss. You bring the gells along, Mr Peasemarsh, sir, and I'll shepherd the boys.'

Speechless with rage and horror, the four children were driven along the streets of Rochester. Tears of anger and shame blinded them, so that when Robert ran right into a passer-by he did not recognize her till a well—known voice said, 'Well, if ever I did! Oh, Master Robert, whatever have you been a doing of now?' And another voice, quite as well known, said, 'Panty; want go own Panty!'

They had run into Martha and the baby!

Martha behaved admirably. She refused to believe a word of the policeman's story, or of Mr Peasemarsh's either, even when they made Robert turn out his pockets in an archway and show the guineas.

'I don't see nothing,' she said. 'You've gone out of your senses, you two! There ain't any gold there - only the poor child's hands, all over crock and dirt, and like the very chimbley. Oh, that I should ever see the day!'

And the children thought this very noble of Martha, even if rather wicked, till they remembered how the Fairy had promised that the servants should never notice any of the fairy gifts. So of course Martha couldn't see the gold, and so was only speaking the truth, and that was quite right, of course, but not extra noble.

It was getting dusk when they reached the police-station. The policeman told his tale to an inspector, who sat in a large bare room with a thing like a clumsy nursery-fender at one end to put prisoners in. Robert wondered whether it was a cell or a dock.

'Produce the coins, officer,' said the inspector.

'Turn out your pockets,' said the constable.

Cyril desperately plunged his hands in his pockets, stood still a moment, and then began to laugh - an odd sort of laugh that hurt, and that felt much more like crying. His pockets were empty. So were the pockets of the others. For of course at sunset all the fairy gold had vanished away.

'Turn out your pockets, and stop that noise,' said the inspector.

Cyril turned out his pockets, every one of the nine which enriched his Norfolk suit. And every pocket was empty.

'Well!' said the inspector.

'I don't know how they done it - artful little beggars! They walked in front of me the 'ole way, so as for me to keep my eye on them and not to attract a crowd and obstruct the traffic.'

'It's very remarkable,' said the inspector, frowning.

40

'If you've quite done a-browbeating of the innocent children,' said Martha, 'I'll hire a private carriage and we'll drive home to their papa's mansion. You'll hear about this again, young man! - I told you they hadn't got any gold, when you were pretending to see it in their poor helpless hands. It's early in the day for a constable on duty not to be able to trust his own eyes. As to the other one, the less said the better; he keeps the Saracen's Head, and he knows best what his liquor's like.'

'Take them away, for goodness' sake,' said the inspector crossly. But as they left the police-station he said, 'Now then!' to the policeman and Mr Pease- marsh, and he said it twenty times as crossly as he had spoken to Martha.

Martha was as good as her word. She took them home in a very grand carriage, because the carrier's cart was gone, and, though she had stood by them so nobly with the police, she was so angry with them as soon as they were alone for 'trapseing into Rochester by themselves', that none of them dared to mention the old man with the pony-cart from the village who was waiting for them in Rochester. And so, after one day of boundless wealth, the children found themselves sent to bed in deep disgrace, and only enriched by two pairs of cotton gloves, dirty inside because of the state of the hands they had been put on to cover, an imitation crocodile-skin purse, and twelve penny buns long since digested.

The thing that troubled them most was the fear that the old gentleman's guinea might have disappeared at sunset with all the rest, so they went down to the village next day to apologize for not meeting him in Rochester, and to see. They found him very friendly. The guinea had NOT disappeared, and he had bored a hole in it and hung it on his watch-chain. As for the guinea the baker took, the children felt they could not care whether it had vanished or not, which was not perhaps very honest, but on the other hand was not wholly unnatural. But afterwards this preyed on Anthea's mind, and at last she secretly sent twelve stamps by post to 'Mr Beale, Baker, Rochester'. Inside she wrote, 'To pay for the buns.' I hope the guinea did disappear, for that pastrycook was really not at all a nice man, and, besides, penny buns are seven for sixpence in all really respectable shops.

CHAPTER 3. BEING WANTED

The morning after the children had been the possessors of boundless wealth, and had been unable to buy anything really useful or enjoyable with it, except two pairs of cotton gloves, twelve penny buns, an imitation crocodile-skin purse, and a ride in a pony-cart, they awoke without any of the enthusiastic happiness which they had felt on the previous day when they remembered how they had had the luck to find a Psammead, or Sand-fairy; and to receive its promise to grant them a new wish every day. For now they had had two wishes, Beauty and Wealth, and neither had exactly made them happy. But the happening of strange things, even if they are not completely pleasant things, is more amusing than those times when nothing happens but meals, and they are not always completely pleasant, especially on the days when it is cold mutton or hash.

There was no chance of talking things over before breakfast, because everyone overslept itself, as it happened, and it needed a vigorous and determined struggle to get dressed so as to be only ten minutes late for breakfast. During this meal some efforts were made to deal with the question of the Psammead in an impartial spirit, but it is very difficult to discuss anything thoroughly and at the same time to attend faithfully to your baby brother's breakfast needs. The Baby was particularly lively that morning. He not only wriggled his body through the bar of his high chair, and hung by his head, choking and purple, but he collared a tablespoon with desperate suddenness, hit Cyril heavily on the head with it, and then cried because it was taken away from him. He put his fat fist in his bread-and-milk, and demanded 'nam', which was only allowed for tea. He sang, he put his feet on the table - he clamoured to 'go walky'. The conversation was something like this:

'Look here - about that Sand-fairy - Look out! - he'll have the milk over.'

Milk removed to a safe distance.

'Yes - about that Fairy - No, Lamb dear, give Panther the narky poon.'

Then Cyril tried. 'Nothing we've had yet has turned out - He nearly had the mustard that time!'

'I wonder whether we'd better wish - Hullo! you've done it now, my boy!' And, in a flash of glass and pink baby-paws, the bowl of golden carp in the middle of the table rolled on its side, and poured a flood of mixed water and goldfish into the Baby's lap and into the laps of the others.

Everyone was almost as much upset as the goldfish: the Lamb only remaining calm. When the pool on the floor had been mopped up, and the leaping, gasping goldfish had been collected and put back in the water, the Baby was taken away to be entirely redressed by Martha, and most of the others had to change completely. The pinafores and jackets that had been bathed in goldfish-and-water were hung out to dry, and then it turned out that Jane must either mend the dress she had torn the day before or appear all day in her best petticoat. It was white and soft and frilly, and trimmed with lace, and very, very pretty, quite as pretty as a frock, if not more so. Only it was NOT a frock, and Martha's word was law. She wouldn't let Jane wear her best frock, and she refused to listen for a moment to Robert's suggestion that Jane should wear her best petticoat and call it a dress.

'It's not respectable,' she said. And when people say that, it's no use anyone's saying anything. You will find this out for yourselves someday.

So there was nothing for it but for Jane to mend her frock. The hole had been torn the day before when she happened to tumble down in the High Street of Rochester, just where a water-cart had passed on its silvery way. She had grazed her knee, and her stocking was much more than grazed, and her dress was cut by the same stone which had attended to the knee and the stocking. Of course the others were not such sneaks as to abandon a comrade in misfortune, so they all sat on the grass-plot round the sundial, and Jane darned away for dear life. The Lamb was still in the hands of Martha having its clothes changed, so conversation was possible.

Anthea and Robert timidly tried to conceal their inmost thought, which was that the Psammead was not to be trusted; but Cyril said:

'Speak out - say what you've got to say - I hate hinting, and "don't know", and sneakish ways like that.'

So then Robert said, as in honour bound: 'Sneak yourself - Anthea and me weren't so goldfishy as you two were, so we got changed quicker, and we've had time to think it over, and if you ask me -'

'I didn't ask you,' said Jane, biting off a needleful of thread as she had always been strictly forbidden to do.

'I don't care who asks or who doesn't,' said Robert, but Anthea and I think the Sammyadd is a spiteful brute. If it can give us our wishes I suppose it can give itself its own, and I feel almost sure it wishes every time that our wishes shan't do us any good. Let's let the tiresome beast alone, and just go and have a jolly good game of forts, on our own, in the chalk-pit.'

(You will remember that the happily situated house where these children were spending their holidays lay between a chalk-quarry and a gravel-pit.)

Cyril and Jane were more hopeful - they generally were.

'I don't think the Sammyadd does it on purpose,' Cyril said; 'and, after all, it WAS silly to wish for boundless wealth. Fifty pounds in two-shilling pieces would have been much more sensible. And

44

wishing to be beautiful as the day was simply donkeyish. I don't want to be disagreeable, but it was. We must try to find a really useful wish, and wish it.'

Jane dropped her work and said:

'I think so too, it's too silly to have a chance like this and not use it. I never heard of anyone else outside a book who had such a chance; there must be simply heaps of things we could wish for that wouldn't turn out Dead Sea fish, like these two things have. Do let's think hard, and wish something nice, so that we can have a real jolly day - what there is left of it.'

Jane darned away again like mad, for time was indeed getting on, and everyone began to talk at once. If you had been there you could not possibly have made head or tail of the talk, but these children were used to talking 'by fours', as soldiers march, and each of them could say what it had to say quite comfortably, and listen to the agreeable sound of its own voice, and at the same time have three-quarters of two sharp ears to spare for listening to what the others said. That is an easy example in multiplication of vulgar fractions, but, as I daresay you can't do even that, I won't ask you to tell me whether $3/4 \times 2 = 1\ 1/2$, but I will ask you to believe me that this was the amount of ear each child was able to lend to the others. Lending ears was common in Roman times, as we learn from Shakespeare; but I fear I am getting too instructive.

When the frock was darned, the start for the gravel-pit was delayed by Martha's insisting on everybody's washing its hands - which was nonsense, because nobody had been doing anything at all, except Jane, and how can you get dirty doing nothing? That is a difficult question, and I cannot answer it on paper. In real life I could very soon show you - or you me, which is much more likely.

During the conversation in which the six ears were lent (there were four children, so THAT sum comes right), it had been decided that fifty pounds in two-shilling pieces was the right wish to have. And the lucky children, who could have anything in the wide world by just wishing for it, hurriedly started for the gravel-pit to express their wishes to the Psammead. Martha caught them at the gate, and insisted on their taking the Baby with them.

'Not want him indeed! Why, everybody 'ud want him, a duck! with all their hearts they would; and you know you promised your ma to take him out every blessed day,' said Martha.

'I know we did,' said Robert in gloom, 'but I wish the Lamb wasn't quite so young and small. It would be much better fun taking him out.'

'He'll mend of his youngness with time,' said Martha; 'and as for his smallness, I don't think you'd fancy carrying of him any more, however big he was. Besides he can walk a bit, bless his precious fat legs, a ducky! He feels the benefit of the new-laid air, so he does, a pet!' With this and a kiss, she plumped the Lamb into Anthea's arms, and went back to make new pinafores on the sewing-machine. She was a rapid performer on this instrument.

The Lamb laughed with pleasure, and said, 'Walky wif Panty,' and rode on Robert's back with yells of joy, and tried to feed Jane with stones, and altogether made himself so agreeable that nobody could long be sorry that he was of the party.

The enthusiastic Jane even suggested that they should devote a week's wishes to assuring the Baby's future, by asking such gifts for him as the good fairies give to Infant Princes in proper fairy-tales, but Anthea soberly reminded her that as the Sand-fairy's wishes only lasted till sunset they could not ensure any benefit to the Baby's later years; and Jane owned that it would be better to wish for fifty pounds in two-shilling pieces, and buy the Lamb a three-pound-fifteen rocking-horse, like those in the Army and Navy Stores list, with part of the money.

It was settled that, as soon as they had wished for the money and got it, they would get Mr Crispin to drive them into Rochester again, taking Martha with them, if they could not get out of taking her. And they would make a list of the things they really wanted before they started. Full of high hopes and excellent resolutions, they went round the safe slow cart-road to the gravel-pits, and as they went in between the mounds of gravel a sudden thought came to them, and would have turned their ruddy cheeks pale if they had been children in a book. Being real live children, it only made them stop and look at each other with rather blank and silly expressions. For now they remembered that yesterday, when they had asked the Psammead for boundless wealth, and it was getting ready to fill the quarry with the minted gold of bright guineas - millions of them - it had told the children to run along outside the quarry for fear they should be buried alive in the heavy splendid treasure. And they had run. And so it happened that they had not had time to mark the spot where the Psammead was, with a ring of stones, as before. And it was this thought that put such silly expressions on their faces.

'Never mind,' said the hopeful Jane, 'we'll soon find him.'

But this, though easily said, was hard in the doing. They looked and they looked, and though they found their seaside spades, nowhere could they find the Sand-fairy.

At last they had to sit down and rest - not at all because they were weary or disheartened, of course, but because the Lamb insisted on being put down, and you cannot look very carefully after anything you may have happened to lose in the sand if you have an active baby to look after at the same time. Get someone to drop your best knife in the sand next time you go to the seaside, and then take your baby brother with you when you go to look for it, and you will see that I am right.

The Lamb, as Martha had said, was feeling the benefit of the country air, and he was as frisky as a sandhopper. The elder ones longed to go on talking about the new wishes they would have when (or if) they found the Psammead again. But the Lamb wished to enjoy himself.

He watched his opportunity and threw a handful of sand into Anthea's face, and then suddenly burrowed his own head in the sand and waved his fat legs in the air. Then of course the sand got into his eyes, as it had into Anthea's, and he howled.

The thoughtful Robert had brought one solid brown bottle of ginger-beer with him, relying on a thirst that had never yet failed him. This had to be uncorked hurriedly - it was the only wet thing within reach, and it was necessary to wash the sand out of the Lamb's eyes somehow. Of course the ginger hurt horribly, and he howled more than ever. And, amid his anguish of kicking, the bottle was upset and the beautiful ginger-beer frothed out into the sand and was lost for ever.

It was then that Robert, usually a very patient brother, so far forgot himself as to say:

'Anybody would want him, indeed! Only they don't; Martha doesn't, not really, or she'd jolly well keep him with her. He's a little nuisance, that's what he is. It's too bad. I only wish everybody DID want him with all their hearts; we might get some peace in our lives.'

The Lamb stopped howling now, because Jane had suddenly remembered that there is only one safe way of taking things out of little children's eyes, and that is with your own soft wet tongue. It is quite easy if you love the Baby as much as you ought to.

Then there was a little silence. Robert was not proud of himself for having been so cross, and the others were not proud of him either. You often notice that sort of silence when someone has said something it ought not to - and everyone else holds its tongue and waits for the one who oughtn't to have said it is sorry.

The silence was broken by a sigh - a breath suddenly let out. The children's heads turned as if there had been a string tied to each nose, and someone had pulled all the strings at once.

And everyone saw the Sand-fairy sitting quite close to them, with the expression which it used as a smile on its hairy face.

'Good-morning,' it said; 'I did that quite easily! Everyone wants him now.'

'It doesn't matter,' said Robert sulkily, because he knew he had been behaving rather like a pig. 'No matter who wants him - there's no one here to - anyhow.'

'Ingratitude,' said the Psammead, 'is a dreadful vice.'

'We're not ungrateful,'Jane made haste to say, 'but we didn't REALLY want that wish. Robert only just said it. Can't you take it back and give us a new one?'

'No - I can't,' the Sand-fairy said shortly; 'chopping and changing - it's not business. You ought to be careful what you do wish. There was a little boy once, he'd wished for a Plesiosaurus instead of an Ichthyosaurus, because he was too lazy to remember the easy names of everyday things, and his father had been very vexed with him, and had made him go to bed before tea-time, and wouldn't let him go out in the nice flint boat along with the other children - it was the annual school-treat next day - and he came and flung himself down near me on the morning of the treat, and he kicked his little prehistoric legs about and said he wished he was dead. And of course then he was.'

'How awful!' said the children all together.

'Only till sunset, of course,' the Psammead said; 'still it was quite enough for his father and mother. And he caught it when he woke up - I can tell you. He didn't turn to stone - I forget why - but there must have been some reason. They didn't know being dead is only being asleep, and you're bound to wake up somewhere or other, either where you go to sleep or in some better place. You may be sure he caught it, giving them such a turn. Why, he wasn't allowed to taste

Megatherium for a month after that. Nothing but oysters and periwinkles, and common things like that.'

All the children were quite crushed by this terrible tale. They looked at the Psammead in horror. Suddenly the Lamb perceived that something brown and furry was near him.

'Poof, poof, poofy,' he said, and made a grab.

'It's not a pussy,' Anthea was beginning, when the Sand-fairy leaped back.

'Oh, my left whisker!' it said; 'don't let him touch me. He's wet.'

Its fur stood on end with horror - and indeed a good deal of the ginger-beer had been spilt on the blue smock of the Lamb.

The Psammead dug with its hands and feet, and vanished in an instant and a whirl of sand.

The children marked the spot with a ring of stones.

'We may as well get along home,' said Robert. 'I'll say I'm sorry; but anyway if it's no good it's no harm, and we know where the sandy thing is for to-morrow.'

The others were noble. No one reproached Robert at all. Cyril picked up the Lamb, who was now quite himself again, and off they went by the safe cart-road.

The cart-road from the gravel-pits joins the road almost directly.

At the gate into the road the party stopped to shift the Lamb from Cyril's back to Robert's. And as they paused a very smart open carriage came in sight, with a coachman and a groom on the box, and inside the carriage a lady - very grand indeed, with a dress all white lace and red ribbons and a parasol all red and white - and a white fluffy dog on her lap with a red ribbon round its neck. She looked at the children, and particularly at the Baby, and she smiled at him. The children were used to this, for the Lamb was, as all the servants said, a 'very taking child'. So they waved their hands politely to the lady and expected her to drive on. But she did not. Instead she made the coachman stop. And she beckoned to Cyril, and when he went up to the carriage she said:

'What a dear darling duck of a baby! Oh, I SHOULD so like to adopt it! Do you think its mother would mind?'

'She'd mind very much indeed,' said Anthea shortly.

'Oh, but I should bring it up in luxury, you know. I am Lady Chittenden. You must have seen my photograph in the illustrated papers. They call me a beauty, you know, but of course that's all nonsense. Anyway -'

She opened the carriage door and jumped out. She had the wonderfullest red high-heeled shoes with silver buckles. 'Let me hold him a minute,' she said. And she took the Lamb and held him very awkwardly, as if she was not used to babies.

Then suddenly she jumped into the carriage with the Lamb in her arms and slammed the door and said, 'Drive on!'

The Lamb roared, the little white dog barked, and the coachman hesitated.

'Drive on, I tell you!' cried the lady; and the coachman did, for, as he said afterwards, it was as much as his place was worth not to.

The four children looked at each other, and then with one accord they rushed after the carriage and held on behind. Down the dusty road went the smart carriage, and after it, at double-quick time, ran the twinkling legs of the Lamb's brothers and sisters.

The Lamb howled louder and louder, but presently his howls changed by slow degree to hiccupy gurgles, and then all was still and they knew he had gone to sleep.

The carriage went on, and the eight feet that twinkled through the dust were growing quite stiff and tired before the carriage stopped at the lodge of a grand park. The children crouched down behind the carriage, and the lady got out. She looked at the Baby as it lay on the carriage seat, and hesitated.

'The darling - I won't disturb it,' she said, and went into the lodge to talk to the woman there about a setting of Buff Orpington eggs that had not turned out well.

The coachman and footman sprang from the box and bent over the sleeping Lamb.

'Fine boy - wish he was mine,' said the coachman.

'He wouldn't favour YOU much,' said the groom sourly; 'too 'andsome.'

The coachman pretended not to hear. He said:

'Wonder at her now - I do really! Hates kids. Got none of her own, and can't abide other folkses'.'

The children, crouching in the white dust under the carriage, exchanged uncomfortable glances.

'Tell you what,' the coachman went on firmly, 'blowed if I don't hide the little nipper in the hedge and tell her his brothers took 'im! Then I'll come back for him afterwards.'

'No, you don't,' said the footman. 'I've took to that kid so as never was. If anyone's to have him, it's me - so there!'

52

'Stow your gab!' the coachman rejoined. 'You don't want no kids, and, if you did, one kid's the same as another to you. But I'm a married man and a judge of breed. I knows a first-rate yearling when I sees him. I'm a-goin' to 'ave him, an' least said soonest mended.'

'I should 'a' thought,' said the footman sneeringly, you'd a'most enough. What with Alfred, an' Albert, an' Louise, an' Victor Stanley, and Helena Beatrice, and another -'

The coachman hit the footman in the chin - the foot- man hit the coachman in the waistcoat - the next minute the two were fighting here and there, in and out, up and down, and all over everywhere, and the little dog jumped on the box of the carriage and began barking like mad.

Cyril, still crouching in the dust, waddled on bent legs to the side of the carriage farthest from the battlefield. He unfastened the door of the carriage - the two men were far too much occupied with their quarrel to notice anything - took the Lamb in his arms, and, still stooping, carried the sleeping baby a dozen yards along the road to where a stile led into a wood. The others followed, and there among the hazels and young oaks and sweet chestnuts, covered by high strong-scented bracken, they all lay hidden till the angry voices of the men were hushed at the angry voice of the red-and-white lady, and, after a long and anxious search, the carriage at last drove away.

'My only hat!' said Cyril, drawing a deep breath as the sound of wheels at last died away. 'Everyone DOES want him now - and no mistake! That Sammyadd has done us again! Tricky brute! For any sake, let's get the kid safe home.'

So they peeped out, and finding on the right hand only lonely white road, and nothing but lonely white road on the left, they took courage, and the road, Anthea carrying the sleeping Lamb.

Adventures dogged their footsteps. A boy with a bundle of faggots on his back dropped his bundle by the roadside and asked to look at the Baby, and then offered to carry him; but Anthea was not to be caught that way twice. They all walked on, but the boy followed, and Cyril and Robert couldn't make him go away till they had more than once invited him to smell their fists. Afterwards a little girl in a blue-and-white checked pinafore actually followed them for a quarter of a mile crying for 'the precious Baby', and then she was only got rid of by threats of tying her to a tree in the wood with all their pocket-handkerchiefs. 'So that the bears can come and eat you as soon as it gets dark,' said Cyril severely. Then she went off crying. It presently seemed wise, to the brothers and sisters of the Baby, who was wanted by everyone, to hide in the hedge whenever they saw anyone coming, and thus they managed to prevent the Lamb from arousing the inconvenient affection of a milkman, a stone-breaker, and a man who drove a cart with a paraffin barrel at the back of it. They were nearly home when the worst thing of all happened. Turning a corner suddenly they came upon two vans, a tent, and a company of gipsies encamped by the side of the road. The vans were hung all round with wicker chairs and cradles, and flower-stands and feather brushes. A lot of ragged children were industriously making dust-pies in the road, two men lay on the grass smoking, and three women were doing the family washing in an old red watering-can with the top broken off.

In a moment all the gipsies, men, women, and children, surrounded Anthea and the Baby.

'Let me hold him, little lady,' said one of the gipsy women, who had a mahogany-coloured face and dust-coloured hair; 'I won't hurt a hair of his head, the little picture!'

'I'd rather not,' said Anthea.

'Let me have him,' said the other woman, whose face was also of the hue of mahogany, and her hair jet-black, in greasy curls. 'I've nineteen of my own, so I have.'

'No,' said Anthea bravely, but her heart beat so that it nearly choked her.

Then one of the men pushed forward.

'Swelp me if it ain't!' he cried, 'my own long-lost cheild! Have he a strawberry mark on his left ear? No? Then he's my own babby, stolen from me in hinnocent hinfancy. 'And 'im over - and we'll not 'ave the law on yer this time.'

He snatched the Baby from Anthea, who turned scarlet and burst into tears of pure rage.

The others were standing quite still; this was much the most terrible thing that had ever happened to them. Even being taken up by the police in Rochester was nothing to this. Cyril was quite white, and his hands trembled a little, but he made a sign to the others to shut up. He was silent a minute, thinking hard. Then he said:

'We don't want to keep him if he's yours. But you see he's used to us. You shall have him if you want him.'

'No, no!' cried Anthea - and Cyril glared at her.

'Of course we want him,' said the women, trying to get the Baby out of the man's arms. The Lamb howled loudly.

'Oh, he's hurt!' shrieked Anthea; and Cyril, in a savage undertone, bade her 'Stow it!'

'You trust to me,' he whispered. 'Look here,' he went on, 'he's awfully tiresome with people he doesn't know very well. Suppose we stay here a bit till he gets used to you, and then when it's bedtime I give you my word of honour we'll go away and let you keep him if you want to. And then when we're gone you can decide which of you is to have him, as you all want him so much.'

'That's fair enough,' said the man who was holding the Baby, trying to loosen the red neckerchief which the Lamb had caught hold of and drawn round his mahogany throat so tight that he could hardly breathe. The gipsies whispered together, and Cyril took the chance to whisper too. He said, 'Sunset! we'll get away then.'

And then his brothers and sisters were filled with wonder and admiration at his having been so clever as to remember this.

'Oh, do let him come to us!' said Jane. 'See we'll sit down here and take care of him for you till he gets used to you.'

'What about dinner?' said Robert suddenly. The others looked at him with scorn. 'Fancy bothering about your beastly dinner when your br - I mean when the Baby' - Jane whispered hotly. Robert carefully winked at her and went on:

'You won't mind my just running home to get our dinner?' he said to the gipsy; 'I can bring it out here in a basket.'

His brother and sisters felt themselves very noble, and despised him. They did not know his thoughtful secret intention. But the gipsies did in a minute. 'Oh yes!' they said; 'and then fetch the police with a pack of lies about it being your baby instead of ours! D'jever catch a weasel asleep?' they asked.

'If you're hungry you can pick a bit along of us,' said the light-haired gipsy woman, not unkindly. 'Here, Levi, that blessed kid'll howl all his buttons off. Give him to the little lady, and let's see if they can't get him used to us a bit.'

So the Lamb was handed back; but the gipsies crowded so closely that he could not possibly stop howling. Then the man with the red handkerchief said:

'Here, Pharaoh, make up the fire; and you girls see to the pot. Give the kid a chanst.' So the gipsies, very much against their will, went off to their work, and the children and the Lamb were left sitting on the grass.

'He'll be all right at sunset,'Jane whispered. 'But, oh, it is awful! Suppose they are frightfully angry when they come to their senses! They might beat us, or leave us tied to trees, or something.'

'No, they won't,' Anthea said. ('Oh, my Lamb, don't cry any more, it's all right, Panty's got oo, duckie!) They aren't unkind people, or they wouldn't be going to give us any dinner.'

'Dinner?' said Robert. 'I won't touch their nasty dinner. It would choke me!'

The others thought so too then. But when the dinner was ready - it turned out to be supper, and happened between four and five - they were all glad enough to take what they could get. It was boiled rabbit, with onions, and some bird rather like a chicken, but stringier about its legs and with a stronger taste. The Lamb had bread soaked in hot water and brown sugar sprinkled on the top. He liked this very much, and consented to let the two gipsy women feed him with it, as he sat on Anthea's lap. All that long hot afternoon Robert and Cyril and Anthea and Jane had to keep the Lamb amused and happy, while the gipsies looked eagerly on. By the time the shadows grew long and black across the meadows he had really 'taken to' the woman with the light hair, and even consented to kiss his hand to the children, and to stand up and bow, with his hand on his chest - 'like a gentleman' - to the two men. The whole gipsy camp was in raptures with him, and his brothers and sisters could not help taking some pleasure in showing off his accomplishments to an audience so interested and enthusiastic. But they longed for sunset.

'We're getting into the habit of longing for sunset,' Cyril whispered. 'How I do wish we could wish something really sensible, that would be of some use, so that we should be quite sorry when sunset came.'

The shadows got longer and longer, and at last there were no separate shadows any more, but one soft glowing shadow over everything; for the sun was out of sight - behind the hill - but he had not really set yet. The people who make the laws about lighting bicycle lamps are the people who decide when the sun sets; he has to do it, too, to the minute, or they would know the reason why!

But the gipsies were getting impatient.

'Now, young uns,' the red-handkerchief man said,'it's time you were laying of your heads on your pillowses - so it is! The kid's all right and friendly with us now - so you just hand him over and sling that hook o' yours like you said.'

The women and children came crowding round the Lamb, arms were held out, fingers snapped invitingly, friendly faces beaming with admiring smiles; but all failed to tempt the loyal Lamb. He clung with arms and legs to Jane, who happened to be holding him, and uttered the gloomiest roar of the whole day.

'It's no good,' the woman said, 'hand the little poppet over, miss. We'll soon quiet him.'

And still the sun would not set.

'Tell her about how to put him to bed,' whispered Cyril; 'anything to gain time - and be ready to bolt when the sun really does make up its silly old mind to set.'

'Yes, I'll hand him over in just one minute,' Anthea began, talking very fast - 'but do let me just tell you he has a warm bath every night and cold in the morning, and he has a crockery rabbit to go into the warm bath with him, and little Samuel saying his prayers in white china on a red cushion for the cold bath; and if you let the soap get into his eyes, the Lamb -'

'Lamb kyes,' said he - he had stopped roaring to listen.

The woman laughed. 'As if I hadn't never bath'd a babby!' she said. 'Come - give us a hold of him. Come to 'Melia, my precious.'

'G'way, ugsie!' replied the Lamb at once.

58

'Yes, but,' Anthea went on, 'about his meals; you really MUST let me tell you he has an apple or a banana every morning, and bread-and-milk for breakfast, and an egg for his tea sometimes, and -'

'I've brought up ten,' said the black-ringleted woman, 'besides the others. Come, miss, 'and 'im over - I can't bear it no longer. I just must give him a hug.'

'We ain't settled yet whose he's to be, Esther,' said one of the men.

'It won't be you, Esther, with seven of 'em at your tail a'ready.'

'I ain't so sure of that,' said Esther's husband.

'And ain't I nobody, to have a say neither?' said the husband of 'Melia.

Zillah, the girl, said, 'An' me? I'm a single girl - and no one but 'im to look after - I ought to have him.'

'Hold yer tongue!'

'Shut your mouth!'

'Don't you show me no more of your imperence!'

Everyone was getting very angry. The dark gipsy faces were frowning and anxious-looking. Suddenly a change swept over them, as if some invisible sponge had wiped away these cross and anxious expressions, and left only a blank.

The children saw that the sun really HAD set. But they were afraid to move. And the gipsies were feeling so muddled, because of the invisible sponge that had washed all the feelings of the last few hours out of their hearts, that they could not say a word.

The children hardly dared to breathe. Suppose the gipsies, when they recovered speech, should be furious to think how silly they had been all day.

It was an awkward moment. Suddenly Anthea, greatly daring, held out the Lamb to the red-handkerchief man.

'Here he is!' she said.

The man drew back. 'I shouldn't like to deprive you, miss,' he said hoarsely.

'Anyone who likes can have my share of him,' said the other man.

'After all, I've got enough of my own,' said Esther.

'He's a nice little chap, though,' said Amelia. She was the only one who now looked affectionately at the whimpering Lamb.

Zillah said, 'If I don't think I must have had a touch of the sun. I don't want him.'

'Then shall we take him away?' said Anthea.

'Well, suppose you do,' said Pharaoh heartily, 'and we'll say no more about it!'

And with great haste all the gipsies began to be busy about their tents for the night. All but Amelia. She went with the children as far as the bend in the road - and there she said:

'Let me give him a kiss, miss - I don't know what made us go for to behave so silly. Us gipsies don't steal babies, whatever they may tell you when you're naughty. We've enough of our own, mostly. But I've lost all mine.'

She leaned towards the Lamb; and he, looking in her eyes, unexpectedly put up a grubby soft paw and stroked her face.

'Poor, poor!' said the Lamb. And he let the gipsy woman kiss him, and, what is more, he kissed her brown cheek in return - a very nice kiss, as all his kisses are, and not a wet one like some babies give. The gipsy woman moved her finger about on his forehead, as if she had been writing something there, and the same with his chest and his hands and his feet; then she said:

'May he be brave, and have the strong head to think with, and the strong heart to love with, and the strong hands to work with, and the strong feet to travel with, and always come safe home to his own.' Then she said something in a strange language no one could understand, and suddenly added:

'Well, I must be saying "so long" - and glad to have made your acquaintance.' And she turned and went back to her home - the tent by the grassy roadside.

The children looked after her till she was out of sight. Then Robert said, 'How silly of her! Even sunset didn't put her right. What rot she talked!'

'Well,' said Cyril, 'if you ask me, I think it was rather decent of her -'

'Decent?' said Anthea; 'it was very nice indeed of her. I think she's a dear.'

'She's just too frightfully nice for anything,' said Jane.

And they went home - very late for tea and unspeakably late for dinner. Martha scolded, of course. But the Lamb was safe.

'I say - it turned out we wanted the Lamb as much as anyone,' said Robert, later.

'Of course.'

'But do you feel different about it now the sun's set?'

'No,' said all the others together.
'Then it's lasted over sunset with us.'

'No, it hasn't,' Cyril explained. 'The wish didn't do anything to US. We always wanted him with all our hearts when we were our proper selves, only we were all pigs this morning; especially you, Robert.' Robert bore this much with a strange calm.

'I certainly THOUGHT I didn't want him this morning,' said he. 'Perhaps I was a pig. But everything looked so different when we thought we were going to lose him.'

CHAPTER 4. WINGS

The next day was very wet - too wet to go out, and far too wet to think of disturbing a Sand-fairy so sensitive to water that he still, after thousands of years, felt the pain of once having had his left whisker wetted. It was a long day, and it was not till the afternoon that all the children suddenly decided to write letters to their mother. It was Robert who had the misfortune to upset the ink-pot - an unusually deep and full one - straight into that part of Anthea's desk where she had long pretended that an arrangement of gum and cardboard painted with Indian ink was a secret drawer. It was not exactly Robert's fault; it was only his misfortune that he chanced to be lifting the ink across the desk just at the moment when Anthea had got it open, and that that same moment should have been the one chosen by the Lamb to get under the table and break his squeaking bird. There was a sharp convenient wire inside the bird, and of course the Lamb ran the wire into Robert's leg at once; and so, without anyone's meaning to, the secret drawer was flooded with ink. At the same time a stream was poured over Anthea's half-finished letter. So that her letter was something like this:

DARLING MOTHER, I hope you are quite well, and I hope Granny is better. The other day we …

Then came a flood of ink, and at the bottom these words in pencil -

It was not me upset the ink, but it took such a time clearing up, so no more as it is post-time. - From your loving daughter, ANTHEA.

Robert's letter had not even been begun. He had been drawing a ship on the blotting-paper while he was trying to think of what to say. And of course after the ink was upset he had to help Anthea to clean out her desk, and he promised to make her another secret drawer, better than the other. And she said, 'Well, make it now.' So it was post-time and his letter wasn't done. And the secret drawer wasn't done either.

Cyril wrote a long letter, very fast, and then went to set a trap for slugs that he had read about in the Home-made Gardener, and when it was post-time the letter could not be found, and it never was found. Perhaps the slugs ate it.

jane's letter was the only one that went. She meant to tell her mother all about the Psammead - in fact -they had all meant to do this - but she spent so long thinking how to spell the word that there was no time to tell the story properly, and it is useless to tell a story unless you do tell it properly, so she had to be contented with this -

MY DEAR MOTHER DEAR,

We are all as as good as we can, like you told us to, and the Lamb has a little cold, but Martha says it is nothing, only he upset the goldfish into himself yesterday morning. When we were up at the sand-pit the other day we went round by the safe way where carts go, and we found a —

Half an hour went by before Jane felt quite sure that they could none of them spell Psammead. And they could not find it in the dictionary either, though they looked. Then Jane hastily finished her letter.

We found a strange thing, but it is nearly post-time, so no more at present from your little girl, JANE.

Ps. - If you could have a wish come true, what would you have?

Then the postman was heard blowing his horn, and Robert rushed out in the rain to stop his cart and give him the letter. And that was how it happened that, though all the children meant to tell their mother about the Sand-fairy, somehow or other she never got to know. There were other reasons why she never got to know, but these come later.

The next day Uncle Richard came and took them all to Maidstone in a wagonette - all except the Lamb. Uncle Richard was the very best kind of uncle. He bought them toys at Maidstone. He took them into a shop and let them choose exactly what they wanted, without any restrictions about price, and no nonsense about things being instructive. It is very wise to let children choose exactly what they like, because they are very foolish and inexperienced, and sometimes they will choose a really instructive thing without meaning to. This happened to Robert, who chose, at the last moment, and in a great hurry, a box with pictures on it of winged bulls with men's heads and winged men with eagles' heads. He thought there would be animals inside, the same as on the box. When he got it home it was a Sunday puzzle about ancient Nineveh! The others chose in haste, and were happy at leisure. Cyril had a model engine, and the girls had two dolls, as well as a china tea-set with forget-me-nots on it, to be 'between them'. The boys' 'between them' was bow and arrows.

Then Uncle Richard took them on the beautiful Medway in a boat, and then they all had tea at a beautiful pastrycook's, and when they reached home it was far too late to have any wishes that day.

They did not tell Uncle Richard anything about the Psammead. I do not know why. And they do not know why. But I daresay you can guess.

The day after Uncle Richard had behaved so handsomely was a very hot day indeed. The people who decide what the weather is to be, and put its orders down for it in the newspapers every morning, said afterwards that it was the hottest day there had been for years. They had ordered it to be 'warmer - some showers', and warmer it certainly was. In fact it was so busy being warmer that it had no time to attend to the order about showers, so there weren't any.

Have you ever been up at five o'clock on a fine summer morning? It is very beautiful. The sunlight is pinky and yellowy, and all the grass and trees are covered with dew-diamonds. And all the shadows go the opposite way to the way they do in the evening, which is very interesting and makes you feel as though you were in a new other world.

Anthea awoke at five. She had made herself wake, and I must tell you how it is done, even if it keeps you waiting for the story to go on.

You get into bed at night, and lie down quite flat on your little back with your hands straight down by your sides. Then you say 'I must wake up at five' (or six, or seven, or eight, or nine, or whatever the time is that you want), and as you say it you push your chin down on to your chest and then bang your head back on the pillow. And you do this as many times as there are ones in the time you want to wake up at. (It is quite an easy sum.) Of course everything depends on your really wanting to get up at five (or six, or seven, or eight, or nine); if you don't really want to, it's all of no use. But if you do - well, try it and see. Of course in this, as in doing Latin proses or getting into mischief, practice makes perfect. Anthea was quite perfect.

At the very moment when she opened her eyes she heard the black-and-gold clock down in the dining-room strike eleven. So she knew it was three minutes to five. The black-and-gold clock always struck wrong, but it was all right when you knew what it meant. It was like a person talking a foreign language. If you know the language it is just as easy to understand as English. And Anthea knew the clock language. She was very sleepy, but she jumped out of bed and put her face and hands into a basin of cold water. This is a fairy charm that prevents your wanting to get back into bed again. Then she dressed, and folded up her nightgown. She did not tumble it together by the sleeves, but folded it by the seams from the hem, and that will show you the kind of well-brought-up little girl she was.

Then she took her shoes in her hand and crept softly down the stairs. She opened the dining-room window and climbed out. It would have been just as easy to go out by the door, but the window was more romantic, and less likely to be noticed by Martha.

'I will always get up at five,' she said to herself. 'It was quite too awfully pretty for anything.'

Her heart was beating very fast, for she was carrying out a plan quite her own. She could not be sure that it was a good plan, but she was quite sure that it would not be any better if she were to tell the others about it. And she had a feeling that, right or wrong, she would rather go through with it alone. She put on her shoes under the iron veranda, on the red-and-yellow shining tiles, and then she ran straight to the sand-pit, and found the Psammead's place, and dug it out; it was very cross indeed.

'It's too bad,' it said, fluffing up its fur like pigeons do their feathers at Christmas time. 'The weather's arctic, and it's the middle of the night.'

'I'm so sorry,' said Anthea gently, and she took off her white pinafore and covered the Sand-fairy up with it, all but its head, its bat's ears, and its eyes that were like a snail's eyes.

'Thank you,' it said, 'that's better. What's the wish this morning?'

'I don't know,' said she; 'that's just it. You see we've been very unlucky, so far. I wanted to talk to you about it. But - would you mind not giving me any wishes till after breakfast? It's so hard to talk to anyone if they jump out at you with wishes you don't really want!'

'You shouldn't say you wish for things if you don't wish for them. In the old days people almost always knew whether it was Megatherium or Ichthyosaurus they really wanted for dinner.'

'I'll try not,' said Anthea, 'but I do wish -'

'Look out!' said the Psammead in a warning voice, and it began to blow itself out.

'Oh, this isn't a magic wish - it's just - I should be so glad if you'd not swell yourself out and nearly burst to give me anything just now. Wait till the others are here.'

'Well, well,' it said indulgently, but it shivered.

'Would you,' asked Anthea kindly - 'would you like to come and sit on my lap? You'd be warmer, and I could turn the skirt of my frock up round you. I'd be very careful.'

Anthea had never expected that it would, but it did.

'Thank you,' it said; 'you really are rather thoughtful.' It crept on to her lap and snuggled down, and she put her arms round it with a rather frightened gentleness. 'Now then!' it said.

'Well then,' said Anthea, 'everything we have wished has turned out rather horrid. I wish you would advise us. You are so old, you must be very wise.'

'I was always generous from a child,' said the Sand-fairy. 'I've spent the whole of my waking hours in giving. But one thing I won't give - that's advice.'

'You see,' Anthea went on, it's such a wonderful thing - such a splendid, glorious chance. It's so good and kind and dear of you to

67

give us our wishes, and it seems such a pity it should all be wasted just because we are too silly to know what to wish for.'

Anthea had meant to say that - and she had not wanted to say it before the others. It's one thing to say you're silly, and quite another to say that other people are.

'Child,' said the Sand-fairy sleepily, 'I can only advise you to think before you speak -'

'But I thought you never gave advice.'

'That piece doesn't count,' it said. 'You'll never take it! Besides, it's not original. It's in all the copy-books.'

'But won't you just say if you think wings would be a silly wish?'

'Wings?' it said. 'I should think you might do worse. Only, take care you aren't flying high at sunset. There was a little Ninevite boy I heard of once. He was one of King Sennacherib's sons, and a traveller brought him a Psammead. He used to keep it in a box of sand on the palace terrace. It was a dreadful degradation for one of us, of course; still the boy was the Assyrian King's son. And one day he wished for wings and got them. But he forgot that they would turn into stone at sunset, and when they did he fell slap on to one of the winged lions at the top of his father's great staircase; and what with HIS stone wings and the lions' stone wings - well, it's not a pretty story! But I believe the boy enjoyed himself very much till then.'

'Tell me,' said Anthea, 'why don't our wishes turn into stone now? Why do they just vanish?'

'Autres temps, autres moeurs,' said the creature.

'Is that the Ninevite language?' asked Anthea, who had learned no foreign language at school except French.

'What I mean is,' the Psammead went on, 'that in the old days people wished for good solid everyday gifts - Mammoths and Pterodactyls and things - and those could be turned into stone as easy as not. But people wish such high-flying fanciful things nowadays. How are you going to turn being beautiful as the day, or being wanted by everybody, into stone? You see it can't be done. And it would never do to have two rules, so they simply vanish. If being beautiful as the day COULD be turned into stone it would last an awfully long time, you know - much longer than you would. just look at the Greek statues. It's just as well as it is. Good-bye. I AM so sleepy.'

It jumped off her lap - dug frantically, and vanished.

Anthea was late for breakfast. It was Robert who quietly poured a spoonful of treacle down the Lamb's frock, so that he had to be taken away and washed thoroughly directly after breakfast. And it was of course a very naughty thing to do; yet it served two purposes - it delighted the Lamb, who loved above all things to be completely sticky, and it engaged Martha's attention so that the others could slip away to the sand-pit without the Lamb.

They did it, and in the lane Anthea, breathless from the scurry of that slipping, panted out -

'I want to propose we take turns to wish. Only, nobody's to have a wish if the others don't think it's a nice wish. Do you agree?'

'Who's to have first wish?' asked Robert cautiously.

'Me, if you don't mind,' said Anthea apologetically. 'And I've thought about it - and it's wings.'

There was a silence. The others rather wanted to find fault, but it was hard, because the word 'wings' raised a flutter of joyous excitement in every breast.

'Not so dusty,' said Cyril generously; and Robert added, 'Really, Panther, you're not quite such a fool as you look.'

Jane said, 'I think it would be perfectly lovely. It's like a bright dream of delirium.' They found the Sand-fairy easily. Anthea said:

'I wish we all had beautiful wings to fly with.'

The Sand-fairy blew himself out, and next moment each child felt a funny feeling, half heaviness and half lightness, on its shoulders. The Psammead put its head on one side and turned its snail's eyes from one to the other.

'Not so dusty,' it said dreamily. 'But really, Robert, you're not quite such an angel as you look.' Robert almost blushed.

The wings were very big, and more beautiful than you can possibly imagine - for they were soft and smooth, and every feather lay neatly in its place. And the feathers were of the most lovely mixed changing colours, like the rainbow, or iridescent glass, or the beautiful scum that sometimes floats on water that is not at all nice to drink.

'Oh - but can we fly?'Jane said, standing anxiously first on one foot and then on the other.

'Look out!' said Cyril; 'you're treading on my wing.'

'Does it hurt?' asked Anthea with interest; but no one answered, for Robert had spread his wings and jumped up, and now he was slowly rising in the air. He looked very awkward in his knickerbocker suit - his boots in particular hung helplessly, and seemed much larger than when he was standing in them. But the others cared but little how he looked - or how they looked, for that matter. For now they all spread out their wings and rose in the air. Of course you all know what flying feels like, because everyone has dreamed about flying, and it seems so beautifully easy - only, you can never remember how you did it; and as a rule you have to do it without wings, in your dreams, which is more clever and uncommon, but not so easy to remember the rule for. Now the four children rose flapping from the ground, and you can't think how good the air felt running against their faces.

Their wings were tremendously wide when they were spread out, and they had to fly quite a long way apart so as not to get in each other's way. But little things like this are easily learned.

All the words in the English Dictionary, and in the Greek Lexicon as well, are, I find, of no use at all to tell you exactly what it feels like to be flying, so I Will not try. But I will say that to look DOWN on the fields and woods, instead of along at them, is something like looking at a beautiful live map, where, instead of silly colours on paper, you have real moving sunny woods and green fields laid out one after the other. As Cyril said, and I can't think where he got hold of such a strange expression, 'It does you a fair treat!' It was most wonderful and more like real magic than any wish the children had had yet. They flapped and flew and sailed on their great rainbow wings, between green earth and blue sky; and they flew right over Rochester and then swerved round towards Maidstone, and presently they all began to feel extremely hungry. Curiously enough, this happened when they were flying rather low, and just as they were crossing an orchard where some early plums shone red and ripe.

They paused on their wings. I cannot explain to you how this is done, but it is something like treading water when you are swimming, and hawks do it extremely well.

'Yes, I daresay,' said Cyril, though no one had spoken. 'But stealing is stealing even if you've got wings.'

'Do you really think so?' said Jane briskly. 'If you've got wings you're a bird, and no one minds birds breaking the commandments. At least, they MAY mind, but the birds always do it, and no one scolds them or sends them to prison.'

It was not so easy to perch on a plum-tree as you might think, because the rainbow wings were so very large; but somehow they all managed to do it, and the plums were certainly very sweet and juicy.

Fortunately, it was not till they had all had quite as many plums as were good for them that they saw a stout man, who looked exactly as though he owned the plum-trees, come hurrying through the orchard gate with a thick stick, and with one accord they disentangled their wings from the plum-laden branches and began to fly.

The man stopped short, with his mouth open. For he had seen the boughs of his trees moving and twitching, and he had said to himself, 'The young varmints - at it again!' And he had come out at once, for the lads of the village had taught him in past seasons that plums want looking after. But when he saw the rainbow wings flutter up out of the plum-tree he felt that he must have gone quite mad, and he did not like the feeling at all. And when Anthea looked down and saw his mouth go slowly open, and stay so, and his face become green and mauve in patches, she called out:

'Don't be frightened,' and felt hastily in her pocket for a threepenny-bit with a hole in it, which she had meant to hang on a ribbon round her neck, for luck. She hovered round the unfortunate plum-owner, and said, 'We have had some of your plums; we thought it wasn't stealing, but now I am not so sure. So here's some money to pay for them.'

She swooped down towards the terror-stricken grower of plums, and slipped the coin into the pocket of his jacket, and in a few flaps she had rejoined the others.

The farmer sat down on the grass, suddenly and heavily.

'Well - I'm blessed!' he said. 'This here is what they call delusions, I suppose. But this here threepenny' - he had pulled it out and bitten it - 'THAT'S real enough. Well, from this day forth I'll be a better man. It's the kind of thing to sober a chap for life, this is. I'm glad it was only wings, though. I'd rather see birds as aren't there, and couldn't be, even if they pretend to talk, than some things as I could name.'

He got up slowly and heavily, and went indoors, and he was so nice to his wife that day that she felt quite happy, and said to herself, 'Law, whatever have a-come to the man!' and smartened herself up and put a blue ribbon bow at the place where her collar fastened on, and looked so pretty that he was kinder than ever. So perhaps the winged children really did do one good thing that day. If so, it was the only one; for really there is nothing like wings for getting you into trouble. But, on the other hand, if you arc in trouble, there is nothing like wings for getting you out of it.

This was the case in the matter of the fierce dog who sprang out at them when they had folded up their wings as small as possible and were going up to a farm door to ask for a crust of bread and cheese, for in spite of the plums they were soon just as hungry as ever again.

Now there is no doubt whatever that, if the four had been ordinary wingless children, that black and fierce dog would have had a good bite out of the brown-stockinged leg of Robert, who was the nearest. But at first growl there was a flutter of wings, and the dog was left to strain at his chain and stand on his hind-legs as if he were trying to fly too.

They tried several other farms, but at those where there were no dogs the people were far too frightened to do anything but scream; and at last when it was nearly four o'clock, and their wings were getting miserably stiff and tired, they alighted on a church-tower and held a council of war.

'We can't possibly fly all the way home without dinner or tea,' said Robert with desperate decision.

'And nobody will give us any dinner, or even lunch, let alone tea,' said Cyril.

'Perhaps the clergyman here might,' suggested Anthea. 'He must know all about angels -'

'Anybody could see we're not that,' said Jane. 'Look at Robert's boots and Squirrel's plaid necktie.'

'Well,' said Cyril firmly, 'if the country you're in won't SELL provisions, you TAKE them. In wars I mean. I'm quite certain you do. And even in other stories no good brother would allow his little sisters to starve in the midst of plenty.'

'Plenty?' repeated Robert hungrily; and the others looked vaguely round the bare leads of the church- tower, and murmured, 'In the midst of?'

'Yes,' said Cyril impressively. 'There is a larder window at the side of the clergyman's house, and I saw things to eat inside - custard pudding and cold chicken and tongue - and pies - and jam. It's rather a high window - but with wings -'

'How clever of you!' said Jane.

'Not at all,' said Cyril modestly; 'any born general - Napoleon or the Duke of Marlborough - would have seen it just the same as I did.'

'It seems very wrong,' said Anthea.

'Nonsense,' said Cyril. 'What was it Sir Philip Sidney said when the soldier wouldn't stand him a drink? - "My necessity is greater than his".'

'We'll club our money, though, and leave it to pay for the things, won't we?' Anthea was persuasive, and very nearly in tears, because it is most trying to feel enormously hungry and unspeakably sinful at one and the same time.

'Some of it,' was the cautious reply.

Everyone now turned out its pockets on the lead roof of the tower, where visitors for the last hundred and fifty years had cut their own and their sweethearts' initials with penknives in the soft lead. There was five-and-sevenpence-halfpenny altogether, and even the upright Anthea admitted that that was too much to pay for four peoples dinners. Robert said he thought eighteen pence.

And half-a-crown was finally agreed to be 'hand- some'.

So Anthea wrote on the back of her last term's report, which happened to be in her pocket, and from which she first tore her own name and that of the school, the following letter:

DEAR REVEREND CLERGYMAN,

We are very hungry indeed because of having to fly all day, and we think it is not stealing when you are starving to death. We are afraid to ask you for fear you should say 'No', because of course you know about angels, but you would not think we were angels. We will only take the nessessities of life, and no pudding or pie, to show you it is not grediness but true starvation that makes us make your larder stand and deliver. But we are not highwaymen by trade.

'Cut it short,' said the others with one accord. And Anthea hastily added:

Our intentions are quite honourable if you only knew. And here is half-a-crown to show we are sinseer and grateful. Thank you for your kind hospitality.
                    FROM Us FOUR.

The half-crown was wrapped in this letter, and all the children felt that when the clergyman had read it he would understand everything, as well as anyone could who had not seen the wings.

'Now,' said Cyril,"of course there's some risk; we'd better fly straight down the other side of the tower and then flutter low across the churchyard and in through the shrubbery. There doesn't seem to be anyone about. But you never know. The window looks out into the shrubbery. It is embowered in foliage, like a window in a story. I'll go in and get the things. Robert and Anthea can take them as I hand them out through the window; and Jane can keep watch - her eyes are sharp - and whistle if she sees anyone about. Shut up, Robert! she can whistle quite well enough for that, anyway. It ought not to be a very good whistle - it'll sound more natural and birdlike. Now then - off we go!'

I cannot pretend that stealing is right. I can only say that on this occasion it did not look like stealing to the hungry four, but appeared in the light of a fair and reasonable business transaction. They had never happened to learn that a tongue - hardly cut into - a chicken and a half, a loaf of bread, and a syphon of soda-water cannot be bought in shops for half-a-crown. These were the necessaries of life, which Cyril handed out of the larder window when, quite unobserved and without hindrance or adventure, he had led the others to that happy spot. He felt that to refrain from jam, apple turnovers, cake, and mixed candied peel was a really heroic act - and I agree with him. He was also proud of not taking the custard pudding - and there I think he was wrong - because if he had taken it there would have been a difficulty about returning the dish; no one, however starving, has a right to steal china pie-dishes with little pink flowers on them. The soda-water syphon was different. They could not do without something to drink, and as the maker's name was on it they felt sure it would be returned to him wherever they might leave it. If they had time they would take it back themselves. The man appeared to live in Rochester, which would not be much out of their way home.

Everything was carried up to the top of the tower, and laid down on a sheet of kitchen paper which Cyril had found on the top shelf of the larder. As he unfolded it, Anthea said, 'I don't think THAT'S a necessity of life.'

'Yes, it is,' said he. 'We must put the things down somewhere to cut them up; and I heard father say the other day people got diseases from germans in rain-water. Now there must be lots of rain-water here - and when it dries up the germans are left, and they'd get into the things, and we should all die of scarlet fever.'

'What are germans?'

'Little waggly things you see with microscopes,' said Cyril, with a scientific air. 'They give you every illness you can think of! I'm sure the paper was a necessary, just as much as the bread and meat and water. Now then! Oh, my eyes, I am hungry!'

I do not wish to describe the picnic party on the top of the tower. You can imagine well enough what it is like to carve a chicken and a tongue with a knife that has only one blade - and that snapped off short about half-way down. But it was done. Eating with your fingers is greasy and difficult - and paper dishes soon get to look very spotty and horrid. But one thing you CAN'T imagine, and that is how soda-water behaves when you try to drink it straight out of a syphon - especially a quite full one. But if imagination will not help you, experience will, and you can easily try it for yourself if you can get a grown-up to give you the syphon. If you want to have a really thorough experience, put the tube in your mouth and press the handle very suddenly and very hard. You had better do it when you are alone - and out of doors is best for this experiment.

However you eat them, tongue and chicken and new bread are very good things, and no one minds being sprinkled a little with soda-water on a really fine hot day. So that everyone enjoyed the dinner very much indeed, and everyone ate as much as it possibly could: first, because it was extremely hungry; and secondly, because, as I said, tongue and chicken and new bread are very nice.

Now, I daresay you will have noticed that if you have to wait for your dinner till long after the proper time, and then eat a great deal more dinner than usual, and sit in the hot sun on the top of a church-tower - or even anywhere else - you become soon and strangely sleepy. Now Anthea and Jane and Cyril and Robert were very like you in many ways, and when they had eaten all they could, and drunk all there was, they became sleepy, strangely and soon - especially Anthea, because she had got up so early.

One by one they left off talking and leaned back, and before it was a quarter of an hour after dinner they had all curled round and tucked themselves up under their large soft warm wings and were fast asleep. And the sun was sinking slowly in the west. (I must say it was in the west, because it is usual in books to say so, for fear careless people should think it was setting in the east. In point of fact, it was not exactly in the west either - but that's near enough.) The sun, I repeat, was sinking slowly in the west, and the children slept warmly and happily on - for wings are cosier than eiderdown quilts to sleep under. The shadow of the church-tower fell across the churchyard, and across the Vicarage, and across the field beyond; and presently there were no more shadows, and the sun had set, and the wings were gone. And still the children slept. But not for long. Twilight is very beautiful, but it is chilly; and you know, however sleepy you are, you wake up soon enough if your brother or sister happens to be up first and pulls your blankets off you. The four wingless children shivered and woke. And there they were - on the top of a church-tower in the dusky twilight, with blue stars coming out by ones and twos and tens and twenties over their heads - miles away from home, with three-and-three-halfpence in their pockets, and a doubtful act about the necessities of life to be accounted for if anyone found them with the soda-water syphon.

They looked at each other. Cyril spoke first, picking up the syphon:

'We'd better get along down and get rid of this beastly thing. It's dark enough to leave it on the clergyman's doorstep, I should think. Come on.'

There was a little turret at the corner of the tower, and the little turret had a door in it. They had noticed this when they were eating, but had not explored it, as you would have done in their place. Because, of course, when you have wings, and can explore the whole sky, doors seem hardly worth exploring.

Now they turned towards it.

'Of course,' said Cyril, 'this is the way down.'

It was. But the door was locked on the inside!

78

And the world was growing darker and darker. And they were miles from home. And there was the soda-water syphon.

I shall not tell you whether anyone cried, nor if so, how many cried, nor who cried. You will be better employed in making up your minds what you would have done if you had been in their place.

CHAPTER 5. NO WINGS

Whether anyone cried or not, there was certainly an interval during which none of the party was quite itself. When they grew calmer, Anthea put her handkerchief in her pocket and her arm round Jane, and said:

'It can't be for more than one night. We can signal with our handkerchiefs in the morning. They'll be dry then. And someone will come up and let us out -'

'And find the syphon,' said Cyril gloomily; 'and we shall be sent to prison for stealing -'

'You said it wasn't stealing. You said you were sure it wasn't.'

'I'm not sure NOW,' said Cyril shortly.

'Let's throw the beastly thing slap away among the trees,' said Robert, 'then no one can do anything to us.'

'Oh yes' - Cyril's laugh was not a lighthearted one - 'and hit some chap on the head, and be murderers as well as - as the other thing.'

'But we can't stay up here all night,' said Jane; 'and I want my tea.'

'You CAN'T want your tea,' said Robert; 'you've only just had your dinner.'

'But I do want it,' she said; 'especially when you begin talking about stopping up here all night. Oh, Panther - I want to go home! I want to go home!'

'Hush, hush,' Anthea said. 'Don't, dear. It'll be all right, somehow. Don't, don't -'

'Let her cry,' said Robert desperately; 'if she howls loud enough, someone may hear and come and let us out.'

'And see the soda-water thing,' said Anthea swiftly. 'Robert, don't be a brute. Oh, Jane, do try to be a man! It's just the same for all of us.'

Jane did try to 'be a man' - and reduced her howls to sniffs.

There was a pause. Then Cyril said slowly, 'Look here. We must risk that syphon. I'll button it up inside my jacket - perhaps no one will notice it. You others keep well in front of me. There are lights in the clergyman's house. They've not gone to bed yet. We must just yell as loud as ever we can. Now all scream when I say three. Robert, you do the yell like the railway engine, and I'll do the coo-ee like father's. The girls can do as they please. One, two, three!'

A fourfold yell rent the silent peace of the evening, and a maid at one of the Vicarage windows paused with her hand on the blind-cord.

'One, two, three!' Another yell, piercing and complex, startled the owls and starlings to a flutter of feathers in the belfry below. The maid fled from the Vicarage window and ran down the Vicarage stairs and into the Vicarage kitchen, and fainted as soon as she had explained to the man-servant and the cook and the cook's cousin that she had seen a ghost. It was quite untrue, of course, but I suppose the girl's nerves were a little upset by the yelling.

'One, two, three!' The Vicar was on his doorstep by this time, and there was no mistaking the yell that greeted him.

'Goodness me,' he said to his wife, 'my dear, someone's being murdered in the church! Give me my hat and a thick stick, and tell Andrew to come after me. I expect it's the lunatic who stole the tongue.'

The children had seen the flash of light when the Vicar opened his front door. They had seen his dark form on the doorstep, and they had paused for breath, and also to see what he would do.

When he turned back for his hat, Cyril said hastily:

'He thinks he only fancied he heard something. You don't half yell! Now! One, two, three!'

It was certainly a whole yell this time, and the Vicar's wife flung her arms round her husband and screamed a feeble echo of it.

'You shan't go!' she said, 'not alone. Jessie!' - the maid unfainted and came out of the kitchen - 'send Andrew at once. There's a dangerous lunatic in the church, and he must go immediately and catch it.'

'I expect he WILL catch it too,' said Jessie to herself as she went through the kitchen door. 'Here, Andrew,' she said, there's someone screaming like mad in the church, and the missus says you're to go along and catch it.'

'Not alone, I don't,' said Andrew in low firm tones. To his master he merely said, 'Yes, sir.'

'You heard those screams?'

'I did think I noticed a sort of something,' said Andrew.

'Well, come on, then,' said the Vicar. 'My dear, I MUST go!' He pushed her gently into the sitting-room, banged the door, and rushed out, dragging Andrew by the arm.

A volley of yells greeted them. As it died into silence Andrew shouted, 'Hullo, you there! Did you call?'

'Yes,' shouted four far-away voices.

'They seem to be in the air,' said the Vicar. 'Very remarkable.'

'Where are you?' shouted Andrew: and Cyril replied in his deepest voice, very slow and loud:

'CHURCH! TOWER! TOP!'

'Come down, then!' said Andrew; and the same voice replied:

'CAN'T! DOOR LOCKED!'

'My goodness!' said the Vicar. 'Andrew, fetch the stable lantern. Perhaps it would be as well to fetch another man from the village.'

'With the rest of the gang about, very likely. No, sir; if this 'ere ain't a trap - well, may I never! There's cook's cousin at the back door now. He's a keeper, sir, and used to dealing with vicious characters. And he's got his gun, sir.'

'Hullo there!' shouted Cyril from the church-tower; 'come up and let us out.'

'We're a-coming,' said Andrew. 'I'm a-going to get a policeman and a gun.'

'Andrew, Andrew,' said the Vicar, 'that's not the truth.'

'It's near enough, sir, for the likes of them.'

So Andrew fetched the lantern and the cook's cousin; and the Vicar's wife begged them all to be very careful.

They went across the churchyard - it was quite dark now - and as they went they talked. The Vicar was certain a lunatic was on the church-tower - the one who had written the mad letter, and taken the cold tongue and things. Andrew thought it was a 'trap'; the cook's cousin alone was calm. 'Great cry, little wool,' said he; 'dangerous chaps is quieter.' He was not at all afraid. But then he had a gun. That was why he was asked to lead the way up the worn steep dark steps of the church-tower. He did lead the way, with the lantern in one hand and the gun in the other. Andrew went next. He pretended afterwards that this was because he was braver than his master, but really it was because he thought of traps, and he did not like the idea of being behind the others for fear someone should come soffly up behind him and catch hold of his legs in the dark. They went on and on, and round and round the little corkscrew staircase - then through the bell-ringers' loft, where the bell-ropes hung with soft furry ends like giant caterpillars - then up another stair into the belfry, where the big quiet bells are - and then on, up a ladder with broad steps - and then up a little stone stair. And at the top of that there was a little door. And the door was bolted on the stair side.

The cook's cousin, who was a gamekeeper, kicked at the door, and said:

'Hullo, you there!'

The children were holding on to each other on the other side of the door, and trembling with anxiousness - and very hoarse with their howls. They could hardly speak, but Cyril managed to reply huskily:

'Hullo, you there!'

'How did you get up there?'

It was no use saying 'We flew up', so Cyril said:

'We got up - and then we found the door was locked and we couldn't get down. Let us out - do.'

'How many of you are there?' asked the keeper.

'Only four,' said Cyril.

'Are you armed?'

'Are we what?'

'I've got my gun handy - so you'd best not try any tricks,' said the keeper. 'If we open the door, will you promise to come quietly down, and no nonsense?'

'Yes - oh YES!' said all the children together.

'Bless me,' said the Vicar, 'surely that was a female voice?'

'Shall I open the door, Sir?' said the keeper. Andrew went down a few steps, 'to leave room for the others' he said afterwards.

'Yes,' said the Vicar, 'open the door. Remember,' he said through the keyhole, 'we have come to release you. You will keep your promise to refrain from violence?'

'How this bolt do stick,' said the keeper; 'anyone 'ud think it hadn't been drawed for half a year.' As a matter of fact it hadn't.

When all the bolts were drawn, the keeper spoke deep-chested words through the keyhole.

'I don't open,' said he, 'till you've gone over to the other side of the tower. And if one of you comes at me I fire. Now!'

'We're all over on the other side,' said the voices.

The keeper felt pleased with himself, and owned himself a bold man when he threw open that door, and, stepping out into the leads, flashed the full light of the stable lantern on to the group of desperadoes standing against the parapet on the other side of the tower.

He lowered his gun, and he nearly dropped the lantern.

'So help me,' he cried, 'if they ain't a pack of kiddies!'

The Vicar now advanced.

'How did you come here?' he asked severely. 'Tell me at once. '

'Oh, take us down,' said Jane, catching at his coat, 'and we'll tell you anything you like. You won't believe us, but it doesn't matter. Oh, take us down!'

The others crowded round him, with the same entreaty. All but Cyril. He had enough to do with the soda-water syphon, which would keep slipping down under his jacket. It needed both hands to keep it steady in its place.

But he said, standing as far out of the lantern light as possible:

'Please do take us down.'

So they were taken down. It is no joke to go down a strange church-tower in the dark, but the keeper helped them - only, Cyril had to be independent because of the soda-water syphon. It would keep trying to get away. Half-way down the ladder it all but escaped. Cyril just caught it by its spout, and as nearly as possible lost his footing. He was trembling and pale when at last they reached the bottom of the winding stair and stepped out on to the flags of the church-porch.

Then suddenly the keeper caught Cyril and Robert each by an arm.

'You bring along the gells, sir,' said he; 'you and Andrew can manage them.'

'Let go!' said Cyril; 'we aren't running away. We haven't hurt your old church. Leave go!'

'You just come along,' said the keeper; and Cyril dared not oppose him with violence, because just then the syphon began to slip again.

So they were all marched into the Vicarage study, and the Vicar's wife came rushing in.

'Oh, William, are you safe?' she cried.

Robert hastened to allay her anxiety.

'Yes,' he said, 'he's quite safe. We haven't hurt him at all. And please, we're very late, and they'll be anxious at home. Could you send us home in your carriage?'

'Or perhaps there's a hotel near where we could get a carriage from,' said Anthea. 'Martha will be very anxious as it is.'

The Vicar had sunk into a chair, overcome by emotion and amazement.

Cyril had also sat down, and was leaning forward with his elbows on his knees because of that soda-water syphon.

'But how did you come to be locked up in the church-tower?' asked the Vicar.

'We went up,' said Robert slowly, 'and we were tired, and we all went to sleep, and when we woke up we found the door was locked, so we yelled.'

'I should think you did!' said the Vicar's wife. 'Frightening everybody out of their wits like this! You ought to be ashamed of yourselves.'

'We are,' said Jane gently.

'But who locked the door?' asked the Vicar.

'I don't know at all,' said Robert, with perfect truth. 'Do please send us home.'

'Well, really,' said the Vicar, 'I suppose we'd better. Andrew, put the horse to, and you can take them home.'

'Not alone, I don't,' said Andrew to himself.

'And,' the Vicar went on, 'let this be a lesson to you …' He went on talking, and the children listened miserably. But the keeper was not listening. He was looking at the unfortunate Cyril. He knew all about poachers of course, so he knew how people look when they're hiding something. The Vicar had just got to the part about trying to grow up to be a blessing to your parents, and not a trouble and a disgrace, when the keeper suddenly said:

'Arst him what he's got there under his jacket'; and Cyril knew that concealment was at an end. So he stood up, and squared his shoulders and tried to look noble, like the boys in books that no one can look in the face of and doubt that they come of brave and noble families and will be faithful to the death, and he pulled out the soda-water syphon and said:

'Well, there you are, then.'

There was a silence. Cyril went on - there was nothing else for it:

'Yes, we took this out of your larder, and some chicken and tongue and bread. We were very hungry, and we didn't take the custard or jam. We only took bread and meat and water - and we couldn't help its being the soda kind -just the necessaries of life; and we left half-a-crown to pay for it, and we left a letter. And we're very sorry. And my father will pay a fine or anything you like, but don't send us to prison. Mother would be so vexed. You know what you said about not being a disgrace. Well, don't you go and do it to us - that's all! We're as sorry as we can be. There!'

'However did you get up to the larder window?' said Mrs Vicar.

'I can't tell you that,' said Cyril firmly.

'Is this the whole truth you've been telling me?' asked the clergyman.

'No,' answered Jane suddenly; 'it's all true, but it's not the whole truth. We can't tell you that. It's no good asking. Oh, do forgive us and take us home!' She ran to the Vicar's wife and threw her arms round her. The Vicar's wife put her arms round Jane, and the keeper whispered behind his hand to the Vicar:

'They're all right, sir - I expect it's a pal they're standing by. Someone put 'em up to it, and they won't peach. Game little kids.'

'Tell me,' said the Vicar kindly, 'are you screening someone else? Had anyone else anything to do with this?'

'Yes,' said Anthea, thinking of the Psammead; 'but it wasn't their fault.'

'Very well, my dears,' said the Vicar, 'then let's say no more about it. Only just tell us why you wrote such an odd letter.'

'I don't know,' said Cyril. 'You see, Anthea wrote it in such a hurry, and it really didn't seem like stealing then. But afterwards, when we found we couldn't get down off the church-tower, it seemed just exactly like it. We are all very sorry -'

'Say no more about it,' said the Vicar's wife; 'but another time just think before you take other people's tongues. Now - some cake and milk before you go home?'

When Andrew came to say that the horse was put to, and was he expected to be led alone into the trap that he had plainly seen from the first, he found the children eating cake and drinking milk and laughing at the Vicar's jokes. Jane was sitting on the Vicar's wife's lap.

So you see they got off better than they deserved.

The gamekeeper, who was the cook's cousin, asked leave to drive home with them, and Andrew was only too glad to have someone to protect him from the trap he was so certain of.

When the wagonette reached their own house, between the chalk-quarry and the gravel-pit, the children were very sleepy, but they felt that they and the keeper were friends for life.

Andrew dumped the children down at the iron gate without a word. 'You get along home,' said the Vicarage cook's cousin, who was a gamekeeper. 'I'll get me home on Shanks' mare.'

So Andrew had to drive off alone, which he did not like at all, and it was the keeper that was cousin to the Vicarage cook who went with the children to the door, and, when they had been swept to bed in a whirlwind of reproaches, remained to explain to Martha and the cook and the housemaid exactly what had happened. He explained so well that Martha was quite amiable the next morning.

After that he often used to come over and see Martha; and in the end - but that is another story, as dear Mr Kipling says.

Martha was obliged to stick to what she had said the night before about keeping the children indoors the next day for a punishment. But she wasn't at all snarky about it, and agreed to let Robert go out for half an hour to get something he particularly wanted. This, of course, was the day's wish.

Robert rushed to the gravel-pit, found the Psammead, and presently wished for - But that, too, is another story.

CHAPTER 6. A CASTLE AND NO DINNER

The others were to be kept in as a punishment for the misfortunes of the day before. Of course Martha thought it was naughtiness, and not misfortune - so you must not blame her. She only thought she was doing her duty. You know grown-up people often say they do not like to punish you, and that they only do it for your own good, and that it hurts them as much as it hurts you - and this is really very often the truth.

Martha certainly hated having to punish the children quite as much as they hated to be punished. For one thing, she knew what a noise there would be in the house all day. And she had other reasons.

'I declare,' she said to the cook, 'it seems almost a shame keeping of them indoors this lovely day; but they are that audacious, they'll be walking in with their heads knocked off some of these days, if I don't put my foot down. You make them a cake for tea to-morrow, dear. And we'll have Baby along of us soon as we've got a bit forrard with our work. Then they can have a good romp with him out of the way. Now, Eliza, come, get on with them beds. Here's ten o'clock nearly, and no rabbits caught!'

People say that in Kent when they mean 'and no work done'.

So all the others were kept in, but Robert, as I have said, was allowed to go out for half an hour to get something they all wanted. And that, of course, was the day's wish. He had no difficulty in finding the Sand-fairy, for the day was already so hot that it had actually, for the first time, come out of its own accord, and it was sitting in a sort of pool of soft sand, stretching itself, and trimming its whiskers, and turning its snail's eyes round and round.

'Ha!' it said when its left eye saw Robert; 'I've been looking out for you. Where are the rest of you? Not smashed themselves up with those wings, I hope?'

'No,' said Robert; 'but the wings got us into a row, just like all the wishes always do. So the others are kept indoors, and I was only let out for half-an-hour - to get the wish. So please let me wish as quickly as I can.'

90

'Wish away,' said the Psammead, twisting itself round in the sand. But Robert couldn't wish away. He forgot all the things he had been thinking about, and nothing would come into his head but little things for himself, like toffee, a foreign stamp album, or a clasp-knife with three blades and a corkscrew. He sat down to think better, but it was no use. He could only think of things the others would not have cared for - such as a football, or a pair of leg-guards, or to be able to lick Simpkins minor thoroughly when he went back to school.

'Well,' said the Psammead at last, 'you'd better hurry up with that wish of yours. Time flies.'

'I know it does,' said Robert. 'I can't think what to wish for. I wish you could give one of the others their wish without their having to come here to ask for it. Oh, DON'T!'

But it was too late. The Psammead had blown itself out to about three times its proper size, and now it collapsed like a pricked bubble, and with a deep sigh leaned back against the edge of its sand-pool, quite faint with the effort.

'There!' it said in a weak voice; 'it was tremendously hard - but I did it. Run along home, or they're sure to wish for something silly before you get there.'

They were - quite sure; Robert felt this, and as he ran home his mind was deeply occupied with the sort of wishes he might find they had wished in his absence. They might wish for rabbits, or white mice, or chocolate, or a fine day to-morrow, or even - and that was most likely - someone might have said, 'I do wish to goodness Robert would hurry up.' Well, he WAS hurrying up, and so they would have their wish, and the day would be wasted. Then he tried to think what they could wish for - something that would be amusing indoors. That had been his own difficulty from the beginning. So few things are amusing indoors when the sun is shining outside and you mayn't go out, however much you want to. Robert was running as fast as he could, but when he turned the corner that ought to have brought him within sight of the architect's nightmare - the ornamental iron-work on the top of the house - he opened his eyes so wide that he had to drop into a walk; for you cannot run with your eyes wide open. Then suddenly he stopped short, for there was no house to be seen. The front-garden railings were gone too, and where the house had stood - Robert rubbed his eyes and looked again. Yes, the others HAD wished - there was no doubt about that - and they must have wished that they lived in a castle; for there the castle stood black and stately, and very tall and broad, with battlements and lancet windows, and eight great towers; and, where the garden and the orchard had been, there were white things dotted like mushrooms. Robert walked slowly on, and as he got nearer he saw that these were tents) and men in armour were walking about among the tents - crowds and crowds of them.

'Oh, crikey!' said Robert fervently. 'They HAVE! They've wished for a castle, and it's being besieged! It's just like that Sand-fairy! I wish we'd never seen the beastly thing!'

At the little window above the great gateway, across the moat that now lay where the garden had been but half an hour ago, someone was waving something pale dust-coloured. Robert thought it was one of Cyril's handkerchiefs. They had never been white since the day when he had upset the bottle of 'Combined Toning and Fixing Solution' into the drawer where they were. Robert waved back, and immediately felt that he had been unwise. For his signal had been seen by the besieging force, and two men in steel-caps were coming towards him. They had high brown boots on their long legs, and they came towards him with such great strides that Robert remembered the shortness of his own legs and did not run away. He knew it would be useless to himself, and he feared it might be irritating to the foe. So he stood still, and the two men seemed quite pleased with him.

'By my halidom,' said one, 'a brave varlet this!'

Robert felt pleased at being CALLED brave, and somehow it made him FEEL brave. He passed over the 'varlet'. It was the way people

92

talked in historical romances for the young, he knew, and it was evidently not meant for rudeness. He only hoped he would be able to understand what they said to him. He had not always been able quite to follow the conversations in the historical romances for the young.

'His garb is strange,' said the other. 'Some outlandish treachery, belike.'

'Say, lad, what brings thee hither?'

Robert knew this meant, 'Now then, youngster, what are you up to here, eh?' - so he said:

'If you please, I want to go home.'

'Go, then!' said the man in the longest boots; 'none hindereth, and nought lets us to follow. Zooks!' he added in a cautious undertone, 'I misdoubt me but he beareth tidings to the besieged.'

'Where dwellest thou, young knave?' inquired the man with the largest steel-cap.

'Over there,' said Robert; and directly he had said it he knew he ought to have said 'Yonder!'

'Ha - sayest so?' rejoined the longest boots. 'Come hither, boy. This is a matter for our leader.'

And to the leader Robert was dragged forthwith - by the reluctant ear.

The leader was the most glorious creature Robert had ever seen. He was exactly like the pictures Robert had so often admired in the historical romances. He had armour, and a helmet, and a horse, and a crest, and feathers, and a shield, and a lance, and a sword. His armour and his weapons were all, I am almost sure, of quite different periods. The shield was thirteenth-century, while the sword was of the pattern used in the Peninsular War. The cuirass was of the time of Charles I, and the helmet dated from the Second Crusade. The arms on the shield were very grand - three red running lions on a blue ground. The tents were of the latest brand and the whole appearance of camp, army, and leader might have been a shock to some. But Robert was dumb with admiration, and it all seemed to him perfectly correct, because he knew no more of heraldry or archaeology than the gifted artists who usually drew the pictures for the historical romances. The scene was indeed 'exactly like a picture'. He admired it all so much that he felt braver than ever.

'Come hither, lad,' said the glorious leader, when the men in Cromwellian steel-caps had said a few low eager words. And he took off his helmet, because he could not see properly with it on. He had a kind face, and long fair hair. 'Have no fear; thou shalt take no scathe,' he said.

Robert was glad of that. He wondered what 'scathe' was, and if it was nastier than the senna tea which he had to take sometimes.

'Unfold thy tale without alarm,' said the leader kindly. 'Whence comest thou, and what is thine intent?'

'My what?' said Robert.

'What seekest thou to accomplish? What is thine errand, that thou wanderest here alone among these rough men-at-arms? Poor child, thy mother's heart aches for thee e'en now, I'll warrant me.'

'I don't think so,' said Robert; 'you see, she doesn't know I'm out.'

The leader wiped away a manly tear, exactly as a leader in a historical romance would have done, and said:

'Fear not to speak the truth, my child; thou hast nought to fear from Wulfric de Talbot.'

94

Robert had a wild feeling that this glorious leader of the besieging party - being himself part of a wish - would be able to understand better than Martha, or the gipsies, or the policeman in Rochester, or the clergyman of yesterday, the true tale of the wishes and the Psammead. The only difficulty was that he knew he could never remember enough 'quothas' and 'beshrew me's', and things like that, to make his talk sound like the talk of a boy in a historical romance. However, he began boldly enough, with a sentence straight out of Ralph de Courcy; or, The Boy Crusader. He said:

'Grammercy for thy courtesy, fair sir knight. The fact is, it's like this - and I hope you're not in a hurry, because the story's rather a breather. Father and mother are away, and when we were down playing in the sand-pits we found a Psammead.'

'I cry thee mercy! A Sammyadd?' said the knight.

'Yes, a sort of - of fairy, or enchanter - yes, that's it, an enchanter; and he said we could have a wish every day, and we wished first to be beautiful.'

'Thy wish was scarce granted,' muttered one of the men-at-arms, looking at Robert, who went on as if he had not heard, though he thought the remark very rude indeed.

'And then we wished for money - treasure, you know; but we couldn't spend it. And yesterday we wished for wings, and we got them, and we had a ripping time to begin with -'

'Thy speech is strange and uncouth,' said Sir Wulfric de Talbot. 'Repeat thy words - what hadst thou?'

'A ripping - I mean a jolly - no - we were contented with our lot - that's what I mean; only, after that we got into an awful fix.'

'What is a fix? A fray, mayhap?'

'No - not a fray. A - a - a tight place.'

'A dungeon? Alas for thy youthful fettered limbs!' said the knight, with polite sympathy.

'It wasn't a dungeon. We just - just encountered undeserved misfortunes,' Robert explained, 'and to-day we are punished by not being allowed to go out. That's where I live,' - he pointed to the castle. 'The others are in there, and they're not allowed to go out. It's all the Psammead's - I mean the enchanter's fault. I wish we'd never seen him.'

'He is an enchanter of might?'

'Oh yes - of might and main. Rather!'

'And thou deemest that it is the spells of the enchanter whom thou hast angered that have lent strength to the besieging party,' said the gallant leader; 'but know thou that Wulfric de Talbot needs no enchanter's aid to lead his followers to victory.'

'No, I'm sure you don't,' said Robert, with hasty courtesy; 'of course not - you wouldn't, you know. But, all the same, it's partly his fault, but we're most to blame. You couldn't have done anything if it hadn't been for us.'

'How now, bold boy?' asked Sir Wulfric haughtily. 'Thy speech is dark, and eke scarce courteous. Unravel me this riddle!'

'Oh,' said Robert desperately, 'of course you don't know it, but you're not REAL at all. You're only here because the others must have been idiots enough to wish for a castle - and when the sun sets you'll just vanish away, and it'll be all right.'

The captain and the men-at-arms exchanged glances, at first pitying, and then sterner, as the longest-booted man said, 'Beware, noble my lord; the urchin doth but feign madness to escape from our clutches. Shall we not bind him?'

'I'm no more mad than you are,' said Robert angrily, 'perhaps not so much - only, I was an idiot to think you'd understand anything. Let me go - I haven't done anything to you.'

'Whither?' asked the knight, who seemed to have believed all the enchanter story till it came to his own share in it. 'Whither wouldst thou wend?'

'Home, of course.' Robert pointed to the castle.

'To carry news of succour? Nay!'

'All right then,' said Robert, struck by a sudden idea; 'then let me go somewhere else.' His mind sought eagerly among his memories of the historical romance.

'Sir Wulfric de Talbot,' he said slowly, 'should think foul scorn to - to keep a chap - I mean one who has done him no hurt - when he wants to cut off quietly - I mean to depart without violence.'

'This to my face! Beshrew thee for a knave!' replied Sir Wulfric. But the appeal seemed to have gone home. 'Yet thou sayest sooth,' he added thoughtfully. 'Go where thou wilt,' he added nobly, 'thou art free. Wulfric de Talbot warreth not with babes, and Jakin here shall bear thee company.' 'All right,' said Robert wildly. 'Jakin will enjoy himself, I think. Come on, Jakin. Sir Wulfric, I salute thee.'

He saluted after the modern military manner, and set off running to the sand-pit, Jakin's long boots keeping up easily.

He found the Fairy. He dug it up, he woke it up,

he implored it to give him one more wish.

'I've done two to-day already,' it grumbled, 'and one was as stiff a bit of work as ever I did.'

'Oh, do, do, do, do, DO!' said Robert, while Jakin looked on with an expression of open-mouthed horror at the strange beast that talked, and gazed with its snail's eyes at him.

'Well, what is it?' snapped the Psammead, with cross sleepiness.

'I wish I was with the others,' said Robert. And the Psammead began to swell. Robert never thought of wishing the castle and the siege away. Of course he knew they had all come out of a wish, but swords and daggers and pikes and lances seemed much too real to be wished away. Robert lost consciousness for an instant. When he opened his eyes the others were crowding round him.

'We never heard you come in,' they said. 'How awfully jolly of you to wish it to give us our wish!'

'Of course we understood that was what you'd done.'

'But you ought to have told us. Suppose we'd wished something silly.'

'Silly?' said Robert, very crossly indeed. 'How much sillier could you have been, I'd like to know? You nearly settled ME - I can tell you.'

Then he told his story, and the others admitted that it certainly had been rough on him. But they praised his courage and cleverness so much that he presently got back his lost temper, and felt braver than ever, and consented to be captain of the besieged force.

'We haven't done anything yet,' said Anthea comfortably; 'we waited for you. We're going to shoot at them through these little loopholes with the bow and arrows uncle gave you, and you shall have first shot.'

'I don't think I would,' said Robert cautiously; 'you don't know what they're like near to. They've got REAL bows and arrows - an awful length - and swords and pikes and daggers, and all sorts of sharp things. They're all quite, quite real. It's not just a - a picture, or a vision, or anything; they can hurt us - or kill us even, I shouldn't wonder. I can feel my ear all sore still. Look here - have you explored the castle? Because I think we'd better let them alone as long as they let us alone. I heard that Jakin man say they weren't going to attack till just before sundown. We can be getting ready for the attack. Are there any soldiers in the castle to defend it?'

'We don't know,' said Cyril. 'You see, directly I'd wished we were in a besieged castle, everything seemed to go upside down, and,when it came straight we looked out of the window, and saw the camp and things and you - and of course we kept on looking at everything. Isn't this room jolly? It's as real as real!'

It was. It was square, with stone walls four feet thick, and great beams for ceiling. A low door at the corner led to a flight of steps, up and down. The children went down; they found themselves in a great arched gatehouse - the enormous doors were shut and barred. There was a window in a little room at the bottom of the round turret up which the stair wound, rather larger than the other windows, and looking through it they saw that the drawbridge was up and the portcullis down; the moat looked very wide and deep. Opposite the great door that led to the moat was another great door, with a little door in it. The children went through this, and found themselves in a big paved courtyard, with the great grey walls of the castle rising dark and heavy on all four sides.

Near the middle of the courtyard stood Martha, moving her right hand backwards and forwards in the air. The cook was stooping down and moving her hands, also in a very curious way. But. the oddest and at the same time most terrible thing was the Lamb, who was sitting on nothing, about three feet from the ground, laughing happily.

The children ran towards him. Just as Anthea was reaching out her arms to take him, Martha said crossly, 'Let him alone - do, miss, when he is good.'

'But what's he DOING?' said Anthea.

'Doing? Why, a-setting in his high chair as good as gold, a precious, watching me doing of the ironing. Get along with you, do - my iron's cold again.'

She went towards the cook, and seemed to poke an invisible fire with an unseen poker - the cook seemed to be putting an unseen dish into an invisible oven.

'Run along with you, do,' she said; 'I'm behindhand as it is. You won't get no dinner if you come a-hindering of me like this. Come, off you goes, or I'll pin a dishcloth to some of your tails.'

'You're sure the Lamb's all right?' asked Jane anxiously.

'Right as ninepence, if you don't come unsettling of him. I thought you'd like to be rid of him for to-day; but take him, if you want him, for gracious' sake.'

'No, no,' they said, and hastened away. They would have to defend the castle presently, and the Lamb was safer even suspended in mid-air in an invisible kitchen than in the guardroom of a besieged castle. They went through the first doorway they came to, and sat down helplessly on a wooden bench that ran along the room inside.

'How awful!' said Anthea and Jane together; and Jane added, 'I feel as if I was in a mad asylum.'

'What does it mean?' Anthea said. 'It's creepy; I don't like it. I wish we'd wished for something plain - a rocking-horse, or a donkey, or something.'

'It's no use wishing NOW,' said Robert bitterly; and Cyril said:

'Do dry up a sec; I want to think.'

He buried his face in his hands, and the others looked about them. They were in a long room with an arched roof. There were wooden tables along it, and one across at the end of the room, on a sort of raised platform. The room was very dim and dark. The floor was strewn with dry things like sticks, and they did not smell nice.

Cyril sat up suddenly and said:

'Look here - it's all right. I think it's like this. You know, we wished that the servants shouldn't notice any difference when we got wishes. And nothing happens to the Lamb unless we specially wish it to. So of course they don't notice the castle or anything. But then the castle is on the same place where our house was - is, I mean - and the servants have to go on being in the house, or else they would notice. But you can't have a castle mixed up with our house - and so we can't see the house, because we see the castle; and they can't see the castle, because they go on seeing the house; and so -'

'Oh, DON'T!' said Jane; 'you make my head go all swimmy, like being on a roundabout. It doesn't matter! Only, I hope we shall be able to see our dinner, that's all - because if it's invisible it'll be unfeelable as well, and then we can't eat it! I KNOW it will, because I tried to feel if I could feel the Lamb's chair, and there was nothing under him at all but air. And we can't eat air, and I feel just as if I hadn't had any breakfast for years and years.'

'It's no use thinking about it,' said Anthea. 'Let's go on exploring. Perhaps we might find something to eat.'

This lighted hope in every breast, and they went on exploring the castle. But though it was the most perfect and delightful castle you can possibly imagine, and furnished in the most complete and beautiful manner, neither food nor men-at-arms were to be found in it. 'If only you'd thought of wishing to be besieged in a castle thoroughly garrisoned and provisioned!' said Jane reproachfully.

'You can't think of everything, you know,' said Anthea. 'I should think it must be nearly dinner-time by now.'

101

It wasn't; but they hung about watching the strange movements of the servants in the middle of the courtyard, because, of course, they couldn't be sure where the dining-room of the invisible house was. Presently they saw Martha carrying an invisible tray across the courtyard, for it seemed that, by the most fortunate accident, the dining-room of the house and the banqueting-hall of the castle were in the same place. But oh, how their hearts sank when they perceived that the tray was invisible!

They waited in wretched silence while Martha went through the form of carving an unseen leg of mutton and serving invisible greens and potatoes with a spoon that no one could see. When she had left the room, the children looked at the empty table, and then at each other.

'This is worse than anything,' said Robert, who had not till now been particularly keen on his dinner.

'I'm not so very hungry,' said Anthea, trying to make the best of things, as usual.

Cyril tightened his belt ostentatiously. Jane burst into tears.

CHAPTER 7. A SIEGE AND BED

The children were sitting in the gloomy banqueting-hall, at the end of one of the long bare wooden tables. There was now no hope. Martha had brought in the dinner, and the dinner was invisible, and unfeelable too; for, when they rubbed their hands along the table, they knew but too well that for them there was nothing there BUT table.

Suddenly Cyril felt in his pocket.

'Right, oh!' he cried. 'Look here! Biscuits.'

Rather broken and crumbled, certainly, but still biscuits. Three whole ones, and a generous handful of crumbs and fragments.

'I got them this morning - cook - and I'd quite forgotten,' he explained as he divided them with scrupulous fairness into four heaps.

They were eaten in a happy silence, though they tasted a little oddly, because they had been in Cyril's pocket all the morning with a hank of tarred twine, some green fir-cones, and a ball of cobbler's wax.

'Yes, but look here, Squirrel,' said Robert; 'you're so clever at explaining about invisibleness and all that. How is it the biscuits are here, and all the bread and meat and things have disappeared?'

'I don't know,' said Cyril after a pause, 'unless it's because WE had them. Nothing about us has changed. Everything's in my pocket all right.'

'Then if we HAD the mutton it would be real,' said Robert. 'Oh, don't I wish we could find it!'

'But we can't find it. I suppose it isn't ours till we've got it in our mouths.'

'Or in our pockets,' said Jane, thinking of the biscuits.

'Who puts mutton in their pockets, goose-girl?' said Cyril. 'But I know - at any rate, I'll try it!'

He leaned over the table with his face about an inch from it, and kept opening and shutting his mouth as if he were taking bites out of air.

'It's no good,' said Robert in deep dejection. 'You'll only - Hullo!'

Cyril stood up with a grin of triumph, holding a square piece of bread in his mouth. It was quite real. Everyone saw it. It is true that, directly he bit a piece off, the rest vanished; but it was all right, because he knew he had it in his hand though he could neither see nor feel it. He took another bite from the air between his fingers, and it turned into bread as he bit. The next moment all the others were following his example, and opening and shutting their mouths an inch or so from the bare-looking table. Robert captured a slice of mutton, and - but I think I will draw a veil over the rest of this painful scene. It is enough to say that they all had enough mutton, and that when Martha came to change the plates she said she had never seen such a mess in all her born days.

The pudding was, fortunately, a plain suet roly-poly, and in answer to Martha's questions the children all with one accord said that they would NOT have treacle on it - nor jam, nor sugar - 'Just plain, please,' they said. Martha said, 'Well, I never - what next, I wonder!' and went away.

Then ensued another scene on which I will not dwell, for nobody looks nice picking up slices of suet pudding from the table in its mouth, like a dog. The great thing, after all, was that they had had dinner; and now everyone felt more courage to prepare for the attack that was to be delivered before sunset. Robert, as captain, insisted on climbing to the top of one of the towers to reconnoitre, so up they all went. And now they could see all round the castle, and could see, too, that beyond the moat, on every side, the tents of the besieging party were pitched. Rather uncomfortable shivers ran down the children's backs as they saw that all the men were very busy cleaning or sharpening their arms, re-stringing their bows, and polishing their shields. A large party came along the road, with horses dragging along the great trunk of a tree; and Cyril felt quite pale, because he knew this was for a battering-ram.

'What a good thing we've got a moat,' he said; 'and what a good thing the drawbridge is up - I should never have known how to work it.'

'Of course it would be up in a besieged castle.'

'You'd think there ought to have been soldiers in it, wouldn't you?' said Robert.

'You see you don't know how long it's been besieged,' said Cyril darkly; 'perhaps most of the brave defenders were killed quite early in the siege and all the provisions eaten, and now there are only a few intrepid survivors - that's us, and we are going to defend it to the death.'

'How do you begin - defending to the death, I mean?' asked Anthea.

'We ought to be heavily armed - and then shoot at them when they advance to the attack.'

'They used to pour boiling lead down on besiegers when they got too close,' said Anthea. 'Father showed me the holes on purpose for pouring it down through at Bodiam Castle. And there are holes like it in the gate-tower here.'

'I think I'm glad it's only a game; it IS only a game, isn't it?' said Jane.

But no one answered.

The children found plenty of strange weapons in the castle, and if they were armed at all it was soon plain that they would be, as Cyril said, 'armed heavily' - for these swords and lances and crossbows were far too weighty even for Cyril's manly strength; and as for the longbows, none of the children could even begin to bend them. The daggers were better; but Jane hoped that the besiegers would not come close enough for daggers to be of any use.

'Never mind, we can hurl them like javelins,' said Cyril, 'or drop them on people's heads. I say - there are lots of stones on the other side of the courtyard. If we took some of those up, just to drop on their heads if they were to try swimming the moat.'

So a heap of stones grew apace, up in the room above the gate; and another heap, a shiny spiky dangerous-looking heap, of daggers and knives.

As Anthea was crossing the courtyard for more stones, a sudden and valuable idea came to her. She went to Martha and said, 'May we have just biscuits for tea? We're going to play at besieged castles, and we'd like the biscuits to provision the garrison. Put mine in my pocket, please, my hands are so dirty. And I'll tell the others to fetch theirs.'

This was indeed a happy thought, for now with four generous handfuls of air, which turned to biscuit as Martha crammed it into their pockets, the garrison was well provisioned till sundown.

They brought up some iron pots of cold water to pour on the besiegers instead of hot lead, with which the castle did not seem to be provided.

The afternoon passed with wonderful quickness. It was very exciting; but none of them, except Robert, could feel all the time that this was real deadly dangerous work. To the others, who had only seen the camp and the besiegers from a distance, the whole thing seemed half a game of make-believe, and half a splendidly distinct and perfectly safe dream. But it was only now and then that Robert could feel this.

When it seemed to be tea-time the biscuits were eaten with water from the deep well in the courtyard, drunk out of horns. Cyril insisted on putting by eight of the biscuits, in case anyone should feel faint in stress of battle.

just as he was putting away the reserve biscuits in a sort of little stone cupboard without a door, a sudden sound made him drop three. It was the loud fierce cry of a trumpet.

'You see it IS real,' said Robert, 'and they are going to attack.'

All rushed to the narrow windows.

'Yes,' said Robert, 'they're all coming out of their tents and moving about like ants. There's that Jakin dancing about where the bridge joins on. I wish he could see me put my tongue out at him! Yah!'

The others were far too pale to wish to put their tongues out at anybody. They looked at Robert with surprised respect. Anthea said:

'You really ARE brave, Robert.'

'Rot!' Cyril's pallor turned to redness now, all in a minute. 'He's been getting ready to be brave all the afternoon. And I wasn't ready, that's all. I shall be braver than he is in half a jiffy.'

'Oh dear!' said Jane, 'what does it matter which of you is the bravest? I think Cyril was a perfect silly to wish for a castle, and I don't want to play.'

'It ISN'T' - Robert was beginning sternly, but Anthea interrupted -

'Oh yes, you do,' she said coaxingly; 'it's a very nice game, really, because they can't possibly get in, and if they do the women and children are always spared by civilized armies.'

'But are you quite, quite sure they ARE civilized?' asked Jane, panting. 'They seem to be such a long time ago.'

'Of course they are.' Anthea pointed cheerfully through the narrow window. 'Why, look at the little flags on their lances, how bright they are - and how fine the leader is! Look, that's him - isn't it, Robert? - on the grey horse.'

Jane consented to look, and the scene was almost too pretty to be alarming. The green turf, the white tents, the flash of pennoned lances, the gleam of armour, and the bright colours of scarf and tunic - it was just like a splendid coloured picture. The trumpets were sounding, and when the trumpets stopped for breath the children could hear the cling-clang of armour and the murmur of voices.

A trumpeter came forward to the edge of the moat, which now seemed very much narrower than at first, and blew the longest and loudest blast they had yet heard. When the blaring noise had died away, a man who was with the trumpeter shouted:

'What ho, within there!' and his voice came plainly to the garrison in the gate-house.

'Hullo there!' Robert bellowed back at once.

'In the name of our Lord the King, and of our good lord and trusty leader Sir Wulfric de Talbot, we summon this castle to surrender - on pain of fire and sword and no quarter. Do ye surrender?'

'No,' bawled Robert, 'of course we don't! Never,

Never, NEVER!'

The man answered back:

'Then your fate be on your own heads.'

'Cheer,' said Robert in a fierce whisper. 'Cheer to show them we aren't afraid, and rattle the daggers to make more noise. One, two, three! Hip, hip, hooray! Again - Hip, hip, hooray! One more - Hip, hip, hooray!' The cheers were rather high and weak, but the rattle of the daggers lent them strength and depth.

There was another shout from the camp across the moat - and then the beleaguered fortress felt that the attack had indeed begun.

It was getting rather dark in the room above the great gate, and Jane took a very little courage as she remembered that sunset couldn't be far off now.

'The moat is dreadfully thin,' said Anthea.

'But they can't get into the castle even if they do swim over,' said Robert. And as he spoke he heard feet on the stair outside - heavy feet and the clank of steel. No one breathed for a moment. The steel and the feet went on up the turret stairs. Then Robert sprang softly to the door. He pulled off his shoes.

'Wait here,' he whispered, and stole quickly and softly after the boots and the spur-clank. He peeped into the upper room. The man was there - and it was Jakin, all dripping with moat-water, and he was fiddling about with the machinery which Robert felt sure worked the drawbridge. Robert banged the door suddenly, and turned the great key in the lock, just as Jakin sprang to the inside of the door. Then he tore downstairs and into the little turret at the foot of the tower where the biggest window was.

'We ought to have defended THIS!' he cried to the others as they followed him. He was just in time. Another man had swum over, and his fingers were on the window-ledge. Robert never knew how the man had managed to climb up out of the water. But he saw the clinging fingers, and hit them as hard as he could with an iron bar that he caught up from the floor. The man fell with a plop-plash into the moat-water. In another moment Robert was outside the little room, had banged its door and was shooting home the enormous bolts, and calling to Cyril to lend a hand.

Then they stood in the arched gate-house, breathing hard and looking at each other. jane's mouth was open.

'Cheer up, jenny,' said Robert - 'it won't last much longer.'

There was a creaking above, and something rattled and shook. The pavement they stood on seemed to tremble. Then a crash told them that the drawbridge had been lowered to its place.

'That's that beast Jakin,' said Robert. 'There's still the portcullis; I'm almost certain that's worked from lower down.'

And now the drawbridge rang and echoed hollowly to the hoofs of horses and the tramp of armed men. 'Up - quick!' cried Robert. 'Let's drop things on them.'

Even the girls were feeling almost brave now. They followed Robert quickly, and under his directions began to drop stones out through the long narrow windows. There was a confused noise below, and some groans.

'Oh dear!' said Anthea, putting down the stone she was just going to drop out. 'I'm afraid we've hurt somebody!'

Robert caught up the stone in a fury.

'I should just hope we HAD!' he said; 'I'd give something for a jolly good boiling kettle of lead. Surrender, indeed!'

And now came more tramping, and a pause, and then the thundering thump of the battering-ram. And the little room was almost quite dark.

'We've held it,' cried Robert, 'we won't surrender! The sun MUST set in a minute. Here - they're all jawing underneath again. Pity there's no time to get more stones! Here, pour that water down on them. It's no good, of course, but they'll hate it.'

'Oh dear!' said Jane; 'don't you think we'd better surrender?'

'Never!' said Robert; 'we'll have a parley if you like, but we'll never surrender. Oh, I'll be a soldier when I grow up - you just see if I don't. I won't go into the Civil Service, whatever anyone says.'

'Let's wave a handkerchief and ask for a parley,' Jane pleaded. 'I don't believe the sun's going to set to-night at all.'

'Give them the water first - the brutes!' said the bloodthirsty Robert. So Anthea tilted the pot over the nearest lead-hole, and poured. They heard a splash below, but no one below seemed to have felt it. And again the ram battered the great door. Anthea paused.

'How idiotic,' said Robert, lying flat on the floor and putting one eye to the lead hole. 'Of course the holes go straight down into the gate-house - that's for when the enemy has got past the door and the portcullis, and almost all is lost. Here, hand me the pot.' He crawled on to the three-cornered window-ledge in the middle of the wall, and, taking the pot from Anthea, poured the water out through the arrow-slit.

And as he began to pour, the noise of the battering-ram and the trampling of the foe and the shouts of 'Surrender!' and 'De Talbot for ever!' all suddenly stopped and went out like the snuff of a candle; the little dark room seemed to whirl round and turn topsy-turvy, and when the children came to themselves there they were safe and sound, in the big front bedroom of their own house - the house with the ornamental nightmare iron-top to the roof.

They all crowded to the window and looked out. The moat and the tents and the besieging force were all gone - and there was the garden with its tangle of dahlias and marigolds and asters and late roses, and the spiky iron railings and the quiet white road.

Everyone drew a deep breath.

'And that's all right!' said Robert. 'I told you so! And, I say, we didn't surrender, did we?'

'Aren't you glad now I wished for a castle?' asked Cyril.

'I think I am NOW,' said Anthea slowly. 'But I wouldn't wish for it again, I think, Squirrel dear!'

'Oh, it was simply splendid!' said Jane unexpectedly. 'I wasn't frightened a bit.'

'Oh, I say!' Cyril was beginning, but Anthea stopped him.

111

'Look here,' she said, 'it's just come into my head. This is the very first thing we've wished for that hasn't got us into a row. And there hasn't been the least little scrap of a row about this. Nobody's raging downstairs, we're safe and sound, we've had an awfully jolly day - at least, not jolly exactly, but you know what I mean. And we know now how brave Robert is - and Cyril too, of course,' she added hastily, 'and Jane as well. And we haven't got into a row with a single grown-up.'

The door was opened suddenly and fiercely.

'You ought to be ashamed of yourselves,' said the voice of Martha, and they could tell by her voice that she was very angry indeed. 'I thought you couldn't last through the day without getting up to some doggery! A person can't take a breath of air on the front doorstep but you must be emptying the wash-hand jug on to their heads! Off you go to bed, the lot of you, and try to get up better children in the morning. Now then - don't let me have to tell you twice. If I find any of you not in bed in ten minutes I'll let you know it, that's all! A new cap, and everything!'

She flounced out amid a disregarded chorus of regrets and apologies. The children were very sorry, but really it was not their faults. You can't help it if you are pouring water on a besieging foe, and your castle suddenly changes into your house - and everything changes with it except the water, and that happens to fall on somebody else's clean cap.

'I don't know why the water didn't change into nothing, though,' said Cyril.

'Why should it?' asked Robert. 'Water's water all the world over.' 'I expect the castle well was the same as ours in the stable-yard,' said Jane. And that was really the case.

'I thought we couldn't get through a wish-day without a row,' said Cyril; 'it was much too good to be true. Come on, Bobs, my military

112

hero. If we lick into bed sharp she won't be so frumious, and perhaps she'll bong us up some supper. I'm jolly hungry! Good-night, kids.'

'Good-night. I hope the castle won't come creeping back in the night,' said Jane.

'Of course it won't,' said Anthea briskly, 'but Martha will - not in the night, but in a minute. Here, turn round, I'll get that knot out of your pinafore strings.'

'Wouldn't it have been degrading for Sir Wulfric de Talbot,' said Jane dreamily, 'if he could have known that half the besieged garrison wore pinafores?'

'And the other half knickerbockers. Yes - frightfully. Do stand still - you're only tightening the knot,' said Anthea.

CHAPTER 8. BIGGER THAN THE BAKER'S BOY

'Look here,' said Cyril. 'I've got an idea.'

'Does it hurt much?' said Robert sympathetically.

'Don't be a jackape! I'm not humbugging.'

'Shut up, Bobs!' said Anthea.

'Silence for the Squirrel's oration,' said Robert.

Cyril balanced himself on the edge of the water-butt in the backyard, where they all happened to be, and spoke.

'Friends, Romans, countrymen - and women - we found a Sammyadd. We have had wishes. We've had wings, and being beautiful as the day - ugh! - that was pretty jolly beastly if you like - and wealth and castles, and that rotten gipsy business with the

Lamb. But we're no forrader. We haven't really got anything worth having for our wishes.'

'We've had things happening,' said Robert; 'that's always something.'

'It's not enough, unless they're the right things,' said Cyril firmly. 'Now I've been thinking -' 'Not really?' whispered Robert.

'In the silent what's-its-names of the night. It's like suddenly being asked something out of history - the date of the Conquest or something; you know it all right all the time, but when you're asked it all goes out of your head. Ladies and gentlemen, you know jolly well that when we're all rotting about in the usual way heaps of things keep cropping up, and then real earnest wishes come into the heads of the beholder -'

'Hear, hear!' said Robert.

'- of the beholder, however stupid he is,' Cyril went on. 'Why, even Robert might happen to think of a really useful wish if he didn't injure his poor little brains trying so hard to think. - Shut up, Bobs, I tell you! - You'll have the whole show over.'

A struggle on the edge of a water-butt is exciting, but damp. When it was over, and the boys were partially dried, Anthea said:

'It really was you began it, Bobs. Now honour is satisfied) do let Squirrel go on. We're wasting the whole morning.'

'Well then,' said Cyril, still wringing the water out of the tails of his jacket, 'I'll call it pax if Bobs will.'

'Pax then,' said Robert sulkily. 'But I've got a lump as big as a cricket ball over my eye.'

Anthea patiently offered a dust-coloured handkerchief, and Robert bathed his wounds in silence. 'Now, Squirrel,' she said.

114

'Well then - let's just play bandits, or forts, or soldiers, or any of the old games. We're dead sure to think of something if we try not to. You always do.'

The others consented. Bandits was hastily chosen for the game. 'It's as good as anything else,' said Jane gloomily. It must be owned that Robert was at first but a half-hearted bandit, but when Anthea had borrowed from Martha the red-spotted handkerchief in which the keeper had brought her mushrooms that morning, and had tied up Robert's head with it so that he could be the wounded hero who had saved the bandit captain's life the day before, he cheered up wonderfully. All were soon armed. Bows and arrows slung on the back look well; and umbrellas and cricket stumps stuck through the belt give a fine impression of the wearer's being armed to the teeth. The white cotton hats that men wear in the country nowadays have a very brigandish effect when a few turkey's feathers are stuck in them. The Lamb's mail-cart was covered with a red-and-blue checked tablecloth, and made an admirable baggage-wagon. The Lamb asleep inside it was not at all in the way. So the banditti set out along the road that led to the sand-pit.

'We ought to be near the Sammyadd,' said Cyril, 'in case we think of anything suddenly.'

It is all very well to make up your minds to play bandits - or chess, or ping-pong, or any other agreeable game - but it is not easy to do it with spirit when all the wonderful wishes you can think of, or can't think of, are waiting for you round the corner. The game was dragging a little, and some of the bandits were beginning to feel that the others were disagreeable things, and were saying so candidly, when the baker's boy came along the road with loaves in a basket. The opportunity was not one to be lost.

'Stand and deliver!' cried Cyril.

'Your money or your life!' said Robert.

And they stood on each side of the baker's boy. Unfortunately, he did not seem to enter into the spirit of the thing at all. He was a baker's boy of an unusually large size. He merely said:

'Chuck it now, d'ye hear!' and pushed the bandits aside most disrespectfully.

Then Robert lassoed him with jane's skipping-rope, and instead of going round his shoulders, as Robert intended, it went round his feet and tripped him up. The basket was upset, the beautiful new loaves went bumping and bouncing all over the dusty chalky road. The girls ran to pick them up, and all in a moment Robert and the baker's boy were fighting it out, man to man, with Cyril to see fair play, and the skipping-rope twisting round their legs like an interested snake that wished to be a peacemaker. It did not succeed; indeed the way the boxwood handles sprang up and hit the fighters on the shins and ankles was not at all peace-making. I know this is the second fight - or contest - in this chapter, but I can't help it. It was that sort of day. You know yourself there are days when rows seem to keep on happening, quite without your meaning them to. If I were a writer of tales of adventure such as those which used to appear in The Boys of England when I was young, of course I should be able to describe the fight, but I cannot do it. I never can see what happens during a fight, even when it is only dogs. Also, if I had been one of these Boys of England writers, Robert would have got the best of it. But I am like George Washington - I cannot tell a lie, even about a cherry-tree, much less about a fight, and I cannot conceal from you that Robert was badly beaten, for the second time that day. The baker's boy blacked his other eye, and, being ignorant of the first rules of fair play and gentlemanly behaviour, he also pulled Robert's hair, and kicked him on the knee. Robert always used to say he could have licked the butcher if it hadn't been for the girls. But I am not sure. Anyway, what happened was this, and very painful it was to self-respecting boys.

Cyril was just tearing off his coat so as to help his brother in proper style, when Jane threw her arms round his legs and began to cry and ask him not to go and be beaten too. That 'too' was very nice for

Robert, as you can imagine - but it was nothing to what he felt when Anthea rushed in between him and the baker's boy, and caught that unfair and degraded fighter round the waist, imploring him not to fight any more.

'Oh, don't hurt my brother any more!' she said in floods of tears. 'He didn't mean it - it's only play. And I'm sure he's very sorry.'

You see how unfair this was to Robert. Because, if the baker's boy had had any right and chivalrous instincts, and had yielded to Anthea's pleading and accepted her despicable apology, Robert could not, in honour, have done anything to him at a future time. But Robert's fears, if he had any, were soon dispelled. Chivalry was a stranger to the breast of the baker's boy. He pushed Anthea away very roughly, and he chased Robert with kicks and unpleasant conversation right down the road to the sand-pit, and there, with one last kick, he landed him in a heap of sand.

'I'D larn you, you young varmint!' he said, and went off to pick up his loaves and go about his business. Cyril, impeded by Jane, could do nothing without hurting her, for she clung round his legs with the strength of despair. The baker's boy went off red and damp about the face; abusive to the last, he called them a pack of silly idiots, and disappeared round the corner. Then jane's grasp loosened. Cyril turned away in silent dignity to follow Robert, and the girls followed him, weeping without restraint.

It was not a happy party that flung itself down in the sand beside the sobbing Robert. For Robert was sobbing - mostly with rage. Though of course I know that a really heroic boy is always dry-eyed after a fight. But then he always wins, which had not been the case with Robert.

Cyril was angry with Jane; Robert was furious with Anthea; the girls were miserable; and not one of the four was pleased with the baker's boy. There was, as French writers say, 'a silence full of emotion'.

Then Robert dug his toes and his hands into the sand and wriggled in his rage. 'He'd better wait till I'm grown up - the cowardly brute! Beast! - I hate him! But I'll pay him out. just because he's bigger than me.'

'You began,' said Jane incautiously.

'I know I did, silly - but I was only rotting - and he kicked me - look here -'

Robert tore down a stocking and showed a purple bruise touched up with red. 'I only wish I was bigger than him, that's all.'

He dug his fingers in the sand, and sprang up, for his hand had touched something furry. It was the Psammead, of course - 'On the look-out to make sillies of them as usual,' as Cyril remarked later. And of course the next moment Robert's wish was granted, and he was bigger than the baker's boy. Oh, but much, much bigger. He was bigger than the big policeman who used to be at the crossing at the Mansion House years ago - the one who was so kind in helping old ladies over the crossing - and he was the biggest man I have ever seen, as well as the kindest. No one had a foot-rule in its pocket, so Robert could not be measured - but he was taller than your father would be if he stood on your mother's head, which I am sure he would never be unkind enough to do. He must have been ten or eleven feet high, and as broad as a boy of that height ought to be. his Norfolk suit had fortunately grown too, and now he stood up in it - with one of his enormous stockings turned down to show the gigantic bruise on his vast leg. Immense tears of fury still stood on his flushed giant face. He looked so surprised, and he was so large to be wearing an Eton collar, that the others could not help laughing.

'The Sammyadd's done us again,' said Cyril.

'Not us - ME,' said Robert. 'If you'd got any decent feeling you'd try to make it make you the same size. You've no idea how silly it feels,' he added thoughtlessly.

'And I don't want to; I can jolly well see how silly it looks,'
Cyril was beginning; but Anthea said:

'Oh, DON'T! I don't know what's the matter with you boys to-day.
Look here, Squirrel, let's play fair. It is hateful for poor old Bobs, all
alone up there. Let's ask the Sammyadd for another wish, and, if it
will, I do really think we ought to be made the same size.'

The others agreed, but not gaily; but when they found the
Psammead, it wouldn't.

'Not I,' it said crossly, rubbing its face with its feet. He's a rude
violent boy, and it'll do him good to be the wrong size for a bit.
What did he want to come digging me out with his nasty wet hands
for? He nearly touched me! He's a perfect savage. A boy of the
Stone Age would have had more sense.'

Robert's hands had indeed been wet - with tears.

'Go away and leave me in peace, do,' the Psammead went on. 'I can't
think why you don't wish for something sensible - something to eat
or drink, or good manners, or good tempers. Go along with you, do!'

It almost snarled as it shook its whiskers, and turned a sulky brown
back on them. The most hopeful felt that further parley was vain.
They turned again to the colossal Robert.

'Whatever shall we do?' they said; and they all said it.

'First,' said Robert grimly, 'I'm going to reason with that baker's boy.
I shall catch him at the end of the road.'

'Don't hit a chap littler than yourself, old man,' said Cyril.

'Do I look like hitting him?' said Robert scornfully. 'Why, I should
KILL him. But I'll give him something to remember. Wait till I pull
up my stocking.' He pulled up his stocking, which was as large as a
small bolster-case, and strode off. His strides were six or seven feet

long, so that it was quite easy for him to be at the bottom of the hill, ready to meet the baker's boy when he came down swinging the empty basket to meet his master's cart, which had been leaving bread at the cottages along the road.

Robert crouched behind a haystack in the farmyard, that is at the corner, and when he heard the boy come whistling along, he jumped out at him and caught him by the collar.

'Now,' he said, and his voice was about four times its usual size, just as his body was four times its, 'I'm going to teach you to kick boys smaller than you.'

He lifted up the baker's boy and sct him on the top of the haystack, which was about sixteen feet from the ground, and then he sat down on the roof of the cowshed and told the baker's boy exactly what he thought of him. I don't think the boy heard it all - he was in a sort of trance of terror. When Robert had said everything he could think of, and some things twice over, he shook the boy and said:

'And now get down the best way you can,' and left him.

I don't know how the baker's boy got down, but I do know that he missed the cart, and got into the very hottest of hot water when he turned up at last at the bakehouse. I am sorry for him, but, after all, it was quite right that he should be taught that English boys mustn't use their feet when they fight, but their fists. Of course the water he got into only became hotter when he tried to tell his master about the boy he had licked and the giant as high as a church, because no one could possibly believe such a tale as that. Next day the tale was believed - but that was too late to be of any use to the baker's boy.

When Robert rejoined the others he found them in the garden. Anthea had thoughtfully asked Martha to let them have dinner out there - because the dining-room was rather small, and it would have been so awkward to have a brother the size of Robert in there. The Lamb, who had slept peacefully during the whole stormy morning, was now found to be sneezing, and Martha said he had a cold and would be better indoors.

'And really it's just as well,' said Cyril, 'for I don't believe he'd ever have stopped screaming if he'd once seen you the awful size you are!'

Robert was indeed what a draper would call an 'out-size' in boys. He found himself able to step right over the iron gate in the front garden.

Martha brought out the dinner - it was cold veal and baked potatoes, with sago pudding and stewed plums to follow.

She of course did not notice that Robert was anything but the usual size, and she gave him as much meat and potatoes as usual and no more. You have no idea how small your usual helping of dinner looks when you are many times your proper size. Robert groaned, and asked for more bread. But Martha would not go on giving more bread for ever. She was in a hurry, because the keeper intended to call on his way to Benenhurst Fair, and she wished to be dressed smartly before he came.

'I wish WE were going to the Fair,' said Robert.

'You can't go anywhere that size,' said Cyril.

'Why not?' said Robert. 'They have giants at fairs, much bigger ones than me.'

'Not much, they don't,' Cyril was beginning, when Jane screamed 'Oh!' with such loud suddenness that they all thumped her on the back and asked whether she had swallowed a plum-stone.

'No,' she said, breathless from being thumped, 'it's - it's not a plum-stone. it's an idea. Let's take Robert to the Fair, and get them to give us money for showing him! Then we really shall get something out of the old Sammyadd at last!'

'Take me, indeed!' said Robert indignantly. 'Much more likely me take you!'

And so it turned out. The idea appealed irresistibly to everyone but Robert, and even he was brought round by Anthea's suggestion that he should have a double share of any money they might make. There was a little old pony-trap in the coach-house - the kind that is called a governess-cart. It seemed desirable to get to the Fair as quickly as possible, so Robert - who could now take enormous steps and so go very fast indeed - consented to wheel the others in this. It was as easy to him now as wheeling the Lamb in the mail-cart had been in the morning. The Lamb's cold prevented his being of the party.

It was a strange sensation being wheeled in a pony-carriage by a giant. Everyone enjoyed the journey except Robert and the few people they passed on the way. These mostly went into what looked like some kind of standing-up fits by the roadside, as Anthea said. just outside Benenhurst, Robert hid in a barn, and the others went on to the Fair.

There were some swings, and a hooting tooting blaring merry-go-round, and a shooting-gallery and coconut shies. Resisting an impulse to win a coconut - or at least to attempt the enterprise - Cyril went up to the woman who was loading little guns before the array of glass bottles on strings against a sheet of canvas.

'Here you are, little gentleman!' she said. 'Penny a shot!'

'No, thank you,' said Cyril, 'we are here on business, not on pleasure. Who's the master?'

'The what?'

'The master - the head - the boss of the show.'

'Over there,' she said, pointing to a stout man in a dirty linen jacket who was sleeping in the sun; 'but I don't advise you to wake him sudden. His temper's contrary, especially these hot days. Better have a shot while you're waiting.'

'It's rather important,' said Cyril. 'It'll be very profitable to him. I think he'll be sorry if we take it away.'

'Oh, if it's money in his pocket,' said the woman. 'No kid now? What is it?'

'It's a GIANT.'

'You ARE kidding?'

'Come along and see,' said Anthea.

The woman looked doubtfully at them, then she called to a ragged little girl in striped stockings and a dingy white petticoat that came below her brown frock, and leaving her in charge of the 'shooting-gallery' she turned to Anthea and said, 'Well, hurry up! But if you ARE kidding, you'd best say so. I'm as mild as milk myself, but my Bill he's a fair terror and -'

Anthea led the way to the barn. 'It really IS a giant,' she said. 'He's a giant little boy - in Norfolks like my brother's there. And we didn't bring him up to the Fair because people do stare so, and they seem to go into kind of standing-up fits when they see him. And we thought perhaps you'd like to show him and get pennies; and if you like to pay us something, you can - only, it'll have to be rather a lot, because we promised him he should have a double share of whatever we made.'

The woman murmured something indistinct, of which the children could only hear the words, 'Swelp me!' 'balmy,' and 'crumpet,' which conveyed no definite idea to their minds. She had taken Anthea's hand, and was holding it very firmly; and Anthea could not help wondering what would happen if Robert should have wandered off or turned his proper size during the interval. But she knew that the Psammead's gifts really did last till sunset, however inconvenient their lasting might be; and she did not think, somehow, that Robert would care to go out alone while he was that size.

When they reached the barn and Cyril called 'Robert!' there was a stir among the loose hay, and Robert began to come out. His hand and arm came first - then a foot and leg. When the woman saw the hand she said 'My!' but when she saw the foot she said 'Upon my civvy!' and when, by slow and heavy degrees, the whole of Robert's enormous bulk was at last completely disclosed, she drew a long breath and began to say many things, compared with which 'balmy' and 'crumpet' seemed quite ordinary. She dropped into understandable English at last.

'What'll you take for him?' she said excitedly. 'Anything in reason. We'd have a special van built - leastways, I know where there's a second-hand one would do up handsome - what a baby elephant had, as died. What'll you take? He's soft, ain't he? Them giants mostly is - but I never see - no, never! What'll you take? Down on the nail. We'll treat him like a king, and give him first-rate grub and a doss fit for a bloomin' dook. He must be dotty or he wouldn't need you kids to cart him about. What'll you take for him?'

'They won't take anything,' said Robert sternly. 'I'm no more soft than you are - not so much, I shouldn't wonder. I'll come and be a show for to-day if you'll give me' - he hesitated at the enormous price he was about to ask - 'if you'll give me fifteen shillings.'

'Done,' said the woman, so quickly that Robert felt he had been unfair to himself, and wished he had asked thirty. 'Come on now - and see my Bill - and we'll fix a price for the season. I dessay you might get as much as two quid a week reg'lar. Come on - and make yourself as small as you can, for gracious' sake!'

This was not very small, and a crowd gathered quickly, so that it was at the head of an enthusiastic procession that Robert entered the trampled meadow where the Fair was held, and passed over the stubbly yellow dusty grass to the door of the biggest tent. He crept in, and the woman went to call her Bill. He was the big sleeping

124

man, and he did not seem at all pleased at being awakened. Cyril, watching through a slit in the tent, saw him scowl and shake a heavy fist and a sleepy head. Then the woman went on speaking very fast. Cyril heard 'Strewth,' and 'biggest draw you ever, so help me!' and he began to share Robert's feeling that fifteen shillings was indeed far too little. Bill slouched up to the tent and entered. When he beheld the magnificent proportions of Robert he said but little - 'Strike me pink!' were the only words the children could afterwards remember - but he produced fifteen shillings, mainly in sixpences and coppers, and handed it to Robert.

'We'll fix up about what you're to draw when the show's over to-night,' he said with hoarse heartiness. 'Lor' love a duck! you'll be that happy with us you'll never want to leave us. Can you do a song now - or a bit of a breakdown?'

'Not to-day,' said Robert, rejecting the idea of trying to sing 'As once in May', a favourite of his mother's, and the only song he could think of at the moment.

'Get Levi and clear them bloomin' photos out. Clear the tent. Stick up a curtain or suthink,' the man went on. 'Lor', what a pity we ain't got no tights his size! But we'll have 'em before the week's out. Young man, your fortune's made. It's a good thing you came to me, and not to some chaps as I could tell you on. I've known blokes as beat their giants, and starved 'em too; so I'll tell you straight, you're in luck this day if you never was afore. 'Cos I'm a lamb, I am - and I don't deceive you.'

'I'm not afraid of anyone's beating ME,' said Robert, looking down on the 'lamb'. Robert was crouched on his knees, because the tent was not big enough for him to stand upright in, but even in that position he could still look down on most people. 'But I'm awfully hungry I wish you'd get me something to eat.'

'Here, 'Becca,' said the hoarse Bill. 'Get him some grub - the best you've got, mind!' Another whisper followed, of which the children only heard, 'Down in black and white - first thing to-morrow.'

Then the woman went to get the food - it was only bread and cheese when it came, but it was delightful to the large and empty Robert; and the man went to post sentinels round the tent, to give the alarm if Robert should attempt to escape with his fifteen shillings.

'As if we weren't honest,' said Anthea indignantly when the meaning of the sentinels dawned on her.

Then began a very strange and wonderful afternoon.

Bill was a man who knew his business. In a very little while, the photographic views, the spyglasses you look at them through, so that they really seem rather real, and the lights you see them by, were all packed away. A curtain - it was an old red-and-black carpet really - was run across the tent. Robert was concealed behind, and Bill was standing on a trestle-table outside the tent making a speech. It was rather a good speech. It began by saying that the giant it was his privilege to introduce to the public that day was the eldest son of the Emperor of San Francisco, compelled through an unfortunate love affair with the Duchess of the Fiji Islands to leave his own country and take refuge in England - the land of liberty - where freedom was the right of every man, no matter how big he was. It ended by the announcement that the first twenty who came to the tent door should see the giant for threepence apiece. 'After that,' said Bill, 'the price is riz, and I don't undertake to say what it won't be riz to. So now's yer time.'

A young man squiring his sweetheart on her afternoon out was the first to come forward. For that occasion his was the princely attitude - no expense spared - money no object. His girl wished to see the giant? Well, she should see the giant, even though seeing the giant cost threepence each and the other entertainments were all penny ones.

The flap of the tent was raised - the couple entered. Next moment a wild shriek from the girl thrilled through all present. Bill slapped his leg. 'That's done the trick!' he whispered to 'Becca. It was indeed a splendid advertisement of the charms of Robert. When the girl came out she was pale and trembling, and a crowd was round the tent.

'What was it like?' asked a bailiff.

'Oh! - horrid! - you wouldn't believe,' she said. 'It's as big as a barn, and that fierce. It froze the blood in my bones. I wouldn't ha' missed seeing it for anything.'

The fierceness was only caused by Robert's trying not to laugh. But the desire to do that soon left him, and before sunset he was more inclined to cry than to laugh, and more inclined to sleep than either. For, by ones and twos and threes, people kept coming in all the afternoon, and Robert had to shake hands with those who wished it, and allow himself to be punched and pulled and patted and thumped, so that people might make sure he was really real.

The other children sat on a bench and watched and waited, and were very bored indeed. It seemed to them that this was the hardest way of earning money that could have been invented. And only fifteen shillings! Bill had taken four times that already, for the news of the giant had spread, and tradespeople in carts, and gentlepeople in carriages, came from far and near. One gentleman with an eyeglass, and a very large yellow rose in his buttonhole, offered Robert, in an obliging whisper, ten pounds a week to appear at the Crystal Palace. Robert had to say 'No'.

'I can't,' he said regretfully. 'It's no use promising what you can't do.'

'Ah, poor fellow, bound for a term of years, I suppose! Well, here's my card; when your time's up come to me.'

'I will - if I'm the same size then,' said Robert truthfully.

'If you grow a bit, so much the better,' said the gentleman.
When he had gone, Robert beckoned Cyril and said:

'Tell them I must and will have an easy. And I want my tea.'

Tea was provided, and a paper hastily pinned on the tent. It said:

CLOSED FOR HALF AN HOUR
WHILE THE GIANT GETS HIS TEA

Then there was a hurried council.

'How am I to get away?' said Robert. 'I've been thinking about it all the afternoon.'

'Why, walk out when the sun sets and you're your right size. They can't do anything to us.'

Robert opened his eyes. 'Why, they'd nearly kill us,' he said, 'when they saw me get my right size. No, we must think of some other way. We MUST be alone when the sun sets.'

'I know,' said Cyril briskly, and he went to the door, outside which Bill was smoking a clay pipe and talking in a low voice to 'Becca. Cyril heard him say - 'Good as havin' a fortune left you.'

'Look here,' said Cyril, 'you can let people come in again in a minute. He's nearly finished his tea. But he must be left alone when the sun sets. He's very queer at that time of day, and if he's worried I won't answer for the consequences.'

'Why - what comes over him?' asked Bill.

'I don't know; it's - it's a sort of a change,' said Cyril candidly. 'He isn't at all like himself - you'd hardly know him. He's very queer indeed. Someone'll get hurt if he's not alone about sunset.' This was true.

'He'll pull round for the evening, I s'pose?'

'Oh yes - half an hour after sunset he'll be quite himself again.'

128

'Best humour him,' said the woman.

And so, at what Cyril judged was about half an hour before sunset, the tent was again closed 'whilst the giant gets his supper'.

The crowd was very merry about the giant's meals and their coming so close together.

'Well, he can pick a bit,' Bill owned. 'You see he has to eat hearty, being the size he is.'

Inside the tent the four children breathlessly arranged a plan of retreat. 'You go NOW,' said Cyril to the girls, 'and get along home as fast as you can. Oh, never mind the beastly pony-cart; we'll get that to-morrow. Robert and I are dressed the same. We'll manage somehow, like Sydney Carton did. Only, you girls MUST get out, or it's all no go. We can run, but you can't - whatever you may think. No, Jane, it's no good Robert going out and knocking people down. The police would follow him till he turned his proper size, and then arrest him like a shot. Go you must! If you don't, I'll never speak to you again. It was you got us into this mess really, hanging round people's legs the way you did this morning. Go, I tell you!'

And Jane and Anthea went.

'We're going home,' they said to Bill. 'We're leaving the giant with you. Be kind to him.' And that, as Anthea said afterwards, was very deceitful, but what were they to do?

When they had gone, Cyril went to Bill.

'Look here,' he said, 'he wants some ears of corn - there's some in the next field but one. I'll just run and get it. Oh, and he says can't you loop up the tent at the back a bit? He says he's stifling for a breath of air. I'll see no one peeps in at him. I'll cover him up, and he can take a nap while I go for the corn. He WILL have it - there's no holding him when he gets like this.'

The giant was made comfortable with a heap of sacks and an old tarpaulin. The curtain was looped up, and the brothers were left alone. They matured their plan in whispers. Outside, the merry-go-round blared out its comic tunes, screaming now and then to attract public notice.

Half a minute after the sun had set, a boy in a Norfolk suit came out past Bill.

'I'm off for the corn,' he said, and mingled quickly with the crowd.

At the same instant a boy came out of the back of the tent past 'Becca, posted there as sentinel.

'I'm off after the corn,' said this boy also. And he, too, moved away quietly and was lost in the crowd. The front-door boy was Cyril; the back-door was Robert - now, since sunset, once more his proper size. They walked quickly through the field, and along the road, where Robert caught Cyril up. Then they ran. They were home as soon as the girls were, for it was a long way, and they ran most of it. It was indeed a very long way, as they found when they had to go and drag the pony-trap home next morning, with no enormous Robert to wheel them in it as if it were a mail-cart, and they were babies and he was their gigantic nursemaid.

I cannot possibly tell you what Bill and 'Becca said when they found that the giant had gone. For one thing, I do not know.

CHAPTER 9. GROWN UP

Cyril had once pointed out that ordinary life is full of occasions on which a wish would be most useful. And this thought filled his mind when he happened to wake early on the morning after the morning after Robert had wished to be bigger than the baker's boy, and had been it. The day that lay between these two days had been occupied entirely by getting the governess-cart home from Benenhurst.

Cyril dressed hastily; he did not take a bath, because tin baths are so noisy, and he had no wish to rouse Robert, and he slipped off alone, as Anthea had once done, and ran through the dewy morning to the sand-pit. He dug up the Psammead very carefully and kindly, and began the conversation by asking it whether it still felt any ill effects from the contact with the tears of Robert the day before yesterday. The Psammead was in a good temper. It replied politely.

'And now, what can I do for you?' it said. 'I suppose you've come here so early to ask for something for yourself, something your brothers and sisters aren't to know about eh? Now, do be persuaded for your own good! Ask for a good fat Megatherium and have done with it.'

'Thank you - not to-day, I think,' said Cyril cautiously. 'What I really wanted to say was - you know how you're always wishing for things when you're playing at anything?'

'I seldom play,' said the Psammead coldly.

'Well, you know what I mean,' Cyril went on impatiently. 'What I want to say is: won't you let us have our wish just when we think of it, and just where we happen to be? So that we don't have to come and disturb you again,' added the crafty Cyril.

'It'll only end in your wishing for something you don't really want, like you did about the castle,' said the Psammead, stretching its brown arms and yawning. 'It's always the same since people left off eating really wholesome things. However, have it your own way. Good-bye.'

'Good-bye,' said Cyril politely.

'I'll tell you what,' said the Psammead suddenly, shooting out its long snail's eyes - 'I'm getting tired of you - all of you. You have no more sense than so many oysters. Go along with you!' And Cyril went.

'What an awful long time babies STAY babies,' said Cyril after the Lamb had taken his watch out of his pocket while he wasn't noticing, and with coos and clucks of naughty rapture had opened the case and used the whole thing as a garden spade, and when even immersion in a wash-hand basin had failed to wash the mould from the works and make the watch go again. Cyril had said several things in the heat of the moment; but now he was calmer, and had even consented to carry the Lamb part of the way to the woods. Cyril had persuaded the others to agree to his plan, and not to wish for anything more till they really did wish it. Meantime it seemed good to go to the woods for nuts, and on the mossy grass under a sweet chestnut-tree the five were sitting. The Lamb was pulling up the moss by fat handfuls, and Cyril was gloomily contemplating the ruins of his watch.

'He does grow,' said Anthea. 'Doesn't oo, precious?'

'Me grow,' said the Lamb cheerfully - 'me grow big boy, have guns an' mouses - an' - an' …' Imagination or vocabulary gave out here. But anyway it was the longest speech the Lamb had ever made, and it charmed everyone, even Cyril, who tumbled the Lamb over and rolled him in the moss to the music of delighted squeals.

'I suppose he'll be grown up someday,' Anthea was saying, dreamily looking up at the blue of the sky that showed between the long straight chestnut-leaves. But at that moment the Lamb, struggling gaily with Cyril, thrust a stoutly-shod little foot against his brother's chest; there was a crack! - the innocent Lamb had broken the glass of father's second-best Waterbury watch, which Cyril had borrowed without leave.

'Grow up someday!' said Cyril bitterly, plumping the Lamb down on the grass. 'I daresay he will when nobody wants him to. I wish to goodness he would -'

'OH, take care!' cried Anthea in an agony of apprehension. But it was too late - like music to a song her words and Cyril's came out together - Anthea - 'Oh, take care!' Cyril - 'Grow up now!'

132

The faithful Psammead was true to its promise, and there, before the horrified eyes of its brothers and sisters, the Lamb suddenly and violently grew up. It was the most terrible moment. The change was not so sudden as the wish-changes usually were. The Baby's face changed first. It grew thinner and larger, lines came in the forehead, the eyes grew more deep-set and darker in colour, the mouth grew longer and thinner; most terrible of all, a little dark moustache appeared on the lip of one who was still - except as to the face - a two-year-old baby in a linen smock and white open-work socks.

'Oh, I wish it wouldn't! Oh, I wish it wouldn't! You boys might wish as well!' They all wished hard, for the sight was enough to dismay the most heartless. They all wished so hard, indeed, that they felt quite giddy and almost lost consciousness; but the wishing was quite vain, for, when the wood ceased to whirl round, their dazzled eyes were riveted at once by the spectacle of a very proper-looking young man in flannels and a straw hat - a young man who wore the same little black moustache which just before they had actually seen growing upon the Baby's lip. This, then, was the Lamb - grown up! Their own Lamb! It was a terrible moment. The grown-up Lamb moved gracefully across the moss and settled himself against the trunk of the sweet chestnut. He tilted the straw hat over his eyes. He was evidently weary. He was going to sleep. The Lamb - the original little tiresome beloved Lamb often went to sleep at odd times and in unexpected places. Was this new Lamb in the grey flannel suit and the pale green necktie like the other Lamb? or had his mind grown up together with his body?

That was the question which the others, in a hurried council held among the yellowing bracken a few yards from the sleeper, debated eagerly.

'Whichever it is, it'll be just as awful,' said Anthea. 'If his inside senses are grown up too, he won't stand our looking after him; and if he's still a baby inside of him how on earth are we to get him to do anything? And it'll be getting on for dinner-time in a minute 'And we haven't got any nuts,' said Jane.

133

'Oh, bother nuts!' said Robert; 'but dinner's different - I didn't have half enough dinner yesterday. Couldn't we tie him to the tree and go home to our dinners and come back afterwards?'

'A fat lot of dinner we should get if we went back without the Lamb!' said Cyril in scornful misery. 'And it'll be just the same if we go back with him in the state he is now. Yes, I know it's my doing; don't rub it in! I know I'm a beast, and not fit to live; you can take that for settled, and say no more about it. The question is, what are we going to do?'

'Let's wake him up, and take him into Rochester or Maidstone and get some grub at a pastrycook's,' said Robert hopefully.

'Take him?' repeated Cyril. 'Yes - do! It's all MY fault - I don't deny that - but you'll find you've got your work cut out for you if you try to take that young man anywhere. The Lamb always was spoilt, but now he's grown up he's a demon - simply. I can see it. Look at his mouth.'

'Well then,' said Robert, 'let's wake him up and see what HE'LL do. Perhaps HE'LL take us to Maidstone and stand Sam. He ought to have a lot of money in the pockets of those extra-special bags. We MUST have dinner, anyway.'

They drew lots with little bits of bracken. It fell to jane's lot to waken the grown-up Lamb.

She did it gently by tickling his nose with a twig of wild honeysuckle. He said 'Bother the flies!' twice, and then opened his eyes.

'Hullo, kiddies!' he said in a languid tone, 'still here? What's the giddy hour? You'll be late for your grub!'

'I know we shall,' said Robert bitterly.

'Then cut along home,' said the grown-up Lamb.

'What about your grub, though?' asked Jane.

'Oh, how far is it to the station, do you think? I've a sort of notion that I'll run up to town and have some lunch at the club.'

Blank misery fell like a pall on the four others. The Lamb - alone - unattended - would go to town and have lunch at a club! Perhaps he would also have tea there. Perhaps sunset would come upon him amid the dazzling luxury of club-land, and a helpless cross sleepy baby would find itself alone amid unsympathetic waiters, and would wail miserably for 'Panty' from the depths of a club arm-chair! The picture moved Anthea almost to tears.

'Oh no, Lamb ducky, you mustn't do that!' she cried incautiously.

The grown-up Lamb frowned. 'My dear Anthea,' he said, 'how often am I to tell you that my name is Hilary or St Maur or Devereux? - any of my baptismal names are free to my little brothers and sisters, but NOT "Lamb" - a relic of foolish and far-off childhood.'

This was awful. He was their elder brother now, was he? Well, of course he was, if he was grown up - since they weren't. Thus, in whispers, Anthea and Robert.

But the almost daily adventures resulting from the Psammead wishes were making the children wise beyond their years.

'Dear Hilary,' said Anthea, and the others choked at the name, 'you know father didn't wish you to go to London. He wouldn't like us to be left alone without you to take care of us. Oh, deceitful beast that I am!' she added to herself.

'Look here,' said Cyril, 'if you're our elder brother, why not behave as such and take us over to Maidstone and give us a jolly good blow-out, and we'll go on the river afterwards?'

'I'm infinitely obliged to you,' said the Lamb courteously, 'but I should prefer solitude. Go home to your lunch - I mean your dinner.

135

Perhaps I may look in about tea-time - or I may not be home till after you are in your beds.'

Their beds! Speaking glances flashed between the wretched four. Much bed there would be for them if they went home without the Lamb.

'We promised mother not to lose sight of you if we took you out,'Jane said before the others could stop her.

'Look here, Jane,' said the grown-up Lamb, putting his hands in his pockets and looking down at her, 'little girls should be seen and not heard. You kids must learn not to make yourselves a nuisance. Run along home now - and perhaps, if you're good, I'll give you each a penny to-morrow.'

'Look here,' said Cyril, in the best 'man to man' tone at his command, 'where are you going, old man? You might let Bobs and me come with you - even if you don't want the girls.'

This was really rather noble of Cyril, for he never did care much about being seen in public with the Lamb, who of course after sunset would be a baby again.

The 'man to man' tone succeeded.

'I shall just run over to Maidstone on my bike,' said the new Lamb airily, fingering the little black moustache. 'I can lunch at The Crown - and perhaps I'll have a pull on the river; but I can't take you all on the machine - now, can I? Run along home, like good children.'

The position was desperate. Robert exchanged a despairing look with Cyril. Anthea detached a pin from her waistband, a pin whose withdrawal left a gaping chasm between skirt and bodice, and handed it furtively to Robert - with a grimace of the darkest and deepest meaning. Robert slipped away to the road. There, sure enough, stood a bicycle - a beautiful new free-wheel. Of course

136

Robert understood at once that if the Lamb was grown up he MUST have a bicycle. This had always been one of Robert's own reasons for wishing to be grown up. He hastily began to use the pin - eleven punctures in the back tyre, seven in the front. He would have made the total twenty-two but for the rustling of the yellow hazel-leaves, which warned him of the approach of the others. He hastily leaned a hand on each wheel, and was rewarded by the 'whish' of what was left of the air escaping from eighteen neat pin-holes.

'Your bike's run down,' said Robert, wondering how he could so soon have learned to deceive.

'So it is,' said Cyril.

'It's a puncture,' said Anthea, stooping down, and standing up again with a thorn which she had got ready for the purpose. 'Look here.'

The grown-up Lamb (or Hilary, as I suppose one must now call him) fixed his pump and blew up the tyre. The punctured state of it was soon evident.

'I suppose there's a cottage somewhere near - where one could get a pail of water?' said the Lamb.

There was; and when the number of punctures had been made manifest, it was felt to be a special blessing that the cottage provided 'teas for cyclists'. It provided an odd sort of tea-and-hammy meal for the Lamb and his brothers. This was paid for out of the fifteen shillings which had been earned by Robert when he was a giant - for the Lamb, it appeared, had unfortunately no money about him. This was a great disappointment for the others; but it is a thing that will happen, even to the most grown-up of us. However, Robert had enough to eat, and that was something. Quietly but persistently the miserable four took it in turns to try to persuade the Lamb (or St Maur) to spend the rest of the day in the woods. There was not very much of the day left by the time he had mended the eighteenth puncture. He looked up from the completed work with a sigh of relief, and suddenly put his tie straight.

137

'There's a lady coming,' he said briskly - 'for goodness' sake, get out of the way. Go home - hide - vanish somehow! I can't be seen with a pack of dirty kids.' His brothers and sisters were indeed rather dirty, because, earlier in the day, the Lamb, in his infant state, had sprinkled a good deal of garden soil over them. The grown-up Lamb's voice was so tyrant-like, as Jane said afterwards, that they actually retreated to the back garden, and left him with his little moustache and his flannel suit to meet alone the young lady, who now came up the front garden wheeling a bicycle.

The woman of the house came out, and the young lady spoke to her - the Lamb raised his hat as she passed him - and the children could not hear what she said, though they were craning round the corner by the pig-pail and listening with all their ears. They felt it to be 'perfectly fair,' as Robert said, 'with that wretched Lamb in that condition.'

When the Lamb spoke in a languid voice heavy with politeness, they heard well enough.

'A puncture?' he was saying. 'Can I not be of any assistance? If you could allow me -?'

There was a stifled explosion of laughter behind the pig-pail - the grown-up Lamb (otherwise Devereux) turned the tail of an angry eye in its direction.

'You're very kind,' said the lady, looking at the Lamb. She looked rather shy, but, as the boys put it, there didn't seem to be any nonsense about her.

'But oh,' whispered Cyril behind the pig-pail, 'I should have thought he'd had enough bicycle-mending for one day - and if she only knew that really and truly he's only a whiny-piny, silly little baby!'

'He's not,' Anthea murmured angrily. 'He's a dear - if people only let him alone. It's our own precious Lamb still, whatever silly idiots may turn him into - isn't he, Pussy?'

138

Jane doubtfully supposed so.

Now, the Lamb - whom I must try to remember to call St Maur - was examining the lady's bicycle and talking to her with a very grown-up manner indeed. No one could possibly have supposed, to see and hear him, that only that very morning he had been a chubby child of two years breaking other people's Waterbury watches. Devereux (as he ought to be called for the future) took out a gold watch when he had mended the lady's bicycle, and all the onlookers behind the pig-pail said 'Oh!' - because it seemed so unfair that the Baby, who had only that morning destroyed two cheap but honest watches, should now, in the grown-upness Cyril's folly had raised him to, have a real gold watch - with a chain and seals!

Hilary (as I will now term him) withered his brothers and sisters with a glance, and then said to the lady - with whom he seemed to be quite friendly:

'If you will allow me, I will ride with you as far as the Cross Roads; it is getting late, and there are tramps about.'

No one will ever know what answer the young lady intended to give to this gallant offer, for, directly Anthea heard it made, she rushed out, knocking against the pig-pail, which overflowed in a turbid stream, and caught the Lamb (I suppose I ought to say Hilary) by the arm. The others followed, and in an instant the four dirty children were visible, beyond disguise.

'Don't let him,' said Anthea to the lady, and she spoke with intense earnestness; 'he's not fit to go with anyone!'

'Go away, little girl!' said St Maur (as we will now call him) in a terrible voice. 'Go home at once!'

'You'd much better not have anything to do with him,' the now reckless Anthea went on. 'He doesn't know who he is. He's something very different from what you think he is.'

'What do you mean?' asked the lady not unnaturally, while Devereux (as I must term the grown-up Lamb) tried vainly to push Anthea away. The others backed her up, and she stood solid as a rock.

'You just let him go with you,' said Anthea, 'you'll soon see what I mean! How would you like to suddenly see a poor little helpless baby spinning along downhill beside you with its feet up on a bicycle it had lost control Of?'

The lady had turned rather pale.

'Who are these very dirty children?' she asked the grown-up Lamb (sometimes called St Maur in these pages).

'I don't know,' he lied miserably.

'Oh, Lamb! how can you?' cried Jane - 'when you know perfectly well you're our own little baby brother that we're so fond of. We're his big brothers and sisters,' she explained, turning to the lady, who with trembling hands was now turning her bicycle towards the gate, 'and we've got to take care of him. And we must get him home before sunset, or I don't know whatever will become of us. You see, he's sort of under a spell - enchanted - you know what I mean!'

Again and again the Lamb (Devereux, I mean) had tried to stop Jane's eloquence, but Robert and Cyril held him, one by each leg, and no proper explanation was possible. The lady rode hastily away, and electrified her relatives at dinner by telling them of her escape from a family of dangerous lunatics. 'The little girl's eyes were simply those of a maniac. I can't think how she came to be at large,' she said.

When her bicycle had whizzed away down the road, Cyril spoke gravely.

'Hilary, old chap,' he said, 'you must have had a sunstroke or something. And the things you've been saying to that lady! Why, if we were to tell you the things you've said when you are yourself again, say to- morrow morning, you wouldn't even understand them - let alone believe them! You trust to me, old chap, and come home now, and if you're not yourself in the morning we'll ask the milkman to ask the doctor to come.'

The poor grown-up Lamb (St Maur was really one of his Christian names) seemed now too bewildered to resist.

'Since you seem all to be as mad as the whole worshipful company of hatters,' he said bitterly, 'I suppose I HAD better take you home. But you're not to suppose I shall pass this over. I shall have something to say to you all to-morrow morning.'

'Yes, you will, my Lamb,' said Anthea under her breath, 'but it won't be at all the sort of thing you think it's going to be.'

In her heart she could hear the pretty, soft little loving voice of the baby Lamb - so different from the affected tones of the dreadful grown-up Lamb (one of whose names was Devereux) - saying, 'Me love Panty - wants to come to own Panty.'

'Oh, let's get home, for goodness' sake,' she said. 'You shall say whatever you like in the morning - if you can,' she added in a whisper. It was a gloomy party that went home through the soft evening. During Anthea's remarks Robert had again made play with the pin and the bicycle tyre and the Lamb (whom they had to call St Maur or Devereux or Hilary) seemed really at last to have had his fill of bicycle-mending. So the machine was wheeled.

The sun was just on the point of setting when they arrived at the White House. The four elder children would have liked to linger in the lane till the complete sunsetting turned the grown-up Lamb (whose Christian names I will not further weary you by repeating) into their own dear tiresome baby brother. But he, in his grown-upness, insisted on going on, and thus he was met in the front garden by Martha.

141

Now you remember that, as a special favour, the Psammead had arranged that the servants in the house should never notice any change brought about by the wishes of the children. Therefore Martha merely saw the usual party, with the baby Lamb, about whom she had been desperately anxious all the afternoon, trotting beside Anthea on fat baby legs, while the children, of course, still saw the grown-up Lamb (never mind what names he was christened by), and Martha rushed at him and caught him in her arms, exclaiming:

'Come to his own Martha, then - a precious poppet!'

The grown-up Lamb (whose names shall now be buried in oblivion) struggled furiously. An expression of intense horror and annoyance was seen on his face. But Martha was stronger than he. She lifted him up and carried him into the house. None of the children will ever forget that picture. The neat grey-flannel-suited grown-up young man with the green tie and the little black moustache - fortunately, he was slightly built, and not tall - struggling in the sturdy arms of Martha, who bore him away helpless, imploring him, as she went, to be a good boy now, and come and have his nice bremmilk! Fortunately, the sun set as they reached the doorstep, the bicycle disappeared, and Martha was seen to carry into the house the real live darling sleepy two-year-old Lamb. The grown-up Lamb (nameless hence- forth) was gone for ever.

'For ever,' said Cyril, 'because, as soon as ever the Lamb's old enough to be bullied, we must jolly well begin to bully him, for his own sake - so that he mayn't grow up like that.'

'You shan't bully him,' said Anthea stoutly; 'not if I can stop it.'

'We must tame him by kindness,' said Jane.

'You see,' said Robert, 'if he grows up in the usual way, there'll be plenty of time to correct him as he goes along. The awful thing to-day was his growing up so suddenly. There was no time to improve him at all.'

142

'He doesn't want any improving,' said Anthea as the voice of the Lamb came cooing through the open door, just as she had heard it in her heart that afternoon:

'Me loves Panty - wants to come to own Panty!'

CHAPTER 10. SCALPS

Probably the day would have been a greater success if Cyril had not been reading The Last of the Mohicans. The story was running in his head at breakfast, and as he took his third cup of tea he said dreamily, 'I wish there were Red Indians in England - not big ones, you know, but little ones, just about the right size for us to fight.'

Everyone disagreed with him at the time, and no one attached any importance to the incident. But when they went down to the sand-pit to ask for a hundred pounds in two-shilling pieces with Queen Victoria's head on, to prevent mistakes - which they had always felt to be a really reasonable wish that must turn out well - they found out that they had done it again! For the Psammead, which was very cross and sleepy, said:

'Oh, don't bother me. You've had your wish.'

'I didn't know it,' said Cyril.

'Don't you remember yesterday?' said the Sand-fairy, still more disagreeably. 'You asked me to let you have your wishes wherever you happened to be, and you wished this morning, and you've got it.'

'Oh, have we?' said Robert. 'What is it?'

'So you've forgotten?' said the Psammead, beginning to burrow. 'Never mind; you'll know soon enough. And I wish you joy of it! A nice thing you've let yourselves in for!'

'We always do, somehow,' said Jane sadly.

And now the odd thing was that no one could remember anyone's having wished for anything that morning. The wish about the Red Indians had not stuck in anyone's head. It was a most anxious morning. Everyone was trying to remember what had been wished for, and no one could, and everyone kept expecting something awful to happen every minute. It was most agitating; they knew, from what the Psammead had said, that they must have wished for something more than usually undesirable, and they spent several hours in most agonizing uncertainty. It was not till nearly dinner-time that Jane tumbled over The Last of the Mohicans - which had, of course, been left face downwards on the floor - and when Anthea had picked her and the book up she suddenly said, 'I know!' and sat down flat on the carpet.

'Oh, Pussy, how awful! It was Indians he wished for - Cyril - at breakfast, don't you remember? He said, "I wish there were Red Indians in England," - and now there are, and they're going about scalping people all over the country, like as not.'

'Perhaps they're only in Northumberland and Durham,' said Jane soothingly. It was almost impossible to believe that it could really hurt people much to be scalped so far away as that.

'Don't you believe it!' said Anthea. 'The Sammyadd said we'd let ourselves in for a nice thing. That means they'll come HERE. And suppose they scalped the Lamb!'

'Perhaps the scalping would come right again at sunset,' said Jane; but she did not speak so hopefully as usual.

'Not it!' said Anthea. 'The things that grow out of the wishes don't go. Look at the fifteen shillings! Pussy, I'm going to break something, and you must let me have every penny of money you've got. The Indians will come HERE, don't you see? That spiteful Psammead as good as said so. You see what my plan is? Come on!'

Jane did not see at all. But she followed her sister meekly into their mother's bedroom.

Anthea lifted down the heavy water-jug - it had a pattern of storks and long grasses on it, which Anthea never forgot. She carried it into the dressing-room, and carefully emptied the water out of it into the bath. Then she took the jug back into the bedroom and dropped it on the floor. You know how a jug always breaks if you happen to drop it by accident. If you happen to drop it on purpose, it is quite different. Anthea dropped that jug three times, and it was as unbroken as ever. So at last she had to take her father's boot-tree and break the jug with that in cold blood. It was heartless work.

Next she broke open the missionary-box with the poker. Jane told her that it was wrong, of course, but Anthea shut her lips very tight and then said:

'Don't be silly - it's a matter of life and death.'

There was not very much in the missionary-box - only seven-and-fourpence - but the girls between them had nearly four shillings. This made over eleven shillings, as you will easily see.

Anthea tied up the money in a corner of her pocket-handkerchief. 'Come on, Jane!' she said, and ran down to the farm. She knew that the farmer was going into Rochester that afternoon. In fact it had been arranged that he was to take the four children with him. They had planned this in the happy hour when they believed that they were going to get that hundred pounds, in two-shilling pieces, out of the Psammead. They had arranged to pay the farmer two shillings each for the ride. Now Anthea hastily explained to him that they could not go, but would he take Martha and the Baby instead? He agreed, but he was not pleased to get only half-a-crown instead of eight shillings.

Then the girls ran home again. Anthea was agitated, but not flurried. When she came to think it over afterwards, she could not help seeing that she had acted with the most far-seeing promptitude, just like a born general. She fetched a little box from her corner drawer, and went to find Martha, who was laying the cloth and not in the best of tempers.

'Look here,' said Anthea. 'I've broken the toilet-jug in mother's room.'

'Just like you - always up to some mischief,' said Martha, dumping down a salt-cellar with a bang.

'Don't be cross, Martha dear,' said Anthea. 'I've got enough money to pay for a new one - if only you'll be a dear and go and buy it for us. Your cousins keep a china-shop, don't they? And I would like you to get it to-day, in case mother comes home to-morrow. You know she said she might, perhaps.'

'But you're all going into town yourselves,' said Martha.

'We can't afford to, if we get the new jug,' said Anthea; 'but we'll pay for you to go, if you'll take the Lamb. And I say, Martha, look here - I'll give you my Liberty box, if you'll go. Look, it's most awfully pretty - all inlaid with real silver and ivory and ebony like King Solomon's temple.'

'I see,' said Martha; 'no, I don't want your box, miss. What you want is to get the precious Lamb off your hands for the afternoon. Don't you go for to think I don't see through you!'

This was so true that Anthea longed to deny it at once - Martha had no business to know so much. But she held her tongue.

Martha set down the bread with a bang that made it jump off its trencher.

'I DO want the jug got,' said Anthea softly. 'You WILL go, won't you?'

'Well, just for this once, I don't mind; but mind you don't get into none of your outrageous mischief while I'm gone - that's all!'

'He's going earlier than he thought,' said Anthea eagerly. 'You'd better hurry and get dressed. Do put on that lovely purple frock,

146

Martha, and the hat with the pink cornflowers, and the yellow-lace collar. Jane'll finish laying the cloth, and I'll wash the Lamb and get him ready.'

As she washed the unwilling Lamb, and hurried him into his best clothes, Anthea peeped out of the window from time to time; so far all was well - she could see no Red Indians. When with a rush and a scurry and some deepening of the damask of Martha's complexion she and the Lamb had been got off, Anthea drew a deep breath.

'HE'S safe!' she said, and, to jane's horror, flung herself down on the floor and burst into floods of tears. Jane did not understand at all how a person could be so brave and like a general, and then suddenly give way and go flat like an air-balloon when you prick it. It is better not to go flat, of course, but you will observe that Anthea did not give way till her aim was accomplished. She had got the dear Lamb out of danger - she felt certain the Red Indians would be round the White House or nowhere - the farmer's cart would not come back till after sunset, so she could afford to cry a little. It was partly with joy that she cried, because she had done what she meant to do. She cried for about three minutes, while Jane hugged her miserably and said at five-second intervals, 'Don't cry, Panther dear!'

Then she jumped up, rubbed her eyes hard with the corner of her pinafore, so that they kept red for the rest of the day, and started to tell the boys. But just at that moment cook rang the dinner-bell, and nothing could be said till they had all been helped to minced beef. Then cook left the room, and Anthea told her tale. But it is a mistake to tell a thrilling tale when people are eating minced beef and boiled potatoes. There seemed somehow to be something about the food that made the idea of Red Indians seem flat and unbelievable. The boys actually laughed, and called Anthea a little silly.

'Why,' said Cyril, 'I'm almost sure it was before I said that, that Jane said she wished it would be a fine day.'

'It wasn't,' said Jane briefly.

'Why, if it was Indians,' Cyril went on - 'salt, please, and mustard - I must have something to make this mush go down - if it was Indians, they'd have been infesting the place long before this - you know they would. I believe it's the fine day.'

'Then why did the Sammyadd say we'd let ourselves in for a nice thing?' asked Anthea. She was feeling very cross. She knew she had acted with nobility and discretion, and after that it was very hard to be called a little silly, especially when she had the weight of a burglared missionary-box and about seven-and-fourpence, mostly in coppers, lying like lead upon her conscience.

There was a silence, during which cook took away the mincy plates and brought in the treacle-pudding. As soon as she had retired, Cyril began again.

'Of course I don't mean to say,' he admitted, 'that it wasn't a good thing to get Martha and the Lamb out of the light for the afternoon; but as for Red Indians - why, you know jolly well the wishes always come that very minute. If there was going to be Red Indians, they'd be here now.'

'I expect they are,' said Anthea; 'they're lurking amid the undergrowth, for anything you know. I do think you're most beastly unkind.'

'Indians almost always DO lurk, really, though, don't they?' put in Jane, anxious for peace.

No, they don't,' said Cyril tartly. 'And I'm not unkind, I'm only truthful. And I say it was utter rot breaking the water-jug; and as for the missionary-box, I believe it's a treason-crime, and I shouldn't wonder if you could be hanged for it, if any of us was to split -'

'Shut up, can't you?' said Robert; but Cyril couldn't. You see, he felt in his heart that if there SHOULD be Indians they would be entirely his own fault, so he did not wish to believe in them. And trying not

148

to believe things when in your heart you are almost sure they are true, is as bad for the temper as anything I know.

'It's simply idiotic,' he said, 'talking about Indians, when you can see for yourselves that it's Jane who's got her wish. Look what a fine day it is - OH - '

He had turned towards the window to point out the fineness of the day - the others turned too - and a frozen silence caught at Cyril, and none of the others felt at all like breaking it. For there, peering round the corner of the window, among the red leaves of the Virginia creeper, was a face - a brown face, with a long nose and a tight mouth and very bright eyes. And the face was painted in coloured patches. It had long black hair, and in the hair were feathers!

Every child's mouth in the room opened, and stayed open. The treacle-pudding was growing white and cold on their plates. No one could move.

Suddenly the feathered head was cautiously withdrawn, and the spell was broken. I am sorry to say that Anthea's first words were very like a girl.

'There, now!' she said. 'I told you so!'

Treacle-pudding had now definitely ceased to charm. Hastily wrapping their portions in a Spectator of the week before the week before last, they hid them behind the crinkled-paper stove-ornament, and fled upstairs to reconnoitre and to hold a hurried council.

'Pax,' said Cyril handsomely when they reached their mother's bedroom. 'Panther, I'm sorry if I was a brute.'

'All right,' said Anthea, 'but you see now!'

No further trace of Indians, however, could be discerned from the windows.

'Well,' said Robert, 'what are we to do?'

'The only thing I can think of,' said Anthea, who was now generally admitted to be the heroine of the day, 'is - if we dressed up as like Indians as we can, and looked out of the windows, or even went out. They might think we were the powerful leaders of a large neighbouring tribe, and - and not do anything to us, you know, for fear of awful vengeance.'

'But Eliza, and the cook?' said Jane.

'You forget - they can't notice anything,' said Robert. 'They wouldn't notice anything out of the way, even if they were scalped or roasted at a slow fire.'

'But would they come right at sunset?'

'Of course. You can't be really scalped or burned to death without noticing it, and you'd be sure to notice it next day, even if it escaped your attention at the time,' said Cyril. 'I think Anthea's right, but we shall want a most awful lot of feathers.'

'I'll go down to the hen-house,' said Robert. 'There's one of the turkeys in there - it's not very well. I could cut its feathers without it minding much. It's very bad - doesn't seem to care what happens to it. Get me the cutting-out scissors.'

Earnest reconnoitring convinced them all that no Indians were in the poultry-yard. Robert went. In five minutes he came back - pale, but with many feathers.

'Look here,' he said, 'this is jolly serious. I cut off the feathers, and when I turned to come out there was an Indian squinting at me from under the old hen-coop. I just brandished the feathers and yelled, and got away before he could get the coop off the top of himself. Panther, get the coloured blankets off our beds, and look slippy, can't you?'

150

It is wonderful how like an Indian you can make yourselves with blankets and feathers and coloured scarves. Of course none of the children happened to have long black hair, but there was a lot of black calico that had been got to cover school-books with. They cut strips of this into a sort of fine fringe, and fastened it round their heads with the amber-coloured ribbons off the girls' Sunday dresses. Then they stuck turkeys' feathers in the ribbons. The calico looked very like long black hair, especially when the strips began to curl up a bit.

'But our faces,' said Anthea, 'they're not at all the right colour. We're all rather pale, and I'm sure I don't know why, but Cyril is the colour of putty.'

'I'm not,' said Cyril.

'The real Indians outside seem to be brownish,' said Robert hastily. 'I think we ought to be really RED - it's sort of superior to have a red skin, if you are one.'

The red ochre cook used for the kitchen bricks seemed to be about the reddest thing in the house. The children mixed some in a saucer with milk, as they had seen cook do for the kitchen floor. Then they carefully painted each other's faces and hands with it, till they were quite as red as any Red Indian need be - if not redder.

They knew at once that they must look very terrible when they met Eliza in the passage, and she screamed aloud. This unsolicited testimonial pleased them very much. Hastily telling her not to be a goose, and that it was only a game, the four blanketed, feathered, really and truly Redskins went boldly out to meet the foe. I say boldly. That is because I wish to be polite. At any rate, they went.

Along the hedge dividing the wilderness from the garden was a row of dark heads, all highly feathered.

'It's our only chance,' whispered Anthea. 'Much better than to wait for their blood-freezing attack. We must pretend like mad. Like that game of cards where you pretend you've got aces when you haven't. Fluffing they call it, I think. Now then. Whoop!'

With four wild war-whoops - or as near them as English children could be expected to go without any previous practice - they rushed through the gate and struck four warlike attitudes in face of the line of Red Indians. These were all about the same height, and that height was Cyril's.

'I hope to goodness they can talk English,' said Cyril through his attitude.

Anthea knew they could, though she never knew how she came to know it. She had a white towel tied to a walking-stick. This was a flag of truce, and she waved it, in the hope that the Indians would know what it was. Apparently they did - for one who was browner than the others stepped forward.

'Ye seek a pow-wow?' he said in excellent English. 'I am Golden Eagle, of the mighty tribe of Rock-dwellers.'
'And I,' said Anthea, with a sudden inspiration, 'am the Black Panther - chief of the - the - the - Mazawattee tribe. My brothers - I don't mean - yes, I do - the tribe - I mean the Mazawattees - are in ambush below the brow of yonder hill.'

'And what mighty warriors be these?' asked Golden Eagle, turning to the others.

Cyril said he was the great chief Squirrel, of the Moning Congo tribe, and, seeing that Jane was sucking her thumb and could evidently think of no name for herself, he added, 'This great warrior is Wild Cat - Pussy Ferox we call it in this land - leader of the vast Phiteezi tribe.'

And thou, valorous Redskin?' Golden Eagle inquired suddenly of Robert, who, taken unawares, could only reply that he was Bobs, leader of the Cape Mounted Police.

'And now,' said Black Panther, 'our tribes, if we just whistle them up, will far outnumber your puny forces; so resistance is useless. Return, therefore, to your own land, O brother, and smoke pipes of peace in your wampums with your squaws and your medicine-men, and dress yourselves in the gayest wigwams, and eat happily of the juicy fresh-caught moccasins.'

'You've got it all wrong,' murmured Cyril angrily. But Golden Eagle only looked inquiringly at her.

'Thy customs are other than ours, O Black Panther,' he said. 'Bring up thy tribe, that we may hold pow-wow in state before them, as becomes great chiefs.'

'We'll bring them up right enough,' said Anthea, 'with their bows and arrows, and tomahawks, and scalping-knives, and everything you can think of, if you don't look sharp and go.'

She spoke bravely enough, but the hearts of all the children were beating furiously, and their breath came in shorter and shorter gasps. For the little real Red Indians were closing up round them - coming nearer and nearer with angry murmurs - so that they were the centre of a crowd of dark, cruel faces.

'It's no go,' whispered Robert. 'I knew it wouldn't be. We must make a bolt for the Psammead. It might help us. If it doesn't - well, I suppose we shall come alive again at sunset. I wonder if scalping hurts as much as they say.'

'I'll wave the flag again,' said Anthea. 'If they stand back, we'll run for it.'

She waved the towel, and the chief commanded his followers to stand back. Then, charging wildly at the place where the line of Indians was thinnest, the four children started to run. Their first rush knocked down some half-dozen Indians, over whose blanketed bodies the children leaped, and made straight for the sand-Pit. This was no time for the safe easy way by which carts go down - right

153

over the edge of the sand-pit they went, among the yellow and pale purple flowers and dried grasses, past the little sand-martins' little front doors, skipping, clinging, bounding, stumbling, sprawling, and finally rolling.

Yellow Eagle and his followers came up with them just at the very spot where they had seen the Psammead that morning.

Breathless and beaten, the wretched children now awaited their fate. Sharp knives and axes gleamed round them, but worse than these was the cruel light in the eyes of Golden Eagle and his followers.

'Ye have lied to us, O Black Panther of the Mazawattees - and thou, too, Squirrel of the Moning Congos. These also, Pussy Ferox of the Phiteezi, and Bobs of the Cape Mounted Police - these also have lied to us, if not with their tongue, yet by their silence. Ye have lied under the cover of the Truce-flag of the Pale-face. Ye have no followers. Your tribes are far away - following the hunting trail. What shall be their doom?' he concluded, turning with a bitter smile to the other Red Indians.

'Build we the fire!' shouted his followers; and at once a dozen ready volunteers started to look for fuel. The four children, each held between two strong little Indians, cast despairing glances round them. Oh, if they could only see the Psammead!

'Do you mean to scalp us first and then roast us?' asked Anthea desperately.

'Of course!' Redskin opened his eyes at her. 'It's always done.'

The Indians had formed a ring round the children, and now sat on the ground gazing at their captives. There was a threatening silence.

Then slowly, by twos and threes, the Indians who had gone to look for firewood came back, and they came back empty-handed. They had not been able to find a single stick of wood, for a fire! No one ever can, as a matter of fact, in that part of Kent.

154

The children drew a deep breath of relief, but it ended in a moan of terror. For bright knives were being brandished all about them. Next moment each child was seized by an Indian; each closed its eyes and tried not to scream. They waited for the sharp agony of the knife. It did not come. Next moment they were released, and fell in a trembling heap. Their heads did not hurt at all. They only felt strangely cool! Wild war-whoops rang in their ears. When they ventured to open their eyes they saw four of their foes dancing round them with wild leaps and screams, and each of the four brandished in his hand a scalp of long flowing black hair. They put their hands to their heads - their own scalps were safe! The poor untutored savages had indeed scalped the children. But they had only, so to speak, scalped them of the black calico ringlets!

The children fell into each other's arms, sobbing and laughing.

'Their scalps are ours,' chanted the chief; 'ill-rooted were their ill-fated hairs! They came off in the hands of the victors - without struggle, without resistance, they yielded their scalps to the conquering Rock-dwellers! Oh, how little a thing is a scalp so lightly won!'

'They'll take our real ones in a minute; you see if they don't,' said Robert, trying to rub some of the red ochre off his face and hands on to his hair.

'Cheated of our just and fiery revenge are we,' the chant went on - 'but there are other torments than the scalping-knife and the flames. Yet is the slow fire the correct thing. O strange unnatural country, wherein a man may find no wood to burn his enemy! - Ah, for the boundless forests of my native land, where the great trees for thousands of miles grow but to furnish firewood wherewithal to burn our foes. Ah, would we were but in our native forest once more!'

Suddenly, like a flash of lightning, the golden gravel shone all round the four children instead of the dusky figures. For every single Indian had vanished on the instant at their leader's word. The

Psammead must have been there all the time. And it had given the Indian chief his wish.

Martha brought home a jug with a pattern of storks and long grasses on it. Also she brought back all Anthea's money.

'My cousin, she give me the jug for luck; she said it was an odd one what the basin of had got smashed.'

'Oh, Martha, you arc a dear!' sighed Anthea, throwing her arms round her.

'Yes,' giggled Martha, 'you'd better make the most of me while you've got me. I shall give your ma notice directly minute she comes back.'

'Oh, Martha, we haven't been so very horrid to you, have we?' asked Anthea, aghast.

'Oh, it ain't that, miss.' Martha giggled more than ever. 'I'm a-goin' to be married. It's Beale the gamekeeper. He's been a-proposin' to me off and on ever since you come home from the clergyman's where you got locked up on the church-tower. And to-day I said the word an' made him a happy man.'

Anthea put the seven-and-fourpence back in the missionary-box, and pasted paper over the place where the poker had broken it. She was very glad to be able to do this, and she does not know to this day whether breaking open a missionary-box is or is not a hanging matter.

CHAPTER 11. THE LAST WISH

Of course you, who see above that this is the eleventh (and last) chapter, know very well that the day of which this chapter tells must be the last on which Cyril, Anthea, Robert, and Jane will have a chance of getting anything out of the Psammead, or Sand-fairy.

But the children themselves did not know this. They were full of rosy visions, and, whereas on other days they had often found it extremely difficult to think of anything really nice to wish for, their brains were now full of the most beautiful and sensible ideas. 'This,' as Jane remarked afterwards, 'is always the way.' Everyone was up extra early that morning, and these plans were hopefully discussed in the garden before breakfast. The old idea of one hundred pounds in modern florins was still first favourite, but there were others that ran it close - the chief of these being the 'pony each' idea. This had a great advantage. You could wish for a pony each during the morning, ride it all day, have it vanish at sunset, and wish it back again next day. Which would be an economy of litter and stabling. But at breakfast two things happened. First, there was a letter from mother. Granny was better, and mother and father hoped to be home that very afternoon. A cheer arose. And of course this news at once scattered all the before-breakfast wish-ideas. For everyone saw quite plainly that the wish for the day must be something to please mother and not to please themselves.

'I wonder what she WOULD like,' pondered Cyril.

'She'd like us all to be good,' said Jane primly.

'Yes - but that's so dull for us,' Cyril rejoined; 'and, besides, I should hope we could be that without sand-fairies to help us. No; it must be something splendid, that we couldn't possibly get without wishing for.'

'Look out,' said Anthea in a warning voice; 'don't forget yesterday. Remember, we get our wishes now just wherever we happen to be when we say "I wish". Don't let's let ourselves in for anything silly - to-day of all days.'

'All right,' said Cyril. 'You needn't jaw.'

157

just then Martha came in with a jug full of hot water for the teapot - and a face full of importance for the children.

'A blessing we're all alive to eat our breakfasses!' she said darkly.

'Why, whatever's happened?' everybody asked.

'Oh, nothing,' said Martha, 'only it seems nobody's safe from being murdered in their beds nowadays.'

'Why,' said Jane as an agreeable thrill of horror ran down her back and legs and out at her toes, 'has anyone been murdered in their beds?'

'Well - not exactly,' said Martha; 'but they might just as well. There's been burglars over at Peasmarsh Place - Beale's just told me - and they've took every single one of Lady Chittenden's diamonds and jewels and things, and she's a-goin' out of one fainting fit into another, with hardly time to say "Oh, my diamonds!" in between. And Lord Chittenden's away in London.'

'Lady Chittenden,' said Anthea; 'we've seen her. She wears a red-and-white dress, and she has no children of her own and can't abide other folkses'.'

'That's her,' said Martha. 'Well, she's put all her trust in riches, and you see how she's served. They say the diamonds and things was worth thousands of thousands of pounds. There was a necklace and a river - whatever that is - and no end of bracelets; and a tarrer and ever so many rings. But there, I mustn't stand talking and all the place to clean down afore your ma comes home.'

'I don't see why she should ever have had such lots of diamonds,' said Anthea when Martha had Bounced off. 'She was rather a nasty lady, I thought. And mother hasn't any diamonds, and hardly any jewels - the topaz necklace, and the sapphire ring daddy gave her when they were engaged, and the garnet star, and the little pearl brooch with great-grandpapa's hair in it - that's about all.'

158

'When I'm grown up I'll buy mother no end of diamonds,' said Robert, 'if she wants them. I shall make so much money exploring in Africa I shan't know what to do with it.'

'Wouldn't it be jolly,' said Jane dreamily, 'if mother could find all those lovely things, necklaces and rivers of diamonds and tarrers?'

'TI—ARAS,' said Cyril.

'Ti—aras, then - and rings and everything in her room when she came home? I wish she would.' The others gazed at her in horror.

'Well, she WILL,' said Robert; 'you've wished, my good Jane - and our only chance now is to find the Psammead, and if it's in a good temper it MAY take back the wish and give us another. If not - well - goodness knows what we're in for! - the police, of course, and - Don't cry, silly! We'll stand by you. Father says we need never be afraid if we don't do anything wrong and always speak the truth.'

But Cyril and Anthea exchanged gloomy glances. They remembered how convincing the truth about the Psammead had been once before when told to the police.

It was a day of misfortunes. Of course the Psammead could not be found. Nor the jewels, though every one Of the children searched their mother's room again and again.

'Of course,' Robert said, 'WE couldn't find them. It'll be mother who'll do that. Perhaps she'll think they've been in the house for years and years, and never know they are the stolen ones at all.'

'Oh yes!' Cyril was very scornful; 'then mother will be a receiver of stolen goods, and you know jolly well what THAT'S worse than.'

Another and exhaustive search of the sand-pit failed to reveal the Psammead, so the children went back to the house slowly and sadly.

'I don't care,' said Anthea stoutly, 'we'll tell mother the truth, and she'll give back the jewels - and make everything all right.'

'Do you think so?' said Cyril slowly. 'Do you think She'll believe us? Could anyone believe about a Sammyadd unless they'd seen it? She'll think we're pretending. Or else she'll think we're raving mad, and then we shall be sent to Bedlam. How would you like it?' - he turned suddenly on the miserable Jane - 'how would you like it, to be shut up in an iron cage with bars and padded walls, and nothing to do but stick straws in your hair all day, and listen to the howlings and ravings of the other maniacs? Make up your minds to it, all of you. It's no use telling mother.'

'But it's true,' said Jane.

'Of course it is, but it's not true enough for grown-up people to believe it,' said Anthea. 'Cyril's right. Let's put flowers in all the vases, and try not to think about diamonds. After all, everything has come right in the end all the other times.'

So they filled all the pots they could find with flowers - asters and zinnias, and loose-leaved late red roses from the wall of the stable-yard, till the house was a perfect bower.

And almost as soon as dinner was cleared away mother arrived, and was clasped in eight loving arms. It was very difficult indeed not to tell her all about the Psammead at once, because they had got into the habit of telling her everything. But they did succeed in not telling her. Mother, on her side, had plenty to tell them - about Granny, and Granny's pigeons, and Auntie Emma's lame tame donkey. She was very delighted with the flowery-boweryness of the house; and everything seemed so natural and pleasant, now that she was home again, that the children almost thought they must have dreamed the Psammead.

But, when mother moved towards the stairs to go UP to her bedroom and take off her bonnet, the eight arms clung round her just as if she only had two children, one the Lamb and the other an octopus.

'Don't go up, mummy darling,' said Anthea; 'let me take your things up for you.'

'Or I will,' said Cyril.

'We want you to come and look at the rose-tree,' said Robert.

'Oh, don't go up!' said Jane helplessly.

'Nonsense, dears,' said mother briskly, 'I'm not such an old woman yet that I can't take my bonnet off in the proper place. Besides, I must wash these black hands of mine.'

So up she went, and the children, following her, exchanged glances of gloomy foreboding.

Mother took off her bonnet - it was a very pretty hat, really, with white roses on it - and when she had taken it off she went to the dressing-table to do her pretty hair.

On the table between the ring-stand and the pincushion lay a green leather case. Mother opened it.

'Oh, how lovely!' she cried. It was a ring, a large pearl with shining many-lighted diamonds set round it. 'Wherever did this come from?' mother asked, trying it on her wedding finger, which it fitted beautifully. 'However did it come here?'

'I don't know,' said each of the children truthfully.

'Father must have told Martha to put it here,' mother said. 'I'll run down and ask her.'

'Let me look at it,' said Anthea, who knew Martha would not be able to see the ring. But when Martha was asked, of course she denied putting the ring there, and so did Eliza and cook.

Mother came back to her bedroom, very much interested and pleased about the ring. But, when she opened the dressing-table drawer and found a long case containing an almost priceless diamond necklace, she was more interested still, though not so pleased. In the wardrobe, when she went to put away her 'bonnet', she found a tiara and several brooches, and the rest of the jewellery turned up in various parts of the room during the next half-hour. The children looked more and more uncomfortable, and now Jane began to sniff.

Mother looked at her gravely.

'Jane,' she said, 'I am sure you know something about this. Now think before you speak, and tell me the truth.'

'We found a Fairy,' said Jane obediently.

'No nonsense, please,' said her mother sharply.

'Don't be silly, Jane,' Cyril interrupted. Then he went on desperately. 'Look here, mother, we've never seen the things before, but Lady Chittenden at Peasmarsh Place lost all her jewellery by wicked burglars last night. Could this possibly be it?'

All drew a deep breath. They were saved.

'But how could they have put it here? And why should they?' asked mother, not unreasonably. 'Surely it would have been easier and safer to make off with it?'

'Suppose,' said Cyril, 'they thought it better to wait for - for sunset - nightfall, I mean, before they went off with it. No one but us knew that you were coming back to-day.'

'I must send for the police at once,' said mother distractedly. 'Oh, how I wish daddy were here!'

'Wouldn't it be better to wait till he DOES come?' asked Robert, knowing that his father would not be home before sunset.

'No, no; I can't wait a minute with all this on my mind,' cried mother. 'All this' was the heap of jewel-cases on the bed. They put them all in the wardrobe, and mother locked it. Then mother called Martha.

'Martha,' she said, 'has any stranger been into MY room since I've been away? Now, answer me truthfully.'

'No, mum,' answered Martha; 'leastways, what I mean to say -'

She stopped.

'Come,' said her mistress kindly; 'I see someone has. You must tell me at once. Don't be frightened. I'm sure you haven't done anything wrong.'

Martha burst into heavy sobs.

'I was a-goin' to give you warning this very day, mum, to leave at the end of my month, so I was - on account of me being going to make a respectable young man happy. A gamekeeper he is by trade, mum - and I wouldn't deceive you - of the name of Beale. And it's as true as I stand here, it Was your coming home in such a hurry, and no warning given, out of the kindness of his heart it was, as he says, "Martha, my beauty," he says - which I ain't and never was, but you know how them men will go on - "I can't see you a-toiling and a-moiling and not lend a 'elping 'and; which mine is a strong arm and it's yours, Martha, my dear," says he. And so he helped me a-cleanin' of the windows, but outside, mum, the whole time, and me in; if I never say another breathing word it's the gospel truth.'

'Were you with him the whole time?' asked her mistress.

163

'Him outside and me in, I was,' said Martha; 'except for fetching up a fresh pail and the leather that that slut of a Eliza 'd hidden away behind the mangle.'

'That will do,' said the children's mother. 'I am not pleased with you, Martha, but you have spoken the truth, and that counts for something.'

When Martha had gone, the children clung round their mother.

'Oh, mummy darling,' cried Anthea, 'it isn't Beale's fault, it isn't really! He's a great dear; he is, truly and honourably, and as honest as the day. Don't let the police take him, mummy! oh, don't, don't, don't!'

It was truly awful. Here was an innocent man accused of robbery through that silly wish of Jane's, and it was absolutely useless to tell the truth. All longed to, but they thought of the straws in the hair and the shrieks of the other frantic maniacs, and they could not do it.

'Is there a cart hereabouts?' asked mother feverishly. 'A trap of any sort? I must drive in to Rochester and tell the police at once.'

All the children sobbed, 'There's a cart at the farm, but, oh, don't go! - don't go! - oh, don't go! - wait till daddy comes home!'

Mother took not the faintest notice. When she had set her mind on a thing she always went straight through with it; she was rather like Anthea in this respect.

'Look here, Cyril,' she said, sticking on her hat with long sharp violet-headed pins, 'I leave you in charge. Stay in the dressing-room. You can pretend to be swimming boats in the bath, or something. Say I gave you leave. But stay there, with the landing door open; I've locked the other. And don't let anyone go into my room. Remember, no one knows the jewels are there except me, and all of you, and the wicked thieves who put them there. Robert, you stay in the garden and watch the windows. If anyone tries to get in you

164

must run and tell the two farm men that I'll send up to wait in the kitchen. I'll tell them there are dangerous characters about - that's true enough. Now, remember, I trust you both. But I don't think they'll try it till after dark, so you're quite safe. Good-bye, darlings.'

And she locked her bedroom door and went off with the key in her pocket.

The children could not help admiring the dashing and decided way in which she had acted. They thought how useful she would have been in organizing escape from some of the tight places in which they had found themselves of late in consequence of their ill-timed wishes.

'She's a born general,' said Cyril - 'but I don't know what's going to happen to us. Even if the girls were to hunt for that beastly Sammyadd and find it, and get it to take the jewels away again, mother would only think we hadn't looked out properly and let the burglars sneak in and nick them - or else the police will think WE'VE got them - or else that she's been fooling them. Oh, it's a pretty decent average ghastly mess this time, and no mistake!'

He savagely made a paper boat and began to float it in the bath, as he had been told to do.

Robert went into the garden and sat down on the worn yellow grass, with his miserable head between his helpless hands.

Anthea and Jane whispered together in the passage downstairs, where the coconut matting was - with the hole in it that you always caught your foot in if you were not careful. Martha's voice could be heard in the kitchen - grumbling loud and long.

'It's simply quite too dreadfully awful,' said Anthea. 'How do you know all the diamonds are there, too? If they aren't, the police will think mother and father have got them, and that they've only given up some of them for a kind of desperate blind. And they'll be put in

165

prison, and we shall be branded outcasts, the children of felons. And it won't be at all nice for father and mother either,' she added, by a candid afterthought.

'But what can WE do?' asked Jane.

'Nothing - at least we might look for the Psammead again. It's a very, very hot day. He may have come out to warm that whisker of his.'

'He won't give us any more beastly wishes to-day,' said Jane flatly. 'He gets crosser and crosser every time we see him. I believe he hates having to give wishes.'

Anthea had been shaking her head gloomily - now she stopped shaking it so suddenly that it really looked as though she were pricking up her ears.

'What is it?' asked Jane. 'Oh, have you thought of something?'

'Our one chance,' cried Anthea dramatically; 'the last lone-lorn forlorn hope. Come on.'

At a brisk trot she led the way to the sand-pit. Oh, joy! - there was the Psammead, basking in a golden sandy hollow and preening its whiskers happily in the glowing afternoon sun. The moment it saw them it whisked round and began to burrow - it evidently preferred its own company to theirs. But Anthea was too quick for it. She caught it by its furry shoulders gently but firmly, and held it.

'Here - none of that!' said the Psammead. 'Leave go of me, will you?'

But Anthea held him fast.

'Dear kind darling Sammyadd,' she said breathlessly.

166

'Oh yes - it's all very well,' it said; 'you want another wish, I expect. But I can't keep on slaving from morning till night giving people their wishes. I must have SOME time to myself.'

'Do you hate giving wishes?' asked Anthea gently, and her voice trembled with excitement.

'Of course I do,' it said. 'Leave go of me or I'll bite! - I really will - I mean it. Oh, well, if you choose to risk it.'

Anthea risked it and held on.

'Look here,' she said, 'don't bite me - listen to reason. If you'll only do what we want to-day, we'll never ask you for another wish as long as we live.'

The Psammead was much moved.

'I'd do anything,' it said in a tearful voice. 'I'd almost burst myself to give you one wish after another, as long as I held out, if you'd only never, never ask me to do it after to-day. If you knew how I hate to blow myself out with other people's wishes, and how frightened I am always that I shall strain a muscle or something. And then to wake up every morning and know you've GOT to do it. You don't know what it is - you don't know what it is, you don't!' Its voice cracked with emotion, and the last 'don't' was a squeak.

Anthea set it down gently on the sand.

'It's all over now,' she said soothingly. 'We promise faithfully never to ask for another wish after to-day.' 'Well, go ahead,' said the Psammead; 'let's get it over.'

'How many can you do?'

'I don't know - as long as I can hold out.'

'Well, first, I wish Lady Chittenden may find she's never lost her jewels.'

The Psammead blew itself out, collapsed, and said, 'Done.'

'I wish, said Anthea more slowly, 'mother mayn't get to the police.'

'Done,' said the creature after the proper interval.

'I wish,' said Jane suddenly, 'mother could forget all about the diamonds.'

'Done,' said the Psammead; but its voice was weaker.

'Wouldn't you like to rest a little?' asked Anthea considerately.

'Yes, please,' said the Psammead; 'and, before we go further, will you wish something for me?'

'Can't you do wishes for yourself?'

'Of course not,' it said; 'we were always expected to give each other our wishes - not that we had any to speak of in the good old Megatherium days. just wish, will you, that you may never be able, any of you, to tell anyone a word about ME.'

'Why?' asked Jane.

'Why, don't you see, if you told grown-ups I should have no peace of my life. They'd get hold of me, and they wouldn't wish silly things like you do, but real earnest things; and the scientific people would hit on some way of making things last after sunset, as likely as not; and they'd ask for a graduated income-tax, and old-age pensions and manhood suffrage, and free secondary education, and dull things like that; and get them, and keep them, and the whole world would be turned topsy-turvy. Do wish it! Quick!'

Anthea repeated the Psammead's wish, and it blew itself out to a larger size than they had yet seen it attain.

'And now,' it said as it collapsed, 'can I do anything more for you?'

'Just one thing; and I think that clears everything up, doesn't it, Jane? I wish Martha to forget about the diamond ring, and mother to forget about the keeper cleaning the windows.'
'It's like the "Brass Bottle",' said Jane.

'Yes, I'm glad we read that or I should never have thought of it.'

'Now,' said the Psammead faintly, 'I'm almost worn out. Is there anything else?'

'No; only thank you kindly for all you've done for us, and I hope you'll have a good long sleep, and I hope we shall see you again someday.'

'Is that a wish?' it said in a weak voice.

'Yes, please,' said the two girls together.

Then for the last time in this story they saw the Psammead blow itself out and collapse suddenly. It nodded to them, blinked its long snail's eyes, burrowed, and disappeared, scratching fiercely to the last, and the sand closed over it.

'I hope we've done right?' said Jane.

'I'm sure we have,' said Anthea. 'Come on home and tell the boys.'

Anthea found Cyril glooming over his paper boats, and told him. Jane told Robert. The two tales were only just ended when mother walked in, hot and dusty. She explained that as she was being driven into Rochester to buy the girls' autumn school-dresses the axle had broken, and but for the narrowness of the lane and the high soft hedges she would have been thrown out. As it was, she was not hurt,

169

but she had had to walk home. 'And oh, my dearest dear chicks,' she said, 'I am simply dying for a cup of tea! Do run and see if the kettle boils!'

'So you see it's all right,'Jane whispered. 'She doesn't remember.'

'No more does Martha,' said Anthea, who had been to ask after the state of the kettle.

As the servants sat at their tea, Beale the gamekeeper dropped in. He brought the welcome news that Lady Chittenden's diamonds had not been lost at all. Lord Chittenden had taken them to be re-set and cleaned, and the maid who knew about it had gone for a holiday. So that was all right.

'I wonder if we ever shall see the Psammead again,' said Jane wistfully as they walked in the garden, while mother was putting the Lamb to bed.

'I'm sure we shall,' said Cyril, 'if you really wished it.'

'We've promised never to ask it for another wish,' said Anthea.

'I never want to,' said Robert earnestly.

They did see it again, of course, but not in this story. And it was not in a sand-pit either, but in a very, very, very different place. It was in a — But I must say no more.

THE PHOENIX AND THE CARPET

CHAPTER 1. THE EGG

It began with the day when it was almost the Fifth of November, and a doubt arose in some breast—Robert's, I fancy—as to the quality of the fireworks laid in for the Guy Fawkes celebration.

'They were jolly cheap,' said whoever it was, and I think it was Robert, 'and suppose they didn't go off on the night? Those Prosser kids would have something to snigger about then.'

'The ones *I* got are all right,' Jane said; 'I know they are, because the man at the shop said they were worth thribble the money—'

'I'm sure thribble isn't grammar,' Anthea said.

'Of course it isn't,' said Cyril; 'one word can't be grammar all by itself, so you needn't be so jolly clever.'

Anthea was rummaging in the corner-drawers of her mind for a very disagreeable answer, when she remembered what a wet day it was, and how the boys had been disappointed of that ride to London and back on the top of the tram, which their mother had promised them as a reward for not having once forgotten, for six whole days, to wipe their boots on the mat when they came home from school.

So Anthea only said, 'Don't be so jolly clever yourself, Squirrel. And the fireworks look all right, and you'll have the eightpence that your tram fares didn't cost to-day, to buy something more with. You ought to get a perfectly lovely Catharine wheel for eightpence.'

'I daresay,' said Cyril, coldly; 'but it's not YOUR eightpence anyhow—'

'But look here,' said Robert, 'really now, about the fireworks. We don't want to be disgraced before those kids next door. They think because they wear red plush on Sundays no one else is any good.'

'I wouldn't wear plush if it was ever so—unless it was black to be beheaded in, if I was Mary Queen of Scots,' said Anthea, with scorn.

Robert stuck steadily to his point. One great point about Robert is the steadiness with which he can stick.

'I think we ought to test them,' he said.

'You young duffer,' said Cyril, 'fireworks are like postage-stamps. You can only use them once.'

'What do you suppose it means by "Carter's tested seeds" in the advertisement?'

There was a blank silence. Then Cyril touched his forehead with his finger and shook his head.

'A little wrong here,' he said. 'I was always afraid of that with poor Robert. All that cleverness, you know, and being top in algebra so often—it's bound to tell—'

'Dry up,' said Robert, fiercely. 'Don't you see? You can't TEST seeds if you do them ALL. You just take a few here and there, and if those grow you can feel pretty sure the others will be—what do you call it?—Father told me—"up to sample". Don't you think we ought to sample the fire-works? Just shut our eyes and each draw one out, and then try them.'

'But it's raining cats and dogs,' said Jane.

'And Queen Anne is dead,' rejoined Robert. No one was in a very good temper. 'We needn't go out to do them; we can just move back the table, and let them off on the old tea-tray we play toboggans with. I don't know what YOU think, but I think it's time we did something, and that would be really useful; because then we shouldn't just HOPE the fireworks would make those Prossers sit up—we should KNOW.'

172

'It WOULD be something to do,' Cyril owned with languid approval.

So the table was moved back. And then the hole in the carpet, that had been near the window till the carpet was turned round, showed most awfully. But Anthea stole out on tip-toe, and got the tray when cook wasn't looking, and brought it in and put it over the hole.

Then all the fireworks were put on the table, and each of the four children shut its eyes very tight and put out its hand and grasped something. Robert took a cracker, Cyril and Anthea had Roman candles; but Jane's fat paw closed on the gem of the whole collection, the Jack-in-the-box that had cost two shillings, and one at least of the party—I will not say which, because it was sorry afterwards—declared that Jane had done it on purpose. Nobody was pleased. For the worst of it was that these four children, with a very proper dislike of anything even faintly bordering on the sneakish, had a law, unalterable as those of the Medes and Persians, that one had to stand by the results of a toss-up, or a drawing of lots, or any other appeal to chance, however much one might happen to dislike the way things were turning out.

'I didn't mean to,' said Jane, near tears. 'I don't care, I'll draw another—'

'You know jolly well you can't,' said Cyril, bitterly. 'It's settled. It's Medium and Persian. You've done it, and you'll have to stand by it—and us too, worse luck. Never mind. YOU'LL have your pocket-money before the Fifth. Anyway, we'll have the Jack-in-the-box LAST, and get the most out of it we can.'

So the cracker and the Roman candles were lighted, and they were all that could be expected for the money; but when it came to the Jack-in-the-box it simply sat in the tray and laughed at them, as Cyril said. They tried to light it with paper and they tried to light it with matches; they tried to light it with Vesuvian fusees from the pocket of father's second-best overcoat that was hanging in the hall. And then Anthea slipped away to the cupboard under the stairs where the brooms and dustpans were kept, and the rosiny fire-lighters that smell so nice and like the woods where pine-trees grow, and the old newspapers and the bees-wax and turpentine, and the

173

horrid an stiff dark rags that are used for cleaning brass and furniture, and the paraffin for the lamps. She came back with a little pot that had once cost sevenpence-halfpenny when it was full of red-currant jelly; but the jelly had been all eaten long ago, and now Anthea had filled the jar with paraffin. She came in, and she threw the paraffin over the tray just at the moment when Cyril was trying with the twenty-third match to light the Jack-in-the-box. The Jack-in-the-box did not catch fire any more than usual, but the paraffin acted quite differently, and in an instant a hot flash of flame leapt up and burnt off Cyril's eyelashes, and scorched the faces of all four before they could spring back. They backed, in four instantaneous bounds, as far as they could, which was to the wall, and the pillar of fire reached from floor to ceiling.

'My hat,' said Cyril, with emotion, 'You've done it this time, Anthea.'

The flame was spreading out under the ceiling like the rose of fire in Mr Rider Haggard's exciting story about Allan Quatermain. Robert and Cyril saw that no time was to be lost. They turned up the edges of the carpet, and kicked them over the tray. This cut off the column of fire, and it disappeared and there was nothing left but smoke and a dreadful smell of lamps that have been turned too low.

All hands now rushed to the rescue, and the paraffin fire was only a bundle of trampled carpet, when suddenly a sharp crack beneath their feet made the amateur firemen start back. Another crack—the carpet moved as if it had had a cat wrapped in it; the Jack-in-the-box had at last allowed itself to be lighted, and it was going off with desperate violence inside the carpet.

Robert, with the air of one doing the only possible thing, rushed to the window and opened it. Anthea screamed, Jane burst into tears, and Cyril turned the table wrong way up on top of the carpet heap. But the firework went on, banging and bursting and spluttering even underneath the table.

Next moment mother rushed in, attracted by the howls of Anthea, and in a few moments the firework desisted and there was a dead silence, and the children stood looking at each other's black faces, and, out of the corners of their eyes, at mother's white one.

The fact that the nursery carpet was ruined occasioned but little surprise, nor was any one really astonished that bed should prove the immediate end of the adventure. It has been said that all roads lead to Rome; this may be true, but at any rate, in early youth I am quite sure that many roads lead to BED, and stop there—or YOU do.

The rest of the fireworks were confiscated, and mother was not pleased when father let them off himself in the back garden, though he said, 'Well, how else can you get rid of them, my dear?'

You see, father had forgotten that the children were in disgrace, and that their bedroom windows looked out on to the back garden. So that they all saw the fireworks most beautifully, and admired the skill with which father handled them.

Next day all was forgotten and forgiven; only the nursery had to be deeply cleaned (like spring-cleaning), and the ceiling had to be whitewashed.

And mother went out; and just at tea-time next day a man came with a rolled-up carpet, and father paid him, and mother said—

'If the carpet isn't in good condition, you know, I shall expect you to change it.' And the man replied—

'There ain't a thread gone in it nowhere, mum. It's a bargain, if ever there was one, and I'm more'n 'arf sorry I let it go at the price; but we can't resist the lydies, can we, sir?' and he winked at father and went away.

Then the carpet was put down in the nursery, and sure enough there wasn't a hole in it anywhere.

As the last fold was unrolled something hard and loud-sounding bumped out of it and trundled along the nursery floor. All the children scrambled for it, and Cyril got it. He took it to the gas. It was shaped like an egg, very yellow and shiny, half-transparent, and it had an odd sort of light in it that changed as you held it in different ways. It was as though it was an egg with a yolk of pale fire that just showed through the stone.

175

'I MAY keep it, mayn't I, mother?' Cyril asked.

And of course mother said no; they must take it back to the man who had brought the carpet, because she had only paid for a carpet, and not for a stone egg with a fiery yolk to it.

So she told them where the shop was, and it was in the Kentish Town Road, not far from the hotel that is called the Bull and Gate. It was a poky little shop, and the man was arranging furniture outside on the pavement very cunningly, so that the more broken parts should show as little as possible. And directly he saw the children he knew them again, and he began at once, without giving them a chance to speak.

'No you don't' he cried loudly; 'I ain't a-goin' to take back no carpets, so don't you make no bloomin' errer. A bargain's a bargain, and the carpet's puffik throughout.'

'We don't want you to take it back,' said Cyril; 'but we found something in it.'

'It must have got into it up at your place, then,' said the man, with indignant promptness, 'for there ain't nothing in nothing as I sell. It's all as clean as a whistle.'

'I never said it wasn't CLEAN,' said Cyril, 'but—'

'Oh, if it's MOTHS,' said the man, 'that's easy cured with borax. But I expect it was only an odd one. I tell you the carpet's good through and through. It hadn't got no moths when it left my 'ands—not so much as an hegg.'

'But that's just it,' interrupted Jane; 'there WAS so much as an egg.'

The man made a sort of rush at the children and stamped his foot.

'Clear out, I say!' he shouted, 'or I'll call for the police. A nice thing for customers to 'ear you a-coming 'ere a-charging me with finding things in goods what I sells. 'Ere, be off, afore I sends you off with a flea in your ears. Hi! constable—'

176

The children fled, and they think, and their father thinks, that they couldn't have done anything else. Mother has her own opinion.

But father said they might keep the egg.

'The man certainly didn't know the egg was there when he brought the carpet,' said he, 'any more than your mother did, and we've as much right to it as he had.'

So the egg was put on the mantelpiece, where it quite brightened up the dingy nursery. The nursery was dingy, because it was a basement room, and its windows looked out on a stone area with a rockery made of clinkers facing the windows. Nothing grew in the rockery except London pride and snails.

The room had been described in the house agent's list as a 'convenient breakfast-room in basement,' and in the daytime it was rather dark. This did not matter so much in the evenings when the gas was alight, but then it was in the evening that the blackbeetles got so sociable, and used to come out of the low cupboards on each side of the fireplace where their homes were, and try to make friends with the children. At least, I suppose that was what they wanted, but the children never would.

On the Fifth of November father and mother went to the theatre, and the children were not happy, because the Prossers next door had lots of fireworks and they had none.

They were not even allowed to have a bonfire in the garden.

'No more playing with fire, thank you,' was father's answer, when they asked him.

When the baby had been put to bed the children sat sadly round the fire in the nursery.

'I'm beastly bored,' said Robert.

'Let's talk about the Psammead,' said Anthea, who generally tried to give the conversation a cheerful turn.

'What's the good of TALKING?' said Cyril. 'What I want is for something to happen. It's awfully stuffy for a chap not to be allowed out in the evenings. There's simply nothing to do when you've got through your homers.'

Jane finished the last of her home-lessons and shut the book with a bang.

'We've got the pleasure of memory,' said she. 'Just think of last holidays.'

Last holidays, indeed, offered something to think of—for they had been spent in the country at a white house between a sand-pit and a gravel-pit, and things had happened. The children had found a Psammead, or sand-fairy, and it had let them have anything they wished for—just exactly anything, with no bother about its not being really for their good, or anything like that. And if you want to know what kind of things they wished for, and how their wishes turned out you can read it all in a book called Five Children and It (It was the Psammead). If you've not read it, perhaps I ought to tell you that the fifth child was the baby brother, who was called the Lamb, because the first thing he ever said was 'Baa!' and that the other children were not particularly handsome, nor were they extra clever, nor extraordinarily good. But they were not bad sorts on the whole; in fact, they were rather like you.

'I don't want to think about the pleasures of memory,' said Cyril; 'I want some more things to happen.'

'We're very much luckier than any one else, as it is,' said Jane. 'Why, no one else ever found a Psammead. We ought to be grateful.'

'Why shouldn't we GO ON being, though?' Cyril asked—'lucky, I mean, not grateful. Why's it all got to stop?'

'Perhaps something will happen,' said Anthea, comfortably. 'Do you know, sometimes I think we are the sort of people that things DO happen to.'

'It's like that in history,' said Jane: 'some kings are full of interesting things, and others—nothing ever happens to them, except their being born and crowned and buried, and sometimes not that.'

'I think Panther's right,' said Cyril: 'I think we are the sort of people things do happen to. I have a sort of feeling things would happen right enough if we could only give them a shove. It just wants something to start it. That's all.'

'I wish they taught magic at school,' Jane sighed. 'I believe if we could do a little magic it might make something happen.'

'I wonder how you begin?' Robert looked round the room, but he got no ideas from the faded green curtains, or the drab Venetian blinds, or the worn brown oil-cloth on the floor. Even the new carpet suggested nothing, though its pattern was a very wonderful one, and always seemed as though it were just going to make you think of something.

'I could begin right enough,' said Anthea; 'I've read lots about it. But I believe it's wrong in the Bible.'

'It's only wrong in the Bible because people wanted to hurt other people. I don't see how things can be wrong unless they hurt somebody, and we don't want to hurt anybody; and what's more, we jolly well couldn't if we tried. Let's get the Ingoldsby Legends. There's a thing about Abra-cadabra there,' said Cyril, yawning. 'We may as well play at magic. Let's be Knights Templars. They were awfully gone on magic. They used to work spells or something with a goat and a goose. Father says so.'

'Well, that's all right,' said Robert, unkindly; 'you can play the goat right enough, and Jane knows how to be a goose.'

'I'll get Ingoldsby,' said Anthea, hastily. 'You turn up the hearthrug.'

So they traced strange figures on the linoleum, where the hearthrug had kept it clean. They traced them with chalk that Robert had nicked from the top of the mathematical master's desk at school. You know, of course, that it is stealing to take a new stick of chalk, but it is not wrong to take a broken piece, so long as you only take

179

one. (I do not know the reason of this rule, nor who made it.) And they chanted all the gloomiest songs they could think of. And, of course, nothing happened. So then Anthea said, 'I'm sure a magic fire ought to be made of sweet-smelling wood, and have magic gums and essences and things in it.'

'I don't know any sweet-smelling wood, except cedar,' said Robert; 'but I've got some ends of cedar-wood lead pencil.'

So they burned the ends of lead pencil. And still nothing happened.

'Let's burn some of the eucalyptus oil we have for our colds,' said Anthea.

And they did. It certainly smelt very strong. And they burned lumps of camphor out of the big chest. It was very bright, and made a horrid black smoke, which looked very magical. But still nothing happened. Then they got some clean tea-cloths from the dresser drawer in the kitchen, and waved them over the magic chalk-tracings, and sang 'The Hymn of the Moravian Nuns at Bethlehem', which is very impressive. And still nothing happened. So they waved more and more wildly, and Robert's tea-cloth caught the golden egg and whisked it off the mantelpiece, and it fell into the fender and rolled under the grate.

'Oh, crikey!' said more than one voice.

And everyone instantly fell down flat on its front to look under the grate, and there lay the egg, glowing in a nest of hot ashes.

'It's not smashed, anyhow,' said Robert, and he put his hand under the grate and picked up the egg. But the egg was much hotter than any one would have believed it could possibly get in such a short time, and Robert had to drop it with a cry of 'Bother!' It fell on the top bar of the grate, and bounced right into the glowing red-hot heart of the fire.

'The tongs!' cried Anthea. But, alas, no one could remember where they were. Everyone had forgotten that the tongs had last been used to fish up the doll's teapot from the bottom of the water-butt, where the Lamb had dropped it. So the nursery tongs were resting between the water-butt and the dustbin, and cook refused to lend the kitchen ones.

'Never mind,' said Robert, 'we'll get it out with the poker and the shovel.'

'Oh, stop,' cried Anthea. 'Look at it! Look! look! look! I do believe something IS going to happen!'

For the egg was now red-hot, and inside it something was moving. Next moment there was a soft cracking sound; the egg burst in two, and out of it came a flame-coloured bird. It rested a moment among the flames, and as it rested there the four children could see it growing bigger and bigger under their eyes.

Every mouth was a-gape, every eye a-goggle.

The bird rose in its nest of fire, stretched its wings, and flew out into the room. It flew round and round, and round again, and where it passed the air was warm. Then it perched on the fender. The children looked at each other. Then Cyril put out a hand towards the bird. It put its head on one side and looked up at him, as you may have seen a parrot do when it is just going to speak, so that the children were hardly astonished at all when it said, 'Be careful; I am not nearly cool yet.'

They were not astonished, but they were very, very much interested.

They looked at the bird, and it was certainly worth looking at. Its feathers were like gold. It was about as large as a bantam, only its beak was not at all bantam-shaped. 'I believe I know what it is,' said Robert. 'I've seen a picture.'

He hurried away. A hasty dash and scramble among the papers on father's study table yielded, as the sum-books say, 'the desired result'. But when he came back into the room holding out a paper, and crying, 'I say, look here,' the others all said 'Hush!' and he hushed obediently and instantly, for the bird was speaking.

'Which of you,' it was saying, 'put the egg into the fire?'

'He did,' said three voices, and three fingers pointed at Robert.

The bird bowed; at least it was more like that than anything else.

'I am your grateful debtor,' it said with a high-bred air.

The children were all choking with wonder and curiosity—all except Robert. He held the paper in his hand, and he KNEW. He said so. He said—

'*I* know who you are.'

And he opened and displayed a printed paper, at the head of which was a little picture of a bird sitting in a nest of flames.

'You are the Phoenix,' said Robert; and the bird was quite pleased.

'My fame has lived then for two thousand years,' it said. 'Allow me to look at my portrait.' It looked at the page which Robert, kneeling down, spread out in the fender, and said—

'It's not a flattering likeness... And what are these characters?' it asked, pointing to the printed part.

'Oh, that's all dullish; it's not much about YOU, you know,' said Cyril, with unconscious politeness; 'but you're in lots of books.'

'With portraits?' asked the Phoenix.

'Well, no,' said Cyril; 'in fact, I don't think I ever saw any portrait of you but that one, but I can read you something about yourself, if you like.'

The Phoenix nodded, and Cyril went off and fetched Volume X of the old Encyclopedia, and on page 246 he found the following:—

'Phoenix—in ornithology, a fabulous bird of antiquity.'

'Antiquity is quite correct,' said the Phoenix, 'but fabulous—well, do I look it?'

Everyone shook its head. Cyril went on—

'The ancients speak of this bird as single, or the only one of its kind.'

'That's right enough,' said the Phoenix.

182

'They describe it as about the size of an eagle.'

'Eagles are of different sizes,' said the Phoenix; 'it's not at all a good description.'

All the children were kneeling on the hearthrug, to be as near the Phoenix as possible.

'You'll boil your brains,' it said. 'Look out, I'm nearly cool now;' and with a whirr of golden wings it fluttered from the fender to the table. It was so nearly cool that there was only a very faint smell of burning when it had settled itself on the table-cloth.

'It's only a very little scorched,' said the Phoenix, apologetically; 'it will come out in the wash. Please go on reading.'

The children gathered round the table.

'The size of an eagle,' Cyril went on, 'its head finely crested with a beautiful plumage, its neck covered with feathers of a gold colour, and the rest of its body purple; only the tail white, and the eyes sparkling like stars. They say that it lives about five hundred years in the wilderness, and when advanced in age it builds itself a pile of sweet wood and aromatic gums, fires it with the wafting of its wings, and thus burns itself; and that from its ashes arises a worm, which in time grows up to be a Phoenix. Hence the Phoenicians gave—'

'Never mind what they gave,' said the Phoenix, ruffling its golden feathers. 'They never gave much, anyway; they always were people who gave nothing for nothing. That book ought to be destroyed. It's most inaccurate. The rest of my body was never purple, and as for my—tail—well, I simply ask you, IS it white?'

It turned round and gravely presented its golden tail to the children.

'No, it's not,' said everybody.

'No, and it never was,' said the Phoenix. 'And that about the worm is just a vulgar insult. The Phoenix has an egg, like all respectable birds. It makes a pile—that part's all right—and it lays its egg, and it burns itself; and it goes to sleep and wakes up in its egg, and comes

183

out and goes on living again, and so on for ever and ever. I can't tell you how weary I got of it—such a restless existence; no repose.'

'But how did your egg get HERE?' asked Anthea.

'Ah, that's my life-secret,' said the Phoenix. 'I couldn't tell it to any one who wasn't really sympathetic. I've always been a misunderstood bird. You can tell that by what they say about the worm. I might tell YOU,' it went on, looking at Robert with eyes that were indeed starry. 'You put me on the fire—' Robert looked uncomfortable.

'The rest of us made the fire of sweet-scented woods and gums, though,' said Cyril.

'And—and it was an accident my putting you on the fire,' said Robert, telling the truth with some difficulty, for he did not know how the Phoenix might take it. It took it in the most unexpected manner.

'Your candid avowal,' it said, 'removes my last scruple. I will tell you my story.'

'And you won't vanish, or anything sudden will you? asked Anthea, anxiously.

'Why?' it asked, puffing out the golden feathers, 'do you wish me to stay here?'

'Oh YES,' said everyone, with unmistakable sincerity.

'Why?' asked the Phoenix again, looking modestly at the table-cloth.

'Because,' said everyone at once, and then stopped short; only Jane added after a pause, 'you are the most beautiful person we've ever seen.' 'You are a sensible child,' said the Phoenix, 'and I will NOT vanish or anything sudden. And I will tell you my tale. I had resided, as your book says, for many thousand years in the wilderness, which is a large, quiet place with very little really good society, and I was becoming weary of the monotony of my existence. But I acquired the habit of laying my egg and burning myself every five hundred years—and you know how difficult it is to break yourself of a habit.'

184

'Yes,' said Cyril; 'Jane used to bite her nails.'

'But I broke myself of it,' urged Jane, rather hurt, 'You know I did.'

'Not till they put bitter aloes on them,' said Cyril.

'I doubt,' said the bird, gravely, 'whether even bitter aloes (the aloe, by the way, has a bad habit of its own, which it might well cure before seeking to cure others; I allude to its indolent practice of flowering but once a century), I doubt whether even bitter aloes could have cured ME. But I WAS cured. I awoke one morning from a feverish dream—it was getting near the time for me to lay that tiresome fire and lay that tedious egg upon it—and I saw two people, a man and a woman. They were sitting on a carpet—and when I accosted them civilly they narrated to me their life-story, which, as you have not yet heard it, I will now proceed to relate. They were a prince and princess, and the story of their parents was one which I am sure you will like to hear. In early youth the mother of the princess happened to hear the story of a certain enchanter, and in that story I am sure you will be interested. The enchanter—'

'Oh, please don't,' said Anthea. 'I can't understand all these beginnings of stories, and you seem to be getting deeper and deeper in them every minute. Do tell us your OWN story. That's what we really want to hear.'

'Well,' said the Phoenix, seeming on the whole rather flattered, 'to cut about seventy long stories short (though *I* had to listen to them all—but to be sure in the wilderness there is plenty of time), this prince and princess were so fond of each other that they did not want any one else, and the enchanter—don't be alarmed, I won't go into his history—had given them a magic carpet (you've heard of a magic carpet?), and they had just sat on it and told it to take them right away from everyone—and it had brought them to the wilderness. And as they meant to stay there they had no further use for the carpet, so they gave it to me. That was indeed the chance of a lifetime!'

'I don't see what you wanted with a carpet,' said Jane, 'when you've got those lovely wings.'

'They ARE nice wings, aren't they?' said the Phoenix, simpering and spreading them out. 'Well, I got the prince to lay out the carpet, and I laid my egg on it; then I said to the carpet, "Now, my excellent carpet, prove your worth. Take that egg somewhere where it can't be hatched for two thousand years, and where, when that time's up, some one will light a fire of sweet wood and aromatic gums, and put the egg in to hatch;" and you see it's all come out exactly as I said. The words were no sooner out of my beak than egg and carpet disappeared. The royal lovers assisted to arrange my pile, and soothed my last moments. I burnt myself up and knew no more till I awoke on yonder altar.'

It pointed its claw at the grate.

'But the carpet,' said Robert, 'the magic carpet that takes you anywhere you wish. What became of that?'

'Oh, THAT?' said the Phoenix, carelessly—'I should say that that is the carpet. I remember the pattern perfectly.'

It pointed as it spoke to the floor, where lay the carpet which mother had bought in the Kentish Town Road for twenty-two shillings and ninepence.

At that instant father's latch-key was heard in the door.

'OH,' whispered Cyril, 'now we shall catch it for not being in bed!'

'Wish yourself there,' said the Phoenix, in a hurried whisper, 'and then wish the carpet back in its place.'

No sooner said than done. It made one a little giddy, certainly, and a little breathless; but when things seemed right way up again, there the children were, in bed, and the lights were out.

They heard the soft voice of the Phoenix through the darkness.

'I shall sleep on the cornice above your curtains,' it said. 'Please don't mention me to your kinsfolk.'

'Not much good,' said Robert, 'they'd never believe us. I say,' he called through the half-open door to the girls; 'talk about adventures

186

and things happening. We ought to be able to get some fun out of a magic carpet AND a Phoenix.'

'Rather,' said the girls, in bed.

'Children,' said father, on the stairs, 'go to sleep at once. What do you mean by talking at this time of night?'

No answer was expected to this question, but under the bedclothes Cyril murmured one.

'Mean?' he said. 'Don't know what we mean. I don't know what anything means.'

'But we've got a magic carpet AND a Phoenix,' said Robert.

'You'll get something else if father comes in and catches you,' said Cyril. 'Shut up, I tell you.'

Robert shut up. But he knew as well as you do that the adventures of that carpet and that Phoenix were only just beginning.

Father and mother had not the least idea of what had happened in their absence. This is often the case, even when there are no magic carpets or Phoenixes in the house.

The next morning—but I am sure you would rather wait till the next chapter before you hear about THAT.

CHAPTER 2. THE TOPLESS TOWER

The children had seen the Phoenix-egg hatched in the flames in their own nursery grate, and had heard from it how the carpet on their own nursery floor was really the wishing carpet, which would take them anywhere they chose. The carpet had transported them to bed just at the right moment, and the Phoenix had gone to roost on the cornice supporting the window-curtains of the boys' room.

'Excuse me,' said a gentle voice, and a courteous beak opened, very kindly and delicately, the right eye of Cyril. 'I hear the slaves below preparing food. Awaken! A word of explanation and arrangement... I do wish you wouldn't—'

The Phoenix stopped speaking and fluttered away crossly to the cornice-pole; for Cyril had hit out, as boys do when they are awakened suddenly, and the Phoenix was not used to boys, and his feelings, if not his wings, were hurt.

'Sorry,' said Cyril, coming awake all in a minute. 'Do come back! What was it you were saying? Something about bacon and rations?'

The Phoenix fluttered back to the brass rail at the foot of the bed.

'I say—you ARE real,' said Cyril. 'How ripping! And the carpet?'

'The carpet is as real as it ever was,' said the Phoenix, rather contemptuously; 'but, of course, a carpet's only a carpet, whereas a Phoenix is superlatively a Phoenix.'

'Yes, indeed,' said Cyril, 'I see it is. Oh, what luck! Wake up, Bobs! There's jolly well something to wake up for today. And it's Saturday, too.'

'I've been reflecting,' said the Phoenix, 'during the silent watches of the night, and I could not avoid the conclusion that you were quite insufficiently astonished at my appearance yesterday. The ancients were always VERY surprised. Did you, by chance, EXPECT my egg to hatch?'

'Not us,' Cyril said.

'And if we had,' said Anthea, who had come in in her nightie when she heard the silvery voice of the Phoenix, 'we could never, never have expected it to hatch anything so splendid as you.'

The bird smiled. Perhaps you've never seen a bird smile?

'You see,' said Anthea, wrapping herself in the boys' counterpane, for the morning was chill, 'we've had things happen to us before;' and she told the story of the Psammead, or sand-fairy.

188

'Ah yes,' said the Phoenix; 'Psammeads were rare, even in my time. I remember I used to be called the Psammead of the Desert. I was always having compliments paid me; I can't think why.'

'Can YOU give wishes, then?' asked Jane, who had now come in too.

'Oh, dear me, no,' said the Phoenix, contemptuously, 'at least—but I hear footsteps approaching. I hasten to conceal myself.' And it did.

I think I said that this day was Saturday. It was also cook's birthday, and mother had allowed her and Eliza to go to the Crystal Palace with a party of friends, so Jane and Anthea of course had to help to make beds and to wash up the breakfast cups, and little things like that. Robert and Cyril intended to spend the morning in conversation with the Phoenix, but the bird had its own ideas about this.

'I must have an hour or two's quiet,' it said, 'I really must. My nerves will give way unless I can get a little rest. You must remember it's two thousand years since I had any conversation—I'm out of practice, and I must take care of myself. I've often been told that mine is a valuable life.' So it nestled down inside an old hatbox of father's, which had been brought down from the box-room some days before, when a helmet was suddenly needed for a game of tournaments, with its golden head under its golden wing, and went to sleep. So then Robert and Cyril moved the table back and were going to sit on the carpet and wish themselves somewhere else. But before they could decide on the place, Cyril said—

'I don't know. Perhaps it's rather sneakish to begin without the girls.'

'They'll be all the morning,' said Robert, impatiently. And then a thing inside him, which tiresome books sometimes call the 'inward monitor', said, 'Why don't you help them, then?'

Cyril's 'inward monitor' happened to say the same thing at the same moment, so the boys went and helped to wash up the tea-cups, and to dust the drawing-room. Robert was so interested that he proposed to clean the front doorsteps—a thing he had never been allowed to do. Nor was he allowed to do it on this occasion. One reason was that it had already been done by cook.

189

When all the housework was finished, the girls dressed the happy, wriggling baby in his blue highwayman coat and three-cornered hat, and kept him amused while mother changed her dress and got ready to take him over to granny's. Mother always went to granny's every Saturday, and generally some of the children went with her; but today they were to keep house. And their hearts were full of joyous and delightful feelings every time they remembered that the house they would have to keep had a Phoenix in it, AND a wishing carpet.

You can always keep the Lamb good and happy for quite a long time if you play the Noah's Ark game with him. It is quite simple. He just sits on your lap and tells you what animal he is, and then you say the little poetry piece about whatever animal he chooses to be.

Of course, some of the animals, like the zebra and the tiger, haven't got any poetry, because they are so difficult to rhyme to. The Lamb knows quite well which are the poetry animals.

'I'm a baby bear!' said the Lamb, snugging down; and Anthea began:

> 'I love my little baby bear,
> I love his nose and toes and hair;
> I like to hold him in my arm,
> And keep him VERY safe and warm.'

And when she said 'very', of course there was a real bear's hug.

Then came the eel, and the Lamb was tickled till he wriggled exactly like a real one:

> 'I love my little baby eel,
> He is so squidglety to feel;
> He'll be an eel when he is big—
> But now he's just—a—tiny SNIG!'

Perhaps you didn't know that a snig was a baby eel? It is, though, and the Lamb knew it.

'Hedgehog now-!' he said; and Anthea went on:

> 'My baby hedgehog, how I like ye,
> Though your back's so prickly-spiky;
> Your front is very soft, I've found,

190

So I must love you front ways round!'

And then she loved him front ways round, while he squealed with pleasure.

It is a very baby game, and, of course, the rhymes are only meant for very, very small people—not for people who are old enough to read books, so I won't tell you any more of them.

By the time the Lamb had been a baby lion and a baby weazel, and a baby rabbit and a baby rat, mother was ready; and she and the Lamb, having been kissed by everybody and hugged as thoroughly as it is possible to be when you're dressed for out-of-doors, were seen to the tram by the boys. When the boys came back, everyone looked at everyone else and said—

'Now!'

They locked the front door and they locked the back door, and they fastened all the windows. They moved the table and chairs off the carpet, and Anthea swept it.

'We must show it a LITTLE attention,' she said kindly. 'We'll give it tea-leaves next time. Carpets like tea-leaves.'

Then everyone put on its out-door things, because as Cyril said, they didn't know where they might be going, and it makes people stare if you go out of doors in November in pinafores and without hats.

Then Robert gently awoke the Phoenix, who yawned and stretched itself, and allowed Robert to lift it on to the middle of the carpet, where it instantly went to sleep again with its crested head tucked under its golden wing as before. Then everyone sat down on the carpet.

'Where shall we go?' was of course the question, and it was warmly discussed. Anthea wanted to go to Japan. Robert and Cyril voted for America, and Jane wished to go to the seaside.

'Because there are donkeys there,' said she.

'Not in November, silly,' said Cyril; and the discussion got warmer and warmer, and still nothing was settled.

'I vote we let the Phoenix decide,' said Robert, at last. So they stroked it till it woke. 'We want to go somewhere abroad,' they said, 'and we can't make up our minds where.'

'Let the carpet make up ITS mind, if it has one,' said the Phoenix.

'Just say you wish to go abroad.'

So they did; and the next moment the world seemed to spin upside down, and when it was right way up again and they were ungiddy enough to look about them, they were out of doors.

Out of doors—this is a feeble way to express where they were. They were out of—out of the earth, or off it. In fact, they were floating steadily, safely, splendidly, in the crisp clear air, with the pale bright blue of the sky above them, and far down below the pale bright sun-diamonded waves of the sea. The carpet had stiffened itself somehow, so that it was square and firm like a raft, and it steered itself so beautifully and kept on its way so flat and fearless that no one was at all afraid of tumbling off. In front of them lay land.

'The coast of France,' said the Phoenix, waking up and pointing with its wing. 'Where do you wish to go? I should always keep one wish, of course—for emergencies—otherwise you may get into an emergency from which you can't emerge at all.'

But the children were far too deeply interested to listen.

'I tell you what,' said Cyril: 'let's let the thing go on and on, and when we see a place we really want to stop at—why, we'll just stop. Isn't this ripping?'

'It's like trains,' said Anthea, as they swept over the low-lying coast-line and held a steady course above orderly fields and straight roads bordered with poplar trees—'like express trains, only in trains you never can see anything because of grown-ups wanting the windows shut; and then they breathe on them, and it's like ground glass, and nobody can see anything, and then they go to sleep.'

'It's like tobogganing,' said Robert, 'so fast and smooth, only there's no door-mat to stop short on—it goes on and on.'

'You darling Phoenix,' said Jane, 'it's all your doing. Oh, look at that ducky little church and the women with flappy cappy things on their heads.'

'Don't mention it,' said the Phoenix, with sleepy politeness.

'OH!' said Cyril, summing up all the rapture that was in every heart. 'Look at it all—look at it—and think of the Kentish Town Road!'

Everyone looked and everyone thought. And the glorious, gliding, smooth, steady rush went on, and they looked down on strange and beautiful things, and held their breath and let it go in deep sighs, and said 'Oh!' and 'Ah!' till it was long past dinner-time.

It was Jane who suddenly said, 'I wish we'd brought that jam tart and cold mutton with us. It would have been jolly to have a picnic in the air.'

The jam tart and cold mutton were, however, far away, sitting quietly in the larder of the house in Camden Town which the children were supposed to be keeping. A mouse was at that moment tasting the outside of the raspberry jam part of the tart (she had nibbled a sort of gulf, or bay, through the pastry edge) to see whether it was the sort of dinner she could ask her little mouse-husband to sit down to. She had had a very good dinner herself. It is an ill wind that blows nobody any good.

'We'll stop as soon as we see a nice place,' said Anthea. 'I've got threepence, and you boys have the fourpence each that your trams didn't cost the other day, so we can buy things to eat. I expect the Phoenix can speak French.'

The carpet was sailing along over rocks and rivers and trees and towns and farms and fields. It reminded everybody of a certain time when all of them had had wings, and had flown up to the top of a church tower, and had had a feast there of chicken and tongue and new bread and soda-water. And this again reminded them how hungry they were. And just as they were all being reminded of this very strongly indeed, they saw ahead of them some ruined walls on a hill, and strong and upright, and really, to look at, as good as new—a great square tower.

'The top of that's just the exactly same size as the carpet,' said Jane. '*I* think it would be good to go to the top of that, because then none of the Abby-what's-its-names—I mean natives—would be able to take the carpet away even if they wanted to. And some of us could go out and get things to eat—buy them honestly, I mean, not take them out of larder windows.'

'I think it would be better if we went—' Anthea was beginning; but Jane suddenly clenched her hands.

'I don't see why I should never do anything I want, just because I'm the youngest. I wish the carpet would fit itself in at the top of that tower—so there!'

The carpet made a disconcerting bound, and next moment it was hovering above the square top of the tower. Then slowly and carefully it began to sink under them. It was like a lift going down with you at the Army and Navy Stores.

'I don't think we ought to wish things without all agreeing to them first,' said Robert, huffishly. 'Hullo! What on earth?'

For unexpectedly and greyly something was coming up all round the four sides of the carpet. It was as if a wall were being built by magic quickness. It was a foot high—it was two feet high—three, four, five. It was shutting out the light—more and more.

Anthea looked up at the sky and the walls that now rose six feet above them.

'We're dropping into the tower,' she screamed. 'THERE WASN'T ANY TOP TO IT. So the carpet's going to fit itself in at the bottom.'

Robert sprang to his feet.

'We ought to have—Hullo! an owl's nest.' He put his knee on a jutting smooth piece of grey stone, and reached his hand into a deep window slit—broad to the inside of the tower, and narrowing like a funnel to the outside.

'Look sharp!' cried everyone, but Robert did not look sharp enough. By the time he had drawn his hand out of the owl's nest—there were no eggs there—the carpet had sunk eight feet below him.

'Jump, you silly cuckoo!' cried Cyril, with brotherly anxiety.

But Robert couldn't turn round all in a minute into a jumping position. He wriggled and twisted and got on to the broad ledge, and by the time he was ready to jump the walls of the tower had risen up thirty feet above the others, who were still sinking with the carpet, and Robert found himself in the embrasure of a window; alone, for even the owls were not at home that day. The wall was smoothish; there was no climbing up, and as for climbing down—Robert hid his face in his hands, and squirmed back and back from the giddy verge, until the back part of him was wedged quite tight in the narrowest part of the window slit.

He was safe now, of course, but the outside part of his window was like a frame to a picture of part of the other side of the tower. It was very pretty, with moss growing between the stones and little shiny gems; but between him and it there was the width of the tower, and nothing in it but empty air. The situation was terrible. Robert saw in a flash that the carpet was likely to bring them into just the same sort of tight places that they used to get into with the wishes the Psammead granted them.

And the others—imagine their feelings as the carpet sank slowly and steadily to the very bottom of the tower, leaving Robert clinging to the wall. Robert did not even try to imagine their feelings—he had quite enough to do with his own; but you can.

As soon as the carpet came to a stop on the ground at the bottom of the inside of the tower it suddenly lost that raft-like stiffness which had been such a comfort during the journey from Camden Town to the topless tower, and spread itself limply over the loose stones and little earthy mounds at the bottom of the tower, just exactly like any ordinary carpet. Also it shrank suddenly, so that it seemed to draw away from under their feet, and they stepped quickly off the edges and stood on the firm ground, while the carpet drew itself in till it was its proper size, and no longer fitted exactly into the inside of the tower, but left quite a big space all round it.

Then across the carpet they looked at each other, and then every chin was tilted up and every eye sought vainly to see where poor Robert had got to. Of course, they couldn't see him.

'I wish we hadn't come,' said Jane.

'You always do,' said Cyril, briefly. 'Look here, we can't leave Robert up there. I wish the carpet would fetch him down.'

The carpet seemed to awake from a dream and pull itself together. It stiffened itself briskly and floated up between the four walls of the tower. The children below craned their heads back, and nearly broke their necks in doing it. The carpet rose and rose. It hung poised darkly above them for an anxious moment or two; then it dropped down again, threw itself on the uneven floor of the tower, and as it did so it tumbled Robert out on the uneven floor of the tower.

'Oh, glory!' said Robert, 'that was a squeak. You don't know how I felt. I say, I've had about enough for a bit. Let's wish ourselves at home again and have a go at that jam tart and mutton. We can go out again afterwards.'

'Righto!' said everyone, for the adventure had shaken the nerves of all. So they all got on to the carpet again, and said—

'I wish we were at home.'

And lo and behold, they were no more at home than before. The carpet never moved. The Phoenix had taken the opportunity to go to sleep. Anthea woke it up gently.

'Look here,' she said.

'I'm looking,' said the Phoenix.

'We WISHED to be at home, and we're still here,' complained Jane.

'No,' said the Phoenix, looking about it at the high dark walls of the tower. 'No; I quite see that.'

'But we wished to be at home,' said Cyril.

'No doubt,' said the bird, politely.

'And the carpet hasn't moved an inch,' said Robert.

'No,' said the Phoenix, 'I see it hasn't.'

'But I thought it was a wishing carpet?'

'So it is,' said the Phoenix.

'Then why—?' asked the children, altogether.

'I did tell you, you know,' said the Phoenix, 'only you are so fond of listening to the music of your own voices. It is, indeed, the most lovely music to each of us, and therefore—'

'You did tell us WHAT?' interrupted an Exasperated.

'Why, that the carpet only gives you three wishes a day and YOU'VE HAD THEM.'

There was a heartfelt silence.

'Then how are we going to get home?' said Cyril, at last.

'I haven't any idea,' replied the Phoenix, kindly. 'Can I fly out and get you any little thing?'

'How could you carry the money to pay for it?'

'It isn't necessary. Birds always take what they want. It is not regarded as stealing, except in the case of magpies.'

The children were glad to find they had been right in supposing this to be the case, on the day when they had wings, and had enjoyed somebody else's ripe plums.

'Yes; let the Phoenix get us something to eat, anyway,' Robert urged—' ('If it will be so kind you mean,' corrected Anthea, in a whisper); 'if it will be so kind, and we can be thinking while it's gone.'

So the Phoenix fluttered up through the grey space of the tower and vanished at the top, and it was not till it had quite gone that Jane said—

'Suppose it never comes back.'

It was not a pleasant thought, and though Anthea at once said, 'Of course it will come back; I'm certain it's a bird of its word,' a further gloom was cast by the idea. For, curiously enough, there was no door to the tower, and all the windows were far, far too high to be reached by the most adventurous climber. It was cold, too, and Anthea shivered.

'Yes,' said Cyril, 'it's like being at the bottom of a well.'

The children waited in a sad and hungry silence, and got little stiff necks with holding their little heads back to look up the inside of the tall grey tower, to see if the Phoenix were coming.

At last it came. It looked very big as it fluttered down between the walls, and as it neared them the children saw that its bigness was caused by a basket of boiled chestnuts which it carried in one claw. In the other it held a piece of bread. And in its beak was a very large pear. The pear was juicy, and as good as a very small drink. When the meal was over everyone felt better, and the question of how to get home was discussed without any disagreeableness. But no one could think of any way out of the difficulty, or even out of the tower; for the Phoenix, though its beak and claws had fortunately been strong enough to carry food for them, was plainly not equal to flying through the air with four well-nourished children.

'We must stay here, I suppose,' said Robert at last, 'and shout out every now and then, and some one will hear us and bring ropes and ladders, and rescue us like out of mines; and they'll get up a subscription to send us home, like castaways.'

'Yes; but we shan't be home before mother is, and then father'll take away the carpet and say it's dangerous or something,' said Cyril.

198

'I DO wish we hadn't come,' said Jane.

And everyone else said 'Shut up,' except Anthea, who suddenly awoke the Phoenix and said—

'Look here, I believe YOU can help us. Oh, I do wish you would!'

'I will help you as far as lies in my power,' said the Phoenix, at once. 'What is it you want now?'

'Why, we want to get home,' said everyone.

'Oh,' said the Phoenix. 'Ah, hum! Yes. Home, you said? Meaning?'

'Where we live—where we slept last night—where the altar is that your egg was hatched on.'

'Oh, there!' said the Phoenix. 'Well, I'll do my best.' It fluttered on to the carpet and walked up and down for a few minutes in deep thought. Then it drew itself up proudly.

'I CAN help you,' it said. 'I am almost sure I can help you. Unless I am grossly deceived I can help you. You won't mind my leaving you for an hour or two?' and without waiting for a reply it soared up through the dimness of the tower into the brightness above.

'Now,' said Cyril, firmly, 'it said an hour or two. But I've read about captives and people shut up in dungeons and catacombs and things awaiting release, and I know each moment is an eternity. Those people always do something to pass the desperate moments. It's no use our trying to tame spiders, because we shan't have time.'

'I HOPE not,' said Jane, doubtfully.

'But we ought to scratch our names on the stones or something.'

'I say, talking of stones,' said Robert, 'you see that heap of stones against the wall over in that corner. Well, I'm certain there's a hole in the wall there—and I believe it's a door. Yes, look here—the stones are round like an arch in the wall; and here's the hole—it's all black inside.'

He had walked over to the heap as he spoke and climbed up to it—dislodged the top stone of the heap and uncovered a little dark space.

Next moment everyone was helping to pull down the heap of stones, and very soon everyone threw off its jacket, for it was warm work.

'It IS a door,' said Cyril, wiping his face, 'and not a bad thing either, if—'

He was going to add 'if anything happens to the Phoenix,' but he didn't for fear of frightening Jane. He was not an unkind boy when he had leisure to think of such things.

The arched hole in the wall grew larger and larger. It was very, very black, even compared with the sort of twilight at the bottom of the tower; it grew larger because the children kept pulling off the stones and throwing them down into another heap. The stones must have been there a very long time, for they were covered with moss, and some of them were stuck together by it. So it was fairly hard work, as Robert pointed out.

When the hole reached to about halfway between the top of the arch and the tower, Robert and Cyril let themselves down cautiously on the inside, and lit matches. How thankful they felt then that they had a sensible father, who did not forbid them to carry matches, as some boys' fathers do. The father of Robert and Cyril only insisted on the matches being of the kind that strike only on the box.

'It's not a door, it's a sort of tunnel,' Robert cried to the girls, after the first match had flared up, flickered, and gone out. 'Stand off—we'll push some more stones down!'

They did, amid deep excitement. And now the stone heap was almost gone—and before them the girls saw the dark archway leading to unknown things. All doubts and fears as to getting home were forgotten in this thrilling moment. It was like Monte Cristo—it was like—

'I say,' cried Anthea, suddenly, 'come out! There's always bad air in places that have been shut up. It makes your torches go out, and then you die. It's called fire-damp, I believe. Come out, I tell you.'

The urgency of her tone actually brought the boys out—and then everyone took up its jacket and fanned the dark arch with it, so as to make the air fresh inside. When Anthea thought the air inside 'must be freshened by now,' Cyril led the way into the arch.

The girls followed, and Robert came last, because Jane refused to tail the procession lest 'something' should come in after her, and catch at her from behind. Cyril advanced cautiously, lighting match after match, and peering before him.

'It's a vaulting roof,' he said, 'and it's all stone—all right, Panther, don't keep pulling at my jacket! The air must be all right because of the matches, silly, and there are—look out—there are steps down.'

'Oh, don't let's go any farther,' said Jane, in an agony of reluctance (a very painful thing, by the way, to be in). 'I'm sure there are snakes, or dens of lions, or something. Do let's go back, and come some other time, with candles, and bellows for the fire-damp.'

'Let me get in front of you, then,' said the stern voice of Robert, from behind. 'This is exactly the place for buried treasure, and I'm going on, anyway; you can stay behind if you like.'

And then, of course, Jane consented to go on.

So, very slowly and carefully, the children went down the steps—there were seventeen of them—and at the bottom of the steps were more passages branching four ways, and a sort of low arch on the right-hand side made Cyril wonder what it could be, for it was too low to be the beginning of another passage.

So he knelt down and lit a match, and stooping very low he peeped in.

'There's SOMETHING,' he said, and reached out his hand. It touched something that felt more like a damp bag of marbles than anything else that Cyril had ever touched.

'I believe it IS a buried treasure,' he cried.

And it was; for even as Anthea cried, 'Oh, hurry up, Squirrel—fetch it out!' Cyril pulled out a rotting canvas bag—about as big as the paper ones the greengrocer gives you with Barcelona nuts in for sixpence.

'There's more of it, a lot more,' he said.

As he pulled the rotten bag gave way, and the gold coins ran and span and jumped and bumped and chinked and clinked on the floor of the dark passage.

I wonder what you would say if you suddenly came upon a buried treasure? What Cyril said was, 'Oh, bother—I've burnt my fingers!' and as he spoke he dropped the match. 'AND IT WAS THE LAST!' he added.

There was a moment of desperate silence. Then Jane began to cry.

'Don't,' said Anthea, 'don't, Pussy—you'll exhaust the air if you cry. We can get out all right.'

'Yes,' said Jane, through her sobs, 'and find the Phoenix has come back and gone away again—because it thought we'd gone home some other way, and—Oh, I WISH we hadn't come.'

Everyone stood quite still—only Anthea cuddled Jane up to her and tried to wipe her eyes in the dark.

'D-DON'T,' said Jane; 'that's my EAR—I'm not crying with my ears.'

'Come, let's get on out,' said Robert; but that was not so easy, for no one could remember exactly which way they had come. It is very difficult to remember things in the dark, unless you have matches with you, and then of course it is quite different, even if you don't strike one.

Everyone had come to agree with Jane's constant wish—and despair was making the darkness blacker than ever, when quite suddenly the floor seemed to tip up—and a strong sensation of being in a whirling lift came upon everyone. All eyes were closed—one's eyes always are in the dark, don't you think? When the whirling feeling stopped, Cyril said 'Earthquakes!' and they all opened their eyes.

They were in their own dingy breakfast-room at home, and oh, how light and bright and safe and pleasant and altogether delightful it seemed after that dark underground tunnel! The carpet lay on the floor, looking as calm as though it had never been for an excursion in its life. On the mantelpiece stood the Phoenix, waiting with an air of modest yet sterling worth for the thanks of the children.

'But how DID you do it?' they asked, when everyone had thanked the Phoenix again and again.

'Oh, I just went and got a wish from your friend the Psammead.'

'But how DID you know where to find it?'

'I found that out from the carpet; these wishing creatures always know all about each other—they're so clannish; like the Scots, you know—all related.'

'But, the carpet can't talk, can it?'

'No.'

'Then how—'

'How did I get the Psammead's address? I tell you I got it from the carpet.'

'DID it speak then?'

'No,' said the Phoenix, thoughtfully, 'it didn't speak, but I gathered my information from something in its manner. I was always a singularly observant bird.'

It was not till after the cold mutton and the jam tart, as well as the tea and bread-and-butter, that any one found time to regret the golden treasure which had been left scattered on the floor of the underground passage, and which, indeed, no one had thought of till now, since the moment when Cyril burnt his fingers at the flame of the last match.

'What owls and goats we were!' said Robert. 'Look how we've always wanted treasure—and now—'

'Never mind,' said Anthea, trying as usual to make the best of it. 'We'll go back again and get it all, and then we'll give everybody presents.'

More than a quarter of an hour passed most agreeably in arranging what presents should be given to whom, and, when the claims of generosity had been satisfied, the talk ran for fifty minutes on what they would buy for themselves.

It was Cyril who broke in on Robert's almost too technical account of the motor-car on which he meant to go to and from school—

'There!' he said. 'Dry up. It's no good. We can't ever go back. We don't know where it is.'

'Don't YOU know?' Jane asked the Phoenix, wistfully.

'Not in the least,' the Phoenix replied, in a tone of amiable regret.

'Then we've lost the treasure,' said Cyril. And they had.

'But we've got the carpet and the Phoenix,' said Anthea.

'Excuse me,' said the bird, with an air of wounded dignity, 'I do SO HATE to seem to interfere, but surely you MUST mean the Phoenix and the carpet?'

CHAPTER 3. THE QUEEN COOK

It was on a Saturday that the children made their first glorious journey on the wishing carpet. Unless you are too young to read at all, you will know that the next day must have been Sunday.

Sunday at 18, Camden Terrace, Camden Town, was always a very pretty day. Father always brought home flowers on Saturday, so that the breakfast-table was extra beautiful. In November, of course, the flowers were chrysanthemums, yellow and coppery coloured. Then there were always sausages on toast for breakfast, and these are rapture, after six days of Kentish Town Road eggs at fourteen a shilling.

On this particular Sunday there were fowls for dinner, a kind of food that is generally kept for birthdays and grand occasions, and there was an angel pudding, when rice and milk and oranges and white icing do their best to make you happy.

After dinner father was very sleepy indeed, because he had been working hard all the week; but he did not yield to the voice that said, 'Go and have an hour's rest.' He nursed the Lamb, who had a horrid cough that cook said was whooping-cough as sure as eggs, and he said—

'Come along, kiddies; I've got a ripping book from the library, called The Golden Age, and I'll read it to you.'

Mother settled herself on the drawing-room sofa, and said she could listen quite nicely with her eyes shut. The Lamb snugged into the 'armchair corner' of daddy's arm, and the others got into a happy heap on the hearth-rug. At first, of course, there were too many feet and knees and shoulders and elbows, but real comfort was actually settling down on them, and the Phoenix and the carpet were put away on the back top shelf of their minds (beautiful things that could be taken out and played with later), when a surly solid knock came at the drawing-room door. It opened an angry inch, and the cook's voice said, 'Please, m', may I speak to you a moment?'

Mother looked at father with a desperate expression. Then she put her pretty sparkly Sunday shoes down from the sofa, and stood up in them and sighed.

'As good fish in the sea,' said father, cheerfully, and it was not till much later that the children understood what he meant.

Mother went out into the passage, which is called 'the hall', where the umbrella-stand is, and the picture of the 'Monarch of the Glen' in a yellow shining frame, with brown spots on the Monarch from the damp in the house before last, and there was cook, very red and damp in the face, and with a clean apron tied on all crooked over the dirty one that she had dished up those dear delightful chickens in. She stood there and she seemed to get redder and damper, and she twisted the corner of her apron round her fingers, and she said very shortly and fiercely—

'If you please ma'am, I should wish to leave at my day month.' Mother leaned against the hatstand. The children could see her looking pale through the crack of the door, because she had been very kind to the cook, and had given her a holiday only the day before, and it seemed so very unkind of the cook to want to go like this, and on a Sunday too.

'Why, what's the matter?' mother said.

'It's them children,' the cook replied, and somehow the children all felt that they had known it from the first. They did not remember having done anything extra wrong, but it is so frightfully easy to displease a cook. 'It's them children: there's that there new carpet in their room, covered thick with mud, both sides, beastly yellow mud, and sakes alive knows where they got it. And all that muck to clean up on a Sunday! It's not my place, and it's not my intentions, so I don't deceive you, ma'am, and but for them limbs, which they is if ever there was, it's not a bad place, though I says it, and I wouldn't wish to leave, but—'

'I'm very sorry,' said mother, gently. 'I will speak to the children. And you had better think it over, and if you REALLY wish to go, tell me to-morrow.'

Next day mother had a quiet talk with cook, and cook said she didn't mind if she stayed on a bit, just to see.

But meantime the question of the muddy carpet had been gone into thoroughly by father and mother. Jane's candid explanation that the mud had come from the bottom of a foreign tower where there was buried treasure was received with such chilling disbelief that the others limited their defence to an expression of sorrow, and of a determination 'not to do it again'. But father said (and mother agreed with him, because mothers have to agree with fathers, and not because it was her own idea) that children who coated a carpet on both sides with thick mud, and when they were asked for an explanation could only talk silly nonsense—that meant Jane's truthful statement—were not fit to have a carpet at all, and, indeed, SHOULDN'T have one for a week!

So the carpet was brushed (with tea-leaves, too) which was the only comfort Anthea could think of, and folded up and put away in the cupboard at the top of the stairs, and daddy put the key in his trousers pocket. 'Till Saturday,' said he.

'Never mind,' said Anthea, 'we've got the Phoenix.'

But, as it happened, they hadn't. The Phoenix was nowhere to be found, and everything had suddenly settled down from the rosy wild beauty of magic happenings to the common damp brownness of ordinary November life in Camden Town—and there was the nursery floor all bare boards in the middle and brown oilcloth round the outside, and the bareness and yellowness of the middle floor showed up the blackbeetles with terrible distinctness, when the poor things came out in the evening, as usual, to try to make friends with the children. But the children never would.

The Sunday ended in gloom, which even junket for supper in the blue Dresden bowl could hardly lighten at all. Next day the Lamb's cough was worse. It certainly seemed very whoopy, and the doctor came in his brougham carriage.

Everyone tried to bear up under the weight of the sorrow which it was to know that the wishing carpet was locked up and the Phoenix mislaid. A good deal of time was spent in looking for the Phoenix.

'It's a bird of its word,' said Anthea. 'I'm sure it's not deserted us. But you know it had a most awfully long fly from wherever it was to near Rochester and back, and I expect the poor thing's feeling tired out and wants rest. I am sure we may trust it.'

The others tried to feel sure of this, too, but it was hard.

No one could be expected to feel very kindly towards the cook, since it was entirely through her making such a fuss about a little foreign mud that the carpet had been taken away.

'She might have told us,' said Jane, 'and Panther and I would have cleaned it with tea-leaves.'

'She's a cantankerous cat,' said Robert.

'I shan't say what I think about her,' said Anthea, primly, 'because it would be evil speaking, lying, and slandering.'

'It's not lying to say she's a disagreeable pig, and a beastly blue-nosed Bozwoz,' said Cyril, who had read The Eyes of Light, and intended to talk like Tony as soon as he could teach Robert to talk like Paul.

And all the children, even Anthea, agreed that even if she wasn't a blue-nosed Bozwoz, they wished cook had never been born.

But I ask you to believe that they didn't do all the things on purpose which so annoyed the cook during the following week, though I daresay the things would not have happened if the cook had been a favourite. This is a mystery. Explain it if you can. The things that had happened were as follows:

Sunday.—Discovery of foreign mud on both sides of the carpet.

Monday.—Liquorice put on to boil with aniseed balls in a saucepan. Anthea did this, because she thought it would be good for the Lamb's cough. The whole thing forgotten, and bottom of saucepan burned out. It was the little saucepan lined with white that was kept for the baby's milk.

Tuesday.—A dead mouse found in pantry. Fish-slice taken to dig grave with. By regrettable accident fish-slice broken. Defence: 'The cook oughtn't to keep dead mice in pantries.'

Wednesday.—Chopped suet left on kitchen table. Robert added chopped soap, but he says he thought the suet was soap too.

Thursday.—Broke the kitchen window by falling against it during a perfectly fair game of bandits in the area.

Friday.—Stopped up grating of kitchen sink with putty and filled sink with water to make a lake to sail paper boats in. Went away and left the tap running. Kitchen hearthrug and cook's shoes ruined.

On Saturday the carpet was restored. There had been plenty of time during the week to decide where it should be asked to go when they did get it back.

Mother had gone over to granny's, and had not taken the Lamb because he had a bad cough, which, cook repeatedly said, was whooping-cough as sure as eggs is eggs.

'But we'll take him out, a ducky darling,' said Anthea. 'We'll take him somewhere where you can't have whooping-cough. Don't be so silly, Robert. If he DOES talk about it no one'll take any notice. He's always talking about things he's never seen.'

So they dressed the Lamb and themselves in out-of-doors clothes, and the Lamb chuckled and coughed, and laughed and coughed again, poor dear, and all the chairs and tables were moved off the carpet by the boys, while Jane nursed the Lamb, and Anthea rushed through the house in one last wild hunt for the missing Phoenix.

'It's no use waiting for it,' she said, reappearing breathless in the breakfast-room. 'But I know it hasn't deserted us. It's a bird of its word.'

'Quite so,' said the gentle voice of the Phoenix from beneath the table.

Everyone fell on its knees and looked up, and there was the Phoenix perched on a crossbar of wood that ran across under the table, and had once supported a drawer, in the happy days before the drawer had been used as a boat, and its bottom unfortunately trodden out by Raggett's Really Reliable School Boots on the feet of Robert.

'I've been here all the time,' said the Phoenix, yawning politely behind its claw. 'If you wanted me you should have recited the ode of invocation; it's seven thousand lines long, and written in very pure and beautiful Greek.'

'Couldn't you tell it us in English?' asked Anthea.

'It's rather long, isn't it?' said Jane, jumping the Lamb on her knee.

'Couldn't you make a short English version, like Tate and Brady?'

'Oh, come along, do,' said Robert, holding out his hand. 'Come along, good old Phoenix.'

'Good old BEAUTIFUL Phoenix,' it corrected shyly.

'Good old BEAUTIFUL Phoenix, then. Come along, come along,' said Robert, impatiently, with his hand still held out.

The Phoenix fluttered at once on to his wrist.

'This amiable youth,' it said to the others, 'has miraculously been able to put the whole meaning of the seven thousand lines of Greek invocation into one English hexameter—a little misplaced some of the words—but—

'Oh, come along, come along, good old beautiful Phoenix!'

'Not perfect, I admit—but not bad for a boy of his age.'

'Well, now then,' said Robert, stepping back on to the carpet with the golden Phoenix on his wrist.

'You look like the king's falconer,' said Jane, sitting down on the carpet with the baby on her lap.

Robert tried to go on looking like it. Cyril and Anthea stood on the carpet.

'We shall have to get back before dinner,' said Cyril, 'or cook will blow the gaff.'

'She hasn't sneaked since Sunday,' said Anthea.

'She—' Robert was beginning, when the door burst open and the cook, fierce and furious, came in like a whirlwind and stood on the corner of the carpet, with a broken basin in one hand and a threat in the other, which was clenched.

'Look 'ere!' she cried, 'my only basin; and what the powers am I to make the beefsteak and kidney pudding in that your ma ordered for your dinners? You don't deserve no dinners, so yer don't.'

'I'm awfully sorry, cook,' said Anthea gently; 'it was my fault, and I forgot to tell you about it. It got broken when we were telling our fortunes with melted lead, you know, and I meant to tell you.'

'Meant to tell me,' replied the cook; she was red with anger, and really I don't wonder—'meant to tell! Well, *I* mean to tell, too. I've held my tongue this week through, because the missus she said to me quiet like, "We mustn't expect old heads on young shoulders," but now I shan't hold it no longer. There was the soap you put in our pudding, and me and Eliza never so much as breathed it to your ma—though well we might—and the saucepan, and the fish-slice, and—My gracious cats alive! what 'ave you got that blessed child dressed up in his outdoors for?'

'We aren't going to take him out,' said Anthea; 'at least—' She stopped short, for though they weren't going to take him out in the Kentish Town Road, they certainly intended to take him elsewhere. But not at all where cook meant when she said 'out'. This confused the truthful Anthea.

'Out!' said the cook, 'that I'll take care you don't;' and she snatched the Lamb from the lap of Jane, while Anthea and Robert caught her by the skirts and apron. 'Look here,' said Cyril, in stern desperation, 'will you go away, and make your pudding in a pie-dish, or a flower-pot, or a hot-water can, or something?'

'Not me,' said the cook, briefly; 'and leave this precious poppet for you to give his deathercold to.'

'I warn you,' said Cyril, solemnly. 'Beware, ere yet it be too late.'

'Late yourself the little popsey-wopsey,' said the cook, with angry tenderness. 'They shan't take it out, no more they shan't.

211

And—Where did you get that there yellow fowl?' She pointed to the Phoenix.

Even Anthea saw that unless the cook lost her situation the loss would be theirs.

'I wish,' she said suddenly, 'we were on a sunny southern shore, where there can't be any whooping-cough.'

She said it through the frightened howls of the Lamb, and the sturdy scoldings of the cook, and instantly the giddy-go-round-and-falling-lift feeling swept over the whole party, and the cook sat down flat on the carpet, holding the screaming Lamb tight to her stout print-covered self, and calling on St Bridget to help her. She was an Irishwoman.

The moment the tipsy-topsy-turvy feeling stopped, the cook opened her eyes, gave one sounding screech and shut them again, and Anthea took the opportunity to get the desperately howling Lamb into her own arms.

'It's all right,' she said; 'own Panther's got you. Look at the trees, and the sand, and the shells, and the great big tortoises. Oh DEAR, how hot it is!'

It certainly was; for the trusty carpet had laid itself out on a southern shore that was sunny and no mistake, as Robert remarked. The greenest of green slopes led up to glorious groves where palm-trees and all the tropical flowers and fruits that you read of in Westward Ho! and Fair Play were growing in rich profusion. Between the green, green slope and the blue, blue sea lay a stretch of sand that looked like a carpet of jewelled cloth of gold, for it was not greyish as our northern sand is, but yellow and changing—opal-coloured like sunshine and rainbows. And at the very moment when the wild, whirling, blinding, deafening, tumbling upside-downness of the carpet-moving stopped, the children had the happiness of seeing three large live turtles waddle down to the edge of the sea and disappear in the water. And it was hotter than you can possibly imagine, unless you think of ovens on a baking-day.

Everyone without an instant's hesitation tore off its London-in-November outdoor clothes, and Anthea took off the Lamb's highwayman blue coat and his three-cornered hat, and then his jersey, and then the Lamb himself suddenly slipped out of his little blue tight breeches and stood up happy and hot in his little white shirt.

'I'm sure it's much warmer than the seaside in the summer,' said Anthea. 'Mother always lets us go barefoot then.'

So the Lamb's shoes and socks and gaiters came off, and he stood digging his happy naked pink toes into the golden smooth sand.

'I'm a little white duck-dickie,' said he—'a little white duck-dickie what swims,' and splashed quacking into a sandy pool.

'Let him,' said Anthea; 'it can't hurt him. Oh, how hot it is!'

The cook suddenly opened her eyes and screamed, shut them, screamed again, opened her eyes once more and said—

'Why, drat my cats alive, what's all this? It's a dream, I expect.

Well, it's the best I ever dreamed. I'll look it up in the dream-book to-morrow. Seaside and trees and a carpet to sit on. I never did!'

'Look here,' said Cyril, 'it isn't a dream; it's real.'

'Ho yes!' said the cook; 'they always says that in dreams.'

'It's REAL, I tell you,' Robert said, stamping his foot. 'I'm not going to tell you how it's done, because that's our secret.' He winked heavily at each of the others in turn. 'But you wouldn't go away and make that pudding, so we HAD to bring you, and I hope you like it.'

'I do that, and no mistake,' said the cook unexpectedly; 'and it being a dream it don't matter what I say; and I WILL say, if it's my last word, that of all the aggravating little varmints—' 'Calm yourself, my good woman,' said the Phoenix.

'Good woman, indeed,' said the cook; 'good woman yourself' Then she saw who it was that had spoken. 'Well, if I ever,' said she; 'this is something like a dream! Yellow fowls a-talking and all! I've heard of such, but never did I think to see the day.'

'Well, then,' said Cyril, impatiently, 'sit here and see the day now. It's a jolly fine day. Here, you others—a council!' They walked along the shore till they were out of earshot of the cook, who still sat gazing about her with a happy, dreamy, vacant smile.

'Look here,' said Cyril, 'we must roll the carpet up and hide it, so that we can get at it at any moment. The Lamb can be getting rid of his whooping-cough all the morning, and we can look about; and if the savages on this island are cannibals, we'll hook it, and take her back. And if not, we'll LEAVE HER HERE.'

'Is that being kind to servants and animals, like the clergyman said?' asked Jane.

'Nor she isn't kind,' retorted Cyril.

'Well—anyway,' said Anthea, 'the safest thing is to leave the carpet there with her sitting on it. Perhaps it'll be a lesson to her, and anyway, if she thinks it's a dream it won't matter what she says when she gets home.'

So the extra coats and hats and mufflers were piled on the carpet. Cyril shouldered the well and happy Lamb, the Phoenix perched on Robert's wrist, and 'the party of explorers prepared to enter the interior'.

The grassy slope was smooth, but under the trees there were tangled creepers with bright, strange-shaped flowers, and it was not easy to walk.

'We ought to have an explorer's axe,' said Robert. 'I shall ask father to give me one for Christmas.'

There were curtains of creepers with scented blossoms hanging from the trees, and brilliant birds darted about quite close to their faces.

'Now, tell me honestly,' said the Phoenix, 'are there any birds here handsomer than I am? Don't be afraid of hurting my feelings—I'm a modest bird, I hope.'

214

'Not one of them,' said Robert, with conviction, 'is a patch upon you!'

'I was never a vain bird,' said the Phoenix, 'but I own that you confirm my own impression. I will take a flight.' It circled in the air for a moment, and, returning to Robert's wrist, went on, 'There is a path to the left.'

And there was. So now the children went on through the wood more quickly and comfortably, the girls picking flowers and the Lamb inviting the 'pretty dickies' to observe that he himself was a 'little white real-water-wet duck!'

And all this time he hadn't whooping-coughed once.

The path turned and twisted, and, always threading their way amid a tangle of flowers, the children suddenly passed a corner and found themselves in a forest clearing, where there were a lot of pointed huts—the huts, as they knew at once, of SAVAGES.

The boldest heart beat more quickly. Suppose they WERE cannibals. It was a long way back to the carpet.

'Hadn't we better go back?' said Jane. 'Go NOW,' she said, and her voice trembled a little. 'Suppose they eat us.'

'Nonsense, Pussy,' said Cyril, firmly. 'Look, there's a goat tied up. That shows they don't eat PEOPLE.'

'Let's go on and say we're missionaries,' Robert suggested.

'I shouldn't advise THAT,' said the Phoenix, very earnestly.

'Why not?'

'Well, for one thing, it isn't true,' replied the golden bird.

It was while they stood hesitating on the edge of the clearing that a tall man suddenly came out of one of the huts. He had hardly any clothes, and his body all over was a dark and beautiful coppery colour—just like the chrysanthemums father had brought home on Saturday. In his hand he held a spear. The whites of his eyes and the white of his teeth were the only light things about him, except that where the sun shone on his shiny brown body it looked white, too. If you will look carefully at the next shiny savage you meet with next to nothing on, you will see at once—if the sun happens to be shining at the time—that I am right about this.

The savage looked at the children. Concealment was impossible. He uttered a shout that was more like 'Oo goggery bag-wag' than anything else the children had ever heard, and at once brown coppery people leapt out of every hut, and swarmed like ants about the clearing. There was no time for discussion, and no one wanted to discuss anything, anyhow. Whether these coppery people were cannibals or not now seemed to matter very little.

Without an instant's hesitation the four children turned and ran back along the forest path; the only pause was Anthea's. She stood back to let Cyril pass, because he was carrying the Lamb, who screamed with delight. (He had not whooping-coughed a single once since the carpet landed him on the island.)

'Gee-up, Squirrel; gee-gee,' he shouted, and Cyril did gee-up. The path was a shorter cut to the beach than the creeper-covered way by which they had come, and almost directly they saw through the trees the shining blue-and-gold-and-opal of sand and sea.

'Stick to it,' cried Cyril, breathlessly.

They did stick to it; they tore down the sands—they could hear behind them as they ran the patter of feet which they knew, too well, were copper-coloured.

The sands were golden and opal-coloured—and BARE. There were wreaths of tropic seaweed, there were rich tropic shells of the kind you would not buy in the Kentish Town Road under at least fifteen pence a pair. There were turtles basking lumpily on the water's edge—but no cook, no clothes, and no carpet.

'On, on! Into the sea!' gasped Cyril. 'They MUST hate water. I've—heard—savages always—dirty.'

Their feet were splashing in the warm shallows before his breathless words were ended. The calm baby-waves were easy to go through. It is warm work running for your life in the tropics, and the coolness of the water was delicious. They were up to their arm-pits now, and Jane was up to her chin.

'Look!' said the Phoenix. 'What are they pointing at?'

The children turned; and there, a little to the west was a head—a head they knew, with a crooked cap upon it. It was the head of the cook.

For some reason or other the savages had stopped at the water's edge and were all talking at the top of their voices, and all were pointing copper-coloured fingers, stiff with interest and excitement, at the head of the cook.

The children hurried towards her as quickly as the water would let them.

'What on earth did you come out here for?' Robert shouted; 'and where on earth's the carpet?'

'It's not on earth, bless you,' replied the cook, happily; 'it's UNDER ME—in the water. I got a bit warm setting there in the sun, and I just says, "I wish I was in a cold bath"—just like that—and next minute here I was! It's all part of the dream.'

Everyone at once saw how extremely fortunate it was that the carpet had had the sense to take the cook to the nearest and largest bath—the sea, and how terrible it would have been if the carpet had taken itself and her to the stuffy little bath-room of the house in Camden Town!

'Excuse me,' said the Phoenix's soft voice, breaking in on the general sigh of relief, 'but I think these brown people want your cook.'

'To—to eat?' whispered Jane, as well as she could through the water which the plunging Lamb was dashing in her face with happy fat hands and feet.

'Hardly,' rejoined the bird. 'Who wants cooks to EAT? Cooks are ENGAGED, not eaten. They wish to engage her.'

'How can you understand what they say?' asked Cyril, doubtfully.

'It's as easy as kissing your claw,' replied the bird. 'I speak and understand ALL languages, even that of your cook, which is difficult and unpleasing. It's quite easy, when you know how it's done. It just comes to you. I should advise you to beach the carpet and land the cargo—the cook, I mean. You can take my word for it, the copper-coloured ones will not harm you now.'

It is impossible not to take the word of a Phoenix when it tells you to. So the children at once got hold of the corners of the carpet, and, pulling it from under the cook, towed it slowly in through the shallowing water, and at last spread it on the sand. The cook, who had followed, instantly sat down on it, and at once the copper-coloured natives, now strangely humble, formed a ring round the carpet, and fell on their faces on the rainbow-and-gold sand. The tallest savage spoke in this position, which must have been very awkward for him; and Jane noticed that it took him quite a long time to get the sand out of his mouth afterwards.

'He says,' the Phoenix remarked after some time, 'that they wish to engage your cook permanently.'

'Without a character?' asked Anthea, who had heard her mother speak of such things.

'They do not wish to engage her as cook, but as queen; and queens need not have characters.'

There was a breathless pause.

'WELL,' said Cyril, 'of all the choices! But there's no accounting for tastes.'

Everyone laughed at the idea of the cook's being engaged as queen; they could not help it.

'I do not advise laughter,' warned the Phoenix, ruffling out his golden feathers, which were extremely wet. 'And it's not their own

218

choice. It seems that there is an ancient prophecy of this copper-coloured tribe that a great queen should some day arise out of the sea with a white crown on her head, and—and—well, you see! There's the crown!'

It pointed its claw at cook's cap; and a very dirty cap it was, because it was the end of the week.

'That's the white crown,' it said; 'at least, it's nearly white—very white indeed compared to the colour THEY are—and anyway, it's quite white enough.'

Cyril addressed the cook. 'Look here!' said he, 'these brown people want you to be their queen. They're only savages, and they don't know any better. Now would you really like to stay? or, if you'll promise not to be so jolly aggravating at home, and not to tell any one a word about to-day, we'll take you back to Camden Town.'

'No, you don't,' said the cook, in firm, undoubting tones. 'I've always wanted to be the Queen, God bless her! and I always thought what a good one I should make; and now I'm going to. IF it's only in a dream, it's well worth while. And I don't go back to that nasty underground kitchen, and me blamed for everything; that I don't, not till the dream's finished and I wake up with that nasty bell a rang-tanging in my ears—so I tell you.'

'Are you SURE,' Anthea anxiously asked the Phoenix, 'that she will be quite safe here?'

'She will find the nest of a queen a very precious and soft thing,' said the bird, solemnly.

'There—you hear,' said Cyril. 'You're in for a precious soft thing, so mind you're a good queen, cook. It's more than you'd any right to expect, but long may you reign.'

Some of the cook's copper-coloured subjects now advanced from the forest with long garlands of beautiful flowers, white and sweet-scented, and hung them respectfully round the neck of their new sovereign.

'What! all them lovely bokays for me!' exclaimed the enraptured cook. 'Well, this here is something LIKE a dream, I must say.'

She sat up very straight on the carpet, and the copper-coloured ones, themselves wreathed in garlands of the gayest flowers, madly stuck parrot feathers in their hair and began to dance. It was a dance such as you have never seen; it made the children feel almost sure that the cook was right, and that they were all in a dream. Small, strange-shaped drums were beaten, odd-sounding songs were sung, and the dance got faster and faster and odder and odder, till at last all the dancers fell on the sand tired out.

The new queen, with her white crown-cap all on one side, clapped wildly.

'Brayvo!' she cried, 'brayvo! It's better than the Albert Edward Music-hall in the Kentish Town Road. Go it again!'

But the Phoenix would not translate this request into the copper-coloured language; and when the savages had recovered their breath, they implored their queen to leave her white escort and come with them to their huts.

'The finest shall be yours, O queen,' said they.

'Well—so long!' said the cook, getting heavily on to her feet, when the Phoenix had translated this request. 'No more kitchens and attics for me, thank you. I'm off to my royal palace, I am; and I only wish this here dream would keep on for ever and ever.'

She picked up the ends of the garlands that trailed round her feet, and the children had one last glimpse of her striped stockings and worn elastic-side boots before she disappeared into the shadow of the forest, surrounded by her dusky retainers, singing songs of rejoicing as they went.

'WELL!' said Cyril, 'I suppose she's all right, but they don't seem to count us for much, one way or the other.'

'Oh,' said the Phoenix, 'they think you're merely dreams. The prophecy said that the queen would arise from the waves with a white crown and surrounded by white dream-children. That's about what they think YOU are!'

'And what about dinner?' said Robert, abruptly.

'There won't be any dinner, with no cook and no pudding-basin,' Anthea reminded him; 'but there's always bread-and-butter.'

'Let's get home,' said Cyril.

The Lamb was furiously unwishful to be dressed in his warm clothes again, but Anthea and Jane managed it, by force disguised as coaxing, and he never once whooping-coughed.

Then everyone put on its own warm things and took its place on the carpet.

A sound of uncouth singing still came from beyond the trees where the copper-coloured natives were crooning songs of admiration and respect to their white-crowned queen. Then Anthea said 'Home,' just as duchesses and other people do to their coachmen, and the intelligent carpet in one whirling moment laid itself down in its proper place on the nursery floor. And at that very moment Eliza opened the door and said—

'Cook's gone! I can't find her anywhere, and there's no dinner ready. She hasn't taken her box nor yet her outdoor things. She just ran out to see the time, I shouldn't wonder—the kitchen clock never did give her satisfaction—and she's got run over or fell down in a fit as likely as not. You'll have to put up with the cold bacon for your dinners; and what on earth you've got your outdoor things on for I don't know. And then I'll slip out and see if they know anything about her at the police-station.'

But nobody ever knew anything about the cook any more, except the children, and, later, one other person.

Mother was so upset at losing the cook, and so anxious about her, that Anthea felt most miserable, as though she had done something very wrong indeed. She woke several times in the night, and at last decided that she would ask the Phoenix to let her tell her mother all about it. But there was no opportunity to do this next day, because the Phoenix, as usual, had gone to sleep in some out-of-the-way spot, after asking, as a special favour, not to be disturbed for twenty-four hours.

The Lamb never whooping-coughed once all that Sunday, and mother and father said what good medicine it was that the doctor had given him. But the children knew that it was the southern shore where you can't have whooping-cough that had cured him. The Lamb babbled of coloured sand and water, but no one took any notice of that. He often talked of things that hadn't happened.

It was on Monday morning, very early indeed, that Anthea woke and suddenly made up her mind. She crept downstairs in her night-gown (it was very chilly), sat down on the carpet, and with a beating heart wished herself on the sunny shore where you can't have whooping-cough, and next moment there she was.

The sand was splendidly warm. She could feel it at once, even through the carpet. She folded the carpet, and put it over her shoulders like a shawl, for she was determined not to be parted from it for a single instant, no matter how hot it might be to wear.

Then trembling a little, and trying to keep up her courage by saying over and over, 'It is my DUTY, it IS my duty,' she went up the forest path.

'Well, here you are again,' said the cook, directly she saw Anthea.

'This dream does keep on!'

The cook was dressed in a white robe; she had no shoes and stockings and no cap and she was sitting under a screen of palm-leaves, for it was afternoon in the island, and blazing hot. She wore a flower wreath on her hair, and copper-coloured boys were fanning her with peacock's feathers.

'They've got the cap put away,' she said. 'They seem to think a lot of it. Never saw one before, I expect.'

222

'Are you happy?' asked Anthea, panting; the sight of the cook as queen quite took her breath away.

'I believe you, my dear,' said the cook, heartily. 'Nothing to do unless you want to. But I'm getting rested now. Tomorrow I'm going to start cleaning out my hut, if the dream keeps on, and I shall teach them cooking; they burns everything to a cinder now unless they eats it raw.'

'But can you talk to them?'

'Lor' love a duck, yes!' the happy cook-queen replied; 'it's quite easy to pick up. I always thought I should be quick at foreign languages. I've taught them to understand "dinner," and "I want a drink," and "You leave me be," already.'

'Then you don't want anything?' Anthea asked earnestly and anxiously.

'Not me, miss; except if you'd only go away. I'm afraid of me waking up with that bell a-going if you keep on stopping here a-talking to me. Long as this here dream keeps up I'm as happy as a queen.'

'Goodbye, then,' said Anthea, gaily, for her conscience was clear now.

She hurried into the wood, threw herself on the ground, and said 'Home'—and there she was, rolled in the carpet on the nursery floor.

'SHE'S all right, anyhow,' said Anthea, and went back to bed. 'I'm glad somebody's pleased. But mother will never believe me when I tell her.'

The story is indeed a little difficult to believe. Still, you might try.

CHAPTER 4. TWO BAZAARS

Mother was really a great dear. She was pretty and she was loving, and most frightfully good when you were ill, and always kind, and almost always just. That is, she was just when she understood things. But of course she did not always understand things. No one understands everything, and mothers are not angels, though a good many of them come pretty near it. The children knew that mother always WANTED to do what was best for them, even if she was not clever enough to know exactly what was the best. That was why all of them, but much more particularly Anthea, felt rather uncomfortable at keeping the great secret from her of the wishing carpet and the Phoenix. And Anthea, whose inside mind was made so that she was able to be much more uncomfortable than the others, had decided that she MUST tell her mother the truth, however little likely it was that her mother would believe it.

'Then I shall have done what's right,' said she to the Phoenix; 'and if she doesn't believe me it won't be my fault—will it?'

'Not in the least,' said the golden bird. 'And she won't, so you're quite safe.'

Anthea chose a time when she was doing her home-lessons—they were Algebra and Latin, German, English, and Euclid—and she asked her mother whether she might come and do them in the drawing-room—'so as to be quiet,' she said to her mother; and to herself she said, 'And that's not the real reason. I hope I shan't grow up a LIAR.'

Mother said, 'Of course, dearie,' and Anthea started swimming through a sea of x's and y's and z's. Mother was sitting at the mahogany bureau writing letters.

'Mother dear,' said Anthea.

'Yes, love-a-duck,' said mother.

'About cook,' said Anthea. '*I* know where she is.'

'Do you, dear?' said mother. 'Well, I wouldn't take her back after the way she has behaved.'

'It's not her fault,' said Anthea. 'May I tell you about it from the beginning?'

Mother laid down her pen, and her nice face had a resigned expression. As you know, a resigned expression always makes you want not to tell anybody anything.

'It's like this,' said Anthea, in a hurry: 'that egg, you know, that came in the carpet; we put it in the fire and it hatched into the Phoenix, and the carpet was a wishing carpet—and—'

'A very nice game, darling,' said mother, taking up her pen. 'Now do be quiet. I've got a lot of letters to write. I'm going to Bournemouth to-morrow with the Lamb—and there's that bazaar.'

Anthea went back to x y z, and mother's pen scratched busily.

'But, mother,' said Anthea, when mother put down the pen to lick an envelope, 'the carpet takes us wherever we like—and—'

'I wish it would take you where you could get a few nice Eastern things for my bazaar,' said mother. 'I promised them, and I've no time to go to Liberty's now.'

'It shall,' said Anthea, 'but, mother—'

'Well, dear,' said mother, a little impatiently, for she had taken up her pen again.

'The carpet took us to a place where you couldn't have whooping-cough, and the Lamb hasn't whooped since, and we took cook because she was so tiresome, and then she would stay and be queen of the savages. They thought her cap was a crown, and—'

'Darling one,' said mother, 'you know I love to hear the things you make up—but I am most awfully busy.'

'But it's true,' said Anthea, desperately.

225

'You shouldn't say that, my sweet,' said mother, gently. And then Anthea knew it was hopeless.

'Are you going away for long?' asked Anthea.

'I've got a cold,' said mother, 'and daddy's anxious about it, and the Lamb's cough.'

'He hasn't coughed since Saturday,' the Lamb's eldest sister interrupted.

'I wish I could think so,' mother replied. 'And daddy's got to go to Scotland. I do hope you'll be good children.'

'We will, we will,' said Anthea, fervently. 'When's the bazaar?'

'On Saturday,' said mother, 'at the schools. Oh, don't talk any more, there's a treasure! My head's going round, and I've forgotten how to spell whooping-cough.'

Mother and the Lamb went away, and father went away, and there was a new cook who looked so like a frightened rabbit that no one had the heart to do anything to frighten her any more than seemed natural to her.

The Phoenix begged to be excused. It said it wanted a week's rest, and asked that it might not be disturbed. And it hid its golden gleaming self, and nobody could find it.

So that when Wednesday afternoon brought an unexpected holiday, and everyone decided to go somewhere on the carpet, the journey had to be undertaken without the Phoenix. They were debarred from any carpet excursions in the evening by a sudden promise to mother, exacted in the agitation of parting, that they would not be out after six at night, except on Saturday, when they were to go to the bazaar, and were pledged to put on their best clothes, to wash themselves to the uttermost, and to clean their nails—not with scissors, which are scratchy and bad, but with flat-sharpened ends of wooden matches, which do no harm to any one's nails.

'Let's go and see the Lamb,' said Jane.

But everyone was agreed that if they appeared suddenly in Bournemouth it would frighten mother out of her wits, if not into a fit. So they sat on the carpet, and thought and thought and thought till they almost began to squint.

'Look here,' said Cyril, 'I know. Please carpet, take us somewhere where we can see the Lamb and mother and no one can see us.'

'Except the Lamb,' said Jane, quickly.

And the next moment they found themselves recovering from the upside-down movement—and there they were sitting on the carpet, and the carpet was laid out over another thick soft carpet of brown pine-needles. There were green pine-trees overhead, and a swift clear little stream was running as fast as ever it could between steep banks—and there, sitting on the pine-needle carpet, was mother, without her hat; and the sun was shining brightly, although it was November—and there was the Lamb, as jolly as jolly and not whooping at all.

'The carpet's deceived us,' said Robert, gloomily; 'mother will see us directly she turns her head.'

But the faithful carpet had not deceived them.

Mother turned her dear head and looked straight at them, and DID NOT SEE THEM!

'We're invisible,' Cyril whispered: 'what awful larks!'

But to the girls it was not larks at all. It was horrible to have mother looking straight at them, and her face keeping the same, just as though they weren't there.

'I don't like it,' said Jane. 'Mother never looked at us like that before. Just as if she didn't love us—as if we were somebody else's children, and not very nice ones either—as if she didn't care whether she saw us or not.'

'It is horrid,' said Anthea, almost in tears.

But at this moment the Lamb saw them, and plunged towards the carpet, shrieking, 'Panty, own Panty—an' Pussy, an' Squiggle—an' Bobs, oh, oh!'

Anthea caught him and kissed him, so did Jane; they could not help it—he looked such a darling, with his blue three-cornered hat all on one side, and his precious face all dirty—quite in the old familiar way.

'I love you, Panty; I love you—and you, and you, and you,' cried the Lamb.

It was a delicious moment. Even the boys thumped their baby brother joyously on the back.

Then Anthea glanced at mother—and mother's face was a pale sea-green colour, and she was staring at the Lamb as if she thought he had gone mad. And, indeed, that was exactly what she did think.

'My Lamb, my precious! Come to mother,' she cried, and jumped up and ran to the baby.

She was so quick that the invisible children had to leap back, or she would have felt them; and to feel what you can't see is the worst sort of ghost-feeling. Mother picked up the Lamb and hurried away from the pinewood.

'Let's go home,' said Jane, after a miserable silence. 'It feels just exactly as if mother didn't love us.'

But they couldn't bear to go home till they had seen mother meet another lady, and knew that she was safe. You cannot leave your mother to go green in the face in a distant pinewood, far from all human aid, and then go home on your wishing carpet as though nothing had happened.

When mother seemed safe the children returned to the carpet, and said 'Home'—and home they went.

'I don't care about being invisible myself,' said Cyril, 'at least, not with my own family. It would be different if you were a prince, or a bandit, or a burglar.'

228

And now the thoughts of all four dwelt fondly on the dear greenish face of mother.

'I wish she hadn't gone away,' said Jane; 'the house is simply beastly without her.'

'I think we ought to do what she said,' Anthea put in. 'I saw something in a book the other day about the wishes of the departed being sacred.'

'That means when they've departed farther off,' said Cyril. 'India's coral or Greenland's icy, don't you know; not Bournemouth. Besides, we don't know what her wishes are.'

'She SAID'—Anthea was very much inclined to cry—'she said, "Get Indian things for my bazaar;" but I know she thought we couldn't, and it was only play.'

'Let's get them all the same,' said Robert. 'We'll go the first thing on Saturday morning.'

And on Saturday morning, the first thing, they went.

There was no finding the Phoenix, so they sat on the beautiful wishing carpet, and said—

'We want Indian things for mother's bazaar. Will you please take us where people will give us heaps of Indian things?'

The docile carpet swirled their senses away, and restored them on the outskirts of a gleaming white Indian town. They knew it was Indian at once, by the shape of the domes and roofs; and besides, a man went by on an elephant, and two English soldiers went along the road, talking like in Mr Kipling's books—so after that no one could have any doubt as to where they were. They rolled up the carpet and Robert carried it, and they walked bodily into the town.

It was very warm, and once more they had to take off their London-in-November coats, and carry them on their arms.

The streets were narrow and strange, and the clothes of the people in the streets were stranger and the talk of the people was strangest of all.

'I can't understand a word,' said Cyril. 'How on earth are we to ask for things for our bazaar?'

'And they're poor people, too,' said Jane; 'I'm sure they are. What we want is a rajah or something.'

Robert was beginning to unroll the carpet, but the others stopped him, imploring him not to waste a wish.

'We asked the carpet to take us where we could get Indian things for bazaars,' said Anthea, 'and it will.'

Her faith was justified.

Just as she finished speaking a very brown gentleman in a turban came up to them and bowed deeply. He spoke, and they thrilled to the sound of English words.

'My ranee, she think you very nice childs. She asks do you lose yourselves, and do you desire to sell carpet? She see you from her palkee. You come see her—yes?'

They followed the stranger, who seemed to have a great many more teeth in his smile than are usual, and he led them through crooked streets to the ranee's palace. I am not going to describe the ranee's palace, because I really have never seen the palace of a ranee, and Mr Kipling has. So you can read about it in his books. But I know exactly what happened there.

The old ranee sat on a low-cushioned seat, and there were a lot of other ladies with her—all in trousers and veils, and sparkling with tinsel and gold and jewels. And the brown, turbaned gentleman stood behind a sort of carved screen, and interpreted what the children said and what the queen said. And when the queen asked to buy the carpet, the children said 'No.'

'Why?' asked the ranee.

And Jane briefly said why, and the interpreter interpreted. The queen spoke, and then the interpreter said—

'My mistress says it is a good story, and you tell it all through without thought of time.'

And they had to. It made a long story, especially as it had all to be told twice—once by Cyril and once by the interpreter. Cyril rather enjoyed himself. He warmed to his work, and told the tale of the Phoenix and the Carpet, and the Lone Tower, and the Queen-Cook, in language that grew insensibly more and more Arabian Nightsy, and the ranee and her ladies listened to the interpreter, and rolled about on their fat cushions with laughter.

When the story was ended she spoke, and the interpreter explained that she had said, 'Little one, thou art a heaven-born teller of tales,' and she threw him a string of turquoises from round her neck.

'OH, how lovely!' cried Jane and Anthea.

Cyril bowed several times, and then cleared his throat and said—

'Thank her very, very much; but I would much rather she gave me some of the cheap things in the bazaar. Tell her I want them to sell again, and give the money to buy clothes for poor people who haven't any.'

'Tell him he has my leave to sell my gift and clothe the naked with its price,' said the queen, when this was translated.

But Cyril said very firmly, 'No, thank you. The things have got to be sold to-day at our bazaar, and no one would buy a turquoise necklace at an English bazaar. They'd think it was sham, or else they'd want to know where we got it.'

So then the queen sent out for little pretty things, and her servants piled the carpet with them.

'I must needs lend you an elephant to carry them away,' she said, laughing.

But Anthea said, 'If the queen will lend us a comb and let us wash our hands and faces, she shall see a magic thing. We and the carpet and all these brass trays and pots and carved things and stuffs and things will just vanish away like smoke.'

The queen clapped her hands at this idea, and lent the children a sandal-wood comb inlaid with ivory lotus-flowers. And they washed their faces and hands in silver basins. Then Cyril made a very polite farewell speech, and quite suddenly he ended with the words—

'And I wish we were at the bazaar at our schools.'

And of course they were. And the queen and her ladies were left with their mouths open, gazing at the bare space on the inlaid marble floor where the carpet and the children had been.

'That is magic, if ever magic was!' said the queen, delighted with the incident; which, indeed, has given the ladies of that court something to talk about on wet days ever since.

Cyril's stories had taken some time, so had the meal of strange sweet foods that they had had while the little pretty things were being bought, and the gas in the schoolroom was already lighted. Outside, the winter dusk was stealing down among the Camden Town houses.

'I'm glad we got washed in India,' said Cyril. 'We should have been awfully late if we'd had to go home and scrub.'

'Besides,' Robert said, 'it's much warmer washing in India. I shouldn't mind it so much if we lived there.'

The thoughtful carpet had dumped the children down in a dusky space behind the point where the corners of two stalls met. The floor was littered with string and brown paper, and baskets and boxes were heaped along the wall.

The children crept out under a stall covered with all sorts of table-covers and mats and things, embroidered beautifully by idle ladies with no real work to do. They got out at the end, displacing a sideboard-cloth adorned with a tasteful pattern of blue geraniums.

The girls got out unobserved, so did Cyril; but Robert, as he cautiously emerged, was actually walked on by Mrs Biddle, who kept the stall. Her large, solid foot stood firmly on the small, solid hand of Robert and who can blame Robert if he DID yell a little?

A crowd instantly collected. Yells are very unusual at bazaars, and everyone was intensely interested. It was several seconds before the three free children could make Mrs Biddle understand that what she was walking on was not a schoolroom floor, or even, as she presently supposed, a dropped pin-cushion, but the living hand of a suffering child. When she became aware that she really had hurt him, she grew very angry indeed. When people have hurt other people by accident, the one who does the hurting is always much the angriest. I wonder why.

'I'm very sorry, I'm sure,' said Mrs Biddle; but she spoke more in anger than in sorrow. 'Come out! whatever do you mean by creeping about under the stalls, like earwigs?'

'We were looking at the things in the corner.'

'Such nasty, prying ways,' said Mrs Biddle, 'will never make you successful in life. There's nothing there but packing and dust.'

'Oh, isn't there!' said Jane. 'That's all you know.'

'Little girl, don't be rude,' said Mrs Biddle, flushing violet.

'She doesn't mean to be; but there ARE some nice things there, all the same,' said Cyril; who suddenly felt how impossible it was to inform the listening crowd that all the treasures piled on the carpet were mother's contributions to the bazaar. No one would believe it; and if they did, and wrote to thank mother, she would think—well, goodness only knew what she would think. The other three children felt the same.

'I should like to see them,' said a very nice lady, whose friends had disappointed her, and who hoped that these might be belated contributions to her poorly furnished stall.

She looked inquiringly at Robert, who said, 'With pleasure, don't mention it,' and dived back under Mrs Biddle's stall.

'I wonder you encourage such behaviour,' said Mrs Biddle. 'I always speak my mind, as you know, Miss Peasmarsh; and, I must say, I am surprised.' She turned to the crowd. 'There is no entertainment here,' she said sternly. 'A very naughty little boy has accidentally hurt himself, but only slightly. Will you please disperse? It will only encourage him in naughtiness if he finds himself the centre of attraction.'

The crowd slowly dispersed. Anthea, speechless with fury, heard a nice curate say, 'Poor little beggar!' and loved the curate at once and for ever.

Then Robert wriggled out from under the stall with some Benares brass and some inlaid sandalwood boxes.

'Liberty!' cried Miss Peasmarsh. 'Then Charles has not forgotten, after all.'

'Excuse me,' said Mrs Biddle, with fierce politeness, 'these objects are deposited behind MY stall. Some unknown donor who does good by stealth, and would blush if he could hear you claim the things. Of course they are for me.'

'My stall touches yours at the corner,' said poor Miss Peasmarsh, timidly, 'and my cousin did promise—'

The children sidled away from the unequal contest and mingled with the crowd. Their feelings were too deep for words—till at last Robert said—

'That stiff-starched PIG!'

'And after all our trouble! I'm hoarse with gassing to that trousered lady in India.'

'The pig-lady's very, very nasty,' said Jane.

It was Anthea who said, in a hurried undertone, 'She isn't very nice, and Miss Peasmarsh is pretty and nice too. Who's got a pencil?'

234

It was a long crawl, under three stalls, but Anthea did it. A large piece of pale blue paper lay among the rubbish in the corner.

She folded it to a square and wrote upon it, licking the pencil at every word to make it mark quite blackly: 'All these Indian things are for pretty, nice Miss Peasmarsh's stall.' She thought of adding, 'There is nothing for Mrs Biddle;' but she saw that this might lead to suspicion, so she wrote hastily: 'From an unknown donna,' and crept back among the boards and trestles to join the others.

So that when Mrs Biddle appealed to the bazaar committee, and the corner of the stall was lifted and shifted, so that stout clergymen and heavy ladies could get to the corner without creeping under stalls, the blue paper was discovered, and all the splendid, shining Indian things were given over to Miss Peasmarsh, and she sold them all, and got thirty-five pounds for them.

'I don't understand about that blue paper,' said Mrs Biddle. 'It looks to me like the work of a lunatic. And saying you were nice and pretty! It's not the work of a sane person.'

Anthea and Jane begged Miss Peasmarsh to let them help her to sell the things, because it was their brother who had announced the good news that the things had come. Miss Peasmarsh was very willing, for now her stall, that had been SO neglected, was surrounded by people who wanted to buy, and she was glad to be helped. The children noted that Mrs Biddle had not more to do in the way of selling than she could manage quite well. I hope they were not glad—for you should forgive your enemies, even if they walk on your hands and then say it is all your naughty fault. But I am afraid they were not so sorry as they ought to have been.

It took some time to arrange the things on the stall. The carpet was spread over it, and the dark colours showed up the brass and silver and ivory things. It was a happy and busy afternoon, and when Miss Peasmarsh and the girls had sold every single one of the little pretty things from the Indian bazaar, far, far away, Anthea and Jane went off with the boys to fish in the fishpond, and dive into the bran-pie, and hear the cardboard band, and the phonograph, and the chorus of singing birds that was done behind a screen with glass tubes and glasses of water.

They had a beautiful tea, suddenly presented to them by the nice curate, and Miss Peasmarsh joined them before they had had more than three cakes each. It was a merry party, and the curate was extremely pleasant to everyone, 'even to Miss Peasmarsh,' as Jane said afterwards.

'We ought to get back to the stall,' said Anthea, when no one could possibly eat any more, and the curate was talking in a low voice to Miss Peas marsh about 'after Easter'.

'There's nothing to go back for,' said Miss Peasmarsh gaily; 'thanks to you dear children we've sold everything.'

'There—there's the carpet,' said Cyril.

'Oh,' said Miss Peasmarsh, radiantly, 'don't bother about the carpet. I've sold even that. Mrs Biddle gave me ten shillings for it. She said it would do for her servant's bedroom.'

'Why,' said Jane, 'her servants don't HAVE carpets. We had cook from her, and she told us so.'

'No scandal about Queen Elizabeth, if YOU please,' said the curate, cheerfully; and Miss Peasmarsh laughed, and looked at him as though she had never dreamed that any one COULD be so amusing. But the others were struck dumb. How could they say, 'The carpet is ours!' For who brings carpets to bazaars?

The children were now thoroughly wretched. But I am glad to say that their wretchedness did not make them forget their manners, as it does sometimes, even with grown-up people, who ought to know ever so much better.

They said, 'Thank you very much for the jolly tea,' and 'Thanks for being so jolly,' and 'Thanks awfully for giving us such a jolly time;' for the curate had stood fish-ponds, and bran-pies, and phonographs, and the chorus of singing birds, and had stood them like a man. The girls hugged Miss Peasmarsh, and as they went away they heard the curate say—

'Jolly little kids, yes, but what about—you will let it be directly after Easter. Ah, do say you will—'

And Jane ran back and said, before Anthea could drag her away, 'What are you going to do after Easter?'

Miss Peasmarsh smiled and looked very pretty indeed. And the curate said—

'I hope I am going to take a trip to the Fortunate Islands.'

'I wish we could take you on the wishing carpet,' said Jane.

'Thank you,' said the curate, 'but I'm afraid I can't wait for that. I must go to the Fortunate Islands before they make me a bishop. I should have no time afterwards.'

'I've always thought I should marry a bishop,' said Jane: 'his aprons would come in so useful. Wouldn't YOU like to marry a bishop, Miss Peasmarsh?'

It was then that they dragged her away.

As it was Robert's hand that Mrs Biddle had walked on, it was decided that he had better not recall the incident to her mind, and so make her angry again. Anthea and Jane had helped to sell things at the rival stall, so they were not likely to be popular.

A hasty council of four decided that Mrs Biddle would hate Cyril less than she would hate the others, so the others mingled with the crowd, and it was he who said to her—

'Mrs Biddle, WE meant to have that carpet. Would you sell it to us? We would give you—'

'Certainly not,' said Mrs Biddle. 'Go away, little boy.'

There was that in her tone which showed Cyril, all too plainly, the hopelessness of persuasion. He found the others and said—

'It's no use; she's like a lioness robbed of its puppies. We must watch where it goes—and—Anthea, I don't care what you say. It's our own carpet. It wouldn't be burglary. It would be a sort of forlorn hope rescue party—heroic and daring and dashing, and not wrong at all.'

The children still wandered among the gay crowd—but there was no pleasure there for them any more. The chorus of singing birds sounded just like glass tubes being blown through water, and the phonograph simply made a horrid noise, so that you could hardly hear yourself speak. And the people were buying things they couldn't possibly want, and it all seemed very stupid. And Mrs Biddle had bought the wishing carpet for ten shillings. And the whole of life was sad and grey and dusty, and smelt of slight gas escapes, and hot people, and cake and crumbs, and all the children were very tired indeed.

They found a corner within sight of the carpet, and there they waited miserably, till it was far beyond their proper bedtime. And when it was ten the people who had bought things went away, but the people who had been selling stayed to count up their money.

'And to jaw about it,' said Robert. 'I'll never go to another bazaar as long as ever I live. My hand is swollen as big as a pudding. I expect the nails in her horrible boots were poisoned.'

Just then some one who seemed to have a right to interfere said—

'Everything is over now; you had better go home.'

So they went. And then they waited on the pavement under the gas lamp, where ragged children had been standing all the evening to listen to the band, and their feet slipped about in the greasy mud till Mrs Biddle came out and was driven away in a cab with the many things she hadn't sold, and the few things she had bought—among others the carpet. The other stall-holders left their things at the school till Monday morning, but Mrs Biddle was afraid some one would steal some of them, so she took them in a cab.

The children, now too desperate to care for mud or appearances, hung on behind the cab till it reached Mrs Biddle's house. When she and the carpet had gone in and the door was shut Anthea said—

238

'Don't let's burgle—I mean do daring and dashing rescue acts—till we've given her a chance. Let's ring and ask to see her.'

The others hated to do this, but at last they agreed, on condition that Anthea would not make any silly fuss about the burglary afterwards, if it really had to come to that.

So they knocked and rang, and a scared-looking parlourmaid opened the front door. While they were asking for Mrs Biddle they saw her. She was in the dining-room, and she had already pushed back the table and spread out the carpet to see how it looked on the floor.

'I knew she didn't want it for her servants' bedroom,' Jane muttered.

Anthea walked straight past the uncomfortable parlourmaid, and the others followed her. Mrs Biddle had her back to them, and was smoothing down the carpet with the same boot that had trampled on the hand of Robert. So that they were all in the room, and Cyril, with great presence of mind, had shut the room door before she saw them.

'Who is it, Jane?' she asked in a sour voice; and then turning suddenly, she saw who it was. Once more her face grew violet—a deep, dark violet. 'You wicked daring little things!' she cried, 'how dare you come here? At this time of night, too. Be off, or I'll send for the police.'

'Don't be angry,' said Anthea, soothingly, 'we only wanted to ask you to let us have the carpet. We have quite twelve shillings between us, and—'

'How DARE you?' cried Mrs Biddle, and her voice shook with angriness.

'You do look horrid,' said Jane suddenly.

Mrs Biddle actually stamped that booted foot of hers. 'You rude, barefaced child!' she said.

Anthea almost shook Jane; but Jane pushed forward in spite of her.

'It really IS our nursery carpet,' she said, 'you ask ANY ONE if it isn't.'

'Let's wish ourselves home,' said Cyril in a whisper.

'No go,' Robert whispered back, 'she'd be there too, and raving mad as likely as not. Horrid thing, I hate her!'

'I wish Mrs Biddle was in an angelic good temper,' cried Anthea, suddenly. 'It's worth trying,' she said to herself.

Mrs Biddle's face grew from purple to violet, and from violet to mauve, and from mauve to pink. Then she smiled quite a jolly smile.

'Why, so I am!' she said, 'what a funny idea! Why shouldn't I be in a good temper, my dears.'

Once more the carpet had done its work, and not on Mrs Biddle alone. The children felt suddenly good and happy.

'You're a jolly good sort,' said Cyril. 'I see that now. I'm sorry we vexed you at the bazaar to-day.'

'Not another word,' said the changed Mrs Biddle. 'Of course you shall have the carpet, my dears, if you've taken such a fancy to it. No, no; I won't have more than the ten shillings I paid.'

'It does seem hard to ask you for it after you bought it at the bazaar,' said Anthea; 'but it really IS our nursery carpet. It got to the bazaar by mistake, with some other things.'

'Did it really, now? How vexing!' said Mrs Biddle, kindly. 'Well, my dears, I can very well give the extra ten shillings; so you take your carpet and we'll say no more about it. Have a piece of cake before you go! I'm so sorry I stepped on your hand, my boy. Is it all right now?'

'Yes, thank you,' said Robert. 'I say, you ARE good.'

'Not at all,' said Mrs Biddle, heartily. 'I'm delighted to be able to give any little pleasure to you dear children.'

And she helped them to roll up the carpet, and the boys carried it away between them.

'You ARE a dear,' said Anthea, and she and Mrs Biddle kissed each other heartily.

'WELL!' said Cyril as they went along the street.

'Yes,' said Robert, 'and the odd part is that you feel just as if it was REAL—her being so jolly, I mean—and not only the carpet making her nice.'

'Perhaps it IS real,' said Anthea, 'only it was covered up with crossness and tiredness and things, and the carpet took them away.'

'I hope it'll keep them away,' said Jane; 'she isn't ugly at all when she laughs.'

The carpet has done many wonders in its day; but the case of Mrs Biddle is, I think, the most wonderful. For from that day she was never anything like so disagreeable as she was before, and she sent a lovely silver tea-pot and a kind letter to Miss Peasmarsh when the pretty lady married the nice curate; just after Easter it was, and they went to Italy for their honeymoon.

CHAPTER 5. THE TEMPLE

'I wish we could find the Phoenix,' said Jane. 'It's much better company than the carpet.'

'Beastly ungrateful, little kids are,' said Cyril.

'No, I'm not; only the carpet never says anything, and it's so helpless. It doesn't seem able to take care of itself. It gets sold, and taken into the sea, and things like that. You wouldn't catch the Phoenix getting sold.'

It was two days after the bazaar. Everyone was a little cross—some days are like that, usually Mondays, by the way. And this was a Monday.

'I shouldn't wonder if your precious Phoenix had gone off for good,' said Cyril; 'and I don't know that I blame it. Look at the weather!'

'It's not worth looking at,' said Robert. And indeed it wasn't.

'The Phoenix hasn't gone—I'm sure it hasn't,' said Anthea. 'I'll have another look for it.'

Anthea looked under tables and chairs, and in boxes and baskets, in mother's work-bag and father's portmanteau, but still the Phoenix showed not so much as the tip of one shining feather.

Then suddenly Robert remembered how the whole of the Greek invocation song of seven thousand lines had been condensed by him into one English hexameter, so he stood on the carpet and chanted—

'Oh, come along, come along, you good old beautiful Phoenix,'

and almost at once there was a rustle of wings down the kitchen stairs, and the Phoenix sailed in on wide gold wings.

'Where on earth HAVE you been?' asked Anthea. 'I've looked everywhere for you.'

'Not EVERYWHERE,' replied the bird, 'because you did not look in the place where I was. Confess that that hallowed spot was overlooked by you.'

'WHAT hallowed spot?' asked Cyril, a little impatiently, for time was hastening on, and the wishing carpet still idle.

'The spot,' said the Phoenix, 'which I hallowed by my golden presence was the Lutron.'

'The WHAT?'

'The bath—the place of washing.'

'I'm sure you weren't,' said Jane. 'I looked there three times and moved all the towels.'

'I was concealed,' said the Phoenix, 'on the summit of a metal column—enchanted, I should judge, for it felt warm to my golden toes, as though the glorious sun of the desert shone ever upon it.'

'Oh, you mean the cylinder,' said Cyril: 'it HAS rather a comforting feel, this weather. And now where shall we go?'

And then, of course, the usual discussion broke out as to where they should go and what they should do. And naturally, everyone wanted to do something that the others did not care about.

'I am the eldest,' Cyril remarked, 'let's go to the North Pole.'

'This weather! Likely!' Robert rejoined. 'Let's go to the Equator.'

'I think the diamond mines of Golconda would be nice,' said Anthea; 'don't you agree, Jane?'

'No, I don't,' retorted Jane, 'I don't agree with you. I don't agree with anybody.'

The Phoenix raised a warning claw.

'If you cannot agree among yourselves, I fear I shall have to leave you,' it said.

'Well, where shall we go? You decide!' said all.

'If I were you,' said the bird, thoughtfully, 'I should give the carpet a rest. Besides, you'll lose the use of your legs if you go everywhere by carpet. Can't you take me out and explain your ugly city to me?'

'We will if it clears up,' said Robert, without enthusiasm. 'Just look at the rain. And why should we give the carpet a rest?'

'Are you greedy and grasping, and heartless and selfish?' asked the bird, sharply.

'NO!' said Robert, with indignation.

'Well then!' said the Phoenix. 'And as to the rain—well, I am not fond of rain myself. If the sun knew *I* was here—he's very fond of shining on me because I look so bright and golden. He always says I repay a little attention. Haven't you some form of words suitable for use in wet weather?'

'There's "Rain, rain, go away,"' said Anthea; 'but it never DOES go.'

'Perhaps you don't say the invocation properly,' said the bird.

> *'Rain, rain, go away,*
> *Come again another day,*
> *Little baby wants to play,'*

said Anthea.

'That's quite wrong; and if you say it in that sort of dull way, I can quite understand the rain not taking any notice. You should open the window and shout as loud as you can—

> *'Rain, rain, go away,*
> *Come again another day;*
> *Now we want the sun, and so,*
> *Pretty rain, be kind and go!*

'You should always speak politely to people when you want them to do things, and especially when it's going away that you want them to do. And to-day you might add—

> *'Shine, great sun, the lovely Phoe-*
> *Nix is here, and wants to be*
> *Shone on, splendid sun, by thee!'*

'That's poetry!' said Cyril, decidedly.

'It's like it,' said the more cautious Robert.

'I was obliged to put in "lovely",' said the Phoenix, modestly, 'to make the line long enough.'

'There are plenty of nasty words just that length,' said Jane; but everyone else said 'Hush!' And then they opened the window and shouted the seven lines as loud as they could, and the Phoenix said

244

all the words with them, except 'lovely', and when they came to that it looked down and coughed bashfully.

The rain hesitated a moment and then went away.

'There's true politeness,' said the Phoenix, and the next moment it was perched on the window-ledge, opening and shutting its radiant wings and flapping out its golden feathers in such a flood of glorious sunshine as you sometimes have at sunset in autumn time. People said afterwards that there had not been such sunshine in December for years and years and years.

'And now,' said the bird, 'we will go out into the city, and you shall take me to see one of my temples.'

'Your temples?'

'I gather from the carpet that I have many temples in this land.'

'I don't see how you CAN find anything out from it,' said Jane: 'it never speaks.'

'All the same, you can pick up things from a carpet,' said the bird; 'I've seen YOU do it. And I have picked up several pieces of information in this way. That papyrus on which you showed me my picture—I understand that it bears on it the name of the street of your city in which my finest temple stands, with my image graved in stone and in metal over against its portal.'

'You mean the fire insurance office,' said Robert. 'It's not really a temple, and they don't—'

'Excuse me,' said the Phoenix, coldly, 'you are wholly misinformed. It IS a temple, and they do.'

'Don't let's waste the sunshine,' said Anthea; 'we might argue as we go along, to save time.'

So the Phoenix consented to make itself a nest in the breast of Robert's Norfolk jacket, and they all went out into the splendid sunshine. The best way to the temple of the Phoenix seemed to be to take the tram, and on the top of it the children talked, while the

Phoenix now and then put out a wary beak, cocked a cautious eye, and contradicted what the children were saying.

It was a delicious ride, and the children felt how lucky they were to have had the money to pay for it. They went with the tram as far as it went, and when it did not go any farther they stopped too, and got off. The tram stops at the end of the Gray's Inn Road, and it was Cyril who thought that one might well find a short cut to the Phoenix Office through the little streets and courts that lie tightly packed between Fetter Lane and Ludgate Circus. Of course, he was quite mistaken, as Robert told him at the time, and afterwards Robert did not forbear to remind his brother how he had said so. The streets there were small and stuffy and ugly, and crowded with printers' boys and binders' girls coming out from work; and these stared so hard at the pretty red coats and caps of the sisters that they wished they had gone some other way. And the printers and binders made very personal remarks, advising Jane to get her hair cut, and inquiring where Anthea had bought that hat. Jane and Anthea scorned to reply, and Cyril and Robert found that they were hardly a match for the rough crowd. They could think of nothing nasty enough to say. They turned a corner sharply, and then Anthea pulled Jane into an archway, and then inside a door; Cyril and Robert quickly followed, and the jeering crowd passed by without seein them.

Anthea drew a long breath.

'How awful!' she said. 'I didn't know there were such people, except in books.'

'It was a bit thick; but it's partly you girls' fault, coming out in those flashy coats.'

'We thought we ought to, when we were going out with the Phoenix,' said Jane; and the bird said, 'Quite right, too'—and incautiously put out his head to give her a wink of encouragement.

And at the same instant a dirty hand reached through the grim balustrade of the staircase beside them and clutched the Phoenix, and a hoarse voice said—

'I say, Urb, blowed if this ain't our Poll parrot what we lost. Thank you very much, lidy, for bringin' 'im home to roost.'

The four turned swiftly. Two large and ragged boys were crouched amid the dark shadows of the stairs. They were much larger than Robert and Cyril, and one of them had snatched the Phoenix away and was holding it high above their heads.

'Give me that bird,' said Cyril, sternly: 'it's ours.'

'Good arternoon, and thankin' you,' the boy went on, with maddening mockery. 'Sorry I can't give yer tuppence for yer trouble—but I've 'ad to spend my fortune advertising for my vallyable bird in all the newspapers. You can call for the reward next year.'

'Look out, Ike,' said his friend, a little anxiously; 'it 'ave a beak on it.'

'It's other parties as'll have the Beak on to 'em presently,' said Ike, darkly, 'if they come a-trying to lay claims on my Poll parrot. You just shut up, Urb. Now then, you four little gells, get out er this.'

'Little girls!' cried Robert. 'I'll little girl you!'

He sprang up three stairs and hit out.

There was a squawk—the most bird-like noise any one had ever heard from the Phoenix—and a fluttering, and a laugh in the darkness, and Ike said—

'There now, you've been and gone and strook my Poll parrot right in the fevvers—strook 'im something crool, you 'ave.'

Robert stamped with fury. Cyril felt himself growing pale with rage, and with the effort of screwing up his brain to make it clever enough to think of some way of being even with those boys. Anthea and Jane were as angry as the boys, but it made them want to cry. Yet it was Anthea who said—

'Do, PLEASE, let us have the bird.'

'Dew, PLEASE, get along and leave us an' our bird alone.'

'If you don't,' said Anthea, 'I shall fetch the police.'

'You better!' said he who was named Urb. 'Say, Ike, you twist the bloomin' pigeon's neck; he ain't worth tuppence.'

'Oh, no,' cried Jane, 'don't hurt it. Oh, don't; it is such a pet.'

'I won't hurt it,' said Ike; 'I'm 'shamed of you, Urb, for to think of such a thing. Arf a shiner, miss, and the bird is yours for life.'

'Half a WHAT?' asked Anthea.

'Arf a shiner, quid, thick 'un—half a sov, then.'

'I haven't got it—and, besides, it's OUR bird,' said Anthea.

'Oh, don't talk to him,' said Cyril and then Jane said suddenly—

'Phoenix—dear Phoenix, we can't do anything. YOU must manage it.'

'With pleasure,' said the Phoenix—and Ike nearly dropped it in his amazement.

'I say, it do talk, suthin' like,' said he.

'Youths,' said the Phoenix, 'sons of misfortune, hear my words.'

'My eyes!' said Ike.

'Look out, Ike,' said Urb, 'you'll throttle the joker—and I see at wunst 'e was wuth 'is weight in flimsies.'00

'Hearken, O Eikonoclastes, despiser of sacred images—and thou, Urbanus, dweller in the sordid city. Forbear this adventure lest a worse thing befall.'

'Luv' us!' said Ike, 'ain't it been taught its schoolin' just!'

'Restore me to my young acolytes and escape unscathed. Retain me—and—'

'They must ha' got all this up, case the Polly got pinched,' said Ike. 'Lor' lumme, the artfulness of them young uns!'

'I say, slosh 'em in the geseech and get clear off with the swag's wot I say,' urged Herbert.

'Right O,' said Isaac.

'Forbear,' repeated the Phoenix, sternly. 'Who pinched the click off of the old bloke in Aldermanbury?' it added, in a changed tone.

'Who sneaked the nose-rag out of the young gell's 'and in Bell Court? Who—'

'Stow it,' said Ike. 'You! ugh! yah!—leave go of me. Bash him off, Urb; 'e'll have my bloomin' eyes outer my ed.'

There were howls, a scuffle, a flutter; Ike and Urb fled up the stairs, and the Phoenix swept out through the doorway. The children followed and the Phoenix settled on Robert, 'like a butterfly on a rose,' as Anthea said afterwards, and wriggled into the breast of his Norfolk jacket, 'like an eel into mud,' as Cyril later said.

'Why ever didn't you burn him? You could have, couldn't you?' asked Robert, when the hurried flight through the narrow courts had ended in the safe wideness of Farringdon Street.

'I could have, of course,' said the bird, 'but I didn't think it would be dignified to allow myself to get warm about a little thing like that. The Fates, after all, have not been illiberal to me. I have a good many friends among the London sparrows, and I have a beak and claws.'

These happenings had somewhat shaken the adventurous temper of the children, and the Phoenix had to exert its golden self to hearten them up.

Presently the children came to a great house in Lombard Street, and there, on each side of the door, was the image of the Phoenix carved in stone, and set forth on shining brass were the words—

PHOENIX FIRE OFFICE

'One moment,' said the bird. 'Fire? For altars, I suppose?'

'*I* don't know,' said Robert; he was beginning to feel shy, and that always made him rather cross.

'Oh, yes, you do,' Cyril contradicted. 'When people's houses are burnt down the Phoenix gives them new houses. Father told me; I asked him.'

'The house, then, like the Phoenix, rises from its ashes? Well have my priests dealt with the sons of men!'

'The sons of men pay, you know,' said Anthea; 'but it's only a little every year.'

'That is to maintain my priests,' said the bird, 'who, in the hour of affliction, heal sorrows and rebuild houses. Lead on; inquire for the High Priest. I will not break upon them too suddenly in all my glory. Noble and honour-deserving are they who make as nought the evil deeds of the lame-footed and unpleasing Hephaestus.'

'I don't know what you're talking about, and I wish you wouldn't muddle us with new names. Fire just happens. Nobody does it—not as a deed, you know,' Cyril explained. 'If they did the Phoenix wouldn't help them, because its a crime to set fire to things. Arsenic, or something they call it, because it's as bad as poisoning people. The Phoenix wouldn't help THEM—father told me it wouldn't.'

'My priests do well,' said the Phoenix. 'Lead on.'

'I don't know what to say,' said Cyril; and the Others said the same.

'Ask for the High Priest,' said the Phoenix. 'Say that you have a secret to unfold that concerns my worship, and he will lead you to the innermost sanctuary.'

So the children went in, all four of them, though they didn't like it, and stood in a large and beautiful hall adorned with Doulton tiles, like a large and beautiful bath with no water in it, and stately pillars supporting the roof. An unpleasing representation of the Phoenix in brown pottery disfigured one wall. There were counters and desks of mahogany and brass, and clerks bent over the desks and walked behind the counters. There was a great clock over an inner doorway.

'Inquire for the High Priest,' whispered the Phoenix.

An attentive clerk in decent black, who controlled his mouth but not his eyebrows, now came towards them. He leaned forward on the counter, and the children thought he was going to say, 'What can I have the pleasure of showing you?' like in a draper's; instead of which the young man said—

'And what do YOU want?'

'We want to see the High Priest.'

'Get along with you,' said the young man.

An elder man, also decent in black coat, advanced.

'Perhaps it's Mr Blank' (not for worlds would I give the name). 'He's a Masonic High Priest, you know.'

A porter was sent away to look for Mr Asterisk (I cannot give his name), and the children were left there to look on and be looked on by all the gentlemen at the mahogany desks. Anthea and Jane thought that they looked kind. The boys thought they stared, and that it was like their cheek.

The porter returned with the news that Mr Dot Dash Dot (I dare not reveal his name) was out, but that Mr—

Here a really delightful gentleman appeared. He had a beard and a kind and merry eye, and each one of the four knew at once that this was a man who had kiddies of his own and could understand what you were talking about. Yet it was a difficult thing to explain.

'What is it?' he asked. 'Mr'—he named the name which I will never reveal—'is out. Can I do anything?'

'Inner sanctuary,' murmured the Phoenix.

'I beg your pardon,' said the nice gentleman, who thought it was Robert who had spoken.

'We have something to tell you,' said Cyril, 'but'—he glanced at the porter, who was lingering much nearer than he need have done—'this is a very public place.'

The nice gentleman laughed.

'Come upstairs then,' he said, and led the way up a wide and beautiful staircase. Anthea says the stairs were of white marble, but I am not sure. On the corner-post of the stairs, at the top, was a beautiful image of the Phoenix in dark metal, and on the wall at each side was a flat sort of image of it.

The nice gentleman led them into a room where the chairs, and even the tables, were covered with reddish leather. He looked at the children inquiringly.

'Don't be frightened,' he said; 'tell me exactly what you want.'

'May I shut the door?' asked Cyril.

The gentleman looked surprised, but he shut the door.

'Now,' said Cyril, firmly, 'I know you'll be awfully surprised, and you'll think it's not true and we are lunatics; but we aren't, and it is. Robert's got something inside his Norfolk—that's Robert, he's my young brother. Now don't be upset and have a fit or anything sir. Of course, I know when you called your shop the "Phoenix" you never thought there was one; but there is—and Robert's got it buttoned up against his chest!'

'If it's an old curio in the form of a Phoenix, I dare say the Board—' said the nice gentleman, as Robert began to fumble with his buttons.

'It's old enough,' said Anthea, 'going by what it says, but—'

'My goodness gracious!' said the gentleman, as the Phoenix, with one last wriggle that melted into a flutter, got out of its nest in the breast of Robert and stood up on the leather-covered table.

'What an extraordinarily fine bird!' he went on. 'I don't think I ever saw one just like it.'

'I should think not,' said the Phoenix, with pardonable pride. And the gentleman jumped.

'Oh, it's been taught to speak! Some sort of parrot, perhaps?'

'I am,' said the bird, simply, 'the Head of your House, and I have come to my temple to receive your homage. I am no parrot'—its beak curved scornfully—'I am the one and only Phoenix, and I demand the homage of my High Priest.'

'In the absence of our manager,' the gentleman began, exactly as though he were addressing a valued customer—'in the absence of our manager, I might perhaps be able—What am I saying?' He turned pale, and passed his hand across his brow. 'My dears,' he said, 'the weather is unusually warm for the time of year, and I don't feel quite myself. Do you know, for a moment I really thought that that remarkable bird of yours had spoken and said it was the Phoenix, and, what's more, that I'd believed it.'

'So it did, sir,' said Cyril, 'and so did you.'

'It really—Allow me.'

A bell was rung. The porter appeared.

'Mackenzie,' said the gentleman, 'you see that golden bird?'

'Yes, sir.'

The other breathed a sigh of relief.

'It IS real, then?'

'Yes, sir, of course, sir. You take it in your hand, sir,' said the porter, sympathetically, and reached out his hand to the Phoenix, who shrank back on toes curved with agitated indignation.

'Forbear!' it cried; 'how dare you seek to lay hands on me?'

The porter saluted.

'Beg pardon, sir,' he said, 'I thought you was a bird.'

253

'I AM a bird—THE bird—the Phoenix.'

'Of course you are, sir,' said the porter. 'I see that the first minute, directly I got my breath, sir.'

'That will do,' said the gentleman. 'Ask Mr Wilson and Mr Sterry to step up here for a moment, please.'

Mr Sterry and Mr Wilson were in their turn overcome by amazement—quickly followed by conviction. To the surprise of the children everyone in the office took the Phoenix at its word, and after the first shock of surprise it seemed to be perfectly natural to everyone that the Phoenix should be alive, and that, passing through London, it should call at its temple.

'We ought to have some sort of ceremony,' said the nicest gentleman, anxiously. 'There isn't time to summon the directors and shareholders—we might do that tomorrow, perhaps. Yes, the board-room would be best. I shouldn't like it to feel we hadn't done everything in our power to show our appreciation of its condescension in looking in on us in this friendly way.'

The children could hardly believe their ears, for they had never thought that any one but themselves would believe in the Phoenix. And yet everyone did; all the men in the office were brought in by twos and threes, and the moment the Phoenix opened its beak it convinced the cleverest of them, as well as those who were not so clever. Cyril wondered how the story would look in the papers next day. He seemed to see the posters in the streets:

PHOENIX FIRE OFFICE
THE PHOENIX AT ITS TEMPLE
MEETING TO WELCOME IT
DELIGHT OF THE MANAGER AND EVERYBODY.

'Excuse our leaving you a moment,' said the nice gentleman, and he went away with the others; and through the half-closed door the children could hear the sound of many boots on stairs, the hum of excited voices explaining, suggesting, arguing, the thumpy drag of heavy furniture being moved about.

The Phoenix strutted up and down the leather-covered table, looking over its shoulder at its pretty back.

'You see what a convincing manner I have,' it said proudly.

And now a new gentleman came in and said, bowing low—

'Everything is prepared—we have done our best at so short a notice; the meeting—the ceremony—will be in the board-room. Will the Honourable Phoenix walk—it is only a few steps—or would it like to be—would it like some sort of conveyance?'

'My Robert will bear me to the board-room, if that be the unlovely name of my temple's inmost court,' replied the bird.

So they all followed the gentleman. There was a big table in the board-room, but it had been pushed right up under the long windows at one side, and chairs were arranged in rows across the room—like those you have at schools when there is a magic lantern on 'Our Eastern Empire', or on 'The Way We Do in the Navy'. The doors were of carved wood, very beautiful, with a carved Phoenix above. Anthea noticed that the chairs in the front rows were of the kind that her mother so loved to ask the price of in old furniture shops, and never could buy, because the price was always nearly twenty pounds each. On the mantelpiece were some heavy bronze candlesticks and a clock, and on the top of the clock was another image of the Phoenix.

'Remove that effigy,' said the Phoenix to the gentlemen who were there, and it was hastily taken down. Then the Phoenix fluttered to the middle of the mantelpiece and stood there, looking more golden than ever. Then everyone in the house and the office came in—from the cashier to the women who cooked the clerks' dinners in the beautiful kitchen at the top of the house. And everyone bowed to the Phoenix and then sat down in a chair.

'Gentlemen,' said the nicest gentleman, 'we have met here today—'

The Phoenix was turning its golden beak from side to side.

'I don't notice any incense,' it said, with an injured sniff. A hurried consultation ended in plates being fetched from the kitchen. Brown sugar, sealing-wax, and tobacco were placed on these, and something from a square bottle was poured over it all. Then a match was applied. It was the only incense that was handy in the Phoenix office, and it certainly burned very briskly and smoked a great deal.

'We have met here today,' said the gentleman again, 'on an occasion unparalleled in the annals of this office. Our respected Phoenix—'

'Head of the House,' said the Phoenix, in a hollow voice.

'I was coming to that. Our respected Phoenix, the Head of this ancient House, has at length done us the honour to come among us. I think I may say, gentlemen, that we are not insensible to this honour, and that we welcome with no uncertain voice one whom we have so long desired to see in our midst.'

Several of the younger clerks thought of saying 'Hear, hear,' but they feared it might seem disrespectful to the bird.

'I will not take up your time,' the speaker went on, 'by recapitulating the advantages to be derived from a proper use of our system of fire insurance. I know, and you know, gentlemen, that our aim has ever been to be worthy of that eminent bird whose name we bear, and who now adorns our mantelpiece with his presence. Three cheers, gentlemen, for the winged Head of the House!'

The cheers rose, deafening. When they had died away the Phoenix was asked to say a few words.

It expressed in graceful phrases the pleasure it felt in finding itself at last in its own temple.

'And,' it went on, 'You must not think me wanting in appreciation of your very hearty and cordial reception when I ask that an ode may be recited or a choric song sung. It is what I have always been accustomed to.'

The four children, dumb witnesses of this wonderful scene, glanced a little nervously across the foam of white faces above the sea of black coats. It seemed to them that the Phoenix was really asking a little too much.

'Time presses,' said the Phoenix, 'and the original ode of invocation is long, as well as being Greek; and, besides, it's no use invoking me when here I am; but is there not a song in your own tongue for a great day such as this?'

Absently the manager began to sing, and one by one the rest joined—

> *'Absolute security!*
> *No liability!*
> *All kinds of property*
> *insured against fire.*
> *Terms most favourable,*
> *Expenses reasonable,*
> *Moderate rates for annual*
> *Insurance.'*

'That one is NOT my favourite,' interrupted the Phoenix, 'and I think you've forgotten part of it.'

The manager hastily began another—

> *'O Golden Phoenix, fairest bird,*
> *The whole great world has often heard*
> *Of all the splendid things we do,*
> *Great Phoenix, just to honour you.'*

'That's better,' said the bird. And everyone sang—

> *'Class one, for private dwelling-house,*
> *For household goods and shops allows;*
> *Provided these are built of brick*
> *Or stone, and tiled and slated thick.'*

'Try another verse,' said the Phoenix, 'further on.'

And again arose the voices of all the clerks and employees and managers and secretaries and cooks—

> *'In Scotland our insurance yields*
> *The price of burnt-up stacks in fields.'*

'Skip that verse,' said the Phoenix.

> *'Thatched dwellings and their whole contents*
> *We deal with—also with their rents;*
> *Oh, glorious Phoenix, look and see*
> *That these are dealt with in class three.*
>
> *'The glories of your temple throng*
> *Too thick to go in any song;*
> *And we attend, O good and wise,*
> *To "days of grace" and merchandise.*
>
> *'When people's homes are burned away*
> *They never have a cent to pay*
> *If they have done as all should do,*
> *O Phoenix, and have honoured you.*
>
> *'So let us raise our voice and sing*
> *The praises of the Phoenix King.*
> *In classes one and two and three,*
> *Oh, trust to him, for kind is he!'*

'I'm sure YOU'RE very kind,' said the Phoenix; 'and now we must be going. An thank you very much for a very pleasant time. May you all prosper as you deserve to do, for I am sure a nicer, pleasanter-spoken lot of temple attendants I have never met, and never wish to meet. I wish you all good-day!'

It fluttered to the wrist of Robert and drew the four children from the room. The whole of the office staff followed down the wide stairs and filed into their accustomed places, and the two most important officials stood on the steps bowing till Robert had buttoned the golden bird in his Norfolk bosom, and it and he and the three other children were lost in the crowd.

The two most important gentlemen looked at each other earnestly and strangely for a moment, and then retreated to those sacred inner rooms, where they toil without ceasing for the good of the House.

And the moment they were all in their places—managers, secretaries, clerks, and porters—they all started, and each looked cautiously round to see if any one was looking at him. For each

258

thought that he had fallen asleep for a few minutes, and had dreamed a very odd dream about the Phoenix and the board-room. And, of course, no one mentioned it to any one else, because going to sleep at your office is a thing you simply MUST NOT do.

The extraordinary confusion of the board-room, with the remains of the incense in the plates, would have shown them at once that the visit of the Phoenix had been no dream, but a radiant reality, but no one went into the board-room again that day; and next day, before the office was opened, it was all cleaned and put nice and tidy by a lady whose business asking questions was not part of. That is why Cyril read the papers in vain on the next day and the day after that; because no sensible person thinks his dreams worth putting in the paper, and no one will ever own that he has been asleep in the daytime.

The Phoenix was very pleased, but it decided to write an ode for itself. It thought the ones it had heard at its temple had been too hastily composed. Its own ode began—

> *'For beauty and for modest worth*
> *The Phoenix has not its equal on earth.'*

And when the children went to bed that night it was still trying to cut down the last line to the proper length without taking out any of what it wanted to say.

That is what makes poetry so difficult.

CHAPTER 6. DOING GOOD

'We shan't be able to go anywhere on the carpet for a whole week, though,' said Robert.

'And I'm glad of it,' said Jane, unexpectedly.

'Glad?' said Cyril; 'GLAD?'

It was breakfast-time, and mother's letter, telling them how they were all going for Christmas to their aunt's at Lyndhurst, and how father and mother would meet them there, having been read by everyone, lay on the table, drinking hot bacon-fat with one corner and eating marmalade with the other.

'Yes, glad,' said Jane. 'I don't want any more things to happen just now. I feel like you do when you've been to three parties in a week—like we did at granny's once—and extras in between, toys and chocs and things like that. I want everything to be just real, and no fancy things happening at all.' 'I don't like being obliged to keep things from mother,' said Anthea. 'I don't know why, but it makes me feel selfish and mean.'

'If we could only get the mater to believe it, we might take her to the jolliest places,' said Cyril, thoughtfully. 'As it is, we've just got to be selfish and mean—if it is that—but I don't feel it is.'

'I KNOW it isn't, but I FEEL it is,' said Anthea, 'and that's just as bad.'

'It's worse,' said Robert; 'if you knew it and didn't feel it, it wouldn't matter so much.'

'That's being a hardened criminal, father says,' put in Cyril, and he picked up mother's letter and wiped its corners with his handkerchief, to whose colour a trifle of bacon-fat and marmalade made but little difference.

'We're going to-morrow, anyhow,' said Robert. 'Don't,' he added, with a good-boy expression on his face—'don't let's be ungrateful for our blessings; don't let's waste the day in saying how horrid it is to keep secrets from mother, when we all know Anthea tried all she knew to give her the secret, and she wouldn't take it. Let's get on the carpet and have a jolly good wish. You'll have time enough to repent of things all next week.'

'Yes,' said Cyril, 'let's. It's not really wrong.'

'Well, look here,' said Anthea. 'You know there's something about Christmas that makes you want to be good—however little you wish

260

it at other times. Couldn't we wish the carpet to take us somewhere where we should have the chance to do some good and kind action? It would be an adventure just the same,' she pleaded.

'I don't mind,' said Cyril. 'We shan't know where we're going, and that'll be exciting. No one knows what'll happen. We'd best put on our outers in case—'

'We might rescue a traveller buried in the snow, like St Bernard dogs, with barrels round our necks,' said Jane, beginning to be interested.

'Or we might arrive just in time to witness a will being signed—more tea, please,' said Robert, 'and we should see the old man hide it away in the secret cupboard; and then, after long years, when the rightful heir was in despair, we should lead him to the hidden panel and—'

'Yes,' interrupted Anthea; 'or we might be taken to some freezing garret in a German town, where a poor little pale, sick child—'

'We haven't any German money,' interrupted Cyril, 'so THAT'S no go. What I should like would be getting into the middle of a war and getting hold of secret intelligence and taking it to the general, and he would make me a lieutenant or a scout, or a hussar.'

When breakfast was cleared away, Anthea swept the carpet, and the children sat down on it, together with the Phoenix, who had been especially invited, as a Christmas treat, to come with them and witness the good and kind action they were about to do.

Four children and one bird were ready, and the wish was wished.

Everyone closed its eyes, so as to feel the topsy-turvy swirl of the carpet's movement as little as possible.

When the eyes were opened again the children found themselves on the carpet, and the carpet was in its proper place on the floor of their own nursery at Camden Town.

'I say,' said Cyril, 'here's a go!'

'Do you think it's worn out? The wishing part of it, I mean?' Robert anxiously asked the Phoenix.

'It's not that,' said the Phoenix; 'but—well—what did you wish—?'

'Oh! I see what it means,' said Robert, with deep disgust; 'it's like the end of a fairy story in a Sunday magazine. How perfectly beastly!'

'You mean it means we can do kind and good actions where we are? I see. I suppose it wants us to carry coals for the cook or make clothes for the bare heathens. Well, I simply won't. And the last day and everything. Look here!' Cyril spoke loudly and firmly. 'We want to go somewhere really interesting, where we have a chance of doing something good and kind; we don't want to do it here, but somewhere else. See? Now, then.'

The obedient carpet started instantly, and the four children and one bird fell in a heap together, and as they fell were plunged in perfect darkness.

'Are you all there?' said Anthea, breathlessly, through the black dark. Everyone owned that it was there.

'Where are we? Oh! how shivery and wet it is! Ugh!—oh!—I've put my hand in a puddle!'

'Has any one got any matches?' said Anthea, hopelessly. She felt sure that no one would have any.

It was then that Robert, with a radiant smile of triumph that was quite wasted in the darkness, where, of course, no one could see anything, drew out of his pocket a box of matches, struck a match and lighted a candle—two candles. And everyone, with its mouth open, blinked at the sudden light.

'Well done Bobs,' said his sisters, and even Cyril's natural brotherly feelings could not check his admiration of Robert's foresight.

'I've always carried them about ever since the lone tower day,' said Robert, with modest pride. 'I knew we should want them some day. I kept the secret well, didn't I?'

'Oh, yes,' said Cyril, with fine scorn. 'I found them the Sunday after, when I was feeling in your Norfolks for the knife you borrowed off me. But I thought you'd only sneaked them for Chinese lanterns, or reading in bed by.'

'Bobs,' said Anthea, suddenly, 'do you know where we are? This is the underground passage, and look there—there's the money and the money-bags, and everything.'

By this time the ten eyes had got used to the light of the candles, and no one could help seeing that Anthea spoke the truth.

'It seems an odd place to do good and kind acts in, though,' said Jane. 'There's no one to do them to.'

'Don't you be too sure,' said Cyril; 'just round the next turning we might find a prisoner who has languished here for years and years, and we could take him out on our carpet and restore him to his sorrowing friends.'

'Of course we could,' said Robert, standing up and holding the candle above his head to see further off; 'or we might find the bones of a poor prisoner and take them to his friends to be buried properly—that's always a kind action in books, though I never could see what bones matter.'

'I wish you wouldn't,' said Jane.

'I know exactly where we shall find the bones, too,' Robert went on. 'You see that dark arch just along the passage? Well, just inside there—'

'If you don't stop going on like that,' said Jane, firmly, 'I shall scream, and then I'll faint—so now then!'

'And *I* will, too,' said Anthea.

Robert was not pleased at being checked in his flight of fancy.

'You girls will never be great writers,' he said bitterly. 'They just love to think of things in dungeons, and chains, and knobbly bare human bones, and—'

263

Jane had opened her mouth to scream, but before she could decide how you began when you wanted to faint, the golden voice of the Phoenix spoke through the gloom.

'Peace!' it said; 'there are no bones here except the small but useful sets that you have inside you. And you did not invite me to come out with you to hear you talk about bones, but to see you do some good and kind action.'

'We can't do it here,' said Robert, sulkily.

'No,' rejoined the bird. 'The only thing we can do here, it seems, is to try to frighten our little sisters.'

'He didn't, really, and I'm not so VERY little,' said Jane, rather ungratefully.

Robert was silent. It was Cyril who suggested that perhaps they had better take the money and go.

'That wouldn't be a kind act, except to ourselves; and it wouldn't be good, whatever way you look at it,' said Anthea, 'to take money that's not ours.'

'We might take it and spend it all on benefits to the poor and aged,' said Cyril.

'That wouldn't make it right to steal,' said Anthea, stoutly.

'I don't know,' said Cyril. They were all standing up now. 'Stealing is taking things that belong to some one else, and there's no one else.'

'It can't be stealing if—'

'That's right,' said Robert, with ironical approval; 'stand here all day arguing while the candles burn out. You'll like it awfully when it's all dark again—and bony.'

'Let's get out, then,' said Anthea. 'We can argue as we go.' So they rolled up the carpet and went. But when they had crept along to the place where the passage led into the topless tower they found the way blocked by a great stone, which they could not move.

264

'There!' said Robert. 'I hope you're satisfied!'

'Everything has two ends,' said the Phoenix, softly; 'even a quarrel or a secret passage.'

So they turned round and went back, and Robert was made to go first with one of the candles, because he was the one who had begun to talk about bones. And Cyril carried the carpet.

'I wish you hadn't put bones into our heads,' said Jane, as they went along.

'I didn't; you always had them. More bones than brains,' said Robert.

The passage was long, and there were arches and steps and turnings and dark alcoves that the girls did not much like passing. The passage ended in a flight of steps. Robert went up them.

Suddenly he staggered heavily back on to the following feet of Jane, and everybody screamed, 'Oh! what is it?'

'I've only bashed my head in,' said Robert, when he had groaned for some time; 'that's all. Don't mention it; I like it. The stairs just go right slap into the ceiling, and it's a stone ceiling. You can't do good and kind actions underneath a paving-stone.'

'Stairs aren't made to lead just to paving-stones as a general rule,' said the Phoenix. 'Put your shoulder to the wheel.'

'There isn't any wheel,' said the injured Robert, still rubbing his head.

But Cyril had pushed past him to the top stair, and was already shoving his hardest against the stone above. Of course, it did not give in the least.

'If it's a trap-door—' said Cyril. And he stopped shoving and began to feel about with his hands.

'Yes, there is a bolt. I can't move it.'

By a happy chance Cyril had in his pocket the oil-can of his father's bicycle; he put the carpet down at the foot of the stairs, and he lay on his back, with his head on the top step and his feet straggling down among his young relations, and he oiled the bolt till the drops of rust and oil fell down on his face. One even went into his mouth—open, as he panted with the exertion of keeping up this unnatural position. Then he tried again, but still the bolt would not move. So now he tied his handkerchief—the one with the bacon-fat and marmalade on it—to the bolt, and Robert's handkerchief to that, in a reef knot, which cannot come undone however much you pull, and, indeed, gets tighter and tighter the more you pull it. This must not be confused with a granny knot, which comes undone if you look at it. And then he and Robert pulled, and the girls put their arms round their brothers and pulled too, and suddenly the bolt gave way with a rusty scrunch, and they all rolled together to the bottom of the stairs—all but the Phoenix, which had taken to its wings when the pulling began.

Nobody was hurt much, because the rolled-up carpet broke their fall; and now, indeed, the shoulders of the boys were used to some purpose, for the stone allowed them to heave it up. They felt it give; dust fell freely on them.

'Now, then,' cried Robert, forgetting his head and his temper, 'push all together. One, two, three!'

The stone was heaved up. It swung up on a creaking, unwilling hinge, and showed a growing oblong of dazzling daylight; and it fell back with a bang against something that kept it upright. Everyone climbed out, but there was not room for everyone to stand comfortably in the little paved house where they found themselves, so when the Phoenix had fluttered up from the darkness they let the stone down, and it closed like a trap-door, as indeed it was.

You can have no idea how dusty and dirty the children were. Fortunately there was no one to see them but each other. The place they were in was a little shrine, built on the side of a road that went winding up through yellow-green fields to the topless tower. Below them were fields and orchards, all bare boughs and brown furrows, and little houses and gardens. The shrine was a kind of tiny chapel with no front wall—just a place for people to stop and rest in and wish to be good. So the Phoenix told them. There was an image that

266

had once been brightly coloured, but the rain and snow had beaten in through the open front of the shrine, and the poor image was dull and weather-stained. Under it was written: 'St Jean de Luz. Priez pour nous.' It was a sad little place, very neglected and lonely, and yet it was nice, Anthea thought, that poor travellers should come to this little rest-house in the hurry and worry of their journeyings and be quiet for a few minutes, and think about being good. The thought of St Jean de Luz—who had, no doubt, in his time, been very good and kind—made Anthea want more than ever to do something kind and good.

'Tell us,' she said to the Phoenix, 'what is the good and kind action the carpet brought us here to do?'

'I think it would be kind to find the owners of the treasure and tell them about it,' said Cyril.

'And give it them ALL?' said Jane.

'Yes. But whose is it?'

'I should go to the first house and ask the name of the owner of the castle,' said the golden bird, and really the idea seemed a good one.

They dusted each other as well as they could and went down the road. A little way on they found a tiny spring, bubbling out of the hillside and falling into a rough stone basin surrounded by draggled hart's-tongue ferns, now hardly green at all. Here the children washed their hands and faces and dried them on their pocket-handkerchiefs, which always, on these occasions, seem unnaturally small. Cyril's and Robert's handkerchiefs, indeed, rather undid the effects of the wash. But in spite of this the party certainly looked cleaner than before.

The first house they came to was a little white house with green shutters and a slate roof. It stood in a prim little garden, and down each side of the neat path were large stone vases for flowers to grow in; but all the flowers were dead now.

Along one side of the house was a sort of wide veranda, built of poles and trellis-work, and a vine crawled all over it. It was wider than our English verandas, and Anthea thought it must look lovely when the green leaves and the grapes were there; but now there were only dry, reddish-brown stalks and stems, with a few withered leaves caught in them.

The children walked up to the front door. It was green and narrow. A chain with a handle hung beside it, and joined itself quite openly to a rusty bell that hung under the porch. Cyril had pulled the bell and its noisy clang was dying away before the terrible thought came to all. Cyril spoke it.

'My hat!' he breathed. 'We don't know any French!'

At this moment the door opened. A very tall, lean lady, with pale ringlets like whitey-brown paper or oak shavings, stood before them. She had an ugly grey dress and a black silk apron. Her eyes were small and grey and not pretty, and the rims were red, as though she had been crying.

She addressed the party in something that sounded like a foreign language, and ended with something which they were sure was a question. Of course, no one could answer it.

'What does she say?' Robert asked, looking down into the hollow of his jacket, where the Phoenix was nestling. But before the Phoenix could answer, the whitey-brown lady's face was lighted up by a most charming smile.

'You—you ar-r-re fr-r-rom the England!' she cried. 'I love so much the England. Mais entrez—entrez donc tous! Enter, then—enter all. One essuyes his feet on the carpet.' She pointed to the mat.

'We only wanted to ask—'

'I shall say you all that what you wish,' said the lady. 'Enter only!'

So they all went in, wiping their feet on a very clean mat, and putting the carpet in a safe corner of the veranda.

'The most beautiful days of my life,' said the lady, as she shut the door, 'did pass themselves in England. And since long time I have not heard an English voice to repeal me the past.'

268

This warm welcome embarrassed everyone, but most the boys, for the floor of the hall was of such very clean red and white tiles, and the floor of the sitting-room so very shiny—like a black looking-glass—that each felt as though he had on far more boots than usual, and far noisier.

There was a wood fire, very small and very bright, on the hearth—neat little logs laid on brass fire-dogs. Some portraits of powdered ladies and gentlemen hung in oval frames on the pale walls. There were silver candlesticks on the mantelpiece, and there were chairs and a table, very slim and polite, with slender legs. The room was extremely bare, but with a bright foreign bareness that was very cheerful, in an odd way of its own. At the end of the polished table a very un-English little boy sat on a footstool in a high-backed, uncomfortable-looking chair. He wore black velvet, and the kind of collar—all frills and lacey—that Robert would rather have died than wear; but then the little French boy was much younger than Robert.

'Oh, how pretty!' said everyone. But no one meant the little French boy, with the velvety short knickerbockers and the velvety short hair.

What everyone admired was a little, little Christmas-tree, very green, and standing in a very red little flower-pot, and hung round with very bright little things made of tinsel and coloured paper. There were tiny candles on the tree, but they were not lighted yet.

'But yes—is it not that it is genteel?' said the lady. 'Sit down you then, and let us see.'

The children sat down in a row on the stiff chairs against the wall, and the lady lighted a long, slim red taper at the wood flame, and then she drew the curtains and lit the little candles, and when they were all lighted the little French boy suddenly shouted, 'Bravo, ma tante! Oh, que c'est gentil,' and the English children shouted 'Hooray!'

Then there was a struggle in the breast of Robert, and out fluttered the Phoenix—spread his gold wings, flew to the top of the Christmas-tree, and perched there.

'Ah! catch it, then,' cried the lady; 'it will itself burn—your genteel parrakeet!'

'It won't,' said Robert, 'thank you.'

And the little French boy clapped his clean and tidy hands; but the lady was so anxious that the Phoenix fluttered down and walked up and down on the shiny walnut-wood table.

'Is it that it talks?' asked the lady.

And the Phoenix replied in excellent French. It said, 'Parfaitement, madame!'

'Oh, the pretty parrakeet,' said the lady. 'Can it say still of other things?'

And the Phoenix replied, this time in English, 'Why are you sad so near Christmas-time?'

The children looked at it with one gasp of horror and surprise, for the youngest of them knew that it is far from manners to notice that strangers have been crying, and much worse to ask them the reason of their tears. And, of course, the lady began to cry again, very much indeed, after calling the Phoenix a bird without a heart; and she could not find her handkerchief, so Anthea offered hers, which was still very damp and no use at all. She also hugged the lady, and this seemed to be of more use than the handkerchief, so that presently the lady stopped crying, and found her own handkerchief and dried her eyes, and called Anthea a cherished angel.

'I am sorry we came just when you were so sad,' said Anthea, 'but we really only wanted to ask you whose that castle is on the hill.'

'Oh, my little angel,' said the poor lady, sniffing, 'to-day and for hundreds of years the castle is to us, to our family. To-morrow it must that I sell it to some strangers—and my little Henri, who ignores all, he will not have never the lands paternal. But what will

270

you? His father, my brother—Mr the Marquis—has spent much of money, and it the must, despite the sentiments of familial respect, that I admit that my sainted father he also—'

'How would you feel if you found a lot of money—hundreds and thousands of gold pieces?' asked Cyril.

The lady smiled sadly.

'Ah! one has already recounted to you the legend?' she said. 'It is true that one says that it is long time; oh! but long time, one of our ancestors has hid a treasure—of gold, and of gold, and of gold—enough to enrich my little Henri for the life. But all that, my children, it is but the accounts of fays—'

'She means fairy stories,' whispered the Phoenix to Robert. 'Tell her what you have found.'

So Robert told, while Anthea and Jane hugged the lady for fear she should faint for joy, like people in books, and they hugged her with the earnest, joyous hugs of unselfish delight.

'It's no use explaining how we got in,' said Robert, when he had told of the finding of the treasure, 'because you would find it a little difficult to understand, and much more difficult to believe. But we can show you where the gold is and help you to fetch it away.'

The lady looked doubtfully at Robert as she absently returned the hugs of the girls.

'No, he's not making it up,' said Anthea; 'it's true, TRUE, TRUE!—and we are so glad.'

'You would not be capable to torment an old woman?' she said; 'and it is not possible that it be a dream.'

'It really IS true,' said Cyril; 'and I congratulate you very much.'

His tone of studied politeness seemed to convince more than the raptures of the others.

'If I do not dream,' she said, 'Henri come to Manon—and you—you shall come all with me to Mr the Curate. Is it not?'

Manon was a wrinkled old woman with a red and yellow handkerchief twisted round her head. She took Henri, who was already sleepy with the excitement of his Christmas-tree and his visitors, and when the lady had put on a stiff black cape and a wonderful black silk bonnet and a pair of black wooden clogs over her black cashmere house-boots, the whole party went down the road to a little white house—very like the one they had left—where an old priest, with a good face, welcomed them with a politeness so great that it hid his astonishment.

The lady, with her French waving hands and her shrugging French shoulders and her trembling French speech, told the story. And now the priest, who knew no English, shrugged HIS shoulders and waved HIS hands and spoke also in French.

'He thinks,' whispered the Phoenix, 'that her troubles have turned her brain. What a pity you know no French!'

'I do know a lot of French,' whispered Robert, indignantly; 'but it's all about the pencil of the gardener's son and the penknife of the baker's niece—nothing that anyone ever wants to say.'

'If *I* speak,' the bird whispered, 'he'll think HE'S mad, too.'

'Tell me what to say.'

'Say "C'est vrai, monsieur. Venez donc voir,"' said the Phoenix; and then Robert earned the undying respect of everybody by suddenly saying, very loudly and distinctly—

'Say vray, mossoo; venny dong vwaw.'

The priest was disappointed when he found that Robert's French began and ended with these useful words; but, at any rate, he saw that if the lady was mad she was not the only one, and he put on a big beavery hat, and got a candle and matches and a spade, and they all went up the hill to the wayside shrine of St John of Luz.

'Now,' said Robert, 'I will go first and show you where it is.'

So they prised the stone up with a corner of the spade, and Robert did go first, and they all followed and found the golden treasure exactly as they had left it. And everyone was flushed with the joy of performing such a wonderfully kind action.

Then the lady and the priest clasped hands and wept for joy, as French people do, and knelt down and touched the money, and talked very fast and both together, and the lady embraced all the children three times each, and called them 'little garden angels,' and then she and the priest shook each other by both hands again, and talked, and talked, and talked, faster and more Frenchy than you would have believed possible. And the children were struck dumb with joy and pleasure.

'Get away NOW,' said the Phoenix softly, breaking in on the radiant dream.

So the children crept away, and out through the little shrine, and the lady and the priest were so tearfully, talkatively happy that they never noticed that the guardian angels had gone.

The 'garden angels' ran down the hill to the lady's little house, where they had left the carpet on the veranda, and they spread it out and said 'Home,' and no one saw them disappear, except little Henri, who had flattened his nose into a white button against the window-glass, and when he tried to tell his aunt she thought he had been dreaming. So that was all right.

'It is much the best thing we've done,' said Anthea, when they talked it over at tea-time. 'In the future we'll only do kind actions with the carpet.'

'Ahem!' said the Phoenix.

'I beg your pardon?' said Anthea.

'Oh, nothing,' said the bird. 'I was only thinking!'

CHAPTER 7. MEWS FROM PERSIA

When you hear that the four children found themselves at Waterloo Station quite un-taken-care-of, and with no one to meet them, it may make you think that their parents were neither kind nor careful. But if you think this you will be wrong. The fact is, mother arranged with Aunt Emma that she was to meet the children at Waterloo, when they went back from their Christmas holiday at Lyndhurst. The train was fixed, but not the day. Then mother wrote to Aunt Emma, giving her careful instructions about the day and the hour, and about luggage and cabs and things, and gave the letter to Robert to post. But the hounds happened to meet near Rufus Stone that morning, and what is more, on the way to the meet they met Robert, and Robert met them, and instantly forgot all about posting Aunt Emma's letter, and never thought of it again until he and the others had wandered three times up and down the platform at Waterloo—which makes six in all—and had bumped against old gentlemen, and stared in the faces of ladies, and been shoved by people in a hurry, and 'by-your-leaved' by porters with trucks, and were quite, quite sure that Aunt Emma was not there. Then suddenly the true truth of what he had forgotten to do came home to Robert, and he said, 'Oh, crikey!' and stood still with his mouth open, and let a porter with a Gladstone bag in each hand and a bundle of umbrellas under one arm blunder heavily into him, and never so much as said, 'Where are you shoving to now?' or, 'Look out where you're going, can't you?' The heavier bag smote him at the knee, and he staggered, but he said nothing.

When the others understood what was the matter I think they told Robert what they thought of him.

'We must take the train to Croydon,' said Anthea, 'and find Aunt Emma.'

'Yes,' said Cyril, 'and precious pleased those Jevonses would be to see us and our traps.'

Aunt Emma, indeed, was staying with some Jevonses—very prim people. They were middle-aged and wore very smart blouses, and they were fond of matinees and shopping, and they did not care about children.

'I know MOTHER would be pleased to see us if we went back,' said Jane.

'Yes, she would, but she'd think it was not right to show she was pleased, because it's Bob's fault we're not met. Don't I know the sort of thing?' said Cyril. 'Besides, we've no tin. No; we've got enough for a growler among us, but not enough for tickets to the New Forest. We must just go home. They won't be so savage when they find we've really got home all right. You know auntie was only going to take us home in a cab.'

'I believe we ought to go to Croydon,' Anthea insisted.

'Aunt Emma would be out to a dead cert,' said Robert. 'Those Jevonses go to the theatre every afternoon, I believe. Besides, there's the Phoenix at home, AND the carpet. I votes we call a four-wheeled cabman.'

A four-wheeled cabman was called—his cab was one of the old-fashioned kind with straw in the bottom—and he was asked by Anthea to drive them very carefully to their address. This he did, and the price he asked for doing so was exactly the value of the gold coin grandpapa had given Cyril for Christmas. This cast a gloom; but Cyril would never have stooped to argue about a cab-fare, for fear the cabman should think he was not accustomed to take cabs whenever he wanted them. For a reason that was something like this he told the cabman to put the luggage on the steps, and waited till the wheels of the growler had grittily retired before he rang the bell.

'You see,' he said, with his hand on the handle, 'we don't want cook and Eliza asking us before HIM how it is we've come home alone, as if we were babies.'

Here he rang the bell; and the moment its answering clang was heard, everyone felt that it would be some time before that bell was answered. The sound of a bell is quite different, somehow, when there is anyone inside the house who hears it. I can't tell you why that is—but so it is.

'I expect they're changing their dresses,' said Jane.

'Too late,' said Anthea, 'it must be past five. I expect Eliza's gone to post a letter, and cook's gone to see the time.'

Cyril rang again. And the bell did its best to inform the listening children that there was really no one human in the house. They rang again and listened intently. The hearts of all sank low. It is a terrible thing to be locked out of your own house, on a dark, muggy January evening.

'There is no gas on anywhere,' said Jane, in a broken voice.

'I expect they've left the gas on once too often, and the draught blew it out, and they're suffocated in their beds. Father always said they would some day,' said Robert cheerfully.

'Let's go and fetch a policeman,' said Anthea, trembling.

'And be taken up for trying to be burglars—no, thank you,' said Cyril. 'I heard father read out of the paper about a young man who got into his own mother's house, and they got him made a burglar only the other day.'

'I only hope the gas hasn't hurt the Phoenix,' said Anthea. 'It said it wanted to stay in the bathroom cupboard, and I thought it would be all right, because the servants never clean that out. But if it's gone and got out and been choked by gas—And besides, directly we open the door we shall be choked, too. I KNEW we ought to have gone to Aunt Emma, at Croydon. Oh, Squirrel, I wish we had. Let's go NOW.'

'Shut up,' said her brother, briefly. 'There's some one rattling the latch inside.' Everyone listened with all its ears, and everyone stood back as far from the door as the steps would allow.

The latch rattled, and clicked. Then the flap of the letter-box lifted itself—everyone saw it by the flickering light of the gas-lamp that shone through the leafless lime-tree by the gate—a golden eye seemed to wink at them through the letter-slit, and a cautious beak whispered—

'Are you alone?'

'It's the Phoenix,' said everyone, in a voice so joyous, and so full of relief, as to be a sort of whispered shout.

'Hush!' said the voice from the letter-box slit. 'Your slaves have gone a-merry-making. The latch of this portal is too stiff for my beak. But at the side—the little window above the shelf whereon your bread lies—it is not fastened.'

'Righto!' said Cyril.

And Anthea added, 'I wish you'd meet us there, dear Phoenix.'

The children crept round to the pantry window. It is at the side of the house, and there is a green gate labelled 'Tradesmen's Entrance', which is always kept bolted. But if you get one foot on the fence between you and next door, and one on the handle of the gate, you are over before you know where you are. This, at least, was the experience of Cyril and Robert, and even, if the truth must be told, of Anthea and Jane. So in almost no time all four were in the narrow gravelled passage that runs between that house and the next.

Then Robert made a back, and Cyril hoisted himself up and got his knicker-bockered knee on the concrete window-sill. He dived into the pantry head first, as one dives into water, and his legs waved in the air as he went, just as your legs do when you are first beginning to learn to dive. The soles of his boots—squarish muddy patches—disappeared.

'Give me a leg up,' said Robert to his sisters.

'No, you don't,' said Jane firmly. 'I'm not going to be left outside here with just Anthea, and have something creep up behind us out of the dark. Squirrel can go and open the back door.'

A light had sprung awake in the pantry. Cyril always said the Phoenix turned the gas on with its beak, and lighted it with a waft of its wing; but he was excited at the time, and perhaps he really did it himself with matches, and then forgot all about it. He let the others in by the back door. And when it had been bolted again the children went all over the house and lighted every single gas-jet they could find. For they couldn't help feeling that this was just the dark dreary winter's evening when an armed burglar might easily be expected to appear at any moment. There is nothing like light when you are afraid of burglars—or of anything else, for that matter.

And when all the gas-jets were lighted it was quite clear that the Phoenix had made no mistake, and that Eliza and cook were really out, and that there was no one in the house except the four children, and the Phoenix, and the carpet, and the blackbeetles who lived in the cupboards on each side of the nursery fire-place. These last were very pleased that the children had come home again, especially when Anthea had lighted the nursery fire. But, as usual, the children treated the loving little blackbeetles with coldness and disdain.

I wonder whether you know how to light a fire? I don't mean how to strike a match and set fire to the corners of the paper in a fire someone has laid ready, but how to lay and light a fire all by yourself. I will tell you how Anthea did it, and if ever you have to light one yourself you may remember how it is done. First, she raked out the ashes of the fire that had burned there a week ago—for Eliza had actually never done this, though she had had plenty of time. In doing this Anthea knocked her knuckle and made it bleed. Then she laid the largest and handsomest cinders in the bottom of the grate. Then she took a sheet of old newspaper (you ought never to light a fire with to-day's newspaper—it will not burn well, and there are other reasons against it), and tore it into four quarters, and screwed each of these into a loose ball, and put them on the cinders; then she got a bundle of wood and broke the string, and stuck the sticks in so that their front ends rested on the bars, and the back ends on the back of the paper balls. In doing this she cut her finger slightly with the string, and when she broke it, two of the sticks jumped up and hit her on the cheek. Then she put more cinders and some bits of coal—no dust. She put most of that on her hands, but there seemed to be enough left for her face. Then she lighted the edges of the paper balls, and waited till she heard the fizz-crack-crack-fizz of the wood as it began to burn. Then she went and washed her hands and face under the tap in the back kitchen.

Of course, you need not bark your knuckles, or cut your finger, or bruise your cheek with wood, or black yourself all over; but otherwise, this is a very good way to light a fire in London. In the real country fires are lighted in a different and prettier way.

But it is always good to wash your hands and face afterwards, wherever you are.

While Anthea was delighting the poor little blackbeetles with the cheerful blaze, Jane had set the table for—I was going to say tea, but the meal of which I am speaking was not exactly tea. Let us call it a tea-ish meal. There was tea, certainly, for Anthea's fire blazed and crackled so kindly that it really seemed to be affectionately inviting the kettle to come and sit upon its lap. So the kettle was brought and tea made. But no milk could be found—so everyone had six lumps of sugar to each cup instead. The things to eat, on the other hand, were nicer than usual. The boys looked about very carefully, and found in the pantry some cold tongue, bread, butter, cheese, and part of a cold pudding—very much nicer than cook ever made when they were at home. And in the kitchen cupboard was half a Christmassy cake, a pot of strawberry jam, and about a pound of mixed candied fruit, with soft crumbly slabs of delicious sugar in each cup of lemon, orange, or citron.

It was indeed, as Jane said, 'a banquet fit for an Arabian Knight.'

The Phoenix perched on Robert's chair, and listened kindly and politely to all they had to tell it about their visit to Lyndhurst, and underneath the table, by just stretching a toe down rather far, the faithful carpet could be felt by all—even by Jane, whose legs were very short.

'Your slaves will not return to-night,' said the Phoenix. 'They sleep under the roof of the cook's stepmother's aunt, who is, I gather, hostess to a large party to-night in honour of her husband's cousin's sister-in-law's mother's ninetieth birthday.'

'I don't think they ought to have gone without leave,' said Anthea, 'however many relations they have, or however old they are; but I suppose we ought to wash up.'

'It's not our business about the leave,' said Cyril, firmly, 'but I simply won't wash up for them. We got it, and we'll clear it away; and then we'll go somewhere on the carpet. It's not often we get a chance of being out all night. We can go right away to the other side of the equator, to the tropical climes, and see the sun rise over the great Pacific Ocean.'

'Right you are,' said Robert. 'I always did want to see the Southern Cross and the stars as big as gas-lamps.'

'DON'T go,' said Anthea, very earnestly, 'because I COULDN'T. I'm SURE mother wouldn't like us to leave the house and I should hate to be left here alone.'

'I'd stay with you,' said Jane loyally.

'I know you would,' said Anthea gratefully, 'but even with you I'd much rather not.'

'Well,' said Cyril, trying to be kind and amiable, 'I don't want you to do anything you think's wrong, BUT—'

He was silent; this silence said many things.

'I don't see,' Robert was beginning, when Anthea interrupted—

'I'm quite sure. Sometimes you just think a thing's wrong, and sometimes you KNOW. And this is a KNOW time.'

The Phoenix turned kind golden eyes on her and opened a friendly beak to say—

'When it is, as you say, a "know time", there is no more to be said. And your noble brothers would never leave you.'

'Of course not,' said Cyril rather quickly. And Robert said so too.

'I myself,' the Phoenix went on, 'am willing to help in any way possible. I will go personally—either by carpet or on the wing—and fetch you anything you can think of to amuse you during the evening. In order to waste no time I could go while you wash up.—Why,' it went on in a musing voice, 'does one wash up teacups and wash down the stairs?'

'You couldn't wash stairs up, you know,' said Anthea, 'unless you began at the bottom and went up feet first as you washed. I wish cook would try that way for a change.'

'I don't,' said Cyril, briefly. 'I should hate the look of her elastic-side boots sticking up.'

'This is mere trifling,' said the Phoenix. 'Come, decide what I shall fetch for you. I can get you anything you like.'

But of course they couldn't decide. Many things were suggested—a rocking-horse, jewelled chessmen, an elephant, a bicycle, a motor-car, books with pictures, musical instruments, and many other things. But a musical instrument is agreeable only to the player, unless he has learned to play it really well; books are not sociable, bicycles cannot be ridden without going out of doors, and the same is true of motor-cars and elephants. Only two people can play chess at once with one set of chessmen (and anyway it's very much too much like lessons for a game), and only one can ride on a rocking-horse. Suddenly, in the midst of the discussion, the Phoenix spread its wings and fluttered to the floor, and from there it spoke.

'I gather,' it said, 'from the carpet, that it wants you to let it go to its old home, where it was born and brought up, and it will return within the hour laden with a number of the most beautiful and delightful products of its native land.'

'What IS its native land?'

'I didn't gather. But since you can't agree, and time is passing, and the tea-things are not washed down—I mean washed up—'

'I votes we do,' said Robert. 'It'll stop all this jaw, anyway. And it's not bad to have surprises. Perhaps it's a Turkey carpet, and it might bring us Turkish delight.'

'Or a Turkish patrol,' said Robert.

'Or a Turkish bath,' said Anthea.

'Or a Turkish towel,' said Jane.

'Nonsense,' Robert urged, 'it said beautiful and delightful, and towels and baths aren't THAT, however good they may be for you. Let it go. I suppose it won't give us the slip,' he added, pushing back his chair and standing up.

'Hush!' said the Phoenix; 'how can you? Don't trample on its feelings just because it's only a carpet.'

'But how can it do it—unless one of us is on it to do the wishing?' asked Robert. He spoke with a rising hope that it MIGHT be necessary for one to go and why not Robert? But the Phoenix quickly threw cold water on his new-born dream.

'Why, you just write your wish on a paper, and pin it on the carpet.'

So a leaf was torn from Anthea's arithmetic book, and on it Cyril wrote in large round-hand the following:

We wish you to go to your dear native home, and bring back the most beautiful and delightful productions of it you can—and not to be gone long, please.

(Signed) CYRIL.
          ROBERT.
          ANTHEA.
          JANE.

Then the paper was laid on the carpet.

'Writing down, please,' said the Phoenix; 'the carpet can't read a paper whose back is turned to it, any more than you can.'

It was pinned fast, and the table and chairs having been moved, the carpet simply and suddenly vanished, rather like a patch of water on a hearth under a fierce fire. The edges got smaller and smaller, and then it disappeared from sight.

'It may take it some time to collect the beautiful and delightful things,' said the Phoenix. 'I should wash up—I mean wash down.'

So they did. There was plenty of hot water left in the kettle, and everyone helped—even the Phoenix, who took up cups by their handles with its clever claws and dipped them in the hot water, and then stood them on the table ready for Anthea to dry them. But the bird was rather slow, because, as it said, though it was not above any sort of honest work, messing about with dish-water was not exactly what it had been brought up to. Everything was nicely washed up, and dried, and put in its proper place, and the dish-cloth washed and hung on the edge of the copper to dry, and the tea-cloth was hung on the line that goes across the scullery. (If you are a duchess's child, or a king's, or a person of high social position's child, you will perhaps not know the difference between a dish-cloth and a tea-cloth; but in that case your nurse has been better instructed than you, and she will tell you all about it.) And just as eight hands and one pair of claws were being dried on the roller-towel behind the scullery door there came a strange sound from the other side of the kitchen wall—the side where the nursery was. It was a very strange sound, indeed—most odd, and unlike any other sounds the children had ever heard. At least, they had heard sounds as much like it as a toy engine's whistle is like a steam siren's.

'The carpet's come back,' said Robert; and the others felt that he was right.

'But what has it brought with it?' asked Jane. 'It sounds like Leviathan, that great beast.'

'It couldn't have been made in India, and have brought elephants? Even baby ones would be rather awful in that room,' said Cyril. 'I vote we take it in turns to squint through the keyhole.'

They did—in the order of their ages. The Phoenix, being the eldest by some thousands of years, was entitled to the first peep. But—

'Excuse me,' it said, ruffling its golden feathers and sneezing softly; 'looking through keyholes always gives me a cold in my golden eyes.'

So Cyril looked.

'I see something grey moving,' said he.

283

'It's a zoological garden of some sort, I bet,' said Robert, when he had taken his turn. And the soft rustling, bustling, ruffling, scuffling, shuffling, fluffling noise went on inside.

'*I* can't see anything,' said Anthea, 'my eye tickles so.'

Then Jane's turn came, and she put her eye to the keyhole.

'It's a giant kitty-cat,' she said; 'and it's asleep all over the floor.'

'Giant cats are tigers—father said so.'

'No, he didn't. He said tigers were giant cats. It's not at all the same thing.'

'It's no use sending the carpet to fetch precious things for you if you're afraid to look at them when they come,' said the Phoenix, sensibly. And Cyril, being the eldest, said—

'Come on,' and turned the handle.

The gas had been left full on after tea, and everything in the room could be plainly seen by the ten eyes at the door. At least, not everything, for though the carpet was there it was invisible, because it was completely covered by the hundred and ninety-nine beautiful objects which it had brought from its birthplace.

'My hat!' Cyril remarked. 'I never thought about its being a PERSIAN carpet.'

Yet it was now plain that it was so, for the beautiful objects which it had brought back were cats—Persian cats, grey Persian cats, and there were, as I have said, 199 of them, and they were sitting on the carpet as close as they could get to each other. But the moment the children entered the room the cats rose and stretched, and spread and overflowed from the carpet to the floor, and in an instant the floor was a sea of moving, mewing pussishness, and the children with one accord climbed to the table, and gathered up their legs, and the people next door knocked on the wall—and, indeed, no wonder, for the mews were Persian and piercing.

'This is pretty poor sport,' said Cyril. 'What's the matter with the bounders?'

'I imagine that they are hungry,' said the Phoenix. 'If you were to feed them—'

'We haven't anything to feed them with,' said Anthea in despair, and she stroked the nearest Persian back. 'Oh, pussies, do be quiet—we can't hear ourselves think.'

She had to shout this entreaty, for the mews were growing deafening, 'and it would take pounds' and pounds' worth of cat's-meat.'

'Let's ask the carpet to take them away,' said Robert. But the girls said 'No.'

'They are so soft and pussy,' said Jane.

'And valuable,' said Anthea, hastily. 'We can sell them for lots and lots of money.'

'Why not send the carpet to get food for them?' suggested the Phoenix, and its golden voice came harsh and cracked with the effort it had to be make to be heard above the increasing fierceness of the Persian mews.

So it was written that the carpet should bring food for 199 Persian cats, and the paper was pinned to the carpet as before.

The carpet seemed to gather itself together, and the cats dropped off it, as raindrops do from your mackintosh when you shake it. And the carpet disappeared.

Unless you have had one-hundred and ninety-nine well-grown Persian cats in one small room, all hungry, and all saying so in unmistakable mews, you can form but a poor idea of the noise that now deafened the children and the Phoenix. The cats did not seem to have been at all properly brought up. They seemed to have no idea of its being a mistake in manners to ask for meals in a strange house—let alone to howl for them—and they mewed, and they mewed, and they mewed, and they mewed, till the children poked

285

their fingers into their ears and waited in silent agony, wondering why the whole of Camden Town did not come knocking at the door to ask what was the matter, and only hoping that the food for the cats would come before the neighbours did—and before all the secret of the carpet and the Phoenix had to be given away beyond recall to an indignant neighbourhood.

The cats mewed and mewed and twisted their Persian forms in and out and unfolded their Persian tails, and the children and the Phoenix huddled together on the table.

The Phoenix, Robert noticed suddenly, was trembling.

'So many cats,' it said, 'and they might not know I was the Phoenix. These accidents happen so quickly. It quite un-mans me.'

This was a danger of which the children had not thought.

'Creep in,' cried Robert, opening his jacket.

And the Phoenix crept in—only just in time, for green eyes had glared, pink noses had sniffed, white whiskers had twitched, and as Robert buttoned his coat he disappeared to the waist in a wave of eager grey Persian fur. And on the instant the good carpet slapped itself down on the floor. And it was covered with rats—three hundred and ninety-eight of them, I believe, two for each cat.

'How horrible!' cried Anthea. 'Oh, take them away!'

'Take yourself away,' said the Phoenix, 'and me.'

'I wish we'd never had a carpet,' said Anthea, in tears.

They hustled and crowded out of the door, and shut it, and locked it. Cyril, with great presence of mind, lit a candle and turned off the gas at the main.

'The rats'll have a better chance in the dark,' he said.

The mewing had ceased. Everyone listened in breathless silence. We all know that cats eat rats—it is one of the first things we read in our little brown reading books; but all those cats eating all those rats—it wouldn't bear thinking of.

Suddenly Robert sniffed, in the silence of the dark kitchen, where the only candle was burning all on one side, because of the draught.

'What a funny scent!' he said.

And as he spoke, a lantern flashed its light through the window of the kitchen, a face peered in, and a voice said—

'What's all this row about? You let me in.'

It was the voice of the police!

Robert tip-toed to the window, and spoke through the pane that had been a little cracked since Cyril accidentally knocked it with a walking-stick when he was playing at balancing it on his nose. (It was after they had been to a circus.)

'What do you mean?' he said. 'There's no row. You listen; everything's as quiet as quiet.' And indeed it was.

The strange sweet scent grew stronger, and the Phoenix put out its beak.

The policeman hesitated.

'They're MUSK-rats,' said the Phoenix. 'I suppose some cats eat them—but never Persian ones. What a mistake for a well-informed carpet to make! Oh, what a night we're having!'

'Do go away,' said Robert, nervously. 'We're just going to bed—that's our bedroom candle; there isn't any row. Everything's as quiet as a mouse.'

A wild chorus of mews drowned his words, and with the mews were mingled the shrieks of the musk-rats. What had happened? Had the cats tasted them before deciding that they disliked the flavour?

'I'm a-coming in,' said the policeman. 'You've got a cat shut up there.'

'A cat,' said Cyril. 'Oh, my only aunt! A cat!'

'Come in, then,' said Robert. 'It's your own look out. I advise you not. Wait a shake, and I'll undo the side gate.'

He undid the side gate, and the policeman, very cautiously, came in. And there in the kitchen, by the light of one candle, with the mewing and the screaming going like a dozen steam sirens, twenty waiting on motor-cars, and half a hundred squeaking pumps, four agitated voices shouted to the policeman four mixed and wholly different explanations of the very mixed events of the evening.

Did you ever try to explain the simplest thing to a policeman?

CHAPTER 8. THE CATS, THE COW, AND THE BURGLAR

The nursery was full of Persian cats and musk-rats that had been brought there by the wishing carpet. The cats were mewing and the musk-rats were squeaking so that you could hardly hear yourself speak. In the kitchen were the four children, one candle, a concealed Phoenix, and a very visible policeman.

'Now then, look here,' said the Policeman, very loudly, and he pointed his lantern at each child in turn, 'what's the meaning of this here yelling and caterwauling. I tell you you've got a cat here, and some one's a ill-treating of it. What do you mean by it, eh?'

It was five to one, counting the Phoenix; but the policeman, who was one, was of unusually fine size, and the five, including the Phoenix, were small. The mews and the squeaks grew softer, and in the comparative silence, Cyril said—

'It's true. There are a few cats here. But we've not hurt them. It's quite the opposite. We've just fed them.'

'It don't sound like it,' said the policeman grimly.

288

'I daresay they're not REAL cats,' said Jane madly, perhaps they're only dream-cats.'

'I'll dream-cat you, my lady,' was the brief response of the force.

'If you understood anything except people who do murders and stealings and naughty things like that, I'd tell you all about it,' said Robert; 'but I'm certain you don't. You're not meant to shove your oar into people's private cat-keepings. You're only supposed to interfere when people shout "murder" and "stop thief" in the street. So there!'

The policeman assured them that he should see about that; and at this point the Phoenix, who had been making itself small on the pot-shelf under the dresser, among the saucepan lids and the fish-kettle, walked on tip-toed claws in a noiseless and modest manner, and left the room unnoticed by any one.

'Oh, don't be so horrid,' Anthea was saying, gently and earnestly. 'We LOVE cats—dear pussy-soft things. We wouldn't hurt them for worlds. Would we, Pussy?'

And Jane answered that of course they wouldn't. And still the policeman seemed unmoved by their eloquence.

'Now, look here,' he said, 'I'm a-going to see what's in that room beyond there, and—'

His voice was drowned in a wild burst of mewing and squeaking. And as soon as it died down all four children began to explain at once; and though the squeaking and mewing were not at their very loudest, yet there was quite enough of both to make it very hard for the policeman to understand a single word of any of the four wholly different explanations now poured out to him.

'Stow it,' he said at last. 'I'm a-goin' into the next room in the execution of my duty. I'm a-goin' to use my eyes—my ears have gone off their chumps, what with you and them cats.'

And he pushed Robert aside, and strode through the door.

'Don't say I didn't warn you,' said Robert.

'It's tigers REALLY,' said Jane. 'Father said so. I wouldn't go in, if I were you.'

But the policeman was quite stony; nothing any one said seemed to make any difference to him. Some policemen are like this, I believe. He strode down the passage, and in another moment he would have been in the room with all the cats and all the rats (musk), but at that very instant a thin, sharp voice screamed from the street outside—

'Murder—murder! Stop thief!'

The policeman stopped, with one regulation boot heavily poised in the air.

'Eh?' he said.

And again the shrieks sounded shrilly and piercingly from the dark street outside.

'Come on,' said Robert. 'Come and look after cats while somebody's being killed outside.' For Robert had an inside feeling that told him quite plainly WHO it was that was screaming.

'You young rip,' said the policeman, 'I'll settle up with you bimeby.'

And he rushed out, and the children heard his boots going weightily along the pavement, and the screams also going along, rather ahead of the policeman; and both the murder-screams and the policeman's boots faded away in the remote distance.

Then Robert smacked his knickerbocker loudly with his palm, and said—

'Good old Phoenix! I should know its golden voice anywhere.'

And then everyone understood how cleverly the Phoenix had caught at what Robert had said about the real work of a policeman being to look after murderers and thieves, and not after cats, and all hearts were filled with admiring affection.

'But he'll come back,' said Anthea, mournfully, 'as soon as it finds the murderer is only a bright vision of a dream, and there isn't one at all really.'

'No he won't,' said the soft voice of the clever Phoenix, as it flew in. 'HE DOES NOT KNOW WHERE YOUR HOUSE IS. I heard him own as much to a fellow mercenary. Oh! what a night we are having! Lock the door, and let us rid ourselves of this intolerable smell of the perfume peculiar to the musk-rat and to the house of the trimmers of beards. If you'll excuse me, I will go to bed. I am worn out.'

It was Cyril who wrote the paper that told the carpet to take away the rats and bring milk, because there seemed to be no doubt in any breast that, however Persian cats may be, they must like milk.

'Let's hope it won't be musk-milk,' said Anthea, in gloom, as she pinned the paper face-downwards on the carpet. 'Is there such a thing as a musk-cow?' she added anxiously, as the carpet shrivelled and vanished. 'I do hope not. Perhaps really it WOULD have been wiser to let the carpet take the cats away. It's getting quite late, and we can't keep them all night.'

'Oh, can't we?' was the bitter rejoinder of Robert, who had been fastening the side door. 'You might have consulted me,' he went on. 'I'm not such an idiot as some people.'

'Why, whatever—'

'Don't you see? We've jolly well GOT to keep the cats all night—oh, get down, you furry beasts!—because we've had three wishes out of the old carpet now, and we can't get any more till to-morrow.'

The liveliness of Persian mews alone prevented the occurrence of a dismal silence.

Anthea spoke first.

'Never mind,' she said. 'Do you know, I really do think they're quieting down a bit. Perhaps they heard us say milk.'

'They can't understand English,' said Jane. 'You forget they're Persian cats, Panther.'

'Well,' said Anthea, rather sharply, for she was tired and anxious, 'who told you "milk" wasn't Persian for milk. Lots of English words are just the same in French—at least I know "miaw" is, and "croquet", and "fiance". Oh, pussies, do be quiet! Let's stroke them as hard as we can with both hands, and perhaps they'll stop.'

So everyone stroked grey fur till their hands were tired, and as soon as a cat had been stroked enough to make it stop mewing it was pushed gently away, and another mewing mouser was approached by the hands of the strokers. And the noise was really more than half purr when the carpet suddenly appeared in its proper place, and on it, instead of rows of milk-cans, or even of milk-jugs, there was a COW. Not a Persian cow, either, nor, most fortunately, a musk-cow, if there is such a thing, but a smooth, sleek, dun-coloured Jersey cow, who blinked large soft eyes at the gas-light and mooed in an amiable if rather inquiring manner.

Anthea had always been afraid of cows; but now she tried to be brave.

'Anyway, it can't run after me,' she said to herself 'There isn't room for it even to begin to run.'

The cow was perfectly placid. She behaved like a strayed duchess till some one brought a saucer for the milk, and some one else tried to milk the cow into it. Milking is very difficult. You may think it is easy, but it is not. All the children were by this time strung up to a pitch of heroism that would have been impossible to them in their ordinary condition. Robert and Cyril held the cow by the horns; and Jane, when she was quite sure that their end of the cow was quite secure, consented to stand by, ready to hold the cow by the tail should occasion arise. Anthea, holding the saucer, now advanced towards the cow. She remembered to have heard that cows, when milked by strangers, are susceptible to the soothing influence of the human voice. So, clutching her saucer very tight, she sought for words to whose soothing influence the cow might be susceptible. And her memory, troubled by the events of the night, which seemed to go on and on for ever and ever, refused to help her with any form of words suitable to address a Jersey cow in.

'Poor pussy, then. Lie down, then, good dog, lie down!' was all that she could think of to say, and she said it.

And nobody laughed. The situation, full of grey mewing cats, was too serious for that. Then Anthea, with a beating heart, tried to milk the cow. Next moment the cow had knocked the saucer out of her hand and trampled on it with one foot, while with the other three she had walked on a foot each of Robert, Cyril, and Jane.

Jane burst into tears. 'Oh, how much too horrid everything is!' she cried. 'Come away. Let's go to bed and leave the horrid cats with the hateful cow. Perhaps somebody will eat somebody else. And serve them right.'

They did not go to bed, but they had a shivering council in the drawing-room, which smelt of soot—and, indeed, a heap of this lay in the fender. There had been no fire in the room since mother went away, and all the chairs and tables were in the wrong places, and the chrysanthemums were dead, and the water in the pot nearly dried up. Anthea wrapped the embroidered woolly sofa blanket round Jane and herself, while Robert and Cyril had a struggle, silent and brief, but fierce, for the larger share of the fur hearthrug.

'It is most truly awful,' said Anthea, 'and I am so tired. Let's let the cats loose.'

'And the cow, perhaps?' said Cyril. 'The police would find us at once. That cow would stand at the gate and mew—I mean moo—to come in. And so would the cats. No; I see quite well what we've got to do. We must put them in baskets and leave them on people's doorsteps, like orphan foundlings.'

'We've got three baskets, counting mother's work one,' said Jane brightening.

'And there are nearly two hundred cats,' said Anthea, 'besides the cow—and it would have to be a different-sized basket for her; and then I don't know how you'd carry it, and you'd never find a doorstep big enough to put it on. Except the church one—and—'

'Oh, well,' said Cyril, 'if you simply MAKE difficulties—'

'I'm with you,' said Robert. 'Don't fuss about the cow, Panther. It's simply GOT to stay the night, and I'm sure I've read that the cow is a remunerating creature, and that means it will sit still and think for hours. The carpet can take it away in the morning. And as for the baskets, we'll do them up in dusters, or pillow-cases, or bath-towels. Come on, Squirrel. You girls can be out of it if you like.'

His tone was full of contempt, but Jane and Anthea were too tired and desperate to care; even being 'out of it', which at other times they could not have borne, now seemed quite a comfort. They snuggled down in the sofa blanket, and Cyril threw the fur hearthrug over them.

'Ah, he said, 'that's all women are fit for—to keep safe and warm, while the men do the work and run dangers and risks and things.'

'I'm not,' said Anthea, 'you know I'm not.' But Cyril was gone.

It was warm under the blanket and the hearthrug, and Jane snuggled up close to her sister; and Anthea cuddled Jane closely and kindly, and in a sort of dream they heard the rise of a wave of mewing as Robert opened the door of the nursery. They heard the booted search for baskets in the back kitchen. They heard the side door open and close, and they knew that each brother had gone out with at least one cat. Anthea's last thought was that it would take at least all night to get rid of one hundred and ninety-nine cats by twos. There would be ninety-nine journeys of two cats each, and one cat over.

'I almost think we might keep the one cat over,' said Anthea. 'I don't seem to care for cats just now, but I daresay I shall again some day.' And she fell asleep. Jane also was sleeping.

It was Jane who awoke with a start, to find Anthea still asleep. As, in the act of awakening, she kicked her sister, she wondered idly why they should have gone to bed in their boots; but the next moment she remembered where they were.

There was a sound of muffled, shuffled feet on the stairs. Like the heroine of the classic poem, Jane 'thought it was the boys', and as she felt quite wide awake, and not nearly so tired as before, she crept gently from Anthea's side and followed the footsteps. They went down into the basement; the cats, who seemed to have fallen into the sleep of exhaustion, awoke at the sound of the approaching footsteps and mewed piteously. Jane was at the foot of the stairs before she saw it was not her brothers whose coming had roused her and the cats, but a burglar. She knew he was a burglar at once, because he wore a fur cap and a red and black charity-check comforter, and he had no business where he was.

If you had been stood in jane's shoes you would no doubt have run away in them, appealing to the police and neighbours with horrid screams. But Jane knew better. She had read a great many nice stories about burglars, as well as some affecting pieces of poetry, and she knew that no burglar will ever hurt a little girl if he meets her when burgling. Indeed, in all the cases Jane had read of, his burglarishness was almost at once forgotten in the interest he felt in the little girl's artless prattle. So if Jane hesitated for a moment before addressing the burglar, it was only because she could not at once think of any remark sufficiently prattling and artless to make a beginning with. In the stories and the affecting poetry the child could never speak plainly, though it always looked old enough to in the pictures. And Jane could not make up her mind to lisp and 'talk baby', even to a burglar. And while she hesitated he softly opened the nursery door and went in.

Jane followed—just in time to see him sit down flat on the floor, scattering cats as a stone thrown into a pool splashes water.

She closed the door softly and stood there, still wondering whether she COULD bring herself to say, 'What's 'oo doing here, Mithter Wobber?' and whether any other kind of talk would do.

Then she heard the burglar draw a long breath, and he spoke.

'It's a judgement,' he said, 'so help me bob if it ain't. Oh, 'ere's a thing to 'appen to a chap! Makes it come 'ome to you, don't it neither? Cats an' cats an' cats. There couldn't be all them cats. Let alone the cow. If she ain't the moral of the old man's Daisy. She's a dream out of when I was a lad—I don't mind 'er so much. 'Ere, Daisy, Daisy?'

The cow turned and looked at him.

'SHE'S all right,' he went on. 'Sort of company, too. Though them above knows how she got into this downstairs parlour. But them cats—oh, take 'em away, take 'em away! I'll chuck the 'ole show—Oh, take 'em away.'

'Burglar,' said Jane, close behind him, and he started convulsively, and turned on her a blank face, whose pale lips trembled. 'I can't take those cats away.'

'Lor' lumme!' exclaimed the man; 'if 'ere ain't another on 'em. Are you real, miss, or something I'll wake up from presently?'

'I am quite real,' said Jane, relieved to find that a lisp was not needed to make the burglar understand her. 'And so,' she added, 'are the cats.'

'Then send for the police, send for the police, and I'll go quiet. If you ain't no realler than them cats, I'm done, spunchuck—out of time. Send for the police. I'll go quiet. One thing, there'd not be room for 'arf them cats in no cell as ever *I* see.'

He ran his fingers through his hair, which was short, and his eyes wandered wildly round the roomful of cats.

'Burglar,' said Jane, kindly and softly, 'if you didn't like cats, what did you come here for?'

'Send for the police,' was the unfortunate criminal's only reply. 'I'd rather you would—honest, I'd rather.'

'I daren't,' said Jane, 'and besides, I've no one to send. I hate the police. I wish he'd never been born.'

'You've a feeling 'art, miss,' said the burglar; 'but them cats is really a little bit too thick.'

296

'Look here,' said Jane, 'I won't call the police. And I am quite a real little girl, though I talk older than the kind you've met before when you've been doing your burglings. And they are real cats—and they want real milk—and—Didn't you say the cow was like somebody's Daisy that you used to know?'

'Wish I may die if she ain't the very spit of her,' replied the man.

'Well, then,' said Jane—and a thrill of joyful pride ran through her—'perhaps you know how to milk cows?'

'Perhaps I does,' was the burglar's cautious rejoinder.

'Then,' said Jane, 'if you will ONLY milk ours—you don't know how we shall always love you.'

The burglar replied that loving was all very well.

'If those cats only had a good long, wet, thirsty drink of milk,' Jane went on with eager persuasion, 'they'd lie down and go to sleep as likely as not, and then the police won't come back. But if they go on mewing like this he will, and then I don't know what'll become of us, or you either.'

This argument seemed to decide the criminal. Jane fetched the wash-bowl from the sink, and he spat on his hands and prepared to milk the cow. At this instant boots were heard on the stairs.

'It's all up,' said the man, desperately, 'this 'ere's a plant. 'ERE'S the police.' He made as if to open the window and leap from it.

'It's all right, I tell you,' whispered Jane, in anguish. 'I'll say you're a friend of mine, or the good clergyman called in, or my uncle, or ANYTHING—only do, do, do milk the cow. Oh, DON'T go—oh—oh, thank goodness it's only the boys!'

It was; and their entrance had awakened Anthea, who, with her brothers, now crowded through the doorway. The man looked about him like a rat looks round a trap.

'This is a friend of mine,' said Jane; 'he's just called in, and he's going to milk the cow for us. ISN'T it good and kind of him?'

She winked at the others, and though they did not understand they played up loyally.

'How do?' said Cyril, 'Very glad to meet you. Don't let us interrupt the milking.'

'I shall 'ave a 'ead and a 'arf in the morning, and no bloomin' error,' remarked the burglar; but he began to milk the cow.

Robert was winked at to stay and see that he did not leave off milking or try to escape, and the others went to get things to put the milk in; for it was now spurting and foaming in the wash-bowl, and the cats had ceased from mewing and were crowding round the cow, with expressions of hope and anticipation on their whiskered faces.

'We can't get rid of any more cats,' said Cyril, as he and his sisters piled a tray high with saucers and soup-plates and platters and pie-dishes, 'the police nearly got us as it was. Not the same one—a much stronger sort. He thought it really was a foundling orphan we'd got. If it hadn't been for me throwing the two bags of cat slap in his eye and hauling Robert over a railing, and lying like mice under a laurel-bush—Well, it's jolly lucky I'm a good shot, that's all. He pranced off when he'd got the cat-bags off his face—thought we'd bolted. And here we are.'

The gentle samishness of the milk swishing into the hand-bowl seemed to have soothed the burglar very much. He went on milking in a sort of happy dream, while the children got a cap and ladled the warm milk out into the pie-dishes and plates, and platters and saucers, and set them down to the music of Persian purrs and lappings.

'It makes me think of old times,' said the burglar, smearing his ragged coat-cuff across his eyes—'about the apples in the orchard at home, and the rats at threshing time, and the rabbits and the ferrets, and how pretty it was seeing the pigs killed.'

Finding him in this softened mood, Jane said—

'I wish you'd tell us how you came to choose our house for your burglaring to-night. I am awfully glad you did. You have been so kind. I don't know what we should have done without you,' she added hastily. 'We all love you ever so. Do tell us.'

The others added their affectionate entreaties, and at last the burglar said—

'Well, it's my first job, and I didn't expect to be made so welcome, and that's the truth, young gents and ladies. And I don't know but what it won't be my last. For this 'ere cow, she reminds me of my father, and I know 'ow 'e'd 'ave 'ided me if I'd laid 'ands on a 'a'penny as wasn't my own.'

'I'm sure he would,' Jane agreed kindly; 'but what made you come here?'

'Well, miss,' said the burglar, 'you know best 'ow you come by them cats, and why you don't like the police, so I'll give myself away free, and trust to your noble 'earts. (You'd best bale out a bit, the pan's getting fullish.) I was a-selling oranges off of my barrow—for I ain't a burglar by trade, though you 'ave used the name so free—an' there was a lady bought three 'a'porth off me. An' while she was a-pickin' of them out—very careful indeed, and I'm always glad when them sort gets a few over-ripe ones—there was two other ladies talkin' over the fence. An' one on 'em said to the other on 'em just like this—

"'I've told both gells to come, and they can doss in with M'ria and Jane, 'cause their boss and his missis is miles away and the kids too. So they can just lock up the 'ouse and leave the gas a-burning, so's no one won't know, and get back bright an' early by 'leven o'clock. And we'll make a night of it, Mrs Prosser, so we will. I'm just a-going to run out to pop the letter in the post." And then the lady what had chosen the three ha'porth so careful, she said: "Lor, Mrs Wigson, I wonder at you, and your hands all over suds. This good gentleman'll slip it into the post for yer, I'll be bound, seeing I'm a customer of his." So they give me the letter, and of course I read the direction what was written on it afore I shoved it into the post. And then when I'd sold my barrowful, I was a-goin' 'ome with the chink in my pocket, and I'm blowed if some bloomin' thievin' beggar didn't nick the lot whilst I was just a-wettin' of my whistle, for callin' of oranges is dry work. Nicked the bloomin' lot 'e did—and me with not a farden to take 'ome to my brother and his missus.'

'How awful!' said Anthea, with much sympathy.

'Horful indeed, miss, I believe yer,' the burglar rejoined, with deep feeling. 'You don't know her temper when she's roused. An' I'm sure I 'ope you never may, neither. And I'd 'ad all my oranges off of 'em. So it came back to me what was wrote on the ongverlope, and I says to myself, "Why not, seein' as I've been done myself, and if they keeps two slaveys there must be some pickings?" An' so 'ere I am. But them cats, they've brought me back to the ways of honestness. Never no more.'

'Look here,' said Cyril, 'these cats are very valuable—very indeed. And we will give them all to you, if only you will take them away.'

'I see they're a breedy lot,' replied the burglar. 'But I don't want no bother with the coppers. Did you come by them honest now? Straight?'

'They are all our very own,' said Anthea, 'we wanted them, but the confidement—'

'Consignment,' whispered Cyril, 'was larger than we wanted, and they're an awful bother. If you got your barrow, and some sacks or baskets, your brother's missus would be awfully pleased. My father says Persian cats are worth pounds and pounds each.'

'Well,' said the burglar—and he was certainly moved by her remarks—'I see you're in a hole—and I don't mind lending a helping 'and. I don't ask 'ow you come by them. But I've got a pal—'e's a mark on cats. I'll fetch him along, and if he thinks they'd fetch anything above their skins I don't mind doin' you a kindness.'

'You won't go away and never come back,' said Jane, 'because I don't think I COULD bear that.'

The burglar, quite touched by her emotion, swore sentimentally that, alive or dead, he would come back.

Then he went, and Cyril and Robert sent the girls to bed and sat up to wait for his return. It soon seemed absurd to await him in a state of wakefulness, but his stealthy tap on the window awoke them readily enough. For he did return, with the pal and the barrow and the sacks. The pal approved of the cats, now dormant in Persian repletion, and they were bundled into the sacks, and taken away on the barrow—mewing, indeed, but with mews too sleepy to attract public attention.

'I'm a fence—that's what I am,' said the burglar gloomily. 'I never thought I'd come down to this, and all acause er my kind 'eart.'

Cyril knew that a fence is a receiver of stolen goods, and he replied briskly—

'I give you my sacred the cats aren't stolen. What do you make the time?'

'I ain't got the time on me,' said the pal—'but it was just about chucking-out time as I come by the "Bull and Gate". I shouldn't wonder if it was nigh upon one now.'

When the cats had been removed, and the boys and the burglar had parted with warm expressions of friendship, there remained only the cow.

'She must stay all night,' said Robert. 'Cook'll have a fit when she sees her.'

'All night?' said Cyril. 'Why—it's tomorrow morning if it's one. We can have another wish!'

So the carpet was urged, in a hastily written note, to remove the cow to wherever she belonged, and to return to its proper place on the nursery floor. But the cow could not be got to move on to the carpet. So Robert got the clothes line out of the back kitchen, and tied one end very firmly to the cow's horns, and the other end to a bunched-up corner of the carpet, and said 'Fire away.'

And the carpet and cow vanished together, and the boys went to bed, tired out and only too thankful that the evening at last was over.

Next morning the carpet lay calmly in its place, but one corner was very badly torn. It was the corner that the cow had been tied on to.

CHAPTER 9. THE BURGLAR'S BRIDE

The morning after the adventure of the Persian cats, the musk-rats, the common cow, and the uncommon burglar, all the children slept till it was ten o'clock; and then it was only Cyril who woke; but he attended to the others, so that by half past ten everyone was ready to help to get breakfast. It was shivery cold, and there was but little in the house that was really worth eating.

Robert had arranged a thoughtful little surprise for the absent servants. He had made a neat and delightful booby trap over the kitchen door, and as soon as they heard the front door click open and knew the servants had come back, all four children hid in the cupboard under the stairs and listened with delight to the entrance—the tumble, the splash, the scuffle, and the remarks of the servants. They heard the cook say it was a judgement on them for leaving the place to itself; she seemed to think that a booby trap was a kind of plant that was quite likely to grow, all by itself, in a dwelling that was left shut up. But the housemaid, more acute, judged that someone must have been in the house—a view confirmed by the sight of the breakfast things on the nursery table.

The cupboard under the stairs was very tight and paraffiny, however, and a silent struggle for a place on top ended in the door bursting open and discharging Jane, who rolled like a football to the feet of the servants.

'Now,' said Cyril, firmly, when the cook's hysterics had become quieter, and the housemaid had time to say what she thought of them, 'don't you begin jawing us. We aren't going to stand it. We know too much. You'll please make an extra special treacle roley for dinner, and we'll have a tinned tongue.'

'I daresay,' said the housemaid, indignant, still in her outdoor things and with her hat very much on one side. 'Don't you come a-threatening me, Master Cyril, because I won't stand it, so I tell you. You tell your ma about us being out? Much I care! She'll be sorry for me when she hears about my dear great-aunt by marriage as brought me up from a child and was a mother to me. She sent for me, she did, she wasn't expected to last the night, from the spasms going to her legs—and cook was that kind and careful she couldn't let me go alone, so—'

'Don't,' said Anthea, in real distress. 'You know where liars go to, Eliza—at least if you don't—'

'Liars indeed!' said Eliza, 'I won't demean myself talking to you.'

'How's Mrs Wigson?' said Robert, 'and DID you keep it up last night?'

The mouth of the housemaid fell open.

'Did you doss with Maria or Emily?' asked Cyril.

'How did Mrs Prosser enjoy herself?' asked Jane.

'Forbear,' said Cyril, 'they've had enough. Whether we tell or not depends on your later life,' he went on, addressing the servants. 'If you are decent to us we'll be decent to you. You'd better make that treacle roley—and if I were you, Eliza, I'd do a little housework and cleaning, just for a change.'

The servants gave in once and for all.

'There's nothing like firmness,' Cyril went on, when the breakfast things were cleared away and the children were alone in the nursery. 'People are always talking of difficulties with servants. It's quite simple, when you know the way. We can do what we like now and they won't peach. I think we've broken THEIR proud spirit. Let's go somewhere by carpet.'

'I wouldn't if I were you,' said the Phoenix, yawning, as it swooped down from its roost on the curtain pole. 'I've given you one or two hints, but now concealment is at an end, and I see I must speak out.'

303

It perched on the back of a chair and swayed to and fro, like a parrot on a swing.

'What's the matter now?' said Anthea. She was not quite so gentle as usual, because she was still weary from the excitement of last night's cats. 'I'm tired of things happening. I shan't go anywhere on the carpet. I'm going to darn my stockings.'

'Darn!' said the Phoenix, 'darn! From those young lips these strange expressions—'

'Mend, then,' said Anthea, 'with a needle and wool.'

The Phoenix opened and shut its wings thoughtfully.

'Your stockings,' it said, 'are much less important than they now appear to you. But the carpet—look at the bare worn patches, look at the great rent at yonder corner. The carpet has been your faithful friend—your willing servant. How have you requited its devoted service?'

'Dear Phoenix,' Anthea urged, 'don't talk in that horrid lecturing tone. You make me feel as if I'd done something wrong. And really it is a wishing carpet, and we haven't done anything else to it—only wishes.'

'Only wishes,' repeated the Phoenix, ruffling its neck feathers angrily, 'and what sort of wishes? Wishing people to be in a good temper, for instance. What carpet did you ever hear of that had such a wish asked of it? But this noble fabric, on which you trample so recklessly' (everyone removed its boots from the carpet and stood on the linoleum), 'this carpet never flinched. It did what you asked, but the wear and tear must have been awful. And then last night—I don't blame you about the cats and the rats, for those were its own choice; but what carpet could stand a heavy cow hanging on to it at one corner?'

'I should think the cats and rats were worse,' said Robert, 'look at all their claws.'

'Yes,' said the bird, 'eleven thousand nine hundred and forty of them—I daresay you noticed? I should be surprised if these had not left their mark.'

'Good gracious,' said Jane, sitting down suddenly on the floor, and patting the edge of the carpet softly; 'do you mean it's WEARING OUT?'

'Its life with you has not been a luxurious one,' said the Phoenix.

'French mud twice. Sand of sunny shores twice. Soaking in southern seas once. India once. Goodness knows where in Persia once. Musk-rat-land once. And once, wherever the cow came from. Hold your carpet up to the light, and with cautious tenderness, if YOU please.'

With cautious tenderness the boys held the carpet up to the light; the girls looked, and a shiver of regret ran through them as they saw how those eleven thoousand nine hundred and forty claws had run through the carpet. It was full of little holes: there were some large ones, and more than one thin place. At one corner a strip of it was torn, and hung forlornly.

'We must mend it,' said Anthea; 'never mind about my stockings. I can sew them up in lumps with sewing cotton if there's no time to do them properly. I know it's awful and no girl would who respected herself, and all that; but the poor dear carpet's more important than my silly stockings. Let's go out now this very minute.'

So out they all went, and bought wool to mend the carpet; but there is no shop in Camden Town where you can buy wishing-wool, no, nor in Kentish Town either. However, ordinary Scotch heather-mixture fingering seemed good enough, and this they bought, and all that day Jane and Anthea darned and darned and darned. The boys went out for a walk in the afternoon, and the gentle Phoenix paced up and down the table—for exercise, as it said—and talked to the industrious girls about their carpet.

'It is not an ordinary, ignorant, innocent carpet from Kidderminster,' it said, 'it is a carpet with a past—a Persian past. Do you know that in happier years, when that carpet was the property of caliphs, viziers, kings, and sultans, it never lay on a floor?'

'I thought the floor was the proper home of a carpet,' Jane interrupted.

'Not of a MAGIC carpet,' said the Phoenix; 'why, if it had been allowed to lie about on floors there wouldn't be much of it left now. No, indeed! It has lived in chests of cedarwood, inlaid with pearl and ivory, wrapped in priceless tissues of cloth of gold, embroidered with gems of fabulous value. It has reposed in the sandal-wood caskets of princesses, and in the rose-attar-scented treasure-houses of kings. Never, never, had any one degraded it by walking on it—except in the way of business, when wishes were required, and then they always took their shoes off. And YOU—'

'Oh, DON'T!' said Jane, very near tears. 'You know you'd never have been hatched at all if it hadn't been for mother wanting a carpet for us to walk on.'

'You needn't have walked so much or so hard!' said the bird, 'but come, dry that crystal tear, and I will relate to you the story of the Princess Zulieka, the Prince of Asia, and the magic carpet.'

'Relate away,' said Anthea—'I mean, please do.'

'The Princess Zulieka, fairest of royal ladies,' began the bird, 'had in her cradle been the subject of several enchantments. Her grandmother had been in her day—'

But what in her day Zulieka's grandmother had been was destined never to be revealed, for Cyril and Robert suddenly burst into the room, and on each brow were the traces of deep emotion. On Cyril's pale brow stood beads of agitation and perspiration, and on the scarlet brow of Robert was a large black smear.

'What ails ye both?' asked the Phoenix, and it added tartly that story-telling was quite impossible if people would come interrupting like that.

'Oh, do shut up, for any sake!' said Cyril, sinking into a chair.

Robert smoothed the ruffled golden feathers, adding kindly—

'Squirrel doesn't mean to be a beast. It's only that the MOST AWFUL thing has happened, and stories don't seem to matter so much. Don't be cross. You won't be when you've heard what's happened.'

'Well, what HAS happened?' said the bird, still rather crossly; and Anthea and Jane paused with long needles poised in air, and long needlefuls of Scotch heather-mixture fingering wool drooping from them.

'The most awful thing you can possibly think of,' said Cyril. 'That nice chap—our own burglar—the police have got him, on suspicion of stolen cats. That's what his brother's missis told me.'

'Oh, begin at the beginning!' cried Anthea impatiently.

'Well, then, we went out, and down by where the undertaker's is, with the china flowers in the window—you know. There was a crowd, and of course we went to have a squint. And it was two bobbies and our burglar between them, and he was being dragged along; and he said, "I tell you them cats was GIVE me. I got 'em in exchange for me milking a cow in a basement parlour up Camden Town way."

'And the people laughed. Beasts! And then one of the policemen said perhaps he could give the name and address of the cow, and he said, no, he couldn't; but he could take them there if they'd only leave go of his coat collar, and give him a chance to get his breath. And the policeman said he could tell all that to the magistrate in the morning. He didn't see us, and so we came away.'

'Oh, Cyril, how COULD you?' said Anthea.

'Don't be a pudding-head,' Cyril advised. 'A fat lot of good it would have done if we'd let him see us. No one would have believed a word we said. They'd have thought we were kidding. We did better than let him see us. We asked a boy where he lived and he told us, and we went there, and it's a little greengrocer's shop, and we bought some Brazil nuts. Here they are.' The girls waved away the Brazil nuts with loathing and contempt.

'Well, we had to buy SOMETHING, and while we were making up our minds what to buy we heard his brother's missis talking. She said when he came home with all them miaoulers she thought there was more in it than met the eye. But he WOULD go out this morning with the two likeliest of them, one under each arm. She said he sent her out to buy blue ribbon to put round their beastly necks, and she said if he got three months' hard it was her dying word that he'd got the blue ribbon to thank for it; that, and his own silly thieving ways, taking cats that anybody would know he couldn't have come by in the way of business, instead of things that wouldn't have been missed, which Lord knows there are plenty such, and—'

'Oh, STOP!' cried Jane. And indeed it was time, for Cyril seemed like a clock that had been wound up, and could not help going on. 'Where is he now?'

'At the police-station,' said Robert, for Cyril was out of breath. 'The boy told us they'd put him in the cells, and would bring him up before the Beak in the morning. I thought it was a jolly lark last night—getting him to take the cats—but now—'

'The end of a lark,' said the Phoenix, 'is the Beak.'

'Let's go to him,' cried both the girls jumping up. 'Let's go and tell the truth. They MUST believe us.'

'They CAN'T,' said Cyril. 'Just think! If any one came to you with such a tale, you couldn't believe it, however much you tried. We should only mix things up worse for him.'

'There must be something we could do,' said Jane, sniffing very much—'my own dear pet burglar! I can't bear it. And he was so nice, the way he talked about his father, and how he was going to be so extra honest. Dear Phoenix, you MUST be able to help us. You're so good and kind and pretty and clever. Do, do tell us what to do.'

The Phoenix rubbed its beak thoughtfully with its claw.

'You might rescue him,' it said, 'and conceal him here, till the law-supporters had forgotten about him.'

308

'That would be ages and ages,' said Cyril, 'and we couldn't conceal him here. Father might come home at any moment, and if he found the burglar here HE wouldn't believe the true truth any more than the police would. That's the worst of the truth. Nobody ever believes it. Couldn't we take him somewhere else?'

Jane clapped her hands.

'The sunny southern shore!' she cried, 'where the cook is being queen. He and she would be company for each other!'

And really the idea did not seem bad, if only he would consent to go.

So, all talking at once, the children arranged to wait till evening, and then to seek the dear burglar in his lonely cell.

Meantime Jane and Anthea darned away as hard as they could, to make the carpet as strong as possible. For all felt how terrible it would be if the precious burglar, while being carried to the sunny southern shore, were to tumble through a hole in the carpet, and be lost for ever in the sunny southern sea.

The servants were tired after Mrs Wigson's party, so everyone went to bed early, and when the Phoenix reported that both servants were snoring in a heartfelt and candid manner, the children got up—they had never undressed; just putting their nightgowns on over their things had been enough to deceive Eliza when she came to turn out the gas. So they were ready for anything, and they stood on the carpet and said—

'I wish we were in our burglar's lonely cell.' and instantly they were.

I think everyone had expected the cell to be the 'deepest dungeon below the castle moat'. I am sure no one had doubted that the burglar, chained by heavy fetters to a ring in the damp stone wall, would be tossing uneasily on a bed of straw, with a pitcher of water and a mouldering crust, untasted, beside him. Robert, remembering the underground passage and the treasure, had brought a candle and matches, but these were not needed.

The cell was a little white-washed room about twelve feet long and six feet wide. On one side of it was a sort of shelf sloping a little towards the wall. On this were two rugs, striped blue and yellow, and a water-proof pillow. Rolled in the rugs, and with his head on the pillow, lay the burglar, fast asleep. (He had had his tea, though this the children did not know—it had come from the coffee-shop round the corner, in very thick crockery.) The scene was plainly revealed by the light of a gas-lamp in the passage outside, which shone into the cell through a pane of thick glass over the door.

'I shall gag him,' said Cyril, 'and Robert will hold him down. Anthea and Jane and the Phoenix can whisper soft nothings to him while he gradually awakes.'

This plan did not have the success it deserved, because the burglar, curiously enough, was much stronger, even in his sleep, than Robert and Cyril, and at the first touch of their hands he leapt up and shouted out something very loud indeed.

Instantly steps were heard outside. Anthea threw her arms round the burglar and whispered—

'It's us—the ones that gave you the cats. We've come to save you, only don't let on we're here. Can't we hide somewhere?'

Heavy boots sounded on the flagged passage outside, and a firm voice shouted—

'Here—you—stop that row, will you?'

'All right, governor,' replied the burglar, still with Anthea's arms round him; 'I was only a-talking in my sleep. No offence.'

It was an awful moment. Would the boots and the voice come in. Yes! No! The voice said—

'Well, stow it, will you?'

And the boots went heavily away, along the passage and up some sounding stone stairs.

'Now then,' whispered Anthea.

'How the blue Moses did you get in?' asked the burglar, in a hoarse whisper of amazement.

'On the carpet,' said Jane, truly.

'Stow that,' said the burglar. 'One on you I could 'a' swallowed, but four—AND a yellow fowl.'

'Look here,' said Cyril, sternly, 'you wouldn't have believed any one if they'd told you beforehand about your finding a cow and all those cats in our nursery.'

'That I wouldn't,' said the burglar, with whispered fervour, 'so help me Bob, I wouldn't.'

'Well, then,' Cyril went on, ignoring this appeal to his brother, 'just try to believe what we tell you and act accordingly. It can't do you any HARM, you know,' he went on in hoarse whispered earnestness. 'You can't be very much worse off than you are now, you know. But if you'll just trust to us we'll get you out of this right enough. No one saw us come in. The question is, where would you like to go?'

'I'd like to go to Boolong,' was the instant reply of the burglar. 'I've always wanted to go on that there trip, but I've never 'ad the ready at the right time of the year.'

'Boolong is a town like London,' said Cyril, well meaning, but inaccurate, 'how could you get a living there?'

The burglar scratched his head in deep doubt.

'It's 'ard to get a 'onest living anywheres nowadays,' he said, and his voice was sad.

'Yes, isn't it?' said Jane, sympathetically; 'but how about a sunny southern shore, where there's nothing to do at all unless you want to.'

'That's my billet, miss,' replied the burglar. 'I never did care about work—not like some people, always fussing about.'

'Did you never like any sort of work?' asked Anthea, severely.

'Lor', lumme, yes,' he answered, 'gardening was my 'obby, so it was. But father died afore 'e could bind me to a nurseryman, an'—'

'We'll take you to the sunny southern shore,' said Jane; 'you've no idea what the flowers are like.'

'Our old cook's there,' said Anthea. 'She's queen—'

'Oh, chuck it,' the burglar whispered, clutching at his head with both hands. 'I knowed the first minute I see them cats and that cow as it was a judgement on me. I don't know now whether I'm a-standing on my hat or my boots, so help me I don't. If you CAN get me out, get me, and if you can't, get along with you for goodness' sake, and give me a chanst to think about what'll be most likely to go down with the Beak in the morning.'

'Come on to the carpet, then,' said Anthea, gently shoving. The others quietly pulled, and the moment the feet of the burglar were planted on the carpet Anthea wished:

'I wish we were all on the sunny southern shore where cook is.'

And instantly they were. There were the rainbow sands, the tropic glories of leaf and flower, and there, of course, was the cook, crowned with white flowers, and with all the wrinkles of crossness and tiredness and hard work wiped out of her face.

'Why, cook, you're quite pretty!' Anthea said, as soon as she had got her breath after the tumble-rush-whirl of the carpet. The burglar stood rubbing his eyes in the brilliant tropic sunlight, and gazing wildly round him on the vivid hues of the tropic land.

'Penny plain and tuppence coloured!' he exclaimed pensively, 'and well worth any tuppence, however hard-earned.'

The cook was seated on a grassy mound with her court of copper-coloured savages around her. The burglar pointed a grimy finger at these.

'Are they tame?' he asked anxiously. 'Do they bite or scratch, or do anything to yer with poisoned arrows or oyster shells or that?'

312

'Don't you be so timid,' said the cook. 'Look'e 'ere, this 'ere's only a dream what you've come into, an' as it's only a dream there's no nonsense about what a young lady like me ought to say or not, so I'll say you're the best-looking fellow I've seen this many a day. And the dream goes on and on, seemingly, as long as you behaves. The things what you has to eat and drink tastes just as good as real ones, and—'

'Look 'ere,' said the burglar, 'I've come 'ere straight outer the pleece station. These 'ere kids'll tell you it ain't no blame er mine.'

'Well, you WERE a burglar, you know,' said the truthful Anthea gently.

'Only because I was druv to it by dishonest blokes, as well you knows, miss,' rejoined the criminal. 'Blowed if this ain't the 'ottest January as I've known for years.'

'Wouldn't you like a bath?' asked the queen, 'and some white clothes like me?'

'I should only look a juggins in 'em, miss, thanking you all the same,' was the reply; 'but a bath I wouldn't resist, and my shirt was only clean on week before last.'

Cyril and Robert led him to a rocky pool, where he bathed luxuriously. Then, in shirt and trousers he sat on the sand and spoke.

'That cook, or queen, or whatever you call her—her with the white bokay on her 'ed—she's my sort. Wonder if she'd keep company!'

'I should ask her.'

'I was always a quick hitter,' the man went on; 'it's a word and a blow with me. I will.'

In shirt and trousers, and crowned with a scented flowery wreath which Cyril hastily wove as they returned to the court of the queen, the burglar stood before the cook and spoke.

'Look 'ere, miss,' he said. 'You an' me being' all forlorn-like, both on us, in this 'ere dream, or whatever you calls it, I'd like to tell you straight as I likes yer looks.'

The cook smiled and looked down bashfully.

'I'm a single man—what you might call a batcheldore. I'm mild in my 'abits, which these kids'll tell you the same, and I'd like to 'ave the pleasure of walkin' out with you next Sunday.'

'Lor!' said the queen cook, "ow sudden you are, mister.'

'Walking out means you're going to be married,' said Anthea. 'Why not get married and have done with it? *I* would.'

'I don't mind if I do,' said the burglar. But the cook said—

'No, miss. Not me, not even in a dream. I don't say anythink ag'in the young chap's looks, but I always swore I'd be married in church, if at all—and, anyway, I don't believe these here savages would know how to keep a registering office, even if I was to show them. No, mister, thanking you kindly, if you can't bring a clergyman into the dream I'll live and die like what I am.'

'Will you marry her if we get a clergyman?' asked the match-making Anthea.

'I'm agreeable, miss, I'm sure,' said he, pulling his wreath straight. "Ow this 'ere bokay do tiddle a chap's ears to be sure!'

So, very hurriedly, the carpet was spread out, and instructed to fetch a clergyman. The instructions were written on the inside of Cyril's cap with a piece of billiard chalk Robert had got from the marker at the hotel at Lyndhurst. The carpet disappeared, and more quickly than you would have thought possible it came back, bearing on its bosom the Reverend Septimus Blenkinsop.

The Reverend Septimus was rather a nice young man, but very much mazed and muddled, because when he saw a strange carpet laid out at his feet, in his own study, he naturally walked on it to examine it more closely. And he happened to stand on one of the thin places that Jane and Anthea had darned, so that he was half on

314

wishing carpet and half on plain Scotch heather-mixture fingering, which has no magic properties at all.

The effect of this was that he was only half there—so that the children could just see through him, as though he had been a ghost. And as for him, he saw the sunny southern shore, the cook and the burglar and the children quite plainly; but through them all he saw, quite plainly also, his study at home, with the books and the pictures and the marble clock that had been presented to him when he left his last situation.

He seemed to himself to be in a sort of insane fit, so that it did not matter what he did—and he married the burglar to the cook. The cook said that she would rather have had a solider kind of a clergyman, one that you couldn't see through so plain, but perhaps this was real enough for a dream.

And of course the clergyman, though misty, was really real, and able to marry people, and he did. When the ceremony was over the clergyman wandered about the island collecting botanical specimens, for he was a great botanist, and the ruling passion was strong even in an insane fit.

There was a splendid wedding feast. Can you fancy Jane and Anthea, and Robert and Cyril, dancing merrily in a ring, hand-in-hand with copper-coloured savages, round the happy couple, the queen cook and the burglar consort? There were more flowers gathered and thrown than you have ever even dreamed of, and before the children took carpet for home the now married-and-settled burglar made a speech.

'Ladies and gentlemen,' he said, 'and savages of both kinds, only I know you can't understand what I'm a saying of, but we'll let that pass. If this is a dream, I'm on. If it ain't, I'm onner than ever. If it's betwixt and between—well, I'm honest, and I can't say more. I don't want no more 'igh London society—I've got some one to put my arm around of; and I've got the whole lot of this 'ere island for my allotment, and if I don't grow some broccoli as'll open the judge's eye at the cottage flower shows, well, strike me pink! All I ask is, as these young gents and ladies'll bring some parsley seed into the dream, and a penn'orth of radish seed, and threepenn'orth of onion, and I wouldn't mind goin' to fourpence or fippence for mixed kale, only I ain't got a brown, so I don't deceive you. And there's one thing more, you might take away the parson. I don't like things what I can see 'alf through, so here's how!' He drained a coconut-shell of palm wine.

It was now past midnight—though it was tea-time on the island.

With all good wishes the children took their leave. They also collected the clergyman and took him back to his study and his presentation clock.

The Phoenix kindly carried the seeds next day to the burglar and his bride, and returned with the most satisfactory news of the happy pair.

'He's made a wooden spade and started on his allotment,' it said, 'and she is weaving him a shirt and trousers of the most radiant whiteness.'

The police never knew how the burglar got away. In Kentish Town Police Station his escape is still spoken of with bated breath as the Persian mystery.

As for the Reverend Septimus Blenkinsop, he felt that he had had a very insane fit indeed, and he was sure it was due to over-study. So he planned a little dissipation, and took his two maiden aunts to Paris, where they enjoyed a dazzling round of museums and picture galleries, and came back feeling that they had indeed seen life. He never told his aunts or any one else about the marriage on the island—because no one likes it to be generally known if he has had insane fits, however interesting and unusual.

CHAPTER 10. THE HOLE IN THE CARPET

Hooray! hooray! hooray!
Mother comes home to-day;
Mother comes home to-day,
Hooray! hooray! hooray!'

Jane sang this simple song directly after breakfast, and the Phoenix shed crystal tears of affectionate sympathy.

'How beautiful,' it said, 'is filial devotion!'

'She won't be home till past bedtime, though,' said Robert. 'We might have one more carpet-day.'

He was glad that mother was coming home—quite glad, very glad; but at the same time that gladness was rudely contradicted by a quite strong feeling of sorrow, because now they could not go out all day on the carpet.

'I do wish we could go and get something nice for mother, only she'd want to know where we got it,' said Anthea. 'And she'd never, never believe it, the truth. People never do, somehow, if it's at all interesting.'

'I'll tell you what,' said Robert. 'Suppose we wished the carpet to take us somewhere where we could find a purse with money in it—then we could buy her something.'

'Suppose it took us somewhere foreign, and the purse was covered with strange Eastern devices, embroidered in rich silks, and full of money that wasn't money at all here, only foreign curiosities, then we couldn't spend it, and people would bother about where we got it, and we shouldn't know how on earth to get out of it at all.'

Cyril moved the table off the carpet as he spoke, and its leg caught in one of Anthea's darns and ripped away most of it, as well as a large slit in the carpet.

'Well, now you HAVE done it,' said Robert.

But Anthea was a really first-class sister. She did not say a word till she had got out the Scotch heather-mixture fingering wool and the darning-needle and the thimble and the scissors, and by that time she had been able to get the better of her natural wish to be thoroughly disagreeable, and was able to say quite kindly—

'Never mind, Squirrel, I'll soon mend it.'

Cyril thumped her on the back. He understood exactly how she had felt, and he was not an ungrateful brother.

'Respecting the purse containing coins,' the Phoenix said, scratching its invisible ear thoughtfully with its shining claw, 'it might be as well, perhaps, to state clearly the amount which you wish to find, as well as the country where you wish to find it, and the nature of the coins which you prefer. It would be indeed a cold moment when you should find a purse containing but three oboloi.'

'How much is an oboloi?'

'An obol is about twopence halfpenny,' the Phoenix replied.

'Yes,' said Jane, 'and if you find a purse I suppose it is only because some one has lost it, and you ought to take it to the policeman.'

'The situation,' remarked the Phoenix, 'does indeed bristle with difficulties.'

'What about a buried treasure,' said Cyril, 'and everyone was dead that it belonged to?'

'Mother wouldn't believe THAT,' said more than one voice.

'Suppose,' said Robert—'suppose we asked to be taken where we could find a purse and give it back to the person it belonged to, and they would give us something for finding it?'

'We aren't allowed to take money from strangers. You know we aren't, Bobs,' said Anthea, making a knot at the end of a needleful of Scotch heather-mixture fingering wool (which is very wrong, and you must never do it when you are darning).

'No, THAT wouldn't do,' said Cyril. 'Let's chuck it and go to the North Pole, or somewhere really interesting.'

318

'No,' said the girls together, 'there must be SOME way.'

'Wait a sec,' Anthea added. 'I've got an idea coming. Don't speak.'

There was a silence as she paused with the darning-needle in the air! Suddenly she spoke:

'I see. Let's tell the carpet to take us somewhere where we can get the money for mother's present, and—and—and get it some way that she'll believe in and not think wrong.'

'Well, I must say you are learning the way to get the most out of the carpet,' said Cyril. He spoke more heartily and kindly than usual, because he remembered how Anthea had refrained from snarking him about tearing the carpet.

'Yes,' said the Phoenix, 'you certainly are. And you have to remember that if you take a thing out it doesn't stay in.'

No one paid any attention to this remark at the time, but afterwards everyone thought of it.

'Do hurry up, Panther,' said Robert; and that was why Anthea did hurry up, and why the big darn in the middle of the carpet was all open and webby like a fishing net, not tight and close like woven cloth, which is what a good, well-behaved darn should be.

Then everyone put on its outdoor things, the Phoenix fluttered on to the mantelpiece and arranged its golden feathers in the glass, and all was ready. Everyone got on to the carpet.

'Please go slowly, dear carpet,' Anthea began; we like to see where we're going.' And then she added the difficult wish that had been decided on.

Next moment the carpet, stiff and raftlike, was sailing over the roofs of Kentish Town.

'I wish—No, I don't mean that. I mean it's a PITY we aren't higher up,' said Anthea, as the edge of the carpet grazed a chimney-pot.

'That's right. Be careful,' said the Phoenix, in warning tones. 'If you wish when you're on a wishing carpet, you DO wish, and there's an end of it.'

So for a short time no one spoke, and the carpet sailed on in calm magnificence over St Pancras and King's Cross stations and over the crowded streets of Clerkenwell.

'We're going out Greenwich way,' said Cyril, as they crossed the streak of rough, tumbled water that was the Thames. 'We might go and have a look at the Palace.'

On and on the carpet swept, still keeping much nearer to the chimney-pots than the children found at all comfortable. And then, just over New Cross, a terrible thing happened.

Jane and Robert were in the middle of the carpet. Part of them was on the carpet, and part of them—the heaviest part—was on the great central darn.

'It's all very misty,' said Jane; 'it looks partly like out of doors and partly like in the nursery at home. I feel as if I was going to have measles; everything looked awfully rum then, remember.'

'I feel just exactly the same,' Robert said.

'It's the hole,' said the Phoenix; 'it's not measles whatever that possession may be.'

And at that both Robert and Jane suddenly, and at once, made a bound to try and get on to the safer part of the carpet, and the darn gave way and their boots went up, and the heavy heads and bodies of them went down through the hole, and they landed in a position something between sitting and sprawling on the flat leads on the top of a high, grey, gloomy, respectable house whose address was 705, Amersham Road, New Cross.

The carpet seemed to awaken to new energy as soon as it had got rid of their weight, and it rose high in the air. The others lay down flat and peeped over the edge of the rising carpet.

'Are you hurt?' cried Cyril, and Robert shouted 'No,' and next moment the carpet had sped away, and Jane and Robert were hidden from the sight of the others by a stack of smoky chimneys.

'Oh, how awful!' said Anthea.

'It might have been worse,' said the Phoenix. 'What would have been the sentiments of the survivors if that darn had given way when we were crossing the river?'

'Yes, there's that,' said Cyril, recovering himself. 'They'll be all right. They'll howl till some one gets them down, or drop tiles into the front garden to attract attention of passersby. Bobs has got my one-and-fivepence—lucky you forgot to mend that hole in my pocket, Panther, or he wouldn't have had it. They can tram it home.'

But Anthea would not be comforted.

'It's all my fault,' she said. 'I KNEW the proper way to darn, and I didn't do it. It's all my fault. Let's go home and patch the carpet with your Etons—something really strong—and send it to fetch them.'

'All right,' said Cyril; 'but your Sunday jacket is stronger than my Etons. We must just chuck mother's present, that's all. I wish—'

'Stop!' cried the Phoenix; 'the carpet is dropping to earth.'

And indeed it was.

It sank swiftly, yet steadily, and landed on the pavement of the Deptford Road. It tipped a little as it landed, so that Cyril and Anthea naturally walked off it, and in an instant it had rolled itself up and hidden behind a gate-post. It did this so quickly that not a single person in the Deptford Road noticed it. The Phoenix rustled its way into the breast of Cyril's coat, and almost at the same moment a well-known voice remarked—

'Well, I never! What on earth are you doing here?'

They were face to face with their pet uncle—their Uncle Reginald.

'We DID think of going to Greenwich Palace and talking about Nelson,' said Cyril, telling as much of the truth as he thought his uncle could believe.

'And where are the others?' asked Uncle Reginald.

'I don't exactly know,' Cyril replied, this time quite truthfully.

'Well,' said Uncle Reginald, 'I must fly. I've a case in the County Court. That's the worst of being a beastly solicitor. One can't take the chances of life when one gets them. If only I could come with you to the Painted Hall and give you lunch at the "Ship" afterwards! But, alas! it may not be.'

The uncle felt in his pocket.

'*I* mustn't enjoy myself,' he said, 'but that's no reason why you shouldn't. Here, divide this by four, and the product ought to give you some desired result. Take care of yourselves. Adieu.'

And waving a cheery farewell with his neat umbrella, the good and high-hatted uncle passed away, leaving Cyril and Anthea to exchange eloquent glances over the shining golden sovereign that lay in Cyril's hand.

'Well!' said Anthea.

'Well!' said Cyril.

'Well!' said the Phoenix.

'Good old carpet!' said Cyril, joyously.

'It WAS clever of it—so adequate and yet so simple,' said the Phoenix, with calm approval.

'Oh, come on home and let's mend the carpet. I am a beast. I'd forgotten the others just for a minute,' said the conscience-stricken Anthea.

They unrolled the carpet quickly and slyly—they did not want to attract public attention—and the moment their feet were on the carpet Anthea wished to be at home, and instantly they were.

The kindness of their excellent uncle had made it unnecessary for them to go to such extremes as Cyril's Etons or Anthea's Sunday jacket for the patching of the carpet.

Anthea set to work at once to draw the edges of the broken darn together, and Cyril hastily went out and bought a large piece of the marble-patterned American oil-cloth which careful house-wives use to cover dressers and kitchen tables. It was the strongest thing he could think of.

Then they set to work to line the carpet throughout with the oil-cloth. The nursery felt very odd and empty without the others, and Cyril did not feel so sure as he had done about their being able to 'tram it' home. So he tried to help Anthea, which was very good of him, but not much use to her.

The Phoenix watched them for a time, but it was plainly growing more and more restless. It fluffed up its splendid feathers, and stood first on one gilded claw and then on the other, and at last it said—

'I can bear it no longer. This suspense! My Robert—who set my egg to hatch—in the bosom of whose Norfolk raiment I have nestled so often and so pleasantly! I think, if you'll excuse me—'

'Yes—DO,' cried Anthea, 'I wish we'd thought of asking you before.'

Cyril opened the window. The Phoenix flapped its sunbright wings and vanished.

'So THAT'S all right,' said Cyril, taking up his needle and instantly pricking his hand in a new place.

Of course I know that what you have really wanted to know about all this time is not what Anthea and Cyril did, but what happened to Jane and Robert after they fell through the carpet on to the leads of the house which was called number 705, Amersham Road.

But I had to tell you the other first. That is one of the most annoying things about stories, you cannot tell all the different parts of them at the same time.

Robert's first remark when he found himself seated on the damp, cold, sooty leads was—

'Here's a go!'

Jane's first act was tears.

'Dry up, Pussy; don't be a little duffer,' said her brother, kindly, 'it'll be all right.'

And then he looked about, just as Cyril had known he would, for something to throw down, so as to attract the attention of the wayfarers far below in the street. He could not find anything. Curiously enough, there were no stones on the leads, not even a loose tile. The roof was of slate, and every single slate knew its place and kept it. But, as so often happens, in looking for one thing he found another. There was a trap-door leading down into the house.

And that trap-door was not fastened.

'Stop snivelling and come here, Jane,' he cried, encouragingly. 'Lend a hand to heave this up. If we can get into the house, we might sneak down without meeting any one, with luck. Come on.'

They heaved up the door till it stood straight up, and, as they bent to look into the hole below, the door fell back with a hollow clang on the leads behind, and with its noise was mingled a blood-curdling scream from underneath.

'Discovered!' hissed Robert. 'Oh, my cats alive!'

They were indeed discovered.

They found themselves looking down into an attic, which was also a lumber-room. It had boxes and broken chairs, old fenders and picture-frames, and rag-bags hanging from nails.

In the middle of the floor was a box, open, half full of clothes. Other clothes lay on the floor in neat piles. In the middle of the piles of clothes sat a lady, very fat indeed, with her feet sticking out straight in front of her. And it was she who had screamed, and who, in fact, was still screaming.

'Don't!' cried Jane, 'please don't! We won't hurt you.'

'Where are the rest of your gang?' asked the lady, stopping short in the middle of a scream.

'The others have gone on, on the wishing carpet,' said Jane truthfully.

'The wishing carpet?' said the lady.

'Yes,' said Jane, before Robert could say 'You shut up!' 'You must have read about it. The Phoenix is with them.'

Then the lady got up, and picking her way carefully between the piles of clothes she got to the door and through it. She shut it behind her, and the two children could hear her calling 'Septimus! Septimus!' in a loud yet frightened way.

'Now,' said Robert quickly; 'I'll drop first.'

He hung by his hands and dropped through the trap-door.

'Now you. Hang by your hands. I'll catch you. Oh, there's no time for jaw. Drop, I say.'

Jane dropped.

Robert tried to catch her, and even before they had finished the breathless roll among the piles of clothes, which was what his catching ended in, he whispered—

'We'll hide—behind those fenders and things; they'll think we've gone along the roofs. Then, when all is calm, we'll creep down the stairs and take our chance.'

They hastily hid. A corner of an iron bedstead stuck into Robert's side, and Jane had only standing room for one foot—but they bore it—and when the lady came back, not with Septimus, but with another lady, they held their breath and their hearts beat thickly.

325

'Gone!' said the first lady; 'poor little things—quite mad, my dear—and at large! We must lock this room and send for the police.'

'Let me look out,' said the second lady, who was, if possible, older and thinner and primmer than the first. So the two ladies dragged a box under the trap-door and put another box on the top of it, and then they both climbed up very carefully and put their two trim, tidy heads out of the trap-door to look for the 'mad children'.

'Now,' whispered Robert, getting the bedstead leg out of his side.

They managed to creep out from their hiding-place and out through the door before the two ladies had done looking out of the trap-door on to the empty leads.

Robert and Jane tiptoed down the stairs—one flight, two flights. Then they looked over the banisters. Horror! a servant was coming up with a loaded scuttle.

The children with one consent crept swiftly through the first open door.

The room was a study, calm and gentlemanly, with rows of books, a writing table, and a pair of embroidered slippers warming themselves in the fender. The children hid behind the window-curtains. As they passed the table they saw on it a missionary-box with its bottom label torn off, open and empty.

'Oh, how awful!' whispered Jane. 'We shall never get away alive.'

'Hush!' said Robert, not a moment too soon, for there were steps on the stairs, and next instant the two ladies came into the room. They did not see the children, but they saw the empty missionary box.

'I knew it,' said one. 'Selina, it WAS a gang. I was certain of it from the first. The children were not mad. They were sent to distract our attention while their confederates robbed the house.'

'I am afraid you are right,' said Selina; 'and WHERE ARE THEY NOW?'

'Downstairs, no doubt, collecting the silver milk-jug and sugar-basin and the punch-ladle that was Uncle Joe's, and Aunt Jerusha's teaspoons. I shall go down.'

'Oh, don't be so rash and heroic,' said Selina. 'Amelia, we must call the police from the window. Lock the door. I WILL—I will—'

The words ended in a yell as Selina, rushing to the window, came face to face with the hidden children.

'Oh, don't!' said Jane; 'how can you be so unkind? We AREN'T burglars, and we haven't any gang, and we didn't open your missionary-box. We opened our own once, but we didn't have to use the money, so our consciences made us put it back and—DON'T! Oh, I wish you wouldn't—'

Miss Selina had seized Jane and Miss Amelia captured Robert. The children found themselves held fast by strong, slim hands, pink at the wrists and white at the knuckles.

'We've got YOU, at any rate,' said Miss Amelia. 'Selina, your captive is smaller than mine. You open the window at once and call "Murder!" as loud as you can.

Selina obeyed; but when she had opened the window, instead of calling 'Murder!' she called 'Septimus!' because at that very moment she saw her nephew coming in at the gate.

In another minute he had let himself in with his latch-key and had mounted the stairs. As he came into the room Jane and Robert each uttered a shriek of joy so loud and so sudden that the ladies leaped with surprise, and nearly let them go.

'It's our own clergyman,' cried Jane.

'Don't you remember us?' asked Robert. 'You married our burglar for us—don't you remember?'

'I KNEW it was a gang,' said Amelia. 'Septimus, these abandoned children are members of a desperate burgling gang who are robbing the house. They have already forced the missionary-box and purloined its contents.'

The Reverend Septimus passed his hand wearily over his brow.

'I feel a little faint,' he said, 'running upstairs so quickly.'

'We never touched the beastly box,' said Robert.

'Then your confederates did,' said Miss Selina.

'No, no,' said the curate, hastily. '*I* opened the box myself. This morning I found I had not enough small change for the Mothers' Independent Unity Measles and Croup Insurance payments. I suppose this is NOT a dream, is it?'

'Dream? No, indeed. Search the house. I insist upon it.'

The curate, still pale and trembling, searched the house, which, of course, was blamelessly free of burglars.

When he came back he sank wearily into his chair.

'Aren't you going to let us go?' asked Robert, with furious indignation, for there is something in being held by a strong lady that sets the blood of a boy boiling in his veins with anger and despair. 'We've never done anything to you. It's all the carpet. It dropped us on the leads. WE couldn't help it. You know how it carried you over to the island, and you had to marry the burglar to the cook.'

'Oh, my head!' said the curate.

'Never mind your head just now,' said Robert; 'try to be honest and honourable, and do your duty in that state of life!'

'This is a judgement on me for something, I suppose,' said the Reverend Septimus, wearily, 'but I really cannot at the moment remember what.'

'Send for the police,' said Miss Selina.

'Send for a doctor,' said the curate.

'Do you think they ARE mad, then,' said Miss Amelia.

'I think I am,' said the curate.

Jane had been crying ever since her capture. Now she said— 'You aren't now, but perhaps you will be, if—And it would serve you jolly well right, too.'

'Aunt Selina,' said the curate, 'and Aunt Amelia, believe me, this is only an insane dream. You will realize it soon. It has happened to me before. But do not let us be unjust, even in a dream. Do not hold the children; they have done no harm. As I said before, it was I who opened the box.'

The strong, bony hands unwillingly loosened their grasp. Robert shook himself and stood in sulky resentment. But Jane ran to the curate and embraced him so suddenly that he had not time to defend himself.

'You're a dear,' she said. 'It IS like a dream just at first, but you get used to it. Now DO let us go. There's a good, kind, honourable clergyman.'

'I don't know,' said the Reverend Septimus; 'it's a difficult problem. It is such a very unusual dream. Perhaps it's only a sort of other life—quite real enough for you to be mad in. And if you're mad, there might be a dream-asylum where you'd be kindly treated, and in time restored, cured, to your sorrowing relatives. It is very hard to see your duty plainly, even in ordinary life, and these dream-circumstances are so complicated—'

'If it's a dream,' said Robert, 'you will wake up directly, and then you'd be sorry if you'd sent us into a dream-asylum, because you might never get into the same dream again and let us out, and so we might stay there for ever, and then what about our sorrowing relatives who aren't in the dreams at all?'

But all the curate could now say was, 'Oh, my head!'

And Jane and Robert felt quite ill with helplessness and hopelessness. A really conscientious curate is a very difficult thing to manage.

And then, just as the hopelessness and the helplessness were getting to be almost more than they could bear, the two children suddenly felt that extraordinary shrinking feeling that you always have when you are just going to vanish. And the next moment they had vanished, and the Reverend Septimus was left alone with his aunts.

'I knew it was a dream,' he cried, wildly. 'I've had something like it before. Did you dream it too, Aunt Selina, and you, Aunt Amelia? I dreamed that you did, you know.'

Aunt Selina looked at him and then at Aunt Amelia. Then she said boldly—

'What do you mean? WE haven't been dreaming anything. You must have dropped off in your chair.'

The curate heaved a sigh of relief.

'Oh, if it's only *I*,' he said; 'if we'd all dreamed it I could never have believed it, never!'

Afterwards Aunt Selina said to the other aunt—

'Yes, I know it was an untruth, and I shall doubtless be punished for it in due course. But I could see the poor dear fellow's brain giving way before my very eyes. He couldn't have stood the strain of three dreams. It WAS odd, wasn't it? All three of us dreaming the same thing at the same moment. We must never tell dear Seppy. But I shall send an account of it to the Psychical Society, with stars instead of names, you know.'

And she did. And you can read all about it in one of the society's fat Blue-books.

Of course, you understand what had happened? The intelligent Phoenix had simply gone straight off to the Psammead, and had wished Robert and Jane at home. And, of course, they were at home at once. Cyril and Anthea had not half finished mending the carpet.

When the joyful emotions of reunion had calmed down a little, they all went out and spent what was left of Uncle Reginald's sovereign in presents for mother. They bought her a pink silk handkerchief, a
330

pair of blue and white vases, a bottle of scent, a packet of Christmas candles, and a cake of soap shaped and coloured like a tomato, and one that was so like an orange that almost any one you had given it to would have tried to peel it—if they liked oranges, of course. Also they bought a cake with icing on, and the rest of the money they spent on flowers to put in the vases.

When they had arranged all the things on a table, with the candles stuck up on a plate ready to light the moment mother's cab was heard, they washed themselves thoroughly and put on tidier clothes.

Then Robert said, 'Good old Psammead,' and the others said so too.

'But, really, it's just as much good old Phoenix,' said Robert. 'Suppose it hadn't thought of getting the wish!'

'Ah!' said the Phoenix, 'it is perhaps fortunate for you that I am such a competent bird.'

'There's mother's cab,' cried Anthea, and the Phoenix hid and they lighted the candles, and next moment mother was home again.

She liked her presents very much, and found their story of Uncle Reginald and the sovereign easy and even pleasant to believe.

'Good old carpet,' were Cyril's last sleepy words.

'What there is of it,' said the Phoenix, from the cornice-pole.

CHAPTER 11. THE BEGINNING OF THE END

'Well, I MUST say,' mother said, looking at the wishing carpet as it lay, all darned and mended and backed with shiny American cloth, on the floor of the nursery—'I MUST say I've never in my life bought such a bad bargain as that carpet.'

A soft 'Oh!' of contradiction sprang to the lips of Cyril, Robert, Jane, and Anthea. Mother looked at them quickly, and said—

'Well, of course, I see you've mended it very nicely, and that was sweet of you, dears.'

'The boys helped too,' said the dears, honourably.

'But, still—twenty-two and ninepence! It ought to have lasted for years. It's simply dreadful now. Well, never mind, darlings, you've done your best. I think we'll have coconut matting next time. A carpet doesn't have an easy life of it in this room, does it?'

'It's not our fault, mother, is it, that our boots are the really reliable kind?' Robert asked the question more in sorrow than in anger.

'No, dear, we can't help our boots,' said mother, cheerfully, 'but we might change them when we come in, perhaps. It's just an idea of mine. I wouldn't dream of scolding on the very first morning after I've come home. Oh, my Lamb, how could you?'

This conversation was at breakfast, and the Lamb had been beautifully good until everyone was looking at the carpet, and then it was for him but the work of a moment to turn a glass dish of syrupy blackberry jam upside down on his young head. It was the work of a good many minutes and several persons to get the jam off him again, and this interesting work took people's minds off the carpet, and nothing more was said just then about its badness as a bargain and about what mother hoped for from coconut matting.

When the Lamb was clean again he had to be taken care of while mother rumpled her hair and inked her fingers and made her head ache over the difficult and twisted house-keeping accounts which cook gave her on dirty bits of paper, and which were supposed to explain how it was that cook had only fivepence-half-penny and a lot of unpaid bills left out of all the money mother had sent her for house-keeping. Mother was very clever, but even she could not quite understand the cook's accounts.

The Lamb was very glad to have his brothers and sisters to play with him. He had not forgotten them a bit, and he made them play all the old exhausting games: 'Whirling Worlds', where you swing the baby round and round by his hands; and 'Leg and Wing', where you swing him from side to side by one ankle and one wrist. There was also climbing Vesuvius. In this game the baby walks up you, and when he is standing on your shoulders, you shout as loud as you can, which is the rumbling of the burning mountain, and then tumble him gently on to the floor, and roll him there, which is the destruction of Pompeii.

'All the same, I wish we could decide what we'd better say next time mother says anything about the carpet,' said Cyril, breathlessly ceasing to be a burning mountain.

'Well, you talk and decide,' said Anthea; 'here, you lovely ducky Lamb. Come to Panther and play Noah's Ark.'

The Lamb came with his pretty hair all tumbled and his face all dusty from the destruction of Pompeii, and instantly became a baby snake, hissing and wriggling and creeping in Anthea's arms, as she said—

> 'I love my little baby snake,
> He hisses when he is awake,
> He creeps with such a wriggly creep,
> He wriggles even in his sleep.'

'Crocky,' said the Lamb, and showed all his little teeth. So Anthea went on—

> 'I love my little crocodile,
> I love his truthful toothful smile;
> It is so wonderful and wide,
> I like to see it—FROM OUTSIDE.'

'Well, you see,' Cyril was saying; 'it's just the old bother. Mother can't believe the real true truth about the carpet, and—'

'You speak sooth, O Cyril,' remarked the Phoenix, coming out from the cupboard where the blackbeetles lived, and the torn books, and the broken slates, and odd pieces of toys that had lost the rest of themselves. 'Now hear the wisdom of Phoenix, the son of the Phoenix—'

'There is a society called that,' said Cyril.

'Where is it? And what is a society?' asked the bird.

'It's a sort of joined-together lot of people—a sort of brotherhood—a kind of—well, something very like your temple, you know, only quite different.'

'I take your meaning,' said the Phoenix. 'I would fain see these calling themselves Sons of the Phoenix.'

'But what about your words of wisdom?'

'Wisdom is always welcome,' said the Phoenix.

'Pretty Polly!' remarked the Lamb, reaching his hands towards the golden speaker.

The Phoenix modestly retreated behind Robert, and Anthea hastened to distract the attention of the Lamb by murmuring—

> *"I love my little baby rabbit;*
> *But oh! he has a dreadful habit*
> *Of paddling out among the rocks*
> *And soaking both his bunny socks.'*

'I don't think you'd care about the sons of the Phoenix, really,' said Robert. 'I have heard that they don't do anything fiery. They only drink a great deal. Much more than other people, because they drink lemonade and fizzy things, and the more you drink of those the more good you get.'

'In your mind, perhaps,' said Jane; 'but it wouldn't be good in your body. You'd get too balloony.'

The Phoenix yawned.

'Look here,' said Anthea; 'I really have an idea. This isn't like a common carpet. It's very magic indeed. Don't you think, if we put Tatcho on it, and then gave it a rest, the magic part of it might grow, like hair is supposed to do?'

'It might,' said Robert; 'but I should think paraffin would do as well—at any rate as far as the smell goes, and that seems to be the great thing about Tatcho.'

But with all its faults Anthea's idea was something to do, and they did it.

It was Cyril who fetched the Tatcho bottle from father's washhand-stand. But the bottle had not much in it.

'We mustn't take it all,' Jane said, 'in case father's hair began to come off suddenly. If he hadn't anything to put on it, it might all drop off before Eliza had time to get round to the chemist's for another bottle. It would be dreadful to have a bald father, and it would all be our fault.'

'And wigs are very expensive, I believe,' said Anthea. 'Look here, leave enough in the bottle to wet father's head all over with in case any emergency emerges—and let's make up with paraffin. I expect it's the smell that does the good really—and the smell's exactly the same.'

So a small teaspoonful of the Tatcho was put on the edges of the worst darn in the carpet and rubbed carefully into the roots of the hairs of it, and all the parts that there was not enough Tatcho for had paraffin rubbed into them with a piece of flannel. Then the flannel was burned. It made a gay flame, which delighted the Phoenix and the Lamb.

'How often,' said mother, opening the door—'how often am I to tell you that you are NOT to play with paraffin? What have you been doing?'

'We have burnt a paraffiny rag,' Anthea answered.

It was no use telling mother what they had done to the carpet. She did not know it was a magic carpet, and no one wants to be laughed at for trying to mend an ordinary carpet with lamp-oil.

'Well, don't do it again,' said mother. 'And now, away with melancholy! Father has sent a telegram. Look!' She held it out, and the children, holding it by its yielding corners, read—

'Box for kiddies at Garrick. Stalls for us, Haymarket. Meet Charing Cross, 6.30.'

'That means,' said mother, 'that you're going to see "The Water Babies" all by your happy selves, and father and I will take you and fetch you. Give me the Lamb, dear, and you and Jane put clean lace in your red evening frocks, and I shouldn't wonder if you found they wanted ironing. This paraffin smell is ghastly. Run and get out your frocks.'

The frocks did want ironing—wanted it rather badly, as it happened; for, being of tomato-Coloured Liberty silk, they had been found very useful for tableaux vivants when a red dress was required for Cardinal Richelieu. They were very nice tableaux, these, and I wish I could tell you about them; but one cannot tell everything in a story. You would have been specially interested in hearing about the tableau of the Princes in the Tower, when one of the pillows burst, and the youthful Princes were so covered with feathers that the picture might very well have been called 'Michaelmas Eve; or, Plucking the Geese'.

Ironing the dresses and sewing the lace in occupied some time, and no one was dull, because there was the theatre to look forward to, and also the possible growth of hairs on the carpet, for which everyone kept looking anxiously. By four o'clock Jane was almost sure that several hairs were beginning to grow.

The Phoenix perched on the fender, and its conversation, as usual, was entertaining and instructive—like school prizes are said to be. But it seemed a little absent-minded, and even a little sad.

'Don't you feel well, Phoenix, dear?' asked Anthea, stooping to take an iron off the fire.

'I am not sick,' replied the golden bird, with a gloomy shake of the head; 'but I am getting old.'

'Why, you've hardly been hatched any time at all.'

'Time,' remarked the Phoenix, 'is measured by heartbeats. I'm sure the palpitations I've had since I've known you are enough to blanch the feathers of any bird.'

'But I thought you lived 500 years,' said Robert, and you've hardly begun this set of years. Think of all the time that's before you.'

'Time,' said the Phoenix, 'is, as you are probably aware, merely a convenient fiction. There is no such thing as time. I have lived in these two months at a pace which generously counterbalances 500 years of life in the desert. I am old, I am weary. I feel as if I ought to lay my egg, and lay me down to my fiery sleep. But unless I'm careful I shall be hatched again instantly, and that is a misfortune which I really do not think I COULD endure. But do not let me intrude these desperate personal reflections on your youthful happiness. What is the show at the theatre to-night? Wrestlers? Gladiators? A combat of cameleopards and unicorns?'

'I don't think so,' said Cyril; 'it's called "The Water Babies", and if it's like the book there isn't any gladiating in it. There are chimney-sweeps and professors, and a lobster and an otter and a salmon, and children living in the water.'

'It sounds chilly.' The Phoenix shivered, and went to sit on the tongs.

'I don't suppose there will be REAL water,' said Jane. 'And theatres are very warm and pretty, with a lot of gold and lamps. Wouldn't you like to come with us?'

'*I* was just going to say that,' said Robert, in injured tones, 'only I know how rude it is to interrupt. Do come, Phoenix, old chap; it will cheer you up. It'll make you laugh like any thing. Mr Bourchier always makes ripping plays. You ought to have seen "Shock-headed Peter" last year.'

'Your words are strange,' said the Phoenix, 'but I will come with you. The revels of this Bourchier, of whom you speak, may help me to forget the weight of my years.' So that evening the Phoenix snuggled inside the waistcoat of Robert's Etons—a very tight fit it seemed both to Robert and to the Phoenix—and was taken to the play.

Robert had to pretend to be cold at the glittering, many-mirrored restaurant where they ate dinner, with father in evening dress, with a very shiny white shirt-front, and mother looking lovely in her grey evening dress, that changes into pink and green when she moves. Robert pretended that he was too cold to take off his great-coat, and so sat sweltering through what would otherwise have been a most thrilling meal. He felt that he was a blot on the smart beauty of the family, and he hoped the Phoenix knew what he was suffering for its sake. Of course, we are all pleased to suffer for the sake of others, but we like them to know it unless we are the very best and noblest kind of people, and Robert was just ordinary.

Father was full of jokes and fun, and everyone laughed all the time, even with their mouths full, which is not manners. Robert thought father would not have been quite so funny about his keeping his over-coat on if father had known all the truth. And there Robert was probably right.

When dinner was finished to the last grape and the last paddle in the finger glasses—for it was a really truly grown-up dinner—the children were taken to the theatre, guided to a box close to the stage, and left.

Father's parting words were: 'Now, don't you stir out of this box, whatever you do. I shall be back before the end of the play. Be good and you will be happy. Is this zone torrid enough for the abandonment of great-coats, Bobs? No? Well, then, I should say you were sickening for something—mumps or measles or thrush or teething. Goodbye.'

He went, and Robert was at last able to remove his coat, mop his perspiring brow, and release the crushed and dishevelled Phoenix. Robert had to arrange his damp hair at the looking-glass at the back of the box, and the Phoenix had to preen its disordered feathers for some time before either of them was fit to be seen.

They were very, very early. When the lights went up fully, the Phoenix, balancing itself on the gilded back of a chair, swayed in ecstasy.

'How fair a scene is this!' it murmured; 'how far fairer than my temple! Or have I guessed aright? Have you brought me hither to lift up my heart with emotions of joyous surprise? Tell me, my Robert,

338

is it not that this, THIS is my true temple, and the other was but a humble shrine frequented by outcasts?'

'I don't know about outcasts,' said Robert, 'but you can call this your temple if you like. Hush! the music is beginning.'

I am not going to tell you about the play. As I said before, one can't tell everything, and no doubt you saw 'The Water Babies' yourselves. If you did not it was a shame, or, rather, a pity.

What I must tell you is that, though Cyril and Jane and Robert and Anthea enjoyed it as much as any children possibly could, the pleasure of the Phoenix was far, far greater than theirs.

'This is indeed my temple,' it said again and again. 'What radiant rites! And all to do honour to me!'

The songs in the play it took to be hymns in its honour. The choruses were choric songs in its praise. The electric lights, it said, were magic torches lighted for its sake, and it was so charmed with the footlights that the children could hardly persuade it to sit still. But when the limelight was shown it could contain its approval no longer. It flapped its golden wings, and cried in a voice that could be heard all over the theatre:

'Well done, my servants! Ye have my favour and my countenance!'

Little Tom on the stage stopped short in what he was saying. A deep breath was drawn by hundreds of lungs, every eye in the house turned to the box where the luckless children cringed, and most people hissed, or said 'Shish!' or 'Turn them out!'

Then the play went on, and an attendant presently came to the box and spoke wrathfully.

'It wasn't us, indeed it wasn't,' said Anthea, earnestly; 'it was the bird.'

The man said well, then, they must keep their bird very quiet. 'Disturbing everyone like this,' he said.

'It won't do it again,' said Robert, glancing imploringly at the golden bird; 'I'm sure it won't.'

'You have my leave to depart,' said the Phoenix gently.

'Well, he is a beauty, and no mistake,' said the attendant, 'only I'd cover him up during the acts. It upsets the performance.'

And he went.

'Don't speak again, there's a dear,' said Anthea; 'you wouldn't like to interfere with your own temple, would you?'

So now the Phoenix was quiet, but it kept whispering to the children. It wanted to know why there was no altar, no fire, no incense, and became so excited and fretful and tiresome that four at least of the party of five wished deeply that it had been left at home.

What happened next was entirely the fault of the Phoenix. It was not in the least the fault of the theatre people, and no one could ever understand afterwards how it did happen. No one, that is, except the guilty bird itself and the four children. The Phoenix was balancing itself on the gilt back of the chair, swaying backwards and forwards and up and down, as you may see your own domestic parrot do. I mean the grey one with the red tail. All eyes were on the stage, where the lobster was delighting the audience with that gem of a song, 'If you can't walk straight, walk sideways!' when the Phoenix murmured warmly—

'No altar, no fire, no incense!' and then, before any of the children could even begin to think of stopping it, it spread its bright wings and swept round the theatre, brushing its gleaming feathers against delicate hangings and gilded woodwork.

It seemed to have made but one circular wing-sweep, such as you may see a gull make over grey water on a stormy day. Next moment it was perched again on the chair-back—and all round the theatre, where it had passed, little sparks shone like tinsel seeds, then little smoke wreaths curled up like growing plants—little flames opened like flower-buds. People whispered—then people shrieked.

340

'Fire! Fire!' The curtain went down—the lights went up.

'Fire!' cried everyone, and made for the doors.

'A magnificent idea!' said the Phoenix, complacently. 'An enormous altar—fire supplied free of charge. Doesn't the incense smell delicious?'

The only smell was the stifling smell of smoke, of burning silk, or scorching varnish.

The little flames had opened now into great flame-flowers. The people in the theatre were shouting and pressing towards the doors.

'Oh, how COULD you!' cried Jane. 'Let's get out.'

'Father said stay here,' said Anthea, very pale, and trying to speak in her ordinary voice.

'He didn't mean stay and be roasted,' said Robert. 'No boys on burning decks for me, thank you.'

'Not much,' said Cyril, and he opened the door of the box.

But a fierce waft of smoke and hot air made him shut it again. It was not possible to get out that way.

They looked over the front of the box. Could they climb down?

It would be possible, certainly; but would they be much better off?

'Look at the people,' moaned Anthea; 'we couldn't get through.'

And, indeed, the crowd round the doors looked as thick as flies in the jam-making season.

'I wish we'd never seen the Phoenix,' cried Jane.

Even at that awful moment Robert looked round to see if the bird had overheard a speech which, however natural, was hardly polite or grateful.

The Phoenix was gone.

'Look here,' said Cyril, 'I've read about fires in papers; I'm sure it's all right. Let's wait here, as father said.'

'We can't do anything else,' said Anthea bitterly.

'Look here,' said Robert, 'I'm NOT frightened—no, I'm not. The Phoenix has never been a skunk yet, and I'm certain it'll see us through somehow. I believe in the Phoenix!'

'The Phoenix thanks you, O Robert,' said a golden voice at his feet, and there was the Phoenix itself, on the Wishing Carpet.

'Quick!' it said. 'Stand on those portions of the carpet which are truly antique and authentic—and—'

A sudden jet of flame stopped its words. Alas! the Phoenix had unconsciously warmed to its subject, and in the unintentional heat of the moment had set fire to the paraffin with which that morning the children had anointed the carpet. It burned merrily. The children tried in vain to stamp it out. They had to stand back and let it burn itself out. When the paraffin had burned away it was found that it had taken with it all the darns of Scotch heather-mixture fingering. Only the fabric of the old carpet was left—and that was full of holes.

'Come,' said the Phoenix, 'I'm cool now.'

The four children got on to what was left of the carpet. Very careful they were not to leave a leg or a hand hanging over one of the holes. It was very hot—the theatre was a pit of fire. Everyone else had got out.

Jane had to sit on Anthea's lap.

'Home!' said Cyril, and instantly the cool draught from under the nursery door played upon their legs as they sat. They were all on the carpet still, and the carpet was lying in its proper place on the nursery floor, as calm and unmoved as though it had never been to the theatre or taken part in a fire in its life.

Four long breaths of deep relief were instantly breathed. The draught which they had never liked before was for the moment quite pleasant. And they were safe. And everyone else was safe. The

342

theatre had been quite empty when they left. Everyone was sure of that.

They presently found themselves all talking at once. Somehow none of their adventures had given them so much to talk about. None other had seemed so real.

'Did you notice—?' they said, and 'Do you remember—?'

When suddenly Anthea's face turned pale under the dirt which it had collected on it during the fire.

'Oh,' she cried, 'mother and father! Oh, how awful! They'll think we're burned to cinders. Oh, let's go this minute and tell them we aren't.'

'We should only miss them,' said the sensible Cyril.

'Well—YOU go then,' said Anthea, 'or I will. Only do wash your face first. Mother will be sure to think you are burnt to a cinder if she sees you as black as that, and she'll faint or be ill or something. Oh, I wish we'd never got to know that Phoenix.'

'Hush!' said Robert; 'it's no use being rude to the bird. I suppose it can't help its nature. Perhaps we'd better wash too. Now I come to think of it my hands are rather—'

No one had noticed the Phoenix since it had bidden them to step on the carpet. And no one noticed that no one had noticed.

All were partially clean, and Cyril was just plunging into his great-coat to go and look for his parents—he, and not unjustly, called it looking for a needle in a bundle of hay—when the sound of father's latchkey in the front door sent everyone bounding up the stairs.

'Are you all safe?' cried mother's voice; 'are you all safe?' and the next moment she was kneeling on the linoleum of the hall, trying to kiss four damp children at once, and laughing and crying by turns, while father stood looking on and saying he was blessed or something.

'But how did you guess we'd come home,' said Cyril, later, when everyone was calm enough for talking.

'Well, it was rather a rum thing. We heard the Garrick was on fire, and of course we went straight there,' said father, briskly. 'We couldn't find you, of course—and we couldn't get in—but the firemen told us everyone was safely out. And then I heard a voice at my ear say, "Cyril, Anthea, Robert, and Jane"—and something touched me on the shoulder. It was a great yellow pigeon, and it got in the way of my seeing who'd spoken. It fluttered off, and then some one said in the other ear, "They're safe at home"; and when I turned again, to see who it was speaking, hanged if there wasn't that confounded pigeon on my other shoulder. Dazed by the fire, I suppose. Your mother said it was the voice of—'

'I said it was the bird that spoke,' said mother, 'and so it was. Or at least I thought so then. It wasn't a pigeon. It was an orange-coloured cockatoo. I don't care who it was that spoke. It was true and you're safe.'

Mother began to cry again, and father said bed was a good place after the pleasures of the stage.

So everyone went there.

Robert had a talk to the Phoenix that night.

'Oh, very well,' said the bird, when Robert had said what he felt, 'didn't you know that I had power over fire? Do not distress yourself. I, like my high priests in Lombard Street, can undo the work of flames. Kindly open the casement.'

It flew out.

That was why the papers said next day that the fire at the theatre had done less damage than had been anticipated. As a matter of fact it had done none, for the Phoenix spent the night in putting things straight. How the management accounted for this, and how many of the theatre officials still believe that they were mad on that night will never be known.

Next day mother saw the burnt holes in the carpet.

'It caught where it was paraffiny,' said Anthea.

'I must get rid of that carpet at once,' said mother.

But what the children said in sad whispers to each other, as they pondered over last night's events, was—

'We must get rid of that Phoenix.'

CHAPTER 12. THE END OF THE END

'Egg, toast, tea, milk, tea-cup and saucer, egg-spoon, knife, butter—that's all, I think,' remarked Anthea, as she put the last touches to mother's breakfast-tray, and went, very carefully up the stairs, feeling for every step with her toes, and holding on to the tray with all her fingers. She crept into mother's room and set the tray on a chair. Then she pulled one of the blinds up very softly.

'Is your head better, mammy dear?' she asked, in the soft little voice that she kept expressly for mother's headaches. 'I've brought your brekkie, and I've put the little cloth with clover-leaves on it, the one I made you.'

'That's very nice,' said mother sleepily.

Anthea knew exactly what to do for mothers with headaches who had breakfast in bed. She fetched warm water and put just enough eau de Cologne in it, and bathed mother's face and hands with the sweet-scented water. Then mother was able to think about breakfast.

'But what's the matter with my girl?' she asked, when her eyes got used to the light.

'Oh, I'm so sorry you're ill,' Anthea said. 'It's that horrible fire and you being so frightened. Father said so. And we all feel as if it was our faults. I can't explain, but—'

'It wasn't your fault a bit, you darling goosie,' mother said. 'How could it be?'

'That's just what I can't tell you,' said Anthea. 'I haven't got a futile brain like you and father, to think of ways of explaining everything.'

Mother laughed.

'My futile brain—or did you mean fertile?—anyway, it feels very stiff and sore this morning—but I shall be quite all right by and by. And don't be a silly little pet girl. The fire wasn't your faults. No; I don't want the egg, dear. I'll go to sleep again, I think. Don't you worry. And tell cook not to bother me about meals. You can order what you like for lunch.'

Anthea closed the door very mousily, and instantly went downstairs and ordered what she liked for lunch. She ordered a pair of turkeys, a large plum-pudding, cheese-cakes, and almonds and raisins.

Cook told her to go along, do. And she might as well not have ordered anything, for when lunch came it was just hashed mutton and semolina pudding, and cook had forgotten the sippets for the mutton hash and the semolina pudding was burnt.

When Anthea rejoined the others she found them all plunged in the gloom where she was herself. For everyone knew that the days of the carpet were now numbered. Indeed, so worn was it that you could almost have numbered its threads.

So that now, after nearly a month of magic happenings, the time was at hand when life would have to go on in the dull, ordinary way and Jane, Robert, Anthea, and Cyril would be just in the same position as the other children who live in Camden Town, the children whom these four had so often pitied, and perhaps a little despised.

'We shall be just like them,' Cyril said.

'Except,' said Robert, 'that we shall have more things to remember and be sorry we haven't got.'

'Mother's going to send away the carpet as soon as she's well enough to see about that coconut matting. Fancy us with coconut-

346

matting—us! And we've walked under live coconut-trees on the island where you can't have whooping-cough.'

'Pretty island,' said the Lamb; 'paint-box sands and sea all shiny sparkly.'

His brothers and sisters had often wondered whether he remembered that island. Now they knew that he did.

'Yes,' said Cyril; 'no more cheap return trips by carpet for us—that's a dead cert.'

They were all talking about the carpet, but what they were all thinking about was the Phoenix.

The golden bird had been so kind, so friendly, so polite, so instructive—and now it had set fire to a theatre and made mother ill.

Nobody blamed the bird. It had acted in a perfectly natural manner. But everyone saw that it must not be asked to prolong its visit. Indeed, in plain English it must be asked to go!

The four children felt like base spies and treacherous friends; and each in its mind was saying who ought not to be the one to tell the Phoenix that there could no longer be a place for it in that happy home in Camden Town. Each child was quite sure that one of them ought to speak out in a fair and manly way, but nobody wanted to be the one.

They could not talk the whole thing over as they would have liked to do, because the Phoenix itself was in the cupboard, among the blackbeetles and the odd shoes and the broken chessmen.

But Anthea tried.

'It's very horrid. I do hate thinking things about people, and not being able to say the things you're thinking because of the way they would feel when they thought what things you were thinking, and wondered what they'd done to make you think things like that, and why you were thinking them.'

Anthea was so anxious that the Phoenix should not understand what she said that she made a speech completely baffling to all. It was not till she pointed to the cupboard in which all believed the Phoenix to be that Cyril understood.

'Yes,' he said, while Jane and Robert were trying to tell each other how deeply they didn't understand what Anthea were saying; 'but after recent eventfulnesses a new leaf has to be turned over, and, after all, mother is more important than the feelings of any of the lower forms of creation, however unnatural.'

'How beautifully you do do it,' said Anthea, absently beginning to build a card-house for the Lamb—'mixing up what you're saying, I mean. We ought to practise doing it so as to be ready for mysterious occasions. We're talking about THAT,' she said to Jane and Robert, frowning, and nodding towards the cupboard where the Phoenix was. Then Robert and Jane understood, and each opened its mouth to speak.

'Wait a minute,' said Anthea quickly; 'the game is to twist up what you want to say so that no one can understand what you're saying except the people you want to understand it, and sometimes not them.'

'The ancient philosophers,' said a golden voice, 'Well understood the art of which you speak.'

Of course it was the Phoenix, who had not been in the cupboard at all, but had been cocking a golden eye at them from the cornice during the whole conversation.

'Pretty dickie!' remarked the Lamb. 'CANARY dickie!'

'Poor misguided infant,' said the Phoenix.

There was a painful pause; the four could not but think it likely that the Phoenix had understood their very veiled allusions, accompanied as they had been by gestures indicating the cupboard. For the Phoenix was not wanting in intelligence.

'We were just saying—' Cyril began, and I hope he was not going to say anything but the truth. Whatever it was he did not say it, for the Phoenix interrupted him, and all breathed more freely as it spoke.

'I gather,' it said, 'that you have some tidings of a fatal nature to communicate to our degraded black brothers who run to and fro for ever yonder.' It pointed a claw at the cupboard, where the blackbeetles lived.

'Canary TALK,' said the Lamb joyously; 'go and show mammy.'

He wriggled off Anthea's lap.

'Mammy's asleep,' said Jane, hastily. 'Come and be wild beasts in a cage under the table.'

But the Lamb caught his feet and hands, and even his head, so often and so deeply in the holes of the carpet that the cage, or table, had to be moved on to the linoleum, and the carpet lay bare to sight with all its horrid holes.

'Ah,' said the bird, 'it isn't long for this world.'

'No,' said Robert; 'everything comes to an end. It's awful.'

'Sometimes the end is peace,' remarked the Phoenix. 'I imagine that unless it comes soon the end of your carpet will be pieces.'

'Yes,' said Cyril, respectfully kicking what was left of the carpet. The movement of its bright colours caught the eye of the Lamb, who went down on all fours instantly and began to pull at the red and blue threads.

'Aggedydaggedygaggedy,' murmured the Lamb; 'daggedy ag ag ag!'

And before any one could have winked (even if they had wanted to, and it would not have been of the slightest use) the middle of the floor showed bare, an island of boards surrounded by a sea of linoleum. The magic carpet was gone, AND SO WAS THE LAMB!

There was a horrible silence. The Lamb—the baby, all alone—had been wafted away on that untrustworthy carpet, so full of holes and magic. And no one could know where he was. And no one could follow him because there was now no carpet to follow on.

Jane burst into tears, but Anthea, though pale and frantic, was dry-eyed.

'It MUST be a dream,' she said.

'That's what the clergyman said,' remarked Robert forlornly; 'but it wasn't, and it isn't.'

'But the Lamb never wished,' said Cyril; 'he was only talking Bosh.'

'The carpet understands all speech,' said the Phoenix, 'even Bosh. I know not this Boshland, but be assured that its tongue is not unknown to the carpet.'

'Do you mean, then,' said Anthea, in white terror, 'that when he was saying "Agglety dag," or whatever it was, that he meant something by it?'

'All speech has meaning,' said the Phoenix.

'There I think you're wrong,' said Cyril; 'even people who talk English sometimes say things that don't mean anything in particular.'

'Oh, never mind that now,' moaned Anthea; 'you think "Aggety dag" meant something to him and the carpet?'

'Beyond doubt it held the same meaning to the carpet as to the luckless infant,' the Phoenix said calmly.

'And WHAT did it mean? Oh WHAT?'

'Unfortunately,' the bird rejoined, 'I never studied Bosh.'

Jane sobbed noisily, but the others were calm with what is sometimes called the calmness of despair. The Lamb was gone—the Lamb, their own precious baby brother—who had never in his happy little life been for a moment out of the sight of eyes that loved him—he was gone. He had gone alone into the great world with no other companion and protector than a carpet with holes in it. The

350

children had never really understood before what an enormously big place the world is. And the Lamb might be anywhere in it!

'And it's no use going to look for him.' Cyril, in flat and wretched tones, only said what the others were thinking.

'Do you wish him to return?' the Phoenix asked; it seemed to speak with some surprise.

'Of course we do!' cried everybody.

'Isn't he more trouble than he's worth?' asked the bird doubtfully.

'No, no. Oh, we do want him back! We do!'

'Then,' said the wearer of gold plumage, 'if you'll excuse me, I'll just pop out and see what I can do.'

Cyril flung open the window, and the Phoenix popped out.

'Oh, if only mother goes on sleeping! Oh, suppose she wakes up and wants the Lamb! Oh, suppose the servants come! Stop crying, Jane. It's no earthly good. No, I'm not crying myself—at least I wasn't till you said so, and I shouldn't anyway if—if there was any mortal thing we could do. Oh, oh, oh!'

Cyril and Robert were boys, and boys never cry, of course. Still, the position was a terrible one, and I do not wonder that they made faces in their efforts to behave in a really manly way.

And at this awful moment mother's bell rang.

A breathless stillness held the children. Then Anthea dried her eyes. She looked round her and caught up the poker. She held it out to Cyril.

'Hit my hand hard,' she said; 'I must show mother some reason for my eyes being like they are. Harder,' she cried as Cyril gently tapped her with the iron handle. And Cyril, agitated and trembling, nerved himself to hit harder, and hit very much harder than he intended.

Anthea screamed.

'Oh, Panther, I didn't mean to hurt, really,' cried Cyril, clattering the poker back into the fender.

'It's—all—right,' said Anthea breathlessly, clasping the hurt hand with the one that wasn't hurt; 'it's—getting—red.'

It was—a round red and blue bump was rising on the back of it. 'Now, Robert,' she said, trying to breathe more evenly, 'you go out—oh, I don't know where—on to the dustbin—anywhere—and I shall tell mother you and the Lamb are out.'

Anthea was now ready to deceive her mother for as long as ever she could. Deceit is very wrong, we know, but it seemed to Anthea that it was her plain duty to keep her mother from being frightened about the Lamb as long as possible. And the Phoenix might help.

'It always has helped,' Robert said; 'it got us out of the tower, and even when it made the fire in the theatre it got us out all right. I'm certain it will manage somehow.'

Mother's bell rang again.

'Oh, Eliza's never answered it,' cried Anthea; 'she never does. Oh, I must go.'

And she went.

Her heart beat bumpingly as she climbed the stairs. Mother would be certain to notice her eyes—well, her hand would account for that. But the Lamb—

'No, I must NOT think of the Lamb, she said to herself, and bit her tongue till her eyes watered again, so as to give herself something else to think of. Her arms and legs and back, and even her tear-reddened face, felt stiff with her resolution not to let mother be worried if she could help it.

She opened the door softly.

'Yes, mother?' she said.

'Dearest,' said mother, 'the Lamb—'

352

Anthea tried to be brave. She tried to say that the Lamb and Robert were out. Perhaps she tried too hard. Anyway, when she opened her mouth no words came. So she stood with it open. It seemed easier to keep from crying with one's mouth in that unusual position.

'The Lamb,' mother went on; 'he was very good at first, but he's pulled the toilet-cover off the dressing-table with all the brushes and pots and things, and now he's so quiet I'm sure he's in some dreadful mischief. And I can't see him from here, and if I'd got out of bed to see I'm sure I should have fainted.'

'Do you mean he's HERE?' said Anthea.

'Of course he's here,' said mother, a little impatiently. 'Where did you think he was?'

Anthea went round the foot of the big mahogany bed. There was a pause.

'He's not here NOW,' she said.

That he had been there was plain, from the toilet-cover on the floor, the scattered pots and bottles, the wandering brushes and combs, all involved in the tangle of ribbons and laces which an open drawer had yielded to the baby's inquisitive fingers.

'He must have crept out, then,' said mother; 'do keep him with you, there's a darling. If I don't get some sleep I shall be a wreck when father comes home.'

Anthea closed the door softly. Then she tore downstairs and burst into the nursery, crying—

'He must have wished he was with mother. He's been there all the time. "Aggety dag—"'

The unusual word was frozen on her lip, as people say in books.

For there, on the floor, lay the carpet, and on the carpet, surrounded by his brothers and by Jane, sat the Lamb. He had covered his face and clothes with vaseline and violet powder, but he was easily recognizable in spite of this disguise.

'You are right,' said the Phoenix, who was also present; 'it is evident that, as you say, "Aggety dag" is Bosh for "I want to be where my mother is," and so the faithful carpet understood it.'

'But how,' said Anthea, catching up the Lamb and hugging him—'how did he get back here?'

'Oh,' said the Phoenix, 'I flew to the Psammead and wished that your infant brother were restored to your midst, and immediately it was so.'

'Oh, I am glad, I am glad!' cried Anthea, still hugging the baby. 'Oh, you darling! Shut up, Jane! I don't care HOW much he comes off on me! Cyril! You and Robert roll that carpet up and put it in the beetle-cupboard. He might say "Aggety dag" again, and it might mean something quite different next time. Now, my Lamb, Panther'll clean you a little. Come on.'

'I hope the beetles won't go wishing,' said Cyril, as they rolled up the carpet.

Two days later mother was well enough to go out, and that evening the coconut matting came home. The children had talked and talked, and thought and thought, but they had not found any polite way of telling the Phoenix that they did not want it to stay any longer.

The days had been days spent by the children in embarrassment, and by the Phoenix in sleep.

And, now the matting was laid down, the Phoenix awoke and fluttered down on to it.

It shook its crested head.

'I like not this carpet,' it said; 'it is harsh and unyielding, and it hurts my golden feet.'

'We've jolly well got to get used to its hurting OUR golden feet,' said Cyril.

'This, then,' said the bird, 'supersedes the Wishing Carpet.'

'Yes,' said Robert, 'if you mean that it's instead of it.'

'And the magic web?' inquired the Phoenix, with sudden eagerness.

'It's the rag-and-bottle man's day to-morrow,' said Anthea, in a low voice; 'he will take it away.'

The Phoenix fluttered up to its favourite perch on the chair-back.

'Hear me!' it cried, 'oh youthful children of men, and restrain your tears of misery and despair, for what must be must be, and I would not remember you, thousands of years hence, as base ingrates and crawling worms compact of low selfishness.'

'I should hope not, indeed,' said Cyril.

'Weep not,' the bird went on; 'I really do beg that you won't weep.

I will not seek to break the news to you gently. Let the blow fall at once. The time has come when I must leave you.'

All four children breathed forth a long sigh of relief.

'We needn't have bothered so about how to break the news to it,' whispered Cyril.

'Ah, sigh not so,' said the bird, gently. 'All meetings end in partings. I must leave you. I have sought to prepare you for this. Ah, do not give way!'

'Must you really go—so soon?' murmured Anthea. It was what she had often heard her mother say to calling ladies in the afternoon.

'I must, really; thank you so much, dear,' replied the bird, just as though it had been one of the ladies.

'I am weary,' it went on. 'I desire to rest—after all the happenings of this last moon I do desire really to rest, and I ask of you one last boon.'

'Any little thing we can do,' said Robert.

Now that it had really come to parting with the Phoenix, whose favourite he had always been, Robert did feel almost as miserable as the Phoenix thought they all did.

'I ask but the relic designed for the rag-and-bottle man. Give me what is left of the carpet and let me go.'

'Dare we?' said Anthea. 'Would mother mind?'

'I have dared greatly for your sakes,' remarked the bird.

'Well, then, we will,' said Robert.

The Phoenix fluffed out its feathers joyously.

'Nor shall you regret it, children of golden hearts,' it said. 'Quick—spread the carpet and leave me alone; but first pile high the fire. Then, while I am immersed in the sacred preliminary rites, do ye prepare sweet-smelling woods and spices for the last act of parting.'

The children spread out what was left of the carpet. And, after all, though this was just what they would have wished to have happened, all hearts were sad. Then they put half a scuttle of coal on the fire and went out, closing the door on the Phoenix—left, at last, alone with the carpet.

'One of us must keep watch,' said Robert, excitedly, as soon as they were all out of the room, 'and the others can go and buy sweet woods and spices. Get the very best that money can buy, and plenty of them. Don't let's stand to a threepence or so. I want it to have a jolly good send-off. It's the only thing that'll make us feel less horrid inside.'

It was felt that Robert, as the pet of the Phoenix, ought to have the last melancholy pleasure of choosing the materials for its funeral pyre.

'I'll keep watch if you like,' said Cyril. 'I don't mind. And, besides, it's raining hard, and my boots let in the wet. You might call and see if my other ones are "really reliable" again yet.'

So they left Cyril, standing like a Roman sentinel outside the door inside which the Phoenix was getting ready for the great change, and they all went out to buy the precious things for the last sad rites.

'Robert is right,' Anthea said; 'this is no time for being careful about our money. Let's go to the stationer's first, and buy a whole packet of lead-pencils. They're cheaper if you buy them by the packet.'

This was a thing that they had always wanted to do, but it needed the great excitement of a funeral pyre and a parting from a beloved Phoenix to screw them up to the extravagance.

The people at the stationer's said that the pencils were real cedar-wood, so I hope they were, for stationers should always speak the truth. At any rate they cost one-and-fourpence. Also they spent sevenpence three-farthings on a little sandal-wood box inlaid with ivory.

'Because,' said Anthea, 'I know sandalwood smells sweet, and when it's burned it smells very sweet indeed.'

'Ivory doesn't smell at all,' said Robert, 'but I expect when you burn it it smells most awful vile, like bones.'

At the grocer's they bought all the spices they could remember the names of—shell-like mace, cloves like blunt nails, peppercorns, the long and the round kind; ginger, the dry sort, of course; and the beautiful bloom-covered shells of fragrant cinnamon. Allspice too, and caraway seeds (caraway seeds that smelt most deadly when the time came for burning them).

Camphor and oil of lavender were bought at the chemist's, and also a little scent sachet labelled 'Violettes de Parme'.

They took the things home and found Cyril still on guard. When they had knocked and the golden voice of the Phoenix had said 'Come in,' they went in.

There lay the carpet—or what was left of it—and on it lay an egg, exactly like the one out of which the Phoenix had been hatched.

The Phoenix was walking round and round the egg, clucking with joy and pride.

'I've laid it, you see,' it said, 'and as fine an egg as ever I laid in all my born days.'

Everyone said yes, it was indeed a beauty.

The things which the children had bought were now taken out of their papers and arranged on the table, and when the Phoenix had been persuaded to leave its egg for a moment and look at the materials for its last fire it was quite overcome.

'Never, never have I had a finer pyre than this will be. You shall not regret it,' it said, wiping away a golden tear. 'Write quickly: "Go and tell the Psammead to fulfil the last wish of the Phoenix, and return instantly".'

But Robert wished to be polite and he wrote—

'Please go and ask the Psammead to be so kind as to fulfil the Phoenix's last wish, and come straight back, if you please.' The paper was pinned to the carpet, which vanished and returned in the flash of an eye.

Then another paper was written ordering the carpet to take the egg somewhere where it wouldn't be hatched for another two thousand years. The Phoenix tore itself away from its cherished egg, which it watched with yearning tenderness till, the paper being pinned on, the carpet hastily rolled itself up round the egg, and both vanished for ever from the nursery of the house in Camden Town.

'Oh, dear! oh, dear! oh, dear!' said everybody.

'Bear up,' said the bird; 'do you think *I* don't suffer, being parted from my precious new-laid egg like this? Come, conquer your emotions and build my fire.'

'OH!' cried Robert, suddenly, and wholly breaking down, 'I can't BEAR you to go!'

The Phoenix perched on his shoulder and rubbed its beak softly against his ear.

'The sorrows of youth soon appear but as dreams,' it said. 'Farewell, Robert of my heart. I have loved you well.'

The fire had burnt to a red glow. One by one the spices and sweet woods were laid on it. Some smelt nice and some—the caraway seeds and the Violettes de Parme sachet among them—smelt worse than you would think possible.

'Farewell, farewell, farewell, farewell!' said the Phoenix, in a far-away voice.

'Oh, GOOD-BYE,' said everyone, and now all were in tears.

The bright bird fluttered seven times round the room and settled in the hot heart of the fire. The sweet gums and spices and woods flared and flickered around it, but its golden feathers did not burn. It seemed to grow red-hot to the very inside heart of it—and then before the eight eyes of its friends it fell together, a heap of white ashes, and the flames of the cedar pencils and the sandal-wood box met and joined above it.

'Whatever have you done with the carpet?' asked mother next day.

'We gave it to some one who wanted it very much. The name began with a P,' said Jane.

The others instantly hushed her.

'Oh, well, it wasn't worth twopence,' said mother.

'The person who began with P said we shouldn't lose by it,' Jane went on before she could be stopped.

'I daresay!' said mother, laughing.

But that very night a great box came, addressed to the children by all their names. Eliza never could remember the name of the carrier who brought it. It wasn't Carter Paterson or the Parcels Delivery.

It was instantly opened. It was a big wooden box, and it had to be opened with a hammer and the kitchen poker; the long nails came squeaking out, and boards scrunched as they were wrenched off. Inside the box was soft paper, with beautiful Chinese patterns on it—blue and green and red and violet. And under the paper—well, almost everything lovely that you can think of. Everything of reasonable size, I mean; for, of course, there were no motors or flying machines or thoroughbred chargers. But there really was almost everything else. Everything that the children had always wanted—toys and games and books, and chocolate and candied cherries and paint-boxes and photographic cameras, and all the presents they had always wanted to give to father and mother and the Lamb, only they had never had the money for them. At the very bottom of the box was a tiny golden feather. No one saw it but Robert, and he picked it up and hid it in the breast of his jacket, which had been so often the nesting-place of the golden bird. When he went to bed the feather was gone. It was the last he ever saw of the Phoenix.

Pinned to the lovely fur cloak that mother had always wanted was a paper, and it said—

'In return for the carpet. With gratitude.—P.'

You may guess how father and mother talked it over. They decided at last the person who had had the carpet, and whom, curiously enough, the children were quite unable to describe, must be an insane millionaire who amused himself by playing at being a rag-and-bone man. But the children knew better.

They knew that this was the fulfilment, by the powerful Psammead, of the last wish of the Phoenix, and that this glorious and delightful boxful of treasures was really the very, very, very end of the Phoenix and the Carpet.

THE STORY OF THE AMULET

CHAPTER 1. THE PSAMMEAD

There were once four children who spent their summer holidays in a white house, happily situated between a sandpit and a chalkpit. One day they had the good fortune to find in the sandpit a strange creature. Its eyes were on long horns like snail's eyes, and it could move them in and out like telescopes. It had ears like a bat's ears, and its tubby body was shaped like a spider's and covered with thick soft fur—and it had hands and feet like a monkey's. It told the children—whose names were Cyril, Robert, Anthea, and Jane—that it was a Psammead or sand-fairy. (Psammead is pronounced Sammy-ad.) It was old, old, old, and its birthday was almost at the very beginning of everything. And it had been buried in the sand for thousands of years. But it still kept its fairylikeness, and part of this fairylikeness was its power to give people whatever they wished for. You know fairies have always been able to do this. Cyril, Robert, Anthea, and Jane now found their wishes come true; but, somehow, they never could think of just the right things to wish for, and their wishes sometimes turned out very oddly indeed. In the end their unwise wishings landed them in what Robert called 'a very tight place indeed', and the Psammead consented to help them out of it in return for their promise never never to ask it to grant them any more wishes, and never to tell anyone about it, because it did not want to be bothered to give wishes to anyone ever any more. At the moment of parting Jane said politely—

'I wish we were going to see you again someday.'

And the Psammead, touched by this friendly thought, granted the wish. The book about all this is called Five Children and It, and it ends up in a most tiresome way by saying—

'The children DID see the Psammead again, but it was not in the sandpit; it was—but I must say no more—'

The reason that nothing more could be said was that I had not then been able to find out exactly when and where the children met the Psammead again. Of course I knew they would meet it, because it was a beast of its word, and when it said a thing would happen, that thing happened without fail. How different from the people who tell us about what weather it is going to be on Thursday next, in London, the South Coast, and Channel!

The summer holidays during which the Psammead had been found and the wishes given had been wonderful holidays in the country, and the children had the highest hopes of just such another holiday for the next summer. The winter holidays were beguiled by the wonderful happenings of The Phoenix and the Carpet, and the loss of these two treasures would have left the children in despair, but for the splendid hope of their next holiday in the country. The world, they felt, and indeed had some reason to feel, was full of wonderful things—and they were really the sort of people that wonderful things happen to. So they looked forward to the summer holiday; but when it came everything was different, and very, very horrid. Father had to go out to Manchuria to telegraph news about the war to the tiresome paper he wrote for—the Daily Bellower, or something like that, was its name. And Mother, poor dear Mother, was away in Madeira, because she had been very ill. And The Lamb—I mean the baby—was with her. And Aunt Emma, who was Mother's sister, had suddenly married Uncle Reginald, who was Father's brother, and they had gone to China, which is much too far off for you to expect to be asked to spend the holidays in, however fond your aunt and uncle may be of you. So the children were left in the care of old Nurse, who lived in Fitzroy Street, near the British Museum, and though she was always very kind to them, and indeed spoiled them far more than would be good for the most grown-up of us, the four children felt perfectly wretched, and when the cab had driven off with Father and all his boxes and guns and the sheepskin, with blankets and the aluminium mess-kit inside it, the stoutest heart quailed, and the girls broke down altogether, and sobbed in each other's arms, while the boys each looked out of one of the long gloomy windows of the parlour, and tried to pretend that no boy would be such a muff as to cry.

I hope you notice that they were not cowardly enough to cry till their Father had gone; they knew he had quite enough to upset him without that. But when he was gone everyone felt as if it had been trying not to cry all its life, and that it must cry now, if it died for it. So they cried.

Tea—with shrimps and watercress—cheered them a little. The watercress was arranged in a hedge round a fat glass salt-cellar, a tasteful device they had never seen before. But it was not a cheerful meal.

After tea Anthea went up to the room that had been Father's, and when she saw how dreadfully he wasn't there, and remembered how every minute was taking him further and further from her, and nearer and nearer to the guns of the Russians, she cried a little more. Then she thought of Mother, ill and alone, and perhaps at that very moment wanting a little girl to put eau-de-cologne on her head, and make her sudden cups of tea, and she cried more than ever. And then she remembered what Mother had said, the night before she went away, about Anthea being the eldest girl, and about trying to make the others happy, and things like that. So she stopped crying, and thought instead. And when she had thought as long as she could bear she washed her face and combed her hair, and went down to the others, trying her best to look as though crying were an exercise she had never even heard of.

She found the parlour in deepest gloom, hardly relieved at all by the efforts of Robert, who, to make the time pass, was pulling Jane's hair—not hard, but just enough to tease.

'Look here,' said Anthea. 'Let's have a palaver.' This word dated from the awful day when Cyril had carelessly wished that there were Red Indians in England—and there had been. The word brought back memories of last summer holidays and everyone groaned; they thought of the white house with the beautiful tangled garden—late roses, asters, marigold, sweet mignonette, and feathery asparagus—of the wilderness which someone had once meant to make into an orchard, but which was now, as Father said, 'five acres of thistles haunted by the ghosts of baby cherry-trees'. They thought of the view across the valley, where the lime-kilns

363

looked like Aladdin's palaces in the sunshine, and they thought of their own sandpit, with its fringe of yellowy grasses and pale-stringy-stalked wild flowers, and the little holes in the cliff that were the little sand-martins' little front doors. And they thought of the free fresh air smelling of thyme and sweetbriar, and the scent of the wood-smoke from the cottages in the lane—and they looked round old Nurse's stuffy parlour, and Jane said—

'Oh, how different it all is!'

It was. Old Nurse had been in the habit of letting lodgings, till Father gave her the children to take care of. And her rooms were furnished 'for letting'. Now it is a very odd thing that no one ever seems to furnish a room 'for letting' in a bit the same way as one would furnish it for living in. This room had heavy dark red stuff curtains—the colour that blood would not make a stain on—with coarse lace curtains inside. The carpet was yellow, and violet, with bits of grey and brown oilcloth in odd places. The fireplace had shavings and tinsel in it. There was a very varnished mahogany chiffonier, or sideboard, with a lock that wouldn't act. There were hard chairs—far too many of them—with crochet antimacassars slipping off their seats, all of which sloped the wrong way. The table wore a cloth of a cruel green colour with a yellow chain-stitch pattern round it. Over the fireplace was a looking-glass that made you look much uglier than you really were, however plain you might be to begin with. Then there was a mantelboard with maroon plush and wool fringe that did not match the plush; a dreary clock like a black marble tomb—it was silent as the grave too, for it had long since forgotten how to tick. And there were painted glass vases that never had any flowers in, and a painted tambourine that no one ever played, and painted brackets with nothing on them.

> 'And maple-framed engravings of the Queen, the Houses of
> Parliament, the Plains of Heaven, and of a blunt-nosed
> woodman's flat return.'

There were two books—last December's Bradshaw, and an odd volume of Plumridge's Commentary on Thessalonians. There were—but I cannot dwell longer on this painful picture. It was indeed, as Jane said, very different.

'Let's have a palaver,' said Anthea again.

'What about?' said Cyril, yawning.

'There's nothing to have ANYTHING about,' said Robert kicking the leg of the table miserably.

'I don't want to play,' said Jane, and her tone was grumpy.

Anthea tried very hard not to be cross. She succeeded.

'Look here,' she said, 'don't think I want to be preachy or a beast in any way, but I want to what Father calls define the situation. Do you agree?'

'Fire ahead,' said Cyril without enthusiasm.

'Well then. We all know the reason we're staying here is because Nurse couldn't leave her house on account of the poor learned gentleman on the top-floor. And there was no one else Father could entrust to take care of us—and you know it's taken a lot of money, Mother's going to Madeira to be made well.'

Jane sniffed miserably.

'Yes, I know,' said Anthea in a hurry, 'but don't let's think about how horrid it all is. I mean we can't go to things that cost a lot, but we must do SOMETHING. And I know there are heaps of things you can see in London without paying for them, and I thought we'd go and see them. We are all quite old now, and we haven't got The Lamb—'

Jane sniffed harder than before.

'I mean no one can say "No" because of him, dear pet. And I thought we MUST get Nurse to see how quite old we are, and let us go out by ourselves, or else we shall never have any sort of a time at all. And I vote we see everything there is, and let's begin by asking Nurse to give us some bits of bread and we'll go to St

James's Park. There are ducks there, I know, we can feed them. Only we must make Nurse let us go by ourselves.'

'Hurrah for liberty!' said Robert, 'but she won't.'

'Yes she will,' said Jane unexpectedly. '*I* thought about that this morning, and I asked Father, and he said yes; and what's more he told old Nurse we might, only he said we must always say where we wanted to go, and if it was right she would let us.'

'Three cheers for thoughtful Jane,' cried Cyril, now roused at last from his yawning despair. 'I say, let's go now.'

So they went, old Nurse only begging them to be careful of crossings, and to ask a policeman to assist in the more difficult cases. But they were used to crossings, for they had lived in Camden Town and knew the Kentish Town Road where the trams rush up and down like mad at all hours of the day and night, and seem as though, if anything, they would rather run over you than not.

They had promised to be home by dark, but it was July, so dark would be very late indeed, and long past bedtime.

They started to walk to St James's Park, and all their pockets were stuffed with bits of bread and the crusts of toast, to feed the ducks with. They started, I repeat, but they never got there.

Between Fitzroy Street and St James's Park there are a great many streets, and, if you go the right way you will pass a great many shops that you cannot possibly help stopping to look at. The children stopped to look at several with gold-lace and beads and pictures and jewellery and dresses, and hats, and oysters and lobsters in their windows, and their sorrow did not seem nearly so impossible to bear as it had done in the best parlour at No. 300, Fitzroy Street.

Presently, by some wonderful chance turn of Robert's (who had been voted Captain because the girls thought it would be good for him—and indeed he thought so himself—and of course Cyril couldn't vote against him because it would have looked like a mean jealousy), they came into the little interesting criss-crossy streets that held the most interesting shops of all—the shops where live things were sold. There was one shop window entirely filled with cages, and all sorts of beautiful birds in them. The children were delighted till they remembered how they had once wished for wings themselves, and had had them—and then they felt how desperately unhappy anything with wings must be if it is shut up in a cage and not allowed to fly.

'It must be fairly beastly to be a bird in a cage,' said Cyril. 'Come on!'

They went on, and Cyril tried to think out a scheme for making his fortune as a gold-digger at Klondyke, and then buying all the caged birds in the world and setting them free. Then they came to a shop that sold cats, but the cats were in cages, and the children could not help wishing someone would buy all the cats and put them on hearthrugs, which are the proper places for cats. And there was the dog-shop, and that was not a happy thing to look at either, because all the dogs were chained or caged, and all the dogs, big and little, looked at the four children with sad wistful eyes and wagged beseeching tails as if they were trying to say, 'Buy me! buy me! buy me! and let me go for a walk with you; oh, do buy me, and buy my poor brothers too! Do! do! do!' They almost said, 'Do! do! do!' plain to the ear, as they whined; all but one big Irish terrier, and he growled when Jane patted him.

'Grrrrr,' he seemed to say, as he looked at them from the back corner of his eye—'YOU won't buy me. Nobody will—ever—I shall die chained up—and I don't know that I care how soon it is, either!'

I don't know that the children would have understood all this, only once they had been in a besieged castle, so they knew how hateful it is to be kept in when you want to get out.

Of course they could not buy any of the dogs. They did, indeed, ask the price of the very, very smallest, and it was sixty-five pounds—but that was because it was a Japanese toy spaniel like the Queen once had her portrait painted with, when she was only

Princess of Wales. But the children thought, if the smallest was all that money, the biggest would run into thousands—so they went on.

And they did not stop at any more cat or dog or bird shops, but passed them by, and at last they came to a shop that seemed as though it only sold creatures that did not much mind where they were—such as goldfish and white mice, and sea-anemones and other aquarium beasts, and lizards and toads, and hedgehogs and tortoises, and tame rabbits and guinea-pigs. And there they stopped for a long time, and fed the guinea-pigs with bits of bread through the cage-bars, and wondered whether it would be possible to keep a sandy-coloured double-lop in the basement of the house in Fitzroy Street.

'I don't suppose old Nurse would mind VERY much,' said Jane. 'Rabbits are most awfully tame sometimes. I expect it would know her voice and follow her all about.'

'She'd tumble over it twenty times a day,' said Cyril; 'now a snake—'

'There aren't any snakes, said Robert hastily, 'and besides, I never could cotton to snakes somehow—I wonder why.'

'Worms are as bad,' said Anthea, 'and eels and slugs—I think it's because we don't like things that haven't got legs.'

'Father says snakes have got legs hidden away inside of them,' said Robert.

'Yes—and he says WE'VE got tails hidden away inside us—but it doesn't either of it come to anything REALLY,' said Anthea. 'I hate things that haven't any legs.'

'It's worse when they have too many,' said Jane with a shudder, 'think of centipedes!'

They stood there on the pavement, a cause of some inconvenience to the passersby, and thus beguiled the time with conversation. Cyril was leaning his elbow on the top of a hutch that had seemed empty when they had inspected the whole edifice of hutches one by one, and he was trying to reawaken the interest of a hedgehog that had curled itself into a ball earlier in the interview, when a small, soft voice just below his elbow said, quietly, plainly and quite unmistakably—not in any squeak or whine that had to be translated—but in downright common English—

'Buy me—do—please buy me!'

Cyril started as though he had been pinched, and jumped a yard away from the hutch.

'Come back—oh, come back!' said the voice, rather louder but still softly; 'stoop down and pretend to be tying up your bootlace—I see it's undone, as usual.'

Cyril mechanically obeyed. He knelt on one knee on the dry, hot dusty pavement, peered into the darkness of the hutch and found himself face to face with—the Psammead!

It seemed much thinner than when he had last seen it. It was dusty and dirty, and its fur was untidy and ragged. It had hunched itself up into a miserable lump, and its long snail's eyes were drawn in quite tight so that they hardly showed at all.

'Listen,' said the Psammead, in a voice that sounded as though it would begin to cry in a minute, 'I don't think the creature who keeps this shop will ask a very high price for me. I've bitten him more than once, and I've made myself look as common as I can. He's never had a glance from my beautiful, beautiful eyes. Tell the others I'm here—but tell them to look at some of those low, common beasts while I'm talking to you. The creature inside mustn't think you care much about me, or he'll put a price upon me far, far beyond your means. I remember in the dear old days last summer you never had much money. Oh—I never thought I should be so glad to see you—I never did.' It sniffed, and shot out its long snail's eyes expressly to drop a tear well away from its fur. 'Tell the others I'm here, and then I'll tell you exactly what to do about buying me.' Cyril tied his bootlace into a hard knot, stood up and addressed the others in firm tones—

'Look here,' he said, 'I'm not kidding—and I appeal to your honour,' an appeal which in this family was never made in vain. 'Don't look at that hutch—look at the white rat. Now you are not to look at that hutch whatever I say.'

He stood in front of it to prevent mistakes.

'Now get yourselves ready for a great surprise. In that hutch there's an old friend of ours—DON'T look!—Yes; it's the Psammead, the good old Psammead! it wants us to buy it. It says you're not to look at it. Look at the white rat and count your money! On your honour don't look!'

The others responded nobly. They looked at the white rat till they quite stared him out of countenance, so that he went and sat up on his hind legs in a far corner and hid his eyes with his front paws, and pretended he was washing his face.

Cyril stooped again, busying himself with the other bootlace and listened for the Psammead's further instructions.

'Go in,' said the Psammead, 'and ask the price of lots of other things. Then say, "What do you want for that monkey that's lost its tail—the mangy old thing in the third hutch from the end." Oh—don't mind MY feelings—call me a mangy monkey—I've tried hard enough to look like one! I don't think he'll put a high price on me—I've bitten him eleven times since I came here the day before yesterday. If he names a bigger price than you can afford, say you wish you had the money.'

'But you can't give us wishes. I've promised never to have another wish from you,' said the bewildered Cyril.

'Don't be a silly little idiot,' said the Sand-fairy in trembling but affectionate tones, 'but find out how much money you've got between you, and do exactly what I tell you.'

Cyril, pointing a stiff and unmeaning finger at the white rat, so as to pretend that its charms alone employed his tongue, explained matters to the others, while the Psammead hunched itself, and bunched itself, and did its very best to make itself look uninteresting. Then the four children filed into the shop.

'How much do you want for that white rat?' asked Cyril.

'Eightpence,' was the answer.

'And the guinea-pigs?'

'Eighteenpence to five bob, according to the breed.'

'And the lizards?'

'Ninepence each.'

'And toads?'

'Fourpence. Now look here,' said the greasy owner of all this caged life with a sudden ferocity which made the whole party back hurriedly on to the wainscoting of hutches with which the shop was lined. 'Lookee here. I ain't agoin' to have you a comin' in here a turnin' the whole place outer winder, an' prizing every animile in the stock just for your larks, so don't think it! If you're a buyer, BE a buyer—but I never had a customer yet as wanted to buy mice, and lizards, and toads, and guineas all at once. So hout you goes.'

'Oh! wait a minute,' said the wretched Cyril, feeling how foolishly yet well-meaningly he had carried out the Psammead's instructions. 'Just tell me one thing. What do you want for the mangy old monkey in the third hutch from the end?'

The shopman only saw in this a new insult.

'Mangy young monkey yourself,' said he; 'get along with your blooming cheek. Hout you goes!'

'Oh! don't be so cross,' said Jane, losing her head altogether, 'don't you see he really DOES want to know THAT!'

'Ho! does 'e indeed,' sneered the merchant. Then he scratched his ear suspiciously, for he was a sharp business man, and he knew the ring of truth when he heard it. His hand was bandaged, and three minutes before he would have been glad to sell the 'mangy old monkey' for ten shillings. Now—'Ho! 'e does, does 'e,' he said, 'then two pun ten's my price. He's not got his fellow that monkey ain't, nor yet his match, not this side of the equator, which he comes from. And the only one ever seen in London. Ought to be in the Zoo. Two pun ten, down on the nail, or hout you goes!'

The children looked at each other—twenty-three shillings and fivepence was all they had in the world, and it would have been merely three and fivepence, but for the sovereign which Father had given to them 'between them' at parting. 'We've only twenty-three shillings and fivepence,' said Cyril, rattling the money in his pocket.

'Twenty-three farthings and somebody's own cheek,' said the dealer, for he did not believe that Cyril had so much money.

There was a miserable pause. Then Anthea remembered, and said—

'Oh! I WISH I had two pounds ten.'

'So do I, Miss, I'm sure,' said the man with bitter politeness; 'I wish you 'ad, I'm sure!'

Anthea's hand was on the counter, something seemed to slide under it. She lifted it. There lay five bright half sovereigns.

'Why, I HAVE got it after all,' she said; 'here's the money, now let's have the Sammy,... the monkey I mean.'

The dealer looked hard at the money, but he made haste to put it in his pocket.

'I only hope you come by it honest,' he said, shrugging his shoulders. He scratched his ear again.

'Well!' he said, 'I suppose I must let you have it, but it's worth thribble the money, so it is—'

He slowly led the way out to the hutch—opened the door gingerly, and made a sudden fierce grab at the Psammead, which the Psammead acknowledged in one last long lingering bite.

372

'Here, take the brute,' said the shopman, squeezing the Psammead so tight that he nearly choked it. 'It's bit me to the marrow, it have.'

The man's eyes opened as Anthea held out her arms.

'Don't blame me if it tears your face off its bones,' he said, and the Psammead made a leap from his dirty horny hands, and Anthea caught it in hers, which were not very clean, certainly, but at any rate were soft and pink, and held it kindly and closely.

'But you can't take it home like that,' Cyril said, 'we shall have a crowd after us,' and indeed two errand boys and a policeman had already collected.

'I can't give you nothink only a paper-bag, like what we put the tortoises in,' said the man grudgingly.

So the whole party went into the shop, and the shopman's eyes nearly came out of his head when, having given Anthea the largest paper-bag he could find, he saw her hold it open, and the Psammead carefully creep into it. 'Well!' he said, 'if that there don't beat cockfighting! But p'raps you've met the brute afore.'

'Yes,' said Cyril affably, 'he's an old friend of ours.'

'If I'd a known that,' the man rejoined, 'you shouldn't a had him under twice the money. 'Owever,' he added, as the children disappeared, 'I ain't done so bad, seeing as I only give five bob for the beast. But then there's the bites to take into account!'

The children trembling in agitation and excitement, carried home the Psammead, trembling in its paper-bag.

When they got it home, Anthea nursed it, and stroked it, and would have cried over it, if she hadn't remembered how it hated to be wet.

When it recovered enough to speak, it said—

'Get me sand; silver sand from the oil and colour shop. And get me plenty.'

They got the sand, and they put it and the Psammead in the round bath together, and it rubbed itself, and rolled itself, and shook itself and scraped itself, and scratched itself, and preened itself, till it felt clean and comfy, and then it scrabbled a hasty hole in the sand, and went to sleep in it.

The children hid the bath under the girls' bed, and had supper. Old Nurse had got them a lovely supper of bread and butter and fried onions. She was full of kind and delicate thoughts.

When Anthea woke the next morning, the Psammead was snuggling down between her shoulder and Jane's.

'You have saved my life,' it said. 'I know that man would have thrown cold water on me sooner or later, and then I should have died. I saw him wash out a guinea-pig's hutch yesterday morning. I'm still frightfully sleepy, I think I'll go back to sand for another nap. Wake the boys and this dormouse of a Jane, and when you've had your breakfasts we'll have a talk.'

'Don't YOU want any breakfast?' asked Anthea.

'I daresay I shall pick a bit presently,' it said; 'but sand is all I care about—it's meat and drink to me, and coals and fire and wife and children.' With these words it clambered down by the bedclothes and scrambled back into the bath, where they heard it scratching itself out of sight.

'Well!' said Anthea, 'anyhow our holidays won't be dull NOW. We've found the Psammead again.'

'No,' said Jane, beginning to put on her stockings. 'We shan't be dull—but it'll be only like having a pet dog now it can't give us wishes.'

'Oh, don't be so discontented,' said Anthea. 'If it can't do anything else it can tell us about Megatheriums and things.'

CHAPTER 2. THE HALF AMULET

Long ago—that is to say last summer—the children, finding themselves embarrassed by some wish which the Psammead had granted them, and which the servants had not received in a proper spirit, had wished that the servants might not notice the gifts which the Psammead gave. And when they parted from the Psammead their last wish had been that they should meet it again. Therefore they HAD met it (and it was jolly lucky for the Psammead, as Robert pointed out). Now, of course, you see that the Psammead's being where it was, was the consequence of one of their wishes, and therefore was a Psammead-wish, and as such could not be noticed by the servants. And it was soon plain that in the Psammead's opinion old Nurse was still a servant, although she had now a house of her own, for she never noticed the Psammead at all. And that was as well, for she would never have consented to allow the girls to keep an animal and a bath of sand under their bed.

When breakfast had been cleared away—it was a very nice breakfast with hot rolls to it, a luxury quite out of the common way—Anthea went and dragged out the bath, and woke the Psammead.

It stretched and shook itself.

'You must have bolted your breakfast most unwholesomely,' it said, 'you can't have been five minutes over it.'

'We've been nearly an hour,' said Anthea. 'Come—you know you promised.'

'Now look here,' said the Psammead, sitting back on the sand and shooting out its long eyes suddenly, 'we'd better begin as we mean to go on. It won't do to have any misunderstanding, so I tell you plainly that—'

'Oh, PLEASE,' Anthea pleaded, 'do wait till we get to the others. They'll think it most awfully sneakish of me to talk to you without them; do come down, there's a dear.'

She knelt before the sand-bath and held out her arms. The Psammead must have remembered how glad it had been to jump into those same little arms only the day before, for it gave a little grudging grunt, and jumped once more.

Anthea wrapped it in her pinafore and carried it downstairs. It was welcomed in a thrilling silence. At last Anthea said, 'Now then!'

'What place is this?' asked the Psammead, shooting its eyes out and turning them slowly round.

'It's a sitting-room, of course,' said Robert.

'Then I don't like it,' said the Psammead.

'Never mind,' said Anthea kindly; 'we'll take you anywhere you like if you want us to. What was it you were going to say upstairs when I said the others wouldn't like it if I stayed talking to you without them?'

It looked keenly at her, and she blushed.

'Don't be silly,' it said sharply. 'Of course, it's quite natural that you should like your brothers and sisters to know exactly how good and unselfish you were.'

'I wish you wouldn't,' said Jane. 'Anthea was quite right. What was it you were going to say when she stopped you?'

'I'll tell you,' said the Psammead, 'since you're so anxious to know. I was going to say this. You've saved my life—and I'm not ungrateful—but it doesn't change your nature or mine. You're still very ignorant, and rather silly, and I am worth a thousand of you any day of the week.'

'Of course you are!' Anthea was beginning but it interrupted her.

'It's very rude to interrupt,' it said; 'what I mean is that I'm not going to stand any nonsense, and if you think what you've done is to give you the right to pet me or make me demean myself by playing with you, you'll find out that what you think doesn't matter a single penny. See? It's what *I* think that matters.'

'I know,' said Cyril, 'it always was, if you remember.'

'Well,' said the Psammead, 'then that's settled. We're to be treated as we deserve. I with respect, and all of you with—but I don't wish to be offensive. Do you want me to tell you how I got into that horrible den you bought me out of? Oh, I'm not ungrateful! I haven't forgotten it and I shan't forget it.'

'Do tell us,' said Anthea. 'I know you're awfully clever, but even with all your cleverness, I don't believe you can possibly know how—how respectfully we do respect you. Don't we?'

The others all said yes—and fidgeted in their chairs. Robert spoke the wishes of all when he said—

'I do wish you'd go on.' So it sat up on the green-covered table and went on.

'When you'd gone away,' it said, 'I went to sand for a bit, and slept. I was tired out with all your silly wishes, and I felt as though I hadn't really been to sand for a year.'

'To sand?' Jane repeated.

'Where I sleep. You go to bed. I go to sand.'

Jane yawned; the mention of bed made her feel sleepy.

'All right,' said the Psammead, in offended tones. 'I'm sure *I* don't want to tell you a long tale. A man caught me, and I bit him. And he put me in a bag with a dead hare and a dead rabbit. And he took me to his house and put me out of the bag into a basket with holes that I could see through. And I bit him again. And then he brought me to this city, which I am told is called the Modern Babylon—though it's not a bit like the old Babylon—and he sold me to the man you bought me from, and then I bit them both. Now, what's your news?'

'There's not quite so much biting in our story,' said Cyril regretfully; 'in fact, there isn't any. Father's gone to Manchuria, and Mother and The Lamb have gone to Madeira because Mother was ill, and don't I just wish that they were both safe home again.'

Merely from habit, the Sand-fairy began to blow itself out, but it stopped short suddenly.

'I forgot,' it said; 'I can't give you any more wishes.'

'No—but look here,' said Cyril, 'couldn't we call in old Nurse and get her to say SHE wishes they were safe home. I'm sure she does.'

'No go,' said the Psammead. 'It's just the same as your wishing yourself if you get some one else to wish for you. It won't act.'

'But it did yesterday—with the man in the shop,' said Robert.

'Ah yes,' said the creature, 'but you didn't ASK him to wish, and you didn't know what would happen if he did. That can't be done again. It's played out.'

'Then you can't help us at all,' said Jane; 'oh—I did think you could do something; I've been thinking about it ever since we saved your life yesterday. I thought you'd be certain to be able to fetch back Father, even if you couldn't manage Mother.'

And Jane began to cry.

'Now DON'T,' said the Psammead hastily; 'you know how it always upsets me if you cry. I can't feel safe a moment. Look here; you must have some new kind of charm.'

'That's easier said than done.'

'Not a bit of it,' said the creature; 'there's one of the strongest charms in the world not a stone's throw from where you bought me yesterday. The man that I bit so—the first one, I mean—went into a shop to ask how much something cost—I think he said it was a concertina—and while he was telling the man in the shop how much too much he wanted for it, I saw the charm in a sort of tray, with a lot of other things. If you can only buy THAT, you will be able to have your heart's desire.'

The children looked at each other and then at the Psammead. Then Cyril coughed awkwardly and took sudden courage to say what everyone was thinking.

'I do hope you won't be waxy,' he said; 'but it's like this: when you used to give us our wishes they almost always got us into some row or other, and we used to think you wouldn't have been pleased if they hadn't. Now, about this charm—we haven't got over and above too much tin, and if we blue it all on this charm and it turns out to be not up to much—well—you see what I'm driving at, don't you?'

'I see that YOU don't see more than the length of your nose, and THAT'S not far,' said the Psammead crossly. 'Look here, I HAD to give you the wishes, and of course they turned out badly, in a sort of way, because you hadn't the sense to wish for what was good for you. But this charm's quite different. I haven't GOT to do this for you, it's just my own generous kindness that makes me tell you about it. So it's bound to be all right. See?'

'Don't be cross,' said Anthea, 'Please, PLEASE don't. You see, it's all we've got; we shan't have any more pocket-money till Daddy comes home—unless he sends us some in a letter. But we DO trust you. And I say all of you,' she went on, 'don't you think it's worth spending ALL the money, if there's even the chanciest chance of getting Father and Mother back safe NOW? Just think of it! Oh, do let's!'

'*I* don't care what you do,' said the Psammead; 'I'll go back to sand again till you've made up your minds.'

'No, don't!' said everybody; and Jane added, 'We are quite mind made-up—don't you see we are? Let's get our hats. Will you come with us?'

'Of course,' said the Psammead; 'how else would you find the shop?'

So everybody got its hat. The Psammead was put into a flat bass-bag that had come from Farringdon Market with two pounds of filleted plaice in it. Now it contained about three pounds and a quarter of solid Psammead, and the children took it in turns to carry it.

'It's not half the weight of The Lamb,' Robert said, and the girls sighed.

The Psammead poked a wary eye out of the top of the basket every now and then, and told the children which turnings to take.

'How on earth do you know?' asked Robert. 'I can't think how you do it.'

And the Psammead said sharply, 'No—I don't suppose you can.'

At last they came to THE shop. It had all sorts and kinds of things in the window—concertinas, and silk handkerchiefs, china vases and tea-cups, blue Japanese jars, pipes, swords, pistols, lace collars, silver spoons tied up in half-dozens, and wedding-rings in a red lacquered basin. There were officers' epaulets and doctors' lancets. There were tea-caddies inlaid with red turtle-shell and brass curly-wurlies, plates of different kinds of money, and stacks of different kinds of plates. There was a beautiful picture of a little girl washing a dog, which Jane liked very much. And in the middle of the window there was a dirty silver tray full of mother-of-pearl card counters, old seals, paste buckles, snuff-boxes, and all sorts of little dingy odds and ends.

The Psammead put its head quite out of the fish-basket to look in the window, when Cyril said—

'There's a tray there with rubbish in it.'

And then its long snail's eyes saw something that made them stretch out so much that they were as long and thin as new slate-pencils. Its fur bristled thickly, and its voice was quite hoarse with excitement as it whispered—

'That's it! That's it! There, under that blue and yellow buckle, you can see a bit sticking out. It's red. Do you see?'

'Is it that thing something like a horse-shoe?' asked Cyril. 'And red, like the common sealing-wax you do up parcels with?' 'Yes, that's it,' said the Psammead. 'Now, you do just as you did before. Ask the price of other things. That blue buckle would do. Then the man will get the tray out of the window. I think you'd better be the one,' it said to Anthea. 'We'll wait out here.'

So the others flattened their noses against the shop window, and presently a large, dirty, short-fingered hand with a very big diamond ring came stretching through the green half-curtains at the back of the shop window and took away the tray.

They could not see what was happening in the interview between Anthea and the Diamond Ring, and it seemed to them that she had had time—if she had had money—to buy everything in the shop before the moment came when she stood before them, her face wreathed in grins, as Cyril said later, and in her hand the charm.

It was something like this: [Drawing omitted.] and it was made of a red, smooth, softly shiny stone.

'I've got it,' Anthea whispered, just opening her hand to give the others a glimpse of it. 'Do let's get home. We can't stand here like stuck-pigs looking at it in the street.'

So home they went. The parlour in Fitzroy Street was a very flat background to magic happenings. Down in the country among the flowers and green fields anything had seemed—and indeed had been—possible. But it was hard to believe that anything really wonderful could happen so near the Tottenham Court Road. But the Psammead was there—and it in itself was wonderful. And it could talk—and it had shown them where a charm could be bought that would make the owner of it perfectly happy. So the four children hurried home, taking very long steps, with their chins stuck out, and their mouths shut very tight indeed. They went so fast that the Psammead was quite shaken about in its fish-bag, but it did not say anything—perhaps for fear of attracting public notice.

They got home at last, very hot indeed, and set the Psammead on the green tablecloth.

'Now then!' said Cyril.

But the Psammead had to have a plate of sand fetched for it, for it was quite faint. When it had refreshed itself a little it said—

'Now then! Let me see the charm,' and Anthea laid it on the green table-cover. The Psammead shot out his long eyes to look at it, then it turned them reproachfully on Anthea and said—

'But there's only half of it here!'

This was indeed a blow.

'It was all there was,' said Anthea, with timid firmness. She knew it was not her fault. 'There should be another piece,' said the Psammead, 'and a sort of pin to fasten the two together.'

'Isn't half any good?'—'Won't it work without the other bit?'—'It cost seven-and-six.'—'Oh, bother, bother, bother!'—'Don't be silly little idiots!' said everyone and the Psammead altogether.

Then there was a wretched silence. Cyril broke it—

'What shall we do?'

'Go back to the shop and see if they haven't got the other half,' said the Psammead. 'I'll go to sand till you come back. Cheer up! Even the bit you've got is SOME good, but it'll be no end of a bother if you can't find the other.'

So Cyril went to the shop. And the Psammead to sand. And the other three went to dinner, which was now ready. And old Nurse was very cross that Cyril was not ready too.

The three were watching at the windows when Cyril returned, and even before he was near enough for them to see his face there was something about the slouch of his shoulders and set of his knickerbockers and the way he dragged his boots along that showed but too plainly that his errand had been in vain.

'Well?' they all said, hoping against hope on the front-door step.

'No go,' Cyril answered; 'the man said the thing was perfect. He said it was a Roman lady's locket, and people shouldn't buy curios if they didn't know anything about arky—something or other, and that he never went back on a bargain, because it wasn't business, and he expected his customers to act the same. He was simply nasty—that's what he was, and I want my dinner.'

It was plain that Cyril was not pleased.

The unlikeliness of anything really interesting happening in that parlour lay like a weight of lead on everyone's spirits. Cyril had his dinner, and just as he was swallowing the last mouthful of apple-pudding there was a scratch at the door. Anthea opened it and in walked the Psammead.

'Well,' it said, when it had heard the news, 'things might be worse. Only you won't be surprised if you have a few adventures before you get the other half. You want to get it, of course.'

'Rather,' was the general reply. 'And we don't mind adventures.'

'No,' said the Psammead, 'I seem to remember that about you. Well, sit down and listen with all your ears. Eight, are there? Right—I am glad you know arithmetic. Now pay attention, because I don't intend to tell you everything twice over.'

As the children settled themselves on the floor—it was far more comfortable than the chairs, as well as more polite to the Psammead, who was stroking its whiskers on the hearth-rug—a sudden cold pain caught at Anthea's heart. Father—Mother—the darling Lamb—all far away. Then a warm, comfortable feeling flowed through her. The Psammead was here, and at least half a charm, and there were to be adventures. (If you don't know what a cold pain is, I am glad for your sakes, and I hope you never may.)

'Now,' said the Psammead cheerily, 'you are not particularly nice, nor particularly clever, and you're not at all good-looking. Still, you've saved my life—oh, when I think of that man and his pail of water!—so I'll tell you all I know. At least, of course I can't do that, because I know far too much. But I'll tell you all I know about this red thing.'

'Do! Do! Do! Do!' said everyone.

'Well, then,' said the Psammead. 'This thing is half of an Amulet that can do all sorts of things; it can make the corn grow, and the waters flow, and the trees bear fruit, and the little new beautiful babies come. (Not that babies ARE beautiful, of course,' it broke off to say, 'but their mothers think they are—and as long as you think a thing's true it IS true as far as you're concerned.)'

Robert yawned.

The Psammead went on.

'The complete Amulet can keep off all the things that make people unhappy—jealousy, bad temper, pride, disagreeableness, greediness, selfishness, laziness. Evil spirits, people called them when the Amulet was made. Don't you think it would be nice to have it?'

'Very,' said the children, quite without enthusiasm.

'And it can give you strength and courage.'

'That's better,' said Cyril.

'And virtue.'

'I suppose it's nice to have that,' said Jane, but not with much interest.

'And it can give you your heart's desire.'

'Now you're talking,' said Robert.

'Of course I am,' retorted the Psammead tartly, 'so there's no need for you to.'

'Heart's desire is good enough for me,' said Cyril.

'Yes, but,' Anthea ventured, 'all that's what the WHOLE charm can do. There's something that the half we've got can win off its own bat—isn't there?' She appealed to the Psammead. It nodded.

'Yes,' it said; 'the half has the power to take you anywhere you like to look for the other half.'

This seemed a brilliant prospect till Robert asked—

'Does it know where to look?'

The Psammead shook its head and answered, 'I don't think it's likely.'

'Do you?'

'No.'

'Then,' said Robert, 'we might as well look for a needle in a bottle of hay. Yes—it IS bottle, and not bundle, Father said so.'

'Not at all,' said the Psammead briskly-, 'you think you know everything, but you are quite mistaken. The first thing is to get the thing to talk.'

'Can it?' Jane questioned. Jane's question did not mean that she thought it couldn't, for in spite of the parlour furniture the feeling of magic was growing deeper and thicker, and seemed to fill the room like a dream of a scented fog.

'Of course it can. I suppose you can read.'

'Oh yes!' Everyone was rather hurt at the question.

'Well, then—all you've got to do is to read the name that's written on the part of the charm that you've got. And as soon as you say the name out loud the thing will have power to do—well, several things.'

There was a silence. The red charm was passed from hand to hand.

'There's no name on it,' said Cyril at last.

'Nonsense,' said the Psammead; 'what's that?'

'Oh, THAT!' said Cyril, 'it's not reading. It looks like pictures of chickens and snakes and things.'

This was what was on the charm: [Hieroglyphics omitted.]

'I've no patience with you,' said the Psammead; 'if you can't read you must find some one who can. A priest now?'

'We don't know any priests,' said Anthea; 'we know a clergyman—he's called a priest in the prayer-book, you know—but he only knows Greek and Latin and Hebrew, and this isn't any of those—I know.'

The Psammead stamped a furry foot angrily.

'I wish I'd never seen you,' it said; 'you aren't any more good than so many stone images. Not so much, if I'm to tell the truth. Is there no wise man in your Babylon who can pronounce the names of the Great Ones?'

'There's a poor learned gentleman upstairs,' said Anthea, 'we might try him. He has a lot of stone images in his room, and iron-looking ones too—we peeped in once when he was out. Old Nurse says he doesn't eat enough to keep a canary alive. He spends it all on stones and things.'

'Try him,' said the Psammead, 'only be careful. If he knows a greater name than this and uses it against you, your charm will be of no use. Bind him first with the chains of honour and upright dealing. And then ask his aid—oh, yes, you'd better all go; you can put me to sand as you go upstairs. I must have a few minutes' peace and quietness.'

So the four children hastily washed their hands and brushed their hair—this was Anthea's idea—and went up to knock at the door of the 'poor learned gentleman', and to 'bind him with the chains of honour and upright dealing'.

CHAPTER 3. THE PAST

The learned gentleman had let his dinner get quite cold. It was mutton chop, and as it lay on the plate it looked like a brown island in the middle of a frozen pond, because the grease of the gravy had become cold, and consequently white. It looked very nasty, and it was the first thing the children saw when, after knocking three times and receiving no reply, one of them ventured to turn the handle and softly to open the door. The chop was on the end of a long table that ran down one side of the room. The table had images on it and queer-shaped stones, and books. And there were glass cases fixed against the wall behind, with little strange things in them. The cases were rather like the ones you see in jewellers' shops.

The 'poor learned gentleman' was sitting at a table in the window, looking at something very small which he held in a pair of fine pincers. He had a round spy-glass sort of thing in one eye—which reminded the children of watchmakers, and also of the long snail's eyes of the Psammead. The gentleman was very long and thin, and his long, thin boots stuck out under the other side of his table. He did not hear the door open, and the children stood hesitating. At last Robert gave the door a push, and they all started back, for in the middle of the wall that the door had hidden was a mummy-case—very, very, very big—painted in red and yellow and green and black, and the face of it seemed to look at them quite angrily.

You know what a mummy-case is like, of course? If you don't you had better go to the British Museum at once and find out. Anyway, it is not at all the sort of thing that you expect to meet in a top-floor front in Bloomsbury, looking as though it would like to know what business YOU had there.

So everyone said, 'Oh!' rather loud, and their boots clattered as they stumbled back.

The learned gentleman took the glass out of his eye and said—'I beg your pardon,' in a very soft, quiet pleasant voice—the voice of a gentleman who has been to Oxford.

'It's us that beg yours,' said Cyril politely. 'We are sorry to disturb you.'

'Come in,' said the gentleman, rising—with the most distinguished courtesy, Anthea told herself. 'I am delighted to see you. Won't you sit down? No, not there; allow me to move that papyrus.'

He cleared a chair, and stood smiling and looking kindly through his large, round spectacles.

'He treats us like grown-ups,' whispered Robert, 'and he doesn't seem to know how many of us there are.'

'Hush,' said Anthea, 'it isn't manners to whisper. You say, Cyril—go ahead.'

'We're very sorry to disturb you,' said Cyril politely, 'but we did knock three times, and you didn't say "Come in", or "Run away now", or that you couldn't be bothered just now, or to come when you weren't so busy, or any of the things people do say when you knock at doors, so we opened it. We knew you were in because we heard you sneeze while we were waiting.'

'Not at all,' said the gentleman; 'do sit down.'

'He has found out there are four of us,' said Robert, as the gentleman cleared three more chairs. He put the things off them carefully on the floor. The first chair had things like bricks that tiny, tiny birds' feet have walked over when the bricks were soft, only the marks were in regular lines. The second chair had round things on it like very large, fat, long, pale beads. And the last chair had a pile of dusty papers on it. The children sat down.

'We know you are very, very learned,' said Cyril, 'and we have got a charm, and we want you to read the name on it, because it isn't in Latin or Greek, or Hebrew, or any of the languages WE know—'

'A thorough knowledge of even those languages is a very fair foundation on which to build an education,' said the gentleman politely.

'Oh!' said Cyril blushing, 'but we only know them to look at, except Latin—and I'm only in Caesar with that.' The gentleman took off his spectacles and laughed. His laugh sounded rusty, Cyril thought, as though it wasn't often used.

'Of course!' he said. 'I'm sure I beg your pardon. I think I must have been in a dream. You are the children who live downstairs, are you not? Yes. I have seen you as I have passed in and out. And you have found something that you think to be an antiquity, and you've brought it to show me? That was very kind. I should like to inspect it.'

'I'm afraid we didn't think about your liking to inspect it,' said the truthful Anthea. 'It was just for US because we wanted to know the name on it—'

'Oh, yes—and, I say,' Robert interjected, 'you won't think it rude of us if we ask you first, before we show it, to be bound in the what-do-you-call-it of—'

'In the bonds of honour and upright dealing,' said Anthea.

'I'm afraid I don't quite follow you,' said the gentleman, with gentle nervousness.

'Well, it's this way,' said Cyril. 'We've got part of a charm. And the Sammy—I mean, something told us it would work, though it's only half a one; but it won't work unless we can say the name that's on it. But, of course, if you've got another name that can lick ours, our charm will be no go; so we want you to give us your word of honour as a gentleman—though I'm sure, now I've seen you, that it's not necessary; but still I've promised to ask you, so we must. Will you please give us your honourable word not to say any name stronger than the name on our charm?'

The gentleman had put on his spectacles again and was looking at Cyril through them. He now said: 'Bless me!' more than once, adding, 'Who told you all this?'

'I can't tell you,' said Cyril. 'I'm very sorry, but I can't.'

Some faint memory of a far-off childhood must have come to the learned gentleman just then, for he smiled. 'I see,' he said. 'It is some sort of game that you are engaged in? Of course! Yes! Well, I will certainly promise. Yet I wonder how you heard of the names of power?'

'We can't tell you that either,' said Cyril; and Anthea said, 'Here is our charm,' and held it out.

With politeness, but without interest, the gentleman took it. But after the first glance all his body suddenly stiffened, as a pointer's does when he sees a partridge.

'Excuse me,' he said in quite a changed voice, and carried the charm to the window. He looked at it; he turned it over. He fixed his spy-glass in his eye and looked again. No one said anything. Only Robert made a shuffling noise with his feet till Anthea nudged him to shut up. At last the learned gentleman drew a long breath.

'Where did you find this?' he asked.

'We didn't find it. We bought it at a shop. Jacob Absalom the name is—not far from Charing Cross,' said Cyril.

'We gave seven-and-sixpence for it,' added Jane.

'It is not for sale, I suppose? You do not wish to part with it?

I ought to tell you that it is extremely valuable—extraordinarily valuable, I may say.'

'Yes,' said Cyril, 'we know that, so of course we want to keep it.'

'Keep it carefully, then,' said the gentleman impressively; 'and if ever you should wish to part with it, may I ask you to give me the refusal of it?'

'The refusal?'

'I mean, do not sell it to anyone else until you have given me the opportunity of buying it.'

'All right,' said Cyril, 'we won't. But we don't want to sell it. We want to make it do things.'

'I suppose you can play at that as well as at anything else,' said the gentleman; 'but I'm afraid the days of magic are over.'

'They aren't REALLY,' said Anthea earnestly. 'You'd see they aren't if I could tell you about our last summer holidays. Only I mustn't. Thank you very much. And can you read the name?'

'Yes, I can read it.'

'Will you tell it us?' 'The name,' said the gentleman, 'is Ur Hekau Setcheh.'

'Ur Hekau Setcheh,' repeated Cyril. 'Thanks awfully. I do hope we haven't taken up too much of your time.'

'Not at all,' said the gentleman. 'And do let me entreat you to be very, very careful of that most valuable specimen.'

They said 'Thank you' in all the different polite ways they could think of, and filed out of the door and down the stairs. Anthea was last. Half-way down to the first landing she turned and ran up again.

The door was still open, and the learned gentleman and the mummy-case were standing opposite to each other, and both looked as though they had stood like that for years.

The gentleman started when Anthea put her hand on his arm.

'I hope you won't be cross and say it's not my business,' she said, 'but do look at your chop! Don't you think you ought to eat it?

391

Father forgets his dinner sometimes when he's writing, and Mother always says I ought to remind him if she's not at home to do it herself, because it's so bad to miss your regular meals.

So I thought perhaps you wouldn't mind my reminding you, because you don't seem to have anyone else to do it.'

She glanced at the mummy-case; IT certainly did not look as though it would ever think of reminding people of their meals.

The learned gentleman looked at her for a moment before he said—

'Thank you, my dear. It was a kindly thought. No, I haven't anyone to remind me about things like that.'

He sighed, and looked at the chop.

'It looks very nasty,' said Anthea.

'Yes,' he said, 'it does. I'll eat it immediately, before I forget.'

As he ate it he sighed more than once. Perhaps because the chop was nasty, perhaps because he longed for the charm which the children did not want to sell, perhaps because it was so long since anyone cared whether he ate his chops or forgot them.

Anthea caught the others at the stair-foot. They woke the Psammead, and it taught them exactly how to use the word of power, and to make the charm speak. I am not going to tell you how this is done, because you might try to do it. And for you any such trying would be almost sure to end in disappointment. Because in the first place it is a thousand million to one against your ever getting hold of the right sort of charm, and if you did, there would be hardly any chance at all of your finding a learned gentleman clever enough and kind enough to read the word for you.

The children and the Psammead crouched in a circle on the floor—in the girls' bedroom, because in the parlour they might have been interrupted by old Nurse's coming in to lay the cloth for tea—and the charm was put in the middle of the circle.

392

The sun shone splendidly outside, and the room was very light. Through the open window came the hum and rattle of London, and in the street below they could hear the voice of the milkman.

When all was ready, the Psammead signed to Anthea to say the word. And she said it. Instantly the whole light of all the world seemed to go out. The room was dark. The world outside was dark—darker than the darkest night that ever was. And all the sounds went out too, so that there was a silence deeper than any silence you have ever even dreamed of imagining. It was like being suddenly deaf and blind, only darker and quieter even than that.

But before the children had got over the sudden shock of it enough to be frightened, a faint, beautiful light began to show in the middle of the circle, and at the same moment a faint, beautiful voice began to speak. The light was too small for one to see anything by, and the voice was too small for you to hear what it said. You could just see the light and just hear the voice.

But the light grew stronger. It was greeny, like glow-worms' lamps, and it grew and grew till it was as though thousands and thousands of glow-worms were signalling to their winged sweethearts from the middle of the circle. And the voice grew, not so much in loudness as in sweetness (though it grew louder, too), till it was so sweet that you wanted to cry with pleasure just at the sound of it. It was like nightingales, and the sea, and the fiddle, and the voice of your mother when you have been a long time away, and she meets you at the door when you get home.

And the voice said—

'Speak. What is it that you would hear?'

I cannot tell you what language the voice used. I only know that everyone present understood it perfectly. If you come to think of it, there must be some language that everyone could understand, if we only knew what it was. Nor can I tell you how the charm spoke, nor whether it was the charm that spoke, or some presence in the charm. The children could not have told you either. Indeed, they could not look at the charm while it was speaking, because the light was too bright. They looked instead at the green radiance on the faded Kidderminster carpet at the edge of the circle. They all felt very quiet, and not inclined to ask questions or fidget with their feet. For this was not like the things that had happened in the country when the Psammead had given them their wishes. That had been funny somehow, and this was not. It was something like Arabian Nights magic, and something like being in church. No one cared to speak.

It was Cyril who said at last—

'Please we want to know where the other half of the charm is.'

'The part of the Amulet which is lost,' said the beautiful voice, 'was broken and ground into the dust of the shrine that held it. It and the pin that joined the two halves are themselves dust, and the dust is scattered over many lands and sunk in many seas.'

'Oh, I say!' murmured Robert, and a blank silence fell. 'Then it's all up?' said Cyril at last; 'it's no use our looking for a thing that's smashed into dust, and the dust scattered all over the place.'

'If you would find it,' said the voice, 'You must seek it where it still is, perfect as ever.'

'I don't understand,' said Cyril.

'In the Past you may find it,' said the voice.

'I wish we MAY find it,' said Cyril.

The Psammead whispered crossly, 'Don't you understand? The thing existed in the Past. If you were in the Past, too, you could find it. It's very difficult to make you understand things. Time and space are only forms of thought.'

'I see,' said Cyril.

'No, you don't,' said the Psammead, 'and it doesn't matter if you don't, either. What I mean is that if you were only made the right way, you could see everything happening in the same place at the same time. Now do you see?'

394

'I'm afraid *I* don't,' said Anthea; 'I'm sorry I'm so stupid.'

'Well, at any rate, you see this. That lost half of the Amulet is in the Past. Therefore it's in the Past we must look for it. I mustn't speak to the charm myself. Ask it things! Find out!'

'Where can we find the other part of you?' asked Cyril obediently.

'In the Past,' said the voice.

'What part of the Past?'

'I may not tell you. If you will choose a time, I will take you to the place that then held it. You yourselves must find it.'

'When did you see it last?' asked Anthea—'I mean, when was it taken away from you?'

The beautiful voice answered—

'That was thousands of years ago. The Amulet was perfect then, and lay in a shrine, the last of many shrines, and I worked wonders. Then came strange men with strange weapons and destroyed my shrine, and the Amulet they bore away with many captives. But of these, one, my priest, knew the word of power, and spoke it for me, so that the Amulet became invisible, and thus returned to my shrine, but the shrine was broken down, and ere any magic could rebuild it one spoke a word before which my power bowed down and was still. And the Amulet lay there, still perfect, but enslaved. Then one coming with stones to rebuild the shrine, dropped a hewn stone on the Amulet as it lay, and one half was sundered from the other. I had no power to seek for that which was lost. And there being none to speak the word of power, I could not rejoin it. So the Amulet lay in the dust of the desert many thousand years, and at last came a small man, a conqueror with an army, and after him a crowd of men who sought to seem wise, and one of these found half the Amulet and brought it to this land. But none could read the name. So I lay still. And this man dying and his son after him, the Amulet was sold by those who came after to a merchant, and from

395

him you bought it, and it is here, and now, the name of power having been spoken, I also am here.'

This is what the voice said. I think it must have meant Napoleon by the small man, the conqueror. Because I know I have been told that he took an army to Egypt, and that afterwards a lot of wise people went grubbing in the sand, and fished up all sorts of wonderful things, older than you would think possible. And of these I believe this charm to have been one, and the most wonderful one of all.

Everyone listened: and everyone tried to think. It is not easy to do this clearly when you have been listening to the kind of talk I have told you about.

At last Robert said—

'Can you take us into the Past—to the shrine where you and the other thing were together. If you could take us there, we might find the other part still there after all these thousands of years.'

'Still there? silly!' said Cyril. 'Don't you see, if we go back into the Past it won't be thousands of years ago. It will be NOW for us—won't it?' He appealed to the Psammead, who said—

'You're not so far off the idea as you usually are!'

'Well,' said Anthea, 'will you take us back to when there was a shrine and you were safe in it—all of you?'

'Yes,' said the voice. 'You must hold me up, and speak the word of power, and one by one, beginning with the first-born, you shall pass through me into the Past. But let the last that passes be the one that holds me, and let him not lose his hold, lest you lose me, and so remain in the Past for ever.'

'That's a nasty idea,' said Robert.

'When you desire to return,' the beautiful voice went on, 'hold me up towards the East, and speak the word. Then, passing through me, you shall return to this time and it shall be the present to you.'

'But how—' A bell rang loudly.

'Oh crikey!' exclaimed Robert, 'that's tea! Will you please make it proper daylight again so that we can go down. And thank you so much for all your kindness.'

'We've enjoyed ourselves very much indeed, thank you!' added Anthea politely.

The beautiful light faded slowly. The great darkness and silence came and these suddenly changed to the dazzlement of day and the great soft, rustling sound of London, that is like some vast beast turning over in its sleep.

The children rubbed their eyes, the Psammead ran quickly to its sandy bath, and the others went down to tea. And until the cups were actually filled tea seemed less real than the beautiful voice and the greeny light.

After tea Anthea persuaded the others to allow her to hang the charm round her neck with a piece of string.

'It would be so awful if it got lost,' she said: 'it might get lost anywhere, you know, and it would be rather beastly for us to have to stay in the Past for ever and ever, wouldn't it?'

CHAPTER 4. EIGHT THOUSAND YEARS AGO

Next morning Anthea got old Nurse to allow her to take up the 'poor learned gentleman's' breakfast. He did not recognize her at first, but when he did he was vaguely pleased to see her.

'You see I'm wearing the charm round my neck,' she said; 'I'm taking care of it—like you told us to.'

'That's right,' said he; 'did you have a good game last night?'

'You will eat your breakfast before it's cold, won't you?' said Anthea. 'Yes, we had a splendid time. The charm made it all dark, and then greeny light, and then it spoke. Oh! I wish you could have heard it—it was such a darling voice—and it told us the other half of it was lost in the Past, so of course we shall have to look for it there!'

The learned gentleman rubbed his hair with both hands and looked anxiously at Anthea.

'I suppose it's natural—youthful imagination and so forth,' he said. 'Yet someone must have... Who told you that some part of the charm was missing?'

'I can't tell you,' she said. 'I know it seems most awfully rude, especially after being so kind about telling us the name of power, and all that, but really, I'm not allowed to tell anybody anything about the—the—the person who told me. You won't forget your breakfast, will you?'

The learned gentleman smiled feebly and then frowned—not a cross-frown, but a puzzle-frown.

'Thank you,' he said, 'I shall always be pleased if you'll look in—any time you're passing you know—at least...'

'I will,' she said; 'goodbye. I'll always tell you anything I MAY tell.'

He had not had many adventures with children in them, and he wondered whether all children were like these. He spent quite five minutes in wondering before he settled down to the fifty-second chapter of his great book on 'The Secret Rites of the Priests of Amen Ra'.

It is no use to pretend that the children did not feel a good deal of agitation at the thought of going through the charm into the Past. That idea, that perhaps they might stay in the Past and never get back again, was anything but pleasing. Yet no one would have dared to suggest that the charm should not be used; and though each was in its heart very frightened indeed, they would all have joined in jeering at the cowardice of any one of them who should have uttered the timid but natural suggestion, 'Don't let's!'

It seemed necessary to make arrangements for being out all day, for there was no reason to suppose that the sound of the dinner-bell would be able to reach back into the Past, and it seemed unwise to excite old Nurse's curiosity when nothing they could say—not even the truth—could in any way satisfy it. They were all very proud to think how well they had understood what the charm and the Psammead had said about Time and Space and things like that, and they were perfectly certain that it would be quite impossible to make old Nurse understand a single word of it. So they merely asked her to let them take their dinner out into Regent's Park—and this, with the implied cold mutton and tomatoes, was readily granted.

'You can get yourselves some buns or sponge-cakes, or whatever you fancy-like,' said old Nurse, giving Cyril a shilling. 'Don't go getting jam-tarts, now—so messy at the best of times, and without forks and plates ruination to your clothes, besides your not being able to wash your hands and faces afterwards.'

So Cyril took the shilling, and they all started off. They went round by the Tottenham Court Road to buy a piece of waterproof sheeting to put over the Psammead in case it should be raining in the Past when they got there. For it is almost certain death to a Psammead to get wet.

The sun was shining very brightly, and even London looked pretty. Women were selling roses from big baskets-full, and Anthea bought four roses, one each, for herself and the others. They were red roses and smelt of summer—the kind of roses you always want so desperately at about Christmas-time when you can only get mistletoe, which is pale right through to its very scent, and holly which pricks your nose if you try to smell it. So now everyone had a rose in its buttonhole, and soon everyone was sitting on the grass in Regent's Park under trees whose leaves would have been clean, clear green in the country, but here were dusty and yellowish, and brown at the edges.

'We've got to go on with it,' said Anthea, 'and as the eldest has to go first, you'll have to be last, Jane. You quite understand about holding on to the charm as you go through, don't you, Pussy?'

'I wish I hadn't got to be last,' said Jane.

'You shall carry the Psammead if you like,' said Anthea. 'That is,' she added, remembering the beast's queer temper, 'if it'll let you.'

The Psammead, however, was unexpectedly amiable.

'*I* don't mind,' it said, 'who carries me, so long as it doesn't drop me. I can't bear being dropped.'

Jane with trembling hands took the Psammead and its fish-basket under one arm. The charm's long string was hung round her neck. Then they all stood up. Jane held out the charm at arm's length, and Cyril solemnly pronounced the word of power.

As he spoke it the charm grew tall and broad, and he saw that Jane was just holding on to the edge of a great red arch of very curious shape. The opening of the arch was small, but Cyril saw that he could go through it. All round and beyond the arch were the faded trees and trampled grass of Regent's Park, where the little ragged children were playing Ring-o'-Roses. But through the opening of it shone a blaze of blue and yellow and red. Cyril drew a long breath and stiffened his legs so that the others should not see that his knees were trembling and almost knocking together. 'Here goes!' he said, and, stepping up through the arch, disappeared. Then followed Anthea. Robert, coming next, held fast, at Anthea's suggestion, to the sleeve of Jane, who was thus dragged safely through the arch. And as soon as they were on the other side of the arch there was no more arch at all and no more Regent's Park either, only the charm in Jane's hand, and it was its proper size again. They were now in a light so bright that they winked and blinked and rubbed their eyes. During this dazzling interval Anthea felt for the charm and pushed it inside Jane's frock, so that it might be quite safe. When their eyes got used to the new wonderful light the children looked around them. The sky was very, very blue, and it sparkled and glittered and dazzled like the sea at home when the sun shines on it.

They were standing on a little clearing in a thick, low forest; there were trees and shrubs and a close, thorny, tangly undergrowth. In front of them stretched a bank of strange black mud, then came the browny-yellowy shining ribbon of a river. Then more dry, caked mud and more greeny-browny jungle. The only things that told that human people had been there were the clearing, a path that led to it, and an odd arrangement of cut reeds in the river.

They looked at each other.

'Well!' said Robert, 'this IS a change of air!'

It was. The air was hotter than they could have imagined, even in London in August.

'I wish I knew where we were,' said Cyril.

'Here's a river, now—I wonder whether it's the Amazon or the Tiber, or what.'

'It's the Nile,' said the Psammead, looking out of the fish-bag.

'Then this is Egypt,' said Robert, who had once taken a geography prize.

'I don't see any crocodiles,' Cyril objected. His prize had been for natural history.

The Psammead reached out a hairy arm from its basket and pointed to a heap of mud at the edge of the water.

'What do you call that?' it said; and as it spoke the heap of mud slid into the river just as a slab of damp mixed mortar will slip from a bricklayer's trowel.

'Oh!' said everybody.

There was a crashing among the reeds on the other side of the water.

'And there's a river-horse!' said the Psammead, as a great beast like an enormous slaty-blue slug showed itself against the black bank on the far side of the stream.

'It's a hippopotamus,' said Cyril; 'it seems much more real somehow than the one at the Zoo, doesn't it?'

'I'm glad it's being real on the other side of the river,' said Jane. And now there was a crackling of reeds and twigs behind them. This was horrible. Of course it might be another hippopotamus, or a crocodile, or a lion—or, in fact, almost anything.

'Keep your hand on the charm, Jane,' said Robert hastily. 'We ought to have a means of escape handy. I'm dead certain this is the sort of place where simply anything might happen to us.'

'I believe a hippopotamus is going to happen to us,' said Jane—'a very, very big one.'

They had all turned to face the danger.

'Don't be silly little duffers,' said the Psammead in its friendly, informal way; 'it's not a river-horse. It's a human.'

It was. It was a girl—of about Anthea's age. Her hair was short and fair, and though her skin was tanned by the sun, you could see that it would have been fair too if it had had a chance. She had every chance of being tanned, for she had no clothes to speak of, and the four English children, carefully dressed in frocks, hats, shoes, stockings, coats, collars, and all the rest of it, envied her more than any words of theirs or of mine could possibly say. There was no doubt that here was the right costume for that climate.

She carried a pot on her head, of red and black earthenware. She did not see the children, who shrank back against the edge of the jungle, and she went forward to the brink of the river to fill her pitcher. As she went she made a strange sort of droning, humming, melancholy noise all on two notes. Anthea could not help thinking that perhaps the girl thought this noise was singing.

The girl filled the pitcher and set it down by the river bank. Then she waded into the water and stooped over the circle of cut reeds. She pulled half a dozen fine fish out of the water within the reeds, killing each as she took it out, and threading it on a long osier that she carried. Then she knotted the osier, hung it on her arm, picked up the pitcher, and turned to come back. And as she turned she saw the four children. The white dresses of Jane and Anthea stood out like snow against the dark forest background. She screamed and the pitcher fell, and the water was spilled out over the hard mud surface and over the fish, which had fallen too. Then the water slowly trickled away into the deep cracks.

'Don't be frightened,' Anthea cried, 'we won't hurt you.'

'Who are you?' said the girl.

Now, once for all, I am not going to be bothered to tell you how it was that the girl could understand Anthea and Anthea could understand the girl. YOU, at any rate, would not understand ME, if I tried to explain it, any more than you can understand about time and space being only forms of thought. You may think what you like. Perhaps the children had found out the universal language which everyone can understand, and which wise men so far have not found. You will have noticed long ago that they were singularly lucky children, and they may have had this piece of luck as well as others. Or it may have been that... but why pursue the question further? The fact remains that in all their adventures the muddle-headed inventions which we call foreign languages never bothered them in the least. They could always understand and be understood. If you can explain this, please do. I daresay I could understand your explanation, though you could never understand mine.

So when the girl said, 'Who are you?' everyone understood at once, and Anthea replied—

'We are children—just like you. Don't be frightened. Won't you show us where you live?'

Jane put her face right into the Psammead's basket, and burrowed her mouth into its fur to whisper—

403

'Is it safe? Won't they eat us? Are they cannibals?'

The Psammead shrugged its fur.

'Don't make your voice buzz like that, it tickles my ears,' it said rather crossly. 'You can always get back to Regent's Park in time if you keep fast hold of the charm,' it said.

The strange girl was trembling with fright.

Anthea had a bangle on her arm. It was a sevenpenny-halfpenny trumpery thing that pretended to be silver; it had a glass heart of turquoise blue hanging from it, and it was the gift of the maid-of-all-work at the Fitzroy Street house. 'Here,' said Anthea, 'this is for you. That is to show we will not hurt you. And if you take it I shall know that you won't hurt us.'

The girl held out her hand. Anthea slid the bangle over it, and the girl's face lighted up with the joy of possession.

'Come,' she said, looking lovingly at the bangle; 'it is peace between your house and mine.'

She picked up her fish and pitcher and led the way up the narrow path by which she had come and the others followed.

'This is something like!' said Cyril, trying to be brave.

'Yes!' said Robert, also assuming a boldness he was far from feeling, 'this really and truly IS an adventure! Its being in the Past makes it quite different from the Phoenix and Carpet happenings.'

The belt of thick-growing acacia trees and shrubs—mostly prickly and unpleasant-looking—seemed about half a mile across. The path was narrow and the wood dark. At last, ahead, daylight shone through the boughs and leaves.

The whole party suddenly came out of the wood's shadow into the glare of the sunlight that shone on a great stretch of yellow sand, dotted with heaps of grey rocks where spiky cactus plants showed gaudy crimson and pink flowers among their shabby, sand-peppered leaves. Away to the right was something that looked like a grey-brown hedge, and from beyond it blue smoke went up to the bluer sky. And over all the sun shone till you could hardly bear your clothes.

'That is where I live,' said the girl pointing.

'I won't go,' whispered Jane into the basket, 'unless you say it's all right.'

The Psammead ought to have been touched by this proof of confidence. Perhaps, however, it looked upon it as a proof of doubt, for it merely snarled—

'If you don't go now I'll never help you again.'

'OH,' whispered Anthea, 'dear Jane, don't! Think of Father and Mother and all of us getting our heart's desire. And we can go back any minute. Come on!'

'Besides,' said Cyril, in a low voice, 'the Psammead must know there's no danger or it wouldn't go. It's not so over and above brave itself. Come on!'

This Jane at last consented to do.

As they got nearer to the browny fence they saw that it was a great hedge about eight feet high, made of piled-up thorn bushes.

'What's that for?' asked Cyril.

'To keep out foes and wild beasts,' said the girl.

'I should think it ought to, too,' said he. 'Why, some of the thorns are as long as my foot.'

There was an opening in the hedge, and they followed the girl through it. A little way further on was another hedge, not so high, also of dry thorn bushes, very prickly and spiteful-looking, and within this was a sort of village of huts.

There were no gardens and no roads. Just huts built of wood and twigs and clay, and roofed with great palm-leaves, dumped down anywhere. The doors of these houses were very low, like the doors of dog-kennels. The ground between them was not paths or streets, but just yellow sand trampled very hard and smooth.

In the middle of the village there was a hedge that enclosed what seemed to be a piece of ground about as big as their own garden in Camden Town.

No sooner were the children well within the inner thorn hedge than dozens of men and women and children came crowding round from behind and inside the huts.

The girl stood protectingly in front of the four children, and said—

'They are wonder-children from beyond the desert. They bring marvellous gifts, and I have said that it is peace between us and them.'

She held out her arm with the Lowther Arcade bangle on it.

The children from London, where nothing now surprises anyone, had never before seen so many people look so astonished.

They crowded round the children, touching their clothes, their shoes, the buttons on the boys' jackets, and the coral of the girls' necklaces.

'Do say something,' whispered Anthea.

'We come,' said Cyril, with some dim remembrance of a dreadful day when he had had to wait in an outer office while his father interviewed a solicitor, and there had been nothing to read but the Daily Telegraph—'we come from the world where the sun never sets. And peace with honour is what we want. We are the great Anglo-Saxon or conquering race. Not that we want to conquer YOU,' he added hastily. 'We only want to look at your houses and your—well, at all you've got here, and then we shall return to our own place, and tell of all that we have seen so that your name may be famed.'

Cyril's speech didn't keep the crowd from pressing round and looking as eagerly as ever at the clothing of the children. Anthea had an idea that these people had never seen woven stuff before, and she saw how wonderful and strange it must seem to people who had never had any clothes but the skins of beasts. The sewing, too, of modern clothes seemed to astonish them very much. They must have been able to sew themselves, by the way, for men who seemed to be the chiefs wore knickerbockers of goat-skin or deerskin, fastened round the waist with twisted strips of hide. And the women wore long skimpy skirts of animals' skins. The people were not very tall, their hair was fair, and men and women both had it short. Their eyes were blue, and that seemed odd in Egypt. Most of them were tattooed like sailors, only more roughly.

'What is this? What is this?' they kept asking touching the children's clothes curiously.

Anthea hastily took off Jane's frilly lace collar and handed it to the woman who seemed most friendly.

'Take this,' she said, 'and look at it. And leave us alone. We want to talk among ourselves.'

She spoke in the tone of authority which she had always found successful when she had not time to coax her baby brother to do as he was told. The tone was just as successful now. The children were left together and the crowd retreated. It paused a dozen yards away to look at the lace collar and to go on talking as hard as it could.

The children will never know what those people said, though they knew well enough that they, the four strangers, were the subject of the talk. They tried to comfort themselves by remembering the girl's promise of friendliness, but of course the thought of the charm was more comfortable than anything else. They sat down on the sand in the shadow of the hedged-round place in the middle of the village, and now for the first time they were able to look about them and to see something more than a crowd of eager, curious faces.

They here noticed that the women wore necklaces made of beads of different coloured stone, and from these hung pendants of odd, strange shapes, and some of them had bracelets of ivory and flint.

'I say,' said Robert, 'what a lot we could teach them if we stayed here!'

'I expect they could teach us something too,' said Cyril. 'Did you notice that flint bracelet the woman had that Anthea gave the collar to? That must have taken some making. Look here, they'll get suspicious if we talk among ourselves, and I do want to know about how they do things. Let's get the girl to show us round, and we can be thinking about how to get the Amulet at the same time. Only mind, we must keep together.'

Anthea beckoned to the girl, who was standing a little way off looking wistfully at them, and she came gladly.

'Tell us how you make the bracelets, the stone ones,' said Cyril.

'With other stones,' said the girl; 'the men make them; we have men of special skill in such work.'

'Haven't you any iron tools?'

'Iron,' said the girl, 'I don't know what you mean.' It was the first word she had not understood.

'Are all your tools of flint?' asked Cyril. 'Of course,' said the girl, opening her eyes wide.

I wish I had time to tell you of that talk. The English children wanted to hear all about this new place, but they also wanted to tell of their own country. It was like when you come back from your holidays and you want to hear and to tell everything at the same time. As the talk went on there were more and more words that the girl could not understand, and the children soon gave up the attempt to explain to her what their own country was like, when they began to see how very few of the things they had always thought they could not do without were really not at all necessary to life.

The girl showed them how the huts were made—indeed, as one was being made that very day she took them to look at it. The way of building was very different from ours. The men stuck long pieces of wood into a piece of ground the size of the hut they wanted to make. These were about eight inches apart; then they put in another row about eight inches away from the first, and then a third row still further out. Then all the space between was filled up with small branches and twigs, and then daubed over with black mud worked with the feet till it was soft and sticky like putty.

The girl told them how the men went hunting with flint spears and arrows, and how they made boats with reeds and clay. Then she explained the reed thing in the river that she had taken the fish out of. It was a fish-trap—just a ring of reeds set up in the water with only one little opening in it, and in this opening, just below the water, were stuck reeds slanting the way of the river's flow, so that the fish, when they had swum sillily in, sillily couldn't get out again. She showed them the clay pots and jars and platters, some of them ornamented with black and red patterns, and the most wonderful things made of flint and different sorts of stone, beads, and ornaments, and tools and weapons of all sorts and kinds.

'It is really wonderful,' said Cyril patronizingly, 'when you consider that it's all eight thousand years ago—'

'I don't understand you,' said the girl.

'It ISN'T eight thousand years ago,' whispered Jane. 'It's NOW—and that's just what I don't like about it. I say, DO let's get home again before anything more happens. You can see for yourselves the charm isn't here.'

'What's in that place in the middle?' asked Anthea, struck by a sudden thought, and pointing to the fence.

'That's the secret sacred place,' said the girl in a whisper. 'No one knows what is there. There are many walls, and inside the insidest one IT is, but no one knows what IT is except the headsmen.'

'I believe YOU know,' said Cyril, looking at her very hard.

'I'll give you this if you'll tell me,' said Anthea taking off a bead-ring which had already been much admired.

'Yes,' said the girl, catching eagerly at the ring. 'My father is one of the heads, and I know a water charm to make him talk in his sleep. And he has spoken. I will tell you. But if they know I have told you they will kill me. In the insidest inside there is a stone box, and in it there is the Amulet. None knows whence it came. It came from very far away.'

'Have you seen it?' asked Anthea.

The girl nodded.

'Is it anything like this?' asked Jane, rashly producing the charm.

The girl's face turned a sickly greenish-white.

'Hide it, hide it,' she whispered. 'You must put it back. If they see it they will kill us all. You for taking it, and me for knowing that there was such a thing. Oh, woe—woe! why did you ever come here?'

'Don't be frightened,' said Cyril. 'They shan't know. Jane, don't you be such a little jack-ape again—that's all. You see what will happen if you do. Now, tell me—' He turned to the girl, but before he had time to speak the question there was a loud shout, and a man bounded in through the opening in the thorn-hedge.

'Many foes are upon us!' he cried. 'Make ready the defences!'

His breath only served for that, and he lay panting on the ground. 'Oh, DO let's go home!' said Jane. 'Look here—I don't care—I WILL!'

She held up the charm. Fortunately all the strange, fair people were too busy to notice HER. She held up the charm. And nothing happened.

'You haven't said the word of power,' said Anthea.

Jane hastily said it—and still nothing happened.

410

'Hold it up towards the East, you silly!' said Robert.

'Which IS the East?' said Jane, dancing about in her agony of terror.

Nobody knew. So they opened the fish-bag to ask the Psammead.

And the bag had only a waterproof sheet in it.

The Psammead was gone.

'Hide the sacred thing! Hide it! Hide it!' whispered the girl.

Cyril shrugged his shoulders, and tried to look as brave as he knew he ought to feel.

'Hide it up, Pussy,' he said. 'We are in for it now. We've just got to stay and see it out.'

CHAPTER 5. THE FIGHT IN THE VILLAGE

Here was a horrible position! Four English children, whose proper date was A.D. 1905, and whose proper address was London, set down in Egypt in the year 6000 B.C. with no means whatever of getting back into their own time and place. They could not find the East, and the sun was of no use at the moment, because some officious person had once explained to Cyril that the sun did not really set in the West at all—nor rise in the East either, for the matter of that.

The Psammead had crept out of the bass-bag when they were not looking and had basely deserted them.

An enemy was approaching. There would be a fight. People get killed in fights, and the idea of taking part in a fight was one that did not appeal to the children.

The man who had brought the news of the enemy still lay panting on the sand. His tongue was hanging out, long and red, like a dog's. The people of the village were hurriedly filling the gaps in the fence with thorn-bushes from the heap that seemed to have been piled there ready for just such a need. They lifted the cluster-thorns with long poles—much as men at home, nowadays, lift hay with a fork.

Jane bit her lip and tried to decide not to cry.

Robert felt in his pocket for a toy pistol and loaded it with a pink paper cap. It was his only weapon.

Cyril tightened his belt two holes.

And Anthea absently took the drooping red roses from the buttonholes of the others, bit the ends of the stalks, and set them in a pot of water that stood in the shadow by a hut door. She was always rather silly about flowers.

'Look here!' she said. 'I think perhaps the Psammead is really arranging something for us. I don't believe it would go away and leave us all alone in the Past. I'm certain it wouldn't.'

Jane succeeded in deciding not to cry—at any rate yet.

'But what can we do?' Robert asked.

'Nothing,' Cyril answered promptly, 'except keep our eyes and ears open. Look! That runner chap's getting his wind. Let's go and hear what he's got to say.'

The runner had risen to his knees and was sitting back on his heels. Now he stood up and spoke. He began by some respectful remarks addressed to the heads of the village. His speech got more interesting when he said—

'I went out in my raft to snare ibises, and I had gone up the stream an hour's journey. Then I set my snares and waited. And I heard the sound of many wings, and looking up, saw many herons circling in the air. And I saw that they were afraid; so I took thought. A beast may scare one heron, coming upon it suddenly,

412

but no beast will scare a whole flock of herons. And still they flew and circled, and would not light. So then I knew that what scared the herons must be men, and men who knew not our ways of going softly so as to take the birds and beasts unawares. By this I knew they were not of our race or of our place. So, leaving my raft, I crept along the river bank, and at last came upon the strangers. They are many as the sands of the desert, and their spear-heads shine red like the sun. They are a terrible people, and their march is towards US. Having seen this, I ran, and did not stay till I was before you.'

'These are YOUR folk,' said the headman, turning suddenly and angrily on Cyril, 'you came as spies for them.'

'We did NOT,' said Cyril indignantly. 'We wouldn't be spies for anything. I'm certain these people aren't a bit like us. Are they now?' he asked the runner.

'No,' was the answer. 'These men's faces were darkened, and their hair black as night. Yet these strange children, maybe, are their gods, who have come before to make ready the way for them.'

A murmur ran through the crowd.

'No, NO,' said Cyril again. 'We are on your side. We will help you to guard your sacred things.'

The headman seemed impressed by the fact that Cyril knew that there WERE sacred things to be guarded. He stood a moment gazing at the children. Then he said—

'It is well. And now let all make offering, that we may be strong in battle.'

The crowd dispersed, and nine men, wearing antelope-skins, grouped themselves in front of the opening in the hedge in the middle of the village. And presently, one by one, the men brought all sorts of things—hippopotamus flesh, ostrich-feathers, the fruit of the date palms, red chalk, green chalk, fish from the river, and ibex from the mountains; and the headman received these gifts. There was another hedge inside the first, about a yard from it, so that there was a lane inside between the hedges. And every now and then one of the headmen would disappear along this lane with full hands and come back with hands empty.

'They're making offerings to their Amulet,' said Anthea. 'We'd better give something too.'

The pockets of the party, hastily explored, yielded a piece of pink tape, a bit of sealing-wax, and part of the Waterbury watch that Robert had not been able to help taking to pieces at Christmas and had never had time to rearrange. Most boys have a watch in this condition. They presented their offerings, and Anthea added the red roses.

The headman who took the things looked at them with awe, especially at the red roses and the Waterbury-watch fragment.

'This is a day of very wondrous happenings,' he said. 'I have no more room in me to be astonished. Our maiden said there was peace between you and us. But for this coming of a foe we should have made sure.'

The children shuddered.

'Now speak. Are you upon our side?'

'YES. Don't I keep telling you we are?' Robert said. 'Look here. I will give you a sign. You see this.' He held out the toy pistol. 'I shall speak to it, and if it answers me you will know that I and the others are come to guard your sacred thing—that we've just made the offerings to.'

'Will that god whose image you hold in your hand speak to you alone, or shall I also hear it?' asked the man cautiously.

'You'll be surprised when you DO hear it,' said Robert. 'Now, then.' He looked at the pistol and said—

'If we are to guard the sacred treasure within'—he pointed to the hedged-in space—'speak with thy loud voice, and we shall obey.'

414

He pulled the trigger, and the cap went off. The noise was loud, for it was a two-shilling pistol, and the caps were excellent.

Every man, woman, and child in the village fell on its face on the sand. The headman who had accepted the test rose first.

'The voice has spoken,' he said. 'Lead them into the ante-room of the sacred thing.'

So now the four children were led in through the opening of the hedge and round the lane till they came to an opening in the inner hedge, and they went through an opening in that, and so passed into another lane.

The thing was built something like this, and all the hedges were of brushwood and thorns: [Drawing of maze omitted.]

'It's like the maze at Hampton Court,' whispered Anthea.

The lanes were all open to the sky, but the little hut in the middle of the maze was round-roofed, and a curtain of skins hung over the doorway.

'Here you may wait,' said their guide, 'but do not dare to pass the curtain.' He himself passed it and disappeared.

'But look here,' whispered Cyril, 'some of us ought to be outside in case the Psammead turns up.'

'Don't let's get separated from each other, whatever we do,' said Anthea. 'It's quite bad enough to be separated from the Psammead. We can't do anything while that man is in there. Let's all go out into the village again. We can come back later now we know the way in. That man'll have to fight like the rest, most likely, if it comes to fighting. If we find the Psammead we'll go straight home.

It must be getting late, and I don't much like this mazy place.'

They went out and told the headman that they would protect the treasure when the fighting began. And now they looked about them and were able to see exactly how a first-class worker in flint flakes and notches an arrow-head or the edge of an axe—an advantage which no other person now alive has ever enjoyed. The boys found the weapons most interesting. The arrow-heads were not on arrows such as you shoot from a bow, but on javelins, for throwing from the hand. The chief weapon was a stone fastened to a rather short stick something like the things gentlemen used to carry about and call life-preservers in the days of the garrotters.

Then there were long things like spears or lances, with flint knives—horribly sharp—and flint battle-axes.

Everyone in the village was so busy that the place was like an ant-heap when you have walked into it by accident. The women were busy and even the children.

Quite suddenly all the air seemed to glow and grow red—it was like the sudden opening of a furnace door, such as you may see at Woolwich Arsenal if you ever have the luck to be taken there—and then almost as suddenly it was as though the furnace doors had been shut. For the sun had set, and it was night.

The sun had that abrupt way of setting in Egypt eight thousand years ago, and I believe it has never been able to break itself of the habit, and sets in exactly the same manner to the present day. The girl brought the skins of wild deer and led the children to a heap of dry sedge.

'My father says they will not attack yet. Sleep!' she said, and it really seemed a good idea. You may think that in the midst of all these dangers the children would not have been able to sleep—but somehow, though they were rather frightened now and then, the feeling was growing in them—deep down and almost hidden away, but still growing—that the Psammead was to be trusted, and that they were really and truly safe. This did not prevent their being quite as much frightened as they could bear to be without being perfectly miserable.

'I suppose we'd better go to sleep,' said Robert. 'I don't know what on earth poor old Nurse will do with us out all night; set the police on our tracks, I expect. I only wish they could find us! A dozen policemen would be rather welcome just now. But it's no use getting into a stew over it,' he added soothingly. 'Good night.'

And they all fell asleep.

They were awakened by long, loud, terrible sounds that seemed to come from everywhere at once—horrible threatening shouts and shrieks and howls that sounded, as Cyril said later, like the voices of men thirsting for their enemies' blood.

'It is the voice of the strange men,' said the girl, coming to them trembling through the dark. 'They have attacked the walls, and the thorns have driven them back. My father says they will not try again till daylight. But they are shouting to frighten us. As though we were savages! Dwellers in the swamps!' she cried indignantly.

All night the terrible noise went on, but when the sun rose, as abruptly as he had set, the sound suddenly ceased.

The children had hardly time to be glad of this before a shower of javelins came hurtling over the great thorn-hedge, and everyone sheltered behind the huts. But next moment another shower of weapons came from the opposite side, and the crowd rushed to other shelter. Cyril pulled out a javelin that had stuck in the roof of the hut beside him. Its head was of brightly burnished copper.

Then the sound of shouting arose again and the crackle of dried thorns. The enemy was breaking down the hedge. All the villagers swarmed to the point whence the crackling and the shouting came; they hurled stones over the hedges, and short arrows with flint heads. The children had never before seen men with the fighting light in their eyes. It was very strange and terrible, and gave you a queer thick feeling in your throat; it was quite different from the pictures of fights in the illustrated papers at home.

It seemed that the shower of stones had driven back the besiegers. The besieged drew breath, but at that moment the shouting and the crackling arose on the opposite side of the village and the crowd hastened to defend that point, and so the fight swayed to and fro across the village, for the besieged had not the sense to divide their forces as their enemies had done.

417

Cyril noticed that every now and then certain of the fighting-men would enter the maze, and come out with brighter faces, a braver aspect, and a more upright carriage.

'I believe they go and touch the Amulet,' he said. 'You know the Psammead said it could make people brave.'

They crept through the maze, and watching they saw that Cyril was right. A headman was standing in front of the skin curtain, and as the warriors came before him he murmured a word they could not hear, and touched their foreheads with something that they could not see. And this something he held in his hands. And through his fingers they saw the gleam of a red stone that they knew.

The fight raged across the thorn-hedge outside. Suddenly there was a loud and bitter cry.

'They're in! They're in! The hedge is down!'

The headman disappeared behind the deer-skin curtain.

'He's gone to hide it,' said Anthea. 'Oh, Psammead dear, how could you leave us!'

Suddenly there was a shriek from inside the hut, and the headman staggered out white with fear and fled out through the maze. The children were as white as he.

'Oh! What is it? What is it?' moaned Anthea. 'Oh, Psammead, how could you! How could you!'

And the sound of the fight sank breathlessly, and swelled fiercely all around. It was like the rising and falling of the waves of the sea.

Anthea shuddered and said again, 'Oh, Psammead, Psammead!'

'Well?' said a brisk voice, and the curtain of skins was lifted at one corner by a furry hand, and out peeped the bat's ears and snail's eyes of the Psammead.

Anthea caught it in her arms and a sigh of desperate relief was breathed by each of the four.

'Oh! which IS the East!' Anthea said, and she spoke hurriedly, for the noise of wild fighting drew nearer and nearer.

'Don't choke me,' said the Psammead, 'come inside.'

The inside of the hut was pitch dark.

'I've got a match,' said Cyril, and struck it. The floor of the hut was of soft, loose sand.

'I've been asleep here,' said the Psammead; 'most comfortable it's been, the best sand I've had for a month. It's all right. Everything's all right. I knew your only chance would be while the fight was going on. That man won't come back. I bit him, and he thinks I'm an Evil Spirit. Now you've only got to take the thing and go.'

The hut was hung with skins. Heaped in the middle were the offerings that had been given the night before, Anthea's roses fading on the top of the heap. At one side of the hut stood a large square stone block, and on it an oblong box of earthenware with strange figures of men and beasts on it.

'Is the thing in there?' asked Cyril, as the Psammead pointed a skinny finger at it.

'You must judge of that,' said the Psammead. 'The man was just going to bury the box in the sand when I jumped out at him and bit him.'

'Light another match, Robert,' said Anthea. 'Now, then quick! which is the East?'

'Why, where the sun rises, of course!'

'But someone told us—'

'Oh! they'll tell you anything!' said the Psammead impatiently, getting into its bass-bag and wrapping itself in its waterproof sheet.

'But we can't see the sun in here, and it isn't rising anyhow,' said Jane.

'How you do waste time!' the Psammead said. 'Why, the East's where the shrine is, of course. THERE!'

It pointed to the great stone.

And still the shouting and the clash of stone on metal sounded nearer and nearer. The children could hear that the headmen had surrounded the hut to protect their treasure as long as might be from the enemy. But none dare to come in after the Psammead's sudden fierce biting of the headman.

'Now, Jane,' said Cyril, very quickly. 'I'll take the Amulet, you stand ready to hold up the charm, and be sure you don't let it go as you come through.'

He made a step forward, but at that instant a great crackling overhead ended in a blaze of sunlight. The roof had been broken in at one side, and great slabs of it were being lifted off by two spears. As the children trembled and winked in the new light, large dark hands tore down the wall, and a dark face, with a blobby fat nose, looked over the gap. Even at that awful moment Anthea had time to think that it was very like the face of Mr Jacob Absalom, who had sold them the charm in the shop near Charing Cross.

'Here is their Amulet,' cried a harsh, strange voice; 'it is this that makes them strong to fight and brave to die. And what else have we here—gods or demons?'

He glared fiercely at the children, and the whites of his eyes were very white indeed. He had a wet, red copper knife in his teeth. There was not a moment to lose.

'Jane, JANE, QUICK!' cried everyone passionately.

Jane with trembling hands held up the charm towards the East, and Cyril spoke the word of power. The Amulet grew to a great arch. Out beyond it was the glaring Egyptian sky, the broken wall, the cruel, dark, big-nosed face with the red, wet knife in its

420

gleaming teeth. Within the arch was the dull, faint, greeny-brown of London grass and trees.

'Hold tight, Jane!' Cyril cried, and he dashed through the arch, dragging Anthea and the Psammead after him. Robert followed, clutching Jane. And in the ears of each, as they passed through the arch of the charm, the sound and fury of battle died out suddenly and utterly, and they heard only the low, dull, discontented hum of vast London, and the peeking and patting of the sparrows on the gravel and the voices of the ragged baby children playing Ring-o'-Roses on the yellow trampled grass. And the charm was a little charm again in Jane's hand, and there was the basket with their dinner and the bathbuns lying just where they had left it.

'My hat!' said Cyril, drawing a long breath; 'that was something like an adventure.'

'It was rather like one, certainly,' said the Psammead.

They all lay still, breathing in the safe, quiet air of Regent's Park.

'We'd better go home at once,' said Anthea presently. 'Old Nurse will be most frightfully anxious. The sun looks about the same as it did when we started yesterday. We've been away twenty-four hours.' 'The buns are quite soft still,' said Cyril, feeling one; 'I suppose the dew kept them fresh.'

They were not hungry, curiously enough.

They picked up the dinner-basket and the Psammead-basket, and went straight home.

Old Nurse met them with amazement.

'Well, if ever I did!' she said. 'What's gone wrong? You've soon tired of your picnic.'

The children took this to be bitter irony, which means saying the exact opposite of what you mean in order to make yourself disagreeable; as when you happen to have a dirty face, and someone says, 'How nice and clean you look!'

'We're very sorry,' began Anthea, but old Nurse said—

'Oh, bless me, child, I don't care! Please yourselves and you'll please me. Come in and get your dinners comf'table. I've got a potato on a-boiling.'

When she had gone to attend to the potatoes the children looked at each other. Could it be that old Nurse had so changed that she no longer cared that they should have been away from home for twenty-four hours—all night in fact—without any explanation whatever?

But the Psammead put its head out of its basket and said—

'What's the matter? Don't you understand? You come back through the charm-arch at the same time as you go through it. This isn't tomorrow!' 'Is it still yesterday?' asked Jane.

'No, it's today. The same as it's always been. It wouldn't do to go mixing up the present and the Past, and cutting bits out of one to fit into the other.'

'Then all that adventure took no time at all?'

'You can call it that if you like,' said the Psammead. 'It took none of the modern time, anyhow.'

That evening Anthea carried up a steak for the learned gentleman's dinner. She persuaded Beatrice, the maid-of-all-work, who had given her the bangle with the blue stone, to let her do it. And she stayed and talked to him, by special invitation, while he ate the dinner.

She told him the whole adventure, beginning with—

'This afternoon we found ourselves on the bank of the River Nile,' and ending up with, 'And then we remembered how to get back, and there we were in Regent's Park, and it hadn't taken any time at all.'

422

She did not tell anything about the charm or the Psammead, because that was forbidden, but the story was quite wonderful enough even as it was to entrance the learned gentleman.

'You are a most unusual little girl,' he said. 'Who tells you all these things?'

'No one,' said Anthea, 'they just happen.'

'Make-believe,' he said slowly, as one who recalls and pronounces a long-forgotten word.

He sat long after she had left him. At last he roused himself with a start.

'I really must take a holiday,' he said; 'my nerves must be all out of order. I actually have a perfectly distinct impression that the little girl from the rooms below came in and gave me a coherent and graphic picture of life as I conceive it to have been in pre-dynastic Egypt. Strange what tricks the mind will play! I shall have to be more careful.'

He finished his bread conscientiously, and actually went for a mile walk before he went back to his work.

CHAPTER 6. THE WAY TO BABYLON

'How many miles to Babylon?
Three score and ten!
Can I get there by candle light?
Yes, and back again!'

Jane was singing to her doll, rocking it to and fro in the house which she had made for herself and it. The roof of the house was the dining-table, and the walls were tablecloths and antimacassars hanging all round, and kept in their places by books laid on their top ends at the table edge.

The others were tasting the fearful joys of domestic tobogganing. You know how it is done—with the largest and best tea-tray and the surface of the stair carpet. It is best to do it on the days when the stair rods are being cleaned, and the carpet is only held by the nails at the top. Of course, it is one of the five or six thoroughly tip-top games that grown-up people are so unjust to—and old Nurse, though a brick in many respects, was quite enough of a standard grown-up to put her foot down on the tobogganing long before any of the performers had had half enough of it. The tea-tray was taken away, and the baffled party entered the sitting-room, in exactly the mood not to be pleased if they could help it.

So Cyril said, 'What a beastly mess!'

And Robert added, 'Do shut up, Jane!'

Even Anthea, who was almost always kind, advised Jane to try another song. 'I'm sick to death of that,' said she.

It was a wet day, so none of the plans for seeing all the sights of London that can be seen for nothing could be carried out. Everyone had been thinking all the morning about the wonderful adventures of the day before, when Jane had held up the charm and it had turned into an arch, through which they had walked straight out of the present time and the Regent's Park into the land of Egypt eight thousand years ago. The memory of yesterday's happenings was still extremely fresh and frightening, so that everyone hoped that no one would suggest another excursion into the past, for it seemed to all that yesterday's adventures were quite enough to last for at least a week. Yet each felt a little anxious that the others should not think it was afraid, and presently Cyril, who really was not a coward, began to see that it would not be at all nice if he should have to think himself one. So he said—

'I say—about that charm—Jane—come out. We ought to talk about it, anyhow.'

'Oh, if that's all,' said Robert.

Jane obediently wriggled to the front of her house and sat there.

She felt for the charm, to make sure that it was still round her neck.

'It ISN'T all,' said Cyril, saying much more than he meant because he thought Robert's tone had been rude—as indeed it had.

'We ought to go and look for that Amulet. What's the good of having a first-class charm and keeping it idle, just eating its head off in the stable.'

'I'M game for anything, of course,' said Robert; but he added, with a fine air of chivalry, 'only I don't think the girls are keen today somehow.'

'Oh, yes; I am,' said Anthea hurriedly. 'If you think I'm afraid, I'm not.'

'I am though,' said Jane heavily; 'I didn't like it, and I won't go there again—not for anything I won't.'

'We shouldn't go THERE again, silly,' said Cyril; 'it would be some other place.'

'I daresay; a place with lions and tigers in it as likely as not.'

Seeing Jane so frightened, made the others feel quite brave. They said they were certain they ought to go.

'It's so ungrateful to the Psammead not to,' Anthea added, a little primly.

Jane stood up. She was desperate.

'I won't!' she cried; 'I won't, I won't, I won't! If you make me I'll scream and I'll scream, and I'll tell old Nurse, and I'll get her to burn the charm in the kitchen fire. So now, then!'

You can imagine how furious everyone was with Jane for feeling what each of them had felt all the morning. In each breast the same thought arose, 'No one can say it's OUR fault.' And they at once began to show Jane how angry they all felt that all the fault was hers. This made them feel quite brave.

> *'Tell-tale tit, its tongue shall be*
> *split,*
> *   And all the dogs in our town shall*
> *have a little bit,'*

sang Robert.

'It's always the way if you have girls in anything.' Cyril spoke in a cold displeasure that was worse than Robert's cruel quotation, and even Anthea said, 'Well, I'M not afraid if I AM a girl,' which of course, was the most cutting thing of all.

Jane picked up her doll and faced the others with what is sometimes called the courage of despair.

'I don't care,' she said; 'I won't, so there! It's just silly going to places when you don't want to, and when you don't know what they're going to be like! You can laugh at me as much as you like. You're beasts—and I hate you all!'

With these awful words she went out and banged the door.

Then the others would not look at each other, and they did not feel so brave as they had done.

Cyril took up a book, but it was not interesting to read. Robert kicked a chair-leg absently. His feet were always eloquent in moments of emotion. Anthea stood pleating the end of the tablecloth into folds—she seemed earnestly anxious to get all the pleats the same size. The sound of Jane's sobs had died away.

Suddenly Anthea said, 'Oh! let it be "pax"—poor little Pussy—you know she's the youngest.'

'She called us beasts,' said Robert, kicking the chair suddenly.

'Well, said Cyril, who was subject to passing fits of justice, 'we began, you know. At least you did.' Cyril's justice was always uncompromising.

'I'm not going to say I'm sorry if you mean that,' said Robert, and the chair-leg cracked to the kick he gave as he said it.

426

'Oh, do let's,' said Anthea, 'we're three to one, and Mother does so hate it if we row. Come on. I'll say I'm sorry first, though I didn't say anything, hardly.'

'All right, let's get it over,' said Cyril, opening the door.'Hi—you—Pussy!'

Far away up the stairs a voice could be heard singing brokenly, but still defiantly—

> *'How many miles (sniff) to Babylon?*
> *Three score and ten! (sniff)*
> *Can I get there by candle light?*
> *Yes (sniff), and back again!'*

It was trying, for this was plainly meant to annoy. But Anthea would not give herself time to think this. She led the way up the stairs, taking three at a time, and bounded to the level of Jane, who sat on the top step of all, thumping her doll to the tune of the song she was trying to sing.

'I say, Pussy, let it be pax! We're sorry if you are—'

It was enough. The kiss of peace was given by all. Jane being the youngest was entitled to this ceremonial. Anthea added a special apology of her own.

'I'm sorry if I was a pig, Pussy dear,' she said—'especially because in my really and truly inside mind I've been feeling a little as if I'd rather not go into the Past again either. But then, do think. If we don't go we shan't get the Amulet, and oh, Pussy, think if we could only get Father and Mother and The Lamb safe back! We MUST go, but we'll wait a day or two if you like and then perhaps you'll feel braver.'

'Raw meat makes you brave, however cowardly you are,' said Robert, to show that there was now no ill-feeling, 'and cranberries—that's what Tartars eat, and they're so brave it's simply awful. I suppose cranberries are only for Christmas time, but I'll ask old Nurse to let you have your chop very raw if you like.'

427

'I think I could be brave without that,' said Jane hastily; she hated underdone meat. 'I'll try.'

At this moment the door of the learned gentleman's room opened, and he looked out.

'Excuse me,' he said, in that gentle, polite weary voice of his, 'but was I mistaken in thinking that I caught a familiar word just now? Were you not singing some old ballad of Babylon?'

'No,' said Robert, 'at least Jane was singing "How many miles," but I shouldn't have thought you could have heard the words for—'

He would have said, 'for the sniffing,' but Anthea pinched him just in time.

'I did not hear ALL the words,' said the learned gentleman. 'I wonder would you recite them to me?'

So they all said together—

> 'How many miles to Babylon?
> Three score and ten!
> Can I get there by candle light?
> Yes, and back again!'

'I wish one could,' the learned gentleman said with a sigh.

'Can't you?' asked Jane.

'Babylon has fallen,' he answered with a sigh. 'You know it was once a great and beautiful city, and the centre of learning and Art, and now it is only ruins, and so covered up with earth that people are not even agreed as to where it once stood.'

He was leaning on the banisters, and his eyes had a far-away look in them, as though he could see through the staircase window the splendour and glory of ancient Babylon.

'I say,' Cyril remarked abruptly. 'You know that charm we showed you, and you told us how to say the name that's on it?'

'Yes!'

428

'Well, do you think that charm was ever in Babylon?'

'It's quite possible,' the learned gentleman replied. 'Such charms have been found in very early Egyptian tombs, yet their origin has not been accurately determined as Egyptian. They may have been brought from Asia. Or, supposing the charm to have been fashioned in Egypt, it might very well have been carried to Babylon by some friendly embassy, or brought back by the Babylonish army from some Egyptian campaign as part of the spoils of war. The inscription may be much later than the charm. Oh yes! it is a pleasant fancy, that that splendid specimen of yours was once used amid Babylonish surroundings.' The others looked at each other, but it was Jane who spoke.

'Were the Babylon people savages, were they always fighting and throwing things about?' For she had read the thoughts of the others by the unerring light of her own fears.

'The Babylonians were certainly more gentle than the Assyrians,' said the learned gentleman. 'And they were not savages by any means. A very high level of culture,' he looked doubtfully at his audience and went on, 'I mean that they made beautiful statues and jewellery, and built splendid palaces. And they were very learned—they had glorious libraries and high towers for the purpose of astrological and astronomical observation.'

'Er?' said Robert.

'I mean for—star-gazing and fortune-telling,' said the learned gentleman, 'and there were temples and beautiful hanging gardens—'

'I'll go to Babylon if you like,' said Jane abruptly, and the others hastened to say 'Done!' before she should have time to change her mind.

'Ah,' said the learned gentleman, smiling rather sadly, 'one can go so far in dreams, when one is young.' He sighed again, and then adding with a laboured briskness, 'I hope you'll have a—a—jolly game,' he went into his room and shut the door.

'He said "jolly" as if it was a foreign language,' said Cyril. 'Come on, let's get the Psammead and go now. I think Babylon seems a most frightfully jolly place to go to.'

So they woke the Psammead and put it in its bass-bag with the waterproof sheet, in case of inclement weather in Babylon. It was very cross, but it said it would as soon go to Babylon as anywhere else. 'The sand is good thereabouts,' it added.

Then Jane held up the charm, and Cyril said—

'We want to go to Babylon to look for the part of you that was lost. Will you please let us go there through you?'

'Please put us down just outside,' said Jane hastily; 'and then if we don't like it we needn't go inside.'

'Don't be all day,' said the Psammead.

So Anthea hastily uttered the word of power, without which the charm could do nothing.

'Ur—Hekau—Setcheh!' she said softly, and as she spoke the charm grew into an arch so tall that the top of it was close against the bedroom ceiling. Outside the arch was the bedroom painted chest-of-drawers and the Kidderminster carpet, and the washhand-stand with the riveted willow-pattern jug, and the faded curtains, and the dull light of indoors on a wet day. Through the arch showed the gleam of soft green leaves and white blossoms. They stepped forward quite happily. Even Jane felt that this did not look like lions, and her hand hardly trembled at all as she held the charm for the others to go through, and last, slipped through herself, and hung the charm, now grown small again, round her neck.

The children found themselves under a white-blossomed, green-leafed fruit-tree, in what seemed to be an orchard of such trees, all white-flowered and green-foliaged. Among the long green grass under their feet grew crocuses and lilies, and strange blue flowers. In the branches overhead thrushes and blackbirds were singing, and the coo of a pigeon came softly to them in the green quietness of the orchard.

'Oh, how perfectly lovely!' cried Anthea.

'Why, it's like home exactly—I mean England—only everything's bluer, and whiter, and greener, and the flowers are bigger.'

The boys owned that it certainly was fairly decent, and even Jane admitted that it was all very pretty.

'I'm certain there's nothing to be frightened of here,' said Anthea.

'I don't know,' said Jane. 'I suppose the fruit-trees go on just the same even when people are killing each other. I didn't half like what the learned gentleman said about the hanging gardens. I suppose they have gardens on purpose to hang people in. I do hope this isn't one.'

'Of course it isn't,' said Cyril. 'The hanging gardens are just gardens hung up—*I* think on chains between houses, don't you know, like trays. Come on; let's get somewhere.'

They began to walk through the cool grass. As far as they could see was nothing but trees, and trees and more trees. At the end of their orchard was another one, only separated from theirs by a little stream of clear water. They jumped this, and went on. Cyril, who was fond of gardening—which meant that he liked to watch the gardener at work—was able to command the respect of the others by telling them the names of a good many trees. There were nut-trees and almond-trees, and apricots, and fig-trees with their big five-fingered leaves. And every now and then the children had to cross another brook.

'It's like between the squares in Through the Looking-glass,' said Anthea.

At last they came to an orchard which was quite different from the other orchards. It had a low building in one corner.

'These are vines,' said Cyril superiorly, 'and I know this is a vineyard. I shouldn't wonder if there was a wine-press inside that place over there.'

At last they got out of the orchards and on to a sort of road, very rough, and not at all like the roads you are used to. It had cypress trees and acacia trees along it, and a sort of hedge of tamarisks, like those you see on the road between Nice and Cannes, or near Littlehampton, if you've only been as far as that.

And now in front of them they could see a great mass of buildings. There were scattered houses of wood and stone here and there among green orchards, and beyond these a great wall that shone red in the early morning sun. The wall was enormously high—more than half the height of St Paul's—and in the wall were set enormous gates that shone like gold as the rising sun beat on them. Each gate had a solid square tower on each side of it that stood out from the wall and rose above it. Beyond the wall were more towers and houses, gleaming with gold and bright colours. Away to the left ran the steel-blue swirl of a great river. And the children could see, through a gap in the trees, that the river flowed out from the town under a great arch in the wall.

'Those feathery things along by the water are palms,' said Cyril instructively.

'Oh, yes; you know everything,' Robert replied. 'What's all that grey-green stuff you see away over there, where it's all flat and sandy?'

'All right,' said Cyril loftily, '*I* don't want to tell you anything. I only thought you'd like to know a palm-tree when you saw it again.'

'Look!' cried Anthea; 'they're opening the gates.'

And indeed the great gates swung back with a brazen clang, and instantly a little crowd of a dozen or more people came out and along the road towards them.

The children, with one accord, crouched behind the tamarisk hedge.

'I don't like the sound of those gates,' said Jane. 'Fancy being inside when they shut. You'd never get out.'

432

'You've got an arch of your own to go out by,' the Psammead put its head out of the basket to remind her. 'Don't behave so like a girl. If I were you I should just march right into the town and ask to see the king.'

There was something at once simple and grand about this idea, and it pleased everyone.

So when the work-people had passed (they WERE work-people, the children felt sure, because they were dressed so plainly—just one long blue shirt thing—of blue or yellow) the four children marched boldly up to the brazen gate between the towers. The arch above the gate was quite a tunnel, the walls were so thick.

'Courage,' said Cyril. 'Step out. It's no use trying to sneak past. Be bold!'

Robert answered this appeal by unexpectedly bursting into 'The British Grenadiers', and to its quick-step they approached the gates of Babylon.

> *'Some talk of Alexander,*
> *And some of Hercules,*
> *Of Hector and Lysander,*
> *And such great names as these.*
> *But of all the gallant heroes...'*

This brought them to the threshold of the gate, and two men in bright armour suddenly barred their way with crossed spears.

'Who goes there?' they said.

(I think I must have explained to you before how it was that the children were always able to understand the language of any place they might happen to be in, and to be themselves understood. If not, I have no time to explain it now.)

'We come from very far,' said Cyril mechanically. 'From the Empire where the sun never sets, and we want to see your King.'

'If it's quite convenient,' amended Anthea. 'The King (may he live for ever!),' said the gatekeeper, 'is gone to fetch home his fourteenth wife. Where on earth have you come from not to know that?'

'The Queen then,' said Anthea hurriedly, and not taking any notice of the question as to where they had come from.

'The Queen,' said the gatekeeper, '(may she live for ever!) gives audience today three hours after sunrising.'

'But what are we to do till the end of the three hours?' asked Cyril.

The gatekeeper seemed neither to know nor to care. He appeared less interested in them than they could have thought possible. But the man who had crossed spears with him to bar the children's way was more human.

'Let them go in and look about them,' he said. 'I'll wager my best sword they've never seen anything to come near our little—village.' He said it in the tone people use for when they call the Atlantic Ocean the 'herring pond'.

The gatekeeper hesitated.

'They're only children, after all,' said the other, who had children of his own. 'Let me off for a few minutes, Captain, and I'll take them to my place and see if my good woman can't fit them up in something a little less outlandish than their present rig. Then they can have a look round without being mobbed. May I go?'

'Oh yes, if you like,' said the Captain, 'but don't be all day.'

The man led them through the dark arch into the town. And it was very different from London. For one thing, everything in London seems to be patched up out of odds and ends, but these houses seemed to have been built by people who liked the same sort of things. Not that they were all alike, for though all were squarish, they were of different sizes, and decorated in all sorts of different ways, some with paintings in bright colours, some with black and silver designs. There were terraces, and gardens, and balconies, and open spaces with trees. Their guide took them to a

434

little house in a back street, where a kind-faced woman sat spinning at the door of a very dark room.

'Here,' he said, 'just lend these children a mantle each, so that they can go about and see the place till the Queen's audience begins. You leave that wool for a bit, and show them round if you like. I must be off now.'

The woman did as she was told, and the four children, wrapped in fringed mantles, went with her all about the town, and oh! how I wish I had time to tell you all that they saw. It was all so wonderfully different from anything you have ever seen. For one thing, all the houses were dazzlingly bright, and many of them covered with pictures. Some had great creatures carved in stone at each side of the door. Then the people—there were no black frock-coats and tall hats; no dingy coats and skirts of good, useful, ugly stuffs warranted to wear. Everyone's clothes were bright and beautiful with blue and scarlet and green and gold.

The market was brighter than you would think anything could be. There were stalls for everything you could possibly want—and for a great many things that if you wanted here and now, want would be your master. There were pineapples and peaches in heaps—and stalls of crockery and glass things, beautiful shapes and glorious colours, there were stalls for necklaces, and clasps, and bracelets, and brooches, for woven stuffs, and furs, and embroidered linen. The children had never seen half so many beautiful things together, even at Liberty's. It seemed no time at all before the woman said—

'It's nearly time now. We ought to be getting on towards the palace. It's as well to be early.' So they went to the palace, and when they got there it was more splendid than anything they had seen yet.

For it was glowing with colours, and with gold and silver and black and white—like some magnificent embroidery. Flight after flight of broad marble steps led up to it, and at the edges of the stairs stood great images, twenty times as big as a man—images of men with wings like chain armour, and hawks' heads, and winged men with the heads of dogs. And there were the statues of great kings.

Between the flights of steps were terraces where fountains played, and the Queen's Guard in white and scarlet, and armour that shone like gold, stood by twos lining the way up the stairs; and a great body of them was massed by the vast door of the palace itself, where it stood glittering like an impossibly radiant peacock in the noon-day sun.

All sorts of people were passing up the steps to seek audience of the Queen. Ladies in richly-embroidered dresses with fringy flounces, poor folks in plain and simple clothes, dandies with beards oiled and curled.

And Cyril, Robert, Anthea and Jane, went with the crowd.

At the gate of the palace the Psammead put one eye cautiously out of the basket and whispered—

'I can't be bothered with queens. I'll go home with this lady. I'm sure she'll get me some sand if you ask her to.'

'Oh! don't leave us,' said Jane. The woman was giving some last instructions in Court etiquette to Anthea, and did not hear Jane.

'Don't be a little muff,' said the Psammead quite fiercely. 'It's not a bit of good your having a charm. You never use it. If you want me you've only got to say the name of power and ask the charm to bring me to you.'

'I'd rather go with you,' said Jane. And it was the most surprising thing she had ever said in her life.

Everyone opened its mouth without thinking of manners, and Anthea, who was peeping into the Psammead's basket, saw that its mouth opened wider than anybody's.

'You needn't gawp like that,' Jane went on. 'I'm not going to be bothered with queens any more than IT is. And I know, wherever it is, it'll take jolly good care that it's safe.'

436

'She's right there,' said everyone, for they had observed that the Psammead had a way of knowing which side its bread was buttered.

She turned to the woman and said, 'You'll take me home with you, won't you? And let me play with your little girls till the others have done with the Queen.'

'Surely I will, little heart!' said the woman.

And then Anthea hurriedly stroked the Psammead and embraced Jane, who took the woman's hand, and trotted contentedly away with the Psammead's bag under the other arm.

The others stood looking after her till she, the woman, and the basket were lost in the many-coloured crowd. Then Anthea turned once more to the palace's magnificent doorway and said—

'Let's ask the porter to take care of our Babylonian overcoats.'

So they took off the garments that the woman had lent them and stood amid the jostling petitioners of the Queen in their own English frocks and coats and hats and boots.

'We want to see the Queen,' said Cyril; 'we come from the far Empire where the sun never sets!'

A murmur of surprise and a thrill of excitement ran through the crowd. The door-porter spoke to a black man, he spoke to someone else. There was a whispering, waiting pause. Then a big man, with a cleanly-shaven face, beckoned them from the top of a flight of red marble steps.

They went up; the boots of Robert clattering more than usual because he was so nervous. A door swung open, a curtain was drawn back. A double line of bowing forms in gorgeous raiment formed a lane that led to the steps of the throne, and as the children advanced hurriedly there came from the throne a voice very sweet and kind.

'Three children from the land where the sun never sets! Let them draw hither without fear.'

437

In another minute they were kneeling at the throne's foot, saying, 'O Queen, live for ever!' exactly as the woman had taught them. And a splendid dream-lady, all gold and silver and jewels and snowy drift of veils, was raising Anthea, and saying—

'Don't be frightened, I really am SO glad you came! The land where the sun never sets! I am delighted to see you! I was getting quite too dreadfully bored for anything!'

And behind Anthea the kneeling Cyril whispered in the ears of the respectful Robert—

'Bobs, don't say anything to Panther. It's no use upsetting her, but we didn't ask for Jane's address, and the Psammead's with her.'

'Well,' whispered Robert, 'the charm can bring them to us at any moment. IT said so.'

'Oh, yes,' whispered Cyril, in miserable derision, 'WE'RE all right, of course. So we are! Oh, yes! If we'd only GOT the charm.'

Then Robert saw, and he murmured, 'Crikey!' at the foot of the throne of Babylon; while Cyril hoarsely whispered the plain English fact—

'Jane's got the charm round her neck, you silly cuckoo.'

'Crikey!' Robert repeated in heart-broken undertones.

CHAPTER 7. 'THE DEEPEST DUNGEON BELOW THE CASTLE MOAT'

The Queen threw three of the red and gold embroidered cushions off the throne on to the marble steps that led up to it.

'Just make yourselves comfortable there,' she said. 'I'm simply dying to talk to you, and to hear all about your wonderful country and how you got here, and everything, but I have to do justice

438

every morning. Such a bore, isn't it? Do you do justice in your own country?'

'No, said Cyril; 'at least of course we try to, but not in this public sort of way, only in private.' 'Ah, yes,' said the Queen, 'I should much prefer a private audience myself—much easier to manage. But public opinion has to be considered. Doing justice is very hard work, even when you're brought up to it.'

'We don't do justice, but we have to do scales, Jane and me,' said Anthea, 'twenty minutes a day. It's simply horrid.'

'What are scales?' asked the Queen, 'and what is Jane?'

'Jane is my little sister. One of the guards-at-the-gate's wife is taking care of her. And scales are music.'

'I never heard of the instrument,' said the Queen. 'Do you sing?'

'Oh, yes. We can sing in parts,' said Anthea.

'That IS magic,' said the Queen. 'How many parts are you each cut into before you do it?'

'We aren't cut at all,' said Robert hastily. 'We couldn't sing if we were. We'll show you afterwards.'

'So you shall, and now sit quiet like dear children and hear me do justice. The way I do it has always been admired. I oughtn't to say that ought I? Sounds so conceited. But I don't mind with you, dears. Somehow I feel as though I'd known you quite a long time already.'

The Queen settled herself on her throne and made a signal to her attendants. The children, whispering together among the cushions on the steps of the throne, decided that she was very beautiful and very kind, but perhaps just the least bit flighty.

The first person who came to ask for justice was a woman whose brother had taken the money the father had left for her. The brother said it was the uncle who had the money. There was a good deal of talk and the children were growing rather bored, when the Queen suddenly clapped her hands, and said—

'Put both the men in prison till one of them owns up that the other is innocent.'

'But suppose they both did it?' Cyril could not help interrupting.

'Then prison's the best place for them,' said the Queen.

'But suppose neither did it.'

'That's impossible,' said the Queen; 'a thing's not done unless someone does it. And you mustn't interrupt.'

Then came a woman, in tears, with a torn veil and real ashes on her head—at least Anthea thought so, but it may have been only road-dust. She complained that her husband was in prison.

'What for?' said the Queen.

'They SAID it was for speaking evil of your Majesty,' said the woman, 'but it wasn't. Someone had a spite against him. That was what it was.'

'How do you know he hadn't spoken evil of me?' said the Queen.

'No one could,' said the woman simply, 'when they'd once seen your beautiful face.'

'Let the man out,' said the Queen, smiling. 'Next case.'

The next case was that of a boy who had stolen a fox. 'Like the Spartan boy,' whispered Robert. But the Queen ruled that nobody could have any possible reason for owning a fox, and still less for stealing one. And she did not believe that there were any foxes in Babylon; she, at any rate, had never seen one. So the boy was released.

The people came to the Queen about all sorts of family quarrels and neighbourly misunderstandings—from a fight between brothers over the division of an inheritance, to the dishonest and unfriendly conduct of a woman who had borrowed a cooking-pot at the last New Year's festival, and not returned it yet.

And the Queen decided everything, very, very decidedly indeed. At last she clapped her hands quite suddenly and with extreme loudness, and said—

'The audience is over for today.'

Everyone said, 'May the Queen live for ever!' and went out.

And the children were left alone in the justice-hall with the Queen of Babylon and her ladies.

'There!' said the Queen, with a long sigh of relief. 'THAT'S over! I couldn't have done another stitch of justice if you'd offered me the crown of Egypt! Now come into the garden, and we'll have a nice, long, cosy talk.'

She led them through long, narrow corridors whose walls they somehow felt, were very, very thick, into a sort of garden courtyard. There were thick shrubs closely planted, and roses were trained over trellises, and made a pleasant shade—needed, indeed, for already the sun was as hot as it is in England in August at the seaside.

Slaves spread cushions on a low, marble terrace, and a big man with a smooth face served cool drink in cups of gold studded with beryls. He drank a little from the Queen's cup before handing it to her.

'That's rather a nasty trick,' whispered Robert, who had been carefully taught never to drink out of one of the nice, shiny, metal cups that are chained to the London drinking fountains without first rinsing it out thoroughly.

The Queen overheard him.

'Not at all,' said she. 'Ritti-Marduk is a very clean man. And one has to have SOME ONE as taster, you know, because of poison.'

The word made the children feel rather creepy; but Ritti-Marduk had tasted all the cups, so they felt pretty safe. The drink was delicious—very cold, and tasting like lemonade and partly like penny ices.

'Leave us,' said the Queen. And all the Court ladies, in their beautiful, many-folded, many-coloured, fringed dresses, filed out slowly, and the children were left alone with the Queen.

'Now,' she said, 'tell me all about yourselves.'

They looked at each other.

'You, Bobs,' said Cyril.

'No—Anthea,' said Robert.

'No—you—Cyril,' said Anthea. 'Don't you remember how pleased the Queen of India was when you told her all about us?'

Cyril muttered that it was all very well, and so it was. For when he had told the tale of the Phoenix and the Carpet to the Ranee, it had been only the truth—and all the truth that he had to tell. But now it was not easy to tell a convincing story without mentioning the Amulet—which, of course, it wouldn't have done to mention—and without owning that they were really living in London, about 2,500 years later than the time they were talking in.

Cyril took refuge in the tale of the Psammead and its wonderful power of making wishes come true. The children had never been able to tell anyone before, and Cyril was surprised to find that the spell which kept them silent in London did not work here. 'Something to do with our being in the Past, I suppose,' he said to himself.

'This is MOST interesting,' said the Queen. 'We must have this Psammead for the banquet tonight. Its performance will be one of the most popular turns in the whole programme. Where is it?'

Anthea explained that they did not know; also why it was that they did not know.

'Oh, THAT'S quite simple,' said the Queen, and everyone breathed a deep sigh of relief as she said it.

'Ritti-Marduk shall run down to the gates and find out which guard your sister went home with.'

442

'Might he'—Anthea's voice was tremulous—'might he—would it interfere with his meal-times, or anything like that, if he went NOW?'

'Of course he shall go now. He may think himself lucky if he gets his meals at any time,' said the Queen heartily, and clapped her hands.

'May I send a letter?' asked Cyril, pulling out a red-backed penny account-book, and feeling in his pockets for a stump of pencil that he knew was in one of them.

'By all means. I'll call my scribe.'

'Oh, I can scribe right enough, thanks,' said Cyril, finding the pencil and licking its point. He even had to bite the wood a little, for it was very blunt.

'Oh, you clever, clever boy!' said the Queen. 'DO let me watch you do it!'

Cyril wrote on a leaf of the book—it was of rough, woolly paper, with hairs that stuck out and would have got in his pen if he had been using one, and ruled for accounts.

'Hide IT most carefully before you come here,' he wrote, 'and don't mention it—and destroy this letter. Everything is going A1. The Queen is a fair treat. There's nothing to be afraid of.'

'What curious characters, and what a strange flat surface!' said the Queen. 'What have you inscribed?'

'I've 'scribed,' replied Cyril cautiously, 'that you are fair, and a—and like a—like a festival; and that she need not be afraid, and that she is to come at once.'

Ritti-Marduk, who had come in and had stood waiting while Cyril wrote, his Babylonish eyes nearly starting out of his Babylonish head, now took the letter, with some reluctance.

'O Queen, live for ever! Is it a charm?' he timidly asked. 'A strong charm, most great lady?'

'YES,' said Robert, unexpectedly, 'it IS a charm, but it won't hurt anyone until you've given it to Jane. And then she'll destroy it, so that it CAN'T hurt anyone. It's most awful strong!—as strong as—Peppermint!' he ended abruptly.

'I know not the god,' said Ritti-Marduk, bending timorously.

'She'll tear it up directly she gets it,' said Robert, 'That'll end the charm. You needn't be afraid if you go now.'

Ritti-Marduk went, seeming only partly satisfied; and then the Queen began to admire the penny account-book and the bit of pencil in so marked and significant a way that Cyril felt he could not do less than press them upon her as a gift. She ruffled the leaves delightedly.

'What a wonderful substance!' she said. 'And with this style you make charms? Make a charm for me! Do you know,' her voice sank to a whisper, 'the names of the great ones of your own far country?'

'Rather!' said Cyril, and hastily wrote the names of Alfred the Great, Shakespeare, Nelson, Gordon, Lord Beaconsfield, Mr Rudyard Kipling, and Mr Sherlock Holmes, while the Queen watched him with 'unbaited breath', as Anthea said afterwards.

She took the book and hid it reverently among the bright folds of her gown.

'You shall teach me later to say the great names,' she said. 'And the names of their Ministers—perhaps the great Nisroch is one of them?'

'I don't think so,' said Cyril. 'Mr Campbell Bannerman's Prime Minister and Mr Burns a Minister, and so is the Archbishop of Canterbury, I think, but I'm not sure—and Dr Parker was one, I know, and—'

'No more,' said the Queen, putting her hands to her ears. 'My head's going round with all those great names. You shall teach them to me later—because of course you'll make us a nice long visit now you have come, won't you? Now tell me—but no, I am quite tired out with your being so clever. Besides, I'm sure you'd like ME to tell YOU something, wouldn't you?'

'Yes,' said Anthea. 'I want to know how it is that the King has gone—'

'Excuse me, but you should say "the King may-he-live-for-ever",' said the Queen gently.

'I beg your pardon,' Anthea hastened to say—'the King may-he-live-for-ever has gone to fetch home his fourteenth wife? I don't think even Bluebeard had as many as that. And, besides, he hasn't killed YOU at any rate.'

The Queen looked bewildered.

'She means,' explained Robert, 'that English kings only have one wife—at least, Henry the Eighth had seven or eight, but not all at once.'

'In our country,' said the Queen scornfully, 'a king would not reign a day who had only one wife. No one would respect him, and quite right too.'

'Then are all the other thirteen alive?' asked Anthea.

'Of course they are—poor mean-spirited things! I don't associate with them, of course, I am the Queen: they're only the wives.'

'I see,' said Anthea, gasping.

'But oh, my dears,' the Queen went on, 'such a to-do as there's been about this last wife! You never did! It really was TOO funny. We wanted an Egyptian princess. The King may-he-live-for-ever has got a wife from most of the important nations, and he had set his heart on an Egyptian one to complete his collection. Well, of course, to begin with, we sent a handsome present of gold. The Egyptian king sent back some horses—quite a few; he's fearfully stingy!—and he said he liked the gold very much, but what they were really short of was lapis lazuli, so of course we sent him some. But by that time he'd begun to use the gold to cover the beams of the roof of the Temple of the Sun-God, and he hadn't nearly enough to finish the job, so we sent some more. And so it went on, oh, for years. You see each journey takes at least six months. And at last we asked the hand of his daughter in marriage.'

'Yes, and then?' said Anthea, who wanted to get to the princess part of the story.

'Well, then,' said the Queen, 'when he'd got everything out of us that he could, and only given the meanest presents in return, he sent to say he would esteem the honour of an alliance very highly, only unfortunately he hadn't any daughter, but he hoped one would be born soon, and if so, she should certainly be reserved for the King of Babylon!'

'What a trick!' said Cyril.

'Yes, wasn't it? So then we said his sister would do, and then there were more gifts and more journeys; and now at last the tiresome, black-haired thing is coming, and the King may-he-live-for-ever has gone seven days' journey to meet her at Carchemish. And he's gone in his best chariot, the one inlaid with lapis lazuli and gold, with the gold-plated wheels and onyx-studded hubs—much too great an honour in my opinion. She'll be here tonight; there'll be a grand banquet to celebrate her arrival. SHE won't be present, of course. She'll be having her baths and her anointings, and all that sort of thing. We always clean our foreign brides very carefully. It takes two or three weeks. Now it's dinnertime, and you shall eat with me, for I can see that you are of high rank.' She led them into a dark, cool hall, with many cushions on the floor. On these they sat and low tables were brought—beautiful tables of smooth, blue stone mounted in gold. On these, golden trays were placed; but there were no knives, or forks, or spoons. The children expected the Queen to call for them; but no. She just ate with her fingers, and as the first dish was a great tray of boiled corn, and meat and raisins all mixed up together, and melted fat poured all over the tray, it was found difficult to follow her example with anything like what we are used to think of as good table manners. There were stewed quinces afterwards, and dates in syrup, and thick yellowy cream. It was the kind of dinner you hardly ever get in Fitzroy Street.

446

After dinner everybody went to sleep, even the children.

The Queen awoke with a start.

'Good gracious!' she cried, 'what a time we've slept! I must rush off and dress for the banquet. I shan't have much more than time.'

'Hasn't Ritti-Marduk got back with our sister and the Psammead yet?' Anthea asked.

'I QUITE forgot to ask. I'm sorry,' said the Queen. 'And of course they wouldn't announce her unless I told them to, except during justice hours. I expect she's waiting outside. I'll see.'

Ritti-Marduk came in a moment later.

'I regret,' he said, 'that I have been unable to find your sister. The beast she bears with her in a basket has bitten the child of the guard, and your sister and the beast set out to come to you. The police say they have a clue. No doubt we shall have news of her in a few weeks.' He bowed and withdrew.

The horror of this threefold loss—Jane, the Psammead, and the Amulet—gave the children something to talk about while the Queen was dressing. I shall not report their conversation; it was very gloomy. Everyone repeated himself several times, and the discussion ended in each of them blaming the other two for having let Jane go. You know the sort of talk it was, don't you? At last Cyril said—

'After all, she's with the Psammead, so SHE'S all right. The Psammead is jolly careful of itself too. And it isn't as if we were in any danger. Let's try to buck up and enjoy the banquet.'

They did enjoy the banquet. They had a beautiful bath, which was delicious, were heavily oiled all over, including their hair, and that was most unpleasant. Then, they dressed again and were presented to the King, who was most affable. The banquet was long; there were all sorts of nice things to eat, and everybody seemed to eat and drink a good deal. Everyone lay on cushions and couches, ladies on one side and gentlemen on the other; and after the eating was done each lady went and sat by some gentleman, who seemed to be her sweetheart or her husband, for they were very affectionate to each other. The Court dresses had gold threads woven in them, very bright and beautiful.

The middle of the room was left clear, and different people came and did amusing things. There were conjurers and jugglers and snake-charmers, which last Anthea did not like at all.

When it got dark torches were lighted. Cedar splinters dipped in oil blazed in copper dishes set high on poles.

Then there was a dancer, who hardly danced at all, only just struck attitudes. She had hardly any clothes, and was not at all pretty. The children were rather bored by her, but everyone else was delighted, including the King.

'By the beard of Nimrod!' he cried, 'ask what you like girl, and you shall have it!'

'I want nothing,' said the dancer; 'the honour of having pleased the King may-he-live-for-ever is reward enough for me.'

And the King was so pleased with this modest and sensible reply that he gave her the gold collar off his own neck.

'I say!' said Cyril, awed by the magnificence of the gift.

'It's all right,' whispered the Queen, 'it's not his best collar by any means. We always keep a stock of cheap jewellery for these occasions. And now—you promised to sing us something. Would you like my minstrels to accompany you?'

'No, thank you,' said Anthea quickly. The minstrels had been playing off and on all the time, and their music reminded Anthea of the band she and the others had once had on the fifth of November—with penny horns, a tin whistle, a tea-tray, the tongs, a policeman's rattle, and a toy drum. They had enjoyed this band very much at the time. But it was quite different when someone else was making the same kind of music. Anthea understood now that Father had not been really heartless and unreasonable when he had told them to stop that infuriating din.

'What shall we sing?' Cyril was asking.

'Sweet and low?' suggested Anthea.

'Too soft—I vote for "Who will o'er the downs". Now then—one, two, three.

> 'Oh, who will o'er the downs so free,
> Oh, who will with me ride,
> Oh, who will up and follow me,
> To win a blooming bride?
>
> Her father he has locked the door,
> Her mother keeps the key;
> But neither bolt nor bar shall keep
> My own true love from me.'

Jane, the alto, was missing, and Robert, unlike the mother of the lady in the song, never could 'keep the key', but the song, even so, was sufficiently unlike anything any of them had ever heard to rouse the Babylonian Court to the wildest enthusiasm.

'More, more,' cried the King; 'by my beard, this savage music is a new thing. Sing again!'

So they sang:

> 'I saw her bower at twilight gray,
> 'Twas guarded safe and sure.
> I saw her bower at break of day,
> 'Twas guarded then no more.
>
> The varlets they were all asleep,
> And there was none to see
> The greeting fair that passed there
> Between my love and me.'

Shouts of applause greeted the ending of the verse, and the King would not be satisfied till they had sung all their part-songs (they only knew three) twice over, and ended up with 'Men of Harlech' in unison. Then the King stood up in his royal robes with his high, narrow crown on his head and shouted—

'By the beak of Nisroch, ask what you will, strangers from the land where the sun never sets!'

'We ought to say it's enough honour, like the dancer did,' whispered Anthea.

'No, let's ask for IT,' said Robert.

'No, no, I'm sure the other's manners,' said Anthea. But Robert, who was excited by the music, and the flaring torches, and the applause and the opportunity, spoke up before the others could stop him.

'Give us the half of the Amulet that has on it the name UR HEKAU SETCHEH,' he said, adding as an afterthought, 'O King, live-for-ever.'

As he spoke the great name those in the pillared hall fell on their faces, and lay still. All but the Queen who crouched amid her cushions with her head in her hands, and the King, who stood upright, perfectly still, like the statue of a king in stone. It was only for a moment though. Then his great voice thundered out—

'Guard, seize them!'

Instantly, from nowhere as it seemed, sprang eight soldiers in bright armour inlaid with gold, and tunics of red and white. Very splendid they were, and very alarming.

'Impious and sacrilegious wretches!' shouted the King. 'To the dungeons with them! We will find a way, tomorrow, to make them speak. For without doubt they can tell us where to find the lost half of It.'

A wall of scarlet and white and steel and gold closed up round the children and hurried them away among the many pillars of the great hall. As they went they heard the voices of the courtiers loud in horror.

450

'You've done it this time,' said Cyril with extreme bitterness.

'Oh, it will come right. It MUST. It always does,' said Anthea desperately.

They could not see where they were going, because the guard surrounded them so closely, but the ground under their feet, smooth marble at first, grew rougher like stone, then it was loose earth and sand, and they felt the night air. Then there was more stone, and steps down.

'It's my belief we really ARE going to the deepest dungeon below the castle moat this time,' said Cyril.

And they were. At least it was not below a moat, but below the river Euphrates, which was just as bad if not worse. In a most unpleasant place it was. Dark, very, very damp, and with an odd, musty smell rather like the shells of oysters. There was a torch—that is to say, a copper basket on a high stick with oiled wood burning in it. By its light the children saw that the walls were green, and that trickles of water ran down them and dripped from the roof. There were things on the floor that looked like newts, and in the dark corners creepy, shiny things moved sluggishly, uneasily, horribly.

Robert's heart sank right into those really reliable boots of his. Anthea and Cyril each had a private struggle with that inside disagreeableness which is part of all of us, and which is sometimes called the Old Adam—and both were victors. Neither of them said to Robert (and both tried hard not even to think it), 'This is YOUR doing.' Anthea had the additional temptation to add, 'I told you so.' And she resisted it successfully.

'Sacrilege, and impious cheek,' said the captain of the guard to the gaoler. 'To be kept during the King's pleasure. I expect he means to get some pleasure out of them tomorrow! He'll tickle them up!'

'Poor little kids,' said the gaoler.

'Oh, yes,' said the captain. 'I've got kids of my own too. But it doesn't do to let domestic sentiment interfere with one's public duties. Good night.'

The soldiers tramped heavily off in their white and red and steel and gold. The gaoler, with a bunch of big keys in his hand, stood looking pityingly at the children. He shook his head twice and went out.

'Courage!' said Anthea. 'I know it will be all right. It's only a dream REALLY, you know. It MUST be! I don't believe about time being only a something or other of thought. It IS a dream, and we're bound to wake up all right and safe.'

'Humph,' said Cyril bitterly. And Robert suddenly said—

'It's all my doing. If it really IS all up do please not keep a down on me about it, and tell Father—Oh, I forgot.'

What he had forgotten was that his father was 3,000 miles and 5,000 or more years away from him.

'All right, Bobs, old man,' said Cyril; and Anthea got hold of Robert's hand and squeezed it.

Then the gaoler came back with a platter of hard, flat cakes made of coarse grain, very different from the cream-and-juicy-date feasts of the palace; also a pitcher of water.

'There,' he said.

'Oh, thank you so very much. You ARE kind,' said Anthea feverishly.

'Go to sleep,' said the gaoler, pointing to a heap of straw in a corner; 'tomorrow comes soon enough.'

'Oh, dear Mr Gaoler,' said Anthea, 'whatever will they do to us tomorrow?'

'They'll try to make you tell things,' said the gaoler grimly, 'and my advice is if you've nothing to tell, make up something. Then

452

perhaps they'll sell you to the Northern nations. Regular savages THEY are. Good night.'

'Good night,' said three trembling voices, which their owners strove in vain to render firm. Then he went out, and the three were left alone in the damp, dim vault.

'I know the light won't last long,' said Cyril, looking at the flickering brazier.

'Is it any good, do you think, calling on the name when we haven't got the charm?' suggested Anthea.

'I shouldn't think so. But we might try.'

So they tried. But the blank silence of the damp dungeon remained unchanged.

'What was the name the Queen said?' asked Cyril suddenly. 'Nisbeth—Nesbit—something? You know, the slave of the great names?'

'Wait a sec,' said Robert, 'though I don't know why you want it. Nusroch—Nisrock—Nisroch—that's it.'

Then Anthea pulled herself together. All her muscles tightened, and the muscles of her mind and soul, if you can call them that, tightened too.

'UR HEKAU SETCHEH,' she cried in a fervent voice. 'Oh, Nisroch, servant of the Great Ones, come and help us!'

There was a waiting silence. Then a cold, blue light awoke in the corner where the straw was—and in the light they saw coming towards them a strange and terrible figure. I won't try to describe it, because the drawing shows it, exactly as it was, and exactly as the old Babylonians carved it on their stones, so that you can see it in our own British Museum at this day. I will just say that it had eagle's wings and an eagle's head and the body of a man.

It came towards them, strong and unspeakably horrible.

'Oh, go away,' cried Anthea; but Cyril cried, 'No; stay!'

The creature hesitated, then bowed low before them on the damp floor of the dungeon.

'Speak,' it said, in a harsh, grating voice like large rusty keys being turned in locks. 'The servant of the Great Ones is YOUR servant. What is your need that you call on the name of Nisroch?'

'We want to go home,' said Robert.

'No, no,' cried Anthea; 'we want to be where Jane is.'

Nisroch raised his great arm and pointed at the wall of the dungeon. And, as he pointed, the wall disappeared, and instead of the damp, green, rocky surface, there shone and glowed a room with rich hangings of red silk embroidered with golden water-lilies, with cushioned couches and great mirrors of polished steel; and in it was the Queen, and before her, on a red pillow, sat the Psammead, its fur hunched up in an irritated, discontented way. On a blue-covered couch lay Jane fast asleep.

'Walk forward without fear,' said Nisroch. 'Is there aught else that the Servant of the great Name can do for those who speak that name?'

'No—oh, no,' said Cyril. 'It's all right now. Thanks ever so.'

'You are a dear,' cried Anthea, not in the least knowing what she was saying. 'Oh, thank you thank you. But DO go NOW!'

She caught the hand of the creature, and it was cold and hard in hers, like a hand of stone.

'Go forward,' said Nisroch. And they went.

'Oh, my good gracious,' said the Queen as they stood before her. 'How did you get here? I KNEW you were magic. I meant to let you out the first thing in the morning, if I could slip away—but thanks be to Dagon, you've managed it for yourselves. You must get away. I'll wake my chief lady and she shall call Ritti-Marduk, and he'll let you out the back way, and—'

454

'Don't rouse anybody for goodness' sake,' said Anthea, 'except Jane, and I'll rouse her.'

She shook Jane with energy, and Jane slowly awoke.

'Ritti-Marduk brought them in hours ago, really,' said the Queen, 'but I wanted to have the Psammead all to myself for a bit. You'll excuse the little natural deception?—it's part of the Babylonish character, don't you know? But I don't want anything to happen to you. Do let me rouse someone.'

'No, no, no,' said Anthea with desperate earnestness. She thought she knew enough of what the Babylonians were like when they were roused. 'We can go by our own magic. And you will tell the King it wasn't the gaoler's fault. It was Nisroch.'

'Nisroch!' echoed the Queen. 'You are indeed magicians.'

Jane sat up, blinking stupidly.

'Hold It up, and say the word,' cried Cyril, catching up the Psammead, which mechanically bit him, but only very slightly.

'Which is the East?' asked Jane.

'Behind me,' said the Queen. 'Why?'

'Ur Hekau Setcheh,' said Jane sleepily, and held up the charm.

And there they all were in the dining-room at 300, Fitzroy Street.

'Jane,' cried Cyril with great presence of mind, 'go and get the plate of sand down for the Psammead.'

Jane went.

'Look here!' he said quickly, as the sound of her boots grew less loud on the stairs, 'don't let's tell her about the dungeon and all that. It'll only frighten her so that she'll never want to go anywhere else.'

'Righto!' said Cyril; but Anthea felt that she could not have said a word to save her life.

'Why did you want to come back in such a hurry?' asked Jane, returning with the plate of sand. 'It was awfully jolly in Babylon, I think! I liked it no end.'

'Oh, yes,' said Cyril carelessly. 'It was jolly enough, of course, but I thought we'd been there long enough. Mother always says you oughtn't to wear out your welcome!'

CHAPTER 8. THE QUEEN IN LONDON

'Now tell us what happened to you,' said Cyril to Jane, when he and the others had told her all about the Queen's talk and the banquet, and the variety entertainment, carefully stopping short before the beginning of the dungeon part of the story.

'It wasn't much good going,' said Jane, 'if you didn't even try to get the Amulet.'

'We found out it was no go,' said Cyril; 'it's not to be got in Babylon. It was lost before that. We'll go to some other jolly friendly place, where everyone is kind and pleasant, and look for it there. Now tell us about your part.'

'Oh,' said Jane, 'the Queen's man with the smooth face—what was his name?'

'Ritti-Marduk,' said Cyril.

'Yes,' said Jane, 'Ritti-Marduk, he came for me just after the Psammead had bitten the guard-of-the-gate's wife's little boy, and he took me to the Palace. And we had supper with the new little Queen from Egypt. She is a dear—not much older than you. She told me heaps about Egypt. And we played ball after supper. And then the Babylon Queen sent for me. I like her too. And she talked to the Psammead and I went to sleep. And then you woke me up. That's all.'

456

The Psammead, roused from its sound sleep, told the same story.

'But,' it added, 'what possessed you to tell that Queen that I could give wishes? I sometimes think you were born without even the most rudimentary imitation of brains.'

The children did not know the meaning of rudimentary, but it sounded a rude, insulting word.

'I don't see that we did any harm,' said Cyril sulkily.

'Oh, no,' said the Psammead with withering irony, 'not at all! Of course not! Quite the contrary! Exactly so! Only she happened to wish that she might soon find herself in your country. And soon may mean any moment.'

'Then it's your fault,' said Robert, 'because you might just as well have made "soon" mean some moment next year or next century.'

'That's where you, as so often happens, make the mistake,' rejoined the Sand-fairy. '*I* couldn't mean anything but what SHE meant by "soon". It wasn't my wish. And what SHE meant was the next time the King happens to go out lion hunting. So she'll have a whole day, and perhaps two, to do as she wishes with. SHE doesn't know about time only being a mode of thought.'

'Well,' said Cyril, with a sigh of resignation, 'we must do what we can to give her a good time. She was jolly decent to us. I say, suppose we were to go to St James's Park after dinner and feed those ducks that we never did feed. After all that Babylon and all those years ago, I feel as if I should like to see something REAL, and NOW. You'll come, Psammead?'

'Where's my priceless woven basket of sacred rushes?' asked the Psammead morosely. 'I can't go out with nothing on. And I won't, what's more.'

And then everybody remembered with pain that the bass bag had, in the hurry of departure from Babylon, not been remembered.

'But it's not so extra precious,' said Robert hastily. 'You can get them given to you for nothing if you buy fish in Farringdon Market.'

'Oh,' said the Psammead very crossly indeed, 'so you presume on my sublime indifference to the things of this disgusting modern world, to fob me off with a travelling equipage that costs you nothing. Very well, I shall go to sand. Please don't wake me.'

And it went then and there to sand, which, as you know, meant to bed. The boys went to St James's Park to feed the ducks, but they went alone.

Anthea and Jane sat sewing all the afternoon. They cut off half a yard from each of their best green Liberty sashes. A towel cut in two formed a lining; and they sat and sewed and sewed and sewed. What they were making was a bag for the Psammead. Each worked at a half of the bag. jane's half had four-leaved shamrocks embroidered on it. They were the only things she could do (because she had been taught how at school, and, fortunately, some of the silk she had been taught with was left over). And even so, Anthea had to draw the pattern for her. Anthea's side of the bag had letters on it—worked hastily but affectionately in chain stitch. They were something like this:

PSAMS TRAVEL CAR

She would have put 'travelling carriage', but she made the letters too big, so there was no room. The bag was made INTO a bag with old Nurse's sewing machine, and the strings of it were Anthea's and Jane's best red hair ribbons. At tea-time, when the boys had come home with a most unfavourable report of the St james's Park ducks, Anthea ventured to awaken the Psammead, and to show it its new travelling bag.

'Humph,' it said, sniffing a little contemptuously, yet at the same time affectionately, 'it's not so dusty.'

The Psammead seemed to pick up very easily the kind of things that people said nowadays. For a creature that had in its time associated with Megatheriums and Pterodactyls, its quickness was really wonderful.

'It's more worthy of me,' it said, 'than the kind of bag that's given away with a pound of plaice. When do you propose to take me out in it?'

'I should like a rest from taking you or us anywhere,' said Cyril. But Jane said—

'I want to go to Egypt. I did like that Egyptian Princess that came to marry the King in Babylon. She told me about the larks they have in Egypt. And the cats. Do let's go there. And I told her what the bird things on the Amulet were like. And she said it was Egyptian writing.'

The others exchanged looks of silent rejoicing at the thought of their cleverness in having concealed from Jane the terrors they had suffered in the dungeon below the Euphrates.

'Egypt's so nice too,' Jane went on, 'because of Doctor Brewer's Scripture History. I would like to go there when Joseph was dreaming those curious dreams, or when Moses was doing wonderful things with snakes and sticks.'

'I don't care about snakes,' said Anthea shuddering.

'Well, we needn't be in at that part, but Babylon was lovely! We had cream and sweet, sticky stuff. And I expect Egypt's the same.'

There was a good deal of discussion, but it all ended in everybody's agreeing to Jane's idea. And next morning directly after breakfast (which was kippers and very nice) the Psammead was invited to get into his travelling carriage.

The moment after it had done so, with stiff, furry reluctance, like that of a cat when you want to nurse it, and its ideas are not the same as yours, old Nurse came in.

'Well, chickies,' she said, 'are you feeling very dull?'

'Oh, no, Nurse dear,' said Anthea; 'we're having a lovely time. We're just going off to see some old ancient relics.'

'Ah,' said old Nurse, 'the Royal Academy, I suppose? Don't go wasting your money too reckless, that's all.'

She cleared away the kipper bones and the tea-things, and when she had swept up the crumbs and removed the cloth, the Amulet was held up and the order given—just as Duchesses (and other people) give it to their coachmen.

'To Egypt, please!' said Anthea, when Cyril had uttered the wonderful Name of Power.

'When Moses was there,' added Jane.

And there, in the dingy Fitzroy Street dining-room, the Amulet grew big, and it was an arch, and through it they saw a blue, blue sky and a running river.

'No, stop!' said Cyril, and pulled down jane's hand with the Amulet in it.

'What silly cuckoos we all are,' he said. 'Of course we can't go. We daren't leave home for a single minute now, for fear that minute should be THE minute.'

'What minute be WHAT minute?' asked Jane impatiently, trying to get her hand away from Cyril.

'The minute when the Queen of Babylon comes,' said Cyril. And then everyone saw it.

For somedays life flowed in a very slow, dusty, uneventful stream.

The children could never go out all at once, because they never knew when the King of Babylon would go out lion hunting and leave his Queen free to pay them that surprise visit to which she was, without doubt, eagerly looking forward.

So they took it in turns, two and two, to go out and to stay in.

The stay-at-homes would have been much duller than they were but for the new interest taken in them by the learned gentleman.

He called Anthea in one day to show her a beautiful necklace of purple and gold beads.

'I saw one like that,' she said, 'in—'

'In the British Museum, perhaps?'

'I like to call the place where I saw it Babylon,' said Anthea cautiously.

'A pretty fancy,' said the learned gentleman, 'and quite correct too, because, as a matter of fact, these beads did come from Babylon.' The other three were all out that day. The boys had been going to the Zoo, and Jane had said so plaintively, 'I'm sure I am fonder of rhinoceroses than either of you are,' that Anthea had told her to run along then. And she had run, catching the boys before that part of the road where Fitzroy Street suddenly becomes Fitzroy Square.

'I think Babylon is most frightfully interesting,' said Anthea. 'I do have such interesting dreams about it—at least, not dreams exactly, but quite as wonderful.'

'Do sit down and tell me,' said he. So she sat down and told. And he asked her a lot of questions, and she answered them as well as she could.

'Wonderful—wonderful!' he said at last. 'One's heard of thought-transference, but I never thought *I* had any power of that sort. Yet it must be that, and very bad for YOU, I should think. Doesn't your head ache very much?'

He suddenly put a cold, thin hand on her forehead.

'No thank you, not at all,' said she.

'I assure you it is not done intentionally,' he went on. 'Of course I know a good deal about Babylon, and I unconsciously communicate it to you; you've heard of thought-reading, but some of the things you say, I don't understand; they never enter my head, and yet they're so astoundingly probable.'

'It's all right,' said Anthea reassuringly. '*I* understand. And don't worry. It's all quite simple really.'

It was not quite so simple when Anthea, having heard the others come in, went down, and before she had had time to ask how they had liked the Zoo, heard a noise outside, compared to which the wild beasts' noises were gentle as singing birds.

'Good gracious!' cried Anthea, 'what's that?'

The loud hum of many voices came through the open window. Words could be distinguished.

"Ere's a guy!'

'This ain't November. That ain't no guy. It's a ballet lady, that's what it is.'

'Not it—it's a bloomin' looney, I tell you.'

Then came a clear voice that they knew.

'Retire, slaves!' it said.

'What's she a saying of?' cried a dozen voices. 'Some blamed foreign lingo,' one voice replied.

The children rushed to the door. A crowd was on the road and pavement.

In the middle of the crowd, plainly to be seen from the top of the steps, were the beautiful face and bright veil of the Babylonian Queen.

'Jimminy!' cried Robert, and ran down the steps, 'here she is!'

'Here!' he cried, 'look out—let the lady pass. She's a friend of ours, coming to see us.'

'Nice friend for a respectable house,' snorted a fat woman with marrows on a handcart.

All the same the crowd made way a little. The Queen met Robert on the pavement, and Cyril joined them, the Psammead bag still on his arm.

'Here,' he whispered; 'here's the Psammead; you can get wishes.'

'*I* wish you'd come in a different dress, if you HAD to come,' said Robert; 'but it's no use my wishing anything.'

'No,' said the Queen. 'I wish I was dressed—no, I don't—I wish THEY were dressed properly, then they wouldn't be so silly.'

The Psammead blew itself out till the bag was a very tight fit for it; and suddenly every man, woman, and child in that crowd felt that it had not enough clothes on. For, of course, the Queen's idea of proper dress was the dress that had been proper for the working-classes 3,000 years ago in Babylon—and there was not much of it.

'Lawky me!' said the marrow-selling woman, 'whatever could a-took me to come out this figure?' and she wheeled her cart away very quickly indeed.

'Someone's made a pretty guy of you—talk of guys,' said a man who sold bootlaces.

'Well, don't you talk,' said the man next to him. 'Look at your own silly legs; and where's your boots?'

'I never come out like this, I'll take my sacred,' said the bootlace-seller. 'I wasn't quite myself last night, I'll own, but not to dress up like a circus.'

The crowd was all talking at once, and getting rather angry. But no one seemed to think of blaming the Queen.

Anthea bounded down the steps and pulled her up; the others followed, and the door was shut. 'Blowed if I can make it out!' they heard. 'I'm off home, I am.'

And the crowd, coming slowly to the same mind, dispersed, followed by another crowd of persons who were not dressed in what the Queen thought was the proper way.

'We shall have the police here directly,' said Anthea in the tones of despair. 'Oh, why did you come dressed like that?'

The Queen leaned against the arm of the horse-hair sofa.

'How else can a queen dress I should like to know?' she questioned.

'Our Queen wears things like other people,' said Cyril.

'Well, I don't. And I must say,' she remarked in an injured tone, 'that you don't seem very glad to see me now I HAVE come. But perhaps it's the surprise that makes you behave like this. Yet you ought to be used to surprises. The way you vanished! I shall never forget it. The best magic I've ever seen. How did you do it?'

'Oh, never mind about that now,' said Robert. 'You see you've gone and upset all those people, and I expect they'll fetch the police. And we don't want to see you collared and put in prison.'

'You can't put queens in prison,' she said loftily. 'Oh, can't you?' said Cyril. 'We cut off a king's head here once.'

'In this miserable room? How frightfully interesting.'

'No, no, not in this room; in history.'

'Oh, in THAT,' said the Queen disparagingly. 'I thought you'd done it with your own hands.'

The girls shuddered.

'What a hideous city yours is,' the Queen went on pleasantly, 'and what horrid, ignorant people. Do you know they actually can't understand a single word I say.'

'Can you understand them?' asked Jane.

464

'Of course not; they speak some vulgar, Northern dialect. I can understand YOU quite well.'

I really am not going to explain AGAIN how it was that the children could understand other languages than their own so thoroughly, and talk them, too, so that it felt and sounded (to them) just as though they were talking English.

'Well,' said Cyril bluntly, 'now you've seen just how horrid it is, don't you think you might as well go home again?' 'Why, I've seen simply nothing yet,' said the Queen, arranging her starry veil. 'I wished to be at your door, and I was. Now I must go and see your King and Queen.'

'Nobody's allowed to,' said Anthea in haste; 'but look here, we'll take you and show you anything you'd like to see—anything you CAN see,' she added kindly, because she remembered how nice the Queen had been to them in Babylon, even if she had been a little deceitful in the matter of Jane and Psammead.

'There's the Museum,' said Cyril hopefully; 'there are lots of things from your country there. If only we could disguise you a little.'

'I know,' said Anthea suddenly. 'Mother's old theatre cloak, and there are a lot of her old hats in the big box.'

The blue silk, lace-trimmed cloak did indeed hide some of the Queen's startling splendours, but the hat fitted very badly. It had pink roses in it; and there was something about the coat or the hat or the Queen, that made her look somehow not very respectable.

'Oh, never mind,' said Anthea, when Cyril whispered this. 'The thing is to get her out before Nurse has finished her forty winks. I should think she's about got to the thirty-ninth wink by now.'

'Come on then,' said Robert. 'You know how dangerous it is. Let's make haste into the Museum. If any of those people you made guys of do fetch the police, they won't think of looking for you there.'

The blue silk coat and the pink-rosed hat attracted almost as much attention as the royal costume had done; and the children were uncommonly glad to get out of the noisy streets into the grey quiet of the Museum.

'Parcels and umbrellas to be left here,' said a man at the counter.

The party had no umbrellas, and the only parcel was the bag containing the Psammead, which the Queen had insisted should be brought.

'I'M not going to be left,' said the Psammead softly, 'so don't you think it.'

'I'll wait outside with you,' said Anthea hastily, and went to sit on the seat near the drinking fountain.

'Don't sit so near that nasty fountain,' said the creature crossly; 'I might get splashed.'

Anthea obediently moved to another seat and waited. Indeed she waited, and waited, and waited, and waited, and waited. The Psammead dropped into an uneasy slumber. Anthea had long ceased to watch the swing-door that always let out the wrong person, and she was herself almost asleep, and still the others did not come back.

It was quite a start when Anthea suddenly realized that they HAD come back, and that they were not alone. Behind them was quite a crowd of men in uniform, and several gentlemen were there. Everyone seemed very angry.

'Now go,' said the nicest of the angry gentlemen. 'Take the poor, demented thing home and tell your parents she ought to be properly looked after.'

'If you can't get her to go we must send for the police,' said the nastiest gentleman.

'But we don't wish to use harsh measures,' added the nice one, who was really very nice indeed, and seemed to be over all the others.

466

'May I speak to my sister a moment first?' asked Robert.

The nicest gentleman nodded, and the officials stood round the Queen, the others forming a sort of guard while Robert crossed over to Anthea.

'Everything you can think of,' he replied to Anthea's glance of inquiry. 'Kicked up the most frightful shine in there. Said those necklaces and earrings and things in the glass cases were all hers—would have them out of the cases. Tried to break the glass—she did break one bit! Everybody in the place has been at her. No good. I only got her out by telling her that was the place where they cut queens' heads off.'

'Oh, Bobs, what a whacker!'

'You'd have told a whackinger one to get her out. Besides, it wasn't. I meant MUMMY queens. How do you know they don't cut off mummies' heads to see how the embalming is done? What I want to say is, can't you get her to go with you quietly?'

'I'll try,' said Anthea, and went up to the Queen.

'Do come home,' she said; 'the learned gentleman in our house has a much nicer necklace than anything they've got here. Come and see it.'

The Queen nodded.

'You see,' said the nastiest gentleman, 'she does understand English.'

'I was talking Babylonian, I think,' said Anthea bashfully.

'My good child,' said the nice gentleman, 'what you're talking is not Babylonian, but nonsense. You just go home at once, and tell your parents exactly what has happened.'

Anthea took the Queen's hand and gently pulled her away. The other children followed, and the black crowd of angry gentlemen stood on the steps watching them. It was when the little party of disgraced children, with the Queen who had disgraced them, had reached the middle of the courtyard that her eyes fell on the bag where the Psammead was. She stopped short.

'I wish,' she said, very loud and clear, 'that all those Babylonian things would come out to me here—slowly, so that those dogs and slaves can see the working of the great Queen's magic.'

'Oh, you ARE a tiresome woman,' said the Psammead in its bag, but it puffed itself out.

Next moment there was a crash. The glass swing doors and all their framework were smashed suddenly and completely. The crowd of angry gentlemen sprang aside when they saw what had done this.

But the nastiest of them was not quick enough, and he was roughly pushed out of the way by an enormous stone bull that was floating steadily through the door. It came and stood beside the Queen in the middle of the courtyard.

It was followed by more stone images, by great slabs of carved stone, bricks, helmets, tools, weapons, fetters, wine-jars, bowls, bottles, vases, jugs, saucers, seals, and the round long things, something like rolling pins with marks on them like the print of little bird-feet, necklaces, collars, rings, armlets, earrings—heaps and heaps and heaps of things, far more than anyone had time to count, or even to see distinctly.

All the angry gentlemen had abruptly sat down on the Museum steps except the nice one. He stood with his hands in his pockets just as though he was quite used to seeing great stone bulls and all sorts of small Babylonish objects float out into the Museum yard.

But he sent a man to close the big iron gates.

A journalist, who was just leaving the museum, spoke to Robert as he passed.

'Theosophy, I suppose?' he said. 'Is she Mrs Besant?'

'YES,' said Robert recklessly.

The journalist passed through the gates just before they were shut.

He rushed off to Fleet Street, and his paper got out a new edition within half an hour.

MRS BESANT AND THEOSOPHY

IMPERTINENT MIRACLE AT THE BRITISH MUSEUM.

People saw it in fat, black letters on the boards carried by the sellers of newspapers. Some few people who had nothing better to do went down to the Museum on the tops of omnibuses. But by the time they got there there was nothing to be seen. For the Babylonian Queen had suddenly seen the closed gates, had felt the threat of them, and had said—

'I wish we were in your house.'

And, of course, instantly they were.

The Psammead was furious.

'Look here,' it said, 'they'll come after you, and they'll find ME. There'll be a National Cage built for me at Westminster, and I shall have to work at politics. Why wouldn't you leave the things in their places?'

'What a temper you have, haven't you?' said the Queen serenely. 'I wish all the things were back in their places. Will THAT do for you?'

The Psammead swelled and shrank and spoke very angrily.

'I can't refuse to give your wishes,' it said, 'but I can Bite. And I will if this goes on. Now then.'

'Ah, don't,' whispered Anthea close to its bristling ear; 'it's dreadful for us too. Don't YOU desert us. Perhaps she'll wish herself at home again soon.'

'Not she,' said the Psammead a little less crossly.

'Take me to see your City,' said the Queen.

The children looked at each other.

'If we had some money we could take her about in a cab. People wouldn't notice her so much then. But we haven't.'

'Sell this,' said the Queen, taking a ring from her finger.

'They'd only think we'd stolen it,' said Cyril bitterly, 'and put us in prison.'

'All roads lead to prison with you, it seems,' said the Queen.

'The learned gentleman!' said Anthea, and ran up to him with the ring in her hand.

'Look here,' she said, 'will you buy this for a pound?'

'Oh!' he said in tones of joy and amazement, and took the ring into his hand. 'It's my very own,' said Anthea; 'it was given to me to sell.'

'I'll lend you a pound,' said the learned gentleman, 'with pleasure; and I'll take care of the ring for you. Who did you say gave it to you?'

'We call her,' said Anthea carefully, 'the Queen of Babylon.'

'Is it a game?' he asked hopefully.

'It'll be a pretty game if I don't get the money to pay for cabs for her,' said Anthea.

'I sometimes think,' he said slowly, 'that I am becoming insane, or that—'

'Or that I am; but I'm not, and you're not, and she's not.'

'Does she SAY that she's the Queen of Babylon?' he uneasily asked.

'Yes,' said Anthea recklessly.

470

'This thought-transference is more far-reaching than I imagined,' he said. 'I suppose I have unconsciously influenced HER, too. I never thought my Babylonish studies would bear fruit like this. Horrible! There are more things in heaven and earth—'

'Yes,' said Anthea, 'heaps more. And the pound is the thing *I* want more than anything on earth.'

He ran his fingers through his thin hair.

'This thought-transference!' he said. 'It's undoubtedly a Babylonian ring—or it seems so to me. But perhaps I have hypnotized myself. I will see a doctor the moment I have corrected the last proofs of my book.'

'Yes, do!' said Anthea, 'and thank you so very much.'

She took the sovereign and ran down to the others.

And now from the window of a four-wheeled cab the Queen of Babylon beheld the wonders of London. Buckingham Palace she thought uninteresting; Westminster Abbey and the Houses of Parliament little better. But she liked the Tower, and the River, and the ships filled her with wonder and delight.

'But how badly you keep your slaves. How wretched and poor and neglected they seem,' she said, as the cab rattled along the Mile End Road.

'They aren't slaves; they're working-people,' said Jane.

'Of course they're working. That's what slaves are. Don't you tell me. Do you suppose I don't know a slave's face when I see it?

Why don't their masters see that they're better fed and better clothed? Tell me in three words.'

No one answered. The wage-system of modern England is a little difficult to explain in three words even if you understand it—which the children didn't.

'You'll have a revolt of your slaves if you're not careful,' said the Queen.

'Oh, no,' said Cyril; 'you see they have votes—that makes them safe not to revolt. It makes all the difference. Father told me so.'

'What is this vote?' asked the Queen. 'Is it a charm? What do they do with it?'

'I don't know,' said the harassed Cyril; 'it's just a vote, that's all! They don't do anything particular with it.'

'I see,' said the Queen; 'a sort of plaything. Well, I wish that all these slaves may have in their hands this moment their fill of their favourite meat and drink.'

Instantly all the people in the Mile End Road, and in all the other streets where poor people live, found their hands full of things to eat and drink. From the cab window could be seen persons carrying every kind of food, and bottles and cans as well. Roast meat, fowls, red lobsters, great yellowy crabs, fried fish, boiled pork, beef-steak puddings, baked onions, mutton pies; most of the young people had oranges and sweets and cake. It made an enormous change in the look of the Mile End Road—brightened it up, so to speak, and brightened up, more than you can possibly imagine, the faces of the people.

'Makes a difference, doesn't it?' said the Queen.

'That's the best wish you've had yet,' said Jane with cordial approval.

just by the Bank the cabman stopped.

'I ain't agoin' to drive you no further,' he said. 'Out you gets.'

They got out rather unwillingly.

'I wants my tea,' he said; and they saw that on the box of the cab was a mound of cabbage, with pork chops and apple sauce, a duck, and a spotted currant pudding. Also a large can.

472

'You pay me my fare,' he said threateningly, and looked down at the mound, muttering again about his tea.

'We'll take another cab,' said Cyril with dignity. 'Give me change for a sovereign, if you please.'

But the cabman, as it turned out, was not at all a nice character. He took the sovereign, whipped up his horse, and disappeared in the stream of cabs and omnibuses and wagons, without giving them any change at all.

Already a little crowd was collecting round the party.

'Come on,' said Robert, leading the wrong way.

The crowd round them thickened. They were in a narrow street where many gentlemen in black coats and without hats were standing about on the pavement talking very loudly.

'How ugly their clothes are,' said the Queen of Babylon. 'They'd be rather fine men, some of them, if they were dressed decently, especially the ones with the beautiful long, curved noses. I wish they were dressed like the Babylonians of my court.'

And of course, it was so.

The moment the almost fainting Psammead had blown itself out every man in Throgmorton Street appeared abruptly in Babylonian full dress.

All were carefully powdered, their hair and beards were scented and curled, their garments richly embroidered. They wore rings and armlets, flat gold collars and swords, and impossible-looking head-dresses.

A stupefied silence fell on them.

'I say,' a youth who had always been fair-haired broke that silence, 'it's only fancy of course—something wrong with my eyes—but you chaps do look so rum.'

'Rum,' said his friend. 'Look at YOU. You in a sash! My hat! And your hair's gone black and you've got a beard. It's my belief we've been poisoned. You do look a jackape.'

'Old Levinstein don't look so bad. But how was it DONE—that's what I want to know. How was it done? Is it conjuring, or what?'

'I think it is chust a ver' bad tream,' said old Levinstein to his clerk; 'all along Bishopsgate I haf seen the gommon people have their hants full of food—GOOT food. Oh yes, without doubt a very bad tream!'

'Then I'm dreaming too, Sir,' said the clerk, looking down at his legs with an expression of loathing. 'I see my feet in beastly sandals as plain as plain.'

'All that goot food wasted,' said old Mr Levinstein. A bad tream—a bad tream.'

The Members of the Stock Exchange are said to be at all times a noisy lot. But the noise they made now to express their disgust at the costumes of ancient Babylon was far louder than their ordinary row. One had to shout before one could hear oneself speak.

'I only wish,' said the clerk who thought it was conjuring—he was quite close to the children and they trembled, because they knew that whatever he wished would come true. 'I only wish we knew who'd done it.'

And, of course, instantly they did know, and they pressed round the Queen.

'Scandalous! Shameful! Ought to be put down by law. Give her in charge. Fetch the police,' two or three voices shouted at once.

The Queen recoiled.

'What is it?' she asked. 'They sound like caged lions—lions by the thousand. What is it that they say?'

'They say "Police!",' said Cyril briefly. 'I knew they would sooner or later. And I don't blame them, mind you.'

'I wish my guards were here!' cried the Queen. The exhausted Psammead was panting and trembling, but the Queen's guards in red and green garments, and brass and iron gear, choked Throgmorton Street, and bared weapons flashed round the Queen.

'I'm mad,' said a Mr Rosenbaum; 'dat's what it is—mad!'

'It's a judgement on you, Rosy,' said his partner. 'I always said you were too hard in that matter of Flowerdew. It's a judgement, and I'm in it too.'

The members of the Stock Exchange had edged carefully away from the gleaming blades, the mailed figures, the hard, cruel Eastern faces.

But Throgmorton Street is narrow, and the crowd was too thick for them to get away as quickly as they wished.

'Kill them,' cried the Queen. 'Kill the dogs!'

The guards obeyed.

'It IS all a dream,' cried Mr Levinstein, cowering in a doorway behind his clerk.

'It isn't,' said the clerk. 'It isn't. Oh, my good gracious! those foreign brutes are killing everybody. Henry Hirsh is down now, and Prentice is cut in two—oh, Lord! and Huth, and there goes Lionel Cohen with his head off, and Guy Nickalls has lost his head now. A dream? I wish to goodness it was all a dream.'

And, of course, instantly it was! The entire Stock Exchange rubbed its eyes and went back to close, to over, and either side of seven-eights, and Trunks, and Kaffirs, and Steel Common, and Contangoes, and Backwardations, Double Options, and all the interesting subjects concerning which they talk in the Street without ceasing.

No one said a word about it to anyone else. I think I have explained before that business men do not like it to be known that they have been dreaming in business hours. Especially mad dreams

475

including such dreadful things as hungry people getting dinners, and the destruction of the Stock Exchange.

The children were in the dining-room at 300, Fitzroy Street, pale and trembling. The Psammead crawled out of the embroidered bag, and lay flat on the table, its leg stretched out, looking more like a dead hare than anything else.

'Thank Goodness that's over,' said Anthea, drawing a deep breath.

'She won't come back, will she?' asked Jane tremulously.

'No,' said Cyril. 'She's thousands of years ago. But we spent a whole precious pound on her. It'll take all our pocket-money for ages to pay that back.'

'Not if it was ALL a dream,' said Robert.

'The wish said ALL a dream, you know, Panther; you cut up and ask if he lent you anything.'

'I beg your pardon,' said Anthea politely, following the sound of her knock into the presence of the learned gentleman, 'I'm so sorry to trouble you, but DID you lend me a pound today?'

'No,' said he, looking kindly at her through his spectacles. 'But it's extraordinary that you should ask me, for I dozed for a few moments this afternoon, a thing I very rarely do, and I dreamed quite distinctly that you brought me a ring that you said belonged to the Queen of Babylon, and that I lent you a sovereign and that you left one of the Queen's rings here. The ring was a magnificent specimen.' He sighed. 'I wish it hadn't been a dream,' he said smiling. He was really learning to smile quite nicely.

Anthea could not be too thankful that the Psammead was not there to grant his wish.

CHAPTER 9. ATLANTIS

You will understand that the adventure of the Babylonian queen in London was the only one that had occupied any time at all. But the children's time was very fully taken up by talking over all the wonderful things seen and done in the Past, where, by the power of the Amulet, they seemed to spend hours and hours, only to find when they got back to London that the whole thing had been briefer than a lightning flash.

They talked of the Past at their meals, in their walks, in the dining-room, in the first-floor drawing-room, but most of all on the stairs. It was an old house; it had once been a fashionable one, and was a fine one still. The banister rails of the stairs were excellent for sliding down, and in the corners of the landings were big alcoves that had once held graceful statues, and now quite often held the graceful forms of Cyril, Robert, Anthea, and Jane.

One day Cyril and Robert in tight white underclothing had spent a pleasant hour in reproducing the attitudes of statues seen either in the British Museum, or in Father's big photograph book. But the show ended abruptly because Robert wanted to be the Venus of Milo, and for this purpose pulled at the sheet which served for drapery at the very moment when Cyril, looking really quite like the Discobolos—with a gold and white saucer for the disc—was standing on one foot, and under that one foot was the sheet.

Of course the Discobolos and his disc and the would-be Venus came down together, and everyone was a good deal hurt, especially the saucer, which would never be the same again, however neatly one might join its uneven bits with Seccotine or the white of an egg.

'I hope you're satisfied,' said Cyril, holding his head where a large lump was rising.

'Quite, thanks,' said Robert bitterly. His thumb had caught in the banisters and bent itself back almost to breaking point.

'I AM so sorry, poor, dear Squirrel,' said Anthea; 'and you were looking so lovely. I'll get a wet rag. Bobs, go and hold your hand under the hot-water tap. It's what ballet girls do with their legs when they hurt them. I saw it in a book.'

'What book?' said Robert disagreeably. But he went.

When he came back Cyril's head had been bandaged by his sisters, and he had been brought to the state of mind where he was able reluctantly to admit that he supposed Robert hadn't done it on purpose.

Robert replying with equal suavity, Anthea hastened to lead the talk away from the accident.

'I suppose you don't feel like going anywhere through the Amulet,' she said.

'Egypt!' said Jane promptly. 'I want to see the pussy cats.'

'Not me—too hot,' said Cyril. 'It's about as much as I can stand here—let alone Egypt.' It was indeed, hot, even on the second landing, which was the coolest place in the house. 'Let's go to the North Pole.'

'I don't suppose the Amulet was ever there—and we might get our fingers frost-bitten so that we could never hold it up to get home again. No thanks,' said Robert.

'I say,' said Jane, 'let's get the Psammead and ask its advice. It will like us asking, even if we don't take it.'

The Psammead was brought up in its green silk embroidered bag, but before it could be asked anything the door of the learned gentleman's room opened and the voice of the visitor who had been lunching with him was heard on the stairs. He seemed to be speaking with the door handle in his hand.

'You see a doctor, old boy,' he said; 'all that about thought-transference is just simply twaddle. You've been over-working. Take a holiday. Go to Dieppe.'

'I'd rather go to Babylon,' said the learned gentleman.

'I wish you'd go to Atlantis some time, while we're about it, so as to give me some tips for my Nineteenth Century article when you come home.'

'I wish I could,' said the voice of the learned gentleman. 'Goodbye. Take care of yourself.'

The door was banged, and the visitor came smiling down the stairs—a stout, prosperous, big man. The children had to get up to let him pass.

'Hullo, Kiddies,' he said, glancing at the bandages on the head of Cyril and the hand of Robert, 'been in the wars?'

'It's all right,' said Cyril. 'I say, what was that Atlantic place you wanted him to go to? We couldn't help hearing you talk.'

'You talk so VERY loud, you see,' said Jane soothingly.

'Atlantis,' said the visitor, 'the lost Atlantis, garden of the Hesperides. Great continent—disappeared in the sea. You can read about it in Plato.'

'Thank you,' said Cyril doubtfully.

'Were there any Amulets there?' asked Anthea, made anxious by a sudden thought.

'Hundreds, I should think. So HE'S been talking to you?'

'Yes, often. He's very kind to us. We like him awfully.'

'Well, what he wants is a holiday; you persuade him to take one. What he wants is a change of scene. You see, his head is crusted so thickly inside with knowledge about Egypt and Assyria and things that you can't hammer anything into it unless you keep hard at it all day long for days and days. And I haven't time. But you live in the house. You can hammer almost incessantly. Just try your hands, will you? Right. So long!'

He went down the stairs three at a time, and Jane remarked that he was a nice man, and she thought he had little girls of his own.

'I should like to have them to play with,' she added pensively.

The three elder ones exchanged glances. Cyril nodded.

'All right. LET'S go to Atlantis,' he said.

'Let's go to Atlantis and take the learned gentleman with us,' said Anthea; 'he'll think it's a dream, afterwards, but it'll certainly be a change of scene.'

'Why not take him to nice Egypt?' asked Jane.

'Too hot,' said Cyril shortly.

'Or Babylon, where he wants to go?'

'I've had enough of Babylon,' said Robert, 'at least for the present. And so have the others. I don't know why,' he added, forestalling the question on Jane's lips, 'but somehow we have. Squirrel, let's take off these beastly bandages and get into flannels. We can't go in our unders.'

'He WISHED to go to Atlantis, so he's got to go some time; and he might as well go with us,' said Anthea.

This was how it was that the learned gentleman, permitting himself a few moments of relaxation in his chair, after the fatigue of listening to opinions (about Atlantis and many other things) with which he did not at all agree, opened his eyes to find his four young friends standing in front of him in a row.

'Will you come,' said Anthea, 'to Atlantis with us?'

'To know that you are dreaming shows that the dream is nearly at an end,' he told himself; 'or perhaps it's only a game, like "How many miles to Babylon?".' So he said aloud: 'Thank you very much, but I have only a quarter of an hour to spare.'

'It doesn't take any time,' said Cyril; 'time is only a mode of thought, you know, and you've got to go some time, so why not with us?'

'Very well,' said the learned gentleman, now quite certain that he was dreaming.

Anthea held out her soft, pink hand. He took it. She pulled him gently to his feet. Jane held up the Amulet.

'To just outside Atlantis,' said Cyril, and Jane said the Name of Power.

'You owl!' said Robert, 'it's an island. Outside an island's all water.'

'I won't go. I WON'T,' said the Psammead, kicking and struggling in its bag.

But already the Amulet had grown to a great arch. Cyril pushed the learned gentleman, as undoubtedly the first-born, through the arch—not into water, but on to a wooden floor, out of doors. The others followed. The Amulet grew smaller again, and there they all were, standing on the deck of a ship whose sailors were busy making her fast with chains to rings on a white quay-side. The rings and the chains were of a metal that shone red-yellow like gold.

Everyone on the ship seemed too busy at first to notice the group of newcomers from Fitzroy Street. Those who seemed to be officers were shouting orders to the men.

They stood and looked across the wide quay to the town that rose beyond it. What they saw was the most beautiful sight any of them had ever seen—or ever dreamed of.

The blue sea sparkled in soft sunlight; little white-capped waves broke softly against the marble breakwaters that guarded the shipping of a great city from the wilderness of winter winds and seas. The quay was of marble, white and sparkling with a veining bright as gold. The city was of marble, red and white. The greater

481

buildings that seemed to be temples and palaces were roofed with what looked like gold and silver, but most of the roofs were of copper that glowed golden-red on the houses on the hills among which the city stood, and shaded into marvellous tints of green and blue and purple where they had been touched by the salt sea spray and the fumes of the dyeing and smelting works of the lower town.

Broad and magnificent flights of marble stairs led up from the quay to a sort of terrace that seemed to run along for miles, and beyond rose the town built on a hill.

The learned gentleman drew a long breath. 'Wonderful!' he said, 'wonderful!'

'I say, Mr—what's your name,' said Robert. 'He means,' said Anthea, with gentle politeness, 'that we never can remember your name. I know it's Mr De Something.'

'When I was your age I was called Jimmy,' he said timidly. 'Would you mind? I should feel more at home in a dream like this if I—Anything that made me seem more like one of you.'

'Thank you—Jimmy,' said Anthea with an effort. It seemed such a cheek to be saying Jimmy to a grown-up man. 'Jimmy, DEAR,' she added, with no effort at all. Jimmy smiled and looked pleased.

But now the ship was made fast, and the Captain had time to notice other things. He came towards them, and he was dressed in the best of all possible dresses for the seafaring life.

'What are you doing here?' he asked rather fiercely. 'Do you come to bless or to curse?'

'To bless, of course,' said Cyril. 'I'm sorry if it annoys you, but we're here by magic. We come from the land of the sun-rising,' he went on explanatorily.

'I see,' said the Captain; no one had expected that he would. 'I didn't notice at first, but of course I hope you're a good omen. It's needed. And this,' he pointed to the learned gentleman, 'your slave, I presume?'

'Not at all,' said Anthea; 'he's a very great man. A sage, don't they call it? And we want to see all your beautiful city, and your temples and things, and then we shall go back, and he will tell his friend, and his friend will write a book about it.'

'What,' asked the Captain, fingering a rope, 'is a book?'

'A record—something written, or,' she added hastily, remembering the Babylonian writing, 'or engraved.'

Some sudden impulse of confidence made Jane pluck the Amulet from the neck of her frock.

'Like this,' she said.

The Captain looked at it curiously, but, the other three were relieved to notice, without any of that overwhelming interest which the mere name of it had roused in Egypt and Babylon.

'The stone is of our country,' he said; 'and that which is engraved on it, it is like our writing, but I cannot read it. What is the name of your sage?'

'Ji-jimmy,' said Anthea hesitatingly.

The Captain repeated, 'Ji-jimmy. Will you land?' he added. 'And shall I lead you to the Kings?'

'Look here,' said Robert, 'does your King hate strangers?'

'Our Kings are ten,' said the Captain, 'and the Royal line, unbroken from Poseidon, the father of us all, has the noble tradition to do honour to strangers if they come in peace.'

'Then lead on, please,' said Robert, 'though I SHOULD like to see all over your beautiful ship, and sail about in her.'

'That shall be later,' said the Captain; 'just now we're afraid of a storm—do you notice that odd rumbling?'

'That's nothing, master,' said an old sailor who stood near; 'it's the pilchards coming in, that's all.'

'Too loud,' said the Captain.

There was a rather anxious pause; then the Captain stepped on to the quay, and the others followed him.

'Do talk to him—Jimmy,' said Anthea as they went; 'you can find out all sorts of things for your friend's book.'

'Please excuse me,' he said earnestly. 'If I talk I shall wake up; and besides, I can't understand what he says.'

No one else could think of anything to say, so that it was in complete silence that they followed the Captain up the marble steps and through the streets of the town. There were streets and shops and houses and markets.

'It's just like Babylon,' whispered Jane, 'only everything's perfectly different.'

'It's a great comfort the ten Kings have been properly brought up—to be kind to strangers,' Anthea whispered to Cyril.

'Yes,' he said, 'no deepest dungeons here.'

There were no horses or chariots in the street, but there were handcarts and low trolleys running on thick log-wheels, and porters carrying packets on their heads, and a good many of the people were riding on what looked like elephants, only the great beasts were hairy, and they had not that mild expression we are accustomed to meet on the faces of the elephants at the Zoo.

'Mammoths!' murmured the learned gentleman, and stumbled over a loose stone.

The people in the streets kept crowding round them as they went along, but the Captain always dispersed the crowd before it grew uncomfortably thick by saying—

'Children of the Sun God and their High Priest—come to bless the City.'

And then the people would draw back with a low murmur that sounded like a suppressed cheer.

Many of the buildings were covered with gold, but the gold on the bigger buildings was of a different colour, and they had sorts of steeples of burnished silver rising above them.

'Are all these houses real gold?' asked Jane.

'The temples are covered with gold, of course,' answered the Captain, 'but the houses are only oricalchum. It's not quite so expensive.'

The learned gentleman, now very pale, stumbled along in a dazed way, repeating:

'Oricalchum—oricalchum.'

'Don't be frightened,' said Anthea; 'we can get home in a minute, just by holding up the charm. Would you rather go back now? We could easily come some other day without you.'

'Oh, no, no,' he pleaded fervently; 'let the dream go on. Please, please do.'

'The High Ji-jimmy is perhaps weary with his magic journey,' said the Captain, noticing the blundering walk of the learned gentleman; 'and we are yet very far from the Great Temple, where today the Kings make sacrifice.'

He stopped at the gate of a great enclosure. It seemed to be a sort of park, for trees showed high above its brazen wall.

The party waited, and almost at once the Captain came back with one of the hairy elephants and begged them to mount.

This they did.

It was a glorious ride. The elephant at the Zoo—to ride on him is also glorious, but he goes such a very little way, and then he goes back again, which is always dull. But this great hairy beast went on and on and on along streets and through squares and gardens. It was a glorious city; almost everything was built of marble, red, or white, or black. Every now and then the party crossed a bridge.

It was not till they had climbed to the hill which is the centre of the town that they saw that the whole city was divided into twenty circles, alternately land and water, and over each of the water circles were the bridges by which they had come.

And now they were in a great square. A vast building filled up one side of it; it was overlaid with gold, and had a dome of silver. The rest of the buildings round the square were of oricalchum. And it looked more splendid than you can possibly imagine, standing up bold and shining in the sunlight.

'You would like a bath,' said the Captain, as the hairy elephant went clumsily down on his knees. 'It's customary, you know, before entering the Presence. We have baths for men, women, horses, and cattle. The High Class Baths are here. Our Father Poseidon gave us a spring of hot water and one of cold.'

The children had never before bathed in baths of gold.

'It feels very splendid,' said Cyril, splashing.

'At least, of course, it's not gold; it's or—what's its name,' said Robert. 'Hand over that towel.'

The bathing hall had several great pools sunk below the level of the floor; one went down to them by steps.

'Jimmy,' said Anthea timidly, when, very clean and boiled-looking, they all met in the flowery courtyard of the Public, 'don't you think all this seems much more like NOW than Babylon or Egypt—? Oh, I forgot, you've never been there.'

'I know a little of those nations, however,' said he, 'and I quite agree with you. A most discerning remark—my dear,' he added awkwardly; 'this city certainly seems to indicate a far higher level of civilization than the Egyptian or Babylonish, and—'

'Follow me,' said the Captain. 'Now, boys, get out of the way.' He pushed through a little crowd of boys who were playing with dried chestnuts fastened to a string.

'Ginger!' remarked Robert, 'they're playing conkers, just like the kids in Kentish Town Road!'

They could see now that three walls surrounded the island on which they were. The outermost wall was of brass, the Captain told them; the next, which looked like silver, was covered with tin; and the innermost one was of oricalchum.

And right in the middle was a wall of gold, with golden towers and gates.

'Behold the Temples of Poseidon,' said the Captain. 'It is not lawful for me to enter. I will await your return here.'

He told them what they ought to say, and the five people from Fitzroy Street took hands and went forward. The golden gates slowly opened.

'We are the children of the Sun,' said Cyril, as he had been told, 'and our High Priest, at least that's what the Captain calls him. We have a different name for him at home.' 'What is his name?' asked a white-robed man who stood in the doorway with his arms extended.

'Ji-jimmy,' replied Cyril, and he hesitated as Anthea had done. It really did seem to be taking a great liberty with so learned a gentleman. 'And we have come to speak with your Kings in the Temple of Poseidon—does that word sound right?' he whispered anxiously.

'Quite,' said the learned gentleman. 'It's very odd I can understand what you say to them, but not what they say to you.'

'The Queen of Babylon found that too,' said Cyril; 'it's part of the magic.'

'Oh, what a dream!' said the learned gentleman.

The white-robed priest had been joined by others, and all were bowing low.

'Enter,' he said, 'enter, Children of the Sun, with your High Ji-jimmy.'

In an inner courtyard stood the Temple—all of silver, with gold pinnacles and doors, and twenty enormous statues in bright gold of men and women. Also an immense pillar of the other precious yellow metal.

They went through the doors, and the priest led them up a stair into a gallery from which they could look down on to the glorious place.

'The ten Kings are even now choosing the bull. It is not lawful for me to behold,' said the priest, and fell face downward on the floor outside the gallery. The children looked down.

The roof was of ivory adorned with the three precious metals, and the walls were lined with the favourite oricalchum.

At the far end of the Temple was a statue group, the like of which no one living has ever seen.

It was of gold, and the head of the chief figure reached to the roof. That figure was Poseidon, the Father of the City. He stood in a great chariot drawn by six enormous horses, and round about it were a hundred mermaids riding on dolphins.

Ten men, splendidly dressed and armed only with sticks and ropes, were trying to capture one of some fifteen bulls who ran this way and that about the floor of the Temple. The children held their breath, for the bulls looked dangerous, and the great horned heads were swinging more and more wildly.

Anthea did not like looking at the bulls. She looked about the gallery, and noticed that another staircase led up from it to a still higher storey; also that a door led out into the open air, where there seemed to be a balcony.

488

So that when a shout went up and Robert whispered, 'Got him,' and she looked down and saw the herd of bulls being driven out of the Temple by whips, and the ten Kings following, one of them spurring with his stick a black bull that writhed and fought in the grip of a lasso, she answered the boy's agitated, 'Now we shan't see anything more,' with—

'Yes we can, there's an outside balcony.'

So they crowded out.

But very soon the girls crept back.

'I don't like sacrifices,' Jane said. So she and Anthea went and talked to the priest, who was no longer lying on his face, but sitting on the top step mopping his forehead with his robe, for it was a hot day.

'It's a special sacrifice,' he said; 'usually it's only done on the justice days every five years and six years alternately. And then they drink the cup of wine with some of the bull's blood in it, and swear to judge truly. And they wear the sacred blue robe, and put out all the Temple fires. But this today is because the City's so upset by the odd noises from the sea, and the god inside the big mountain speaking with his thunder-voice. But all that's happened so often before. If anything could make ME uneasy it wouldn't be THAT.'

'What would it be?' asked Jane kindly.

'It would be the Lemmings.'

'Who are they—enemies?'

'They're a sort of rat; and every year they come swimming over from the country that no man knows, and stay here awhile, and then swim away. This year they haven't come. You know rats won't stay on a ship that's going to be wrecked. If anything horrible were going to happen to us, it's my belief those Lemmings would know; and that may be why they've fought shy of us.'

'What do you call this country?' asked the Psammead, suddenly putting its head out of its bag.

'Atlantis,' said the priest.

'Then I advise you to get on to the highest ground you can find. I remember hearing something about a flood here. Look here, you'—it turned to Anthea; 'let's get home. The prospect's too wet for my whiskers.' The girls obediently went to find their brothers, who were leaning on the balcony railings.

'Where's the learned gentleman?' asked Anthea.

'There he is—below,' said the priest, who had come with them. 'Your High Ji-jimmy is with the Kings.'

The ten Kings were no longer alone. The learned gentleman—no one had noticed how he got there—stood with them on the steps of an altar, on which lay the dead body of the black bull. All the rest of the courtyard was thick with people, seemingly of all classes, and all were shouting, 'The sea—the sea!'

'Be calm,' said the most kingly of the Kings, he who had lassoed the bull. 'Our town is strong against the thunders of the sea and of the sky!'

'I want to go home,' whined the Psammead.

'We can't go without HIM,' said Anthea firmly.

'Jimmy,' she called, 'Jimmy!' and waved to him. He heard her, and began to come towards her through the crowd. They could see from the balcony the sea-captain edging his way out from among the people. And his face was dead white, like paper.

'To the hills!' he cried in a loud and terrible voice. And above his voice came another voice, louder, more terrible—the voice of the sea.

The girls looked seaward.

Across the smooth distance of the sea something huge and black rolled towards the town. It was a wave, but a wave a hundred feet in height, a wave that looked like a mountain—a wave rising higher and higher till suddenly it seemed to break in two—one half of it rushed out to sea again; the other—

'Oh!' cried Anthea, 'the town—the poor people!'

'It's all thousands of years ago, really,' said Robert but his voice trembled. They hid their eyes for a moment. They could not bear to look down, for the wave had broken on the face of the town, sweeping over the quays and docks, overwhelming the great storehouses and factories, tearing gigantic stones from forts and bridges, and using them as battering rams against the temples. Great ships were swept over the roofs of the houses and dashed down halfway up the hill among ruined gardens and broken buildings. The water ground brown fishing-boats to powder on the golden roofs of Palaces.

Then the wave swept back towards the sea.

'I want to go home,' cried the Psammead fiercely.

'Oh, yes, yes!' said Jane, and the boys were ready—but the learned gentleman had not come.

Then suddenly they heard him dash up to the inner gallery, crying—

'I MUST see the end of the dream.' He rushed up the higher flight.

The others followed him. They found themselves in a sort of turret—roofed, but open to the air at the sides.

The learned gentleman was leaning on the parapet, and as they rejoined him the vast wave rushed back on the town. This time it rose higher—destroyed more.

'Come home,' cried the Psammead; 'THAT'S the LAST, I know it is! That's the last—over there.' It pointed with a claw that trembled.

'Oh, come!' cried Jane, holding up the Amulet.

'I WILL SEE the end of the dream,' cried the learned gentleman.

'You'll never see anything else if you do,' said Cyril. 'Oh, JIMMY!' appealed Anthea. 'I'll NEVER bring you out again!'

'You'll never have the chance if you don't go soon,' said the Psammead.

'I WILL see the end of the dream,' said the learned gentleman obstinately.

The hills around were black with people fleeing from the villages to the mountains. And even as they fled thin smoke broke from the great white peak, and then a faint flash of flame. Then the volcano began to throw up its mysterious fiery inside parts. The earth trembled; ashes and sulphur showered down; a rain of fine pumice-stone fell like snow on all the dry land. The elephants from the forest rushed up towards the peaks; great lizards thirty yards long broke from the mountain pools and rushed down towards the sea. The snows melted and rushed down, first in avalanches, then in roaring torrents. Great rocks cast up by the volcano fell splashing in the sea miles away.

'Oh, this is horrible!' cried Anthea. 'Come home, come home!'

'The end of the dream,' gasped the learned gentleman.

'Hold up the Amulet,' cried the Psammead suddenly. The place where they stood was now crowded with men and women, and the children were strained tight against the parapet. The turret rocked and swayed; the wave had reached the golden wall.

Jane held up the Amulet.

'Now,' cried the Psammead, 'say the word!'

And as Jane said it the Psammead leaped from its bag and bit the hand of the learned gentleman.

At the same moment the boys pushed him through the arch and all followed him.

He turned to look back, and through the arch he saw nothing but a waste of waters, with above it the peak of the terrible mountain with fire raging from it.

He staggered back to his chair.

'What a ghastly dream!' he gasped. 'Oh, you're here, my—er—dears. Can I do anything for you?'

'You've hurt your hand,' said Anthea gently; 'let me bind it up.'

The hand was indeed bleeding rather badly.

The Psammead had crept back to its bag. All the children were very white.

'Never again,' said the Psammead later on, 'will I go into the Past with a grown-up person! I will say for you four, you do do as you're told.'

'We didn't even find the Amulet,' said Anthea later still.

'Of course you didn't; it wasn't there. Only the stone it was made of was there. It fell on to a ship miles away that managed to escape and got to Egypt. *I* could have told you that.'

'I wish you had,' said Anthea, and her voice was still rather shaky. 'Why didn't you?'

'You never asked me,' said the Psammead very sulkily. 'I'm not the sort of chap to go shoving my oar in where it's not wanted.'

'Mr Ji-jimmy's friend will have something worth having to put in his article now,' said Cyril very much later indeed.

'Not he,' said Robert sleepily. 'The learned Ji-jimmy will think it's a dream, and it's ten to one he never tells the other chap a word about it at all.'

Robert was quite right on both points. The learned gentleman did. And he never did.

CHAPTER 10. THE LITTLE BLACK GIRL AND JULIUS CAESAR

A great city swept away by the sea, a beautiful country devastated by an active volcano—these are not the sort of things you see every day of the week. And when you do see them, no matter how many other wonders you may have seen in your time, such sights are rather apt to take your breath away. Atlantis had certainly this effect on the breaths of Cyril, Robert, Anthea, and Jane.

They remained in a breathless state for somedays. The learned gentleman seemed as breathless as anyone; he spent a good deal of what little breath he had in telling Anthea about a wonderful dream he had. 'You would hardly believe,' he said, 'that anyone COULD have such a detailed vision.'

But Anthea could believe it, she said, quite easily.

He had ceased to talk about thought-transference. He had now seen too many wonders to believe that.

In consequence of their breathless condition none of the children suggested any new excursions through the Amulet. Robert voiced the mood of the others when he said that they were 'fed up' with Amulet for a bit. They undoubtedly were.

As for the Psammead, it went to sand and stayed there, worn out by the terror of the flood and the violent exercise it had had to take in obedience to the inconsiderate wishes of the learned gentleman and the Babylonian queen.

The children let it sleep. The danger of taking it about among strange people who might at any moment utter undesirable wishes was becoming more and more plain.

And there are pleasant things to be done in London without any aid from Amulets or Psammeads. You can, for instance visit the Tower of London, the Houses of Parliament, the National Gallery, the Zoological Gardens, the various Parks, the Museums at South Kensington, Madame Tussaud's Exhibition of Waxworks, or the Botanical Gardens at Kew. You can go to Kew by river steamer—and this is the way that the children would have gone if they had gone at all. Only they never did, because it was when they were discussing the arrangements for the journey, and what they should take with them to eat and how much of it, and what the whole thing would cost, that the adventure of the Little Black Girl began to happen.

The children were sitting on a seat in St James's Park. They had been watching the pelican repulsing with careful dignity the advances of the seagulls who are always so anxious to play games with it. The pelican thinks, very properly, that it hasn't the figure for games, so it spends most of its time pretending that that is not the reason why it won't play.

The breathlessness caused by Atlantis was wearing off a little. Cyril, who always wanted to understand all about everything, was turning things over in his mind.

'I'm not; I'm only thinking,' he answered when Robert asked him what he was so grumpy about. 'I'll tell you when I've thought it all out.'

'If it's about the Amulet I don't want to hear it,' said Jane.

'Nobody asked you to,' retorted Cyril mildly, 'and I haven't finished my inside thinking about it yet. Let's go to Kew in the meantime.'

'I'd rather go in a steamer,' said Robert; and the girls laughed.

'That's right,' said Cyril, 'BE funny. I would.'

495

'Well, he was, rather,' said Anthea.

'I wouldn't think, Squirrel, if it hurts you so,' said Robert kindly.

'Oh, shut up,' said Cyril, 'or else talk about Kew.'

'I want to see the palms there,' said Anthea hastily, 'to see if they're anything like the ones on the island where we united the Cook and the Burglar by the Reverend Half-Curate.'

All disagreeableness was swept away in a pleasant tide of recollections, and 'Do you remember...?' they said. 'Have you forgotten...?'

'My hat!' remarked Cyril pensively, as the flood of reminiscence ebbed a little; 'we have had some times.'

'We have that,' said Robert.

'Don't let's have any more,' said Jane anxiously.

'That's what I was thinking about,' Cyril replied; and just then they heard the Little Black Girl sniff. She was quite close to them.

She was not really a little black girl. She was shabby and not very clean, and she had been crying so much that you could hardly see, through the narrow chink between her swollen lids, how very blue her eyes were. It was her dress that was black, and it was too big and too long for her, and she wore a speckled black-ribboned sailor hat that would have fitted a much bigger head than her little flaxen one. And she stood looking at the children and sniffing.

'Oh, dear!' said Anthea, jumping up. 'Whatever is the matter?'

She put her hand on the little girl's arm. It was rudely shaken off.

'You leave me be,' said the little girl. 'I ain't doing nothing to you.'

'But what is it?' Anthea asked. 'Has someone been hurting you?'

'What's that to you?' said the little girl fiercely. 'YOU'RE all right.'

496

'Come away,' said Robert, pulling at Anthea's sleeve. 'She's a nasty, rude little kid.'

'Oh, no,' said Anthea. 'She's only dreadfully unhappy. What is it?' she asked again.

'Oh, YOU'RE all right,' the child repeated; 'YOU ain't agoin' to the Union.'

'Can't we take you home?' said Anthea; and Jane added, 'Where does your mother live?'

'She don't live nowheres—she's dead—so now!' said the little girl fiercely, in tones of miserable triumph. Then she opened her swollen eyes widely, stamped her foot in fury, and ran away. She ran no further than to the next bench, flung herself down there and began to cry without even trying not to.

Anthea, quite at once, went to the little girl and put her arms as tight as she could round the hunched-up black figure.

'Oh, don't cry so, dear, don't, don't!' she whispered under the brim of the large sailor hat, now very crooked indeed. 'Tell Anthea all about it; Anthea'll help you. There, there, dear, don't cry.'

The others stood at a distance. One or two passers-by stared curiously.

The child was now only crying part of the time; the rest of the time she seemed to be talking to Anthea.

Presently Anthea beckoned Cyril.

'It's horrible!' she said in a furious whisper, 'her father was a carpenter and he was a steady man, and never touched a drop except on a Saturday, and he came up to London for work, and there wasn't any, and then he died; and her name is Imogen, and she's nine come next November. And now her mother's dead, and she's to stay tonight with Mrs Shrobsall—that's a landlady that's been kind—and tomorrow the Relieving Officer is coming for her, and she's going into the Union; that means the Workhouse. It's too terrible. What can we do?'

'Let's ask the learned gentleman,' said Jane brightly.

And as no one else could think of anything better the whole party walked back to Fitzroy Street as fast as it could, the little girl holding tight to Anthea's hand and now not crying any more, only sniffing gently.

The learned gentleman looked up from his writing with the smile that had grown much easier to him than it used to be. They were quite at home in his room now; it really seemed to welcome them. Even the mummy-case appeared to smile as if in its distant superior ancient Egyptian way it were rather pleased to see them than not.

Anthea sat on the stairs with Imogen, who was nine come next November, while the others went in and explained the difficulty.

The learned gentleman listened with grave attention.

'It really does seem rather rough luck,' Cyril concluded, 'because I've often heard about rich people who wanted children most awfully—though I know *I* never should—but they do. There must be somebody who'd be glad to have her.'

'Gipsies are awfully fond of children,' Robert hopefully said. 'They're always stealing them. Perhaps they'd have her.'

'She's quite a nice little girl really,' Jane added; 'she was only rude at first because we looked jolly and happy, and she wasn't. You understand that, don't you?'

'Yes,' said he, absently fingering a little blue image from Egypt. 'I understand that very well. As you say, there must be some home where she would be welcome.' He scowled thoughtfully at the little blue image.

Anthea outside thought the explanation was taking a very long time.

She was so busy trying to cheer and comfort the little black girl that she never noticed the Psammead who, roused from sleep by her voice, had shaken itself free of sand, and was coming crookedly up the stairs. It was close to her before she saw it. She picked it up and settled it in her lap.

'What is it?' asked the black child. 'Is it a cat or a organ-monkey, or what?'

And then Anthea heard the learned gentleman say—

'Yes, I wish we could find a home where they would be glad to have her,' and instantly she felt the Psammead begin to blow itself out as it sat on her lap.

She jumped up lifting the Psammead in her skirt, and holding Imogen by the hand, rushed into the learned gentleman's room.

'At least let's keep together,' she cried. 'All hold hands—quick!'

The circle was like that formed for the Mulberry Bush or Ring-o'-Roses. And Anthea was only able to take part in it by holding in her teeth the hem of her frock which, thus supported, formed a bag to hold the Psammead.

'Is it a game?' asked the learned gentleman feebly. No one answered.

There was a moment of suspense; then came that curious upside-down, inside-out sensation which one almost always feels when transported from one place to another by magic. Also there was that dizzy dimness of sight which comes on these occasions.

The mist cleared, the upside-down, inside-out sensation subsided, and there stood the six in a ring, as before, only their twelve feet, instead of standing on the carpet of the learned gentleman's room, stood on green grass. Above them, instead of the dusky ceiling of the Fitzroy Street floor, was a pale blue sky. And where the walls had been and the painted mummy-case, were tall dark green trees, oaks and ashes, and in between the trees and under them tangled bushes and creeping ivy. There were beech-trees too, but there was nothing under them but their own dead red drifted leaves, and here and there a delicate green fern-frond.

And there they stood in a circle still holding hands, as though they were playing Ring-o'-Roses or the Mulberry Bush. Just six people hand in hand in a wood. That sounds simple, but then you must remember that they did not know WHERE the wood was, and what's more, they didn't know WHEN then wood was. There was a curious sort of feeling that made the learned gentleman say—

'Another dream, dear me!' and made the children almost certain that they were in a time a very long while ago. As for little Imogen, she said, 'Oh, my!' and kept her mouth very much open indeed.

'Where are we?' Cyril asked the Psammead.

'In Britain,' said the Psammead.

'But when?' asked Anthea anxiously.

'About the year fifty-five before the year you reckon time from,' said the Psammead crossly. 'Is there anything else you want to know?' it added, sticking its head out of the bag formed by Anthea's blue linen frock, and turning its snail's eyes to right and left. 'I've been here before—it's very little changed.' 'Yes, but why here?' asked Anthea.

'Your inconsiderate friend,' the Psammead replied, 'wished to find some home where they would be glad to have that unattractive and immature female human being whom you have picked up—gracious knows how. In Megatherium days properly brought-up children didn't talk to shabby strangers in parks. Your thoughtless friend wanted a place where someone would be glad to have this undesirable stranger. And now here you are!'

'I see we are,' said Anthea patiently, looking round on the tall gloom of the forest. 'But why HERE? Why NOW?'

'You don't suppose anyone would want a child like that in YOUR times—in YOUR towns?' said the Psammead in irritated tones. 'You've got your country into such a mess that there's no room for half your children—and no one to want them.'

'That's not our doing, you know,' said Anthea gently.

'And bringing me here without any waterproof or anything,' said the Psammead still more crossly, 'when everyone knows how damp and foggy Ancient Britain was.'

'Here, take my coat,' said Robert, taking it off. Anthea spread the coat on the ground and, putting the Psammead on it, folded it round so that only the eyes and furry ears showed.

'There,' she said comfortingly. 'Now if it does begin to look like rain, I can cover you up in a minute. Now what are we to do?'

The others who had stopped holding hands crowded round to hear the answer to this question. Imogen whispered in an awed tone—

'Can't the organ monkey talk neither! I thought it was only parrots!'

'Do?' replied the Psammead. 'I don't care what you do!' And it drew head and ears into the tweed covering of Robert's coat.

The others looked at each other.

'It's only a dream,' said the learned gentleman hopefully; 'something is sure to happen if we can prevent ourselves from waking up.'

And sure enough, something did.

The brooding silence of the dark forest was broken by the laughter of children and the sound of voices.

'Let's go and see,' said Cyril.

'It's only a dream,' said the learned gentleman to Jane, who hung back; 'if you don't go with the tide of a dream—if you resist—you wake up, you know.'

There was a sort of break in the undergrowth that was like a silly person's idea of a path. They went along this in Indian file, the learned gentleman leading.

Quite soon they came to a large clearing in the forest. There were a number of houses—huts perhaps you would have called them—with a sort of mud and wood fence.

'It's like the old Egyptian town,' whispered Anthea.

And it was, rather.

Some children, with no clothes on at all, were playing what looked like Ring-o'-Roses or Mulberry Bush. That is to say, they were dancing round in a ring, holding hands. On a grassy bank several women, dressed in blue and white robes and tunics of beast-skins sat watching the playing children.

The children from Fitzroy Street stood on the fringe of the forest looking at the games. One woman with long, fair braided hair sat a little apart from the others, and there was a look in her eyes as she followed the play of the children that made Anthea feel sad and sorry.

'None of those little girls is her own little girl,' thought Anthea.

The little black-clad London child pulled at Anthea's sleeve.

'Look,' she said, 'that one there—she's precious like mother; mother's 'air was somethink lovely, when she 'ad time to comb it out. Mother wouldn't never a-beat me if she'd lived 'ere—I don't suppose there's e'er a public nearer than Epping, do you, Miss?'

In her eagerness the child had stepped out of the shelter of the forest. The sad-eyed woman saw her. She stood up, her thin face lighted up with a radiance like sunrise, her long, lean arms stretched towards the London child.

'Imogen!' she cried—at least the word was more like that than any other word—'Imogen!'

There was a moment of great silence; the naked children paused in their play, the women on the bank stared anxiously.

'Oh, it IS mother—it IS!' cried Imogen-from-London, and rushed across the cleared space. She and her mother clung together—so closely, so strongly that they stood an instant like a statue carved in stone.

Then the women crowded round. 'It IS my Imogen!' cried the woman.

'Oh it is! And she wasn't eaten by wolves. She's come back to me. Tell me, my darling, how did you escape? Where have you been? Who has fed and clothed you?'

'I don't know nothink,' said Imogen.

'Poor child!' whispered the women who crowded round, 'the terror of the wolves has turned her brain.'

'But you know ME?' said the fair-haired woman.

And Imogen, clinging with black-clothed arms to the bare neck, answered—

'Oh, yes, mother, I know YOU right 'nough.'

'What is it? What do they say?' the learned gentleman asked anxiously.

'You wished to come where someone wanted the child,' said the Psammead. 'The child says this is her mother.'

'And the mother?'

'You can see,' said the Psammead.

'But is she really? Her child, I mean?'

'Who knows?' said the Psammead; 'but each one fills the empty place in the other's heart. It is enough.'

'Oh,' said the learned gentleman, 'this is a good dream. I wish the child might stay in the dream.'

The Psammead blew itself out and granted the wish. So Imogen's future was assured. She had found someone to want her.

'If only all the children that no one wants,' began the learned gentleman—but the woman interrupted. She came towards them.

'Welcome, all!' she cried. 'I am the Queen, and my child tells me that you have befriended her; and this I well believe, looking on your faces. Your garb is strange, but faces I can read. The child is bewitched, I see that well, but in this she speaks truth. Is it not so?'

The children said it wasn't worth mentioning.

I wish you could have seen all the honours and kindnesses lavished on the children and the learned gentleman by those ancient Britons.

You would have thought, to see them, that a child was something to make a fuss about, not a bit of rubbish to be hustled about the streets and hidden away in the Workhouse. It wasn't as grand as the entertainment at Babylon, but somehow it was more satisfying.

'I think you children have some wonderful influence on me,' said the learned gentleman. 'I never dreamed such dreams before I knew you.'

It was when they were alone that night under the stars where the Britons had spread a heap Of dried fern for them to sleep on, that Cyril spoke.

'Well,' he said, 'we've made it all right for Imogen, and had a jolly good time. I vote we get home again before the fighting begins.'

'What fighting?' asked Jane sleepily.

'Why, Julius Caesar, you little goat,' replied her kind brother. 'Don't you see that if this is the year fifty-five, Julius Caesar may happen at any moment.'

'I thought you liked Caesar,' said Robert.

'So I do—in the history. But that's different from being killed by his soldiers.'

504

'If we saw Caesar we might persuade him not to,' said Anthea.

'YOU persuade CAESAR,' Robert laughed.

The learned gentleman, before anyone could stop him, said, 'I only wish we could see Caesar some time.'

And, of course, in just the little time the Psammead took to blow itself out for wish-giving, the five, or six counting the Psammead, found themselves in Caesar's camp, just outside Caesar's tent. And they saw Caesar. The Psammead must have taken advantage of the loose wording of the learned gentleman's wish, for it was not the same time of day as that on which the wish had been uttered among the dried ferns. It was sunset, and the great man sat on a chair outside his tent gazing over the sea towards Britain—everyone knew without being told that it was towards Britain. Two golden eagles on the top of posts stood on each side of the tent, and on the flaps of the tent which was very gorgeous to look at were the letters S.P.Q.R.

The great man turned unchanged on the newcomers the august glance that he had turned on the violet waters of the Channel. Though they had suddenly appeared out of nothing, Caesar never showed by the faintest movement of an eyelid, by the least tightening of that firm mouth, that they were not some long expected embassy. He waved a calm hand towards the sentinels, who sprang weapons in hand towards the newcomers.

'Back!' he said in a voice that thrilled like music. 'Since when has Caesar feared children and students?'

To the children he seemed to speak in the only language they knew; but the learned gentleman heard—in rather a strange accent, but quite intelligibly—the lips of Caesar speaking in the Latin tongue, and in that tongue, a little stiffly, he answered—

'It is a dream, O Caesar.'

'A dream?' repeated Caesar. 'What is a dream?'

'This,' said the learned gentleman.

'Not it,' said Cyril, 'it's a sort of magic. We come out of another time and another place.'

'And we want to ask you not to trouble about conquering Britain,' said Anthea; 'it's a poor little place, not worth bothering about.'

'Are you from Britain?' the General asked. 'Your clothes are uncouth, but well woven, and your hair is short as the hair of Roman citizens, not long like the hair of barbarians, yet such I deem you to be.' 'We're not,' said Jane with angry eagerness; 'we're not barbarians at all. We come from the country where the sun never sets, and we've read about you in books; and our country's full of fine things—St Paul's, and the Tower of London, and Madame Tussaud's Exhibition, and—' Then the others stopped her.

'Don't talk nonsense,' said Robert in a bitter undertone.

Caesar looked at the children a moment in silence. Then he called a soldier and spoke with him apart. Then he said aloud—

'You three elder children may go where you will within the camp. Few children are privileged to see the camp of Caesar. The student and the smaller girl-child will remain here with me.'

Nobody liked this; but when Caesar said a thing that thing was so, and there was an end to it. So the three went.

Left alone with Jane and the learned gentleman, the great Roman found it easy enough to turn them inside out. But it was not easy, even for him, to make head or tail of the insides of their minds when he had got at them.

The learned gentleman insisted that the whole thing was a dream, and refused to talk much, on the ground that if he did he would wake up.

Jane, closely questioned, was full of information about railways, electric lights, balloons, men-of-war, cannons, and dynamite.

'And do they fight with swords?' asked the General.

'Yes, swords and guns and cannons.'

Caesar wanted to know what guns were.

'You fire them,' said Jane, 'and they go bang, and people fall down dead.'

'But what are guns like?'

Jane found them hard to describe.

'But Robert has a toy one in his pocket,' she said. So the others were recalled.

The boys explained the pistol to Caesar very fully, and he looked at it with the greatest interest. It was a two-shilling pistol, the one that had done such good service in the old Egyptian village.

'I shall cause guns to be made,' said Caesar, 'and you will be detained till I know whether you have spoken the truth. I had just decided that Britain was not worth the bother of invading. But what you tell me decides me that it is very much worth while.'

'But it's all nonsense,' said Anthea. 'Britain is just a savage sort of island—all fogs and trees and big rivers. But the people are kind. We know a little girl there named Imogen. And it's no use your making guns because you can't fire them without gunpowder, and that won't be invented for hundreds of years, and we don't know how to make it, and we can't tell you. Do go straight home, dear Caesar, and let poor little Britain alone.'

'But this other girl-child says—' said Caesar.

'All Jane's been telling you is what it's going to be,' Anthea interrupted, 'hundreds and hundreds of years from now.'

'The little one is a prophetess, eh?' said Caesar, with a whimsical look. 'Rather young for the business, isn't she?'

'You can call her a prophetess if you like,' said Cyril, 'but what Anthea says is true.'

'Anthea?' said Caesar. 'That's a Greek name.'

507

'Very likely,' said Cyril, worriedly. 'I say, I do wish you'd give up this idea of conquering Britain. It's not worth while, really it isn't!'

'On the contrary,' said Caesar, 'what you've told me has decided me to go, if it's only to find out what Britain is really like. Guards, detain these children.'

'Quick,' said Robert, 'before the guards begin detaining. We had enough of that in Babylon.'

Jane held up the Amulet away from the sunset, and said the word. The learned gentleman was pushed through and the others more quickly than ever before passed through the arch back into their own times and the quiet dusty sitting-room of the learned gentleman.

It is a curious fact that when Caesar was encamped on the coast of Gaul—somewhere near Boulogne it was, I believe—he was sitting before his tent in the glow of the sunset, looking out over the violet waters of the English Channel. Suddenly he started, rubbed his eyes, and called his secretary. The young man came quickly from within the tent.

'Marcus,' said Caesar. 'I have dreamed a very wonderful dream. Some of it I forget, but I remember enough to decide what was not before determined. Tomorrow the ships that have been brought round from the Ligeris shall be provisioned. We shall sail for this three-cornered island. First, we will take but two legions.

This, if what we have heard be true, should suffice. But if my dream be true, then a hundred legions will not suffice. For the dream I dreamed was the most wonderful that ever tormented the brain even of Caesar. And Caesar has dreamed some strange things in his time.'

'And if you hadn't told Caesar all that about how things are now, he'd never have invaded Britain,' said Robert to Jane as they sat down to tea.

508

'Oh, nonsense,' said Anthea, pouring out; 'it was all settled hundreds of years ago.'

'I don't know,' said Cyril. 'Jam, please. This about time being only a thingummy of thought is very confusing. If everything happens at the same time—'

'It CAN'T!' said Anthea stoutly, 'the present's the present and the past's the past.'

'Not always,' said Cyril.

'When we were in the Past the present was the future. Now then!' he added triumphantly.

And Anthea could not deny it.

'I should have liked to see more of the camp,' said Robert.

'Yes, we didn't get much for our money—but Imogen is happy, that's one thing,' said Anthea. 'We left her happy in the Past. I've often seen about people being happy in the Past, in poetry books. I see what it means now.'

'It's not a bad idea,' said the Psammead sleepily, putting its head out of its bag and taking it in again suddenly, 'being left in the Past.'

Everyone remembered this afterwards, when—

CHAPTER 11. BEFORE PHARAOH

It was the day after the adventure of Julius Caesar and the Little Black Girl that Cyril, bursting into the bathroom to wash his hands for dinner (you have no idea how dirty they were, for he had been playing shipwrecked mariners all the morning on the leads at the back of the house, where the water-cistern is), found Anthea leaning her elbows on the edge of the bath, and crying steadily into it.

'Hullo!' he said, with brotherly concern, 'what's up now? Dinner'll be cold before you've got enough salt-water for a bath.'

'Go away,' said Anthea fiercely. 'I hate you! I hate everybody!'

There was a stricken pause.

'*I* didn't know,' said Cyril tamely.

'Nobody ever does know anything,' sobbed Anthea.

'I didn't know you were waxy. I thought you'd just hurt your fingers with the tap again like you did last week,' Cyril carefully explained.

'Oh—fingers!' sneered Anthea through her sniffs.

'Here, drop it, Panther,' he said uncomfortably. 'You haven't been having a row or anything?'

'No,' she said. 'Wash your horrid hands, for goodness' sake, if that's what you came for, or go.'

Anthea was so seldom cross that when she was cross the others were always more surprised than angry.

Cyril edged along the side of the bath and stood beside her. He put his hand on her arm.

'Dry up, do,' he said, rather tenderly for him. And, finding that though she did not at once take his advice she did not seem to resent it, he put his arm awkwardly across her shoulders and rubbed his head against her ear.

'There!' he said, in the tone of one administering a priceless cure for all possible sorrows. 'Now, what's up?'

'Promise you won't laugh?'

'I don't feel laughish myself,' said Cyril, dismally.

'Well, then,' said Anthea, leaning her ear against his head, 'it's Mother.'

510

'What's the matter with Mother?' asked Cyril, with apparent want of sympathy. 'She was all right in her letter this morning.'

'Yes; but I want her so.'

'You're not the only one,' said Cyril briefly, and the brevity of his tone admitted a good deal.

'Oh, yes,' said Anthea, 'I know. We all want her all the time. But I want her now most dreadfully, awfully much. I never wanted anything so much. That Imogen child—the way the ancient British Queen cuddled her up! And Imogen wasn't me, and the Queen was Mother. And then her letter this morning! And about The Lamb liking the salt bathing! And she bathed him in this very bath the night before she went away—oh, oh, oh!'

Cyril thumped her on the back.

'Cheer up,' he said. 'You know my inside thinking that I was doing? Well, that was partly about Mother. We'll soon get her back. If you'll chuck it, like a sensible kid, and wash your face, I'll tell you about it. That's right. You let me get to the tap. Can't you stop crying? Shall I put the door-key down your back?'

'That's for noses,' said Anthea, 'and I'm not a kid any more than you are,' but she laughed a little, and her mouth began to get back into its proper shape. You know what an odd shape your mouth gets into when you cry in earnest.

'Look here,' said Cyril, working the soap round and round between his hands in a thick slime of grey soapsuds. 'I've been thinking. We've only just PLAYED with the Amulet so far. We've got to work it now—WORK it for all it's worth. And it isn't only Mother either. There's Father out there all among the fighting. I don't howl about it, but I THINK—Oh, bother the soap!' The grey-lined soap had squirted out under the pressure of his fingers, and had hit Anthea's chin with as much force as though it had been shot from a catapult.

'There now,' she said regretfully, 'now I shall have to wash my face.'

511

'You'd have had to do that anyway,' said Cyril with conviction. 'Now, my idea's this. You know missionaries?'

'Yes,' said Anthea, who did not know a single one.

'Well, they always take the savages beads and brandy, and stays, and hats, and braces, and really useful things—things the savages haven't got, and never heard about. And the savages love them for their kind generousness, and give them pearls, and shells, and ivory, and cassowaries. And that's the way—'

'Wait a sec,' said Anthea, splashing. 'I can't hear what you're saying. Shells and—'

'Shells, and things like that. The great thing is to get people to love you by being generous. And that's what we've got to do. Next time we go into the Past wc'll rcgularly fit out the expedition. You remember how the Babylonian Queen froze on to that pocket-book? Well, we'll take things like that. And offer them in exchange for a sight of the Amulet.'

'A sight of it is not much good.'

'No, silly. But, don't you see, when we've seen it we shall know where it is, and we can go and take it in the night when everybody is asleep.'

'It wouldn't be stealing, would it?' said Anthea thoughtfully, 'because it will be such an awfully long time ago when we do it. Oh, there's that bell again.'

As soon as dinner was eaten (it was tinned salmon and lettuce, and a jam tart), and the cloth cleared away, the idea was explained to the others, and the Psammead was aroused from sand, and asked what it thought would be good merchandise with which to buy the affection of say, the Ancient Egyptians, and whether it thought the Amulet was likely to be found in the Court of Pharaoh.

But it shook its head, and shot out its snail's eyes hopelessly.

'I'm not allowed to play in this game,' it said. 'Of course I COULD find out in a minute where the thing was, only I mayn't.

512

But I may go so far as to own that your idea of taking things with you isn't a bad one. And I shouldn't show them all at once. Take small things and conceal them craftily about your persons.'

This advice seemed good. Soon the table was littered over with things which the children thought likely to interest the Ancient Egyptians. Anthea brought dolls, puzzle blocks, a wooden tea-service, a green leather case with Necessaire written on it in gold letters. Aunt Emma had once given it to Anthea, and it had then contained scissors, penknife, bodkin, stiletto, thimble, corkscrew, and glove-buttoner. The scissors, knife, and thimble, and penknife were, of course, lost, but the other things were there and as good as new. Cyril contributed lead soldiers, a cannon, a catapult, a tin-opener, a tie-clip, and a tennis ball, and a padlock—no key. Robert collected a candle ('I don't suppose they ever saw a self-fitting paraffin one,' he said), a penny Japanese pin-tray, a rubber stamp with his father's name and address on it, and a piece of putty.

Jane added a key-ring, the brass handle of a poker, a pot that had held cold-cream, a smoked pearl button off her winter coat, and a key—no lock.

'We can't take all this rubbish,' said Robert, with some scorn. 'We must just each choose one thing.'

The afternoon passed very agreeably in the attempt to choose from the table the four most suitable objects. But the four children could not agree what was suitable, and at last Cyril said—

'Look here, let's each be blindfolded and reach out, and the first thing you touch you stick to.'

This was done.

Cyril touched the padlock.

Anthea got the Necessaire.

Robert clutched the candle.

Jane picked up the tie-clip.

'It's not much,' she said. 'I don't believe Ancient Egyptians wore ties.'

'Never mind,' said Anthea. 'I believe it's luckier not to really choose. In the stories it's always the thing the wood-cutter's son picks up in the forest, and almost throws away because he thinks it's no good, that turns out to be the magic thing in the end; or else someone's lost it, and he is rewarded with the hand of the King's daughter in marriage.'

'I don't want any hands in marriage, thank you.' said Cyril firmly.

'Nor yet me,' said Robert. 'It's always the end of the adventures when it comes to the marriage hands.'

'ARE we ready?' said Anthea.

'It IS Egypt we're going to, isn't it?—nice Egypt?' said Jane. 'I won't go anywhere I don't know about—like that dreadful big-wavy burning-mountain city,' she insisted.

Then the Psammead was coaxed into its bag. 'I say,' said Cyril suddenly, 'I'm rather sick of kings. And people notice you so in palaces. Besides the Amulet's sure to be in a Temple. Let's just go among the common people, and try to work ourselves up by degrees. We might get taken on as Temple assistants.'

'Like beadles,' said Anthea, 'or vergers. They must have splendid chances of stealing the Temple treasures.'

'Righto!' was the general rejoinder. The charm was held up. It grew big once again, and once again the warm golden Eastern light glowed softly beyond it.

As the children stepped through it loud and furious voices rang in their ears. They went suddenly from the quiet of Fitzroy Street dining-room into a very angry Eastern crowd, a crowd much too angry to notice them. They edged through it to the wall of a house and stood there. The crowd was of men, women, and children. They were of all sorts of complexions, and pictures of them might have been coloured by any child with a shilling paint-box. The

514

colours that child would have used for complexions would have been yellow ochre, red ochre, light red, sepia, and indian ink. But their faces were painted already—black eyebrows and lashes, and some red lips. The women wore a sort of pinafore with shoulder straps, and loose things wound round their heads and shoulders. The men wore very little clothing—for they were the working people—and the Egyptian boys and girls wore nothing at all, unless you count the little ornaments hung on chains round their necks and waists. The children saw all this before they could hear anything distinctly.

Everyone was shouting so.

But a voice sounded above the other voices, and presently it was speaking in a silence.

'Comrades and fellow workers,' it said, and it was the voice of a tall, coppery-coloured man who had climbed into a chariot that had been stopped by the crowd. Its owner had bolted, muttering something about calling the Guards, and now the man spoke from it. 'Comrades and fellow workers, how long are we to endure the tyranny of our masters, who live in idleness and luxury on the fruit of our toil? They only give us a bare subsistence wage, and they live on the fat of the land. We labour all our lives to keep them in wanton luxury. Let us make an end of it!'

A roar of applause answered him.

'How are you going to do it?' cried a voice.

'You look out,' cried another, 'or you'll get yourself into trouble.'

'I've heard almost every single word of that,' whispered Robert, 'in Hyde Park last Sunday!'

'Let us strike for more bread and onions and beer, and a longer mid-day rest,' the speaker went on. 'You are tired, you are hungry, you are thirsty. You are poor, your wives and children are pining for food. The barns of the rich are full to bursting with the corn we want, the corn our labour has grown. To the granaries!'

515

'To the granaries!' cried half the crowd; but another voice shouted clear above the tumult, 'To Pharaoh! To the King! Let's present a petition to the King! He will listen to the voice of the oppressed!'

For a moment the crowd swayed one way and another—first towards the granaries and then towards the palace. Then, with a rush like that of an imprisoned torrent suddenly set free, it surged along the street towards the palace, and the children were carried with it. Anthea found it difficult to keep the Psammead from being squeezed very uncomfortably.

The crowd swept through the streets of dull-looking houses with few windows, very high up, across the market where people were not buying but exchanging goods. In a momentary pause Robert saw a basket of onions exchanged for a hair comb and five fish for a string of beads. The people in the market seemed better off than those in the crowd; they had finer clothes, and more of them. They were the kind of people who, nowadays, would have lived at Brixton or Brockley.

'What's the trouble now?' a languid, large-eyed lady in a crimped, half-transparent linen dress, with her black hair very much braided and puffed out, asked of a date-seller.

'Oh, the working-men—discontented as usual,' the man answered. 'Listen to them. Anyone would think it mattered whether they had a little more or less to eat. Dregs of society!' said the date-seller.

'Scum!' said the lady.

'And I've heard THAT before, too,' said Robert.

At that moment the voice of the crowd changed, from anger to doubt, from doubt to fear. There were other voices shouting; they shouted defiance and menace, and they came nearer very quickly. There was the rattle of wheels and the pounding of hoofs. A voice shouted, 'Guards!'

'The Guards! The Guards!' shouted another voice, and the crowd of workmen took up the cry. 'The Guards! Pharaoh's Guards!' And swaying a little once more, the crowd hung for a moment as it were balanced. Then as the trampling hoofs came nearer the workmen fled dispersed, up alleys and into the courts of houses, and the Guards in their embossed leather chariots swept down the street at the gallop, their wheels clattering over the stones, and their dark-coloured, blue tunics blown open and back with the wind of their going.

'So THAT riot's over,' said the crimped-linen-dressed lady; 'that's a blessing! And did you notice the Captain of the Guard? What a very handsome man he was, to be sure!'

The four children had taken advantage of the moment's pause before the crowd turned to fly, to edge themselves and drag each other into an arched doorway.

Now they each drew a long breath and looked at the others.

'We're well out of THAT,' said Cyril.

'Yes,' said Anthea, 'but I do wish the poor men hadn't been driven back before they could get to the King. He might have done something for them.'

'Not if he was the one in the Bible he wouldn't,' said Jane. 'He had a hard heart.' 'Ah, that was the Moses one,' Anthea explained. 'The Joseph one was quite different. I should like to see Pharaoh's house. I wonder whether it's like the Egyptian Court in the Crystal Palace.'

'I thought we decided to try to get taken on in a Temple,' said Cyril in injured tones.

'Yes, but we've got to know someone first. Couldn't we make friends with a Temple doorkeeper—we might give him the padlock or something. I wonder which are temples and which are palaces,' Robert added, glancing across the market-place to where an enormous gateway with huge side buildings towered towards the

517

sky. To right and left of it were other buildings only a little less magnificent.

'Did you wish to seek out the Temple of Amen Ra?' asked a soft voice behind them, 'or the Temple of Mut, or the Temple of Khonsu?'

They turned to find beside them a young man. He was shaved clean from head to foot, and on his feet were light papyrus sandals. He was clothed in a linen tunic of white, embroidered heavily in colours. He was gay with anklets, bracelets, and armlets of gold, richly inlaid. He wore a ring on his finger, and he had a short jacket of gold embroidery something like the Zouave soldiers wear, and on his neck was a gold collar with many amulets hanging from it. But among the amulets the children could see none like theirs.

'It doesn't matter which Temple,' said Cyril frankly.

'Tell me your mission,' said the young man. 'I am a divine father of the Temple of Amen Ra and perhaps I can help you.'

'Well,' said Cyril, 'we've come from the great Empire on which the sun never sets.'

'I thought somehow that you'd come from some odd, out-of-the-way spot,' said the priest with courtesy.

'And we've seen a good many palaces. We thought we should like to see a Temple, for a change,' said Robert.

The Psammead stirred uneasily in its embroidered bag.

'Have you brought gifts to the Temple?' asked the priest cautiously.

'We HAVE got some gifts,' said Cyril with equal caution. 'You see there's magic mixed up in it. So we can't tell you everything. But we don't want to give our gifts for nothing.'

'Beware how you insult the god,' said the priest sternly. 'I also can do magic. I can make a waxen image of you, and I can say words which, as the wax image melts before the fire, will make you dwindle away and at last perish miserably.'

'Pooh!' said Cyril stoutly, 'that's nothing. *I* can make FIRE itself!'

'I should jolly well like to see you do it,' said the priest unbelievingly.

'Well, you shall,' said Cyril, 'nothing easier. Just stand close round me.'

'Do you need no preparation—no fasting, no incantations?' The priest's tone was incredulous.

'The incantation's quite short,' said Cyril, taking the hint; 'and as for fasting, it's not needed in MY sort of magic. Union Jack, Printing Press, Gunpowder, Rule Britannia! Come, Fire, at the end of this little stick!'

He had pulled a match from his pocket, and as he ended the incantation which contained no words that it seemed likely the Egyptian had ever heard he stooped in the little crowd of his relations and the priest and struck the match on his boot. He stood up, shielding the flame with one hand.

'See?' he said, with modest pride. 'Here, take it into your hand.'

'No, thank you,' said the priest, swiftly backing. 'Can you do that again?'

'Yes.'

'Then come with me to the great double house of Pharaoh. He loves good magic, and he will raise you to honour and glory. There's no need of secrets between initiates,' he went on confidentially. 'The fact is, I am out of favour at present owing to a little matter of failure of prophecy. I told him a beautiful princess would be sent to him from Syria, and, lo! a woman thirty years old arrived. But she WAS a beautiful woman not so long ago. Time is only a mode of thought, you know.'

The children thrilled to the familiar words.

'So you know that too, do you?' said Cyril.

'It is part of the mystery of all magic, is it not?' said the priest. 'Now if I bring you to Pharaoh the little unpleasantness I spoke of will be forgotten. And I will ask Pharaoh, the Great House, Son of the Sun, and Lord of the South and North, to decree that you shall lodge in the Temple. Then you can have a good look round, and teach me your magic. And I will teach you mine.'

This idea seemed good—at least it was better than any other which at that moment occurred to anybody, so they followed the priest through the city.

The streets were very narrow and dirty. The best houses, the priest explained, were built within walls twenty to twenty-five feet high, and such windows as showed in the walls were very high up. The tops of palm-trees showed above the walls. The poor people's houses were little square huts with a door and two windows, and smoke coming out of a hole in the back.

'The poor Egyptians haven't improved so very much in their building since the first time we came to Egypt,' whispered Cyril to Anthea.

The huts were roofed with palm branches, and everywhere there were chickens, and goats, and little naked children kicking about in the yellow dust. On one roof was a goat, who had climbed up and was eating the dry palm-leaves with snorts and head-tossings of delight. Over every house door was some sort of figure or shape.

'Amulets,' the priest explained, 'to keep off the evil eye.'

'I don't think much of your "nice Egypt",' Robert whispered to Jane; 'it's simply not a patch on Babylon.'

'Ah, you wait till you see the palace,' Jane whispered back.

The palace was indeed much more magnificent than anything they had yet seen that day, though it would have made but a poor show beside that of the Babylonian King. They came to it through a great square pillared doorway of sandstone that stood in a high brick wall. The shut doors were of massive cedar, with bronze hinges, and were studded with bronze nails. At the side was a little door and a wicket gate, and through this the priest led the children. He seemed to know a word that made the sentries make way for him.

Inside was a garden, planted with hundreds of different kinds of trees and flowering shrubs, a lake full of fish, with blue lotus flowers at the margin, and ducks swimming about cheerfully, and looking, as Jane said, quite modern.

'The guard-chamber, the store-houses, the queen's house,' said the priest, pointing them out.

They passed through open courtyards, paved with flat stones, and the priest whispered to a guard at a great inner gate.

'We are fortunate,' he said to the children, 'Pharaoh is even now in the Court of Honour. Now, don't forget to be overcome with respect and admiration. It won't do any harm if you fall flat on your faces. And whatever you do, don't speak until you're spoken to.'

'There used to be that rule in our country,' said Robert, 'when my father was a little boy.'

At the outer end of the great hall a crowd of people were arguing with and even shoving the Guards, who seemed to make it a rule not to let anyone through unless they were bribed to do it. The children heard several promises of the utmost richness, and wondered whether they would ever be kept.

All round the hall were pillars of painted wood. The roof was of cedar, gorgeously inlaid. About half-way up the hall was a wide, shallow step that went right across the hall; then a little farther on another; and then a steep flight of narrower steps, leading right up to the throne on which Pharaoh sat. He sat there very splendid, his red and white double crown on his head, and his sceptre in his hand. The throne had a canopy of wood and wooden pillars painted in bright colours. On a low, broad bench that ran all round the hall sat the friends, relatives, and courtiers of the King, leaning on richly-covered cushions.

The priest led the children up the steps till they all stood before the throne; and then, suddenly, he fell on his face with hands outstretched. The others did the same, Anthea falling very carefully because of the Psammead.

'Raise them,' said the voice of Pharaoh, 'that they may speak to me.'

The officers of the King's household raised them.

'Who are these strangers?' Pharaoh asked, and added very crossly, 'And what do you mean, Rekh-mara, by daring to come into my presence while your innocence is not established?'

'Oh, great King,' said the young priest, 'you are the very image of Ra, and the likeness of his son Horus in every respect. You know the thoughts of the hearts of the gods and of men, and you have divined that these strangers are the children of the children of the vile and conquered Kings of the Empire where the sun never sets. They know a magic not known to the Egyptians. And they come with gifts in their hands as tribute to Pharaoh, in whose heart is the wisdom of the gods, and on his lips their truth.'

'That is all very well,' said Pharaoh, 'but where are the gifts?'

The children, bowing as well as they could in their embarrassment at finding themselves the centre of interest in a circle more grand, more golden and more highly coloured than they could have imagined possible, pulled out the padlock, the Necessaire, and the tie-clip. 'But it's not tribute all the same,' Cyril muttered. 'England doesn't pay tribute!'

Pharaoh examined all the things with great interest when the chief of the household had taken them up to him. 'Deliver them to the Keeper of the Treasury,' he said to one near him. And to the children he said—

'A small tribute, truly, but strange, and not without worth. And the magic, O Rekh-mara?'

'These unworthy sons of a conquered nation...' began Rekh-mara.

'Nothing of the kind!' Cyril whispered angrily.

'... of a vile and conquered nation, can make fire to spring from dry wood—in the sight of all.'

'I should jolly well like to see them do it,' said Pharaoh, just as the priest had done.

So Cyril, without more ado, did it.

'Do more magic,' said the King, with simple appreciation.

'He cannot do any more magic,' said Anthea suddenly, and all eyes were turned on her, 'because of the voice of the free people who are shouting for bread and onions and beer and a long mid-day rest. If the people had what they wanted, he could do more.'

'A rude-spoken girl,' said Pharaoh. 'But give the dogs what they want,' he said, without turning his head. 'Let them have their rest and their extra rations. There are plenty of slaves to work.'

A richly-dressed official hurried out.

'You will be the idol of the people,' Rekh-mara whispered joyously; 'the Temple of Amen will not contain their offerings.'

Cyril struck another match, and all the court was overwhelmed with delight and wonder. And when Cyril took the candle from his pocket and lighted it with the match, and then held the burning candle up before the King the enthusiasm knew no bounds.

'Oh, greatest of all, before whom sun and moon and stars bow down,' said Rekh-mara insinuatingly, 'am I pardoned? Is my innocence made plain?'

'As plain as it ever will be, I daresay,' said Pharaoh shortly. 'Get along with you. You are pardoned. Go in peace.' The priest went with lightning swiftness.

'And what,' said the King suddenly, 'is it that moves in that sack?

Show me, oh strangers.'

There was nothing for it but to show the Psammead.

'Seize it,' said Pharaoh carelessly. 'A very curious monkey. It will be a nice little novelty for my wild beast collection.'

And instantly, the entreaties of the children availing as little as the bites of the Psammead, though both bites and entreaties were fervent, it was carried away from before their eyes.

'Oh, DO be careful!' cried Anthea. 'At least keep it dry! Keep it in its sacred house!'

She held up the embroidered bag.

'It's a magic creature,' cried Robert; 'it's simply priceless!'

'You've no right to take it away,' cried Jane incautiously. 'It's a shame, a barefaced robbery, that's what it is!'

There was an awful silence. Then Pharaoh spoke.

'Take the sacred house of the beast from them,' he said, 'and imprison all. Tonight after supper it may be our pleasure to see more magic. Guard them well, and do not torture them—yet!'

'Oh, dear!' sobbed Jane, as they were led away. 'I knew exactly what it would be! Oh, I wish you hadn't!'

'Shut up, silly,' said Cyril. 'You know you WOULD come to Egypt. It was your own idea entirely. Shut up. It'll be all right.'

'I thought we should play ball with queens,' sobbed Jane, 'and have no end of larks! And now everything's going to be perfectly horrid!'

The room they were shut up in WAS a room, and not a dungeon, as the elder ones had feared. That, as Anthea said, was one comfort. There were paintings on the wall that at any other time would have been most interesting. And a sort of low couch, and chairs. When they were alone Jane breathed a sigh of relief. 'Now we can get home all right,' she said.

'And leave the Psammead?' said Anthea reproachfully.

'Wait a sec. I've got an idea,' said Cyril. He pondered for a few moments. Then he began hammering on the heavy cedar door. It opened, and a guard put in his head.

'Stop that row,' he said sternly, 'or—'

'Look here,' Cyril interrupted, 'it's very dull for you isn't it? Just doing nothing but guard us. Wouldn't you like to see some magic? We're not too proud to do it for you. Wouldn't you like to see it?'

'I don't mind if I do,' said the guard.

'Well then, you get us that monkey of ours that was taken away, and we'll show you.'

'How do I know you're not making game of me?' asked the soldier. 'Shouldn't wonder if you only wanted to get the creature so as to set it on me. I daresay its teeth and claws are poisonous.' 'Well, look here,' said Robert. 'You see we've got nothing with us? You just shut the door, and open it again in five minutes, and we'll have got a magic—oh, I don't know—a magic flower in a pot for you.'

'If you can do that you can do anything,' said the soldier, and he went out and barred the door.

Then, of course, they held up the Amulet. They found the East by holding it up, and turning slowly till the Amulet began to grow big, walked home through it, and came back with a geranium in full scarlet flower from the staircase window of the Fitzroy Street house.

'Well!' said the soldier when he came in. 'I really am—!'

'We can do much more wonderful things than that—oh, ever so much,' said Anthea persuasively, 'if we only have our monkey. And here's twopence for yourself.'

The soldier looked at the twopence.

'What's this?' he said.

Robert explained how much simpler it was to pay money for things than to exchange them as the people were doing in the market. Later on the soldier gave the coins to his captain, who, later still, showed them to Pharaoh, who of course kept them and was much struck with the idea. That was really how coins first came to be used in Egypt. You will not believe this, I daresay, but really, if you believe the rest of the story, I don't see why you shouldn't believe this as well.

'I say,' said Anthea, struck by a sudden thought, 'I suppose it'll be all right about those workmen? The King won't go back on what he said about them just because he's angry with us?'

'Oh, no,' said the soldier, 'you see, he's rather afraid of magic. He'll keep to his word right enough.'

'Then THAT'S all right,' said Robert; and Anthea said softly and coaxingly—

'Ah, DO get us the monkey, and then you'll see some lovely magic. Do—there's a nice, kind soldier.'

'I don't know where they've put your precious monkey, but if I can get another chap to take on my duty here I'll see what I can do,' he said grudgingly, and went out.

'Do you mean,' said Robert, 'that we're going off without even TRYING for the other half of the Amulet?'

'I really think we'd better,' said Anthea tremulously. 'Of course the other half of the Amulet's here somewhere or our half wouldn't have brought us here. I do wish we could find it. It is a pity we don't know any REAL magic. Then we could find out. I do wonder where it is—exactly.'

If they had only known it, something very like the other half of the Amulet was very near them. It hung round the neck of someone, and that someone was watching them through a chink, high up in the wall, specially devised for watching people who were imprisoned. But they did not know.

There was nearly an hour of anxious waiting. They tried to take an interest in the picture on the wall, a picture of harpers playing very odd harps and women dancing at a feast. They examined the painted plaster floor, and the chairs were of white painted wood with coloured stripes at intervals.

But the time went slowly, and everyone had time to think of how Pharaoh had said, 'Don't torture them—YET.'

'If the worst comes to the worst,' said Cyril, 'we must just bunk, and leave the Psammead. I believe it can take care of itself well enough. They won't kill it or hurt it when they find it can speak and give wishes. They'll build it a temple, I shouldn't wonder.'

'I couldn't bear to go without it,' said Anthea, 'and Pharaoh said "After supper", that won't be just yet. And the soldier WAS curious. I'm sure we're all right for the present.'

All the same, the sounds of the door being unbarred seemed one of the prettiest sounds possible.

'Suppose he hasn't got the Psammead?' whispered Jane.

But that doubt was set at rest by the Psammead itself; for almost before the door was open it sprang through the chink of it into Anthea's arms, shivering and hunching up its fur.

'Here's its fancy overcoat,' said the soldier, holding out the bag, into which the Psammead immediately crept.

'Now,' said Cyril, 'what would you like us to do? Anything you'd like us to get for you?'

'Any little trick you like,' said the soldier. 'If you can get a strange flower blooming in an earthenware vase you can get anything, I suppose,' he said. 'I just wish I'd got two men's loads of jewels from the King's treasury. That's what I've always wished for.'

At the word 'WISH' the children knew that the Psammead would attend to THAT bit of magic. It did, and the floor was littered with a spreading heap of gold and precious stones.

'Any other little trick?' asked Cyril loftily. 'Shall we become invisible? Vanish?'

'Yes, if you like,' said the soldier; 'but not through the door, you don't.'

He closed it carefully and set his broad Egyptian back against it.

'No! no!' cried a voice high up among the tops of the tall wooden pillars that stood against the wall. There was a sound of someone moving above.

The soldier was as much surprised as anybody.

'That's magic, if you like,' he said.

And then Jane held up the Amulet, uttering the word of Power. At the sound of it and at the sight of the Amulet growing into the great arch the soldier fell flat on his face among the jewels with a cry of awe and terror.

The children went through the arch with a quickness born of long practice. But Jane stayed in the middle of the arch and looked back.

The others, standing on the dining-room carpet in Fitzroy Street, turned and saw her still in the arch. 'Someone's holding her,' cried Cyril. 'We must go back.'

But they pulled at Jane's hands just to see if she would come, and, of course, she did come.

Then, as usual, the arch was little again and there they all were.

'Oh, I do wish you hadn't!' Jane said crossly. 'It WAS so interesting. The priest had come in and he was kicking the soldier, and telling him he'd done it now, and they must take the jewels and flee for their lives.'

'And did they?'

'I don't know. You interfered,' said Jane ungratefully. 'I SHOULD have liked to see the last of it.'

As a matter of fact, none of them had seen the last of it—if by 'it' Jane meant the adventure of the Priest and the Soldier.

CHAPTER 12. THE SORRY-PRESENT AND THE EXPELLED LITTLE BOY

'Look here, said Cyril, sitting on the dining-table and swinging his legs; 'I really have got it.'

'Got what?' was the not unnatural rejoinder of the others.

Cyril was making a boat with a penknife and a piece of wood, and the girls were making warm frocks for their dolls, for the weather was growing chilly.

'Why, don't you see? It's really not any good our going into the Past looking for that Amulet. The Past's as full of different times as—as the sea is of sand. We're simply bound to hit upon the wrong time. We might spend our lives looking for the Amulet and never see a sight of it. Why, it's the end of September already. It's like looking for a needle in—'

'A bottle of hay—I know,' interrupted Robert; 'but if we don't go on doing that, what ARE we to do?'

'That's just it,' said Cyril in mysterious accents. 'Oh, BOTHER!'

Old Nurse had come in with the tray of knives, forks, and glasses, and was getting the tablecloth and table-napkins out of the chiffonier drawer.

'It's always meal-times just when you come to anything interesting.'

'And a nice interesting handful YOU'D be, Master Cyril,' said old Nurse, 'if I wasn't to bring your meals up to time. Don't you begin grumbling now, fear you get something to grumble AT.'

'I wasn't grumbling,' said Cyril quite untruly; 'but it does always happen like that.'

'You deserve to HAVE something happen,' said old Nurse. 'Slave, slave, slave for you day and night, and never a word of thanks. ...'

'Why, you do everything beautifully,' said Anthea.

'It's the first time any of you's troubled to say so, anyhow,' said Nurse shortly.

'What's the use of SAYING?' inquired Robert. 'We EAT our meals fast enough, and almost always two helps. THAT ought to show you!'

'Ah!' said old Nurse, going round the table and putting the knives and forks in their places; 'you're a man all over, Master Robert. There was my poor Green, all the years he lived with me I never could get more out of him than "It's all right!" when I asked him if he'd fancied his dinner. And yet, when he lay a-dying, his last words to me was, "Maria, you was always a good cook!"' She ended with a trembling voice.

'And so you are,' cried Anthea, and she and Jane instantly hugged her.

When she had gone out of the room Anthea said—

'I know exactly how she feels. Now, look here! Let's do a penance to show we're sorry we didn't think about telling her before what nice cooking she does, and what a dear she is.'

'Penances are silly,' said Robert.

'Not if the penance is something to please someone else. I didn't mean old peas and hair shirts and sleeping on the stones. I mean we'll make her a sorry-present,' explained Anthea. 'Look here! I vote Cyril doesn't tell us his idea until we've done something for old Nurse. It's worse for us than him,' she added hastily, 'because he knows what it is and we don't. Do you all agree?'

The others would have been ashamed not to agree, so they did. It was not till quite near the end of dinner—mutton fritters and blackberry and apple pie—that out of the earnest talk of the four came an idea that pleased everybody and would, they hoped, please Nurse.

Cyril and Robert went out with the taste of apple still in their mouths and the purple of blackberries on their lips—and, in the case of Robert, on the wristband as well—and bought a big sheet of cardboard at the stationers. Then at the plumber's shop, that has tubes and pipes and taps and gas-fittings in the window, they bought a pane of glass the same size as the cardboard. The man cut it with a very interesting tool that had a bit of diamond at the end, and he gave them, out of his own free generousness, a large piece of putty and a small piece of glue.

While they were out the girls had floated four photographs of the four children off their cards in hot water. These were now stuck in a row along the top of the cardboard. Cyril put the glue to melt in a jampot, and put the jampot in a saucepan and saucepan on the fire, while Robert painted a wreath of poppies round the photographs. He painted rather well and very quickly, and poppies are easy to do if you've once been shown how. Then Anthea drew some printed letters and Jane coloured them. The words were:

> 'With all our loves to shew
> We like the thigs to eat.'

And when the painting was dry they all signed their names at the bottom and put the glass on, and glued brown paper round the edge and over the back, and put two loops of tape to hang it up by.

Of course everyone saw when too late that there were not enough letters in 'things', so the missing 'n' was put in. It was impossible, of course, to do the whole thing over again for just one letter.

'There!' said Anthea, placing it carefully, face up, under the sofa. 'It'll be hours before the glue's dry. Now, Squirrel, fire ahead!'

531

'Well, then,' said Cyril in a great hurry, rubbing at his gluey hands with his pocket handkerchief. 'What I mean to say is this.'

There was a long pause.

'Well,' said Robert at last, 'WHAT is it that you mean to say?'

'It's like this,' said Cyril, and again stopped short.

'Like WHAT?' asked Jane.

'How can I tell you if you will all keep on interrupting?' said Cyril sharply.

So no one said any more, and with wrinkled frowns he arranged his ideas.

'Look here,' he said, 'what I really mean is—we can remember now what we did when we went to look for the Amulet. And if we'd found it we should remember that too.'

'Rather!' said Robert. 'Only, you see we haven't.'

'But in the future we shall have.'

'Shall we, though?' said Jane.

'Yes—unless we've been made fools of by the Psammead. So then, where we want to go to is where we shall remember about where we did find it.'

'I see,' said Robert, but he didn't.

'*I* don't,' said Anthea, who did, very nearly. 'Say it again, Squirrel, and very slowly.'

'If,' said Cyril, very slowly indeed, 'we go into the future—after we've found the Amulet—'

'But we've got to find it first,' said Jane.

'Hush!' said Anthea.

'There will be a future,' said Cyril, driven to greater clearness by the blank faces of the other three, 'there will be a time AFTER we've found it. Let's go into THAT time—and then we shall remember HOW we found it. And then we can go back and do the finding really.'

'I see,' said Robert, and this time he did, and I hope YOU do.

'Yes,' said Anthea. 'Oh, Squirrel, how clever of you!'

'But will the Amulet work both ways?' inquired Robert.

'It ought to,' said Cyril, 'if time's only a thingummy of whatsitsname. Anyway we might try.'

'Let's put on our best things, then,' urged Jane. 'You know what people say about progress and the world growing better and brighter. I expect people will be awfully smart in the future.'

'All right,' said Anthea, 'we should have to wash anyway, I'm all thick with glue.'

When everyone was clean and dressed, the charm was held up.

'We want to go into the future and see the Amulet after we've found it,' said Cyril, and Jane said the word of Power. They walked through the big arch of the charm straight into the British Museum.

They knew it at once, and there, right in front of them, under a glass case, was the Amulet—their own half of it, as well as the other half they had never been able to find—and the two were joined by a pin of red stone that formed a hinge.

'Oh, glorious!' cried Robert. 'Here it is!'

'Yes,' said Cyril, very gloomily, 'here it is. But we can't get it out.'

'No,' said Robert, remembering how impossible the Queen of Babylon had found it to get anything out of the glass cases in the Museum—except by Psammead magic, and then she hadn't been able to take anything away with her; 'no—but we remember where we got it, and we can—'

'Oh, DO we?' interrupted Cyril bitterly, 'do YOU remember where we got it?'

'No,' said Robert, 'I don't exactly, now I come to think of it.'

Nor did any of the others!

'But WHY can't we?' said Jane.

'Oh, *I* don't know,' Cyril's tone was impatient, 'some silly old enchanted rule I suppose. I wish people would teach you magic at school like they do sums—or instead of. It would be some use having an Amulet then.'

'I wonder how far we are in the future,' said Anthea; the Museum looks just the same, only lighter and brighter, somehow.'

'Let's go back and try the Past again,' said Robert.

'Perhaps the Museum people could tell us how we got it,' said Anthea with sudden hope. There was no one in the room, but in the next gallery, where the Assyrian things are and still were, they found a kind, stout man in a loose, blue gown, and stockinged legs.

'Oh, they've got a new uniform, how pretty!' said Jane.

When they asked him their question he showed them a label on the case. It said, 'From the collection of—.' A name followed, and it was the name of the learned gentleman who, among themselves, and to his face when he had been with them at the other side of the Amulet, they had called Jimmy.

'THAT'S not much good,' said Cyril, 'thank you.'

'How is it you're not at school?' asked the kind man in blue. 'Not expelled for long I hope?'

'We're not expelled at all,' said Cyril rather warmly.

'Well, I shouldn't do it again, if I were you,' said the man, and they could see he did not believe them. There is no company so little pleasing as that of people who do not believe you.

'Thank you for showing us the label,' said Cyril. And they came away.

As they came through the doors of the Museum they blinked at the sudden glory of sunlight and blue sky. The houses opposite the Museum were gone. Instead there was a big garden, with trees and flowers and smooth green lawns, and not a single notice to tell you not to walk on the grass and not to destroy the trees and shrubs and not to pick the flowers. There were comfortable seats all about, and arbours covered with roses, and long, trellised walks, also rose-covered. Whispering, splashing fountains fell into full white marble basins, white statues gleamed among the leaves, and the pigeons that swept about among the branches or pecked on the smooth, soft gravel were not black and tumbled like the Museum pigeons are now, but bright and clean and sleek as birds of new silver. A good many people were sitting on the seats, and on the grass babies were rolling and kicking and playing—with very little on indeed. Men, as well as women, seemed to be in charge of the babies and were playing with them.

'It's like a lovely picture,' said Anthea, and it was. For the people's clothes were of bright, soft colours and all beautifully and very simply made. No one seemed to have any hats or bonnets, but there were a great many Japanese-looking sunshades. And among the trees were hung lamps of coloured glass.

'I expect they light those in the evening,' said Jane. 'I do wish we lived in the future!'

They walked down the path, and as they went the people on the benches looked at the four children very curiously, but not rudely or unkindly. The children, in their turn, looked—I hope they did not stare—at the faces of these people in the beautiful soft clothes. Those faces were worth looking at. Not that they were all handsome, though even in the matter of handsomeness they had the advantage of any set of people the children had ever seen. But it

535

was the expression of their faces that made them worth looking at. The children could not tell at first what it was.

'I know,' said Anthea suddenly. 'They're not worried; that's what it is.'

And it was. Everybody looked calm, no one seemed to be in a hurry, no one seemed to be anxious, or fretted, and though some did seem to be sad, not a single one looked worried.

But though the people looked kind everyone looked so interested in the children that they began to feel a little shy and turned out of the big main path into a narrow little one that wound among trees and shrubs and mossy, dripping springs.

It was here, in a deep, shadowed cleft between tall cypresses, that they found the expelled little boy. He was lying face downward on the mossy turf, and the peculiar shaking of his shoulders was a thing they had seen, more than once, in each other. So Anthea kneeled down by him and said—

'What's the matter?'

'I'm expelled from school,' said the boy between his sobs.

This was serious. People are not expelled for light offences.

'Do you mind telling us what you'd done?'

'I—I tore up a sheet of paper and threw it about in the playground,' said the child, in the tone of one confessing an unutterable baseness. 'You won't talk to me any more now you know that,' he added without looking up.

'Was that all?' asked Anthea.

'It's about enough,' said the child; 'and I'm expelled for the whole day!'

'I don't quite understand,' said Anthea, gently. The boy lifted his face, rolled over, and sat up.

'Why, whoever on earth are you?' he said.

536

'We're strangers from a far country,' said Anthea. 'In our country it's not a crime to leave a bit of paper about.'

'It is here,' said the child. 'If grown-ups do it they're fined. When we do it we're expelled for the whole day.'

'Well, but,' said Robert, 'that just means a day's holiday.'

'You MUST come from a long way off,' said the little boy. 'A holiday's when you all have play and treats and jolliness, all of you together. On your expelled days no one'll speak to you. Everyone sees you're an Expelleder or you'd be in school.'

'Suppose you were ill?'

'Nobody is—hardly. If they are, of course they wear the badge, and everyone is kind to you. I know a boy that stole his sister's illness badge and wore it when he was expelled for a day. HE got expelled for a week for that. It must be awful not to go to school for a week.'

'Do you LIKE school, then?' asked Robert incredulously.

'Of course I do. It's the loveliest place there is. I chose railways for my special subject this year, there are such splendid models and things, and now I shall be all behind because of that torn-up paper.'

'You choose your own subject?' asked Cyril.

'Yes, of course. Where DID you come from? Don't you know ANYTHING?'

'No,' said Jane definitely; 'so you'd better tell us.'

'Well, on Midsummer Day school breaks up and everything's decorated with flowers, and you choose your special subject for next year. Of course you have to stick to it for a year at least. Then there are all your other subjects, of course, reading, and painting, and the rules of Citizenship.'

'Good gracious!' said Anthea.

'Look here,' said the child, jumping up, 'it's nearly four. The expelledness only lasts till then. Come home with me. Mother will tell you all about everything.'

'Will your mother like you taking home strange children?' asked Anthea.

'I don't understand,' said the child, settling his leather belt over his honey-coloured smock and stepping out with hard little bare feet. 'Come on.'

So they went.

The streets were wide and hard and very clean. There were no horses, but a sort of motor carriage that made no noise. The Thames flowed between green banks, and there were trees at the edge, and people sat under them, fishing, for the stream was clear as crystal. Everywhere there were green trees and there was no smoke. The houses were set in what seemed like one green garden.

The little boy brought them to a house, and at the window was a good, bright mother-face. The little boy rushed in, and through the window they could see him hugging his mother, then his eager lips moving and his quick hands pointing.

A lady in soft green clothes came out, spoke kindly to them, and took them into the oddest house they had ever seen. It was very bare, there were no ornaments, and yet every single thing was beautiful, from the dresser with its rows of bright china, to the thick squares of Eastern-looking carpet on the floors. I can't describe that house; I haven't the time. And I haven't heart either, when I think how different it was from our houses. The lady took them all over it. The oddest thing of all was the big room in the middle. It had padded walls and a soft, thick carpet, and all the chairs and tables were padded. There wasn't a single thing in it that anyone could hurt itself with.

'What ever's this for?—lunatics?' asked Cyril.

The lady looked very shocked.

'No! It's for the children, of course,' she said. 'Don't tell me that in your country there are no children's rooms.'

'There are nurseries,' said Anthea doubtfully, 'but the furniture's all cornery and hard, like other rooms.'

'How shocking!' said the lady;'you must be VERY much behind the times in your country! Why, the children are more than half of the people; it's not much to have one room where they can have a good time and not hurt themselves.'

'But there's no fireplace,' said Anthea.

'Hot-air pipes, of course,' said the lady. 'Why, how could you have a fire in a nursery? A child might get burned.'

'In our country,' said Robert suddenly, 'more than 3,000 children are burned to death every year. Father told me,' he added, as if apologizing for this piece of information, 'once when I'd been playing with fire.'

The lady turned quite pale.

'What a frightful place you must live in!' she said. 'What's all the furniture padded for?' Anthea asked, hastily turning the subject.

'Why, you couldn't have little tots of two or three running about in rooms where the things were hard and sharp! They might hurt themselves.'

Robert fingered the scar on his forehead where he had hit it against the nursery fender when he was little.

'But does everyone have rooms like this, poor people and all?' asked Anthea.

'There's a room like this wherever there's a child, of course,' said the lady. 'How refreshingly ignorant you are!—no, I don't mean ignorant, my dear. Of course, you're awfully well up in ancient History. But I see you haven't done your Duties of Citizenship Course yet.'

'But beggars, and people like that?' persisted Anthea 'and tramps and people who haven't any homes?'

'People who haven't any homes?' repeated the lady. 'I really DON'T understand what you're talking about.'

'It's all different in our country,' said Cyril carefully; and I have read it used to be different in London. Usedn't people to have no homes and beg because they were hungry? And wasn't London very black and dirty once upon a time? And the Thames all muddy and filthy? And narrow streets, and—'

'You must have been reading very old-fashioned books,' said the lady. 'Why, all that was in the dark ages! My husband can tell you more about it than I can. He took Ancient History as one of his special subjects.'

'I haven't seen any working people,' said Anthea.

'Why, we're all working people,' said the lady; 'at least my husband's a carpenter.'

'Good gracious!' said Anthea; 'but you're a lady!'

'Ah,' said the lady, 'that quaint old word! Well, my husband WILL enjoy a talk with you. In the dark ages everyone was allowed to have a smoky chimney, and those nasty horses all over the streets, and all sorts of rubbish thrown into the Thames. And, of course, the sufferings of the people will hardly bear thinking of. It's very learned of you to know it all. Did you make Ancient History your special subject?'

'Not exactly,' said Cyril, rather uneasily. 'What is the Duties of Citizenship Course about?'

'Don't you REALLY know? Aren't you pretending—just for fun? Really not? Well, that course teaches you how to be a good citizen, what you must do and what you mayn't do, so as to do your full share of the work of making your town a beautiful and happy place for people to live in. There's a quite simple little thing they teach the tiny children. How does it go...?

'I must not steal and I must learn,
Nothing is mine that I do not earn.
I must try in work and play
To make things beautiful every day.
I must be kind to everyone,
And never let cruel things be done.
I must be brave, and I must try
When I am hurt never to cry,
And always laugh as much as I can,
And be glad that I'm going to be a man
To work for my living and help the rest
And never do less than my very best.'

'That's very easy,' said Jane. '*I* could remember that.'

'That's only the very beginning, of course,' said the lady; 'there are heaps more rhymes. There's the one beginning—

'I must not litter the beautiful street
With bits of paper or things to eat;
I must not pick the public flowers,
They are not MINE, but they are OURS.'

'And "things to eat" reminds me—are you hungry? Wells, run and get a tray of nice things.'

'Why do you call him "Wells"?' asked Robert, as the boy ran off.

'It's after the great reformer—surely you've heard of HIM? He lived in the dark ages, and he saw that what you ought to do is to find out what you want and then try to get it. Up to then people had always tried to tinker up what they'd got. We've got a great many of the things he thought of. Then "Wells" means springs of clear water. It's a nice name, don't you think?'

Here Wells returned with strawberries and cakes and lemonade on a tray, and everybody ate and enjoyed.

'Now, Wells,' said the lady, 'run off or you'll be late and not meet your Daddy.'

Wells kissed her, waved to the others, and went.

'Look here,' said Anthea suddenly, 'would you like to come to OUR country, and see what it's like? It wouldn't take you a minute.'

The lady laughed. But Jane held up the charm and said the word.

'What a splendid conjuring trick!' cried the lady, enchanted with the beautiful, growing arch.

'Go through,' said Anthea.

The lady went, laughing. But she did not laugh when she found herself, suddenly, in the dining-room at Fitzroy Street.

'Oh, what a HORRIBLE trick!' she cried. 'What a hateful, dark, ugly place!'

She ran to the window and looked out. The sky was grey, the street was foggy, a dismal organ-grinder was standing opposite the door, a beggar and a man who sold matches were quarrelling at the edge of the pavement on whose greasy black surface people hurried along, hastening to get to the shelter of their houses.

'Oh, look at their faces, their horrible faces!' she cried. 'What's the matter with them all?'

'They're poor people, that's all,' said Robert.

'But it's NOT all! They're ill, they're unhappy, they're wicked! Oh, do stop it, there's dear children. It's very, very clever. Some sort of magic-lantern trick, I suppose, like I've read of. But DO stop it. Oh! their poor, tired, miserable, wicked faces!'

The tears were in her eyes. Anthea signed to Jane. The arch grew, they spoke the words, and pushed the lady through it into her own time and place, where London is clean and beautiful, and the Thames runs clear and bright, and the green trees grow, and no one is afraid, or anxious, or in a hurry. There was a silence. Then—

542

'I'm glad we went,' said Anthea, with a deep breath.

'I'll never throw paper about again as long as I live,' said Robert.

'Mother always told us not to,' said Jane.

'I would like to take up the Duties of Citizenship for a special subject,' said Cyril. 'I wonder if Father could put me through it. I shall ask him when he comes home.'

'If we'd found the Amulet, Father could be home NOW,' said Anthea, 'and Mother and The Lamb.'

'Let's go into the future AGAIN,' suggested Jane brightly. 'Perhaps we could remember if it wasn't such an awful way off.'

So they did. This time they said, 'The future, where the Amulet is, not so far away.'

And they went through the familiar arch into a large, light room with three windows. Facing them was the familiar mummy-case. And at a table by the window sat the learned gentleman. They knew him at once, though his hair was white. He was one of the faces that do not change with age. In his hand was the Amulet—complete and perfect.

He rubbed his other hand across his forehead in the way they were so used to.

'Dreams, dreams!' he said; 'old age is full of them!'

'You've been in dreams with us before now,' said Robert, 'don't you remember?'

'I do, indeed,' said he. The room had many more books than the Fitzroy Street room, and far more curious and wonderful Assyrian and Egyptian objects. 'The most wonderful dreams I ever had had you in them.'

'Where,' asked Cyril, 'did you get that thing in your hand?'

'If you weren't just a dream,' he answered, smiling, you'd remember that you gave it to me.'

543

'But where did we get it?' Cyril asked eagerly.

'Ah, you never would tell me that,' he said, 'You always had your little mysteries. You dear children! What a difference you made to that old Bloomsbury house! I wish I could dream you oftener. Now you're grown up you're not like you used to be.'

'Grown up?' said Anthea.

The learned gentleman pointed to a frame with four photographs in it.

'There you are,' he said.

The children saw four grown-up people's portraits—two ladies, two gentlemen—and looked on them with loathing.

'Shall we grow up like THAT?' whispered Jane. 'How perfectly horrid!'

'If we're ever like that, we sha'n't know it's horrid, I expect,' Anthea with some insight whispered back. 'You see, you get used to yourself while you're changing. It's—it's being so sudden makes it seem so frightful now.'

The learned gentleman was looking at them with wistful kindness. 'Don't let me undream you just yet,' he said. There was a pause.

'Do you remember WHEN we gave you that Amulet?' Cyril asked suddenly.

'You know, or you would if you weren't a dream, that it was on the 3rd December, 1905. I shall never forget THAT day.'

'Thank you,' said Cyril, earnestly; 'oh, thank you very much.'

'You've got a new room,' said Anthea, looking out of the window, 'and what a lovely garden!'

'Yes,' said he, 'I'm too old now to care even about being near the Museum. This is a beautiful place. Do you know—I can hardly believe you're just a dream, you do look so exactly real. Do you

544

know...' his voice dropped, 'I can say it to YOU, though, of course, if I said it to anyone that wasn't a dream they'd call me mad; there was something about that Amulet you gave me—something very mysterious.'

'There was that,' said Robert.

'Ah, I don't mean your pretty little childish mysteries about where you got it. But about the thing itself. First, the wonderful dreams I used to have, after you'd shown me the first half of it! Why, my book on Atlantis, that I did, was the beginning of my fame and my fortune, too. And I got it all out of a dream! And then, "Britain at the Time of the Roman Invasion"—that was only a pamphlet, but it explained a lot of things people hadn't understood.'

'Yes,' said Anthea, 'it would.'

'That was the beginning. But after you'd given me the whole of the Amulet—ah, it was generous of you!—then, somehow, I didn't need to theorize, I seemed to KNOW about the old Egyptian civilization. And they can't upset my theories'—he rubbed his thin hands and laughed triumphantly—'they can't, though they've tried. Theories, they call them, but they're more like—I don't know—more like memories. I KNOW I'm right about the secret rites of the Temple of Amen.'

'I'm so glad you're rich,' said Anthea. 'You weren't, you know, at Fitzroy Street.'

'Indeed I wasn't,' said he, 'but I am now. This beautiful house and this lovely garden—I dig in it sometimes; you remember, you used to tell me to take more exercise? Well, I feel I owe it all to you—and the Amulet.'

'I'm so glad,' said Anthea, and kissed him. He started.

'THAT didn't feel like a dream,' he said, and his voice trembled.

'It isn't exactly a dream,' said Anthea softly, 'it's all part of the Amulet—it's a sort of extra special, real dream, dear Jimmy.'

'Ah,' said he, 'when you call me that, I know I'm dreaming. My little sister—I dream of her sometimes. But it's not real like this. Do you remember the day I dreamed you brought me the Babylonish ring?'

'We remember it all,' said Robert. 'Did you leave Fitzroy Street because you were too rich for it?'

'Oh, no!' he said reproachfully. 'You know I should never have done such a thing as that. Of course, I left when your old Nurse died and—what's the matter!'

'Old Nurse DEAD?' said Anthea. 'Oh, NO!'

'Yes, yes, it's the common lot. It's a long time ago now.'

Jane held up the Amulet in a hand that twittered.

'Come!' she cried, 'oh, come home! She may be dead before we get there, and then we can't give it to her. Oh, come!'

'Ah, don't let the dream end now!' pleaded the learned gentleman.

'It must,' said Anthea firmly, and kissed him again.

'When it comes to people dying,' said Robert, 'good-bye! I'm so glad you're rich and famous and happy.'

'DO come!' cried Jane, stamping in her agony of impatience. And they went. Old Nurse brought in tea almost as soon as they were back in Fitzroy Street. As she came in with the tray, the girls rushed at her and nearly upset her and it.

'Don't die!' cried Jane, 'oh, don't!' and Anthea cried, 'Dear, ducky, darling old Nurse, don't die!'

'Lord, love you!' said Nurse, 'I'm not agoin' to die yet a while, please Heaven! Whatever on earth's the matter with the chicks?'

'Nothing. Only don't!'

She put the tray down and hugged the girls in turn. The boys thumped her on the back with heartfelt affection.

'I'm as well as ever I was in my life,' she said. 'What nonsense about dying! You've been a sitting too long in the dusk, that's what it is. Regular blind man's holiday. Leave go of me, while I light the gas.'

The yellow light illuminated four pale faces. 'We do love you so,' Anthea went on, 'and we've made you a picture to show you how we love you. Get it out, Squirrel.'

The glazed testimonial was dragged out from under the sofa and displayed.

'The glue's not dry yet,' said Cyril, 'look out!'

'What a beauty!' cried old Nurse. 'Well, I never! And your pictures and the beautiful writing and all. Well, I always did say your hearts was in the right place, if a bit careless at times. Well! I never did! I don't know as I was ever pleased better in my life.'

She hugged them all, one after the other. And the boys did not mind it, somehow, that day.

'How is it we can remember all about the future, NOW?' Anthea woke the Psammead with laborious gentleness to put the question. 'How is it we can remember what we saw in the future, and yet, when we WERE in the future, we could not remember the bit of the future that was past then, the time of finding the Amulet?'

'Why, what a silly question!' said the Psammead, 'of course you cannot remember what hasn't happened yet.'

'But the FUTURE hasn't happened yet,' Anthea persisted, 'and we remember that all right.'

'Oh, that isn't what's happened, my good child,' said the Psammead, rather crossly, 'that's prophetic vision. And you remember dreams, don't you? So why not visions? You never do seem to understand the simplest thing.'

It went to sand again at once.

Anthea crept down in her nightgown to give one last kiss to old Nurse, and one last look at the beautiful testimonial hanging, by its tapes, its glue now firmly set, in glazed glory on the wall of the kitchen.

'Good-night, bless your loving heart,' said old Nurse, 'if only you don't catch your deather-cold!'

CHAPTER 13. THE SHIPWRECK ON THE TIN ISLANDS

'Blue and red,' said Jane softly, 'make purple.'

'Not always they don't,' said Cyril, 'it has to be crimson lake and Prussian blue. If you mix Vermilion and Indigo you get the most loathsome slate colour.'

'Sepia's the nastiest colour in the box, I think,' said Jane, sucking her brush.

They were all painting. Nurse in the flush of grateful emotion, excited by Robert's border of poppies, had presented each of the four with a shilling paint-box, and had supplemented the gift with a pile of old copies of the Illustrated London News.

'Sepia,' said Cyril instructively, 'is made out of beastly cuttlefish.'

'Purple's made out of a fish, as well as out of red and blue,' said Robert. 'Tyrian purple was, I know.'

'Out of lobsters?' said Jane dreamily. 'They're red when they're boiled, and blue when they aren't. If you mixed live and dead lobsters you'd get Tyrian purple.'

'*I* shouldn't like to mix anything with a live lobster,' said Anthea, shuddering.

'Well, there aren't any other red and blue fish,' said Jane; 'you'd have to.'

'I'd rather not have the purple,' said Anthea.

'The Tyrian purple wasn't that colour when it came out of the fish, nor yet afterwards, it wasn't,' said Robert; 'it was scarlet really, and Roman Emperors wore it. And it wasn't any nice colour while the fish had it. It was a yellowish-white liquid of a creamy consistency.'

'How do you know?' asked Cyril.

'I read it,' said Robert, with the meek pride of superior knowledge.

'Where?' asked Cyril.

'In print,' said Robert, still more proudly meek.

'You think everything's true if it's printed,' said Cyril, naturally annoyed, 'but it isn't. Father said so. Quite a lot of lies get printed, especially in newspapers.'

'You see, as it happens,' said Robert, in what was really a rather annoying tone, 'it wasn't a newspaper, it was in a book.'

'How sweet Chinese white is!' said Jane, dreamily sucking her brush again.

'I don't believe it,' said Cyril to Robert.

'Have a suck yourself,' suggested Robert.

'I don't mean about the Chinese white. I mean about the cream fish turning purple and—'

'Oh!' cried Anthea, jumping up very quickly, 'I'm tired of painting. Let's go somewhere by Amulet. I say let's let IT choose.'

Cyril and Robert agreed that this was an idea. Jane consented to stop painting because, as she said, Chinese white, though certainly sweet, gives you a queer feeling in the back of the throat if you paint with it too long.

The Amulet was held up. 'Take us somewhere,' said Jane, 'anywhere you like in the Past—but somewhere where you are.' Then she said the word.

Next moment everyone felt a queer rocking and swaying—something like what you feel when you go out in a fishing boat. And that was not wonderful, when you come to think of it, for it was in a boat that they found themselves. A queer boat, with high bulwarks pierced with holes for oars to go through. There was a high seat for the steersman, and the prow was shaped like the head of some great animal with big, staring eyes. The boat rode at anchor in a bay, and the bay was very smooth. The crew were dark, wiry fellows with black beards and hair. They had no clothes except a tunic from waist to knee, and round caps with knobs on the top. They were very busy, and what they were doing was so interesting to the children that at first they did not even wonder where the Amulet had brought them. And the crew seemed too busy to notice the children. They were fastening rush baskets to a long rope with a great piece of cork at the end, and in each basket they put mussels or little frogs. Then they cast out the rope, the baskets sank, but the cork floated. And all about on the blue water were other boats and all the crews of all the boats were busy with ropes and baskets and frogs and mussels.

'Whatever are you doing?' Jane suddenly asked a man who had rather more clothes than the others, and seemed to be a sort of captain or overseer. He started and stared at her, but he had seen too many strange lands to be very much surprised at these queerly-dressed stowaways.

'Setting lines for the dye shell-fish,' he said shortly. 'How did you get here?'

'A sort of magic,' said Robert carelessly. The Captain fingered an Amulet that hung round his neck.

'What is this place?' asked Cyril.

'Tyre, of course,' said the man. Then he drew back and spoke in a low voice to one of the sailors.

'Now we shall know about your precious cream-jug fish,' said Cyril.

'But we never SAID come to Tyre,' said Jane.

'The Amulet heard us talking, I expect. I think it's MOST obliging of it,' said Anthea.

'And the Amulet's here too,' said Robert. 'We ought to be able to find it in a little ship like this. I wonder which of them's got it.'

'Oh—look, look!' cried Anthea suddenly. On the bare breast of one of the sailors gleamed something red. It was the exact counterpart of their precious half-Amulet.

A silence, full of emotion, was broken by Jane.

'Then we've found it!' she said. 'Oh do let's take it and go home!'

'Easy to say "take it",' said Cyril; 'he looks very strong.'

He did—yet not so strong as the other sailors.

'It's odd,' said Anthea musingly, 'I do believe I've seen that man somewhere before.'

'He's rather like our learned gentleman,' said Robert, 'but I'll tell you who he's much more like—' At that moment that sailor looked up. His eyes met Robert's—and Robert and the others had no longer any doubt as to where they had seen him before. It was Rekh-mara, the priest who had led them to the palace of Pharaoh—and whom Jane had looked back at through the arch, when he was counselling Pharaoh's guard to take the jewels and fly for his life.

Nobody was quite pleased, and nobody quite knew why.

Jane voiced the feelings of all when she said, fingering THEIR Amulet through the folds of her frock, 'We can go back in a minute if anything nasty happens.'

For the moment nothing worse happened than an offer of food—figs and cucumbers it was, and very pleasant.

'I see,' said the Captain, 'that you are from a far country. Since you have honoured my boat by appearing on it, you must stay here till morning. Then I will lead you to one of our great ones. He loves strangers from far lands.'

'Let's go home,' Jane whispered, 'all the frogs are drowning NOW. I think the people here are cruel.'

But the boys wanted to stay and see the lines taken up in the morning.

'It's just like eel-pots and lobster-pots,' said Cyril, 'the baskets only open from outside—I vote we stay.'

So they stayed.

'That's Tyre over there,' said the Captain, who was evidently trying to be civil. He pointed to a great island rock, that rose steeply from the sea, crowned with huge walls and towers. There was another city on the mainland.

'That's part of Tyre, too,' said the Captain; 'it's where the great merchants have their pleasure-houses and gardens and farms.'

'Look, look!' Cyril cried suddenly; 'what a lovely little ship!'

A ship in full sail was passing swiftly through the fishing fleet. The Captain's face changed. He frowned, and his eyes blazed with fury.

'Insolent young barbarian!' he cried. 'Do you call the ships of Tyre LITTLE? None greater sail the seas. That ship has been on a three years' voyage. She is known in all the great trading ports from here to the Tin Islands. She comes back rich and glorious. Her very anchor is of silver.'

'I'm sure we beg your pardon,' said Anthea hastily. 'In our country we say "little" for a pet name. Your wife might call you her dear little husband, you know.'

'I should like to catch her at it,' growled the Captain, but he stopped scowling.

'It's a rich trade,' he went on. 'For cloth ONCE dipped, second-best glass, and the rough images our young artists carve for practice, the barbarian King in Tessos lets us work the silver mines. We get so much silver there that we leave them our iron anchors and come back with silver ones.'

'How splendid!' said Robert. 'Do go on. What's cloth once dipped?'

'You MUST be barbarians from the outer darkness,' said the Captain scornfully. 'All wealthy nations know that our finest stuffs are twice dyed—dibaptha. They're only for the robes of kings and priests and princes.'

'What do the rich merchants wear,' asked Jane, with interest, 'in the pleasure-houses?'

'They wear the dibaptha. OUR merchants ARE princes,' scowled the skipper.

'Oh, don't be cross, we do so like hearing about things. We want to know ALL about the dyeing,' said Anthea cordially.

'Oh, you do, do you?' growled the man. 'So that's what you're here for? Well, you won't get the secrets of the dye trade out of ME.'

He went away, and everyone felt snubbed and uncomfortable. And all the time the long, narrow eyes of the Egyptian were watching, watching. They felt as though he was watching them through the darkness, when they lay down to sleep on a pile of cloaks.

Next morning the baskets were drawn up full of what looked like whelk shells.

553

The children were rather in the way, but they made themselves as small as they could. While the skipper was at the other end of the boat they did ask one question of a sailor, whose face was a little less unkind than the others.

'Yes,' he answered, 'this is the dye-fish. It's a sort of murex—and there's another kind that they catch at Sidon and then, of course, there's the kind that's used for the dibaptha. But that's quite different. It's—'

'Hold your tongue!' shouted the skipper. And the man held it.

The laden boat was rowed slowly round the end of the island, and was made fast in one of the two great harbours that lay inside a long breakwater. The harbour was full of all sorts of ships, so that Cyril and Robert enjoyed themselves much more than their sisters. The breakwater and the quays were heaped with bales and baskets, and crowded with slaves and sailors. Farther along some men were practising diving.

'That's jolly good,' said Robert, as a naked brown body cleft the water.

'I should think so,' said the skipper. 'The pearl-divers of Persia are not more skilful. Why, we've got a fresh-water spring that comes out at the bottom of the sea. Our divers dive down and bring up the fresh water in skin bottles! Can your barbarian divers do as much?'

'I suppose not,' said Robert, and put away a wild desire to explain to the Captain the English system of waterworks, pipes, taps, and the intricacies of the plumbers' trade.

As they neared the quay the skipper made a hasty toilet. He did his hair, combed his beard, put on a garment like a jersey with short sleeves, an embroidered belt, a necklace of beads, and a big signet ring.

'Now,' said he, 'I'm fit to be seen. Come along?'

'Where to?' said Jane cautiously.

554

'To Pheles, the great sea-captain, said the skipper, 'the man I told you of, who loves barbarians.'

Then Rekh-mara came forward, and, for the first time, spoke.

'I have known these children in another land,' he said. 'You know my powers of magic. It was my magic that brought these barbarians to your boat. And you know how they will profit you. I read your thoughts. Let me come with you and see the end of them, and then I will work the spell I promised you in return for the little experience you have so kindly given me on your boat.'

The skipper looked at the Egyptian with some disfavour.

'So it was YOUR doing,' he said. 'I might have guessed it. Well, come on.'

So he came, and the girls wished he hadn't. But Robert whispered—

'Nonsense—as long as he's with us we've got some chance of the Amulet. We can always fly if anything goes wrong.'

The morning was so fresh and bright; their breakfast had been so good and so unusual; they had actually seen the Amulet round the Egyptian's neck. One or two, or all these things, suddenly raised the children's spirits. They went off quite cheerfully through the city gate—it was not arched, but roofed over with a great flat stone—and so through the street, which smelt horribly of fish and garlic and a thousand other things even less agreeable. But far worse than the street scents was the scent of the factory, where the skipper called in to sell his night's catch. I wish I could tell you all about that factory, but I haven't time, and perhaps after all you aren't interested in dyeing works. I will only mention that Robert was triumphantly proved to be right. The dye WAS a yellowish-white liquid of a creamy consistency, and it smelt more strongly of garlic than garlic itself does.

While the skipper was bargaining with the master of the dye works the Egyptian came close to the children, and said, suddenly and softly—

'Trust me.'

'I wish we could,' said Anthea.

'You feel,' said the Egyptian, 'that I want your Amulet. That makes you distrust me.'

'Yes,' said Cyril bluntly.

'But you also, you want my Amulet, and I am trusting you.'

'There's something in that,' said Robert.

'We have the two halves of the Amulet,' said the Priest, 'but not yet the pin that joined them. Our only chance of getting that is to remain together. Once part these two halves and they may never be found in the same time and place. Be wise. Our interests are the same.'

Before anyone could say more the skipper came back, and with him the dye-master. His hair and beard were curled like the men's in Babylon, and he was dressed like the skipper, but with added grandeur of gold and embroidery. He had necklaces of beads and silver, and a glass amulet with a man's face, very like his own, set between two bull's heads, as well as gold and silver bracelets and armlets. He looked keenly at the children. Then he said—

'My brother Pheles has just come back from Tarshish. He's at his garden house—unless he's hunting wild boar in the marshes. He gets frightfully bored on shore.'

'Ah,' said the skipper, 'he's a true-born Phoenician. "Tyre, Tyre for ever! Oh, Tyre rules the waves!" as the old song says. I'll go at once, and show him my young barbarians.'

'I should,' said the dye-master. 'They are very rum, aren't they? What frightful clothes, and what a lot of them! Observe the covering of their feet. Hideous indeed.'

Robert could not help thinking how easy, and at the same time pleasant, it would be to catch hold of the dye-master's feet and tip him backward into the great sunken vat just near him. But if he had, flight would have had to be the next move, so he restrained his impulse.

There was something about this Tyrian adventure that was different from all the others. It was, somehow, calmer. And there was the undoubted fact that the charm was there on the neck of the Egyptian.

So they enjoyed everything to the full, the row from the Island City to the shore, the ride on the donkeys that the skipper hired at the gate of the mainland city, and the pleasant country—palms and figs and cedars all about. It was like a garden—clematis, honeysuckle, and jasmine clung about the olive and mulberry trees, and there were tulips and gladiolus, and clumps of mandrake, which has bell-flowers that look as though they were cut out of dark blue jewels. In the distance were the mountains of Lebanon. The house they came to at last was rather like a bungalow—long and low, with pillars all along the front. Cedars and sycamores grew near it and sheltered it pleasantly.

Everyone dismounted, and the donkeys were led away.

'Why is this like Rosherville?' whispered Robert, and instantly supplied the answer.

'Because it's the place to spend a happy day.'

'It's jolly decent of the skipper to have brought us to such a ripping place,' said Cyril.

'Do you know,' said Anthea, 'this feels more real than anything else we've seen? It's like a holiday in the country at home.'

The children were left alone in a large hall. The floor was mosaic, done with wonderful pictures of ships and sea-beasts and fishes. Through an open doorway they could see a pleasant courtyard with flowers.

'I should like to spend a week here,' said Jane, 'and donkey ride every day.'

Everyone was feeling very jolly. Even the Egyptian looked pleasanter than usual. And then, quite suddenly, the skipper came back with a joyous smile. With him came the master of the house. He looked steadily at the children and nodded twice.

'Yes,' he said, 'my steward will pay you the price. But I shall not pay at that high rate for the Egyptian dog.'

The two passed on.

'This,' said the Egyptian, 'is a pretty kettle of fish.'

'What is?' asked all the children at once.

'Our present position,' said Rekh-mara. 'Our seafaring friend,' he added, 'has sold us all for slaves!'

A hasty council succeeded the shock of this announcement. The Priest was allowed to take part in it. His advice was 'stay', because they were in no danger, and the Amulet in its completeness must be somewhere near, or, of course, they could not have come to that place at all. And after some discussion they agreed to this.

The children were treated more as guests than as slaves, but the Egyptian was sent to the kitchen and made to work.

Pheles, the master of the house, went off that very evening, by the King's orders, to start on another voyage. And when he was gone his wife found the children amusing company, and kept them talking and singing and dancing till quite late. 'To distract my mind from my sorrows,' she said.

'I do like being a slave,' remarked Jane cheerfully, as they curled up on the big, soft cushions that were to be their beds.

It was black night when they were awakened, each by a hand passed softly over its face, and a low voice that whispered—

'Be quiet, or all is lost.'

So they were quiet.

558

'It's me, Rekh-mara, the Priest of Amen,' said the whisperer. 'The man who brought us has gone to sea again, and he has taken my Amulet from me by force, and I know no magic to get it back. Is there magic for that in the Amulet you bear?'

Everyone was instantly awake by now.

'We can go after him,' said Cyril, leaping up; 'but he might take OURS as well; or he might be angry with us for following him.'

'I'll see to THAT,' said the Egyptian in the dark. 'Hide your Amulet well.'

There in the deep blackness of that room in the Tyrian country house the Amulet was once more held up and the word spoken.

All passed through on to a ship that tossed and tumbled on a wind-blown sea. They crouched together there till morning, and Jane and Cyril were not at all well. When the dawn showed, dove-coloured, across the steely waves, they stood up as well as they could for the tumbling of the ship. Pheles, that hardy sailor and adventurer, turned quite pale when he turned round suddenly and saw them.

'Well!' he said, 'well, I never did!'

'Master,' said the Egyptian, bowing low, and that was even more difficult than standing up, 'we are here by the magic of the sacred Amulet that hangs round your neck.'

'I never did!' repeated Pheles. 'Well, well!'

'What port is the ship bound for?' asked Robert, with a nautical air.

But Pheles said, 'Are you a navigator?' Robert had to own that he was not.

'Then,' said Pheles, 'I don't mind telling you that we're bound for the Tin Isles. Tyre alone knows where the Tin Isles are. It is a splendid secret we keep from all the world. It is as great a thing to us as your magic to you.'

He spoke in quite a new voice, and seemed to respect both the children and the Amulet a good deal more than he had done before.

'The King sent you, didn't he?' said Jane.

'Yes,' answered Pheles, 'he bade me set sail with half a score brave gentlemen and this crew. You shall go with us, and see many wonders.' He bowed and left them.

'What are we going to do now?' said Robert, when Pheles had caused them to be left along with a breakfast of dried fruits and a sort of hard biscuit.

'Wait till he lands in the Tin Isles,' said Rekh-mara, 'then we can get the barbarians to help us. We will attack him by night and tear the sacred Amulet from his accursed heathen neck,' he added, grinding his teeth.

'When shall we get to the Tin Isles?' asked Jane.

'Oh—six months, perhaps, or a year,' said the Egyptian cheerfully.

'A year of THIS?' cried Jane, and Cyril, who was still feeling far too unwell to care about breakfast, hugged himself miserably and shuddered. It was Robert who said—

'Look here, we can shorten that year. Jane, out with the Amulet! Wish that we were where the Amulet will be when the ship is twenty miles from the Tin Island. That'll give us time to mature our plans.'

It was done—the work of a moment—and there they were on the same ship, between grey northern sky and grey northern sea. The sun was setting in a pale yellow line. It was the same ship, but it was changed, and so were the crew. Weather-worn and dirty were the sailors, and their clothes torn and ragged. And the children saw that, of course, though they had skipped the nine months, the ship had had to live through them. Pheles looked thinner, and his face was rugged and anxious.

'Ha!' he cried, 'the charm has brought you back! I have prayed to it daily these nine months—and now you are here? Have you no magic that can help?'

'What is your need?' asked the Egyptian quietly.

'I need a great wave that shall whelm away the foreign ship that follows us. A month ago it lay in wait for us, by the pillars of the gods, and it follows, follows, to find out the secret of Tyre—the place of the Tin Islands. If I could steer by night I could escape them yet, but tonight there will be no stars.'

'My magic will not serve you here,' said the Egyptian.

But Robert said, 'My magic will not bring up great waves, but I can show you how to steer without stars.'

He took out the shilling compass, still, fortunately, in working order, that he had bought off another boy at school for fivepence, a piece of indiarubber, a strip of whalebone, and half a stick of red sealing-wax.

And he showed Pheles how it worked. And Pheles wondered at the compass's magic truth.

'I will give it to you,' Robert said, 'in return for that charm about your neck.'

Pheles made no answer. He first laughed, snatched the compass from Robert's hand, and turned away still laughing.

'Be comforted,' the Priest whispered, 'our time will come.'

The dusk deepened, and Pheles, crouched beside a dim lantern, steered by the shilling compass from the Crystal Palace.

No one ever knew how the other ship sailed, but suddenly, in the deep night, the look-out man at the stern cried out in a terrible voice—

'She is close upon us!'

'And we,' said Pheles, 'are close to the harbour.' He was silent a moment, then suddenly he altered the ship's course, and then he stood up and spoke.

'Good friends and gentlemen,' he said, 'who are bound with me in this brave venture by our King's command, the false, foreign ship is close on our heels. If we land, they land, and only the gods know whether they might not beat us in fight, and themselves survive to carry back the tale of Tyre's secret island to enrich their own miserable land. Shall this be?'

'Never!' cried the half-dozen men near him. The slaves were rowing hard below and could not hear his words.

The Egyptian leaped upon him; suddenly, fiercely, as a wild beast leaps. 'Give me back my Amulet,' he cried, and caught at the charm. The chain that held it snapped, and it lay in the Priest's hand.

Pheles laughed, standing balanced to the leap of the ship that answered the oarstroke.

'This is no time for charms and mummeries,' he said. 'We've lived like men, and we'll die like gentlemen for the honour and glory of Tyre, our splendid city. "Tyre, Tyre for ever! It's Tyre that rules the waves." I steer her straight for the Dragon rocks, and we go down for our city, as brave men should. The creeping cowards who follow shall go down as slaves—and slaves they shall be to us—when we live again. Tyre, Tyre for ever!'

A great shout went up, and the slaves below joined in it.

'Quick, the Amulet,' cried Anthea, and held it up. Rekh-mara held up the one he had snatched from Pheles. The word was spoken, and the two great arches grew on the plunging ship in the shrieking wind under the dark sky. From each Amulet a great and beautiful green light streamed and shone far out over the waves. It illuminated, too, the black faces and jagged teeth of the great rocks that lay not two ships' lengths from the boat's peaked nose.

'Tyre, Tyre for ever! It's Tyre that rules the waves!' the voices of the doomed rose in a triumphant shout. The children scrambled through the arch, and stood trembling and blinking in the Fitzroy Street parlour, and in their ears still sounded the whistle of the wind, and the rattle of the oars, the crash of the ships bow on the rocks, and the last shout of the brave gentlemen-adventurers who went to their deaths singing, for the sake of the city they loved.

'And so we've lost the other half of the Amulet again,' said Anthea, when they had told the Psammead all about it.

'Nonsense, pooh!' said the Psammead. 'That wasn't the other half. It was the same half that you've got—the one that wasn't crushed and lost.'

'But how could it be the same?' said Anthea gently.

'Well, not exactly, of course. The one you've got is a good many years older, but at any rate it's not the other one. What did you say when you wished?'

'I forget,' said Jane.

'I don't,' said the Psammead. 'You said, "Take us where YOU are"—and it did, so you see it was the same half.'

'I see,' said Anthea.

'But you mark my words,' the Psammead went on, 'you'll have trouble with that Priest yet.'

'Why, he was quite friendly,' said Anthea.

'All the same you'd better beware of the Reverend Rekh-mara.'

'Oh, I'm sick of the Amulet,' said Cyril, 'we shall never get it.'

'Oh yes we shall,' said Robert. 'Don't you remember December 3rd?'

'Jinks!' said Cyril, 'I'd forgotten that.'

'I don't believe it,' said Jane, 'and I don't feel at all well.'

'If I were you,' said the Psammead, 'I should not go out into the Past again till that date. You'll find it safer not to go where you're likely to meet that Egyptian any more just at present.'

'Of course we'll do as you say,' said Anthea soothingly, 'though there's something about his face that I really do like.'

'Still, you don't want to run after him, I suppose,' snapped the Psammead. 'You wait till the 3rd, and then see what happens.'

Cyril and Jane were feeling far from well, Anthea was always obliging, so Robert was overruled. And they promised. And none of them, not even the Psammead, at all foresaw, as you no doubt do quite plainly, exactly what it was that WOULD happen on that memorable date.

CHAPTER 14. THE HEART'S DESIRE

If I only had time I could tell you lots of things. For instance, how, in spite of the advice of the Psammead, the four children did, one very wet day, go through their Amulet Arch into the golden desert, and there find the great Temple of Baalbec and meet with the Phoenix whom they never thought to see again. And how the Phoenix did not remember them at all until it went into a sort of prophetic trance—if that can be called remembering. But, alas! I HAVEN'T time, so I must leave all that out though it was a wonderfully thrilling adventure. I must leave out, too, all about the visit of the children to the Hippodrome with the Psammead in its travelling bag, and about how the wishes of the people round about them were granted so suddenly and surprisingly that at last the Psammead had to be taken hurriedly home by Anthea, who consequently missed half the performance. Then there was the time when, Nurse having gone to tea with a friend out Ivalunk way, they were playing 'devil in the dark'—and in the midst of that most creepy pastime the postman's knock frightened Jane nearly out of her life. She took in the letters, however, and put them in the back of the hat-stand drawer, so that they should be safe. And safe they were, for she never thought of them again for weeks and weeks.

One really good thing happened when they took the Psammead to a magic-lantern show and lecture at the boys' school at Camden Town. The lecture was all about our soldiers in South Africa. And the lecturer ended up by saying, 'And I hope every boy in this room has in his heart the seeds of courage and heroism and self-sacrifice, and I wish that every one of you may grow up to be noble and brave and unselfish, worthy citizens of this great Empire for whom our soldiers have freely given their lives.'

And, of course, this came true—which was a distinct score for Camden Town.

As Anthea said, it was unlucky that the lecturer said boys, because now she and Jane would have to be noble and unselfish, if at all, without any outside help. But Jane said, 'I daresay we are already because of our beautiful natures. It's only boys that have to be made brave by magic'—which nearly led to a first-class row.

And I daresay you would like to know all about the affair of the fishing rod, and the fish-hooks, and the cook next door—which was amusing from some points of view, though not perhaps the cook's—but there really is no time even for that.

The only thing that there's time to tell about is the Adventure of Maskelyne and Cooke's, and the Unexpected Apparition—which is also the beginning of the end.

It was Nurse who broke into the gloomy music of the autumn rain on the window panes by suggesting a visit to the Egyptian Hall, England's Home of Mystery. Though they had good, but private reasons to know that their own particular personal mystery was of a very different brand, the four all brightened at the idea. All children, as well as a good many grown-ups, love conjuring.

'It's in Piccadilly,' said old Nurse, carefully counting out the proper number of shillings into Cyril's hand, 'not so very far down on the left from the Circus. There's big pillars outside, something like Carter's seed place in Holborn, as used to be Day and Martin's blacking when I was a gell. And something like Euston Station, only not so big.'

'Yes, I know,' said everybody.

So they started.

But though they walked along the left-hand side of Piccadilly they saw no pillared building that was at all like Carter's seed warehouse or Euston Station or England's Home of Mystery as they remembered it.

At last they stopped a hurried lady, and asked her the way to Maskelyne and Cooke's.

'I don't know, I'm sure,' she said, pushing past them. 'I always shop at the Stores.' Which just shows, as Jane said, how ignorant grown-up people are.

It was a policeman who at last explained to them that England's Mysteries are now appropriately enough enacted at St George's Hall.

So they tramped to Langham Place, and missed the first two items in the programme. But they were in time for the most wonderful magic appearances and disappearances, which they could hardly believe—even with all their knowledge of a larger magic—was not really magic after all.

'If only the Babylonians could have seen THIS conjuring,' whispered Cyril. 'It takes the shine out of their old conjurer, doesn't it?'

'Hush!' said Anthea and several other members of the audience.

Now there was a vacant seat next to Robert. And it was when all eyes were fixed on the stage where Mr Devant was pouring out glasses of all sorts of different things to drink, out of one kettle with one spout, and the audience were delightedly tasting them, that Robert felt someone in that vacant seat. He did not feel someone sit down in it. It was just that one moment there was no one sitting there, and the next moment, suddenly, there was someone.

Robert turned. The someone who had suddenly filled that empty place was Rekh-mara, the Priest of Amen!

Though the eyes of the audience were fixed on Mr David Devant, Mr David Devant's eyes were fixed on the audience. And it happened that his eyes were more particularly fixed on that empty chair. So that he saw quite plainly the sudden appearance, from nowhere, of the Egyptian Priest.

'A jolly good trick,' he said to himself, 'and worked under my own eyes, in my own hall. I'll find out how that's done.' He had never seen a trick that he could not do himself if he tried.

By this time a good many eyes in the audience had turned on the clean-shaven, curiously-dressed figure of the Egyptian Priest.

'Ladies and gentlemen,' said Mr Devant, rising to the occasion, 'this is a trick I have never before performed. The empty seat, third from the end, second row, gallery—you will now find occupied by an Ancient Egyptian, warranted genuine.'

He little knew how true his words were.

And now all eyes were turned on the Priest and the children, and the whole audience, after a moment's breathless surprise, shouted applause. Only the lady on the other side of Rekh-mara drew back a little. She KNEW no one had passed her, and, as she said later, over tea and cold tongue, 'it was that sudden it made her flesh creep.'

Rekh-mara seemed very much annoyed at the notice he was exciting.

'Come out of this crowd,' he whispered to Robert. 'I must talk with you apart.'

'Oh, no,' Jane whispered. 'I did so want to see the Mascot Moth, and the Ventriloquist.'

'How did you get here?' was Robert's return whisper.

'How did you get to Egypt and to Tyre?' retorted Rekh-mara. 'Come, let us leave this crowd.'

'There's no help for it, I suppose,' Robert shrugged angrily. But they all got up.

'Confederates!' said a man in the row behind. 'Now they go round to the back and take part in the next scene.'

'I wish we did,' said Robert.

'Confederate yourself!' said Cyril. And so they got away, the audience applauding to the last.

In the vestibule of St George's Hall they disguised Rekh-mara as well as they could, but even with Robert's hat and Cyril's Inverness cape he was too striking a figure for foot-exercise in the London streets. It had to be a cab, and it took the last, least money of all of them. They stopped the cab a few doors from home, and then the girls went in and engaged old Nurse's attention by an account of the conjuring and a fervent entreaty for dripping-toast with their tea, leaving the front door open so that while Nurse was talking to them the boys could creep quietly in with Rekh-mara and smuggle him, unseen, up the stairs into their bedroom.

When the girls came up they found the Egyptian Priest sitting on the side of Cyril's bed, his hands on his knees, looking like a statue of a king.

'Come on,' said Cyril impatiently. 'He won't begin till we're all here. And shut the door, can't you?'

When the door was shut the Egyptian said—

'My interests and yours are one.'

'Very interesting,' said Cyril, 'and it'll be a jolly sight more interesting if you keep following us about in a decent country with no more clothes on than THAT!'

'Peace,' said the Priest. 'What is this country? and what is this time?'

'The country's England,' said Anthea, 'and the time's about 6,000 years later than YOUR time.'

'The Amulet, then,' said the Priest, deeply thoughtful, 'gives the power to move to and fro in time as well as in space?'

'That's about it,' said Cyril gruffly. 'Look here, it'll be tea-time directly. What are we to do with you?'

'You have one-half of the Amulet, I the other,' said Rekh-mara. 'All that is now needed is the pin to join them.'

'Don't you think it,' said Robert. 'The half you've got is the same half as the one we've got.'

'But the same thing cannot be in the same place and the same time, and yet be not one, but twain,' said the Priest. 'See, here is my half.' He laid it on the Marcella counterpane. 'Where is yours?'

Jane watching the eyes of the others, unfastened the string of the Amulet and laid it on the bed, but too far off for the Priest to seize it, even if he had been so dishonourable. Cyril and Robert stood beside him, ready to spring on him if one of his hands had moved but ever so little towards the magic treasure that was theirs. But his hands did not move, only his eyes opened very wide, and so did everyone else's for the Amulet the Priest had now quivered and shook; and then, as steel is drawn to the magnet, it was drawn across the white counterpane, nearer and nearer to the Amulet, warm from the neck of Jane. And then, as one drop of water mingles with another on a rain-wrinkled window-pane, as one bead of quick-silver is drawn into another bead, Rekh-mara's Amulet slipped into the other one, and, behold! there was no more but the one Amulet!

'Black magic!' cried Rekh-mara, and sprang forward to snatch the Amulet that had swallowed his. But Anthea caught it up, and at the same moment the Priest was jerked back by a rope thrown over his head. It drew, tightened with the pull of his forward leap, and

569

bound his elbows to his sides. Before he had time to use his strength to free himself, Robert had knotted the cord behind him and tied it to the bedpost. Then the four children, overcoming the priest's wrigglings and kickings, tied his legs with more rope.

'I thought,' said Robert, breathing hard, and drawing the last knot tight, 'he'd have a try for OURS, so I got the ropes out of the box-room, so as to be ready.'

The girls, with rather white faces, applauded his foresight.

'Loosen these bonds!' cried Rekh-mara in fury, 'before I blast you with the seven secret curses of Amen-Ra!'

'We shouldn't be likely to loose them AFTER,' Robert retorted.

'Oh, don't quarrel!' said Anthea desperately. 'Look here, he has just as much right to the thing as we have. This,' she took up the Amulet that had swallowed the other one, 'this has got his in it as well as being ours. Let's go shares.'

'Let me go!' cried the Priest, writhing.

'Now, look here,' said Robert, 'if you make a row we can just open that window and call the police—the guards, you know—and tell them you've been trying to rob us. NOW will you shut up and listen to reason?'

'I suppose so,' said Rekh-mara sulkily.

But reason could not be spoken to him till a whispered counsel had been held in the far corner by the washhand-stand and the towel-horse, a counsel rather long and very earnest.

At last Anthea detached herself from the group, and went back to the Priest.

'Look here,' she said in her kind little voice, 'we want to be friends. We want to help you. Let's make a treaty. Let's join together to get the Amulet—the whole one, I mean. And then it shall belong to you as much as to us, and we shall all get our hearts' desire.'

570

'Fair words,' said the Priest, 'grow no onions.'

'WE say, "Butter no parsnips",' Jane put in. 'But don't you see we WANT to be fair? Only we want to bind you in the chains of honour and upright dealing.'

'Will you deal fairly by us?' said Robert.

'I will,' said the Priest. 'By the sacred, secret name that is written under the Altar of Amen-Ra, I will deal fairly by you. Will you, too, take the oath of honourable partnership?'

'No,' said Anthea, on the instant, and added rather rashly. 'We don't swear in England, except in police courts, where the guards are, you know, and you don't want to go there. But when we SAY we'll do a thing—it's the same as an oath to us—we do it. You trust us, and we'll trust you.' She began to unbind his legs, and the boys hastened to untie his arms.

When he was free he stood up, stretched his arms, and laughed.

'Now,' he said, 'I am stronger than you and my oath is void. I have sworn by nothing, and my oath is nothing likewise. For there IS no secret, sacred name under the altar of Amen-Ra.'

'Oh, yes there is!' said a voice from under the bed. Everyone started—Rekh-mara most of all.

Cyril stooped and pulled out the bath of sand where the Psammead slept. 'You don't know everything, though you ARE a Divine Father of the Temple of Amen,' said the Psammead shaking itself till the sand fell tinkling on the bath edge. 'There IS a secret, sacred name beneath the altar of Amen-Ra. Shall I call on that name?'

'No, no!' cried the Priest in terror.

'No,' said Jane, too. 'Don't let's have any calling names.'

'Besides,' said Rekh-mara, who had turned very white indeed under his natural brownness, 'I was only going to say that though there isn't any name under—'

'There IS,' said the Psammead threateningly.

'Well, even if there WASN'T, I will be bound by the wordless oath of your strangely upright land, and having said that I will be your friend—I will be it.'

'Then that's all right,' said the Psammead; 'and there's the tea-bell. What are you going to do with your distinguished partner? He can't go down to tea like that, you know.'

'You see we can't do anything till the 3rd of December,' said Anthea, 'that's when we are to find the whole charm. What can we do with Rekh-mara till then?'

'Box-room,' said Cyril briefly, 'and smuggle up his meals. It will be rather fun.'

'Like a fleeing Cavalier concealed from exasperated Roundheads,' said Robert. 'Yes.'

So Rekh-mara was taken up to the box-room and made as comfortable as possible in a snug nook between an old nursery fender and the wreck of a big four-poster. They gave him a big rag-bag to sit on, and an old, moth-eaten fur coat off the nail on the door to keep him warm. And when they had had their own tea they took him some. He did not like the tea at all, but he liked the bread and butter, and cake that went with it. They took it in turns to sit with him during the evening, and left him fairly happy and quite settled for the night.

But when they went up in the morning with a kipper, a quarter of which each of them had gone without at breakfast, Rekh-mara was gone! There was the cosy corner with the rag-bag, and the moth-eaten fur coat—but the cosy corner was empty.

'Good riddance!' was naturally the first delightful thought in each mind. The second was less pleasing, because everyone at once remembered that since his Amulet had been swallowed up by theirs—which hung once more round the neck of Jane—he could have no possible means of returning to his Egyptian past. Therefore he must be still in England, and probably somewhere quite near them, plotting mischief.

The attic was searched, to prevent mistakes, but quite vainly.

'The best thing we can do,' said Cyril, 'is to go through the half Amulet straight away, get the whole Amulet, and come back.'

'I don't know,' Anthea hesitated. 'Would that be quite fair? Perhaps he isn't really a base deceiver. Perhaps something's happened to him.'

'Happened?' said Cyril, 'not it! Besides, what COULD happen?'

'I don't know,' said Anthea. 'Perhaps burglars came in the night, and accidentally killed him, and took away the—all that was mortal of him, you know—to avoid discovery.'

'Or perhaps,' said Cyril, 'they hid the—all that was mortal, in one of those big trunks in the box-room. SHALL WE GO BACK AND LOOK?' he added grimly.

'No, no!' Jane shuddered. 'Let's go and tell the Psammead and see what it says.'

'No,' said Anthea, 'let's ask the learned gentleman. If anything has happened to Rekh-mara a gentleman's advice would be more useful than a Psammead's. And the learned gentleman'll only think it's a dream, like he always does.'

They tapped at the door, and on the 'Come in' entered. The learned gentleman was sitting in front of his untasted breakfast.

Opposite him, in the easy chair, sat Rekh-mara!

'Hush!' said the learned gentleman very earnestly, 'please, hush! or the dream will go. I am learning... Oh, what have I not learned in the last hour!'

'In the grey dawn,' said the Priest, 'I left my hiding-place, and finding myself among these treasures from my own country, I remained. I feel more at home here somehow.'

'Of course I know it's a dream,' said the learned gentleman feverishly, 'but, oh, ye gods! what a dream! By jove!...'

'Call not upon the gods,' said the Priest, 'lest ye raise greater ones than ye can control. Already,' he explained to the children, 'he and I are as brothers, and his welfare is dear to me as my own.'

'He has told me,' the learned gentleman began, but Robert interrupted. This was no moment for manners.

'Have you told him,' he asked the Priest, 'all about the Amulet?'

'No,' said Rekh-mara.

'Then tell him now. He is very learned. Perhaps he can tell us what to do.'

Rekh-mara hesitated, then told—and, oddly enough, none of the children ever could remember afterwards what it was that he did tell. Perhaps he used some magic to prevent their remembering.

When he had done the learned gentleman was silent, leaning his elbow on the table and his head on his hand.

'Dear Jimmy,' said Anthea gently, 'don't worry about it. We are sure to find it today, somehow.'

'Yes,' said Rekh-mara, 'and perhaps, with it, Death.'

'It's to bring us our hearts' desire,' said Robert.

'Who knows,' said the Priest, 'what things undreamed-of and infinitely desirable lie beyond the dark gates?'

'Oh, DON'T,' said Jane, almost whimpering.

The learned gentleman raised his head suddenly.

'Why not,' he suggested, 'go back into the Past? At a moment when the Amulet is unwatched. Wish to be with it, and that it shall be under your hand.'

It was the simplest thing in the world! And yet none of them had ever thought of it.

'Come,' cried Rekh-mara, leaping up. 'Come NOW!'

'May—may I come?' the learned gentleman timidly asked. 'It's only a dream, you know.'

'Come, and welcome, oh brother,' Rekh-mara was beginning, but Cyril and Robert with one voice cried, 'NO.'

'You weren't with us in Atlantis,' Robert added, 'or you'd know better than to let him come.'

'Dear Jimmy,' said Anthea, 'please don't ask to come. We'll go and be back again before you have time to know that we're gone.'

'And he, too?'

'We must keep together,' said Rekh-mara, 'since there is but one perfect Amulet to which I and these children have equal claims.'

Jane held up the Amulet—Rekh-mara went first—and they all passed through the great arch into which the Amulet grew at the Name of Power.

The learned gentleman saw through the arch a darkness lighted by smoky gleams. He rubbed his eyes. And he only rubbed them for ten seconds.

The children and the Priest were in a small, dark chamber. A square doorway of massive stone let in gleams of shifting light, and the sound of many voices chanting a slow, strange hymn. They stood listening. Now and then the chant quickened and the light grew brighter, as though fuel had been thrown on a fire.

'Where are we?' whispered Anthea.

'And when?' whispered Robert.

'This is some shrine near the beginnings of belief,' said the Egyptian shivering. 'Take the Amulet and come away. It is cold here in the morning of the world.'

And then Jane felt that her hand was on a slab or table of stone, and, under her hand, something that felt like the charm that had so long hung round her neck, only it was thicker. Twice as thick.

'It's HERE!' she said, 'I've got it!' And she hardly knew the sound of her own voice.

'Come away,' repeated Rekh-mara.

'I wish we could see more of this Temple,' said Robert resistingly.

'Come away,' the Priest urged, 'there is death all about, and strong magic. Listen.'

The chanting voices seemed to have grown louder and fiercer, and light stronger.

'They are coming!' cried Rekh-mara. 'Quick, quick, the Amulet!'

Jane held it up.

'What a long time you've been rubbing your eyes!' said Anthea; 'don't you see we've got back?' The learned gentleman merely stared at her.

'Miss Anthea—Miss Jane!' It was Nurse's voice, very much higher and squeaky and more exalted than usual.

'Oh, bother!' said everyone. Cyril adding, 'You just go on with the dream for a sec, Mr Jimmy, we'll be back directly. Nurse'll come up if we don't. SHE wouldn't think Rekh-mara was a dream.'

Then they went down. Nurse was in the hall, an orange envelope in one hand, and a pink paper in the other.

'Your Pa and Ma's come home. "Reach London 11.15. Prepare rooms as directed in letter", and signed in their two names.'

'Oh, hooray! hooray! hooray!' shouted the boys and Jane. But Anthea could not shout, she was nearer crying.

'Oh,' she said almost in a whisper, 'then it WAS true. And we HAVE got our hearts' desire.'

'But I don't understand about the letter,' Nurse was saying. 'I haven't HAD no letter.'

'OH!' said Jane in a queer voice, 'I wonder whether it was one of those... they came that night—you know, when we were playing "devil in the dark"—and I put them in the hat-stand drawer, behind the clothes-brushes and'—she pulled out the drawer as she spoke—'and here they are!'

There was a letter for Nurse and one for the children. The letters told how Father had done being a war-correspondent and was coming home; and how Mother and The Lamb were going to meet him in Italy and all come home together; and how The Lamb and Mother were quite well; and how a telegram would be sent to tell the day and the hour of their home-coming.

'Mercy me!' said old Nurse. 'I declare if it's not too bad of You, Miss Jane. I shall have a nice to-do getting things straight for your Pa and Ma.'

'Oh, never mind, Nurse,' said Jane, hugging her; 'isn't it just too lovely for anything!'

'We'll come and help you,' said Cyril. 'There's just something upstairs we've got to settle up, and then we'll all come and help you.'

'Get along with you,' said old Nurse, but she laughed jollily. 'Nice help YOU'D be. I know you. And it's ten o'clock now.'

There was, in fact, something upstairs that they had to settle. Quite a considerable something, too. And it took much longer than they expected.

A hasty rush into the boys' room secured the Psammead, very sandy and very cross.

'It doesn't matter how cross and sandy it is though,' said Anthea, 'it ought to be there at the final council.'

'It'll give the learned gentleman fits, I expect,' said Robert, 'when he sees it.'

But it didn't.

'The dream is growing more and more wonderful,' he exclaimed, when the Psammead had been explained to him by Rekh-mara. 'I have dreamed this beast before.'

'Now,' said Robert, 'Jane has got the half Amulet and I've got the whole. Show up, Jane.'

Jane untied the string and laid her half Amulet on the table, littered with dusty papers, and the clay cylinders marked all over with little marks like the little prints of birds' little feet. Robert laid down the whole Amulet, and Anthea gently restrained the eager hand of the learned gentleman as it reached out yearningly towards the 'perfect specimen'.

And then, just as before on the Marcella quilt, so now on the dusty litter of papers and curiosities, the half Amulet quivered and shook, and then, as steel is drawn to a magnet, it was drawn across the dusty manuscripts, nearer and nearer to the perfect Amulet, warm from the pocket of Robert. And then, as one drop of water mingles with another when the panes of the window are wrinkled with rain, as one bead of mercury is drawn into another bead, the half Amulet, that was the children's and was also Rekh-mara's,—slipped into the whole Amulet, and, behold! there was only one—the perfect and ultimate Charm.

'And THAT'S all right,' said the Psammead, breaking a breathless silence.

'Yes,' said Anthea, 'and we've got our hearts' desire. Father and Mother and The Lamb are coming home today.'

'But what about me?' said Rekh-mara.

'What IS your heart's desire?' Anthea asked.

'Great and deep learning,' said the Priest, without a moment's hesitation. 'A learning greater and deeper than that of any man of
578

my land and my time. But learning too great is useless. If I go back to my own land and my own age, who will believe my tales of what I have seen in the future? Let me stay here, be the great knower of all that has been, in that our time, so living to me, so old to you, about which your learned men speculate unceasingly, and often, HE tells me, vainly.'

'If I were you,' said the Psammead, 'I should ask the Amulet about that. It's a dangerous thing, trying to live in a time that's not your own. You can't breathe an air that's thousands of centuries ahead of your lungs without feeling the effects of it, sooner or later. Prepare the mystic circle and consult the Amulet.'

'Oh, WHAT a dream!' cried the learned gentleman. 'Dear children, if you love me—and I think you do, in dreams and out of them—prepare the mystic circle and consult the Amulet!'

They did. As once before, when the sun had shone in August splendour, they crouched in a circle on the floor. Now the air outside was thick and yellow with the fog that by some strange decree always attends the Cattle Show week. And in the street costers were shouting. 'Ur Hekau Setcheh,' Jane said the Name of Power. And instantly the light went out, and all the sounds went out too, so that there was a silence and a darkness, both deeper than any darkness or silence that you have ever even dreamed of imagining. It was like being deaf or blind, only darker and quieter even than that.

Then out of that vast darkness and silence came a light and a voice. The light was too faint to see anything by, and the voice was too small for you to hear what it said. But the light and the voice grew. And the light was the light that no man may look on and live, and the voice was the sweetest and most terrible voice in the world. The children cast down their eyes. And so did everyone.

'I speak,' said the voice. 'What is it that you would hear?'

There was a pause. Everyone was afraid to speak.

'What are we to do about Rekh-mara?' said Robert suddenly and abruptly. 'Shall he go back through the Amulet to his own time, or—'

'No one can pass through the Amulet now,' said the beautiful, terrible voice, 'to any land or any time. Only when it was imperfect could such things be. But men may pass through the perfect charm to the perfect union, which is not of time or space.'

'Would you be so very kind,' said Anthea tremulously, 'as to speak so that we can understand you? The Psammead said something about Rekh-mara not being able to live here, and if he can't get back—' She stopped, her heart was beating desperately in her throat, as it seemed.

'Nobody can continue to live in a land and in a time not appointed,' said the voice of glorious sweetness. 'But a soul may live, if in that other time and land there be found a soul so akin to it as to offer it refuge, in the body of that land and time, that thus they two may be one soul in one body.'

The children exchanged discouraged glances. But the eyes of Rekh-mara and the learned gentleman met, and were kind to each other, and promised each other many things, secret and sacred and very beautiful.

Anthea saw the look. 'Oh, but,' she said, without at all meaning to say it, 'dear Jimmy's soul isn't at all like Rekh-mara's. I'm certain it isn't. I don't want to be rude, but it ISN'T, you know. Dear Jimmy's soul is as good as gold, and—'

'Nothing that is not good can pass beneath the double arch of my perfect Amulet,' said the voice. 'If both are willing, say the word of Power, and let the two souls become one for ever and ever more.'

'Shall I?' asked Jane.

'Yes.'

'Yes.'

The voices were those of the Egyptian Priest and the learned gentleman, and the voices were eager, alive, thrilled with hope and the desire of great things.

So Jane took the Amulet from Robert and held it up between the two men, and said, for the last time, the word of Power.

'Ur Hekau Setcheh.'

The perfect Amulet grew into a double arch; the two arches leaned to each other making a great A.

'A stands for Amen,' whispered Jane; 'what he was a priest of.'

'Hush!' breathed Anthea.

The great double arch glowed in and through the green light that had been there since the Name of Power had first been spoken—it glowed with a light more bright yet more soft than the other light—a glory and splendour and sweetness unspeakable. 'Come!' cried Rekh-mara, holding out his hands.

'Come!' cried the learned gentleman, and he also held out his hands.

Each moved forward under the glowing, glorious arch of the perfect Amulet.

Then Rekh-mara quavered and shook, and as steel is drawn to a magnet he was drawn, under the arch of magic, nearer and nearer to the learned gentleman. And, as one drop of water mingles with another, when the window-glass is rain-wrinkled, as one quick-silver bead is drawn to another quick-silver bead, Rekh-mara, Divine Father of the Temple of Amen-Ra, was drawn into, slipped into, disappeared into, and was one with Jimmy, the good, the beloved, the learned gentleman.

And suddenly it was good daylight and the December sun shone. The fog has passed away like a dream.

The Amulet was there—little and complete in jane's hand, and there were the other children and the Psammead, and the learned gentleman. But Rekh-mara—or the body of Rekh-mara—was not there any more. As for his soul...

'Oh, the horrid thing!' cried Robert, and put his foot on a centipede as long as your finger, that crawled and wriggled and squirmed at the learned gentleman's feet.

'THAT,' said the Psammead, 'WAS the evil in the soul of Rekh-mara.'

There was a deep silence.

'Then Rekh-mara's HIM now?' said Jane at last.

'All that was good in Rekh-mara,' said the Psammead.

'HE ought to have his heart's desire, too,' said Anthea, in a sort of stubborn gentleness.

'HIS heart's desire,' said the Psammead, 'is the perfect Amulet you hold in your hand. Yes—and has been ever since he first saw the broken half of it.'

'We've got ours,' said Anthea softly.

'Yes,' said the Psammead—its voice was crosser than they had ever heard it—'your parents are coming home. And what's to become of ME? I shall be found out, and made a show of, and degraded in every possible way. I KNOW they'll make me go into Parliament—hateful place—all mud and no sand. That beautiful Baalbec temple in the desert! Plenty of good sand there, and no politics! I wish I were there, safe in the Past—that I do.'

'I wish you were,' said the learned gentleman absently, yet polite as ever.

The Psammead swelled itself up, turned its long snail's eyes in one last lingering look at Anthea—a loving look, she always said, and thought—and—vanished.

'Well,' said Anthea, after a silence, 'I suppose it's happy. The only thing it ever did really care for was SAND.'

582

'My dear children,' said the learned gentleman, 'I must have fallen asleep. I've had the most extraordinary dream.'

'I hope it was a nice one,' said Cyril with courtesy.

'Yes.... I feel a new man after it. Absolutely a new man.'

There was a ring at the front-door bell. The opening of a door. Voices.

'It's THEM!' cried Robert, and a thrill ran through four hearts.

'Here!' cried Anthea, snatching the Amulet from Jane and pressing it into the hand of the learned gentleman. 'Here—it's yours—your very own—a present from us, because you're Rekhmara as well as... I mean, because you're such a dear.'

She hugged him briefly but fervently, and the four swept down the stairs to the hall, where a cabman was bringing in boxes, and where, heavily disguised in travelling cloaks and wraps, was their hearts' desire—three-fold—Mother, Father, and The Lamb.

'Bless me!' said the learned gentleman, left alone, 'bless me! What a treasure! The dear children! It must be their affection that has given me these luminous apercus. I seem to see so many things now—things I never saw before! The dear children! The dear, dear children!'

Biography of Edith Bland, nee Nesbit

(15 August 1858 – 4 May 1924) An English author and poet whose children's works were published under the name of **E. Nesbit**. She wrote or collaborated on over 60 books of fiction for children, several of which have been adapted for film and television. She was also a political activist and co-founded the Fabian Society, a precursor to the modern Labor Party.

Nesbit was born in 1858 at 38 Lower Kennington Lane in Kennington, Surrey (now part of Greater London), the daughter of an agricultural chemist, John Collis Nesbit, who died in March 1862, before her fourth birthday. Her sister Mary's ill health meant that the family moved around constantly for some years, living variously in Brighton, Buckinghamshire, France (Dieppe, Rouen, Paris, Tours, Poitiers, Angoulême, Bordeaux, Arcachon, Pau, Bagnères-de-Bigorre, and Dinan in Brittany), Spain and Germany, before settling for three years at Halstead Hall in Halstead in north-west Kent, a location which later inspired *The Railway Children* (this distinction has also been claimed by the Derbyshire town of New Mills).

When Nesbit was 17, the family moved again, this time back to London, living variously in South East London at Eltham, Lewisham, Grove Park and Lee.

19-year-old Nesbit met bank clerk Hubert Bland in 1877. Seven months pregnant, she married Bland on 22 April 1880, though she did not immediately live with him, as Bland initially continued to live with his mother. Their marriage was a stormy one. Early on Edith discovered another woman believed she was Hubert's fiancée and had also borne him a child. A more serious blow came later when Edith discovered that her good friend, Alice Hoatson, was pregnant with Hubert's child. Edith had already agreed to adopt Hoatson's child and allow Hoatson to live with her as their housekeeper. When she discovered the truth, Edith quarreled violently with her husband and suggested that Hoatson and the baby should leave; Hubert threatened to leave Edith if she disowned the baby and its mother. Hoatson remained with them as a housekeeper and secretary and became pregnant by Hubert again 13 years later. Edith again adopted Hoatson's child.

Nesbit's children were Paul Bland (1880–1940), to whom *The Railway Children* was dedicated; Iris Bland (1881-1950s); Fabian Bland (1885–1900); Rosamund Bland (1886-?), to whom The Book of Dragons was dedicated; and John Bland (1899 -?) to whom The House of Arden was dedicated. Her son Fabian died aged 15 after a tonsil operation, and Nesbit dedicated a number of books to him: *Five Children And It* and its sequels, as well as *The Story of the Treasure Seekers* and its sequels. Nesbit's daughter Rosamund collaborated with her on the book Cat Tales.

Nesbit was a follower of the utopian socialist William Morris and she and her husband Hubert were among the founders of the Fabian Society in 1884. Their son Fabian was named after the society. They also jointly edited the Society's journal *Today*; Hoatson was the Society's assistant secretary. Nesbit and Bland also dallied briefly with the Social Democratic Federation, but rejected it as too radical. Nesbit was an active lecturer and prolific writer on socialism during the 1880s. Nesbit also wrote with her husband under the name "Fabian Bland", though this activity dwindled as her success as a children's author grew.

Nesbit lived from 1899 to 1920 in Well Hall House, Eltham, Kent (now in south-east Greater London), which appears in fictional guise in several of her books, especially *The Red House*. She and her husband entertained a large circle of friends, colleagues and admirers at their grand "Well Hall House".

On 20 February 1917, some three years after Bland died, Nesbit married Thomas "the Skipper" Tucker. They were married in Woolwich, where he was a ship's engineer on the Woolwich Ferry.

She was a guest speaker at the London School of Economics, which had been founded by other Fabian Society members.

Towards the end of her life she moved to a house called "Crowlink" in Friston, East Sussex, and later to "The Long Boat" at Jesson, St Mary's Bay, New Romney, East Kent where, suffering from lung cancer, she died in 1924 and was buried in the churchyard of St Mary in the Marsh. Her husband Thomas died at the same address on 17 May 1935. Edith's son, Paul Bland, was one of the executor's of Thomas Tucker's will.

Nesbit published approximately 40 books for children, including novels, collections of stories and picture books. Collaborating with others, she published almost as many more.

According to her biographer Julia Briggs, Nesbit was "the first modern writer for children": "(Nesbit) helped to reverse the great tradition of children's literature inaugurated by [Lewis] Carroll, [George] MacDonald and Kenneth Grahame, in turning away from their secondary worlds to the tough truths to be won from encounters with things-as-they-are, previously the province of adult novels." Briggs also credits Nesbit with having invented the children's adventure story. Noël Coward was a great admirer of hers and, in a letter to an early biographer Noel Streatfeild, wrote "she had an economy of phrase, and an unparalleled talent for evoking hot summer days in the English countryside."

Among Nesbit's best-known books are *The Story of the Treasure Seekers* (1898) and *The Wouldbegoods* (1899), which both recount stories about the Bastables, a middle class family that has fallen on relatively hard times. The Railway Children is also extremely well known. Her children's writing also included numerous plays and collections of verse.

She created an innovative body of work that combined realistic, contemporary children in real-world settings with magical objects - what would now be classed as contemporary fantasy - and adventures and sometimes travel to fantastic worlds. In doing so, she was a direct or indirect influence on many subsequent writers, including P. L. Travers (author of *Mary Poppins*), Edward Eager, Diana Wynne Jones and J. K. Rowling. C. S. Lewis wrote of her influence on his *Narnia* series and mentions the Bastable children in *The Magician's Nephew*. Michael Moorcock would go on to write a series of steampunk novels with an adult Oswald Bastable (of *The Treasure Seekers*) as the lead character.

Nesbit also wrote for adults, including eleven novels, short stories and four collections of horror stories.

Printed in Great Britain
by Amazon

61787885R00332